Blackbird Adventure Stories

The Persephone Gate

K.C. Russell

The Grimpen Press

Dedicated to:

L.A.W.

who liked to drive her red VW at night in the rain with the headlights off

and

All Lost Worlds

Contents

Prologue

The Jewel in the Heart of the Lie

Her message was shocking and suitably mysterious.

"M is dead. The funeral is this morning. Santa Barbara. If you could meet me in the Marea Hotel parking lot at about one, I may have some time for you – PG."

And then on the other side of the torn slip of paper, *"And there is something you need to see..."*

The note in its square envelope had been slipped under my hotel room door sometime in the night. I had no idea how she even knew I was in town. I had told no one about this impromptu visit.

That alone was very PG.

M dead. *God.*

I had to think about this.

I was short of breath. The stuffy little room spun and banked. I stood there in my hotel robe and wiped my face.

I had arrived in southern California with no intention of looking her up. Before that morning, I doubted I would ever see PG again.

"Wrong," I said to the empty place. "Wrong about everything maybe."

I brought the note up to my face. Vanilla with a hint of something else. I ran a fingertip along the line of perfectly formed words. She had touched this, right here.

Never been a big fan of Los Angeles and as soon as an emergency meeting with my literary agent was behind me I planned to be on a plane back home. I still didn't know what the meeting was all about. The office there had been enigmatic. This was one of those big partnership setups with a bunch of agents in a common building, a couple receptionists out front. Like a big dentist's office only instead of teeth they struggled to pull books out of cranky, little known writers.

Probably forever little known.

Something urgent about a revised contract, the young woman had said, in a tone which had made my pulse race. Her voice had not been familiar. Lawyers were involved.

Well, who cares. They were paying for it. The plane ticket had been waiting for me. This hotel had been my bright idea.

I leaned against the room door and tightened the robe. The back of my head bounced off the little fisheye lens. Before me, gray light suffused through the elegant curtains. Oh so elegant. It was almost eight. I heard the room service cart in the hallway and my stomach grumbled. I had forgotten to order anything, of course.

It was nuts to stay in a big place like this, I thought, what the hell was it called. *Tides.* Right across from the beach, now swept by rain.

I squinted in the gray light at the ornate chairs, the fussy writing table, the gaudy headboard. Lots of carved wood at the *Tides.* Tiny antique television, with a picture tube, which I had never turned on. I pretty much hated the whole place.

But it was right next to the beach. I could go down the elevator, walk out the side door, take off my shoes and with a mere one step be walking on sand. Beach sand. I have never actually done that, you understand, in an actually real sense of things. Walk in the sand barefoot.

The thing is when you are born and raised in the middle of the country the *beach* is a powerful idea. Just the thought of it, something you have never seen, always out there. All that space. Freedom itself. To walk on the *beach.* Barefoot, right? What would that even feel like? The sand, shells, seabirds, the sky, the almost impossible to imagine ocean itself. When you get back they all ask, did you go to the *beach*? If I was a taking a trip to California of course I was going to stay at the *beach.*

And M, whom I actually met at PG's birthday party in Carmel the previous summer (and who did not like me one little bit) had died just in time for this unannounced visit.

Pieces of a puzzle were trying to fall into place.

I braced myself on the windowsill.

There were entire worlds in motion out there in the clouds, all invisible to me. Empires were falling. Unseen tectonic financial and cultural plates the size of continents were shifting under my feet like razor sharp shards of oiled slate, coal black, and silent as falling snow. It was all happening as I breathed.

PG had made her feelings about my little project very clear the previous October, when I first mentioned it to her. She hated it. She turned down all requests for a formal interview. She stopped answering phone messages or email. She had cut me off cold. My last ditch attempt was as old-school as she liked to sometimes be. I wrote her a letter with my aunt Matilda's fountain pen.

Just tell me the story, I had written in my poor, cramped hand. *You know your name will never be mentioned.*

But the story... *The story should be told. And you're the one to do it. I know exactly the approach to take. It will be fiction, but true. A core of reality surrounded by a shell of make believe.*

At the time I thought that sounded kind of cool.

I had used the Santa Barbara address, months ago.

Silence.

Well, it had been a gamble. It could all very well be fantasy. She was quite capable of fabricating the entire, as she liked to say, "Epic saga of lust, loneliness, beauty, evil, death, insanity, and money. Piles and piles of money."

With a sigh of frustration, I pushed aside the curtains.

City of Fog. The Gray Metropolis.

There were people on the wet sidewalk far below. They looked like Monopoly markers or animated, perfectly detailed chess pieces. If only I could make the pawns do what I want. . .

The hair stood up on the back of my neck. I burst out laughing in the hollow room. I let the curtain drop.

Really should have seen this one coming.

For pity's sake.

I wiped my face. I laughed again and the window fogged.

If I were to make my way to my agent's office at the appointed time, they would of course be glad to see me as always but a little puzzled. Meeting? Gosh, we're not showing anything scheduled. Anyway, great to see you, what have you been up to, let's have lunch!

I tied my robe tight and brushed back my hair, sticky with sweat now.

So, let's see. Did I ever mention the name of my agent in her presence? All those conversations we had over the past two years. I wracked my brain. *Probably.* The efficient, well-spoken young woman who called me at home, who rushed me into this trip. Had I ever talked to her before? Those calls sure sounded real, the office ambiance in the background.

It was PG. It was her.

Hell yes.

No meeting and no lawyers.

I was sure.

As I stepped onto the cold tiles there was a rustle behind me.

There was now another piece of paper at the bottom of the door. I made sure my robe was completely closed and bent over and picked the thing up.

hey asshole yur fukked it said in pencil so heavy the paper was ripped. **go back to oklahoma while u can hick faggot.**

My heart began to pound. I tried not to show any reaction to those who might at that moment be watching. I put the charming item in my backpack with the other.

Well now.

I looked around the hotel room. A neutral space no longer. Now officially hostile territory along with all of southern California. I made an effort to calm down. I forced myself to stop staring at the bottom of the door. After a minute my pulse stopped thudding in my ears but the storm light through the window reactivated my airline headache.

What fun.

I vetoed a shower. Just get out. I made my way to the coffee shop in the lobby.

There was a small newsstand at the register. One of the tabloids had a familiar face on the front page, in the little corner box they liked for obituaries.

Already, I thought. There she was from about ten years ago. *Mysterious Billionaire Dies*, it read. *What were her last words?*

Gritting my teeth, I bought the thing and ordered coffee. I was alone in the place.

No laptop for me, just a tiny tablet computer I got on Amazon for thirty bucks. When the time comes I trash it with a propane torch, a lesson I learned from PG. The shop's wifi was first rate.

I first looked up the location of the Marea Hotel. Right on the water, of course.

Now the news. I did a quick scan and *whoa*. Social media was lit up like a North Korean state execution. There was the anti-M faction and the pro-M camp and the government-conspiracy underground and the mothership-is-here club.

From M's page on a well-known personal bulletin board site:

"Now u see the result of evil! And all of there acts will come bk to them! Godam bitch !" Flenzer

From a certain photo posting site:

"Check out this whore! Look at that face! Dead at last. DEAD!" Iamnotafraidofyou.

A forum titled 'Die_M_DieDieDie':

"What a relief! Now we will see how deep the rot goes. I am expecting indictments from DOJ any moment. Have they raided her house yet? They need to get going, like fast. That PG is pretty slippery. My inside sources (I would love to tell you) indicate massive operations are spinning up and the target is her compound in Santa Barbara and all her companies and all of that weirdo PG's stuff. Some kind of genius, right? Shit. Everything she's ever done has crashed big time and anyway, well, there's a lot I cannot divulge. Anyone in the Santa Barbara area, click this link to get a map to her house. Go! We need you all there!" Warrior4Peace

A forum titled 'Citizens For Reality':

"This is it, friends. Look. This is hard for me. I can hardly type. I will be getting rather drunk soon as in right now. They are going to ransack everything she ever owned. It will all fall. We all know how much hate there is, we all have experienced something like this. I can't tell you how much I fear for PG. She was always the target. I know she's super rich and all but good God there's an actual army after her now. I would give anything to know what's really happening. Check my blog for updates." NotASusan

I rated the professional troll level to be rather high. Russian and Far East operatives were in full swing. Damn fine compliment, I thought.

M, that gorgeous unknowable woman, woulda loved it all.

As for that newspaper article.

Apparently, there had been an eavesdropper in the hospital room with M and PG. A nurse? A microphone? The wording was deliberately vague.

On her deathbed in the lavish room, M, they breathlessly reported, whispered her final words to PG who reacted with surprise and had then nodded.

Their relationship was hinted at. Friends? Lovers? They seemed to settle on *partners.*

The short article went on to remind the reader that M had been a controversial figure, always in trouble with the government, with the tax people. The exact reasons were never specified, only insinuated. There had been something with the FBI. An investigation? There were no details. Something with the State Department. Something with governments behind the Iron Curtain during the Cold War. And the amazing Hollywood connection going all the way back to the Golden Age.

Wind gusted through the coffee shop and a rack of picture postcards fell off the counter. The world swayed. Suddenly chilled, an abyss had opened up before me. I grabbed my backpack.

In the fresh air I decided to take a drive up the coast.

Perhaps I would run into someone I knew.

The Spring Meeting

There was a snake in the road at the railroad crossing in the sand dunes, a silver and red creature of ancient provenance curled up on the wet pavement. I blinked and it was gone.

I was on the final turn into the parking lot of the hotel *Marea.*

The old hotel, almost lost in its misty stand of eucalyptus a few yards from the ocean, seemed a little threadbare to me but this was probably a calculated effect. The overwrought Italianate style was so confusing. I knew it was larger and much more extensive than it appeared to the casual eye.

There were several secret wings I had heard about. Tucked against the beach, it was a place of serious privacy, conspiracy theories, myths. I also knew it had changed owners recently with the price rumored to be in the forty to forty-five million range. I made a quick mental calculation. PG could buy the ugly joint two hundred fifty times over.

In the gusting wind of a spring rainstorm I stopped under a tall curving palm tree. If there was ever one specific spot that summed up *California,* that old dream America once had, it could have been right here.

Look up. That's the Pacific Ocean in front of you, blue and icy gray. The entire Earth curves away in the scudding clouds and if you point due east there will be nothing but space between your fingertip and Tokyo. You can smell flowers. Even in the rain the breeze is a perfectly balanced phenomenon of warmth and low humidity.

Squint in the dazzling sunlight just peeking through the clouds then walk over and touch it, the *sea.* Raise your wet fingertips to your lips. Cold, salty, seductive, full of secret life. Take ten steps back and catch your heel on the steel tracks embedded in the sand. The *Starlight* passes this way. You are surrounded by palm trees and green ice plant clogged with purple flowers. Then more flowers, flowers everywhere on a spreading verdant hillside gently curving up to where you can see the sun shining down brightly.

Those clouds drifting by are almost close enough to touch, soft and cottony and unthreatening, clouds from a storybook. People in passing vehicles smile and wave. Ramshackle pickups loaded with landscaping gear, sleek silver eurosedans, and bouncy hybrids. From all a quick nod and friendly tip of the hand. Just don't get in their way.

I pulled myself together.

It was unfinished, this sandy lot. There were ragged borders. On the very edge of the continent creation was occurring. This simple Midwestern boy did not belong in such a place, this much I knew, and I was on my guard in the lovely soft light.

Rounding the final curve through the shaggy eucalyptus trees I thought for a second I had stumbled onto a movie set. In the afternoon gloom, there was a spotlight projecting onto the side of the old building and a brace of crooked scaffolding casting spider web shadows over the porte cochere.

Startled, I took my foot off the gas and coasted. For an instant it looked like there was a huge predatory nightmare creature crouched over the building, a creature with bottomless eyes and hungry claws.

I shook my head. I'm the alien here.

A door opened. I saw bright light spilling from a chandelier and a milling crowd of well-dressed people. The door closed.

And there she was.

PG was waiting for me, unsurprisingly, as if she knew exactly when I was arriving. A seemingly slight woman with intense dark eyes. She waved as I drove past. As I walked back, she came down the steps with her hand extended.

"Right on time," she said, barely smiling, as we shook hands. Her voice was tight and feathery. She was wearing a gray skirt and matching top, a black leather jacket, and as always, old blue boating shoes, complete with frayed lace holes. Never any other kind. I remembered: Sperry Top-Siders.

The idea, she had explained once, was to look businesslike and also like you might decide to take off on a run if the mood struck. Or a quick jaunt in your sloop. Maybe to Catalina. Maybe to Hawaii.

Even coming from a funeral. Such was the culture of Silicon Valley where she had spent most of her life.

"Wonderful to see you, PG."

Her smile increased slightly. Her eyes stayed on the ground.

"I was waving for you to stop," she said. "We can leave now. We should get back to M's."

She never had bodyguards. No entourage. No secretary. Just herself.

No purse or, famously, a cellphone. There were some things she simply refused to do.

Like talk to the media.

We silently got in my rental and I turned on the wipers for a moment and turned up the heater. Her perfume was subtle. Michael Kors? PG turned sideways in the seat and tucked up her legs. The Topsiders bumped the transmission handle. She pulled the seat belt across her chest and held it in one hand. She did not fasten it. Just held it.

I turned the heater to full and powered back up the road.

We were on 101 before she said anything.

"Everyone's gone now." Her voice was flinty.

I kept my eyes on the road.

"I'm sorry, PG."

"This won't make any sense to you but the final battle has begun."

In a flash a black Porsche slalomed around us.

I mentally flipped him off and got into the left lane without signaling. Through the blowing trees the dusty old off-ramp came up fast. I braked hard and turned down to the maze of stop signs. She kept talking.

"I have no one else to tell this to. No one in the world. I have as of this morning resigned from the boards of all seven corporations. You know the names. My life here is over."

She let her head rest against the back of the seat. She looked incredibly young and vibrant and immensely tired. Her eyes were as disconcertingly intelligent as ever. Active. Searching.

"Turn left here. Then about a half mile and turn right on Johnson."

The drizzle turned to rain. The kind of slow, end-of-winter rain that lasted for days in these parts. The wipers slapped.

"I see you have your notebook," she said after a moment in the jostling car. She sounded more relaxed now. We passed a nursery full of palm trees in pots.

"Is it okay?"

"Yes. Are you ready?"

"What's going to happen?"

"Better if you see it. There should be a record."

It was as if we had just been talking yesterday. My theory is that PG can save the state of any conversation, retrieve it on demand, and restart seamlessly, weeks or months later. Awesome skill for business. Combine that with her near-mythical ability to make people feel at ease. And her smile, well, I knew just the word. *Kind.* You would very much look forward to a meeting with PG. You would love for meetings and phone conversations to just keep going and going.

Call it the PG Factor.

"We are creatures who want things," she said into the noisy interior. "I want to tell this to someone. You want to hear it. At least that's what you said before. Will you write a book, you think?"

"If I do, it will be completely fictionalized. Dates. Towns. All that. Absolutely no last names."

"Oh, I'm not worried. I trust you," she said. "And maybe fiction is a good way to go. Even though I know nothing about writing it seems to me, now that I think about it, you can get more insight into people that way. Am I right?"

"It's work but it's possible."

"Yes. Assuming one is capable of being insightful. Do you consider yourself to be insightful?"

She was curled up in the seat like a kitten and she had a playful expression but she was not playing.

"I like to think," I said in as steady a voice as I could, "that I am capable..."

"Say yes."

"Yes."

"I thought so. I bet it would work as a novel," she said.

I stopped for a red light.

"I had the idea it might work as a novel."

"We're on the same page. See, you have good ideas."

"It just came to me. That happens a lot to writers."

"The good writers. You're a good one. What type of audience might this novel have?"

Green light. I made the turn. It gave me a moment to think.

"Novels don't have audiences. They have readers," I said.

"Ah."

"One book, one reader."

She smiled. "Very good." She let go of the seatbelt. "Keep going up this way. The road will get narrow."

Johnson Street began going seriously uphill. Then it got steeper. And then so steep I couldn't understand how they were able to pave it. Chaparral began to scrape the car doors and branches of overgrown eucalyptus trees, drooping with rain, slapped the roof. The narrow slit of sky above was unbroken gray.

"It took us a long time to get the road this way."

"It's like this on purpose?" The road leveled off and the sagebrush and mesquite grew thicker.

"Oh, everything's on purpose. Watch out."

A man carrying a dining room chair in each hand appeared in the rain-blurred windshield. He turned sideways to give us more room. He looked like the gardener. The chairs looked like Ethan Allen.

"Hmm," PG said. "Now, your mysterious readers. How do you visualize them?"

"Well, my readers are diverse. They have one thing in common, however. They are very smart. Brainy."

"Really."

"Yep. It's a safe assumption they're smarter than me. So I have to do the work. I have to do a good job."

"Interesting. We're almost there. Go slow."

Foot off the gas, we came to a blind curve in the dark chaparral and there was movement in the trees. People. Heads turned towards us. I slowed the car to a crawl.

People stood in a circle, backs to each other. There were seven, four women, three men. Their faces registered anger, shock, and grief. One woman was openly weeping. Tall, blonde, about PG's age.

A guy in a Cathartt jacket banged out of the front door with a heavy item on a dolly. Looked like a water heater. A man with white hair was prying out one of the front windows.

PG had her door open before I could stop.

The people saw her and broke out of the circle and formed a line. I hung back. PG went to each in turn, shook their hands and hugged them. Then she went into M's house, walking around a guy dragging out a large rolled-up rug down the mahogany steps.

The seven people swiveled their heads and stared hard at me. I tried to stand straighter and decided that hiding behind the car was lame. I stepped out into the open. Their eyes followed every move I made. They were not from the hotel, the funeral. It was their clothes. They looked like they'd been up all night. Not happy to see me, either.

"Who are you?" It was the woman who had been weeping.

"I'm just an observer."

"Are you a journalist?" said a woman in a tight black jacket and I could hear the sneer. Short black hair, commanding blue eyes. Those eyes did not blink.

I was careful with my words.

"No, ma'am. I worked as a reporter for a while right out of college but I have never been a journalist."

It's possible the tiniest conceivable smile crossed her face. The thin fellow beside her brushed back his gray hair and nodded.

M's front door banged open again and PG appeared dragging a chest of drawers, foot high, two feet long, and so heavy she could only lift one end. I ran and picked up the other end. White oak and simple brass hardware, perhaps fifty pounds. A sizeable jewelry box from an earlier era. We set it on the gravel.

"He's all right," PG said. The group seemed to relax a bit.

She opened the top of the box. It unfolded in a clever telescoping way. I saw necklaces. Pearls glowed in the dusky light. Silver and gold chains, emeralds and rubies in large settings. There was a double handful of them.

PG removed each of the eight drawers and set them on the ground. Bracelets, brooches, and pins. Watches. Two drawers were jammed with rings, more silver and gold.

PG picked up one of the rings, kissed it, and put it deep in her jacket pocket.

I bent close.

"I just need to see," I said.

"Go ahead," PG said. "Take whatever you want."

I kept my hands to myself.

One drawer contained four neat rows of large gold coins but the final drawer was startling. It took me a moment to figure out what I was seeing.

It was full of diamonds. Loose, tumbling, sparkling diamonds, none smaller than a marble. A few looked a half inch in diameter. PG stirred them with her finger and touched a concealed latch. The front of the drawer hinged down and all the diamonds spilled brightly onto the wet sand.

A secret compartment popped open. PG took out a bundle of what looked like credit cards bound with a rubber band. She handed it to the tall blonde woman who did not look at it.

"She remembered all of you. And all this." PG half turned. "Goodbye."

I caught her expression and followed her to the side of the house.

At the back corner where copper rain pipes converged she pushed open a wooden gate and we stepped under the fragrant branches of a flowering orange tree.

The back of the house was a wide grass lawn stretching before a long six-bay garage. Wood framed, white siding, kind of a nineteen twenties look. Five of the garage doors were open. There were vehicles inside. The sixth bay, wider than the others, remained closed.

PG walked quickly to the open garage doors.

"You didn't take anything," she said.

"No, ma'am."

She nodded.

We got to the first open door. There was a black Mercedes two-seater inside.

"I want to ask a favor of you."

"Sure. Anything."

"You might find it difficult, this favor. But first let me explain what's happening." Her voice was less strained now. "We have very little time. All of M's assets are being distributed. Before the sun rises tomorrow everything must be destroyed. It has to be this way. The men in the house are the craftsmen who built it. I wanted them to have the chance to get their items back if they wished. Most did not. The people in the group are the CEOs and presidents of M's companies. All privately owned. These companies are being." She searched for the word. This was unlike her. "Transitioned. This is in addition to her personal accounts. Banks. Brokerages."

"I see. One question, if I may. Were those real diamonds?"

"Oh yes. All flawless. They have an interesting history."

Something passed over us, invisible in the clouds. Something that buzzed like angry hornet. PG didn't seem to notice.

"And what you took from that drawer?" I also wanted to ask about the ring but right then decided not to.

"Just their personal inheritances filtered through other companies in certain Gulf states. Basically debit cards. Ten million each."

She smiled at my raised eyebrows.

"Now about that favor."

"Yes, ma'am."

"What kind of car do you have again, back home?"

I could tell she was bothered by not being able to remember.

"Nineteen ninety-seven Subaru," I said.

"And how many miles on it?"

"Four hundred eighty-eight thousand."

"That is *excellent*."

"It is an exceptional car."

She waved down the row of open doors.

"Mercedes. Nissan GT-R. Jeep. That was hers. I'm the speed demon."

The Grand Cherokee looked several years older than the others. And each garage bay had its own workbench and rolling tool box. And a collection of specialized front end tools, a compressor, and hydraulic engine lift.

"My usual vehicle lately."

A red Corvette. Then the last, a midnight blue Tesla.

"They are all going to whoever wants them. Paper work's on the front seat with the keys. I know you need a car. You can have whichever one you want but as a favor to me I'd like you to take the one that's in here."

The final garage bay had a different construction. Steel I-beams and concrete walls that looked bomb proof. The door was riveted steel plate.

"Sure, PG, thank you." I admit I gaped. What could possibly be in there? Something incredibly valuable.

"Remember I said it might be difficult."

She was looking at me with concern now.

"All right, no problem. Go ahead."

She turned to the blank concrete wall and raised both her hands to chest level, palms out. She moved her hands in a circle, synchronized, then independently. She made a fist with her right hand and letters with her left. I saw an 'A' and a 'C.'

Gesture recognition. A motor whined and a section of the concrete wall withdrew and slid down. There had been no visible seam. Behind it a large monitor glowed into life. PG put both hands flat out and the screen went dark.

"One more test. It will show two numbers then the operation."

There was an electronic tone and a ten or twelve digit number appeared. It was immediately replaced by another which then vanished. The word *Multiply* filled the screen and then a keypad. It all went by too fast for me to even count the number of digits.

PG tapped numbers into the touch screen. I shook my head. This was part of the legend and I was actually seeing it.

A much larger motor rumbled somewhere above.

"Thanks. A problem only PG could solve."

"Not anymore. They have a free app." She rubbed her forehead.

"They?"

A voice issued from a speaker bolted to the concrete. Female voice, clear and almost humorous.

"*Welcome back, PG.*"

"Thank you, Tess. How has everything been?"

"*No intrusions.*"

"Very good. Tess, open the door, please. Then I will be saying goodbye."

"*Opening.*" There was a pause. "*Do you really mean goodbye, PG?*"

"Yes, Tess. This is goodbye."

I heard more heavy relays activating.

"*All comm links have been severed. Purging sensor logs and buffers. All data is now erased. Checking. All volumes empty.*"

"Thank you, Tess. Goodbye."

"*Goodbye, PG,*" Tess said. "*God be with you.*"

The hair stood up on the back of my neck.

PG reached into the bay and disengaged a small object. It had been embedded into the concrete like a mounting bolt. It was the size of a ball point pen. She brought it up to her eyes and then dropped it. She stepped on it and ground it under her shoe.

I had to see. I got to my knees.

There was a smear of particles on the cement floor. I touched them and there was a glint.

"Glass," I said.

My voice was drowned out by the sound of a large motor. I pushed myself off the ground. The final garage door began to slowly lever up. It was at least a foot thick. We both stepped around to the front.

I saw what was in there. A car. PG beamed at me.

"Sapphire, actually. Tess is fine. That was just one of her interfaces. Now, what do you think?"

The garage was open before me. There was a car. Um.

"Well now," I said. "Look at that. It's red. A red Volkswagen Beetle."

The old car had a faded, weathered paint job. I could feel PG looking at me.

"Ah," I said. "*That* is a nineteen sixty-seven. That much I know."

"Right." She sounded impressed.

"I can tell by the taillights." That GT-R was right back there. Oh well. "Sixty-seven VW. This is a classic, PG."

"Yes."

"Your car from college, I bet. You kept it exactly the same."

"Mostly. Changed a few things under the hood." She pulled the keys from her jacket and held them out to me. "I want you to have it."

"Ma'am, it's too much."

"You're probably the only person in the world who understands. And I can't keep it." The true weight of the events of the past few days was suddenly present in her face.

I took the keys.

"Let's go get your things from that rental and then we'll go someplace where we can talk."

I looked down. The rear bumper was badly bent in, a big punch right in the center. The mounting brackets were both sprung. There was rust under the crumpled chrome. Long time ago.

"Got hit pretty good there."

"Yep."

"And you never fixed it?"

'Nope." She grinned and for a moment I saw twenty year old Gabrielle away from home for the first time and astonished by the world. "I'll tell you later."

I opened the driver's door. "Let's see now." Interior smelled clean and new. I clambered in, tight fit no matter what, right. I pulled the lever and the seat slid back as far as it would go. Vinyl looked original. My knees stuck up. Just deal with it. I adjusted the tiny rear view mirror and scanned the dash. Big round speedometer. 71222 on the odometer. Pull-out knobs for headlights and wipers. And the radio. Original AM with chrome buttons. *Sapphire* by Motorola. That right there was a collector's item.

PG got in next to me.

"You know how it works?"

"We might not have very many super-duper electric cars in Oklahoma but we do have VW Bugs. You could say we know value in automobiles."

"The key goes there."

"Yes, ma'am," I said, not really sure of anything. OK, don't screw up, I thought.

Clutch in, stick in neutral. Pull choke out. Pump the pedal? Negative. PG's car would not have a crap carb. Switch on. Gas gauge needle twitched.

Hit the starter. *Whoa.*

Damn engine fired up instantly and she laughed at my reaction. Nice and smooth and high pitched. I knew the procedure. I pushed the choke in halfway. RPMs moderated.

"Perfect," she said with an appreciative nod. "Think you can find reverse?"

Motor had a wasp-like sound and it jumped at the slightest touch of my shoe on the pedal.

"Of course. Done this before."

Oh please don't grind the gears, I thought. Concentrate.

Clutch all the way in. I waggled the stick. Clutch? *All* the way in. Push stick to right. Hit the stop. Check clutch: Still in. Deep breath. Push stick against stop, good spring tension, then final clutch check. Status: IN. Now *do it.* Stick down and to the right, yeah, I could feel it. Sucker went into reverse with a snap.

"Slicker'n snot." I exhaled.

"What? You did it!"

Now, I thought, in the potent contralto tone of the engine, back the car out of the garage. Very. Slowly.

"Come on, let's go." PG bounced on her seat.

I placed my foot on the gas and sent the RPMs soaring and I yelled silently. *Careful!* I eased out the clutch and the car rolled backwards. I got the feel of it. Super sensitive accelerator. But.

"You're doing fine."

"Just a little nervous."

We rolled over the rain soaked lawn and went around the front of the house. The group of CEOs was gone. The jewelry box, the drawers, and contents, also gone. I did want to comb the gravel for loose diamonds but I kept going.

At my rental, I got my backpack and tossed it on the backseat. She eyed it closely. Approvingly, I thought.

There was a line of contractor's trucks on the hill. A man was moving a leather sofa on a small wheeled platform. A loud metallic pounding came from the house. It sounded like the plumbing was being stripped out.

PG looked straight ahead.

As we made our way down the main drive, lined with cars and pickups, PG seemed to unclench a little. The house vanished behind the dripping trees. We were free.

She never looked back.

As we slowly wound our way down the narrow street, I told PG about the little snake in the road at the hotel.

She looked at me sharply. "M would have been impressed. The snake is the symbol of immortality." She sat up straighter. "Perhaps it is a sign the gods have smiled upon your endeavors."

"Does it matter which god?"

"Yes it does."

Santa Barbara at sundown. Drivers were acting angry at the rain, offended by wet pavement. The VW's wipers ticked back and forth like a metronome.

"I don't like this town very much. Sorry."

Traffic was fairly light it seemed to me which was good because I was still getting the hang of the VW. The thing had *torque.* I kept chirping the tires, slamming us back in the seats. Since when do old Beetles do that? Whatever it was, PG was getting a kick of my attempt to drive it. Our shoulders kept bumping.

"It is now about five o'clock. Later, at midnight, we will go back to M's, and you will see just what this place is really like. I know you're getting impatient, but just one more thing."

"I'm not impatient. I am very curious."

"Well, I feel very relaxed with you. I like your curiosity. Despite what you probably think about me, I could take you back to that hotel and spend the next two weeks screwing your brains out. But I'm a virgin. Amazing, huh? I'm a virgin for life."

I let the windshield wipers fill in the silence for a moment. I wanted to protest about what I thought about her, but I said, "Two weeks?"

"Yep."

"You do know how to make it hard for a guy to concentrate on shifting."

For some reason this made her laugh so hard she almost slid out of the seat.

We made another side trip.

At the McDonald's drive-through she got French fries and one of their small apple pies in a cardboard sleeve.

"This is what I had all the time in college," she said around the fries. "I was always so hungry. I loved fast food. My complexion was terrible. When I taste the fries and the apple pie, which is *really* hot, when I taste them together, I can somehow remember that time just perfectly. This is *so* good."

Our destination was a small donut shop in a deserted shopping center. Puddles of water in the old parking lot reflected neon signs, traffic lights, the last patch of blue sky. We were the only customers in the place. Smelled like fresh bread, cinnamon, and sugar. Smelled good. We got coffee.

I knew I would get a few hours. She would tell me what she wanted to tell me and then I would be kicked back out in the cold.

But it was all right. Knew what I was doing.

I got out my pencil.

The Time of Having Friends

PG said: *"My memory isn't as good as it used to be. I've noticed distortions creeping in. I will get some things wrong here.*

"I'm sure the mansions I visited were probably not really as huge and wondrous as I remember them. The sun probably wasn't as bright, the wind as sharp, or the rain as dramatic. And perhaps even the snowy footprints were just a kind of dream. I can still hardly believe that snow.

"But one thing I don't doubt. I hold them inviolate in my memory.

"Once upon a time when I was very young my friends and I went Christmas shopping. I was home from college.

"Barbara had a cute turned-up nose and held my left arm. Linda was tall and had gorgeous blonde hair. Her arm was around my waist."

It was the day after Thanksgiving. The air was dry and full of electricity. The previous night there had been rings around the moon and the warm wind had knocked trash cans off curbs all across the San Gabriel Valley.

Three young women, arm in arm, crossed the north parking lot of the Eastland Shopping Center as the sun disappeared behind the trees along Citrus Avenue. Rivulets of brilliant amber light streamed across the tops of hundreds of dusty cars.

"I can't see," said the one in the middle. "No matter where I look the sun's in my eyes."

"Don't worry, we got you," said Linda. "In fact, we love you."

"We love Gabrielle like nobody's business," said Barbara. "Okay, step up here!"

They both lifted Gabrielle up onto the sidewalk.

The store had one the new designs. Blank exterior walls pierced by glass doors filled with fluorescent light. Just inside, there was a large Christmas tree saturated with bright white bulbs. Behind it they could see a large crowd milling around.

"Boy, look at that," said Linda.

"Just a few people," said Barbara. "I mean, a few thousand."

They detached from each other and entered the store. It smelled of hot electronics, pine trees, and human sweat. Linda's hand lingered on Gabrielle's arm for a moment.

"I'm over here," she said.

Barbara took off for the record department which was full of high schoolers, most of them boys wearing plaid shirts with the sleeves rolled up. The few girls there had on tight jeans and either t-shirts or white, frilly peasant-style tops.

Gabrielle was surprised how little she wanted to go over there.

Muted Christmas music, *Holly Jolly Christmas,* played tastefully behind the chatter of the wall of television sets. They were all tuned to *Eyewitness News.*

There was a crowd gathered around something in the back corner, maybe something new and interesting. A bright light came on over it.

"Let's go see what that is." Gabrielle stood on her tip toes.

"I have to find something for my mom," Linda said with a sigh. Then she was off towards the small electronics department, all the male heads turning in her direction, as usual.

"Okay. I'll be over here," Gabrielle said as Linda disappeared into the echoing store.

Gabrielle didn't have to check to know exactly how much money she had. Seven dollars. Seven dollars for Christmas. There was nothing in the huge store she could buy for her mother. Maybe a pack of gum at the register. A magazine. Or, she thought, I could make her something. Make her a Christmas card like a little kid. Here, Mom, Merry Christmas.

Suddenly, Gabrielle really wanted to leave. But she wandered to the back of the store where the excited crowd milled. It smelled like sweat and overheated dust.

There was a device on a pedestal illuminated by a high-intensity spotlight. Large, shiny, and flat, it looked like a bulky turntable with a chrome cover. The sign said it was a video disc player. People in heavy coats bent close and whispered. A machine that played movies? Real movies? A small boy in a Dodgers hat reached out and pushed one of the silver rectangular buttons on the slim face of it. His mother yanked him back.

Well, Gabrielle thought, *this* is more like it.

She slipped through the crowd.

The video disc itself on a display stand was as big as a dinner plate and absolutely beautiful. Silvery and iridescent, an amazing artifact from the fantastic future.

She looked around for Linda. She wanted Linda to see it. But Linda was on the far side of the store searching for the right radio-cassette tape player.

Gabrielle got as close as she could and peered into the small plastic window in the top of the player where the disc went. Maybe she could see the laser. No, it wasn't plugged in. Or maybe it's just a mock-up.

She realized there was someone standing on the other side of the display, a woman who had just walked up. They both noticed each other at the same moment.

"That's not for sale," the woman said.

She is maybe in her thirties, I don't know, Gabrielle thought, and very nice looking. Short blonde hair. Dark blue turtleneck sweater. New jeans, almost black. No make-up that she can see.

"You into movies?" she asks. The woman studied Gabrielle's face closely. "Eighteen hundred dollars seems like a lot of money just to watch a movie in your living room."

"Oh, no, I don't care about movies very much. I like electronics."

"You're kidding. A cute young lady like you? Electronics?"

"I'm majoring in electronic engineering. Up there."

"Up?" A bright flicker of attention crossed her face.

Gabrielle named a small college town on the central coast. "I really like it."

"Yes." The woman smiled to herself for an instant. "It's so beautiful there. Pretty far from home, though." she said, still looking at Gabrielle intently.

"I hardly notice. Too busy."

"Too busy with all the engineering," she said, nodding. "Of electronics. Speaking of which, this contraption here. Care to give me your professional opinion?"

"It's interesting."

"Yes." She rolled her eyes a little, still smiling. Then she had an idea. "Tell me about, you know, the innards. The electronic parts. How it works."

"Oh, the whole thing will be obsolete really soon. I mean, it's analog. Analog video."

"You're not serious. Analog? Good lord."

Gabrielle saw the mischievous look in her eyes and laughed. "Yes, the whole thing's kind of a kludge."

"A what?"

"Rube Goldberg. Like a quick fix."

"Oh. I get it." She gave the player a hard look. "Huh. But it does work, apparently. Even if it is soon to be obsolete analog."

Gabrielle shrugged. "I suppose so."

"Could you explain something, if you don't mind?"

"I'd love to."

"You love talking about technical things, right?"

"Oh, yes. I hardly ever get the chance. No one cares."

"Well, I care. You can call me M, by the way."

"M?"

Her smile increased as Gabrielle said her name. "Just M."

"Gabrielle," she said and held out her hand.

They shook hands. M's hand was thin and strong and the skin of her palm was soft. M's eyes were a dark blue with a little green around the edges and her short blonde hair, kind of a sandy blonde, curled around her ears in a way that seemed perfect. And she was wearing perfume which Gabrielle thought was amazingly sophisticated.

Gabrielle realized she had looked a bit too long and looked down, shyly. M, she noticed, did the same thing. They both spent an instant looking at each other's shoes. Gabrielle turned her right foot away so the ripped fabric on the edge of her old Topsiders wasn't so obvious.

"Anyway," M said, "my question, um. I forgot what I was going to say."

"About something technical?"

"Yes, yes," she said and smiled. "What was that word?"

Gabrielle smiled now. "Kludge?"

"No, I got that one all right. Started with an *a*."

"Analog?"

"Yes. It's what makes this thing a kludge, right? Love kludge, by the way. Great word."

"Analog is like the groove on a record. The audio signal is recorded as a wavy groove in a piece of plastic. It takes all this delicate equipment to play back the signal and turn it into sound again."

"Yes, and that's analog?"

"The groove in the plastic is physically analogous to the sound. Analog means the signal is a voltage or current that varies over time. It's subject to noise and interference. Dust. And it degrades easily. Like the way a record can get scratched. What you want is a system with no moving parts."

"That makes sense."

"Really?"

"I have no idea how you could play movies without any moving parts." Her eyes were now more friendly than amused. "But I'm definitely understanding most of what you're saying. So this thing plays television the same way a record player plays music."

"Pretty much. Except instead of a needle it uses a laser beam shooting through the disc."

"So an actual laser is in this? And you can have it in your house?" She seemed genuinely impressed. "I know they call it a laser disc player but I just assumed it was the usual hype."

"Well, it's kind of small. The laser, I mean."

"I should hope so. The whole thing sounds way too complicated. I can see why the price was so high."

"It's complicated if you have to work on it. Probably fairly easy to use."

"Good. Because I just bought it." Her blue eyes sparkled in the dull, noisy store.

"You... really?"

"Uh huh. They didn't want to sell it, either. This is one of only three in all of L.A. It's a prototype. They're probably afraid the company will get mad at them. So I just shoved money in their faces. I mean, they're a business, right?"

"Well, yeah."

"So this," she brushed a speck of dust from the player, "is mine. They're supposed to bring out a box for it. And all the wires, too. Whatever they are." M regarded the mass of red, white, yellow, and black cables emanating from the rear of the thing.

"I just had an idea. How would you like to make some money?"

"Money?"

"Yeah, like a job. Help me set this baby up. I mean, look at all this." She threaded her fingers through the wires and shuddered as if it were a nest of snakes. "How do you connect this to a tv set? I sure couldn't do it. What's more, my tv is different than the run of the mill. The manager offered to send a guy to my house but I'd rather have you do it by a long shot. I'll bet this would be a cinch for you."

"I guess so."

"Sure. And it wouldn't take very long. Just an hour at most. I'll pay you seventy-five dollars. Just in time for Christmas."

"Okay." *Wow*, she thought.

"Is that enough? It has to cover your gas. It's kind of a drive from here, I mean, where are we, Covina? I'll write out directions. You sure?"

"I'm sure."

"Good." She said comfortably and pointed. "You, I trust."

Gabrielle felt herself blush. M, she saw, pretended not to notice.

"Hey Mike," M said to the overweight, middle-aged man coming out of an office door. "I already have someone to help with the set up. But thanks for the offer."

"Sure, M. Whatever you want." He was tired looking and red-faced, as if he had been yelling at someone. His clothes were wrinkled. He was looking at M with a mixture of eagerness to please and exasperation.

M, on the other hand, seemed mildly amused. "And make sure the box has plenty of padding," she said. "A kludge needs a lot of padding."

"A what? No, no, this isn't a kludge. I told you all about it. It's state of the art. How'd you know what a kludge is?"

"Mike, do you really think I have no technical knowledge? Come on." She shook her head. "Mike."

"Yes?"

"The box. I do have to get going."

"We're still looking for it," Mike said, and hurried back into the office.

M smiled at Gabrielle and patted the player.

"Well this," she said, "is going to be fun."

They got in Barbara's car, a perfectly clean white Buick that belonged to her mother, and headed for Gabrielle's house, Linda riding shotgun,

Gabrielle in the back seat. She liked to scrunch in the gap between the two front seats. She found the green glow of the instruments to be comforting. The car had a digital clock right above the air conditioning vents. When it reached the end of an hour, which it did, 6:59, right then, they all stopped talking and watched the blue-green fluorescent numbers change.

Linda used the pause to bring it up.

"That lady you were talking to."

"Uh huh."

"What was that?"

"She bought that big video disc player and I'm going to her house to help set it up."

"Video?" Linda said. "Disc?"

"You're going to her house?" Barbara said.

"Yep. She's going to pay me seventy-five dollars."

"Dang, that's pretty good. Where is this," Barbara asked as they stopped for the light at Badillo, "that you're going?"

"Up in Pasadena. I have the directions."

"Pasadena? Like where in Pasadena. Up in the hills?"

"I think so. Above there. I'll have to check my mom's *Thomas Guide*."

"Gabrielle," Linda said. "That lady."

The lights bordering the marquee for the Covina Theater flashed across Linda's face. A lot of the bulbs were burned out. Teenagers in bulky coats waited in groups in front of the ticket booth. *Every Which Way But Loose* and *Heaven Can Wait*.

"I think she thinks you're cute."

"I'm not cute."

Barbara shook her head. "You are cute as a bug."

"My cheeks are fat."

"You have a round face."

"I have pimples. Including this one on my nose."

"Such imperfections only accentuate your innate cuteness."

"I," Gabrielle said and waited for Linda to stop laughing, "have to wear glasses."

"Glasses are sexy," Linda said.

"They are?"

"If you're cute they are," Barbara said. They waited at School Street. "Because they draw attention to your cuteness. Oh, and your tits are amazing."

"Yes, they are," Linda said. "And that lady seemed like she liked you."

"I know."

Barbara stopped for a light.

"She's a little older. Very attractive."

"Honey," Linda said. "We know all about you. We know you don't like boys."

"I like boys."

"You don't like to touch boys."

"Well... I don't like to touch anyone."

"Really? That's good," Barbara said.

"It is?" Linda said.

"Her tragic avoidance of human contact will protect her. Ironic."

"I guess." Linda shook her head.

"Oh, come on. I'm not like that."

Barbara grinned as they rolled over railroad tracks.

"Have you ever had an orgasm?"

"A what?"

"Oh my *God*," Linda exclaimed.

"*You* know," Barbara said. They were passing tract houses with brightly lit windows. She made a right, then left. Most of the houses had large, spreading trees in the generous front yards. "That feeling you get. When you feel it."

Linda was almost choking with laughter. "Oh! I feel it!"

"I didn't know that's what they were called," Gabrielle said, raising her voice a bit. Both of them were laughing now. "I've never heard that word before. Sue me."

"So what got you off?" Barbara said.

"Barbara!" Linda said in amazement.

"No, it's all right," Gabrielle said. "I remember. It was that tv show. *The Avengers*. Sundays on channel nine at four o'clock. I was watching it in my room. You know that actress?"

"*The Avengers*? Um," Linda said. "The British lady. Mrs. Peel? I like that show."

"Right. Mrs. Peel. She was in this all leather suit thing, whatever you call it, all leather from head to toe, and she was jumping around and doing karate type moves. And I really liked it. So I started doing the same moves there in my bedroom. And I kept doing it. And..."

"And?" Barbara said.

"And it happened."

Linda turned around. "You felt the feeling? That you felt?"

"I guess so."

Barbara turned left onto a short cul-de-sac which ran alongside the train tracks. She nearly hit the curb because she was laughing so hard and stopped in front of Gabrielle's house. There were no lights on. Gabrielle's mother worked a second job part-time in the evenings at a department store. She would not be home until midnight. The day after Thanksgiving was getting to be a very busy shopping day. In the warm, idling car, Linda turned all the way around in the seat.

"We don't care if you get off on girls. We just don't think it's a good idea for you to go to this stranger's house by yourself," Linda said.

"I don't get off on girls."

"Oh, we didn't think that, did we, Barbara?"

"Of course not, Linda," Barbara said.

"Look, all that. It's not for me," Gabrielle said, looking at the dark street. "I'm fine by myself. I don't need anyone."

"When you see a couple walking together, you know," Barbara said, "holding hands. What do you feel?"

"That will never be me."

"It might be," Linda said.

"I'm just not a part of that. All that luvie-dovie stuff."

"But." Linda said.

"I have my own world. It's fine."

"You mean school?" Barbara said.

"Yes. I'm a whole year ahead. It's exciting."

"If you say so."

"I'm fine."

"Well, we know how smart you are," Barbara said.

"Promise us you'll be careful if you go to this house," Linda said.

"I promise."

"Your mom will have a *cow.*"

In her front yard, the leafless skeletal branches of the liquid amber tree whipped in the chill wind against the gray sky. Gabrielle let the warm air from the dash heater vent blow over her face

"I'm not going to tell her. I have no intention of making her worry about nothing. I'll leave Sunday night, as usual, go up to this place and do the little job, get paid seventy-five bucks, and then take off from there. It's easy now that the 134 goes all the way through to the 101."

She shivered and pulled her sweatshirt tight.

"If I get to school really late it doesn't matter because my first class on Mondays isn't until one. And it's just a literature class they make you take. Early American writers like Walt Whitman. Nothing to it."

"It still sounds pretty weird," Barbara said. "I mean, who else is there at this house? Is it like the *Aadam's Family*? Will Lurch be there to take your coat?"

"I didn't ask. Probably no one."

"I like Walt Whitman," Linda said. "Run at the first sign of trouble.."

"I will."

"No, be paranoid," Barbara said. "Like, leave the car running so you can make a quick getaway.

"It'll be okay."

She opened the door and got out. The warmth instantly evaporated in the cold dry electric air. She closed the door with a solid thump.

Linda rolled down her window. "I'll call you tomorrow."

"Sure, bye."

Her friends waved as they left. Neither one, she noticed, had volunteered to go with her. Take a second car, maybe.

It was just as well, she thought. They were pulling away from each other like all her high school friends.

"High school was years ago," she said.

Leaves blew across the walkway. She made a mental note to rake the yard in the morning, in addition to the list of fix-it jobs she already wanted to take care of for her mom before leaving.

In the dark silent house, Gabrielle checked the fridge. A couple slices of pumpkin pie sat on a plate covered in plastic wrap. Her mother had brought them from work, her regular job at the local school district. Gabrielle didn't touch them. They didn't do Thanksgiving anymore.

She decided to stay up. She did not turn on the tv set. She was completely out of the habit of watching television. She stayed in her room reading the latest *Scientific American* from the school library.

About eleven, she heard her mother's car pull in. A few minutes later, there was a knock on the bedroom door.

"How'd it go, Mom?"

Her mother, tired around the eyes but otherwise maintaining with that burst of adrenaline that comes from staying up late, said "Promise me, Gabrielle."

"Okay."

"You'll graduate and get a good job so you won't have to do this."

"I promise. I already talked to a guy in the placement office. Did I tell you?"

Her mother kicked off her shoes. "Ah," she said. "Placement office?"

"Yep. There's a possibility of a summer job with Intel."

"Intel. Never heard of it."

"They make computer stuff."

"Good. Maybe they'll replace me with a computer. I'm going to take a shower and go to bed, sweetie. Intel, whoever they are, sounds terrific."

"Tomorrow's Saturday. You can sleep in." She thought her mother looked great, like she had just fought a battle and won big.

"Oh, I fully intend to sleep in," her mom said. "Probably til next year. Good night, smart girl."

Her house felt snug and secure around her. The floorboards creaked in the familiar way under her mother's feet. The pipes in the walls thumped when the shower came on. The back door rattled in the fading Santa Ana. When she turned off the desk lamp, the streetlight out front found the gaps in her curtains and spread bars of orange light across her bed covers. Like always.

But it wasn't home anymore. They had got on after her father died. Close to three years now. She remembered long days and evenings in hospital waiting rooms. The constant smell of disinfectant and the fluorescent lights and the hushed voices of nurses and other people like her waiting in the same place. Waiting for good news which they knew would not come in a cancer ward but they waited for it anyway.

You get on. You just have to.

She waved to her mother Sunday evening as another storm rolled across southern California. In the red slashing light, her mom made a quick wave back and went inside. They no longer needed long goodbyes. She would be back before too long, anyway. Fall quarter was just about over. There were only two weeks left until finals, then Christmas break. Almost a month off. And she fully intended to get a holiday job in that very mall she had just visited.

She shifted into second and turned left on Lark Ellen.

Gabrielle knew the house was no longer home for her mom. She can't wait to get out of there, she thought. She's waiting for me to finish school and move on. Then she will be able to put it behind her. All this. And she will leave too.

She turned north on Citrus and headed for the 210. Her car growled. I don't want to put my dad behind me, she thought. I don't want my mom to leave.

She ran a stop sign, speed shifted, and veered onto the westbound freeway. She slammed the stick into third and quickly found fourth. She pressed the gas pedal to the floor.

Okay, she thought as the engine roared. Pasadena. Let's do this silly little job. Because I need the money.

The little car bounced down the concrete lanes. The four cylinder engine was smooth and powerful. The slip of paper M's directions was tucked under her jacket on the passenger seat. She had no need to look at it again.

"Barbara was right. This *is* pretty weird. Well, get in and get out quick, I guess."

But she found she was curious.

She stayed on the 210 as it wound through Pasadena and curved north.

The note said: *"Now go a ways up Angeles Crest until you pass an old gas station with no windows, then start looking for Lupine Lane on your left. Turn in there, go about half a mile, then left again on Pine Ridge. My driveway is pretty close. You'll see two stone posts with big brass balls on top. Press the button and the gate will open. Just come on in."*

As it became full-on night, Gabrielle passed the old gas station, a dirty white building with black smears on the walls. All the windows had been broken out. As she rolled by, she thought she saw something move in one of the empty black rectangles. Her Volkswagen was buffeted and she gripped the wheel.

Just the wind, she thought. I'm sure that was it.

Lupine Lane appeared and she whipped the car left without slowing down.

The road went up and she downshifted. In her headlights the vegetation went from foothill scrub of sage and Manzanita to small evergreens. Pinyon pine and then much taller trees. Fir trees, her father would have called them.

The road leveled off and the lights of La Cañada and Eagle Rock shone through the branches. There were no other houses she could see and no lights at all in the hills. It was easy to find Pine Ridge. It was the only other road, hemmed in by the large trees. She kept the car in second and glided left again. She noticed she was driving alongside a fence now. Welded steel tubing eight feet high, camouflaged by the brush. And it seemed to be topped by what looked like barbed wire.

She let her foot slip off the clutch.

There they were, ash white against the dark woods. Two massive posts of rough-chiseled granite. And there was a shiny metal sphere atop each one the size of a beach ball. That's copper, not brass, she thought. A heck of a lot of copper.

Gabrielle stopped well short of the drive. She could see the gate. More tubular steel, with signs wired to it. Large plastic signs with big letters.

No Trespassing. Keep Out. No Parking. If you are reading this the police have already been called. And if it wasn't obvious, *Get Lost.*

The curving drive beyond the gate was marked by glowing lights in fixtures close to the ground. The branches of the trees swayed in the surging wind. She could see something through the dense stand of trees. The edge of a roof. There was a soft light there, an upper window.

Well, I did come all this way, she thought. Now I'll have to get gas in Santa Barbara for sure. And it's fifty-five cents a gallon there.

She had twenty-six dollars and thirty-five cents. (Her mom had slipped her a twenty.) This had to cover gas and food for the next three weeks, until she came home again for Christmas break. After that, because her December rent was already paid, all she had to worry about were the school fees for winter quarter – which she could cover from her savings account, currently standing at almost two hundred – and rent for January, February, March. And textbooks. And gas and food. And Christmas.

"May as well get paid."

She pulled into the entrance. There was a white push-button set into the left post. She put the stick in neutral, rolled down her window and reached out. Raindrops tickled the back of her hand. She placed her fingertip on the button. And hesitated.

"Oh, hell," she said and pushed it.

A drive chain rattled somewhere and the gate slid quickly out of the way.

She put it into first and slowly entered between the stone posts. The headlights were lost in swaying dry grass and tangled brush. The s-curve of the drive made it hard to judge distance. As soon as her car crossed the threshold there was a thud behind her. The gate was already back in place.

She let the clutch out and moved forward.

Through a gap in the trees she caught a glimpse of the front of the house. She saw an oversized double door of oak, brightly illuminated by recessed lights in the overhanging eave. For an instant, it looked like several people were standing there, one in a bright yellow jacket. She lost sight of them as the drive curved and when it curved back she was entering a wide, paved parking area. The people, if they had existed, were gone.

The house was three stories, with an all-wood exterior. Gabrielle knew she had no vocabulary for architecture, but it looked to her like a modern mountain cabin that had been extended up in layers. She liked the proportions and the way the front door was framed by tall narrow windows on both sides, and these windows were subdivided into smaller glass squares at the top and bottom.

She knew it was all a kind of language. There was a message in everything. The texture of the materials, like the wood she didn't know the name of, the colors selected, the specific proportions of the boards which made up the walls and the structure of the roof. And the roof itself. The shingles, the metal edging – more copper – and the chimney just visible on the right from which smoke was issuing. The lighting. The curtains or blinds or whatever you called them, in the windows with their own colors and textures.

Maybe message was the wrong word, she thought. It was *information*. All linked to other realms of human life. Economics. Social structure. Civilization itself.

The sudden glimpse of the true scale made her eyes lose focus for a moment. But it wasn't infinite, she thought. It was human, after all. There were boundaries to the complexity.

"I can figure that out," she said. She stopped the car in the center of the circular drive.

Movement startled her. There was a woman standing at the front door.

"It *is* you!" It was M, wearing an old white t-shirt, worn blue jeans, and old sandals. She was beaming with her artfully cut blonde hair framing her face. "Oh my God, Gabrielle! You made it! And in the middle of the night in a *huge* storm."

Gabrielle switched off the engine and headlights and got out, taking her jacket with her. The drizzle had turned cold. She pulled her straggly wet hair back. A dribble of water ran down her neck.

"Hi," Gabrielle said, and started to put on her jacket. A gust of wind almost yanked it out of her hand. She thought M looked like a movie star.

"Oh, don't bother with that. Come on in where it's warm. I got the fire going in the library and it's just for you. Did you have any trouble finding me?"

"Oh, no, not at all. Once I saw the old gas station I knew I was on the right track."

M opened the heavy door for her. The entry room was paneled in oak that seemed to glow in the warm light. There were stained glass windows with an intricate abstract design above the inner door. The floor was more wood, solid-sounding and dark. And behind it all a clean, reassuring smell, vanilla and orange.

Gabrielle had never seen anything like it. Maybe in movies about rich people.

"That's a scary little place, isn't it? Been out of business since the Johnson administration, I think."

"That long? Are you a Pasadena native, then?"

"Hmm? Oh, no," M answered absently. "Right this way. We have the whole place to ourselves."

Gabrielle decided not to ask the question which had just occurred to her.

Beyond the inner door was a long hallway. She could see stairs at the end. It was the same paneling and indirect lighting in the high ceiling. She glanced at her shoes. The floor was perfectly clean.

"Oh, for heaven's sake, don't worry about tracking dirt in. You are my guest." M brushed the hair from her forehead. "Let me give you a quick tour of my dream house. I know you are far too young to be interested in boring old stuff like mortgages. I'm telling you I got the greatest deal of all time. I'm so excited about the future. It's going to be wonderful."

"Thanks. Your house is beautiful. And it's so big."

"Bigger inside than it seems, isn't it? I don't know how that actually works. An illusion, I guess. And it's possible to get lost in here."

"You got lost in your own house?"

She looked directly at Gabrielle and smiled. "Yeah. It was fun afterwards. Not so much when it happening."

"I can imagine."

"Yeah. So to keep oriented, always look for the door with the crazy stained glass transom. Or maybe it's clerestory, I forget. And the first door to your right is the library."

M pushed the heavy wooden door open. The walls inside were angled differently. Gabrielle quickly scanned the edge of the floor, which was covered in deep, cream colored carpeting. Octagonal, she thought. Each wall was completely covered by shelves of books, built-in, the multi-colored spines stretching to the ceiling. One wall segment housed the fireplace where large chunks of wood were burning. The smell was pleasant. Cedar. The fire had just started, she noticed. She liked the contrast of the soft carpeting with the solid wood of the bookshelves.

"I guess I have a few books," M said.

"Yes. Thirty-four hundred." She blinked. "And five."

"Oh." M stepped back and regarded Gabrielle, almost warily. "That's right. How the hell did you do that?"

"I don't know."

"You just counted them that quickly? You actually just did that. That is the correct number. Three thousand four hundred and sixteen in this room. That's as of last month when the inventory was done. I keep very close tabs on it."

"I've always been able to do things like that." You missed eleven, she thought. *Fail.*

"That's wild, Gabrielle."

"Just a trick. It comes in handy sometimes."

"Trick? Well, sure. Being a genius might be useful every now and then."

"It doesn't make me a genius."

M made a puzzled face. "You just counted all those books in the blink of an eye. I think you qualify."

Gabrielle started to say, "No," but stopped and just nodded.

"You don't like being called that."

"Not really. It's just something my brain does."

M squinted and looked serious. "I see. You can't be a genius because your brain does it."

"No, I mean," Gabrielle laughed, "It's not conscious on my part. I didn't learn it. I didn't work to figure it out. It just happens."

"So it doesn't count unless you had to work for it."

Gabrielle couldn't read her expression.

M backed out of the room. She walked to the next door on the right and opened it. "Bathroom." She closed it. Gabrielle got an impression of a lot of white tile.

M went to the first door on the other side of the hall and waved at it.

"The kitchen is through here. Help yourself to whatever you want. I'm not really into cooking myself." She went to the next door on the left. "But you have to have a kitchen, right? Can't have a house without a kitchen." She opened the second door. "Media room."

"Media?"

"Fancy name for television. The kludge is in there. Your old friend. Plenty of time for that thing. Come *on.*" M started up the stairs and Gabrielle followed. The stairs turned back on themselves once, then the other way again. "They keep going up, don't they?"

They reached the top. It was another hall. Much shorter, with another set of stairs at the end. More dark paneling.

"This first room doesn't have a name. Just an extra room." It was a comfortably carpeted space with several full, freestanding bookcases made of painted wood, an overstuffed sofa, a floor lamp, and a large, uncurtained window. Looking west, Gabrielle figured. She could just see the glow of the city lights on the base of the clouds. Rain pattered loudly against the glass.

"*Listen* to that. You got here just in time." M stopped and looked at her, blonde hair flaring. "So you have to earn the title of genius. Or is it that you just don't like being labeled. That I can understand."

"Both, I guess."

"Hmm." M waved at the rest of the hall. "Those two doors are bedrooms. That last one is a bathroom. And the master bedroom is at the top of the stairs." She shrugged. "Not that interesting. You don't strike me as the kind of young woman who would be impressed by closet space. Or great big bathrooms."

"They're okay."

"Eh. Girly stuff. Let's go back to the media room. Boy, it is really raining."

Back down the oddly twisted stairs, M suddenly said. "What kind of hostess am I? Let me get you something to drink. How about hot cocoa?"

"Sure, that would be great."

"Coming right up. One of the few things I *can* create. I'm pretty sure this was supposed to be the dining room. I have no use whatsoever for a dining room. So I put the tv in here with a bunch of pillows. It's perfect. Right off the kitchen. Make yourself comfortable and I'll be right back." She opened the door and Gabrielle went inside.

The media room was long with a whole wall of windows. There were dark red curtains, neatly tied back. At the far end, a large television set rested on a stand made of the same dark oak. And sitting on a crooked pile of pillows was the laser disc player, a rat's nest of multicolored wires beside it.

There was an array of bookcases, solid oak this time, filled with all manner of paperbacks and magazines tucked into cardboard organizers. She pulled one out. It was an entire year's worth of *Sky and Telescope*. The one next to it was full of *Popular Electronics*. There was a whole shelf of *Science* and another of *Nature*. The books were all fiction, though, which she was not interested in at all. She just glanced at them. Popular writers she had heard of but never read. Stephen King. James Michener.

She looked around the strange room. Lightning flickered silently outside.

"Now, this thing," she said. "Better be able to do this."

She started pulling apart the tangle of wires. Several had familiar RCA type connectors and a few that were new to her. She climbed over the pillows and got behind the big bulky television set. Lots of connectors there. No antenna hookup. The video disc player did not come with an owner's manual. No instructions anywhere.

It was largest tv set Gabrielle had ever seen in someone's house. It wasn't absolutely the biggest. That would have been the incredible display in use at the Jet Propulsion Lab she once saw on a tour.

"And that's almost right next door," she said.

This set had no brand name. The case was formed sheet metal, not plastic. There were no controls she could see. No knobs or buttons. There was a small plastic bulb right below the screen that looked like a lens. That was all. It was really just a picture tube in a metal box.

"So I'll just have to guess."

Through the windows, a light suddenly came on outside revealing the backyard, a small area of grass sloping away to an abrupt cliff. Perched on the edge of the cliff was a wooden platform with a single step all around, another octagon shape, which looked unfinished. The light went off and the yard disappeared into impenetrable darkness.

M came out of the kitchen carrying a silver tray. There were white mugs and items wrapped in paper napkins. "Time for a snack. Here." The door swung shut behind her. Gabrielle caught a glimpse of bright white appliances and stainless steel surfaces.

"Thank you." Gabrielle picked up a cup and sipped it carefully. The hot cocoa was intensely chocolate without being overly sweet. And there were other flavors she didn't quite have words for. Elusive and some borderline unpleasant. Citrus. Cinnamon. *Fish?*

"This is really good."

"It only took me my entire life to figure out how to get it right and I intend to enjoy it. Now try one of these. Cheese and crackers. The cheese is supposed to go well with chocolate. First time I've tried it."

"Cheese and chocolate?"

"I know, huh? It sounds kind of weird."

"Sounds interesting." It was a round slice of white cheese on a round cracker. She popped it into her mouth. M did the same. The cheese was tangy and salty and with a sip of cocoa became something new.

"That guy at the cheese shop wasn't lying," M said. "For once."

"The cheese is really strong."

"Yeah, a lot of them are strong but pretty much the same, you know? All sour and salty," M said. "This is unusual. What the heck are these flavors? Nutmeg and lime. Concentrated gardenia with sage and thyme. Lemon. Huh."

Gabrielle nodded. This was complicated and interesting. Gardenia? She took another piece. "Thanks. I was really hungry."

"You looked famished. You should take the rest of it. And there's plenty more cocoa."

"Okay. Well, I was looking at your tv."

"I knew it. You have it figured out already?"

"I think we'll just use the component video. It's fairly simple."

"Component video. Yeah, man, I love it."

"What kind of tv set is this?"

"It's an *M*."

"That's a brand?"

"Yep. One of a kind. Custom made for me by a place in Palo Alto."

"I've never heard of anyone doing that before. Must have been expensive."

"Probably. I don't remember."

The lights flickered for an instant.

"Notice anything different about it?"

"Well, I don't see how you turn it on. Or change channels."

"No channels. We can't get a signal from Mount Wilson anyway so I had them leave out the channel thingy. This is why I wanted the laser disc super kludge-master. Even if it is *horribly* analog."

Gabrielle laughed. "I guess you do need something."

"So far there is only one movie," M said and took a large flat sleeve from a bookcase. She opened it. "Behold."

It was the beautiful disc from the store. The sleeve had a picture like a movie poster. *Jaws.*

"At least it's a decent movie."

"Really? I've never seen it."

"You've . . . My *God*, Gabrielle. You just go to classes all the time? Here, get this hooked up and we'll watch it. You'll love *Jaws.*"

"Okay. Just a part of it, though. I still have to drive to school."

"You're driving there tonight? Now? Almost two hundred miles? Are you serious? In this weather? I'd assumed you'd be going back home from here."

The lights flickered again for a much longer time. Gabrielle could hear the whine of the heating system fans struggling to come back to speed.

"Nope. Back to normal tomorrow. I have two classes starting at one."

"Oh. Well, that's not too bad. You have time, I guess. You do miss all the traffic driving at night. Let's try to get this thing going while we still have power."

Gabrielle took the three video outputs from the player, red, green, and blue, and routed them to the three connections on the back of the tv that seemed similar, purple, orange, and pink. Red was kind of like purple, she thought, but green definitely wasn't orange. And blue wasn't like anything.

"What could it hurt?" she whispered as she stepped back over the pillows.

"What? What could what?"

"Um, I might have a couple of the colors backward. It can't hurt anything. We just need to turn it on to see."

"Ohh, this is interesting. I had no idea you could mix the colors up." M brushed an invisible speck of dust from the player and lifted the disc up, flat, like an offering. "Shall we . . . load the disc?" She was grinning like a kid.

"Do you know how to open the top of the, uh, kludge-master?" Gabrielle said.

"I'm afraid to touch it."

Gabrielle pushed a chrome square on the top edge. "Let's try this one." Nothing happened. "Maybe the power needs to be on."

"Power! This I know." M clicked a round button that had a red dot. The machine whirred and the main display lit up with fluorescent blue-green numbers and then went blank except for a blinking hyphen. "Ah ha. The machine awaits your command, master."

Gabrielle laughed. "Okay, well, I command thee to open." She clicked the square button again. There was a satisfying motor sound and the cover popped open an inch. She opened it the rest of the way. "Gosh."

"Goody! How does it go in?" M said.

"You just set it in on that spindle there and close the cover. But," Gabrielle said, "which side is up on this thing?"

"There must be some way to tell," M said.

And the lights went out.

Gabrielle blinked. She half turned and felt for the player. She wanted to close the top before she bumped into it and broke something. She reached out and found nothing. The darkness was total except for a very faint glow from the windows.

"Well, son of a fucking bitch," M said casually. The house thrummed under the rain. They both stood still for a moment.

Gabrielle heard her close the disc's sleeve and place it back on its shelf. M's perfume was suddenly very strong. She heard her clothes rustle.

"Is that you? I'm sorry, Gabrielle." M brushed past her shoulder. "The rule of thumb is if it doesn't come back on in ten seconds it will probably be ten hours. Let's go to the library if we can find it. Just across the hall."

"I can't see the door."

M brushed against her again and this time her hand slipped around Gabrielle's arm. "Right over here, just past the bookcase."

They took a few steps, arms linked. Gabrielle could feel the warmth of M's face near her's. M pulled her a little tighter.

The door, slightly lighter than the rest of the room, appeared before her. "I see it now. Thanks."

M gently let go. "Good."

Gabrielle felt M's index finger linger for an instant on her bare arm. It was very fast. Gabrielle, surprised, thought about whether she should react. She decided to ignore it. Probably nothing, she thought. Why would anyone want to touch me, anyway? A tingle, a spark of heat, ran down her back and diffused into the lower half of her body. She shook her head with a snap and it was gone.

M opened the door to the hall.

"Gabrielle, don't worry, I will definitely pay you the amount we agreed on no matter what. I'm sure you have that thing set up correctly. We don't need to test anything." They stepped in to the hall. The air was already getting cold. Orange light from the fire flickered under the library door. "I did kind of want to see *Jaws*, though."

Inside, the library was warm and filled with soft firelight. Gabrielle thought the rows of books looked very comforting. "I guess I should get going," she said. "It's a ways to drive." She felt suddenly very weary and her shoulders slumped.

"It's already very late," M said. Her face was warmly lit by the fire. "You would have to be completely nuts to start on a two hundred mile trip right now. I think you should stay here and get an early start. Didn't you tell me your first class was at one?" She placed a split chunk of cedar on the fire with consideration. "The thought of you in that little hippie car way up on 101 on this night."

"Okay," Gabrielle said. She smiled at 'hippie car'.

"If anything were to happen I would have to answer to your mother. Can you even imagine?"

"Okay, I'll stay."

"Well," M said, brushing off her hands, "Thank God. You're so *independent*. Why don't you get your things and I'll fix up the sofa here. This is the nicest room. The front bathroom's right there, after all."

"Thank you."

"I'm just being a good hostess."

Gabrielle went out the front door into the cool blowing night air and down the walkway. Lightning flashed. Branches swayed and the air smelled of wet brush. At her car, the rain was coming down in sheets and the hood of her sweatshirt was quickly soaked. She tapped her glasses to knock off the drops and looked up.

Darkened, M's house was mysterious and fascinating, composed of many levels, yet not frightening. Nevertheless, she paused with the tiny dome light shining on her soggy shoes and the rain pelting the car's interior. She shrugged. Hippie cars don't care if they get wet.

Maybe this is a little weird, she thought, but M seems so normal. Even if she lied about being alone here. There are probably lots of reasons someone might do that. It's none of my business.

There was movement in one of the top windows. A flicker of something that was gone when she looked.

She tossed her backpack over her shoulder, closed the car door and followed the shadowy path back to the house. The front door closed behind her with a heavy click. The lightless hall was warm and had a comfortable echo to it.

There were towels in the front bathroom. Amazingly soft towels. She buried her face in one and rubbed her wet hair and behind her ears which made her whole body shiver. She couldn't tell what color the towels were. Everything was grayish amber in the reflected firelight. They smelled clean. Just clean. Not reeking of industrial disinfectant like the sandpapery towels they handed out in the gym.

Gabrielle found a little tag on one towel and tipped it towards the dim light. She lifted her glasses. *Yves Delorme.* She took out her math notebook, the current one, and wrote that down on the first page. There were two small bottles of perfume beside the sink. She wrote down *Chanel No. 5* and *Fracas.* The cube of soap had a face molded into it, a classical Greek figure, like Venus, and the name *Pre de Provence.* She was beginning to get an idea of what she wanted to get her mom for Christmas.

There was more hot chocolate waiting for her by the fire in a porcelain cup. A pillow and two blankets of the type she thought were called *comforters* were stacked on the sofa. The sofa itself was rather small, covered in dark fabric that looked absolutely black in the firelight. She sipped the cocoa. Then she gulped it.

A door closed on the floor above. Then fast steps in the hall. M poked her head in.

"Remember, the kitchen is right there," she pointed, "and you already found the bathroom. So just make yourself comfortable. I myself am going to turn in. Is everything all right?"

"This is really nice, M. I'm pretty sure I've never spent the night in a library before."

"This is my favorite room. And you're more than welcome. When do you think you'll be taking off?"

"I should get going by seven. Maybe a little earlier. I want to get there by noon."

M nodded. "Have to find a place to park."

"Yeah. It's Monday. It'll be jammed. But it might open up a bit around lunchtime."

"Do you live on campus?"

"Oh, no. That's way too expensive. I'm renting a room in this old house by the train tracks. Actually, it's not even a room. It's a corner of the basement. By the washing machine."

"You live in a basement? You do at least get a bed? Okay. And you share the kitchen and bathroom?"

"It's not that bad. Hardly ever there."

"At least you get a washing machine. I've been up that way a few times. Didn't go to school there." She looked away. "Went somewhere else. But I know the area. What's your favorite place?"

"The library."

"Of course."

"And the best part of the library is the Stacks."

"The Stacks?" Gabrielle could hear M smile. "Sounds intriguing."

"Where most of the real books are. Non-fiction. I guess that's what I like. It's a great place to do homework."

"Then, being in here is perfect. We . . . I have a few books you might like. Not all non-fiction. That whole section is technical. Astronomy.

46

Biology. I'm not as mathematically orientcd as some people but I like them."

The fire had burned low. Wind rattled the windows again.

"Too bad there's no light to read," M said.

The cedar crackled. Her face was bright in the dark room.

"Well, I get up pretty early. Probably before you do. I will leave your fee on the kitchen counter before I go. Do not forget it, all right? The gate out there will open when you drive close to it."

"Okay. Thanks."

"If I miss you tomorrow, remember you are always welcome here. I'll be very disappointed if you don't come back for a visit."

"I will. Don't know when, but I will. Good night."

M left, pulling the door firmly shut.

Alone in the warm room, Gabrielle unfolded one of the comforters and spread it over the sofa. She placed the pillow at the end closest to the fireplace. The house creaked above her and there was a loud thump. Something just blew in, she thought, or a window got left open.

M was funny, she thought. There was a phrase Barbara sometimes used. Off the wall.

M was *off the wall.*

She sat down and took off her wet shoes and socks and set them in front of the fire. They might dry a little. Anything would be an improvement.

She was comfortable in the dark room. She wiggled her toes in the deep carpet. She stretched, watched her dancing shadow on the bookcases, and went into the bathroom. She left the door open to get a little light.

She took off all her clothes except for her white cotton panties. She decided to skip taking a shower. Better in the morning. She took the still damp towel and wiped her face and arms and legs. She put the towel back on the bar. Then, mostly naked, she stood in front of the fire.

"Interesting," she whispered.

Something caught her eye. There was a dark garment draped across the back of the armchair. She ran her hand over it. The same material as the towels, charcoal gray or black. Had it been there all along? She picked it up. Not a towel. It was a bathrobe. She slipped it on. Warm, heavy, and so oversized it dragged on the carpet. She pulled it tight around her waist and crossed her arms under her breasts. It felt wonderful.

She looked out the window on the right side of the fireplace. Her car, a gray shape, was just visible. She liked that.

Outside, the left window was almost total darkness, but she could see a structure of some kind. Now that the fire was almost out, her eyes were adjusting. There was the yard of black grass and a platform with a small roof. The ground dropped off behind it. It was the gazebo she had seen before perched on the edge of a cliff.

Probably nice in the spring, she thought. Not a night like this.

Suddenly cold, she found her empty cup. Maybe there was more hot chocolate. For a moment she thought the hall door was locked and her heart began pounding until she realized you had to push in hard to get the knob to turn. It was very dark in the hall with only a faint glow from the flower window. Her eyes were more dark adapted now but she still had to feel for the handle of the kitchen door.

When she turned it, the house rustled above her.

Something heavy was being dragged across a floor. Mattress, chairs, boxes of china. Her imagination pictured an entire room's furniture suddenly in motion and she paused in the doorway. Silence, except for the rattling window back in the library.

Probably just a broken tree branch sliding down the roof, she thought.

The kitchen was rather small with a functional, restaurant-style layout. There was a bulky stove and oven next to a wide double-door refrigerator and a long narrow table with tubular legs along one wall, all stainless steel. She could see by the pilot light flames beside each burner.

A small sauce pan still had some cocoa. She removed the skin that had formed, licked it off her fingertip, and poured the cocoa into her cup while holding it over the metal sink. Enough for half a cup. On the long table there was a plate covered with a cloth napkin. More of the cheese appetizers. She ate two almost without chewing and took a big sip of the cocoa. It was delicious, warming food.

She took her cup and two more of the cheese things back to the library. She made sure to close all the doors behind her.

She stirred the fire with the poker. The glowing coals were almost out but still giving off nice warmth. She ate the cheese things and drained what little was left of the cocoa. She tossed the heavy robe over the chair and unfolded the second comforter. She pulled it over her and she curled up on the sofa. She took off her glasses and placed at the base of the reading lamp on the small end table. She took off her old Timex and set it there also. *9:45.*

She could make herself wake up at any time she wanted. Six exactly, she thought. Six in the morning. She reached out and touched her watch and glasses. Now she was certain where they were and could find them in the dark without thinking. She snuggled down under the clean-smelling comforter.

She closed her eyes and smiled to herself. After all this, am I going to be able to sleep?

M's unquiet house murmured all around her. She thought she could discern individual voices but she doubted they were real. There was a snap from the fireplace as the last ember died.

The window rattled loudly and she opened her eyes.

There was a flicker of light outside. It was shining on the window frame. Orange firelight. It grew brighter and projected a wavering red-orange rectangle on the wall of books. As she watched, a figure crossed in front of the light.

She reached for her glasses, put them on, and grabbed her watch. *10:25.* She threw off the comforter, got up, and put on the robe. Then she carefully approached the window.

There was a torch burning on one side of the gazebo steps, a bright flame on top of a pole, about head high, nearly guttering in the wind. She watched it for a moment, not understanding how it was staying lit, when something moved at the edge of the light.

Someone wearing a yellow nylon windbreaker walked out of the shadows and crossed in front of the gazebo. It was a young woman, Gabrielle saw, straight blonde hair just touching her shoulders and wearing very short pants that looked like severely cut-off blue jeans. And no shoes. Her back to Gabrielle, she stood in the wet grass in her bare feet. Her hair was sodden and water ran off the back of the windbreaker.

She slowly raised her hand over her head and turned it palm up with her fingers curled. As if commanded, a small flame appeared at the top of a second pole on the other side of the steps. It grew stronger and brighter and made red tracers of the falling rain. She lowered her head and made a small bow in thanks.

Then she slowly ascended the three steps, the well-defined muscles of her long legs firm and strong, and placed her bare feet on the unpainted boards delicately, almost reverently. When she got to the center of the platform she turned slowly around, her arms at her sides, her shoulders tense. The half-unzipped windbreaker billowed.

Gabrielle saw her face for the first time. She had large eyes and a wide mouth. Her hair blew loosely around her brow. She was not smiling. There was some kind of irregularity on the left side of her face around the cheekbone.

Just the bad light, Gabrielle thought and said, "She must be freezing." The glass fogged.

The young woman suddenly unzipped her jacket completely and it blew open. She was not wearing anything under it. Gabrielle held her breath. With her right hand, she touched her left breast and her right, just brushed her nipples with her fingertips. Then she closed her eyes, her mouth open. Gabrielle could see her begin to breathe heavily.

Gabrielle finally left out her breath. She took big gulps of air. "What is she *doing*," she whispered and wedged herself against the side of the fireplace and the window sill where she could still see everything and not breathe on the glass.

The blonde woman dipped her head forward. There was a flash of red light behind the gazebo, bright on all the wet wood. The light just as quickly vanished as if a door had opened and closed.

Gabrielle froze. There was now someone else standing behind the structure. She could make out an upturned face. Another girl, she thought. This one had dark hair, very long, dark, and silky hair, and she was staring at the blonde girl. She began to walk carefully around to the front. She passed under one the torches and Gabrielle saw how tall she was. She was also barefoot, and wearing similar cut-off jeans and a black t-shirt. Gabrielle thought her hair was amazing. Dead straight, it reached almost to her ankles and gave off reddish glints. It flowed around her like a cape. She reached the gazebo steps and paused.

What in the world is this, Gabrielle thought. She felt nervous for the blonde woman, almost frightened.

The blonde woman suddenly realized she was being stalked and spun around. Startled, she stepped back. The tall girl climbed the steps quickly. They locked eyes.

Gabrielle relaxed a little. She could see the blonde woman was not really frightened.

This was something else.

The blonde woman shrugged her shoulders sharply and the yellow windbreaker fell to the boards. She was now topless in the blowing rain and torchlight. The tall one took a step forward, then another, her arms at her sides, hands open.

Now they were standing very close together, face to face, with firelight dancing over their skin. Gabrielle could see the tall girl's silky hair moving in the blonde woman's breath.

Gabrielle had to remind herself to breathe.

The tall girl kissed the blonde woman lightly on the cheek then put her hands on her shoulders and pulled her closer and kissed her neck. The blonde woman turned her head away from the kiss and when the tall girl straightened up, she mischievously kissed her quickly on the mouth. Gabrielle saw her smile and close her eyes again. Her arms encircled the tall girl's waist, she tipped her head to the right and opened her mouth slightly. The tall girl tipped her head the other way and placed her mouth on the blonde woman's mouth, not pressed together, just open, and they held still like that, as if they were breathing each other's breath, until the blonde woman moved her hands down to the tall girl's jeans. She slipped her hands into the back pockets and pressed and massaged. The tall girl brought her tight and they kissed, Gabrielle thought, hungrily, as if they were starving.

"Those are two girls," Gabrielle said out loud. "Those are definitely two girls." There was a buzzing in her ears.

The blonde woman grabbed the bottom of the tall girl's t-shirt and abruptly lifted. They pulled apart and the shirt was tugged off and tossed away without a look. They embraced. The tall girl looked down at their breasts pressed together while the blonde woman looked off at one of the torches, eyes half open, breathing hard. She put her hands back on the tall girl's back pockets, gripped hard, and thrust her hips forward. She bumped the tall girl, she did it again, and the tall girl began to do the same.

They synchronized their bumping and then the blonde woman stopped, dipped her head, and let her hands drop. She shook the wet hair off her face, eyes still closed, and she smiled and nodded at something the tall girl said.

The tall girl buried her face in the blonde woman's neck.

Gabrielle finally looked away from them because it had begun to snow. Large fluffy snowflakes were falling through the torch flames and the bright yellow light dimmed to dark red. She saw snow on top of the tall girl's head, on her black hair. Her bare shoulders were dotted with snow. The blonde woman brushed it off.

"They must really be freezing," she whispered.

The tall one tipped her head back to untangle her hair. Then she took the blonde girl's face in her hands and kissed her for a long time.

Gabrielle could see them talking and smiling. Snow covered the gazebo steps. They both picked up their wet clothes from the floorboards and walked holding hands and wearing only their cut-off jeans, down to the lawn. They went between the torches and into the darkness to Gabrielle's right.

Both torches suddenly went out and Gabrielle jerked back from the window. Behind her, there was a sound outside in the hall.

"They came in the front door," she whispered. "Hurry."

She got to the sofa just as the doorknob started to turn. She slipped under the comforter as quietly as she could, still wearing the robe and her glasses, and pulled it up to her chin. There was a loud whisper from the hall that sounded like swearing.

Pull up then turn, she thought and almost giggled.

The door opened. They entered. Gabrielle could feel the change in the air pressure. She felt their presence.

She did not close her eyes but she still couldn't see a damn thing. The arm of the sofa was in the way. She heard the shush of bare feet on carpeting and the hallway door closed with a sigh. There was a low creaking and a soft click. Then silence.

Gabrielle listened hard. Finally she poked her head up over the back of the sofa. Dark rows of books looked over an empty room. She got up and pulled the robe tight around her. They were gone.

She went to the hallway door and ran her hand down the jamb. It was not completely closed. Because they were trying to be really quiet, she thought. And the doorknob was wet.

Then she saw the footprints in the carpeting. She could just make them out in the faint glow of the fireplace. Two sets of feet. She knelt down and felt one. The indentation was damp. And one of the them had really tiny feet, she noticed. They went from the door to the second wall of bookshelves and ended there.

A secret door? That's what the click was, she surmised. A secret passage. I wonder how you open it.

None of my business. Really none of my business.

She felt along the edge of the middle shelf with the back of her index finger. A wet spot on the right end.

She touched this, she thought. Right here. Hell. I'll probably never come here again. I'll never be able to sleep now, anyway.

She pulled on the wet shelf. No movement. A harder pull. Not budging. The she pushed and the whole bookcase moved slightly. She pushed again with all of her ninety-nine pounds. There was a soft click. She let up and the wall of books opened into a gaping chill cavity.

The room inside was tiny and almost lightless and there was a something taking up all the space, a structure painted black. She banged her hand on metal. She felt a steel rod running vertically, then a flat surface. She had never seen a spiral staircase before but that's what her mind's eye told her it was.

A floorboard creaked somewhere above. They're up there, she thought. A secret room. A secret bedroom. Very private. Two girls in a bedroom. Doing what people do in bedrooms. I guess that really happens. I guess I've never really thought of that before. I don't think I have.

So what am I doing? There's no way I'm going up these stairs which I can't even see. Why? What would I do? Peek under the door?

She thought, *yes*.

She tried to look up into the stairwell. The house is pretty new, she thought. There won't be a gap at the bottom of the door. Besides, what can you see from there? They would be in the bed. Right? Not on the floor, at any rate.

She thought about it some more.

Okay, I don't actually know where they'd be, exactly.

I don't know. I don't know anything.

Like cooking or the ability to tell someone's age by their appearance or the semiotics of upper middle class suburban architecture she knew that sex was another field of human activity – an extensive field – about which her knowledge was somewhat deficient. She felt herself blushing in the darkness.

Okay, she thought. Not deficient. More like nonexistent.

Her highly organized mind paused for a few seconds. Did sex belong in a subcategory (like cooking) or did it deserve its own top level slot? It *is* a bodily function, obviously (she considered). See related subjects: menstruation, reproductive system, hygiene, social conventions. Does it belong there?

Bodily functions, then.

No, she knew she was making an error. There was a lot more to sex than bodily operations. There were relationships. Fundamental emotions. Like, um, what? Desire. Lust. Even love. (She felt confident she could distinguish between them.) But emotions in conjunction with the physical body. My body.

She tightened her robe and stepped back from the staircase in the near total darkness.

"This is too much," she whispered. It was almost like calculating a transcendental number, like *pi*, which could propel her into a mental state externally almost identical to a *petit mal* epileptic seizure.

Wait, she thought, not like a transcendental – and just thinking that word caused a red warning light to appear in her mind's eye – this is more like that lecture. A talk put on by the Science Department. She hadn't paid very close attention at the time, it was on a warm afternoon in the previous spring quarter and attended by all of six students. A moment later her mind found the title and gave it to her: 'Chaotic Systems and Strange Attractors.' She remembered it now. The simple equations that produced interesting computer printouts they projected on the screen, the main one a swirling vortex that could be a whirlpool or colliding galaxies or the pattern on the wing of a butterfly. Sensitivity to initial conditions. There might be an answer there, somewhere.

"Strange attractors," she whispered and grabbed the cold steel railing. "At least I have some idea what I'm dealing with."

She started up. The stairs were very quiet. She pulled up the hem of her oversized robe and made sure to put both feet on each step before going to the next. She lost sight of the glow from the library fire and because the ceiling was invisible began to unconsciously duck her head. She counted the steps and because she knew the rise of the steps was always the same, about ten inches, she had some inkling how far up she was. After twelve steps, one full rotation, she began to feel for a break in the railing. A landing, a door. But it was two full turns. Then three.

Three and a half turns and the stairs ended. Finally, a flat area. She felt the outlines of a door and located the door knob, a commercial style handle. She gave the handle light pressure. Locked.

All but blind, at the top of the spiral staircase, she tried to visualize the mechanism. It seemed to have a looseness, an out-of-adjustment feel. She pushed on the door and the latch moved.

Suddenly below her, halfway down the stairs, a door opened. A shaft of yellow light shone into the stairwell. A candle. A whisper. The shadow of a head bobbed on unpainted drywall.

"No," said a voice. A female voice.

Then from inside another whisper, "What did she do, go back to sleep?"

"I know it opened."

"Well, she's not out there."

The door closed and all the light vanished. Gabrielle let herself breathe and let up on the still half-latched door. Her shoulders were getting sore. She let go and the door swung open into her hand.

Good grief, she thought. The place is so slap-dash none of the doors work right.

In total darkness, she waved her hands in front of her face. It did not sound like a room. It sounded *tighter*. She carefully extended her right foot and her big toe touched a carpeted riser. More stairs.

She went up two steps and stopped to listen. The house creaked around her. Either the drop in temperature outside or the poor construction, she couldn't tell. At least it's fairly warm in here, she thought.

And they were talking about me.

A couple more steps and she saw a glow directly above. She saw spots of ghostly blue-green on the ceiling of a room. There were many glowing dots of luminous paint laid out like the constellations. Her eyes now fully dark-adapted – after the candlelight exposure – she was able to avoid tripping over the last step.

She was impressed by this ceiling. She recognized ghostly Orion and Cygnus. She crossed her arms in the bulky sound-absorbing robe. Stars were way down the list of things to learn.

"Hmm," she said

A voice close by said, "Hush."

In shock, she froze and the hair stood up on the back of her neck. She looked down from the glowing stars. She was standing at the foot of a bed. There were people in the bed. There were definitely people in the bed. She could make out shapes under a dark, voluminous blanket.

Just don't move, she thought.

Someone in the bed, probably the husher, adjusted the covers and, it appeared, rolled close to a second shape, presumably the one who needed to be hushed. Gabrielle got the impression of blonde hair. Not the same as the blonde girl in the gazebo. This was a different blonde.

Gabrielle, fairly confident of her invisibility, put her hands on her hips. Now wait a minute, she thought. I don't know these are actually girls. I mean, I can't see them. Can barely see my hands. This could be anyone.

The one on top, the husher, began to rock the bed. There was a giggle from under the covers. On the far left side of the bed where the blanket was being pulled away an arm poked out. It was another person. For a total of three. The third one rolled out from under the heavy blanket and stood up, their back to her.

Gabrielle did the only thing she could think of. She crouched. She bent her knees until she was even with the blanket foot bulge of the first two. Number Three was also a girl, she saw barely. Tangled dark hair and wearing only white panties, a faint patch in the darkness. Number Three opened the bedroom door and stepped into the hall.

Leave it open, leave it open, whoever you are, Gabrielle yelled in her mind.

The door was left open.

Gabrielle heard another door open and close. Bathroom, probably. She didn't think there was much danger of the two in the bed noticing her.

She stood, knees burning, and went into the hall.

She knew the bathroom was to the right because Number Three went that way. Where were the stairs? There *have* to be regular stairs somewhere, not just the spiral staircase. Oh let there be regular stairs.

She went to the right. Heel to toe, very slow, she thought. She gathered up the robe. Another two steps. She could just make out a rectangle at the end of the hall darker than the walls adjacent. In the other direction, the hallway ended in a plain undecorated wall. She was right in front of the bathroom door. She heard the toilet paper roll spin.

Number Three was doing number two in the dark and she had to clamp her hand over her mouth to stifle the giggles.

Flush, she thought. Flush the toilet like a good girl. Flush and I can run down the stairs. She risked another step. Why don't you flush?

The bathroom door knob made a scraping sound. Gabrielle, an arm's length from the lightless safety of the stairwell, froze again. She didn't hold her breath. She couldn't. Her thudding heart made the robe shake.

The bathroom door opened and the young woman came out. Her gaze, it seemed, passed right through her. She went lightly back to the bedroom and closed the door behind her.

"Wow, wow," Gabrielle whispered in dark freedom. She stared at the bedroom door for a moment. "Oh, hurry up."

She started down, still holding up her robe with one hand and the railing with the other. After the first step into total darkness, it was easy. Nine steps down then double back and nine more. She was in the top hallway. There were two doors on each side and a curtained window at the far end admitting a dim glow. She figured this was the level of the first secret room. Those two were probably asleep by now, she thought. She walked the hall as quietly as she could to the next set of stairs. No sound came from any of the closed doors.

"So everyone's asleep. Good," she whispered. She went down the next set of nine plus nine steps. Another hall and more doors. "God, this house," she said. She knew what it reminded her of. A dormitory. She had never lived in her college dorms. Far too expensive. She didn't like them anyway. They made her feel suffocated.

There were more stairs at the far end. The last ones, she hoped. Before she could move there was a sound. Someone was coming up those stairs right in front of her. A shuffling sound. She backed up the previous nine steps and froze on the landing. She couldn't run all the way back up. There was no way out. She sighed and peeked around the handrail.

It was M, recognizable by her height. She slowly ascended into the hall. Weary, Gabrielle thought. M stopped at the first door on her left, looked around the hall, seemed to peer at the dark stairwell where Gabrielle was hiding, and went in. Gabrielle heard the door latch and the click of the lock.

She didn't move.

Nothing. No sound.

Okay, she thought. Hurry.

She tiptoed as fast as she could past M's door and went down the stairs in the dark house. She found herself in the hall outside the library, the flower window with the front door at the far end, the cold carpeting under her feet. At the library, she remembered to pull up on the knob.

Inside, the secret bookcase door hung open. She didn't want to touch it. Hurry. She got her watch and put it on. *12:15.* Her backpack with the car keys rested by the sofa where she left it but her clothes were no longer draped over the back of the easy chair. It was a frantic moment before she saw them. Her clothes were folded neatly, professionally, on the chair cushion. Her socks were folded on her shoes. They were dry and smelled clean and fresh. Even her shoes were dry.

She flung off the heavy robe.

"Hobbits," she said softly and got dressed.

A minute later she was at the front door, certain she was forgetting something. When she touched the doorknob, it came to her. She set down her backpack and went back to the kitchen.

On the long stainless steel table was a piece of note paper with writing on it and next to that, something covered with a cloth napkin. Under the note was money. Twenty dollar bills. Four of them. It was much too dark to read the note so she folded it and the money all up together and put the whole thing in her front pocket.

Gabrielle immediately felt guilty. She overpays me and I'm skipping out, she thought. *Although* M didn't exactly tell the truth about being alone in the house. And she was leaving early, isn't that what she said? So I'm not really skipping out. Not on her, exactly.

There was a pastry underneath the napkin. It smelled wonderful, and she started to put it into her sweatshirt pocket, felt how flaky and crumbly it was, and wrapped it up.

And then she left the house.

In the cold wet air, as she closed the front door behind her, she felt doubly guilty. First, for leaving early. For not doing what she said she was going to do. And for taking the napkin. Stealing it.

I'll make it up to her, she thought, I will think of something.

The wind was still gusting. There was a buildup of snow, real snow, on her windshield but nothing was falling from the sky. A few tiny patches remained on the ground. It was concentrated around the back of the house, against the hills, where the gazebo was.

She opened the car door and the dome light came on, the little bulb surprisingly bright. She set the pastry on the driver's seat and swung the backpack onto the back seat. She wiped the melting slush away from the wiper blades, dried her hands on her sweatshirt, carefully picked up the pastry, and got in.

She felt much better sitting in hcr car. She pulled the door in and gave it a tug. The dome light went out. The darkness, right then, felt like protection.

"That's the first time I've seen it snow," she said, and then thought, first time I've seen a lot of things.

She put the key into the ignition switch. "Wait, do I have to pee? Yes I do." She looked at the door of the dark house.

"Oh, just handle it."

She pulled out the choke, waggled the stick back and forth to make sure it was in neutral, and turned the key. There was the grinding whine of the starter and the engine started with a growl. She pushed the choke in halfway and shifted into reverse. She didn't touch the headlights. She backed up the driveway, through the s-curve, certain the noise of the engine was waking everyone up and in seconds they would all be pouring out. But the front door did not fly open. There was no movement in any of the many windows. Then the house disappeared behind the swaying branches.

When she got close to the gate, she stopped. "Wait. It's not going to work. Power's out." She rolled up close. "Maybe I can pull it..."

In the mirror, the gate opened with a thrashing of the drive chain, just as M said it would.

"Must have battery back-up." She backed out between the stone pillars and onto the street. She drove out of the path and turned the wheel to face downhill and put the car in neutral. Gravity brought her to a gentle stop and she began to roll forward quietly down the street. A trick for saving gas. Now she finally pulled out the headlight switch and slipped the transmission into second. The pavement was wet but there was no sign of snow. No snow anywhere. She rolled the window halfway down and let the wind blow across her face.

When the stone pillars were out of view, she slumped back into the seat.

"Well, eighty dollars. That's not bad," she said. It was five dollars too much and it bothered her to be in anyone's debt. Plus the nice napkin. She filed it all away as a future task and accelerated.

She unwrapped the pastry as she swung onto Highway 2 and took a bite. It was flaky and buttery and full of chocolate. She thought, one of them actually made this? She got to the 210 and accelerated. With one eye on the freeway, she ate the whole thing and gathered up the napkin and funneled the crumbs into her mouth, thinking, I wonder which one.

The freeway was almost empty. She held it right at sixty. It was nice to be able to cruise through the interchange at the 405 without any hassles. Then she was on the 101, and once past North Hollywood the streetlights became sparse. A light above each off-ramp and that was it.

In her rumbling car seat, she wanted to think about her classes. Her finals for math, inorganic chemistry, and physics looked to be *non-trivial*, as one of her favorite professors liked to say.

Instead, she thought about the gazebo.

When the 101 reached the ocean it turned northward and ran alongside an elevated rail line soaring over the fringes of downtown Ventura. For a good stretch, the freeway and the train tracks curved together gracefully in the late night mist and Gabrielle found herself driving side by side with a freight train, its headlight rotating and sending out a powerful arcing beam.

The train was slowing and she was accelerating and she came up even with the locomotive. She could feel the thunder of it through her seat and she modulated the throttle to stay with it. The engineer was sitting with his arm hanging out the open window and he flipped his hand up from the wrist.

Thrilled, she quickly rolled her window down and waved back, mindful of making her wave just like his. Casual. Confident.

She rolled the window back up against the wet sea air. I could build that machine, she thought. Give me enough time and I could create one. I could generate one from raw materials, from dirt and rocks. Minerals. Ore. I know how to do it.

She smiled at herself and her midnight thoughts. The massive locomotive and its train veered away under her roadway and it was quite close for a few impressive seconds. She caught a final glimpse of the engineer. He was younger than she had thought and he looked back at her, not making a face, not smiling. Just interested. Look at that girl in the old VW. And then he was gone in the departing rumble.

Gabrielle felt her mind getting close to making some sort of connection, something important, but distracted by changing lanes, the thought slipped away from her. She found it really annoying when this happened and she tried to regain the thread but it was no dice. She swore silently to herself. Why do I have to forget things? I don't see why that happens.

Santa Barbara, and the gas station by the big tree, was a half hour ahead. The little side trip above Pasadena had used a lot more gas than she had estimated. A hair over a quarter of a tank left. She let the car's velocity bleed off to fifty miles an hour where she knew she'd get the maximum mileage. Maximum boredom, too.

Materials, she thought. The locomotive. She saw the contents of her thoughts as *objects*, alive with color and motion, linked by bright lines to other objects and further realms of thought and memory.

She shook her head. What am I missing? She realized with a surprise there was quite a lot of new stuff. It all had a fresh feel. She had no idea how such mental constructs could have a taste and smell and even texture but they certainly did and she was too busy with it all to analyze her own analysis. And the new stuff with their new colors and textures and even emotions, now.

Emotions she did not understand.

She wasn't sure what she was feeling or what was even possible to feel.

She tried to keep thinking about steel and copper but by the time she rolled into foggy Santa Barbara with its long series of traffic lights, she was back to thinking about the gazebo again. The air was cold and wet.

Filling up the tank required $4.90 at the station beside the huge tree. She hooked the nozzle back onto the pump and used the restroom. The college guy taking the money smiled at her like he always did and asked her how the car was running.

"Perfect," she said. His shirt had *Tony* embroidered on it but she didn't think he looked like a *Tony*. He had curly red hair and his face was a mass of acne. He looked like an engineering major. There was a math book on the counter next to the register. Part of a calculus sequence. The inside of the office had a funny, sweet smell, like burning cloth. It was kind of familiar – walking around her town she would detect it – but she had no idea what it was. Maybe the coffee.

"Hope you know what you're doing. Check the oil?"

"I did before I left," Gabrielle said. Actually she had completely forgotten.

"Oookay." He gave two nickels back for her five. "You want some coffee?" He gave a look at the fog-shrouded streetlights. "On the house."

"Thanks, but," she said, "it just makes me pee." She stepped back around to the car door.

He shrugged. A noisy pickup with a bed full of gardening tools pulled up to the other island. One of the fluorescent lights above flickered and went out.

"Hell, peeing is the only thing that keeps me awake," he said.

She laughed and waved and got back in the car. I am certainly popular today, she thought. Kind of makes it hard to think straight.

Back on the 101, she admired the fuel gauge. She liked the needle pegged above the full mark. Just stay there, she thought. She knew she'd use less than half getting to the house which meant she'd have a little getting-around-town gas. She could drive to school. Maybe for one day.

But nothing wrong with just walking.

She slumped back in the seat. She was the only vehicle going north on the rumbling highway. Thankfully, no glaring headlights in the rear view mirror. She squeezed her eyes shut. Still had a long way to go, along the beach where the wind could come out of nowhere and blast you off the road. Then up steep Gaviota Pass.

And when she finally got to her basement in the house by the train tracks, there would be her little bed with its old red blanket and her pillow. Her books would be there. And her well-used notebooks. And her stack of t-shirts. All waited in silence.

She shook her head and rubbed her eyes with a finger.

Stay awake.

In the dimly lit Gaviota tunnel the northbound lanes became a claustrophobic tube chiseled out of granite. There was no shoulder and she was separated from the open-air southbound side by a rock wall. The tunnel curved around the mountainside, making it impossible to see any distance ahead. It was antiquated and confusing and always made her nervous.

She shifted into third gear for the long climb and the engine dropped into a nice purr. She was an expert at this. She liked to keep it at about forty-five and the Volkswagen usually cruised all the way to the summit with no problem but on some nights, strangely, it struggled. She sighed, her mind wandered, as the freeway curved.

Guess it was something to think about. Humidity? Barometric pressure?

As she looked at her hand on the stick shift there was flash of light in front of her in her lane impossibly directly ahead. Her head snapped up. Her hands froze on the steering wheel. A pair of headlights came around the bend and high-beams blinded her. The car flashed past inches away. Pinto. The wrong-way driver honked his horn at her, and was gone, speeding downhill.

After a while, Gabrielle remembered to breathe. Her hands remained clamped on the wheel and her right foot somehow maintained the correct pressure on the gas pedal. There were still no other vehicles.

That guy could have killed me.

Her first thought was: I must never tell Mom. God, no. She would never let me out of the house again. I must never tell anyone.

The tunnel ended. There was sky at the edge of the canyon. Yes. The highway climbed steep and straight. At the top of the pass, she caught a glimpse of the stars sailing clear above broken clouds. She needed fresh air. She got her left hand off the steering wheel and rolled her window down. The wind smelled of wet grass. She looked at her hand.

Well, I don't see any shaking. I'm fine.

I was in the right lane, like always, she thought. The slow lane. I'm never in the left lane. I would never be passing anyone in that stupid tunnel. Never. This car can barely get out of its own way. And that drunk idiot thought *he* was in the right lane so there was no chance of running into him. Not that scary, really.

It took her a couple miles to remember to shift back into fourth gear.

Just like that, she thought.

The pavement was rutted and had wandering, eroded grooves. Her excellent automobile handled them with agility.

Just like that. You get one second to see it coming. No time to get scared. No time to do anything. And then it's over.

She was suddenly impatient to see the stars. She wanted to see them right that moment. She switched off the dashboard lights, then, on a straight stretch, she clicked off the headlights. The darkness was *wonderful.* It was her element. She was a ship flying alone through space.

A bright green meteor swept across the sky like an emerald welding arc and thc clouds wcrc thrown into vast, spherical, three dimensional relief. For an instant, she saw the physical world clearly. Indifferent. Incomprehensible. Infinite. And she was running right through the middle of it.

With a sense of careening through space, she turned the headlights back on, breathing hard. There was a streak of green in her eyes. She didn't feel tired at all. Her mind seemed to buzz.

She thought again about the gazebo and the unquiet house. The situation there seemed more clear. The two girls were in a relationship, as everyone now put it. She knew that could happen. She had never given that kind of relationship much thought. It was something no one ever talked about, not ever.

But now she thought about it.

"Maybe I'm stupid," she said to the rumble of the freeway. "Get organized."

In her mind's eye, she saw a great structure of data labeled, 'Human Sexuality, Female.'

Parts were clear, the parts she knew, while the vast majority was opaque. Jutting up beside this structure, in her imagination, was another one labeled 'Solid State Physics.'

The two subjects were comparable in size and complexity.

"More homework, I guess."

Why did people have to be so complicated?

At four-fifteen, she rolled into the town which was just beginning to stir. There were trucks fueling up at the gas station by the off ramp. A taxi sped past. There was still no light in the overcast sky. She saw no reason to bother going to her house and so she turned north, towards the largely unused upper campus entrance. In the big parking lot, she killed the engine and coasted into the space closest to the library. Her's was the only car in the entire, wide expanse.

Still just over half a tank of gas. Not too bad. She watched the rain sweep over the pavement. It would be hours before the library opened. But the cafeteria opened at seven and she could at least get coffee and maybe a doughnut if they were on the ball, which they usually weren't. The wind rocked the little car.

The campus buildings huddled in the rain. The science building, very well known to her, and the industrial-looking Quonset huts of the art department and the low profile Ag building, neither of which she had ever set foot in. On the left was the English building with its courtyard and small, reinforced windows. It was rumored to have been constructed from the same plans used for buildings at San Quentin prison. All the windows were dark, the walls rain-streaked state university beige.

It felt good to be back although it did not feel like home. No place felt like home anymore.

As usual, she tried to analyze her feelings.

She felt adrift. She knew she was lonely and she didn't care. She didn't think there was any help for it, so why worry? Just keep working. Work was good. Work neutralized loneliness. She knew plans were being made regarding her. Some made by people she knew, like her academic adviser, and some by total strangers. Plans she had little or no ability to influence or even anticipate. She felt curious, slightly nervous, and a little excited. The unknown future loomed.

She remembered the note. The dome light seemed very bright.

"Gabrielle, it was wonderful and exciting having you as a guest. I insist you pay me a visit the next time you are in town. I want to continue our fascinating discussion of the coming digital revolution... M."

Gabrielle put the slip of paper in the glove box, thinking, if I ever go back to that house, I won't go alone.

The sky brightened through the rain dappled windshield.

The sunlight was golden.

"Oh my God, Gabrielle. That sounds completely insane."

"No, it was kind of interesting."

"I can't believe you did it," Linda said.

It was halfway between Christmas and New Year's. They were in Gabrielle's car westbound on the sun drenched Foothill Freeway. Gabrielle had the afternoon off from her holiday job at a shoe store in the mall. She had only a few days left there, anyway. Linda was working part-time as a waitress while attending the local community college.

"Wait until you see it. Really neat place. New, but falling apart a little. A lot of the doors didn't work."

"Well, naturally," Linda said. "The death cult living there is far too busy with all the human sacrifices to fix things like doors."

Gabrielle laughed. She had told Linda all about the house. The media room. The kitchen. The library with its secret bookcase door. And the spiral staircase, which she had climbed without encountering anyone at all.

"There's no cult. Just M."

"That weird rich lady who had eyes for you."

"She's okay. She's pretty funny."

"I see."

"Not as funny as you."

"Why, thank you."

Gabrielle took the sweeping transition to the northbound freeway, easily passing several lumbering semi's, and moved back to the right lane, the engine humming powerfully. The clear sunlight swept over them brilliantly.

"It's just a little ways."

"And when we get there, then what?"

"You can see it."

"That's it? We're not going to stop and say hi?"

"Wasn't going to."

"But! What if they see us driving by and then we don't stop. How *rude*. And then an entire, well-funded death cult will be after us. To teach us a lesson. A lesson in *manners*. They know your car. The license plate. We'd be as good as dead."

"Okay."

"Now, by okay, you mean we're going to stop and say hi? Hmm. I see your plan, Gabrielle."

"My plan?"

"When, *not if,* things go bad, you're going to use me as a human shield."

"A what?"

"It was on *Starsky and Hutch* last week. You toss me to the cult and run for it. Well, it was a fate I accepted when I decided to accompany you."

"I would never do anything like that to you. Look, if anything happens to me, you can have my car. Just take it. Leave me there."

"And then watch the cult members rip you to pieces in the rear view mirror?" Linda shrugged. "All right. That's different. I've always wanted a car. I mean, not one of these things. You know, a *real* car. But this would do."

"Linda."

"Yes, death cult survivor?"

"We're almost there."

They got off the freeway and turned towards the hills.

"This is a nice area. This is Pasadena still?"

The day was bright with fast moving clouds in a sharp blue sky. Only the edge of chill in the air betrayed the fact that it was the first week of winter. The old gas station didn't look scary at all. Just a dirty abandoned building. Gabrielle found the first turn. The narrow street curved exactly as she remembered.

"What?" Linda said, studying her.

"It looks different. Smaller, I guess, now that I can see everything. We turn left here."

"There's a house around here?"

Gabrielle scanned the steep hills covered with dry brush and stands of live oak.

"It's right after this turn."

She dropped into second and whipped the car left. She saw the driveway entrance and froze. She stopped the car in the middle of the lane. A chill ran down her back and became a lump of ice in her stomach.

"What is it? What?"

"Hang on." Gabrielle turned the wheel hard and pulled onto the shoulder. She shut off the engine.

The stone pillars were uprooted and collapsed against each other forming a crooked archway. They were covered with dead tendrils of ivy. The copper spheres were gone. Streaks of rust running down the granite faces showed where the bolts had been. The steel gate and all the signs were gone. The massive fence of tubular steel was gone. The entrance was overgrown with dry grass and clumps of wild buckwheat. Beyond, the branches of the trees reached to the ground, intertwined. Gabrielle could not see the driveway. The whole place looked like it had been abandoned for years.

"Are you going to tell me what is going on?"

Gabrielle had to clear her throat. "This is it."

"What? That?"

"That's the driveway."

"What driveway? Those are the pillars you saw?"

"Yes."

"And you drove between them last month?"

"I sure did." Gabrielle could hear the blood pounding in her ears. "Come on." She opened her door.

They both got out.

"Wait," Linda said, alarmed. "Maybe it's just, you know, the wrong place. I mean, it was night time, wasn't it?"

Gabrielle was standing in the middle of the street. She tucked her keys as far down into her pocket as she could. "Let's go through."

"Wait! Oh, my God. You're not going in there."

Gabrielle went to the shadowy space where the pillars touched. The branches of an oak tree had grown around the rock. From all appearances, no one had passed through there in decades. How did they do that?

"You can see where the copper spheres were."

"Yeah, about a hundred years ago."

Gabrielle glared at her.

"Okay. Maybe not that long. Maybe the nineteen twenties."

Gabrielle studied the streak of rust on the granite. Could that be paint? She took off her glasses and scraped at the brown stains with her fingernail in the clear sunlight. It did not come off. It wasn't paint. Some chemical, she thought. She could not believe it was actually rust. It couldn't be. She put her glasses back on.

"I can't see the house," she said. "This has to be a trick."

"Of course it's a trick. And we should sit in the car and discuss it with the doors locked."

Gabrielle knew she should be able to see the sharp corner of the roof from the entrance. Scanning through the branches, she could see only blue sky. She stepped between the pillars and pushed aside the tall dry grass. She scuffed her shoe.

"It's just *dirt*," she said.

Linda was close behind her. "Have you noticed that not a single car has passed by since we stopped? And listen. It's so quiet. Where are the birds?"

"It's winter."

"That's another thing," Linda said. "It doesn't feel like winter. Feels like summer."

Gabrielle took another step. "There's a gap right here. Hold your arms up and just go through."

"Okay. Perhaps early fall." Linda stepped into the gap. "If anything happens to you, your mom will really be upset. So I'll protect you."

"*You'll* protect me?"

"It's what the sidekick does."

Gabrielle peered under the post. There was a tangle of downed trees behind. It was an effective barrier. She stepped into the debris and with her other foot hopped onto a tree trunk.

"Are you actually going in there?"

"Look. Pavement. I knew it." She ducked her head, jumped off the tree trunk, and started picking her way through the branches, brittle and sharp. The asphalt was broken and large sections were missing. The curving driveway was now a rutted dirt track. Nothing of the house was visible through the pines. She carefully jumped clear of the deadfall.

"Where *is* it?" she said.

"Where is what? I'm not sure I can go through there. I keep forgetting to tell you. I'm not very outdoorsy."

"It's just a little ways," Gabrielle called back. "Once you get past this pile of trees it's easy. Looks like it was all pushed up to keep people out."

"Then how inconsiderate of us to be doing this. We should respect their paranoid yet perfectly reasonable wishes. Ow! I'm bleeding. My flawless legs. Ruined." There was thrashing.

Gabrielle saw the path of the driveway was the same, at least. She walked along the curve, afraid of what she would see. She came past the trees. She stood there in the open, perfectly still. She could feel heart pounding.

Linda came up behind her. "I got at least three scratches. And it's getting cold. You're awfully quiet."

"Look."

"Okay." Linda dropped her arms to her sides. "What am I looking at?"

"Tell me what you see."

Linda scrunched up her face and said, "All right, I will. I see a big dirt field covered with weeds. Nice view to the west."

"Do you see a house with three storys?"

"That's a negative. There is no house."

"But there was. A mansion. Almost new."

"Gabrielle, there's nothing there."

"There *was.*"

"Houses don't disappear."

Gabrielle started walking. Her face felt cold and there was a strange tightness in her abdomen. "This was where I parked and there was a lawn and a brick walkway."

The dirt was compacted but she could see traces of tire tracks. Heavy equipment.

"The front door was right here." She waved her hands in the air. "This is so. I don't know."

"It looks like it was cleared off a few years ago in order to build something but they never got around to it," Linda said, trying to avoid the clumps of puncture weed. "My dad's a general contractor. Remember?"

Gabrielle walked to the center of the building's footprint according to memory. Kitchen. Library. Spiral staircase. The bright sun made her eyes water.

"Do you feel okay?"

"Kind of dizzy." She walked to the edge of the cliff where the city lights had been visible through the window of the media room. "This is incredible. I can't even think. I'm really glad you're here to see this, Linda."

"Even though I can't see it."

"It's so strange. Reality changing when you're not looking. Oh, wait!" She started for the other side of the lot.

"What is it?"

Gabrielle jogged across the uneven dirt. "Right over here," she said, crossing the space where the library and fireplace had been, "was a little platform. A gazebo, you know, with a round roof. And there were these torches on poles."

"Tiki torches."

"Right! That's the word."

The ground had been cleared of rocks and brush and rolled flat. And what in the night had given the impression of being a huge canyon was actually a shallow gully, clogged with scraggly oaks and masses of columbine.

So she could have walked up this ravine and then just climbed up behind the gazebo, she thought. The dark-haired one. No need for tunnels or trapdoors.

"You mean the torches were burning?"

"Yes," Gabrielle said carefully. "For a little while."

"There was no one there?"

"Didn't see anyone."

"Huh. This was night, right? Well, would've been freezing."

"I know. Especially when it started snowing."

"*Snow?* It actually snowed?"

"For about half an hour. An inch or so."

"Holy cow! Oh, that *is* freaky. Snow in Pasadena. I have never seen it snow."

"Yeah. It was the first time for me too." Gabrielle let her gaze drift down to the gully, to the jumble of vegetation. Something tickled her eye, as her dad might have said. Twenty feet down something non-natural was wedged in a bank of mud and rye grass. "I need to look at that."

"And I will absolutely watch you do so from right here as you scramble down that crumbling hill full of deadly snakes and poison ivy. You can count on me. What is it?"

Gabrielle plucked the fist-sized object from the brush. She crab-walked up the bank and held it out to Linda.

"Ew! What?"

"Fine, Bambi, you don't have to touch it."

"Well, I need to know what it is I'm touching."

"It's the burner from one of those torches. See here." She put her finger on the cylinder of aluminum stained with carbon. "This is the igniter. And this is the gas valve. You could operate it by remote control. That does explain what I saw."

"And what was that?"

"Oh," Gabrielle said and turned away so as to not lie directly to her friend's face. "Just the torches going on by themselves."

"Anything else?"

"Nothing else." Gabrielle studied the burner.

"Okay. Whatever it was must have been something embarrassing. I've known you since the second grade. I can always tell. Did that M lady try to pull something?"

"No, she was all right."

"Then what? You can tell Auntie Linda anything."

"Yeah."

"Because I'm not giving up."

"Okay, okay." She dropped the valve on the dirt.

"Was it something, like, awful?"

"I'll tell you. You're the faithful sidekick. So you have to keep it secret."

"Absolute secrecy." Linda held out her hand palm up.

Gabrielle placed her hand on hers. They each wiggled their fingers. "Absolute secrecy. All right. After I went to bed..."

"Wait, wait, wait. *Bed?* You spent the night in this house?"

"No, not the whole night."

"Oh, you just went to *bed* for a little while. Good grief, Gabrielle."

"It wasn't like that."

"Of course not. So what embarrassing thing happened while you were *in bed.* God, I can't believe I'm asking this." Linda held her face in her hands.

"It got really late and M insisted I sleep on the sofa in the library and get an early start. It was raining and snowing, remember? And the power went out. The library was right about here," she said, pointing at the featureless dirt in the sunlight. "It was really comfortable and there was a fire in the fireplace."

"The power went out? You don't say."

"Well, it did. I fell asleep and something woke me up. Something outside the house. It was the light from this torch and one other shining through the windows."

"Well, that's weird but not embarrassing. So then what?"

"The torches were right beside the gazebo."

"Which was right where we're standing."

"And there were people in the gazebo."

"Okay. You said there was no one there. Wow." Linda was wide-eyed. "You never lie."

Gabrielle backed up and started walking back to the blocked driveway.

"Oh my God, I bet I can guess."

"Yeah." Gabrielle walked faster. Linda jogged to catch up.

"So there was a couple? And they were, like, doing it?"

"Yeah."

"In the snow?"

"Yep."

They began to navigate the dead fall at the granite posts.

"Well, you know, big deal. It's a little embarrassing, I guess. Was there something strange about them?" Linda batted away low branches.

"No not really."

"Like, were they weird looking? Missing body parts? That would kind of create a mental reaction."

Gabrielle laughed. "No, they weren't like that." She ducked under the post. Linda was right behind her.

"They were something else, right? Finally, we're getting to it."

Gabrielle opened the car door and got in. Linda got in on her side. They both slammed their doors shut simultaneously. The interior of the Volkswagen was warm.

"It was two girls," Gabrielle said.

"Girls?"

"Females. Women."

"Female women. I see."

"Yeah."

"Female women comma girls period." Linda was grinning. "Were they cute?"

"Kinda."

"I guess you're right. That would be embarrassing."

"Exactly," Gabrielle said, feeling even more embarrassed. "Now let's get out of here."

She started the car and made a fast U-turn in the empty street. Fallen leaves blew around the windshield. She did not look back at the ruined entryway of the vanished house. On the way back, they didn't talk much and Linda wouldn't stop grinning and Gabrielle found this really annoying.

PG pushed back.

The doughnut shop was a bleary-eyed pocket of fluorescent brightness in the night of Santa Barbara. We were the only customers and had been for at least an hour.

"It's eleven forty-five. We need to get back." She stood up and stretched. It was a very youthful gesture.

I glanced at my watch. 11:46. Only off by a minute.

"What will I be seeing?"

"Just the way things really are. Better let me drive."

"You don't think I can drive your car around this crazy town at night?"

"No." She wasn't quite smiling. "That's not it."

I gave her the single key.

"I want you to concentrate on observing. I want you to see and then write what you see."

The rain had stopped. She just gazed at me, still pretty much all business even at midnight on the day she buried her best friend. I thought all that and then immediately doubted myself. We got in the VW and PG fired it up, popped the clutch, and punched every red light going back.

M's lovely Craftsman style bungalow had been reduced to a dark skeletal shell of old lumber with a collapsing roof. No doors, windows, siding, or trim remained. No lights shone. A horde of college students in wet clothes were moving though the house like swarming ants armed with smartphones, stepping through walls where the lath and plaster had been smashed away, pounding on the few cabinets and bits of shelving left. When one of them managed to break something with a crash, there was a collective roar of laughter and swearing. Most of the voices sounded female. One of them paused at a window opening, a guy. He was wearing a black t-shirt with *Suck It, Bitch* printed on it in huge pink letters. He saw us and ducked back inside. I heard him say something to the others in the darkness and there was a shriek of triumph that was definitely female.

PG grabbed my arm when I opened the car door.

"You wanted me to see," I said.

Her face was worried but she let go.

"At midnight," she said, "which is six minutes from now, they start up." She nodded to the shadows to the left of the house, where the hidden driveway was. I could make out the blades of a couple bulldozers, monster D-10s, the cab sitting way above the angled-up track. The caterpillar track was higher than my head. And there were bigger machines behind them.

"If they finish by sunrise, they get the bonus."

I nodded. "Big bonus?"

"Seven figures."

"Well then I'll make sure to stay out of their way."

As I reached the house the first D-10 roared to life. A cloud of diesel exhaust floated overhead. And I heard another sound. Helicopter. On a night like this? The chopper moved away, came back, searching in the near zero visibility. Whoever that was, was completely crazy.

I got to the porch and several figures in the front room ran back into the wooden maze of turn-of-the-last-century framing studs. I heard laughing whispers, snorts of disgust when I entered. A brick was thrown at me. It clipped my thigh. One person stood in the middle of the shadowy room. Couldn't see the face. Got an impression of a guy, fifty pounds overweight with shoulder length hair all combed over from left to right.

"Hey. What are you doing here?" he said. Outside, with a thunderous rattle, the first bulldozer began to move.

Midnight. The vibration made my knees itch.

"Hey," I said, "got a call that my house was being ransacked by a bunch of berserk UC students. You wouldn't know anything about that, would you?"

"Sure do," he said and giggled. Student? At least thirty years old, I guessed.

I waited for a moment. The D-10 was halfway to the house.

"Well, why don't you go ahead and fill me in, Chester. You got about seven seconds before that thing removes the front of the building."

I could see him nod in the floodlights of the machine. "We win," he said matter of factly, turned, and headed for the back of the house.

"You what?"

There was a shattering crash as the porch was severed from the house and pounded into a pile of century old sticks, dry as dust. It was deafening. The second D-10, screaming out of nowhere, came blasting through the living room wall and sent me scrambling backwards, barely keeping my feet. The ceiling came down in a rain of plaster, then the roof, a shredded fragrant tangle of cedar. The hardwood floor would be next. I'd end up buried under dried out lumber and ancient rock wool insulation.

The bluish LED floodlights atop the screaming machines played over the ruins and I could at least get an idea of where to run. Down the center hall to the back of the house, tripping over forests of thin wooden slats that had been a bathroom wall, past the gutted kitchen and small office.

Noisy darkness. I had to feel along the wall and hope the floor wouldn't suddenly go away and drop me into the basement.

I found them. Three people with their glowing phones standing close together in the empty master bedroom room. There was a stub of a candle burning on the floor at their feet. They were holding hands. Black shirts and pants.

The two bulldozers made a double pass and destroyed the living room. A cloud of dust blew past me. I smelled soot from the collapsing chimney.

The three were watching me intently.

"Hi there," I said as calmly as I could. "Mind if I ask you a few questions? I'm a writer..."

"We know who you are," said the one on the right, a woman. There was a second woman along with my old pal Chester. Both women seemed middle-aged, very short hair, deeply winkled faces. The candle was guttering.

"Well, I'm so glad. And could I ask your name?"

"Susan."

"Okay, nice to meet you. And how about you," I said to the other woman.

"Susan," she said.

"The two Susans, huh?"

This made Chester giggle again.

"Look, I don't know the official program but I'm gonna go out on a limb and say they're bulldozing the house. Why? Why are they doing this?"

"Ask *her*," the first Susan said.

"Her? All right. Another question. What's with the candle?" It was just a flickering stub in a brass holder.

Chester started to say something and got a hard stare from second Susan. He shut up.

The first Susan said, "Watch the candle."

"What's it gonna do?"

"Just watch."

She swung her leg and stood directly over the candle. Suddenly the other Susan got in front of her, grabbed her shoulders and kissed her. The first Susan dipped her knees and there was a splashing sound. I jumped back a step. She peed on the candle. It instantly went out in a glurt of liquid wax on the beautiful oak floor. The only light was Chester's phone and the ever-closer bulldozer floodlights.

The Susans pushed apart. "There," number one said. "Extinguished. Just like her. Just like that bitch whore. Just like that fucking asshole cunt. Dead and soon to be eaten by maggots."

"You clearly have strong feelings about her. What was her name again?"

"Fuck you."

"Now, hold on."

"I said fuck you."

There was a resounding crash as the bulldozers took out the kitchen and front bathroom. And another sound. The helicopter was back, hovering. I could feel the chop of the rotors in my chest. My breath was sucked out. The bulldozer floodlights must have clued the pilot.

"He doesn't know anything," said the other Susan. "Should we tell him?"

"We don't have permission," I barely heard the other one say.

An intense blue-white light flooded the demolished end of the house.

Bits of wood and insulation pelted my face. The engines screamed.

The hell with this.

"You lovely people," I yelled, "have a nice evening!" None of them moved.

I went out the back and around the side to where the driveway connected to the parking loop. The helicopter was hovering over the spot where the porch had been. PG was standing in the middle of the loop. The brilliant arc light found her. Silhouetted in the blinding arc light, PG raised her right hand, extended her middle finger, and waggled it.

I ran hard. The helicopter made a funny chugging noise, as if the pilot had let go of the collective for a second or had been bumped. Just behind the arc light, I saw a large object fall from the open door. It was a bag, a black plastic bag, and it hit the pavement with a soggy thud and split open. Garbage, smelly garbage.

PG never moved. She continued to slowly wag the bird at whoever was up there. The intense light swung over the half-demolished house. I felt the heat of it on my forehead. Then it snapped off. The copter swung away and was immediately swallowed by clouds.

PG dropped her hand. I saw she was staring at a large vehicle coming up the hill towards us. A black limo. Coming in fast. Halogen headlights pinned us both.

"These assholes are not slowing down, PG," I said.

She said nothing. The look about her eyes wasn't anger. It was a combination of *it's finally happening* and *let's get this show on the road*.

She was smiling.

The limo was very close. There was no room to drive around us. I stepped in front of PG and she glared at me in irritation.

"Sorry, I'm more expendable than you."

I heard the limo's engine drop to idle. The driver had yanked his foot off the gas. The big vehicle, tires crunching on plaster and glass, came to a stop with its bumper touching my knee.

The driver's door opened and the guy got halfway out. Pudgy. Thick glasses. Over the roar of the bulldozers, I heard someone in the back seat yelling at him. Female voice.

I tried to sound dangerous.

"If I were you, sir, I'd get the hell back in there."

He gave me a startled look, glanced nervously at the person behind him, and slumped back down.

I stood in the open door and looked over his shoulder. The armored window in the seat back whirred up. No problem. I just reached around and pulled on the handle. The extra wide passenger door opened. VIPs never think to lock it.

"Careful," PG said from behind.

I shrugged. There was one person in the back seat. I detected *Subterfuge* and very strong body odor, like a wet muskrat. Too dark to make out a face. I could see a long black dress and shoes. Then one of the shoes flew up and hit me in the forehead. I staggered back and they pulled the door shut. As blood ran down to my chin, the limo backed slowly down the driveway, like an eel slithering back into its cave.

"You're bleeding," PG said and handed me a tissue. "I'm glad that happened."

"Thanks." I tried to keep the blood out of my eye.

"What I mean is, it will make the next part a little more believable. Here." She handed me another tissue.

Behind us, the two bulldozers had almost completed the destruction of M's house. One of them headed for the six-stall garage. Another machine with a huge articulated arm grabbed gigantic fistfuls of wood and shingles and flooring and chucked it all into the back of a dump truck. There was a line of waiting dump trucks extending out of sight down the hill. There was no sign of the berserk college students or the Susans.

PG stepped away from me.

"You don't want to stay and make sure they finish by sunrise?"

"I have someone assisting me." She nodded at a car tucked way back in the shadows. I hadn't noticed it. Black sedan, couldn't tell the make which was probably the idea. The driver sat motionless and when the floodlight beams hit him I got the impression of a man with a young-looking face but gray hair, hollow cheeks, unblinking eyes. A face from a bad dream.

The fog was returning and I started shivering.

"Let's get out of here, PG."

The limo was nowhere to be seen as we drove around the split garbage bag made our way back to the 101. PG was more tense than tired. She held her knees together with her clasped hands.

"North or south, I said. The street was lined with palm trees. In the falling mist I saw something move between the trees just at the edge of the VW's headlights. PG noticed it too and as she began to speak a brick flew out of the darkness.

I veered but no good. The brick bounced, loud as a gunshot, off the hood. I hit the gas and the little car burned rubber.

A metallic object came sailing out from the trees. The gallon can of paint just missed us and I saw it splash open on the pavement behind us. I gunned it to the end of the long stretch.

Past the palm trees, intersection coming up, I took my foot off the gas and the Volkswagen slowed with a lurch. The engine became almost silent. Open yards on both sides, nothing moving. In neutral, we coasted to a streetlight. There was a gouge in the hood crusted with brick dust.

"Good compression."

"Sorry, I should have warned you."

Damn engine was so smooth I couldn't tell if it was still running. I put my hand on the stick. Okay. The rear view mirror. Shit.

The street behind us was full of people. They waved their fists and phones at us and ran back and forth, ghostly figures against the blank fog.

Without taking my eyes off them, I stopped at a stop sign.

"North or south?"

"South. Not far. Someone is picking me up."

The street behind us was now completely empty. This made me very uneasy. I scanned right then left. One thirty in the morning, no other vehicles except well-spaced cars on 101 visible beyond the trees. I moved through the stop.

"Feels like lightning's gonna strike." I said and she looked at me in surprise.

I made sure to stop at each stop sign. Right then left. No one following. The final turn took us under the concrete edifice of the freeway then up the southbound on-ramp, a steep climb, the VW powered up without effort, and when the 101 opened up before us I felt relief.

In the right lane, *finally* fourth gear.

I kept it at fifty-five on the long cement ribbon. Only one pair of headlights behind us, half a mile back.

Streetlights were only over the off and on-ramps, between them was darkness, and as we passed one I saw movement in the shadows under the blowing eucalyptus branches. Hit the gas again.

In the mirror I saw someone run across both southbound lanes, hop the galvanized center divider, then continue across the northbound side. They were followed by others, all running.

"Those are little kids," I whispered.

PG only said, "Keep going."

The Pacific was a vast expanse of total darkness on our right. A lone streetlight appeared in the mist.

"That one."

"All right."

I slowed for the off-ramp. We went down sharply hemmed in by piles of boulders on both sides. As the 101 went out of view I checked the mirror again. Those headlights were closer.

PG directed us down a lightless track of ancient asphalt. Sand had blown over the shoulder

"Where does this go?"

"There's an area of vacant land. Nice lots. Makes a good heliport. The road connects up with the freeway if you keep on this way."

"Thanks." Headlights behind us. They took the off-ramp. "Are they waiting for you?"

"No. I have to signal them. What is it?" She looked back.

"They were way back there a few minutes ago. Might be able to out run them."

"There isn't time."

The vehicle came up fast in the utter darkness and then matched our speed. Newer SUV from the height of the headlights. They were studying us.

"I'm gonna go," I said.

"Go," PG said.

Red lights flashed.

"Look at that," I said.

PG stared at the police lights and I swear for an instant she smiled. Then she sat straight in her seat.

"You gonna pull over?"

"Don't say a word. Not a single word. You understand me, ma'am?"

She nodded.

I slowed down, signaled, and moved over to the edge of the sand. The police vehicle got real close, almost touching, centered on our left taillight. I came to a careful stop. The SUV's headlights filled the VW.

Old incandescent bulbs, I thought, from the color. And that visibar.

I rolled my window down. I did not turn off the engine. But I did put both hands on top of the steering wheel. There were no buildings around us at all. No lights except for cars on the 101 angling off into the distance. We were totally alone.

After about a minute I heard their door open. I could see insignia but the glare of the headlights kept me from getting a good view. Someone got out and a flashlight came on. The beam swept across our faces, the back seat, and settled on PG.

They walked up close to my window, hard shoes on tarmac, a barely silhouetted shape. The beam found me now. Then he stepped into his own headlights.

"License and registration."

Hoarse voice. One hand on the five cell flashlight, the other on the hilt of his gun. Police Special. I could see most of his uniform. Sunglasses hung from a pocket. Crooked name plate. Smith. Thick middle aged guy, heavy brows. Stocky but not linebacker stocky. He looked strong but slow.

"Is there a problem, Officer?"

"License and registration. Right now."

"I'm sorry, what was I doing wrong?"

"Do you know how fast you were going?"

I laughed. His thick face showed dismay then reformed into anger.

"Let me explain, Officer Smith."

"Sir, exit the vehicle. *Immediately.*"

He took a step back and unsnapped his holster. Yeah.

"Right out of college," I said and grinned, "I got this great job as a reporter for a newspaper. They put me on the police beat. This was Denver. I loved it. Get up at three in the morning. Stay up four, five days in a row. You see a side of the city you never knew existed."

"Sir, exit the vehicle."

He pulled his gun, kept it pointed down.

"I got to know all the officers pretty well. Two years I did that. Learned a lot. The point is..."

"Get out of the car *now*."

He raised the weapon. The barrel was pointed at my forehead.

"Hey, Smith. Shut up."

I saw him blink. I leaned out the window.

"The point is, fat-ass, if *you* are a real cop, I'm Chelsea Clinton. Have a nice evening."

With his gun pointed at my head I put the VW in gear and drove away, as unhurried as I could make it. Didn't look back but I could feel that damned black barrel track me.

Second gear and I floored it. The car roared and the front end almost lifted off. No headlights back there. I saw a lonely on-ramp under a solitary streetlight. I ran all three stop signs and we once again found ourselves on the southbound 101. Kept it at sixty. After five minutes the adrenaline tapered off.

"You all right, PG?"

"Oh I'm fine."

Her tone made me laugh.

"How sure were you?"

"Ninety percent."

She kept an eye on the long curving freeway behind us. We were the only vehicle. The little car bounced confidently.

"If I'm wrong we'll be swarmed before we get to Ventura."

"Ninety percent?"

"Yeah. This car is something else."

She nodded to herself and closed her eyes.

On the outskirts of Ventura we found an all-night McDonald's. PG used the payphone. We sat at a back table and had French fires, hot apple pies, and coffee. There was a small tv going behind the register. The middle-aged counter person was transfixed by it.

"Now that I made a phone call they know where I am."

I thought, confused, bleary eyed, of course they know where you are so they can pick you up. I was dizzy.

The counterperson glanced at PG, then back at the tv.

"Hey, that's you," he said and covered his mouth.

I got up. He watched me approach and stepped back.

"Hi," I said.

He pointed at the tv. Cable news, crisis logo. The crawl at the bottom of the screen said, 'Treasury SWAT team raids Santa Barbara house.' There was jumpy footage of helmeted, flack-vested men carrying large weapons stumbling through the wreckage of M's house. A quick shot of the bulldozers, another of the hollow-faced man in the car. Then a still of PG from years ago. Her hair was shorter. *Fugitive*, it said.

The man shrugged and smiled. Retiree.

"Don't worry. Refill?"

"That's all right. Thanks."

We sat in silence and almost finished our coffee and then a helicopter landed in the street outside, in the middle of the big intersection beyond the parking lot. Strobe lights mingled with the red and green traffic lights. PG got up as I gaped.

"Best advice I can give you. Keep moving. Don't stay on any one highway for very long. Don't use your phone. Better if you didn't have one."

She pushed open the glass door and began walking fast. I ran to keep up.

"They don't know who you are or where you live. I want to keep it that way as long as possible."

She jogged over the sidewalk and the waiting chopper flashed its spotlight. I heard the turbine spin up. PG came back and held out her hand. I took it.

"Good job."

I nodded thanks.

She ran into the intersection. The cockpit door opened for her and as soon as she was in the chopper lifted straight up into the low clouds. Power lines swayed in the wind.

I heard the machine clatter as it moved off. Keeping it low, I thought, and it headed due east where the sky was starting to brighten. Then I heard that buzzing hornet sound again. Right overhead.

I got the keys out. Had to get gas. Had to get going.

It was four-thirty in the morning. My mind was full of images spinning like the rotor of that helicopter. In the misty parking lot I tried to think.

PG and M's enemies were of a nature, scale, and strength I was clearly ignorant of. A few data points. They could manufacture fake cops. There was more than one Susan. Still no idea who that had been in the limo. And that sound up there.

I rubbed the cut on my forehead.

They could send an OH-6 to pick her up in the middle of a street in Ventura. They could send a drone to watch over her. Or was it.

I shielded my wet face with both hands and ran, panting, for the VW. The buzzing high above was just audible.

Wrong they.

The Summer Meeting

My first morning in Hawaii.

Flight to Kauai, limo, hotel of some sort. Rushed. The Nā Kai, a compound of cottages. Warm and humid. But the humidity was different than what I usually experienced at home. It seemed softer somehow, almost silky. I got used to it right away. It made you want to take off your clothes.

No communication except a note on my pillow.

I'll find you. Don't lose your kō pac.

At the Nā Kai there were no keys. Guests were issued a silver token on a lanyard. Looked like a worn coin with ancient Hawaiian symbols. Did they even have coins back then? When you approached a door you were authorized to enter, it unlocked itself. Walk away and it locked back up behind you. And *always* locked when you were inside your unit.

If it didn't unlock, well, move along, stranger.

I decided to have a look around.

The front door to my flower bedecked cottage clicked behind me. There was another cottage right behind and a discreet connecting passage. Most of the other cottages that I could see in the wide expanse of the Nā Kai were isolated and surrounded by carefully opaque hedges. And the whole estate had a twelve foot fence around it, on top of a five foot berm, all camouflaged by flowering vines.

The buildings had a rather modest look. Single level, classic Hawaiian style from the nineteen-forties. More show-biz, I thought.

"So rich people like security, privacy, convenience, and a lack of stairs," I said to the young woman who had just arrived in an electric vehicle with a basket of breakfast items. Pineapple slices, papaya, fragrant rolls, carafe of coffee.

Her nametag said *Praise.*

She smiled and said, "Aloha," and drove away on the slender concrete path that stretched over the perfectly green lawn.

I stashed the basket just inside the front door. Okay, now I was hungry. She'll find me, or I'll find her.

Walked away from the cottage and went the other way on the path. Sandals, short pants, new Hawaiian shirt. Forgot my sunglasses but no problem. The sky was filling with clouds.

I found the other cottages fascinating. Several looked quite lived in. Long term rentals? A whole world I knew nothing about. Striving not to look too nosy, I thought I saw a hot tub behind one of them. My unit did not have this amenity. Never been in a hot tub.

The path went through a stand of hardwood trees I could not name and another low building came into view. Pool behind a fence, restaurant with outdoor seating where no one was sitting. The pool had no water. I heard raised voices inside.

This place had the look of a classic American coffee shop. I pushed open the glass door. There were two diners, one of them PG.

I took a look at her.

My first reaction was, oh shit.

PG was hunched over an empty plate and a full wine glass. She was sloshed. A waitress stood at her side shielding her from the one other diner at the neighboring table, a middle-aged man in a thin blue shirt. The shirt was stretched to the tearing point over his flabby arms and protruding pot belly. His thighs bulged from tiny swim trunks. A G-string. His jowls were twisted into a sneer.

I noticed two other attendants stationed at the end of the room beside the door to the unfilled pool. Sizeable gentlemen in tasteful Hawaiian shirts. Neither was smiling.

"And you actually thought," the man in blue said, and cleared his throat. Australian. He spit on the floor.

"Robert!" the waitress said sharply. Late twenties, purple streak in her dark hair. Only brushed her shoulders. Athletic. Dark eyes. "Where do you think you are, Robert?"

"Look!" He swayed in his chair.

He was plastered, too. I went to PG's table.

"Robert, are you talking back to me?" the waitress said.

Robert stared at his plate. Belgian waffle. And a big glass of something brown. Not iced tea.

PG, still hunched, turned her head and saw me. She didn't make eye contact but I detected a lessening of tension in her shoulders.

Robert seemed to orient himself in his chair. Or perhaps he was just listening to the voices in his head.

"S and P, Nasdaq, Hang Seng, all off twelve percent or more."

PG exhaled. I sat down.

"Twelve percent. And you did it, you bizarre idiot."

"Robert!" The waitress' nametag said *Janice*.

"You dumped billions. You destroyed wealth on a global scale."

"Oh hogshit," PG said. When she was drunk her voice got sharper. Never realized that before. "You just don't know what you're doing."

"Securities trader for over thirty years."

"Got sucked in, huh. Amateur move," PG muttered.

"And what in God's name do you have against Germany? Good God, PG, they've announced they're pulling out of Schengen. Euro down *twenty* percent. A Euro short? Everyone knows it. You asshole."

"Oh, not me." She squinted at her wine sideways. "That wasn't me. But yeah. That was something." She smiled and nodded to herself.

"You destroy everything you touch." Robert took a big gulp of booze. "You miserable little dyke."

PG said quietly, "What did you say?"

Janice whispered, "Shhh," and stroked the back of PG's hand.

"And who," Robert started.

"Robert," Janice said calmly. "One more word, I snap my fingers, and Sam and Frodo will pick you up and throw you in the pool. That pool."

There was now a crazy look in Robert's eyes. His stomach giggled.

"Oh I see."

Janice sighed like an exasperated school teacher.

"And who is this, PG? Your new playmate? What do you call them these days in Hollywood? Oh I'm sorry. San Francisco's more your style, isn't it. Yes. He's a bit old, don't you think? Over the hill. And, well, wearing the wrong kind of pants, I dare say. Now Janice here –"

I stood up and my chair tipped over and crashed. I fixed Robert in my eyes and walked around the table. As I passed Janice I heard her whisper.

"Who *is* that?"

PG grinned.

"My biographer," she said.

I walked up to Robert and faced him across the table. He sneered.

"And what are *you* going to do?"

"Funny you should ask."

I tipped over his glass and when his bulging eyes darted down I grabbed his sweaty ears and slammed his face into his waffle. I pulled his head up and slammed it down again. His nose hit the edge of his maple syrup covered plate. He gasped for air. I was going for number three when a massive forearm appeared before me. I let go.

It was one of the big guys. I raised my hands.

"I'm out."

The other big guy helped coughing, gasping Robert to his feet and turned his flabby blue bulk towards the kitchen door.

Someone tugged on the waistband of my shorts.

"This way," Janice said.

Outside in the cool breeze all three of us got into a waiting electric vehicle driven by Praise. Janice helped PG into the back and sat with her arm around her. Praise sped away down the concrete ribbon and once out of visual range of the coffee shop veered onto the grass and cut between the backyards of several very lived-in cottages. We pulled up at the unit connected to mine. PG staggered with Janice to the back door, the garden door, draped with plumeria and white naupaka blooms. When they were inside, Praise patted my arm and put it into reverse.

As we headed around the building she said, "Sorry you had problems."

"All part of the job."

"Oh, what do you do? Do you work for one of her companies?"

"No, I'm nothing."

A look from her.

"I'm just a writer. Self-employed."

"Ah."

We stopped at my front door.

"Probably just as well," she said. "She's dismantling everything. Selling off all the assets she can. No one can figure out why. When she converted all her Laguna shares we all knew the shit was going to hit the fan, market-wise."

Laguna Limited was M's holding company.

Praise saw something in my expression.

"Wharton, class of '15," she said. "I'm one of the owners of Nā Kai."

"Oh. Well, wonderful to meet you." I jumped out of the vehicle.

"Thank you. And I hope you enjoy your stay."

"Oh yes ma'am."

She smiled and waved as she drove away.

The door unlocked for me. As I stood at the louvered glass window I heard the door lock back up. The flowers outside rustled in the breeze.

The interior was comfortable. Homey, from the previous century. Bamboo flooring and wicker recliner. Louvered-glass windows. The dining table and chairs in the very modern kitchen had chrome legs.

"Yeah, you know, you could live here."

And there were new items on the table. A dish under a large stainless cover. I peeked and laughed. Belgian waffles topped with strawberries and whipped cream. Two pitchers of syrup. And a bottle of white wine. A California Riesling. There was a note folded under the bottle.

"*Enjoy your breakfast. I'll be in touch about the meeting. —PG.*"

"Sometimes you scare me, PG."

I took a bite of the waffle. Strawberry juice and syrup ran down my chin.

How did she do that? Could be a coincidence. Maybe everyone at Nā

Kai had waffles every day. But the safe bet?

I opened the wine. Good for jet lag, right?

"Just an observer. So observe."

I took the glass of wine to the shower. Never done that before. The tiles making up the floor had little lights in them and I walked in a glowing path through warm wooden walls. The shower was heavenly.

"Tray slick. No such thing as coincidences," I said as I put on the hotel robe, a light cotton kimono. I heard the back door click.

I found Janice in the living room. She locked eyes with me.

"She's asleep." Her eyes darted. "You took a shower."

"I had syrup on me."

She took my hand and untied her robe simultaneously. She kissed the inside of my wrist and pressed her tongue into the pulse point. Then she kissed my arm.

"I can taste it."

She opened her mouth onto the crook of my elbow and her tongue probed deeply. She let her kimono drop to the floor. Her body was flushed. She stood on her toes and kissed me on the cheek. She untied my robe, pulled it open, and then took my face in her hands, tipped her head sideways, and put her mouth on mine. Soft, probing, then hungrily, her tongue thrust eagerly, her hot skin covered in sweat pressed onto me. My robe fell. She pulled back and took a deep breath.

"PG says hi." She locked eyes with me again. "You gonna just stand there?"

The sun was halfway down the sky and shining through the rose-framed, rain dripping bedroom window when Janice opened her eyes. She was sprawled across my chest and made no move to disentangle herself. Her hair smelled of flowers.

"Mind if I ask you something?" she said.

"Thought you were asleep."

"That would be rude. No, I was just resting. It's been such an eventful day."

"That it has."

"But I need to ask you an important question."

"Go ahead."

"And you have to tell the truth."

The tension increased across my body. She chuckled.

"Here's the question. Persephone Gabrielle. Do you love her?"

"Well, yes."

"You want to be with her always. You never stop thinking about her. About her face, the fragrance of her hair, what it feels like to be beside her. Her heart beating. You feel complete. Some part of you that was always missing is found. You didn't even know it was missing and you realize you've been scarching for it your entire life. And yet you know, behind all this, you know she will never be yours. She will never love you. You know this for a fact. And you go on like that."

Janice got up and put her robe back on.

"You have no reason to be jealous of me," she said.

"Janice."

She stood straight and brushed back her hair. Then she looked right at me and her dark eyes did not waver.

"I know her body. But she's giving you the key to her soul. You have no idea how much I envy you."

She went quickly into the bathroom. I heard water running. I rolled onto my side and closed my eyes. After a while the water stopped. As Janice came back out I heard the sharp intake of her breath. The back door opened.

PG, in a blue kimono, walked into the bedroom. She smiled warmly at us.

"Sorry I'm late. Shall we begin the meeting?"

She sloughed off the kimono, stood there naked, then lifted the covers and slipped into the bed beside me. She slid close enough to bump my shoulder.

"Nice and warm."

"Um, PG."

"Where's your notebook?"

Janice put her hands on her hips and her expression went from incredulous to amused. Then I saw her get an idea and her face was illuminated by a crooked grin. She sat on the bed by our feet.

"Okay you two. Knock it off. Move."

She pulled the silk sheets and cotton blanket down, uncovering more of me than PG, and plopped herself down between us. She got under the covers and brought them up to her chin and tugged the pillows together.

"Okay. Go ahead with your meeting. If required I will be available for translation services."

PG pulled her covers up also.

"Fine with me," she said.

"Great. And how about you?"

"Sure. Can you really do that? Translate, I mean."

"I'm not really a waitress."

"Ah. Well." Didn't think so.

"What?" she said.

"Hang on. Notebook."

"Told you," PG said. laughing.

I rolled out and walked to the living room and got my notebook and pencil. Coming back in they watched me, two smiling heads poking above the blanket. The rain outside was heavy and steady. I saw Janice's kimono on the floor.

As I slipped under the sheets I asked, red faced, "Something wrong?"

"How do you walk around with that thing between your legs?" PG said as Janice giggled.

"Normally, I don't –"

"I believe I can be of help here," Janice said.

"Please," PG said.

"If you look closely you will perceive it isn't really between the legs but more in front. Sticking out."

"Ah, right. I didn't want to look that closely. But you are correct."

"The problem," Janice said, "is when walking or running, say, from a jealous husband, it flops around."

"Flops?"

"Flops. Get in the wrong rhythm and the flopping could hurt."

"Wow. Poor boys."

"You gotta be careful. You could really whip the little dude, huh?

"Whip it," PG said.

"I'm just going to take notes if you don't mind," I said as they laughed. "As I was saying I don't normally walk around naked."

"Not even at home?" PG said. "By yourself?"

"No. I just don't."

"Is that an Oklahoma thing?"

"I believe it is a regional trait."

"Will you be all right taking notes in bed with two naked women?"

"Oh, he'll manage," Janice said. "Are the notes for your book?"

"Yes."

"Am I going to be in it?" she said seriously.

"If it's all right."

"Sure. Just don't use my real name."

"Okay."

"Call me Janice."

"No problem. You'll be Janice."

"That's the name of my aunt in North Carolina."

"Let me make a note of that."

"This is going to be so fun," Janice said. She raised her eyebrows at me and pulled the sheets tight under her chin. "What do we do now?"

"I'm just telling stories from when I was young and a college student. He pretends to find them interesting."

"Is it all right for me to be here?"

"Of course."

"Thank you."

"Hope you don't fall asleep."

"Oh no chance of that." Janice grinned at me again. She was loving this. "I promise I'll be quiet."

"Okay. You remember where we left off? Back in that donut shop." PG turned on her side and snuggled closer to Janice. I could tell they were holding each other under the covers.

"In your car with Linda driving out of the hills," I said. "Christmas vacation. First week of winter. The next school term was about to start."

Janice slid her other hand stealthily between the sheets and gently took hold of me. Her eyelids fluttered. If PG noticed she did not let on.

"I remember I always liked winter quarter best," PG said as rain pattered the flowered window.

The River Arcady

Gabrielle liked Winter Quarter best.

A sizable portion of the incoming freshman class always dropped out after Fall thus freeing up space in the hallways and parking lots. Not to mention the library. And the weather was predictably cold and rainy, which she loved. She thought this was interesting, that she liked wet, dreary, gray days. She smiled to herself as she sat on the well-worn linoleum floor of the science building waiting for her class.

Her fellow students waiting for Advanced Topics in Physics lined the hallway on both sides of her. They were all guys – she was used to being the only female student in science and engineering classes – but their clothes were like hers. Warm, dark in color, not new but not threadbare. All had large backpacks, navy blue or deep brown, full of books and supplies, parked at their feet. Their shoes were likewise sensible and unobtrusive and Gabrielle liked to think this one clothing detail over all the others was a good way to get a quick read on someone's personality.

Their shoes were, in general, either athletically inclined or intended for outdoor use away from sidewalks and streets. Well fitting. Kind of pricey but not in a pretentious or flashy way, just competent and down to earth. Which, she thought, was how they liked to think of themselves.

Her own shoes, dark blue canvas deck shoes for use on boats, had holes along the edges where the rubber sole joined the fabric top and she camouflaged this by wearing dark socks so her toes wouldn't be visible.

She sat cross legged and held her backpack in front of her, all snug for the moment. She felt fairly comfortable around her fellow students. After three years none were more than acquaintances.

That was just the way it was.

She scanned the crowded hallway. Few students talked and if they did it was almost a whisper. From the ones walking by there was the shush of nylon coats and blue jeans. There was a shriek of laughter from the far end of the hall near the entrance.

A group of students milled there. One of the girls was wearing a dirty pink jacket and the guy she was close to had on a bulky leather coat with several shiny chains draped from the pockets. Lightweight chains like the kind used on bicycle locks. They were laughing and looking around self-consciously.

The student sitting next to Gabrielle shifted his backpack. He was one of the back row guys. He shook his head. "Art majors."

Gabrielle nodded and watched them. The entrance door opened and another group of earth-tone clothed students entered along with someone in a yellow windbreaker, a bright spark of color. It was a blonde girl, her hair mostly tucked under the collar. Through a break in the mass of dark flannel and polyester, her long, tanned legs flashed under her cut-off jeans. Most of the male heads snapped around at the brief sight.

Then it was 9:50 and the classes began to let out and there were groans and sighs as the students pushed themselves up.

It was just someone in a yellow rain shell, she thought, whatever those are called. She kept her eyes on the end of the hallway as she went into the classroom.

Advanced Topics was a catch-all name for a greatly feared graduate level class in the Physics department. It was required for the master's degree program and the topic was determined by whoever the professor was that quarter. Their permission was needed to enroll. Among the graduate students there was an undercurrent of anxiety about upcoming quarters and who might be teaching what. Sometimes, it was an older professor, such as Dr. Andersen and his love of crystals, or Dr. Bluth and her *obsession* with the aerodynamics of hummingbird wings. It might be a younger instructor with a new subject like Mr. Eidoremstein and his chaotic current flow in semiconductors.

Students had ways of dealing with these charming characters. The older ones could be distracted by questions, or even confused. The younger ones could be flattered and sometimes sent off wandering into long digressions.

However, Advanced Topics: The Physics of the Transistor was taught by someone from the Engineering department named Dr. Rimmler, who was definitely not young, unfortunately far from old, and whose sole purpose in life seemed to be inflicting pain and humiliation on fifteen arrogant, highly competitive physics graduate students, all male. And one lone undergraduate, the only female in the class, and the only Engineering major. She was taking the class because her advisor, a certain Dr. Rimmler, recommended it to her. It wasn't required. He just thought she might like it. For fun.

She sat in the front row.

They all filed in and Gabrielle thought they all seemed a bit nervous. As usual, the professor was late. Everyone took their seats in silence. The hallway outside quieted down until there was only one voice audible, a piercing male laugh.

"Rimmler," someone in the back row said. "Rhymes with Himmler."

Several others began a low level chant. "*Rimmler, Rimmler.*"

The professor's hard leather shoes made a serious, grown-up sound approaching the door. Everyone shut up.

Dr. Rimmler was a slight, wiry man of impossible-to-determine middle age in a white short-sleeved shirt complete with a pocket protector full of pens. He did not look at the class as he entered.

"Stop doing that," he said in a high, strong voice, and slapped a bundle of papers on the wide black counter which filled the front of the science classroom. He glanced at the top sheet and turned to the chalkboard.

"I have your midterms," he said. "Here is the distribution."

Gabrielle was amazed how quiet it was. The only sound was the scrape of the chalk. Dr. Rimmler wrote everyone's score anonymously on the board under the letter grade they received.

A	B	C	D	F
93	89	79	68	58
91	85	75	67	
	85	75	66	
	81	74	65	
	80			

Someone in the back row sighed loudly.

"Your pain is understandable," Dr. Rimmler said cheerfully. "But this is only the first midterm. So do not give up. Think of it as a diagnostic." He picked up the stack of test papers and suddenly looked up. "Shoot. Forgot one." He smiled impishly.

A+

105

"We don't normally grade higher than A because this is not the Art Department. They have lots of A-pluses. But in our case, one person got a perfect score and then answered the extra credit problem correctly as well. In fact, this was the only one who got the extra credit right."

Several students whistled.

"Yes. So, I think just for this test we had an A-plus. On the final grade an A would be the maximum possible. That is departmental policy. Now, that extra credit problem came from the next section of the syllabus. You could have read ahead. It was worth five points and could have been quite useful for several of you. And in fact several of you got it half right. So we will begin our discussion with this problem."

He handed the stack of tests to the student to the guy on Gabrielle's right. She thought his name was Eddie. The test papers were folded lengthwise, names on the outside. He found his paper and passed the stack to her. She picked hers out and passed them to Daniel on her left.

Daniel stuffed the folded paper into his notebook. "Perhaps I will look at it later," he said quietly. "Much later. After I'm drunk."

"Does being drunk help?"

"Affirmative," whispered Eddie. He had also shoved his test away without looking at it.

Maybe graduate students aren't supposed to look at their tests, she thought. She unfolded her test paper. Across the top in red felt pen: *A+ 105* and below, *Well Done!* She quickly folded it back up and put it away. Well, she thought. Well.

Dr. Rimmler unfolded a hanging chart with a large schematic, covered with labels, and on the board wrote: *On a breadboard you have an op-amp set up with the following parameters.* He listed them. *At the exact moment you apply power to the circuit a crack appears on the case of the op-amp and photons (950nm) enter. The beam of photons strikes the Darlington stage transistor, Q12, right smack in the gate. As the photons impact, at that exact moment:*

What is the gain of the op-amp?

"So this is part of our journey through the transistor and it may have been a new way of looking at it for most of you. You would have been well served by reading ahead, as I said before. But interestingly, even the one person who got it right did *not* read it, I think, because they solved it in a way I have never seen before. Something new, maybe, which would be pretty rare. And so perhaps, if we ask politely," he looked directly at Gabrielle, "she might tell us how she did it."

"I knew it," Eddie said. "Gabrielle."

Daniel nodded vigorously. "Gabrielle."

"Look, she's blushing! *Gabrielle.*"

All the other students began to chant her name. "*Gabrielle, Gabrielle.*"

"Oh, come on," she said.

"All right," Dr Rimmler said. "Thank you, gentlemen. Now, Gabrielle, you might be in demand as a tutor for your fellow students if you want. Full time job, I'd say. Charge appropriately." He turned back to the board. "Our problem here..."

"I could see it," she said.

Dr Rimmler thought for a second. "Okay, could you tell us what you mean by that?" He held out the chalk for her.

She froze for a moment. Then she said, "Sure, I'll try."

She stood up and heard the sound of notebooks opening and pens clicking. There was movement in the corner of her eye. Someone in a bright yellow windbreaker was just stepping away from the open classroom door. When she snapped her head to look, they were gone.

The next day, the professor of her last class, a class she was beginning to really dislike, Introduction to Philosophy for Non-Humanities Majors, announced after taking attendance, "It's just too nice a Friday afternoon to sit inside." He scratched his cheek and the beard he was trying to grow.

There was an immediate increase in tension in the classroom. The big guy sitting directly in front of Gabrielle – in this class, she sat in the back row – had just opened his thin, spiral-bound notebook. He now slammed it shut.

This was the kind of professor who was quite sure teaching philosophy outside under a tree, with a pleasant breeze and butterflies flitting about, made him cool and irresistibly attractive. However, it was winter, cold, and gusty. No butterflies. They all looked at each other and there was simultaneous eye rolling.

"You don't really feel like being here. I don't feel like being here. We've finished the midterm. I'll see you all on Monday."

He closed his brand new briefcase, stood, and walked out the door, looking straight ahead. The girl who sat all alone in the front row, Andrea, Gabrielle thought her name was, rose and followed him closely her chin held high.

No one moved. Pencils and Bic pens hovered motionless over college-ruled paper. The big guy in front of Gabrielle said, "It's a trick."

No one laughed. There was total silence for ten seconds and then a sudden frenzy of packing notebooks and writing implements shoved back into folders and book bags and backpacks. No one spoke, not even whispering. Gabrielle could hear panting. Everyone worked with the efficiency of lifelong students, with fearful glances at the open door.

Gabrielle took her time. She didn't care if the professor came back and she was stuck there for another hour and a half. It was Friday. Her fellow students left quickly and then she was alone in the room. This was a class where no one said hello and no one ever looked in her direction.

Many classes were like this. Probably most of them, if she cared to think about it. At least, the general education classes which everyone had to take. Show up, take class in silence, get out. Just the way it was. But the whole school wasn't like that, she thought. No, not the whole school. The sound of footsteps faded from the hallway outside.

Gabrielle zipped up her backpack. The library closed at five on Fridays. And there was also the student union. It was a three story cast-concrete building with a bowling alley, an ice cream shop, and a crafts center. It would also be pretty much deserted. And all that stuff required money, anyway. Forget it.

The leafless branches of the trees outside danced in the wind. This gave her an idea. She would go home, the basement laundry room, and then go for a walk. Cold and windy was perfect. Her house was just a few blocks away from downtown and there were areas she had not explored. She could read the signs and look in store windows. Not actually buy anything, of course.

"Good, I'll do that," she said and the instant she did she saw something and froze. "Wow, oh, this is great!"

Shining brightly on the chair in front of her were four quarters and a dime. The big guy, who always wore flannel shirts and a big flannel jacket and worn-out Levi's, the layers must have muffled the sound of the coins slipping out. It was like he had given the class a tip.

She swept it all into her hand. "I know just what I want."

"That's all? You don't want a hamburger?"

"Just the large fries."

"Anything to drink?"

"No."

"You know, the apple pies are on special. Thirty-nine cents. Want that?"

Apple pie with fries? There was something interesting about that.

"Yeah, okay."

"All right. Your total is a dollar nine cents. Ketchup?"

"Sure. Could I get."

"Extra? No prob."

In her cradling hands she held the fries, glistening with salt, and the slim, sizzling hot apple pie in its paper sleeve, and five packets of ketchup, against her chest and went to the far bench, by the windows. The aroma of the fries rose in a wonderful stream across her face and the apple pie radiated heat through her sweatshirt and t-shirt and seemed to warm the entire upper half of her body.

Alone at the back bench, she carefully, slowly, set it all down. She arranged the fries in their red holder in front of her, angled just right, and unfolded a napkin flat on the plastic table. She made herself refrain from touching them.

She calculated the very hot apple pie would be the right temperature to eat in about a minute thirty seconds but the fries would be too cool by then. She could see the proper timing in her mind, a bright construction of colors and anti-colors in highly dynamic movement. Action and intensity. Velocity and force vectors. She tore the corner off one of the ketchup packets and squirted it onto the napkin. She breathed in. Then out.

"Now."

She pulled the longest French fry from the holder. Wonderful. It was as long as her hand, hot, golden brown, square cross section, with a curve she could describe with the function . . .

She dipped it in the ketchup and bit off half. Salty, sweet. She chewed once and mashed the fry into the roof of her mouth. The savory flavor and vinegary aroma suffused into her sinuses and her eyes watered. She swallowed and ate the second half. No ketchup this time – she only had so much. She picked up the apple pie and held it to her nose. She closed her eyes. Deep fried sugary apples and crispy crust. Yes, it would go perfectly with the fries. Fascinating. She set the pie down next to the napkin. She wanted to be able to smell it while eating. Another fry with plenty of ketchup. She put it all in her mouth and chewed slowly, allowing herself to look around.

Her eyes watered.

There was someone sitting on the bench to her right. A girl with curly black hair that framed her face and bounced when she moved. She had two large soft drinks and was watching the door. She looked like a student.

Gabrielle found it startling that she didn't notice her sit down but she shrugged and tried to not let it distract her. She opened the second packet of ketchup.

Then on her left someone spoke in a soft voice.

Gabrielle glanced. Two women. They had a tray with a pile of yellow-wrapped cheeseburgers and fries and drinks, enough for several people. They were both tall. One had lank, shoulder-tickling blonde hair, and seemed somewhat older than the typical student, although Gabrielle reminded herself she wasn't a good judge of age. The other, with long brown hair, had sharp features and very dark eyes.

Student: probably.

They were sitting close together and talking in whispers. The blonde woman took a French fry and held it out for the brunette, who leaned forward and bit off half. The blonde took her half and popped it into her mouth. They chewed slowly and gazed at each other.

Gabrielle ate two fries at once. Her stomach grumbled and it was so loud that the curly-haired girl turned her head. She ate two more and felt the apple pie with the back of her hand. Getting close.

Then the fries were half gone. One packet of ketchup left. She considered stopping and taking them home for later. But the pie she wanted now. She opened the little flap at the end of the stiff paper sleeve and slipped the flat, flaky tart into her hand. Just nibble, she thought, or you'll burn your tongue.

As she brought it up to her mouth, the blonde woman on her left coughed and began to unwrap one of her several cheeseburgers. Gabrielle turned at the sound and the woman smiled at her and opened her mouth to say something.

"Oh, hi." It was the curly-haired girl on her right.

Surprised, Gabrielle turned her head the other way, apple pie still poised at her lips.

"You know, I don't think my friend is coming and the ice here is melting. You can have it if you want. I haven't touched it."

"Really?"

"You may as well take it. It's Coke, if that's all right."

"Yeah, sure, thanks."

"Great. It would just go to waste otherwise. My name's Audra." Audra had bright green eyes.

"Gabrielle."

One of the women on her left sniffed loudly and in her peripheral vision, Gabrielle saw the two exchange looks with Audra. I guess they know each other, she thought, as she sipped the Coke. She quickly took two gulps.

Then the two women stood up and the blonde one helped the other into her tight, black leather jacket, tugging the waist down. She saw Gabrielle watching.

"Hi, my name's Debbie, by the way," she said with a big smile.

"Gabrielle." She thought Debbie seemed very friendly.

"Hi. We got like way more stuff than we could possibly eat and we can't really take it with us. If you're hungry, for heaven's sake, help yourself. We have to get going."

"Gosh. Thanks." There were three cheeseburgers and at least that many fries.

"Well, good. We have to go visit a friend who just can't stand fast food."

"Don't worry, I like fast food just fine."

"Me, too," Debbie said, laughing. "This is my friend Holly, by the way."

Holly, in the leather jacket, had been watching Debbie talk, completely focused on her face and the movement of her mouth, and now her vacuous smile vanished and she glanced back at Gabrielle. Then she went back to staring at Debbie as if the rest of the world was just too miserable to contemplate.

"Hi," Gabrielle said.

Holly gave no indication of hearing.

"Anyway, nice meeting you, Gabrielle."

"Thanks, Debbie. Nice meeting you. And you too, Holly."

Debbie smiled again. Holly made a 'tsk' sound and they walked away, holding hands.

"Hmm," Audra said. "Watch this."

When the two reached the door, Audra put the back of her hand to her mouth and made a slurpy kissing noise, very loud in the empty restaurant.

Instantly, Holly broke away. Her face turned bright red and she locked eyes with Audra across the room. She went to the center of the order area, in front of the register, where a middle-aged woman in was digging through her purse. Gabrielle could see something building, like a wave coming up from her feet and about to break on the rocks. Holly's hands became fists.

"Go to hell, you little *bitch!*"

Her voice made Gabrielle's left ear ring.

Audra wiggled the fingers of her kissing hand.

Holly took a step forward, found herself blocked by a row of tables. She stared at Audra for a full ten seconds, and walked quickly to the door, held open by a worried looking Debbie. When the door had closed, Gabrielle a scream in the parking lot, an all-consuming scream of rage.

The high school student behind the counter just nodded and smiled. The woman with the purse shook her head.

Audra said, "How rude." She stood up, leaving her untouched drink. "Better make sure they're not slashing my tires." She went to the door and looked out, waved to the high school student. "Sorry, Tommy."

"That's cool," he said and grinned as she left.

Gabrielle felt her pulse rate begin to slow. She tried to breathe normally. She finished the Coke and grabbed the one Audra had left. Her hands were shaking a bit. She drank a third of it in a series of gulps. It was really good.

She knew something was up. They clearly knew each other. If they were gazebo girls, she thought, and just wanted to get into my pants, this was the wrong approach.

It was possible, she thought. Pants. It had never happened before but it was possible. Audra was adorable and she also liked Debbie. However, I have to admit, she thought, I'm not sure about Holly.

She giggled and pulled their tray over. There were actually four orders of fries and they were getting cold. They didn't have any ketchup. She unwrapped one of the cheeseburgers and took out the pickle. Who doesn't like ketchup?

"How interesting. How very interesting," she said.

So what was the game?

She saved two of the cheeseburgers for Saturday. She knew the fries wouldn't keep very well so she ate all of them. She still had half of the apple pie. That was a lot. That was plenty.

Stomach full for the first time in many days, she drove back to her house near the railroad tracks and parked on the narrow street lined with palm trees and shaggy eucalyptus. Being early afternoon, there were several open spots and she parallel parked between a white Toyota and a huge Dodge station wagon, its tires almost flat, wood decal sides covered with dirt that the rain was unable to wash away.

She got her backpack and locked the door. There was gas to go to the grocery store on Sunday, the quietest time, and not much more. Driving was going to be curtailed, she knew. That was fine. The school was only a couple miles up. Easy to walk that. She hated spending money on gas.

That left nothing to do. She went up the driveway and opened the kitchen door. It was unlocked, as always.

She sat in the living room, the *parlor*, of the ancient but still elegant Victorian house, on one end of a third-hand sofa, the cushions covered with a heavy cotton blanket. The room was perpetually dark. There was a big reclining chair that smelled funky and in the corner next to the kitchen door, a crooked book case with an empty glass vase on the top shelf, ghostly white from long dried water.

One of her housemates, Elliot, Art major, was home, and he sat on the other end of the sofa. He was always home. She wasn't sure he actually attended classes. He had a scraggly beard which wasn't an *intentional* beard, as he told her once, so much as a result of having really sensitive skin and of being afraid to shave more than a couple times a month. Elliot usually steered any conversation to the subject of his personal hygiene which was always excellent motivation for Gabrielle to suddenly remember homework she had in the basement.

They watched the big black and white tv set. The town got exactly one television channel and for the first time in two years Gabrielle watched a television show from beginning to end, a rerun of *The Love Boat*.

She had never seen the show before. Her reaction was, as the *Pacific Princess* sailed off into the theme-songed sunset, "You know, that was pretty good."

"You're kidding."

"No."

"Gabrielle."

"What?"

"That's schlock tv."

"But I liked the people on it. Everyone was always smiling and joking around."

"Yeah, that's true."

"And wearing nice clothes."

"I guess so."

"Right. And no one had a gun. No one got shot. And the captain seemed like a nice guy. It would have been more interesting if they had showed more about how the ship worked. Do they ever go down to the engine room?"

"Um, I don't think so. It supposed to be a soap."

"Soap?"

"Soap opera."

"A what?"

He sat up. "You've never heard of a soap opera?"

"Something that weird would definitely stick in my mind."

"Wow."

"I know what an opera is, I guess."

"Of course."

"An opera about soap? You're saying this is real?"

"Yes. They're these little shows on in the afternoon. All about relationships."

"Relationships."

"Yeah, and the stories go on and on forever. They never get to an end."

"Usually stories end at some point."

"Not these."

"Where does the soap come in?"

Elliot thought hard and then shook his head. "Honest to God, Gabrielle, I don't know."

"Well. I'm glad I don't watch tv anymore."

"Really?"

"It's too much work."

He nodded seriously and then had an idea. "If we had a better tv set I'd bet you'd like it more."

Gabrielle thought about it. "There are better units out there."

"I know! I've seen them. *Huge* screens. All Japanese now."

"When everything is converted to digital you'll be able to have tv screens as big as you want. Perfect color. Billions of pixels. I just don't know what you'd watch on the things."

"Wait," Elliot said and leaned forward. "Converted to what?"

"Digital. Instead of," she waved at the Magnavox, "analog."

"I have no idea what that is."

"It'll be a while. Like twenty years."

"Oh. Still. That sounds great." He thought again. "What's a pixel?"

"An image element. The dots on the screen. Red, green, blue."

"Ah. Okay. Sure."

"They make up the image. This tv doesn't have them. It has scanning lines."

Elliot nodded slowly. "You'd think I'd know that. Pixel. That's kind of cute."

"Yep." Gabrielle could tell by the way his eyes were moving back and forth that he was working himself up to say something embarrassing like ask her out on a date. She jumped up. "Well, see you tomorrow. Long day today."

"Yeah, sure."

"Oh, I almost forgot. Do you think it would be okay if I parked my car in the driveway? I'm going to start walking to school."

"Walk?"

"Using the car too much."

"Gotcha. Yeah, you don't want it sitting in the street for a long time. Doesn't look good."

"Would it be okay?"

"Don't see why not. Brian and Mark can just park behind you. There's room for everyone if you park at an angle. Why do you want to walk?"

"Save money. Save my tires. Plus I feel like an idiot driving in circles in the parking lot looking for a spot. It's getting bad. It's always full."

"I could give you a ride."

"On your motorcycle?" Gabrielle mentally kicked herself for forgetting about the motorcycle. But she saw a solution.

"On Tuesdays and Thursdays. Only have eight units. After fall quarter, I have to take it easy."

"I have to be there by seven."

"Seven? Seven o'clock in the *morning*?"

"Uh huh. I have to make sure I'm there when the library opens."

"Oh, the library. Yeah, that makes sense. Not sure I can make seven o'clock. Um."

"What?"

"Just curious. I've been here three years. Where *is* the library, anyway?"

Saturday, she slept in until noon. The open rafters of the floor overhead creaked all morning under the weight of her other roommates, Mark and Brian. They spent some time yelling at each other and there was stomping. Then the house was quiet and she went up the stairs to her bathroom.

When she came out, she glanced into the parlor, saw Elliot staring at the tv, and slipped outside onto the driveway. She cleaned her car with a damp rag. The windshield, the steering wheel, the shift knob, the mirrors.

Gabrielle knew before she parked her car for the week she really needed to get to the grocery store.

She locked the car doors and went back inside. The quiet afternoon passed with notes and pencil sketches of optical circuits. A cold cheeseburger and half an apple pie made a fine dinner and she fell asleep curled up by the grumbling dryer, loaded with Mark's jeans and sweatshirts.

Sunday morning.

Alone in the silent house, she had breakfast of the last leftover cheeseburger kept safe overnight under her pile of t-shirts. In the kitchen, she yanked on the chrome latch of the massive white refrigerator and heaved the door open. It was quite full. There was a gallon of milk and a big carton of orange juice. There were several styrofoam trays holding what looked like steaks. A couple were huge, the size of dinner plates. There was fresh lettuce and a bunch of carrots and stalks of celery. None of this stuff was hers.

Her area of the fridge marked off by masking tape with a 'G' scrawled on it, had only scraps left. She took out all the items to see which were still edible. Possibly edible. She placed everything on the heavy, oak kitchen table. She had three eggs, about two weeks old. They kept trying to roll off the table because the kitchen floor dipped to the south. Two slices of bread in their folded-over plastic bag. They were still good. Bread kept forever. A piece of cheese, the yellow kind, wrapped in a paper napkin. One end was dried and cracked, the other end covered with green mold. So that was okay. But the apple was a total loss. It had collapsed down onto itself and she had to use a paper towel to get it out. It had a strong, fermented smell. That left the hamburger, wrapped in butcher paper, also two weeks old. She unfolded the heavy white paper and the smell hit her before she could see it. It was gray lump of liquefied meat. She hesitated. There was a slightly pink spot on one end.

"Maybe if I cook the heck out of it."

She regretfully wrapped it back up and placed it in the trash can. That was enough for a whole hamburger, she thought, why didn't I cook it when it was good? She stared at the trash can. Can't afford to waste food like that.

Of the four students who lived in the house, Gabrielle was the only one who even attempted to cook on a regular basis. It was far less expensive than fast food or any other kind of restaurant. Of course, some skill was required. But Gabrielle thought the reason most college students did not cook for themselves, aside from simple lack of access to a kitchen, was the fear of wasting food. The inhibition against wasting food was greater than the reluctance to spend scarce money. You could buy a Russet potato for fifteen cents and bake it or buy a bag of potato chips for fifty-nine cents. Students who lived in houses with full kitchens would just buy the chips. Can't mess up potato chips.

Gabrielle thought cooking was fairly easy and she didn't waste much even back when she was starting out. She could make hamburgers and scrambled eggs and was learning all the various ways of cooking potatoes. Baking potatoes and mashed potatoes were no problem, but frying them required cooking oil and made a big mess. Nevertheless, they were so delicious she made the effort at least once a month. She had recently discovered that onions were very good with fried potatoes and they were now also on her mental shopping list, maybe. Nothing fresh lasted more than a few days. Vegetables were usually limited to canned peas and green beans. But maybe an onion would be okay. It would be a nice treat.

She had her own salt and pepper shakers, made of green plastic. She had a stainless steel skillet and an aluminum pot with a lid that almost fit. She had her own can opener and chrome spatula, and a set of silverware: two forks, one spoon, and one butter knife. Her most treasured tool was an old steak knife with a missing handle. The wooden part had long ago splintered and fallen off. No matter. She just held it by the rivets. The blade was still sharp as could be. It was all she needed.

She had twenty-three dollars to spend at the grocery store and she wanted that to last through the whole month of February. Three weeks. So she figured she could spend no more than eight dollars for the week ahead, max. She closed the fridge and put on her sweatshirt.

She went to her car. The morning was cool and cloudy and the air smelled of wet grass.

She drove up the main street, the wipers slapping back and forth to clear the mist. She was behind a white Cadillac which rocked from side to side on its springs like a boat in rough seas.

She had a pretty clear plan. Just buy what you need and get out. No browsing. Browsing just wasted money. The gas gauge was on full and she intended to kcep it that way as long as possible. She had thought of a system. Park in the driveway of the house. Start the engine every three days to keep the battery charged. Don't drive at all (except to the grocery store) until the trip home at the quarter break in the beginning of March, which wasn't much of a break. More like a long weekend. Then Spring Quarter. The very last quarter. And that was it. The last quarter. But so much to do.

Good, she thought. Everything just right. I can concentrate on classes. Just school. Can't let up now. Whatever that was at McDonald's, I can't worry about it.

She shook her head. What*ever* that was.

The Cadillac turned right and was gone down an alley lined with steel trash cans. Out of the mist, a pickup truck with no muffler roared past her in the left lane. The paint on it was oxidized blue. Black smoke poured from the back. She could see the loose end of the exhaust pipe dangling underneath. The rust rotted pipe bounced on the pavement and sent up sparks. The truck blew through the intersection right before her, where the light had just turned red. She took her foot off the gas and held her breath but no car pulled out of the cross street to t-bone it. The crappy truck was gone in the fog in a few seconds.

She sat at the red light, shaking her head. Just like the tunnel, she thought. Her decision to cut back on driving now seemed like a good and prudent one, not just financially necessary.

She made a left and then turned right into the bank parking lot. Her favorite grocery store was a little place tucked away from the street in an dilapidated shopping center. The bank seemed to be doing okay but most of the other storefronts were empty. A fabric supplier, a furniture store, a tiny doughnut shop. All of their windows were soaped-up or covered with real estate signs. She supposed this meant that her favorite grocery store was probably next to go. But they had good prices and she liked the lack of crowds, especially on a Sunday morning.

And one of the employees was interesting. A girl with long blonde hair who usually worked in the back, in the meat department. She had seen her a couple times back there, putting cuts of steak onto little styrofoam trays. Maybe she would be there this morning.

It was as good a reason as any.

She navigated the large cracks in the asphalt and went past a row of dusty student cars, an orange Gremlin, a Chevy Malibu with dented fenders, and a small blue Toyota. She went to the back end of the lot. She froze. The bad muffler truck was there, parked next to a second pick-up with a white bumper. But no driver. No people visible anywhere. They must have gone inside.

She parked as far from the two trucks as she could, switched off the engine, and got out. The area was hushed with mist, scented with eucalyptus. She zipped her sweatshirt up. Vehicles passing over on the main street were barely audible. She stuck the keys in her pocket and slammed her door shut.

As she approached the store doors they opened with a loud whine. It made her wince. Some poor electric motor that never hurt anyone, she thought. Someone came out with a grocery bag in their arms, a young woman walking quickly.

"Oh, hey." It was Audra. "How's it going?" She grinned.

"Hi," Gabrielle said. "I thought I was the only one who shopped here."

One of the pick-up trucks started up roughly and the driver began gunning the engine. That truck. All four of six cylinders, Gabrielle thought, and no muffler. Audra gave the truck a scowl.

"I never thanked you for that," she said over the noise. "That large Coke."

"Oh, sure. Don't worry about it," Audra said. "*Shit.*" The truck was very loud.

"Well, anyway, thanks. It was really good." Gabrielle has to raise her voice.

"And *I* never said I was sorry about, you know."

"That's okay."

"Well, good grief, I couldn't believe it. She should be locked up. Wait until I tell you about her."

The truck driver kept revving the engine. Gabrielle could just make out a shadow in the cab. Another cylinder caught. Now you can drive it to the junkyard, she thought. Raw exhaust fumes blew over them.

"Jeez. Well, I better get this stuff in the fridge." She brushed back her curly hair.

"Okay. Well, I guess I'll see you."

"Oh, no doubt. Bye, Gabrielle," she said, smiling. She started off into the middle of the parking lot.

Kind of in a hurry, Gabrielle thought, and entered the store. The door closed off the hoarse roar of the truck. She blinked away the fumes. The light inside was dim. On the ceiling, two out three fluorescent lights were dark or flickering. There were no other customers. A woman stood patiently at one of the cash registers, the checker, face blank as if lost in thought. Not a student, Gabrielle thought. A bit older. Dark curly hair tied back.

Normally, there was music playing. The store was dead silent. The truck was a faint buzz outside.

In a hurry to put something in the fridge or maybe she doesn't like me. But she's funny. She reminds me of Linda. Someone you just trust, you could tell right off the bat. Unless I'm full of it.

She grabbed one of the plastic baskets from the stack and walked to the vegetable aisle. Canned peas, creamed corn, 'French cut' green beans, her favorite. She had decided to stick with canned food instead of fresh. No chance of Dinty Moore beef stew going bad because someone forgot to cook it. And Dinty Moore was really good. So was Chef Boyardee Mini Ravioli. She put a can of green beans and peas in the basket. Six dollars ninety-two cents left, she thought. Just like that, the money's gone. Wonder if bread is on special. There has to be something cheap.

Yeah, I'm probably full of it, she thought.

She added another can of Del Monte French Style green beans to the basket – why not - and headed for the bakery section, straight back from the doors. She paused at the head of the breakfast aisle. She couldn't help looking at the rows of colorful boxes, so tempting, so expensive. Cocoa Krispies, her favorite, was a dollar seventy-nine. And of course she would need milk. And did she have sugar in the house? Well, forget it. It would use up almost half her budget. Cheap bread, she thought, concentrate on that.

She surveyed the bakery. There wasn't much of a selection, just one staggered shelf display, chipped and spotted with rust like every grocery store she had ever been in. She got the plain wheat bread in a plastic bag. Thirty-nine cents. She shrugged and got another.

She heard the ragged noise of the truck through the glass doors. It had moved close to the front of the store. The sound rose to a crescendo.

Someone screamed outside. The scream was cut off and she felt it like a punch in the stomach. Her fingers weakened and she almost lost her grip on the basket handle. A man in a dark coat ran past. There was shouting, a male voice.

The dark-haired checker left her register and peered out the door, leaning, not wanting to get too far away.

"She was just in here," she said. She covered her mouth.

Someone from the back of the store, the young woman with long blonde hair, ran past the registers and slammed the exit door open, not waiting for the old electric motor. She had a towel in her hands. The door swung loose.

Gabrielle, heart pounding, set the basket on the unmopped floor. She took a step, then ran. Six steps. She stood in the open door and looked. The blonde woman and two other people were standing over someone lying on the ground. A brown paper grocery bag, ripped in half, was nearby. A jar of spaghetti sauce rolled away and stopped. A man in a plaid coat was kneeling.

It was Audra, lying flat on her back. Gabrielle couldn't see her face. Audra's left arm came up and she seemed to wave at the sky. Then her arm slowly settled down, hesitant, reluctant. Her hand made a fist, came to rest on the pavement. The fingers relaxed.

Gabrielle stepped outside. The air was very cold. The young blonde woman, towel under her elbow, was clutching her stomach. She stepped back, seemed to stagger. The man bent closer. Gabrielle still couldn't see Audra's face.

The other person, a middle-aged woman in a knee-length coat, said, "We have to call a amba-lance."

The man nodded and Gabrielle heard him say, "Won't do no good."

Gabrielle walked up quickly and got around the man. Audra's eyes were closed, her mouth slightly open. Her skin looked gray. Her head was surrounded by an area of wetness and Gabrielle realized she was stepping in it. Gabrielle's mind began to race and it felt like a chunk of ice had materialized in her abdomen. Audra's sweater was soaked down the front with her blood and blood was puddled around her shoulders. Her curly hair was tangled and limp with her blood which was running in bright red streamers along a crack in the pavement to a storm drain. That's all of it, Gabrielle thought. That's all of her blood. All there was. I'm looking at all the blood she ever had. She's dead, she thought, she's dead.

She looked at Audra's face again. Her jaw was crooked. Out of joint. And her neck had something stuck to it on the left side. Gabrielle made herself look closely. What had looked like a foreign object was actually a large flap of skin awash with blood. Audra's throat had been ripped open below the curve of her jaw.

"Her heart stopped," the man said. "I'm sorry."

"No," said the woman.

"He was fuckin' drunk. That's what it looked like to me."

"Who was?" Gabrielle was surprised how calm her voice sounded.

"In that truck. He knocked her down and hit the gas."

"The other truck," Gabrielle said.

"Yeah, that's ours. Was she a friend of yours?"

The remaining pickup was the Ford with the white rear bumper. Gabrielle thought furiously. The other truck. The bad muffler truck. Dodge. Dark green. No body damage. Broken exhaust pipe. Went right past me, she thought. Did I look at the license plate? She tried to call up the memory but it slipped away like a rivulet of mercury. License plate, *concentrate*, license plate.

No good.

It was the exhaust pipe that did it, she thought. That killed her. And the way her hand just stopped. That was her death. I saw her die.

She swallowed hard and her right ankle buckled.

"Don't," the man said.

"I was just talking," she said. "To her."

The memory drifted back and she snagged it. The back of the Dodge snapped into perfect resolution.

"Yes, she was a friend of mine."

She remembered in perfect detail. The license plate was covered with mud. She couldn't read it.

"Her name was Audra."

The man took the towel from the blonde girl and covered Audra's head and shoulders with it. "I suppose the police will be here in a few minutes."

Using both of his hands, he took Audra's left hand. He draped her arm over her chest. He did the same with her right arm.

That's the way they do it, Gabrielle thought. When they put you in a coffin. She knew that.

"You'd better come inside."

It was the blonde girl suddenly beside her. She's beautiful, Gabrielle thought distantly. Her name tag said 'Rushel.' She had been joined by the dark haired checker. "Come on."

They each took one of Gabrielle's arms and led her back into the store. They gripped her elbows firmly. The checker's dark hair smelled like apples. There were still no other customers. Only a couple vehicles had passed the whole time. No one seemed to have noticed the event. The checker pulled the broken door in as much as she could. It no longer fit in the jamb.

"My God, that's horrible. I just saw her," the checker said. "And there's still no ambulance. What a time for the phone to stop working."

"You looked like you about to keel over," the blonde girl said. "Where'd you park? Did you know her? You should get out of here before the cops come."

"Yeah, you didn't see anything, right?" the checker said. "It's not like you're a witness or anything."

Gabrielle wiped sweat from her forehead. "No, I didn't see anything." She thought her voice sounded weak.

"You should get out of here then. Those people outside saw it all. Let them talk to the police." Then, to the blonde girl, she said, "We should close. Really. We should close."

"You want to sit down for a while?" said the blonde girl. She looked around. They were standing in front of the registers. There were no chairs.

Fluorescent blue-green zeros flickered across Gabrielle's field of vision. Her hands were numb.

"I'm fine."

"You know, to rest?"

"I'll be okay."

"Did you park out back? Sit in your car until you feel better."

"I will. Thanks."

The checker took Gabrielle's arm and led her past the registers to the emergency exit at the side of the building.

"Were you really a friend of hers? God, that's awful."

"We. I just talked to her."

"I don't think she even had ID. No purse."

"God," said the blonde girl. She turned to Gabrielle. "Don't worry about anything here." She kicked aside empty cardboard boxes labeled *Premium Beef* and pushed open the door. The alarm did not go off. One more thing that no longer worked, Gabrielle thought.

"That your car? If you go out that little driveway back there it takes right to the street. Through those houses."

"Okay. I know. Thanks."

The emergency door slammed behind her. She could hear a siren, very far away, over the thudding of her pulse. She couldn't see Audra around the corner of the cinder block wall. She took a step towards the corner, then stopped. Just get in the car, she thought. The knot in her stomach seemed heavier and she couldn't quite feel her feet. Floating. How I feel now, there's word for it, she thought. I'll think of it in a minute. First, unlock the car. Just unlock it.

She tugged her keys out of her pocket and they almost slipped through her fingers.

"No, come on."

She worked the key with numb fingers and it somehow went in. She stopped. Which way do you turn it to unlock, she thought. Which way? She pushed the button with her thumb and it opened. She felt herself tipped backwards and grabbed the edge of the roof.

"Good grief, stop it. There's nothing wrong with you. Nothing wrong with you."

She slid into the driver's seat and closed the door. The familiar interior smell of it flooded over her. The damp carpeting. The musty headliner. Sitting in her car, the reward for two years of working boring part time jobs, usually made her feel better. Not now. There was a metallic taste in her mouth. She started breathing hard and let her head rest on the steering wheel. No puking allowed in my car, she thought. That's a rule. After a minute the nausea faded.

The girl in the store was right. It has nothing to do with me. I didn't see anything. I didn't know her. They don't need me. Be rational.

She turned the key and the engine started.

It didn't feel right to just leave. But she also wanted to get out of there. Moving through the midst of houses and palm trees, she felt the knot in her stomach relax a bit. Then she was on the main street in the full glare of lifting fog. Lost in the familiar movements of driving she felt comforted.

By the time she got back to her house with it's tall, pointed roof, she had a splitting headache. She parked in the driveway, made sure the door was locked, her backpack was safe on the passenger seat, and went in the kitchen door. No key required, of course. The lock had been broken for forever. No one ever used the front door, which had a nice window built into it of wavy stained glass. She had never even seen that door open. Household legend held that the landlady had had the door nailed shut to keep college students from stealing everything. But there were no nails and Gabrielle thought it was simply hard to open because the foundation of the house was crumbling on the east side and the whole building sloped that way.

Her housemates did not seem to be home, although the tv was playing in the parlor. The room was smelled of sweaty socks. Thick purple curtains were permanently drawn over the one large window and fastened to the frame with thumbtacks by the landlady, Mrs. Rosenberg. The story was, the previous curtains disappeared in nineteen sixty-seven after a graduation party. Someone ripped them off the brass rod, pulled the screws right out of the oak trim, and vomited an entire case of Budweiser onto the heavy red fabric. Then they were buried in the front yard next to the eucalyptus tree. The curtains, that is. And there *was* a funny depression in the grass there. So Gabrielle figured this legend was probably true.

Elliot never turned off the tv. The oval screen glowed blue and white. There was a commercial on for a local car dealership. American Motors.

The kitchen, as always, smelled of overheated coffee from the steel percolator with the broken switch. Brian the English major loved coffee. She picked the percolator up and shook it. And as always, no coffee left. It would have helped with the headache.

She walked around the kitchen table and down the short hallway to her door and opened it. Inside, on the small landing, she locked her door behind her. That was one lock she made sure actually worked. Then she stepped carefully down the steep set of wooden stairs to her basement room. There was a washing machine, a dryer with a missing timer dial, and her bed, consisting of a narrow mattress on top of a piece of plywood, all set on plastic milk crates. There was her old blanket of red wool she had brought from home, along with her pillow. The wall behind her bed was compacted dirt and rock up to her eye level, then century-old blackened wood. On tiptoes, she could reach up and touch the kitchen floor joists. Above the dirt level, just below the floor, a small window of frosted glass admitted grainy light. If she squinted through the glass she could make out the front tire of her car. She really liked that. All of her things were within visual range.

She spread the blanket out and lay down with her shoes on. The lumpy mattress fit her body perfectly. The wool was musty and familiar. She took off her glasses and set them on the nightstand, a cardboard box with a gooseneck lamp. She bunched up the pillow, hers since she was nine, and closed her eyes. The room was warm and smelled of dryer sheets. Someone running the dryer? She thought she should get the clothes out and pile them on the sofa in the front room, the usual procedure, because otherwise someone might knock on the door but all she wanted was to rest for a second. Just a second. She shivered and curled up tight.

She awoke from a dream of falling through bright blue sky, falling and turning, now in clouds, falling towards the wet, black pavement. As she opened her eyes, the dream came into focus and she saw Audra's hand move for the last time.

Gabrielle pushed herself up. The room was dark. Only faint light through the tiny window. The floorboards creaked above her head. There were voices coming from the kitchen.

This is the same day, she thought. That was this morning. It's still today.

She stretched her legs until her shoes poked out from under the scratchy blanket. She felt as if she had run ten miles. Her entire body was sore, especially her neck, and yet every part of her was electric with waves of energy. She threw the blanket off and swung her feet onto the concrete floor. The air was chill. Her breath fogged when she exhaled. Her face was sweaty and her hair was sticking to her cheeks.

Feel funny. Sick. Not sick.

She stood in the dark room. She breathed in. Then out. Her ears tingled. She brushed her hair back.

No, I don't feel bad, she thought. Not hungry, either. But I definitely have to pee.

All her housemates were in the kitchen, their backs to her as they huddled around the old stove. She was able to avoid being seen and ducked into her bathroom, across the hall from her door. When she came out, Brian the English major said, "There she is! We saw your car but not you."

The bright bare ceiling bulb, glass shade long since broken, bored into her eyes. Elliot's face seemed drawn and tired and Brian looked heavier than ever. He was still trying to grow a beard.

"I fell asleep."

"Slept all day, huh?"

"Pretty much. Had a headache."

"Are you not feeling good? Hungry?" Elliot said.

"We're going to make something," Mark the graphic arts major said. "We are going to make." He held up a small white box. "Spaghetti!"

Gabrielle nodded. "That would be good."

"Excellent," Brian said. "I'm sure we have enough for everyone. I thought we could make Sunday the day we all have dinner together."

"Kind of a tradition," Elliot said.

"Sure," Gabrielle said.

"And we could talk about things," Brian said. "Like who's going take out the trash. Or mow the lawn."

Mark sighed. "It's the middle of winter. The grass is dead."

"At the moment."

"Are you making dinner now?" Gabrielle asked trying to keep them from changing the subject.

"Yes. Behold." Mark said, pointing.

"The big pot on the stove?"

"Yes."

"A pot of water."

"Yes."

"It takes all three of you to boil water." The way she said it, it wasn't a question.

They all looked at each other.

"Yes," Elliot said.

"It's harder than it looks," Mark said. "Actually. Because, you know, the stove."

"The stove?" she said slowly.

"It's tricky to light."

"I believe we do possess the skill required to boil water," Brian said.

Gabrielle had to smile at that. "Well, skill is good."

"Skill," Brian continued. "The result of learning. Observe. Understand. Integrate."

"Right," Gabrielle said. "Never heard it put that way, but that's right."

Brian smiled and almost puffed up at her approval. "I need more challenges in the English department."

"Switch to engineering. They'll challenge you. Just finished midterms in everything including physics and the *next* midterms are only two weeks away already."

"At least you're not bored," Mark said.

"At least you'll get a job after graduation," Elliot said.

"I guess so." Gabrielle adjusted her glasses. "This is going to take a while, right? I gotta go over my notes."

"We'll yell. Don't worry."

"There's just one thing," Gabrielle said, and pointed. "To boil water, you have to light the stove."

"Pilot light's broken," Elliot said.

"Yes, we were looking for matches. There don't seem to be any matches in the house. You don't have any, do you?"

"Sorry. Maybe ask Mrs. Rosenberg."

"I will ask Rosie only as a last resort. She doesn't like me."

"Or me," said Mark.

"Really?" Elliot said. "I get along great with her."

"And matches?" Mark said. "She'll think we're up to something."

"Yeah, after how many generations of students?" Brian said. "Gee, why would she think that? That stove is older than the university. And the house is older than..."

"The hills?" Mark said.

"The very state of California itself, I'm pretty sure," Brian said. "Dang, well, let me check my car."

Back in her basement, Gabrielle sat on the edge of her bed in the glow of the gooseneck lamp. She realized she felt much better. Maybe talking to someone helped, she thought. Maybe talking to anyone about anything. The cobwebbed window between the floor joists was completely lightless. "It gets dark so early," she said, and reached for her notebooks.

That was this morning, she thought. It was today that it happened. This is still the same day.

She let her notebook stay where it was.

After a while, the guys called her up for dinner. She nibbled at the garlic bread and sipped her water and although she praised the spaghetti and the thin red sauce as delicious, she found she had lost her appetite. But it was all right. The guys were really hungry so nothing went to waste. They all talked about sports and tv shows and other things she had no interest in so she excused herself quickly.

The house telephone was in the kitchen, on the counter close to the door, a massive, black phone with a chipped dial permanently sitting on a curly-paged phone book from nineteen seventy-five. When Gabrielle no longer heard the footsteps of her roommates above her, she came up the stairs. The kitchen was dark and smelled of tomato sauce.

She went to the phone and picked up the handset. The dial tone seemed very loud. She put her fingertip into the number one hole, and paused. She pushed the dial around and watched it spin back with its comforting whirring sound. She paused. Her mom should be home. It was Sunday evening. Good time to call. She dialed the next three digits and stopped again, finger poised on the last number. What am I going to say? Hi, Mom. I'm upset because someone I know died today. I saw someone die. No, she wasn't really a friend. Just someone.

Childish, she thought. It would just make her mom upset, too. Her mom would worry non-stop about crazy people in trucks.

Nope. Don't do it.

She hung up the phone and walked through the quiet, darkened house down to her basement room. The entire week stretched before her and the thought of it was numbing.

She stuck to her plan.

Monday morning. Two miles to the university. She left the house at five forty-five, the sky speckled with stars. It was going to be warm later. She tucked her hands into the pockets of her sweatshirt. She felt she could walk forever.

Classes were subdued. The hallways, jammed with students, were almost quiet.

Tuesday morning, her legs were so stiff she had trouble getting out of bed and she decided to drive in just that one day. After her jogging class (she walked most of the course), for fifty cents she bought a small bottle of Coke from a vending machine. It was the only food she had eaten since the garlic bread. The soft drink tasted flat and moldy, the bottle was filthy and covered with scratches, and she dumped it in a trash can.

Students playing with a Frisbee on the lawn in front of the library broke a window on the second floor, the study hall with the long tables. The two guys ran past her, laughing, close enough for her to smell them. They haven't had a shower in weeks, she thought. Her stomach churned.

Wednesday morning, she went back to walking. The muscles in her left calf kept cramping up and making her toes curl painfully in her shoe. She ignored it. As she walked, her wire-framed glasses kept sliding down her nose and coming off her ears.

She stopped in the middle of a long block of modern houses with new landscaping. The old sidewalk with its tipped and crooked slabs had been dug out and repoured. It now looked like every generic suburban street she had ever seen. For a moment, she lost track of where she was. Her glasses came loose again and fell into her hands. She examined them. She couldn't see anything wrong with the spindly wire things.

She felt the side of her head. I've lost so much weight that my glasses don't fit anymore, she thought. My head's skinnier. I didn't know that was even possible.

She bent the frames to make them a little tighter and kept going.

The day of classes passed quickly. It was getting hard to stay focused.

Finally, Thursday morning, after her now tortuous jogging class, in the familiar world of Advanced Topics, she found it almost impossible to follow Dr. Rimmler as he explicated the mysteries of the transistor depletion zone.

She caught herself dozing off. This bothered her. Thank God, she thought, Dr. Rimmler didn't notice. Only Daniel seemed to realize something was wrong. He got her attention and raised his eyebrows. She raised her eyebrows back at him and went back to taking notes. There were only ten students left in the class now. It was kind of relaxing.

After the class ended at eleven, she went to the cafeteria next to the graphic arts building and bought a grilled cheese. She could only eat half of it.

Four days without food and I still have no appetite, she thought. At least the sandwich tasted all right. She wiped the oily cheese from her fingers and a wave of nausea hit her. She stood at the corner of one of the concrete planters in the plaza and leaned over the dirt, waiting to see if she would throw up. One of the students sitting there, a girl with long blonde hair done in that feathered style like that actress, slid away on her tight jeans when she saw Gabrielle's face. The pukey feeling passed and she shouldered her backpack in the low, yellow sunlight and said, "Sorry." The girl tossed her hair and turned away.

By that evening, back in her dark and dryer-sheet-smelling basement room, she felt better. Definitely. Clear-headed and stronger. The next day was Friday, usually an easy day. She planned to go grocery shopping, again, over the weekend. There had to be another grocery store somewhere, maybe south of downtown. She felt a subdued excitement at the prospect of exploring a new part of town. Great idea, she thought, and easily fell asleep.

Her dreams that night were long and complex but in the chill, stiff-jointed morning she could not recall any details, only a sense of having traveled a great distance and, just before opening her eyes, finally arriving at a destination of profound mystery. She sat up in her bed hugging her blanket. The washing machine, dryer, the open wooden ceiling and walls seemed to take on a strange lack of solidity in the silvery light from the small window.

The feeling of mystery persisted as she showered. Her arms looked like sticks so she closed her eyes until she put her robe on and got dressed in her jeans, t-shirt, and sweatshirt. The jeans wouldn't stay on her hips. She doubled up the bottom of her t-shirt and tucked it in tightly and the effort exhausted her. She suddenly decided to drive the car. Feel like I should, she thought. Keep the battery charged.

The kitchen seemed different. I'm in a new place, she theorized. I know where everything is but I have never seen this place before. The place smelled of burnt coffee. This seemed vaguely familiar. She ran her fingers over the chipped tiles of the counter.

In the front room, she wondered where Elliot was. Did Elliot even have a room? She left the television set running, volume at minimum. It seemed like bad luck to turn it off. The bluish screen flickered incessantly in her peripheral vision.

Outside, she checked the sky but there were no obvious signs or portents, just wisps of clouds in the soft blue winter dawn. As she opened the car door she saw that the backs of her hands were wrinkled and her fingernails were gray.

"Well I guess that's different."

The driver's seat was comfortable and the car started instantly. Nice and smooth. Almost time to change the oil, she thought, and I should adjust the valves to be on the safe side but that would require buying valve cover gaskets. So just take it easy. She had to strain to get it into reverse. She carefully backed down the concrete driveway and then out into the narrow street. As usual, all the parked cars made it impossible to see if there was traffic coming so she went very slowly. They'd have time to stop when she appeared in front of them, she hoped. If you hear screeching brakes, stop. Easy.

Maybe I won't go to school, she thought. Ditch it. I've never done that. I want to go somewhere. Drive up the coast. I've never been up there. It's supposed to be beautiful. That's a good idea.

She drove to the university and parked in the empty lower lot by the theater.

Where am I? She struggled to remember. Friday. Winter.

She went back to the plaza and sat on the top step of the university's activity area which overlooked an elevated platform. The 'student activity plaza' (as the university catalog called it) had curved steps for seating. There were big, swaying eucalyptus trees and students in coats and jackets reading magazines and having brown-bag lunches.

The sun was warm and the air was cool. With her backpack leaning on her shoes, she pulled her knees in tight and shivered in her sweatshirt. She gripped her wrists. Pulse: slow and irregular.

Classes. Concentrate. What were they again? Her two classes on Fridays were of the blessed type that rarely required participation on her part. They were both humanities electives needed for graduation which she had put off taking for years in favor of science and her core major. In these two classes she could mostly sit back and watch.

There was the (so far) innocuous Survey of Shakespeare at ten, and then there was a break. Then at one-thirty that most annoying class of her entire college career, good old Introduction to Philosophy for Non-Humanities Majors. Hour and a half.

Shakespeare passed quickly. Over in the blink of an eye, it seemed. It's not that I don't like Shakespeare, she thought. I just don't have the time to like it. Him.

The philosophy classroom was already in shadow when she got there. She took her seat at the back and unpacked her dedicated humanities notebook. Sixty pages, spiral-bound, good for at least two quarters. Each class would get five or six pages, which is all the little things needed.

The girl with curly brown hair, Annie, came in and sat in the back corner. Gabrielle thought she seemed irritated. A half dozen other students came in, reluctantly, and big plaid guy sat right in front of her, muttering, "Why am I here?"

Andrea came in and sat in the center front. She didn't look happy either.

"Hey, Onn-drea," Annie said, "where's your boyfriend?"

Gabrielle was surprised when Andrea, instead of being mad, turned around and laughed. "He's coming. He's upset about something."

"Oh, that's too bad."

"No. He's an asshole," she said and turned back.

Annie covered her mouth, laughing.

There was the sound of hard-soled shoes in the hallway. Everyone got out their pens and pencils. Townsend, cheeks pinker than ever, strode into the room and slammed his briefcase on the front desk. He opened it with a loud snap of latches, took out a sheet of paper which Gabrielle assumed was the class list, made a few marks without calling roll or even looking up, and then sniffed, cleared his throat. "Yes," he said, "yes."

He reached into the briefcase and took out a cylindrical object, bright red with a white label. A smiling cartoon face was printed on the side. Townsend sighed and regarded them all with an expression that seemed sad. He sat on the edge of his desk and held the cylinder up.

"Do you know what *this is*?"

The eight students, all science and engineering majors, held perfectly still. Multi-year veterans of dozens of all types of college classes run by a huge diversity of professors and instructors and teaching assistants, they all knew a trap when they saw one. Still, there was nothing to be done.

Gabrielle saw a brief data burst between her fellow students, head turning and eyebrow raising, as silent negotiations took place.

Townsend seemed to sense this activity but by the look of confusion in his rapidly moving eyes he was several processor cycles behind them. The big guy in front of Gabrielle shrugged and raised his hand. Townsend smiled gratefully and pointed at him.

"Um," the student said

Townsend's smile didn't falter. "Yes?"

"I know what that is."

"Okay."

"What that *appears* to be."

Townsend nodded with a slight squint, as if thinking, ah, this one gets it. "And what is that?"

"Um, this is probably wrong," he said, "but that appears to be a can of Tingles potato chips."

The tension broke. Shoulders relaxed, fists unclenched, and breath held was released. The student was the hero of the hour. Annie smiled at him. Gabrielle wrote *Tingles* at the top of the page. *And here comes the doubletalk.*

"You're not wrong," Townsend said. "'There is nothing outside the text,' as a great man once said."

The big guy shrugged, hell yeah, not wrong.

"I seem to be in a non-obfuscatory mood," Townsend said. "Well, it's Friday. Again." He slipped off the edge of his desk, stood up straight and took the plastic lid off the can of chips. He frowned at the metal pull tab and tried to engage it with his thumbnail but it slipped off with a loud ping.

"Here." Andrea reached up, shaking her head. She wiggled her fingers.

Townsend's frown deepened.

"Come *on*."

He reluctantly gave her the Tingles and she popped off the top in one quick move. She flicked it away and the thin aluminum disk clattered musically onto an empty desk. She shot the can back up. Townsend took it impatiently without looking at her.

Gabrielle could smell the chips. Her mouth began to water.

"Let's conclude our module on semiotics with a discussion of this artifact."

He handed the can to the student in the first row who usually spent the class with his head on the desk. He self-consciously shook back his long hair, seemed to study the bright red can, and took out one chip which he placed on his desk in front of him. He passed the can to Annie, two seats behind, and she did the same, holding the curved chip by the edges. Neither of them seemed interested in eating them. Annie leaned out of her chair and handed the can over to Gabrielle. She had never seen Tingles before and the can was heavier than she expected. The saddle-shaped chips were stacked perfectly inside. Wonderful smell and interesting mathematics.

Gabrielle took out the top chip. She smelled it and popped it into her mouth. She let it dissolve on her tongue for a moment and then she chewed it up. Salty and crispy and delicious French fry taste. She got another one and passed the can forward to the big guy. He reached back awkwardly. The instant he touched it, she grabbed it back and got out several more chips. Then it was too hard to reach into the can with her fingers so she dumped out a bunch onto her desk. She counted thirteen. Yeah, should be good. The big guy turned around and watched her, grinning. She gave him the can, much lighter now. "Sorry," she said, mouth full. Her stomach growled.

"Uh, thanks." He shook a single chip out and passed it to the student a couple desks up, a young woman with graying hair in an old Army jacket.

Gabrielle looked up. Townsend was glaring at her. She swallowed.

"This is going to be fun," Townsend said, frowning. "Here we are, creatures adrift in an ocean of signs. They define us, they form us. This is our true reality. We think we are in control, don't we? But he who controls the signs controls reality itself. Including us. So we go into a supermarket and we see it from a distance, a bright red cylinder sitting on its end on a shelf, red to attract attention amidst the company of many other items. A compact object, portable, sturdy-looking, you could sit on it without breaking what's inside, and what in the world could *be* inside? Well, we're not close enough to see the picture of the potato chip on the label, so only in the context of other items on the nearby shelves can we tell. It is not tennis balls."

The class tittered.

"*Context.* The chips aisle. Food, *fun* food, a snack food, industrially produced by huge machines, and all nicely intact, as well. It's good packaging, really well done. You don't have a lot of little broken bits at the bottom of the can, the can which protects them and also informs us of their unique aspect in the chip world. *Uniformity.*"

The Tingles were back in Andrea's hands. She also took out a single chip and then gave the can to Townsend. He looked inside. The chips were almost half gone. He tipped the can over and picked one out.

Gabrielle ate another one, trying to be really quiet but she crunched it.

Townsend held a Tingle up. "Interesting shape, isn't it? That double curve. I don't know what you call that."

Gabrielle quickly swallowed and raised her hand. She didn't wait for him to notice and said, "Hyperbolic paraboloid."

"Hyper..."

"Paraboloid."

Surprised and unsmiling, Townsend put the chip back in the can and went around to the back of his desk. He looked at an open folder and then seemed to study Gabrielle's face.

"Ah. Well, thank you."

Annie and the big guy shared a look.

Gabrielle, not wanting to look up, took short notes, a bare minimum. She knew if she concentrated she would be able to remember it all anyway but she did not want to concentrate:

"Some who say" - 2. computers copyrights patents - just combinations. No authors or inventors. Nothing is original.

"What do you think" - 3. no individuals. Individuals are a myth, a failed ideology. Only the mass of signs interacting. Identity: illusory. Consciousness: illusory. There is no mind. No meaning. We are animals, without meaning. Impossible to get outside the sign-system. Meaning only exists in relation to other meaning, so no ultimate reality. This make-believe system is all there is.

Townsend began to write terms on the chalkboard. *Context. Reader. Sign-system.*

Gabrielle ate the rest of her Tingles silently. She copied whatever Townsend put up on the board without trying to follow it. Townsend seemed to get tired after the halfway point. He reminded them all about the quiz on Monday and also their term papers or presentations were due the second week before finals. Don't let it go. Three pages minimum, typed, must follow the department style sheet, there are copies of which in the office. Unless they ran out. Twenty-five percent of their grade. On any topic they wished as long as it was in the field of philosophy.

Gabrielle sighed. She had no idea what to write about. Or present about.

"All right. Enjoy your weekend. Next week, after the quiz, we start our section on post-structuralism and critical theory. It will be somewhat challenging."

Swell.

"That's the great thing about these Friday afternoon classes, huh?" he said, slammed his briefcase shut, and without another word walked out of the classroom. Andrea jumped up and followed.

Annie breathed, "Run, On-drea," and laughed.

In the sudden shuffling as they all packed up, the big guy, smiling sympathetically, said to Gabrielle, "You gonna drop the class? It's not too late."

"No I can't. Need this to graduate."

"Well," he said, looking at Annie, "good luck."

"Yeah," Annie said. "You know what your paper's going to be?"

"No. Not yet."

Annie nodded and hefted her backpack. "Me neither." She gave a look to the big guy and they went out the door together.

Gabrielle was alone in the classroom. She wrestled her notebook into her backpack beside her heavy project binder. She thought about maybe working on her optical processor, which was at a difficult juncture. She was still stuck on the accumulator design, the photonic equivalent of high speed transistor arrays. Been stuck there awhile although she was starting to have ideas. She started to pull out the binder, then stopped, weary.

"Maybe later," she whispered.

There was the whole weekend ahead with nothing to do. Saturday night was usually good. Her housemates probably wouldn't be home and she could work in the living room without the tv blaring. She could sit in the old recliner and be comfortable instead of working hunched over the edge of her bed while kneeling on the floor.

Or of course, she thought, I could always work on my philosophy paper.

She zipped the backpack shut and swung it over her shoulder. "Nah." She went out into the empty, echoing hall, not hurrying, and down the stairs.

She crossed the lobby and exited the English building. On the deserted, curving inner campus street, under gray skies, she felt a little more energetic. Those potato chips had been pretty good.

Fog was rolling up the street from the west. It already covered the school from the theater to the Architecture building. The tops of the palm trees were swathed in mist. Gabrielle loved the way the fog could just appear when you weren't looking.

Alone and in a good mood, she headed for the north end of the school and her usual Friday evening destination.

The general quietude of the school was one of the pleasant surprises Gabrielle had when she arrived. It was so different from the high school blizzard of dances and courts and rallies and then more dances. The whole yearbook thing. And all the clubs. Key Club. She still had no idea what the heck that was.

And if you were a good student and had friends and were liked by the teachers you were damn well expected to participate in *something*. So she joined the Math Club. One meeting per month. They made her the vice president which she loved because the vice president didn't do anything.

The faculty advisor, Mr. Stumpe, always wore a black nylon jacket, white socks, and massive hiking boots, and had a chronic sinus condition rendering him unable to speak more than a couple words without coughing or clearing his throat loudly, but he did organize a tour of the Jet Propulsion Lab. So overall it was okay.

Now this school here, she supposed, had a football team and a basketball team and lots of other teams, like any large university. Gabrielle could not remember ever hearing about them. No one ever mentioned any big games, any wins or losses. In her very first quarter, she had asked her organic chemistry lab partner, a junior named Shannon, whom she did not think had ever brushed his teeth in his entire life, "You know, we never hear about the football team. Do we even have one?"

"Yeah, we do. But nobody gives a shit." He had scratched his proto-beard and looked straight at her so she had no chance of escaping his breath and said, "Thank God. Sick of that stuff. High school's *over*, man."

And that seemed to be the prevailing mindset.

There were probably lots of clubs. She never heard about them. There was a student body organization with a president. They had meetings. She never heard about them. There was even a yearbook put out each year. A college yearbook. She had never seen one.

Gabrielle loved it.

The library was a plain, rectangular two-story structure with a brightly lit main entrance and an odd monolithic four-story addition on the southwest corner, a massive cube with no windows, just blank walls. University beige.

Gabrielle thought the entrance seemed welcoming as she pushed a door open, a warm glow in the chill mist. Beyond another set of doors, the reading room lay empty. She barely gave it a glance. That was the regular library, as she thought of it. Long wooden tables under fluorescent lights. Popular books perched on varnished oak shelves. It was awful. She spent very little time in the regular library.

To her left was the check-out counter, unoccupied at present, and then the restrooms. Just past the men's room was a nondescript door, propped open with a brick. Beyond this door was darkness. Fascinating darkness.

This was the best part of the entire library. The windowless cube. The Stacks. Gabrielle could see poorly illuminated steel shelves jammed with books from concrete floor to concrete ceiling and a steel staircase, painted forest green. She walked through the door and took a deep breath. Old books and more old books. Weak lights under wire cages, close enough to touch. No windows and at three o'clock on a Friday afternoon no people. Her footsteps were soft and muffled.

She loved the Stacks, home to most of the non-fiction. All the books she cared about.

On the shelf at her right hand, *Learn Magic Tricks*. She snatched it up. She slipped her backpack off her shoulder and quickly walked up the stairs, her deck shoes making a soft ponging on the steel steps. On the second level, she headed straight for the far end of the aisle and went up another set of stairs, Third level, back end of the building, deep in the core. Thousands of books surrounded her, their spines unreadable in the gloom.

She made the familiar conscious effort not to *count*.

Here were the electronics books. *Op-Amp Circuits. Easy Transistor Projects*. She picked up *The Active Filter Cookbook*, then put it back. She just wasn't in the mood.

Restless, she thought, so what's around here, anyway.

There was something on this level she saw once a while back. Just a glance, and she filed it away at the time.

Down low, second to the bottom shelf, lost in the shadows.

Human Sexuality, Vol. 1 and 2 and *Human Sexual Response*. Scholarly books. Then what seemed like the self-help department with a lot of soft-cover books like, *Am I Normal?* and *Your Feelings, My Body.*

She crouched, looked over her shoulder, and began to pull that one out. Then she noticed another book pushed far back, out of sight.

Oh, someone was trying to hide it, she thought. No *way*.

It was a thin paperback, a book of photographs. It was so tightly jammed in she had to snag it with her fingernail to pry it out. The cover was a grainy picture of a woman shown from the neck down, wearing a worn t-shirt and weathered jeans. With one hand she was pulling down at the neckline of the shirt. The other hand was on her thigh, the fingers reaching between her legs. *You Know You Like It* was the title.

She dropped the book of magic tricks on top of this fascinating item and stood up, looking all around. Happy that there was no one to see her, she walked back to the other side and went up the final set of stairs to the fourth level, the very top of the Stacks.

There was a quiet area in the far corner, filled with books no one was interested in, like typography, photography, and similar boring art subjects. There was a study desk built into the shelving. Very private, the desk was nothing more than a varnished plank of pine with a seat of unpainted, splintery plywood. It was out of range of the ceiling lights and too small to be of any use. It was Gabrielle's favorite spot in the entire school.

With the very interesting picture book in hand, she happily turned off the main aisle and went left and stopped. There was someone sitting in her spot, pushed back as far as possible from the light. In her very spot. Gabrielle stared in annoyance. *Damn* it.

The intruder leaned out of the shadows at the sound of her approach. Yellow. It was a young woman wearing a bright yellow windbreaker.

When she saw Gabrielle, she smiled.

"Oh, there you are," she said softly. "I hoped you were up here somewhere." She slid lightly off of the tiny bench and extended her hand. She was wearing cut-off blue jeans and white running shoes without socks. Her legs were long and tanned. She had blue eyes and, as Gabrielle remembered, an irregularity around her left cheek bone. An old injury, she thought, and tried to make her focus on it as fast as possible but the young woman missed nothing and in that instant of realization, Gabrielle thought she saw a look of tolerance and humor.

"My name is Catherine," she said.

"Gabrielle." She took her hand.

"Nice to finally meet you. I didn't get the chance down south."

Her windbreaker was unzipped down to the last inch so it was billowing off her shoulders. Under it she had on a bright blue top made of a sheer, translucent material. It could have been painted on her skin.

Gabrielle, surprised, stared at her chest and she felt Catherine's grip on her hand increase. She cleared her throat.

Catherine's expression went from friendly and laughing to nervous and she looked past her. That evening they were alone in the Stacks. Gabrielle felt a layer of sweat form between their hands. Catherine pulled away until she only had hold of Gabrielle index finger.

Gabrielle felt her fingertip being massaged and she had to clear her throat.

Catherine smiled again, more composed. She looked at Gabrielle intently. Gabrielle saw Catherine study her eyes, her mouth. Catherine leaned closer and said, "I like it here, but do you want to go someplace?"

She did want to.

"Okay."

"Where's your place?"

Gabrielle felt Catherine squeeze the tip of her finger with a rolling motion.

"Um, down by the train."

"By a train?"

"No."

"You live on a train?"

"No." Now Gabrielle was laughing. "Near the station. Next to the tracks."

"I have a place at the beach."

"Really?"

"Maybe we can go there later."

"Okay, I wanted to..."

"Let's go to your place for now." She uncoupled from Gabrielle's finger. "I can't wait to see it."

Gabrielle took a deep breath. The one from the gazebo. I'm just going to go off with her, she thought. Just like that. She suddenly felt flush. She thought of something else and smiled.

"What are you thinking?"

"Oh, I'm just glad I drove the car today." She picked up her backpack by the top strap and left the picture book face down on a shelf.

They both remained silent as they walked down the three sets of stairs. Gabrielle found she had to slow down to keep Catherine by her side. They went past the still empty check-out counter and as they entered the lobby Catherine zipped up her windbreaker.

When they got outside, Catherine started walking faster and Gabrielle had to play catch up. Catherine also stopped smiling altogether and looked around the campus with a critical expression.

"I'm parked over by the theater," Gabrielle said.

Catherine made a quick nod.

"They're building a new library." Gabrielle pointed behind them. "When it's finished, no more Stacks."

"I like the Stacks."

"It's the only place I'm really comfortable."

"I did feel safe in there."

"You found my favorite spot."

"I did?"

"Where you were sitting."

"That teensy desk? Why didn't you tell me?"

"I guess I was kind of surprised."

"I thought it would be perfect."

"It's nice and quiet."

"No, I mean, as I sat there, I thought it would be perfect."

"Perfect?"

"For something else."

"For what? It's a desk."

"At some point, we'll go back and I'll show you."

"At some point?"

"At some point in the future."

Gabrielle could only nod. She had no idea what Catherine was talking about. But the future.

As they approached Gabrielle's car sitting all by itself in the middle of the large lot, Catherine said, "Do you like coffee?"

Gabrielle unlocked the passenger door and then slid into the driver's seat. Catherine sat down with a hop.

"Sure."

She's sitting in my car, she thought. She's sitting there for the first time. She gave in and just watched her. In the tiny vehicle, their shoulders were almost touching. And Catherine was wearing perfume, the one from their bathroom. *Fracas.*

It filled the space between them. She felt herself flush again. She wanted to drink it in. Catherine's windbreaker, now back to being unzipped, was a glowing, crinkly mass. Gabrielle knew it was the long-wave ultraviolet from the streetlights causing the nylon to fluoresce.

Catherine's glowing eyes darted about in curiosity and amusement. Her hair tumbling about the jacket collar looked soft and silky. The corners of her mouth turned up slightly.

She searched for me, Gabrielle thought. She looked all through the Stacks and she found me. And that must have been her outside Rimmler's class. So she's been searching for some time. Obviously, more is going on, she realized. That's safe to assume. Maybe a lot more.

Gabrielle let go of the stick shift and turned in the seat. She thought, I'm going to try something.

She reached up and ran her fingers through Catherine's hair over her left ear. Catherine closed her eyes and tipped her head to press against Gabrielle's hand. When she opened her eyes they gleamed and she looked down.

"You weren't listening at all," she said.

"Hm?" She put her hand back on the stick. I touched her, she thought.

"I said there's this great little place on that big one-way street that I can't remember the name of."

"Sure."

"And they have these wonderful pastries, too. Because I'm starving. And then we can go back to your place."

Gabrielle put the car into reverse and backed out of the spot. Coffee. Can't be all that expensive, right?

"You're very confident," Catherine said.

"Me? I don't feel confident."

"Well, you are."

"All right. I guess I did not know that."

Catherine waited until they pulled onto the street to say, "I bet there are a lot of things about yourself you don't know."

Gabrielle kept quiet and followed directions. On the big one-way street, she passed empty buildings and had no trouble finding a parking spot beside a line of newly planted trees. *Le Petit Cafe* was warmly lit. Through the large windows, Gabrielle could see dark wood and tastefully handwritten menu signs. The prices were horrible. Sandwiches started at four ninety-nine and a small coffee was over a dollar. Her eyes glazed over at the other items. French names. All delicious looking, but Gabrielle thought it was the kind of place she would never normally go into. She knew exactly how much money she had in her pocket.

Catherine said, "I hope they have something left. I've been thinking about this all day. They have *real* éclairs. And they actually know how to make coffee the right way."

The place was redolent of roasted coffee and baking bread. There was room just inside the door for two high, round tables, each with a pair of tall chairs, all wrought iron. An elderly man in a gray hat sat there, gazing out the window, a single tiny white cup near his hand.

"Are you hungry at all?" She saw the empty trays in the display case. "Well, heck fire."

The man in a white apron standing behind the case smiled at her in recognition. "I had a feeling I would see you sometime today," he said. Gabrielle thought his beard was at least more grown-in looking. "I held a little back just for this purpose."

"Really?" Catherine said.

He slid a cabinet panel open and brought out a tray of pastries the size and shape of fat fingers. Some were toasted brown, some coated in dark chocolate.

"These have been waiting patiently all day just for you. So let's say half price."

"Oh, *oui! Merci!* Wow, I'll take 'em all. Someone will be hungry enough to eat them, right?" She nudged Gabrielle.

"Right."

"Any coffee left? Could I have two large and we're in a car so do you have lids? You know, for the cups?"

"We always have coffee," he said. "Lids, yeah, well." He opened several drawers around the shiny coffee machine. "They didn't come in. Sorry, no lids. Here you go." He set two large styrofoam cups on the case top, full to the brim with coffee.

"I guess we'll just have to be careful," Catherine said.

The man set a paper bag containing the éclairs next to the cups. "Anything else? The total is seventeen twenty five."

"What?" Gabrielle said in surprise.

"I got it." Catherine pulled a twenty from the pocket of her shorts.

"That's too much."

"Don't worry about it." She handed over the money. The man set the paper bag with the éclairs on the counter and handed Catherine her change.

Catherine stared at Gabrielle. "I said don't worry about it."

"Okay."

"Really? I know what you're doing. You think you're going to pay me back or something. Keep a tab in your head for however long it takes. I know you are one of the very few people in the entire world who could actually do that. Don't. I got it."

"Okay."

"I'm God damned serious."

"I said okay. And thank you."

"Good. You're welcome. Here." She handed the bag of éclairs to her and picked up both cups of coffee. She said goodbye to the man, who had remained expressionless, and walked backwards into the door to push it open.

"It's such a nice evening, don't you think?"

"I love this weather," Gabrielle said with relief. "Here, let me get the door."

"Overcast makes me feel safe. Like I'm hidden. I guess it won't rain for a week or so. I won't spill. Trust me."

Gabrielle opened the passenger door for her. "Oh, I trust you. At home it's like summer never ends sometimes. Any cool weather is such a relief." She closed the door and went to the other side and got in.

"Where's home?"

Gabrielle put the key in the ignition. "I was born and raised in Covina. That's down south."

"Covina. That's a pretty name. Don't you think that phrase is funny? Born and raised. Like you came off a farm. We raise cows and chickens and really smart girls."

"I guess someone has to take care of you until you're old enough." Gabrielle opened the paper bag and smelled. Chocolate and coffee.

"And now you're old enough. You're on your own. You can do whatever you want. Do you feel free?" Catherine sipped from the cup.

"I feel." Gabrielle started the car. "Like everyone is making plans for me. They're creating a program for me and I'm supposed to follow it."

"And you don't want to follow it?"

"I might. Might not. Why not tell me what it is and let me decide?"

"Hmm. Here, this is yours."

Gabrielle took the full cup in her right hand. She sipped. "That is pretty good."

"I'll shift," Catherine said. She grabbed the stick shift with her left hand.

"No. Thanks..."

"You said you trusted me, right? You drive and I'll shift. Just tell me what gear you want."

Gabrielle sat still for a moment, the éclairs in one hand and the overflowing cup of hot coffee in the other.

"You only have to work the pedals, okay? And the steering wheel, I mean, obviously. So first? As in, gear?"

Gabrielle dropped the éclairs onto her lap and took the steering wheel with one hand. She took a big sip and stepped on the clutch. "First."

"Okay, wait. Left and up, right?" She pushed the stick all the way to the left. "Right?" She pushed it up and a high-pitched whining noise came from under the car.

"Straight up."

"That *is* straight up."

"Try not to push it to the left at all."

"I didn't."

"Push up with the flat of your hand without gripping too hard."

"Hmm."

The stick went smoothly into first gear.

"I felt it go in!" Catherine's shoulder rubbed against Gabrielle's. She took a long sip from her cup. "That's a good trick. I get it."

Gabrielle gulped coffee. Super hot. She coughed. "All I've ever had is a stick shift. My dad taught me. What kind of car do you have?"

"Oh, I don't have a car."

"You don't?"

"Nope. I don't drive. Never driven a car."

"You don't drive?" Gabrielle's foot on the clutch was getting numb.

"Don't even have a license." She grinned and reached all the way over to Gabrielle's left and pulled up on the switch. The right turn signal started blinking. "All clear over here. Ready?"

Gabrielle checked the mirror and saw with relief the entire block was clear behind them on the three-lane one-way street. "Okay." She let out the clutch slowly while giving it a little gas and they pulled out into the lane. "Normally it takes two hands to steer it." They hit ten miles an hour.

"You're doing fine. Third gear?"

"No, second gear." The engine reached a peak and Gabrielle took her foot off the gas and pushed in the clutch. They both lurched forward in their seats.

"Why not third?"

"Just *second*, please."

Behind them, the signal turned green and traffic began to move towards them.

"Are you mad?" They had slowed to walking speed. The turn signal was still blinking.

"Third will stall it."

"Oh."

"Just pull straight back on it. That would be second."

"I don't know."

"What?"

"I'm just not into this anymore." Headlights began to shine into the car through the rear window.

"Catherine!"

"Just kidding. Straight back, right?"

The transmission made a good thump and the engine lugged. Gabrielle feathered the clutch and they sped up. She moved into the center lane. A red pick-up flashed by them on the left. Didn't see him, she thought, crap, okay. She let go of the wheel for an instant to turn off the blinker.

"Third?"

"No, no, it's okay. Second's good up to forty. It's the power gear."

"You don't want me to shift anymore?"

"Okay, fine, third. And be ready to drop back into second."

"Great. All right, where's third gear anyway?"

A huge, boxy Cadillac powered by on their right and let out a long blast of its horn.

"Swine."

"Over to the right and up," Gabrielle said. "We were kind of in his way."

"Like this?"

"Yep, oh wait."

The signal they were approaching turned yellow. Gabrielle put in the clutch and said, "Neutral."

"What the hell's neutral?"

"Never mind." She stopped just as the light turned red. "Ready for first."

"This is really tiring. My whole upper body is sore."

"It's going to turn green."

"There sure is a lot of traffic, huh?"

"Yes, a lot."

"You have to be on your toes."

"I know. *First.*"

"Oh, all right. Hey, it worked again!"

The light went green and Gabrielle drove through the intersection. "We have to move over. Second."

"Ready."

"Second now!"

"Gosh. You don't have to yell."

"I wasn't yelling."

"Fine. *There.* Your precious second gear."

They were on a long, dark block. Gabrielle flicked up the turn signal to move right and looked over her shoulder. A new Sirocco flew past them.

"Nice car."

"Rich kids."

"There is such a thing?"

Gabrielle slid into the right lane. The light in front of them turned yellow and she made a wide right turn just as it went red. It was a relief to get off the main thoroughfare.

"What street is this?"

"Just the main street."

The street went from four wide lanes to two narrow lanes with cars parallel parked on both sides. Warm light shone from the small houses. They all had small front yards, plain grass or landscaped. There were a few driveways and garages but many houses did not have parking. The multitude of large trees blocking the streetlights gave the area a secretive feel.

"You live up here?"

"Just a little ways down."

There were no more headlights behind them.

"I like this. It would be easy to hide here."

Gabrielle nodded and sipped her coffee. "It's easy to get lost."

On her street, Gabrielle drove past her house and found a parking place not too far away, between a blue Ford Falcon with rusty doors and a fairly new four-door Olds, both common student cars. She pulled up beside the Ford.

"Okay, I have to parallel park. You should let me shift now."

"No."

"It would be easier if I did it."

"No."

"All *right.*" Gabrielle took a big gulp of her coffee. At least it wasn't boiling hot anymore. "Do you know how to put it in reverse?"

"You shouldn't drink so fast. And, no, I do not know how to put it in reverse, as you phrase it. What is reverse?"

"Makes to car back up."

"Huh. What are these gear thingies, anyway? Have you ever seen them? I'm sorry but it all seems unnecessarily complicated."

"I just want to park the car."

"So park it."

Gabrielle swallowed more coffee. The cup was half full. "I need to use both hands on the steering wheel."

"Uh huh."

"I can't do it with one hand."

"Uh huh."

"Could you hold my coffee?"

"Sorry, I'm shifting."

Gabrielle took another gulp of coffee.

"It's really good coffee. You should savor it."

"It's okay." Gabrielle poured the last of it into her mouth, closed her eyes and swallowed.

"Oh my God, I've never ever seen anybody do that."

"Reverse." Gabrielle tossed the empty cup over her shoulder.

"What?"

"All the way over to the right, then push down hard. There's a spring. Then back towards you. You really have to push." She took the steering wheel in both hands and pushed down the clutch pedal. "See the diagram on the knob? We're going for 'R.'"

"Oh, *spiffy*. A little picture. It actually shows it." Catherine gripped the smooth shift knob and squeezed. Gabrielle could see her knuckles strain. She pulled the stick to the right. "It just stops."

"Push harder. And pull towards you."

"Wait. Can't." The muscles of Catherine's left arm bulged. The stick snapped into her knee and went into reverse with a thump.

"You did it."

"Wow. How on earth do you drive this thing?"

Gabrielle turned the wheel all the way to the right and started backing up. "Just takes practice." She turned the wheel the other way and the car came up even with the curb. They were very close to the chrome bumper of the Olds. "First."

"First what?"

Now Gabrielle laughed.

"Gear thingie!"

"I'm getting pretty tired." She pushed the stick up and it snapped out of her hand with a twanging sound. "That could've broken my arm." She grabbed it again and pushed it left and up.

Gabrielle rolled forward a couple feet. The car was centered in the space. She let out her breath. "Okay." She pushed in the headlight switch, and the tiny speedometer light went out, and then clicked the key to the left. The engine stopped. It was very dark in the car.

"We made it." Catherine said and laughed. "That was fun! Here, you deserve an éclair." She snatched the paper sack from Gabrielle's lap and took out one the small pastries, partially wrapped in wax paper. "Oh my gosh, I think it's coffee. This is so good. Have a bite." She held it in front of

Gabrielle's face.

"I'm not really hungry."

"How come?"

"Don't know. No appetite lately."

"Just taste it."

"Save it for later."

"Well, I can't wait." Catherine took a small bite. "Yes. Oh my God. Oh my *God*." She bounced in the seat and shook her head. "This is *so good*." She wrapped it back up and dropped it in the bag. "Save it for you."

"Thanks."

"So, this is where you live?"

They were positioned between the yellowish streetlights which were hidden in the trees. Weak spots of lights played over Catherine's face as she looked intently at Gabrielle.

"So dark. I kind of like it."

"Because you could get lost."

"Right." Gabrielle opened her door. "My house is right back there."

Catherine got out without speaking with her cup and the éclairs. Gabrielle got her backpack from the backseat. They both closed their doors and Catherine came around. She looked up and down the quiet, empty street and stood very close. Gabrielle inhaled her perfume and the aroma of chocolate and coffee.

"Well," Catherine said.

"My house is that one," Gabrielle said.

"Uh huh." Catherine's windbreaker was glowing again. She unzipped it completely.

"It's right over there."

"I know."

She ran her fingers through Gabrielle's hair and then along the curve of her left ear. Standing still, Gabrielle stumbled back against the car door.

"Um," she said.

"You okay?" Catherine was grinning.

"Let's go inside."

"Sure. I like it inside."

They stepped up to the sidewalk and went back up the street to the house. Catherine zipped her windbreaker back up as she walked. The house was dark except for the blue glow of a television screen in the front room leaking past the heavy curtains. Gabrielle went around to the right side of the house.

"You have a driveway," Catherine said. "Why didn't you park in the driveway?"

"Someone might park behind me."

"And you don't want to get trapped. Why aren't we going in the front door?"

"It doesn't work. It's stuck and the landlady doesn't want to fix it. So we use the kitchen door."

The concrete driveway ran alongside the house and ended at the front of another house in the back, much larger and older-looking.

"Landlady lives back there," Gabrielle said.

The front door and windows of the back house had fancy trim work. Even in the darkness, the peeling paint was clearly visible. The windows were completely dark.

"This is the kitchen door." It had a frosted glass window. There was a single light on inside. "It's never locked." She opened the door and walked up the two concrete steps. She found the light switch, a brass plate with buttons, and hit it with the heel of her hand. The light on the high ceiling came on, one low wattage bulb.

"The landlady doesn't trust college students, huh?"

"Well, she kind of trusts me."

"Because you're a girl."

Gabrielle set her backpack on the round kitchen table. "I have three roommates, all guys, and they're not allowed to touch anything."

Catherine set the bag next to her pack. "It is her house."

"Yep. Mrs. Rosenberg. We call her Rosie for short."

"But not so she can hear you."

"That wouldn't be a good idea."

Catherine scanned the room. "Small, but then these old places had fairly efficient layouts. That fridge is from the early fifties. Does it get cold?" She pulled on the heavy chrome latch. The wire shelf in the center had a piece of masking tape across the front edge. 'G's stuff' was written on it. "Not bad. Here." She put the éclairs on Gabrielle's shelf and slammed the door. She gave the refrigerator a pat on its rounded off corner.

"Your roommates won't mess with your things?"

"No, they never have."

"That's a good sign."

"Yeah, I guess."

"It means they want the cute girl to like them. They probably screw with each other's stuff all the time. You could do good work in this kitchen. Your oven is a classic. That's just postwar. Wedgewood. They keep perfect temperature." She opened the oven door and gave the interior a hard look. "Small, but okay."

Gabrielle nodded, fascinated. "What about the sink?"

"The crown jewel of the kitchen. A French style farmhouse sink. Looks like twenty generations of students have been throwing pots and pans into it. Not to mention throwing up, right?"

"No one here's like that. I've never seen alcohol here."

"Wow."

"No one has any money. No rich kids here. And I don't think anyone cares that much about it anyway."

"No one cares about booze? This place is definitely different. I'll bet that changes when they stop being so poor. Money will change you."

"Money changes people," Gabrielle said.

"You never know what the effect will be. Sometimes it turns out great. Sometimes it kills you."

"You mean a lot of money. Not just making a living."

"Oh, just a normal amount will do it."

Gabrielle picked up her backpack. "So the solution is what? Stay poor?"

"Just know who you are. Be true to yourself."

"Know yourself."

"Know who you are. Be true to that. And defend it," Catherine said. She pointed at one of the closed doors down the narrow, unlighted hallway. "Bathroom?"

"That door is the basement stairs. That other one. That's the girl's bathroom."

"And since you're the only girl it's all yours."

"Yes it is."

"Well, this is a nice set up. A little chilly."

"Furnace doesn't work."

"Ah, of course not."

The uneven oak floorboards creaked as Catherine went into the bathroom.

Gabrielle quickly grabbed her backpack from the table and opened the door to the stairs. The basement was pitch dark but she knew the way down. She went fast.

She skirted the washer and dryer, dropped the backpack on her bed, and switched on the gooseneck lamp on her nightstand which was an upside down cardboard box. Her thin red blanket had a hole in one corner. She folded it under. Her rug was bunched up. She flattened it out.

Her collection of shirts was splayed out in a mass on top of the other cardboard box that served as a dresser. She usually just yanked out the one she wanted without worrying about neatness. She looked at it in frustration and shoved them into a more vertical pile.

A third box which contained her electronics projects and tools she pushed down to the foot of the bed. She was pretty sure Catherine would not be too interested in a wire-wrapped stereo amplifier or a digital frequency counter, with green LED seven-segment displays, on a real printed circuit board she had made herself.

"There." She evened out the few items she had on hangers, all hooked onto an overhead water pipe against the wall.

She went back up the stairs.

From the doorway, her basement room looked almost inviting. She heard Catherine come out of the bathroom. She stepped into the creaky-floor hall just behind her.

"I didn't flush," Catherine said quietly, "because I was afraid to."

"No, you can."

"I didn't think I should."

"It actually works."

"Huh. Well." She glanced back at the closed bathroom door.

"I'll flush in a minute."

"Okay. I'm sorry."

Catherine went into the dim front room where the tv set was playing and stopped in surprise. "Hi! What'cha watchin'?"

It was Elliot. "Oh, uh, hi. I fell asleep."

"Couldn't have been very interesting, I guess."

"No, it never is. But I think Rockford Files is on tonight."

"Never seen that. Have you been here the whole time?" she said with a raised eyebrow look at Gabrielle.

"I'll be right back," Gabrielle said. "Elliot, this is Catherine. Catherine, Elliot."

As they said hello to each other, Gabrielle went to the bathroom. Flushing was, as always, an anxious moment. There was a long crack in the bowl of the toilet, from top to bottom on the front edge. The toilet looked like it was ready to split in two. But it held together one more time and gurgled as it refilled.

Gabrielle came back to the square, high-ceiling parlor. Where one entertained guests, she remembered. The floor lamp was still missing its light bulb. Elliot sat on one end of the sofa, slumped down. Catherine sat on the other end, hands in her lap. Gabrielle sat on the only place remaining, the dusty easy chair with the ripped out seat. She listened.

"You don't have cable?"

"Cable tv? That would be great but she'd *never* pay for tv."

"Mrs. Rosenberg?"

"You know her?" He switched to a high-pitched voice. "'Vy vould I pay for some ting dat's free, hah?'"

"That sounds like Rosie," Catherine said. "You know, on cable, there's this one channel that's nothing but news. Twenty-four hours a day, nothing but news."

Elliot giggled at her. "How is that possible?"

"Beats me."

"There isn't that much news."

"I *know*."

"In the entire world. That's crazy. Man, they're doomed."

"Cable News Network."

"Huh."

"Everyone figures they'll go under any day now."

Elliot made an effort to sit up. "Be interesting to see that, though."

"It's kind of cool at first. Then you suddenly realize you've been watching the news for like hours and you get up and run out of the house. It's addictive."

"Hm." Elliot slumped back down. There was a loud commercial for a car dealership. He looked at his watch. "Well, it's only six. Nothing comes on until seven-thirty. Oh, hi, Gabrielle."

"Hi."

"Didn't see you. Um, are you making anything for dinner?"

"I don't have any food."

"Damn. Me neither. Maybe I'll go over to Susan's."

"I thought you broke up with her."

"Oh, yeah, we definitely broke up. She threw a lamp at me."

"I hope it was a small lamp," Gabrielle said sympathetically.

"Nah. It was a big floor lamp like ours. With a big heavy base. You can throw those things pretty far," he said thoughtfully.

"Oh my God, Elliot!"

"Don't worry. I know how these things work. It was a long time ago," he said.

"It was just last week. You told me."

"Yeah, that might be long enough. You never met her, did you?"

"Uh, no," Gabrielle said.

"Well, I don't mean to be crass."

"Of course not."

"Or rude."

"Of course not." Catherine said it this time.

"But she's a redhead, right?"

Catherine snapped her head around and stared hard at him.

"I don't mean to be a jerk, but I like girls like that."

"Ah," Catherine said, not taking her eyes off him.

"So," Gabrielle said, watching Catherine's reaction, "You think she has a lot of stuff to eat."

"Yeah, I don't know how she can afford it but like her fridge is always jammed with everything you could imagine. I mean like weird kinds of cheese no one ever heard of. Damn. Now I'm really hungry." He pushed himself off the sofa and went to the stairs to the second floor. "But." He turned. "Am I hungry enough to face her?" He went up the stairs to the other bathroom.

When he was out of hearing range, Catherine said, "He's kind of cute for a male."

Gabrielle laughed at 'male.' "He has a crush on me."

"Can't blame him," Catherine said. "Well. There's nothing on tv and there's nothing for dinner. Except those éclairs."

"Save them for later."

"Because you're not hungry."

"I can have them for breakfast."

"Okay. I guess there's enough."

"Enough?"

"For both of us," she said. She wiggled her fingers in her lap. Her eyes were intense and glistening in the blue light. "I mean, I figured on staying here tonight."

Gabrielle tried to get her thoughts under control. "Do." She cleared her throat. "Do you want to see my room?"

"Sure." Catherine got up from the sagging sofa.

Gabrielle rolled off the worn-out chair. "I'm in the basement."

"Sounds nice and private."

They passed through the kitchen and as Gabrielle opened the door to her stairs, Catherine said, "You're very good at not asking questions."

"Would you answer them?" Gabrielle started down. The air was scented with fabric softener.

"I think it's more like you already know the answers."

"Maybe. It seems complicated."

"Oh, it's complicated. It's definitely complicated," Catherine said quickly, as if she had revealed too much. They stood at the top of the basement steps. "This is where you live? Cozy. What's the rent?"

"Sixteen-fifty."

"*Sixteen hundred dollars?*" Catherine gasped.

"Sixteen dollars. And fifty cents." Gabrielle pulled the door closed and turned the tab on the knob to lock it.

"Oh," Catherine said, relieved. "Oh, good. Wow, cheap." She carefully walked down the creaking steps.

"Yeah. Probably not for much longer. Too bad. I really like it down here."

"I like your little lamp. The lighting's perfect. There's no one on the other side of these walls, right?"

"Just the foundation."

"And." She lifted the lid of the washing machine. "No one's coming down here to get their laundry?"

"Not tonight. Saturday's laundry day."

"Ah, you have a window. It's tiny."

"That's the driveway. You can't see through that glass."

"No, you can't," she said. "You can't see through that at all. And it's already dark. Nice."

Catherine unzipped her yellow windbreaker and shrugged it off her shoulders. As it fell behind her, she caught it with her foot and tossed it up onto the washing machine. "Very nice."

Her top clung to her like a layer of bright blue film. Gabrielle started to ask if she would like to sit down. What she did was look at Catherine's breasts. Catherine turned towards her and Gabrielle thought, seemed to throw her shoulders back. Her smile vanished and her intense look returned. In one smooth move, she wrapped her arms around Gabrielle and pulled their bodies together at the waist.

Gabrielle could feel Catherine's hands clasp on her lower back as if to lock her in. Her chin came up to Catherine's collar bone. She drank in the scent of her skin and hair, the silky hair which trickled over her shoulders. When Catherine exhaled, she breathed in her breath and held it for a moment in wonderment. She could clearly feel Catherine's heart beating. There is so much, she thought. There is so much of her.

She concentrated on the place where Catherine's ear lobe gracefully joined the curve of her neck. What a beautiful thing. Catherine, lips slightly parted, was looking down and Gabrielle could feel her gaze, a pulse of heat, explore her mouth and then travel down the stretched-out front of her shirt where her breasts were pressed together.

"You can touch me," she said. "If you want."

"I am touching you."

Catherine giggled. "I mean, you know, any way you want."

Gabrielle looked at Catherine's face from inches away. Her eyes were dark blue shading to violet, with flecks of gold, and they were never still. She could see the pupils making sub-millimeter adjustments in the dim light. Her lips, parted slightly, moved with every breath she took. They had tiny wrinkles, she saw, and were very close. The area around her left cheekbone she carefully did not look at.

Gabrielle realized this was probably the closest she had physically been to another human being since early childhood. She felt Catherine's leg muscles constantly working, balancing, shifting. She felt the muscles of Catherine's abdomen and back and arms doing similar tasks, a perfectly operating system of fantastic complexity thrumming with hidden energy. Her chest rose and fell smoothly, now firmly pressed against her own. She focused on Catherine's throat where her pulse was visible like a fluttering bird's wing under the skin. She put her finger on the spot.

"You are so alive," she said.

Catherine's gaze suddenly danced and darted about Gabrielle's face, locked onto her eyes. There was an intensity that was almost frightening. Hunger, she thought. Gabrielle could take it for only a moment. She realized she had been holding her breath.

Catherine tipped her head to the left, and then her lips were on hers, Catherine's mouth open slightly, Gabrielle's closed at first then opening a little. So soft, she thought. Then she pressed harder. She saw Catherine close her eyes and she remembered, right, you're supposed to do that.

Eyes closed, she opened her mouth more and suddenly Catherine's tongue gently probed between her lips. She tilted her head all the way over and their mouths fitted together. Catherine gently pivoted her head in a circular motion, slowly, inexorably, grinding her mouth into Gabrielle's. Gabrielle felt her entire body grow warm and flushed. Catherine's tongue explored her mouth, the inside of her lips, all around her teeth. Insistent. Greedy. Gabrielle could feel her swallow. She is drinking me, she thought.

Gabrielle then thought, like *this*, and slipped her tongue into Catherine's mouth. I am tasting another person, she thought. Salt. But also cinnamon. And then orange. She moved her tongue in concert with Catherine's, sliding in and out.

Catherine exhaled through her nose with a deep groan and adjusted her body more fully to Gabrielle's. Pressed back into the edge of the bed at knee level, Gabrielle almost lost her balance. Catherine held her. She placed her right hand on the back of Gabrielle's neck and cradled her head. Her left hand stole around to the small of Gabrielle's back.

Catherine took a deep breath through her nose and finally lifted her mouth from Gabrielle's.

"Have you ever been to bed with anyone before?"

"No."

"Would you like to go to bed with me?"

"Yes."

Catherine pulled back the thin blanket. There was a faded green sheet underneath, tucked tightly around the mattress. "You have one pillow, one sheet, and this blanket, and that's it?"

"Yes."

Catherine didn't say anything. She kicked off her sneakers. One landed on the dryer with a bump. She crossed her arms, took hold of the filmy blue top, and lifted it inside out over her head.

"I like to keep my socks on," she said. "In case it gets cold."

Gabrielle slipped out of her shoes. "I don't have any socks. They wore out."

Catherine smiled and grabbed the bottom of Gabrielle's red university t-shirt and tugged it up. Gabrielle lifted her arms to help. Her shirt was stripped from her body and dropped on the floor.

Catherine began to undo her cotton shorts and Gabrielle closed her eyes. Then she thought, I'm being silly, and opened them.

A woman stood naked before her except for socks. A woman with goosebumps.

Gabrielle quickly took off her jeans and let them fall into a heap. She took off her glasses, folded them, and set them on the nightstand box. She stood there, feeling suddenly shy.

"So, let's go to bed," Catherine said. She clicked off the gooseneck lamp. They both laughed a little.

Gabrielle got in and slid her feet down into the cold. She shivered. Catherine climbed in beside her, their feet playfully bumping, then their knees. It was warm all of a sudden. The bed creaked and sagged. The scratchy blanket barely covered them and the bed was so narrow they could only lay on their sides.

Gabrielle, in the humorous fluffing of the blanket and pillow, managed to find Catherine's face and kissed her. Brief, then intense. They clasped hands. The bed was entirely too small and they laughed again.

They tried it face to face for a while. Then Catherine rolled over and Gabrielle was behind her. This worked perfectly well. Then Catherine rolled back over and Gabrielle tucked herself under her chin. They lost track of time. The faint light from the tiny window did not change. The night house above remained silent. They lost track of time again.

The night settled over them.

A blackbird began to sing, a long and involved song, and Gabrielle felt Catherine stir.

I fell asleep, it's late, Gabrielle thought. It was totally dark.

"Do you hear that?" Catherine said softly.

"Yes."

The blackbird was right outside the window. The beautiful song continued.

"She's telling a story," Catherine whispered in her ear. "She singing about her life and how much she loves the world and how she got lost once. But she searched and searched. There was the sun and the moving air and clouds and the moon and stars. Flowers and grass and the river. And after a long time, she found her way again and was no longer afraid. Out there in the night."

"I wish I could hear it like that."

"Every night, she tells her story to the wind. And the wind carries it away and never forgets. She never wants to leave, ever, even though she knows she will have to one day."

"She will?"

"Do me a favor, Gabrielle."

Gabrielle moved up so her face was even with Catherine's.

"Don't talk of endings."

The blackbird finished her song and the night was once again unbroken.

"I only want beginnings."

"Only beginnings." Gabrielle pulled her arm from beneath the blanket and placed her hand on Catherine's left cheek. In the warm darkness she felt Catherine close her eyes and turn her head into the pillow.

"My scar," she whispered.

"Does it hurt?"

"Not any more. It was a long time ago. I was only two and a half." She nestled her face into Gabrielle's hand. "My father tried to cut off my head with a chainsaw. But my mother shot him. She's still in jail."

"God!"

"The saw barely touched me. One of the doctors told me everything when I was in high school. It ripped out most of my cheekbone."

"Catherine."

"I don't remember it. I remember hospitals. I remember the way they smell. I guess I had a lot of surgery."

"That's horrible."

"I was so young. That helped with the healing, they said." She rolled away from Gabrielle's hand. "I was disfigured. Back then. But I'm fine now. You can hardly see it."

"I'm sorry. I didn't mean to make you talk about it."

"It's ancient history," Catherine said. "I kind of like talking about it with people I trust. Can I ask you something?"

"Yes."

"You touched my neck. You covered my neck with your hand. This hand."

She kissed Gabrielle's hand several times.

"Uh," Gabrielle whispered.

"What was that? What were you doing?"

"I guess I wanted to protect you."

"Protect me? From what?" Catherine slid beneath the blanket and nestled herself on Gabrielle's chest.

"Evil," Gabrielle said.

"You think you can protect me from evil?" Catherine's voice came from under the blanket.

"Yes."

Catherine sighed in the darkness. "You beautiful girl. You don't know what evil is."

Gabrielle felt her breathing become slow and steady. She wasn't sleepy at all herself and decided to stay awake the rest of the night. The blackbird sang again, far away now. Such a little thing, she thought, with so much life in it. There is so much of everything. She looked at the faint gray rectangle of the window and thought, not yet. Don't hurry.

A low frequency vibration came from the floor and Gabrielle immediately knew what it was. The vibration increased.

"Oh, I forgot all about that," she whispered. "Midnight train."

"Hm?"

The train's horn blasted through the basement wall, the ceiling, the foundation. It sounded like it was right outside. Catherine jerked her arm up and the blanket flew up and draped itself over the dryer. Before Gabrielle could react, Catherine rolled off the bed and flopped onto the rug.

"Oh!" she said loudly. "Shit, man."

"Sorry. I'm sorry. I forgot all about the train."

Gabrielle helped her up and got the blanket.

"Holy crap. Is it always like that?"

The vibration slowed and stopped.

"Yeah. You get used to it."

"No way."

"I usually sleep through it."

"No. Way."

They both lay back down. Gabrielle covered them both with the blanket.

"Well," Catherine said. "I'm pretty much awake. How about you?"

"Me too."

"Good," she said.

And it was.

When morning light did come, Gabrielle hesitated to move at all. That was it, she thought as she watched her friend sleep. The first time. My first time.

Someone in the kitchen above slammed a door and a sprinkle of dust rained down. A speck landed on Catherine's cheek and she opened her eyes.

"Morning," she said.

"Morning," Gabrielle said. "I guess it's time to get up."

"You're so funny."

Later, when they got dressed and finally made their way up the stairs it was after nine. Foggy gray light filled the house. Catherine ducked into the bathroom while Gabrielle headed for the fridge. Brian was standing at the stove, wearing a blue flannel bathrobe, tending a pot. He said, "Good morning," without looking up.

Gabrielle grabbed the paper bag of éclairs and tore it open. The éclairs were only finger-sized so she ate two at once. Chocolate and coffee. She ate a third.

Brian watched her. "You're eating something."

"Mm."

"Finally. You were down to, what, sixty pounds?"

"Mm. Mm."

"Oh, she's *fine*," Catherine said as she came in. She was wearing white panties and one of Gabrielle's t-shirts. Her tousled hair almost covered her face.

Brian gaped at her.

"She just needed a few hours of sex."

Brian just stared.

Gabrielle swallowed and smiled. "Bathroom," she said.

"You all didn't make coffee, did you?" Catherine said.

"I, we, we're out of coffee so I thought I'd make tea," Brian said.

"Tea's all right but you really need coffee."

In the bathroom, Gabrielle used the toilet and stood before the sink. She pulled up her shirt halfway. She looked at herself in the antique mirror with its black flecked edges where the silver was eroding. She wasn't completely surprised. She knew she had lost weight, but it was still a shock. Her hip bones jutted from her sides in a way she did not know was possible. Her belly was concave and her ribs sharply defined. She dropped her shirt quickly.

But I feel great, she thought. More than great.

The door popped open and Catherine came in. She carefully closed it behind her and then turned on the hot and cold water at the sink. She came very close. "Oops," she whispered. "I can't believe I did that."

"It's all right."

"No, it's not all right. You don't know. It could change everything."

"I don't think he's awake though. Maybe hungover."

She nodded. "I hope so. You're probably right. He didn't look like he got it. Most guys won't unless you stick it in their faces. Which I kind of just did."

"I know these guys pretty well. He'll forget about it."

"Okay. Okay, good." Catherine kissed her. "I'm making you breakfast. You don't have *anything*." She said and slipped out.

When Gabrielle came out of the bathroom she found Catherine fully dressed in her yellow windbreaker in the process of opening all the kitchen cabinets.

"How can you not have sugar?" She slammed an old painted plywood door. "Mice yes. Sugar no."

Brian was leaning against the kitchen door with his cup of tea. "I guess we used it all."

"You're drinking that without sugar, aren't you?"

He nodded.

"Wow. Yuck. I did find this." She showed Gabrielle a tiny plastic container. "Cinnamon. I'm guessing this dates from the last time a girl lived in this house. About a hundred years ago. Right?"

"It's too early," Brian mumbled, "to exaggerate."

"Clever. You have half a loaf of white bread. Bleah. A tub of margarine, yuk. One orange, two eggs, and no milk. Are your neighbors nice? How about Mrs. Rosenberg?"

"Rosie?" Brian seemed to think about it. "She's very nice. Maybe she likes females better than males."

"Oh?"

"Just an observation I have made."

"I see."

"She thinks boys smell bad," Gabrielle said.

Brian laughed. "Well, Elliot definitely smells like something."

"We don't know what," Gabrielle said.

"And if we did know, the result would be..."

"Insanity. So let us not think about it."

"For our own safety," Brian said, "and that of the world."

"All right, let's go," Catherine said, laughing. She picked up a water glass that had been drying on the edge of the sink. "Brian, don't touch anything."

"Touch? You wound me, dear lady."

Outside, under the overcast sky, Catherine laughed again. "He's funny. You could do something with that guy." They walked to the house that was tucked behind theirs.

"Brian?"

"Yeah. I'm just saying you could. Not saying do it. Is Rosie awake, do you think?"

"According to Elliot she never sleeps at all."

They walked up the front steps. Patches of chalky white paint remained on the door frame and the beveled glass window had a star-shaped hole in it. Catherine poked her finger at it. "Huh. Okay, be nice."

"I'm always nice."

"I was talking to myself." She knocked gently and then poked at the hole again. There was movement in the shadows beyond and Gabrielle waved. A shape waved back and the door opened.

"Ah, Gabrielle, how are you?" Mrs. Rosenberg said. Her voice was sharp edged. "Those dirty boys causing you trouble?" She was an inch shorter than Gabrielle and three times heavier. She was dressed all in gray and her shiny black hair was cut in a pageboy style with perfectly straight bangs across her forehead.

"Oh, no, everything's fine, Mrs. Rosenberg." Gabrielle thought she saw her landlady and Catherine exchange a quick look. "This is my friend, Catherine."

Mrs. Rosenberg's expression softened. "Catherine," she said as if making a discovery. "Gabrielle's friend."

"We were wondering if we could borrow a cup of milk, right?"

"Yes," Catherine said. "And if it's not too much trouble maybe a little sugar. Because they don't have *anything*."

"Ah, sure, come on in. Whatever you need I got it." She shuffled back to let them in. "Come on in the kitchen. You see that?" She pointed her chin at the hole in the glass. "Know what that is? A bullet did that. Not a bad shot, eh?"

"Oh my God," Gabrielle exclaimed.

"Yeah. A friend of mine. Someone who knows nothing about firearms. Twenty-two caliber. I laughed."

In the front room – the parlor, Gabrielle thought – she saw a short sofa with bulky embroidered cushions and carved wood armrests. There was a coffee table with curved legs and a large cabinet, she didn't know the exact name, that had glass doors covering a display of plates with a bright blue pattern on them. Heavy curtains blocked any light from the outside world. Everything was shiny clean in the gloom. Not a single light bulb burned anywhere. The dark Victorian room led to a brighter, mid-twentieth century kitchen.

Catherine and Gabrielle sat in chairs with red plastic seats and wobbly legs around a table of red Formica. There was a gouge across the middle repaired with black tape. A chrome-plated percolator sat in the center on a folded blue towel. Mrs. Rosenberg poured coffee into three tiny cups of paper thin china with gold rims. She settled lightly into her chair.

"Ah, thank you," Catherine said as she gulped.

"So Catherine, what you gonna make? I know you're doing the cooking because Gabrielle can't cook."

"I can cook."

"Sure." Catherine nodded.

"I cook all the time."

"All they have is, get this, half a loaf of bread and two eggs."

"Uh huh," Mrs. Rosenberg said grimly.

"And salt and pepper."

"Because those boys ate everything. Gabrielle goes to the store and brings food home and they steal it. That's why she's so skinny."

"They don't do that."

"You don't let them in your bathroom, do you? Forgive my curiosity. I'm a pervert. That bathroom is only for you. And Catherine."

"No, they're very good about it."

"You sure?"

"I'm sure."

"You say the word and they're out. In the street. Like dogs."

"You don't have to do that."

Mrs. Rosenberg squinted at her. "All right then. What'a ya makin'?"

A short time later, they left Mrs. Rosenberg's house with Catherine carrying a silver tray loaded with a carton of milk, cream in a small cup, a pink box of sugar, a small yet heavy bottle of dark maple syrup, some flour in an ancient square metal canister, half a stick of butter wrapped in wax paper, two fresh eggs, and in miniature cups which Mrs. Rosenberg called *espresso* cups, small amounts of baking powder, baking soda, and dark, wonderful-smelling vanilla extract.

Gabrielle was pretty sure she had never heard the word 'espresso' before and had no idea what baking powder was. Better start taking notes, she thought.

"That was the longest conversation I've ever had with her," she said as they reached their kitchen door. "She doesn't like boys very much, does she?"

Catherine giggled. "She's a sister."

"A sister? Oh."

"Yes indeedy."

"Huh. But." Gabrielle opened the door.

"It's easy."

"Easy for you." They stepped up into the dark but now warm kitchen.

Gabrielle switched on the light.

"Well," Catherine announced. "We were going to have French toast but now, pancakes! And we have real maple syrup."

Gabrielle watched as Catherine made pancakes from scratch. She put some of the flour into a red plastic bowl. Then she cracked an egg into it.

"How much flour?"

"Just the right amount."

"And one egg?"

"All we need."

"You're not measuring anything."

"Oh yes I am. Just watch."

Catherine shook salt from the shaker into the palm of her hand, took a pinch and added it to the bowl. She carefully returned the unused salt to the shaker through the little holes. Then a half-teaspoon of the baking powder and finally the milk. She pour in a good glug, stirred, poured in a bit more. She stirred gently and the batter became smooth and silky.

"See? Just the right amount. Are you writing this down?"

"Yeah."

"Well, someone *should* record this. I'm really good." She pointed at the batter. "Let that rest. Now. Hm. Where did I see that thing?" She opened one of the lower cabinets and brought out an old cast iron skillet. There was a layer of rust around the rim. "This will do. I think." She rinsed it out in the sink. "No one's touched this since Eisenhower. We'll get into the proper way to take care of cast iron later. For now, I'm really hungry. Are you hungry?"

"A little. I ate all the éclairs."

"I'm glad you did. Aren't they the best?" She turned on a burner valve and lit it with a match from a red box. The match filled the kitchen with an acrid, sulfurous odor. "These old stoves are great. You all should clean it, though."

"Okay."

"That would make Mrs. Rosenberg happy. And we need to keep her happy."

"Yes we do."

"We should give her something for letting us take all this." Catherine nodded. "Yes, we'll do that today. So keep that in mind."

"Okay. I have no idea what to get her."

"Just keep it in mind as we look around. We'll find a nice gift for her."

"So, look around? Where are we going?"

"You'll see. All right." Catherine opened drawers and found a spatula, forks, and a butter knife.

"That should be just hot enough."

Catherine made pancakes and Gabrielle took notes:

Skillet has to be quite hot. Water droplets dance on the surface.

Melt butter in skillet then put in 2 spoonfuls of batter.

Always use real butter. Never never use margarine!

The first pancake is never very good. No one knows why. (research project!)

When it's time to flip, the edge pulls away a tiny bit. C says the boxes of pancake mix say to wait until the large bubbles pop but the pros use the edge method.

A griddle would be better than a skillet. Lateral access.

After the flip, you can see the batter cook on the edge – it looks shiny and wet then turns to a matte finish in a few seconds. Remove pancake right before it looks done. Minimize over cooking.

However, even burned pancakes taste good.

Brian goes back to his room. He doesn't get any.

Elliot doesn't like maple syrup. He wants Log Cabin. Catherine says no. He takes his pancakes into the front room to watch tv.

It will take me a long time to be able to cook like her. Just a few techniques, she says. I tell her cooking is similar to solid state electronics. She just looks at me.

So after a breakfast of pancakes covered with melted butter and dark maple syrup, Gabrielle felt the need to get out of the stuffy house with its constantly running tv set. She found herself standing by her car with Catherine in her fully zipped up windbreaker.

"This car is your real home," she said.

"Huh?"

"You're not used to big breakfasts. It makes you fuzzy headed."

"I'm sleepy."

"I'm going to get you used to it. Don't worry. It's one of my goals. You'll wonder how you lived without it."

Gabrielle smiled. "You mean breakfast?"

"Why yes. Breakfast. Of course." Catherine ran her hand over the round top of the Volkswagen. "Now, let's stay focused on Mrs. Rosenberg. We must find a nice thank-you gift. Then lunch. Then, we'll see."

"That's a protocol," Gabrielle said, rubbing her eyes. "Doing things in a specific order."

Catherine thought. "Protocol. For Mrs. Rosenberg."

"The Rosenberg protocol."

"Ooh!" Catherine glanced up and down the sidewalk. Uneven concrete slabs. Palm trees in fog. Nothing moving. Gabrielle stood still as she bumped into her.

"I love it when you talk like that."

"I do it a lot."

"Let's get in the car."

"I was..."

"Get in."

"Oh."

"Hurry."

Later, when they got going in the bright foggy light, Gabrielle said, "I've had this car for years and I've never been in the back seat before. It's pretty comfortable."

"It is, isn't it?" She kept her hand on Gabrielle's thigh as they went down the quiet Saturday morning street.

"I never knew."

"We mustn't let it go to waste."

"No, we can't waste it."

"We won't."

Gabrielle felt Catherine's hand move firmly. "Fourth?" she asked.

"In a second."

"Second gear?"

"No, wait to see if we make the light."

"Then second?"

Gabrielle was laughing now. "See? It's staying green." They rolled through the intersection. "Okay, fourth," she said as Catherine deflected her hand pulled the stick straight back.

"You just like shifting." Gabrielle let out the clutch.

"I do," Catherine said. She put her hand back on Gabrielle's leg.

They turned onto a highway, crested a hill, and entered a long valley. The slopes of the volcanic mountains on their left were a vibrant green in the slacking winter rain. Before them was clear, cold air. On the horizon, beneath wicked cloud wrack, the great gray sea stretched.

"Before yesterday, I would have had trouble understanding."

Catherine moved her hand deeper.

"You like shifting for yourself," she said.

"I've always shifted for myself."

"It's much better to have someone else shift for you."

"If you say so."

"It's really the way it should be."

"I guess you're right."

"You guess?"

"Well, this has all been such a surprise."

Catherine let her head rest on Gabrielle's shoulder. The little car bounced confidently down the cracked and pot-holed highway. "And there may be more surprises to come."

Following Catherine's directions, Gabrielle took an off-ramp and parked on a quaint street a block from the marina of the small bay town. There were several tourist shops Catherine called 'cute' selling 'artsy' items. They checked every shop. Gabrielle noticed that as soon as they walked into the presence of other people – she found herself thinking of them as 'regular' people – Catherine pulled away, would not take her hand, and kept herself clearly separate.

In the last store, she picked out a tall, thin vase of multicolored glass, took a quick glance at the price sticker on the bottom, shrugged and handed it to Gabrielle.

"Think Rosie would like that? It kind of matches the color of that window in the front door."

"With the hole."

"The bullet hole. From a friend of hers."

"Someone shot her house." Gabrielle saw the price and her eyes widened. Fifty-five dollars.

"That happens."

"Shooting?"

"More than that."

"More?"

Catherine waited for a middle-aged couple to move out hearing range. She spoke into Gabrielle's ear. "It's your life. Your one and only life. You fight for what you want."

Gabrielle nodded.

"Sometimes it gets crazy."

Catherine paid for the vase with a hundred dollar bill. The woman at the register took it without visible reaction behind her thick eyeglasses. They drove away from the stores and stopped at a long, narrow park by the water. They walked down the sidewalk and talked about the sailboats moored in the inlet, protected by a long stretch of sand dunes. They had lunch at a tiny cafe at the other end of town. They sat at a table outside, despite the chilly weather, and Catherine ordered for both of them in French. They had soup made with lots of onions and melted cheese on top along with the best coffee Gabrielle had ever tasted. She shivered in her sweatshirt and when her stomach growled loudly, Catherine laughed.

"This is real food. Your body can tell."

"It's so good." She slurped the last of the onion soup from the bowl. "It's expensive."

"I got it. You pay for nothing."

"I'll pay you back."

"No, you won't, I told you. This is your reward. Remind me to fill up your gas tank."

"Reward?"

"For not asking questions."

They departed from the cafe, Catherine left a five dollar tip for a fourteen dollar bill, and they drove around the end of the bay to a long, gravel beach. They passed by the rectangular bulk of the huge power plant, nearly featureless except for three gigantic smoke stacks topped by pulsing red lights bright against the overcast. Gabrielle walked to water's edge to get an unobstructed view of the place.

"You like that?" Catherine said with a pinched expression.

"I love it." Gabrielle held out her hand, palm up. The rain tickled. "It's like its alive."

"It's awful."

"I think it's beautiful," Gabrielle retorted. "It makes life here possible."

"Whatever. You are so weird."

Gabrielle looked at her in amazement. "Yes. *This* makes me weird."

Catherine laughed.

They walked up and then down the beach. Catherine refused to hold hands as long as there were any people present. She said, "Sometimes there are seals and otters playing here but I don't see anything. Oh, well."

"You want to go back to the house? It's kind of cold."

"You don't do much, do you? Just school."

Gabrielle didn't want to say she couldn't afford to do anything so she said, "I have to do really well. Everything depends on it."

Catherine nodded and walked back to the car. They drove towards the highway and true to her word, Catherine had Gabrielle pull into a gas station and paid for a fill-up. Seven and a half gallons at sixty-one cents. Then, as they were about to get back on the highway, she said, "Stop. Just thought of something. Go the other way," and directed Gabrielle to a large supermarket just off the main street. "You need to stock up."

Gabrielle pulled in between a metallic green Volvo with Proposition 13 bumper stickers and a shiny new Datsun. Rich kids' grocery store, she thought.

"May as well," she said. "I still have nineteen dollars left."

"What? You can't use your money, I told you."

"You're going to pay for my groceries?"

"I used up the last of your stuff this morning. I'm paying you back."

"Um. I. All right."

"Good. And we have to pay back Mrs. Rosenberg, too."

As they entered the store, Catherine said, "Never argue with me."

"I wasn't."

"Well, don't."

"I wasn't."

The store was brightly lit and the floor was very clean. It was warm and she smelled baking bread. There was soft classical music playing. All the other customers, ninety-five percent female, Gabrielle figured, were wearing nice clothes and seemed to study the items on the shelves instead of just grabbing them. All the prices were a good ten to twelve percent higher than College Costs Less.

Catherine spent several moments selecting a shopping cart. One had bad wheels. Another a dirty handle. She found a good one. "I'll tell you exactly what to get."

When they finished scouring the store the shopping cart was overflowing and it took the checker, a tall, bald man in an apron who never smiled, a good ten minutes to ring it all up. Gabrielle was absolutely astonished by the final tally. *$169.80.*

"Are you okay?" Catherine said as she gave the man two hundreds.

"This will never fit in the kitchen."

"We'll make it fit."

"I don't see how."

"Just start eating."

It almost didn't fit in the car. The back seat was overflowing with grocery bags piled on top of each other, including one bag which contained a coffee percolator, a toaster, a small cutting board, and a set of stainless utensils. A spatula, tongs, a slotted spoon, and a large knife. Catherine had to sit with a bulging, close-to-ripping paper bag between her feet. It contained two large bottle of ketchup, two loaves of French bread in paper sleeves, two large boxes of Cocoa Krispies, and two bottles of wine. It was the first time Gabrielle had ever purchased alcohol and she found it exciting. Although Catherine paid for it, she thought. So not really. She shook her head.

Catherine held on to the heavy bag and let Gabrielle do the shifting.

Gabrielle parked in the driveway. It was too much to carry in from the street.

"You still have a big Sunday dinner?" Catherine asked as she carried a bag of vegetables into the kitchen. Lettuce, celery, carrots, and something with curly, dark green leaves Gabrielle didn't know the name of and had no idea how to cook.

"I guess so. Brian made spaghetti last week. It was kind of fun." Even though I wasn't exactly hungry, she thought. Not even a week ago.

"If you don't mind, I'd like to cook Sunday dinner for everyone tomorrow."

"That would be really nice."

"It would be, you know, a way of sharing some of this with the guys."

"I'm sure they wouldn't mind."

"Because all this is yours. Just yours."

When they finished unloading the car, the table and all the counters were covered with bulging brown paper bags. Gabrielle stepped back to regard it all. I have a coffee maker now, she thought.

"I have to move the car," she said.

"You are so paranoid about that." Catherine was giving the cabinets a calculating look.

"I know. Sorry. It bugs me."

Gabrielle went out to her car, feeling slightly guilty. Well, she's much better at putting away groceries than I am, she thought. Catherine actually seems to enjoy it.

She backed out of the driveway very carefully, inch by inch.

The situation was as bad as she had feared. Every place a car could be parked had a vehicle in it. Using a spiral search pattern, she soon found herself well away from the house. There was, at least, very little traffic so it was easy to get through the stop signs.

She decided to circle, using the small triangular park near the train station as the waypoint. On her third orbit, she finally got lucky. Before her, a lumbering, green Pontiac pulled away from a perfect place at the tip of the park. She downshifted and slid into the spot. She got as close to the curb as she could. The angle of the streets made it impossible for anyone to park in front of her.

This is it, she thought. I'm leaving the car here. She shut down the trusty four cylinder engine.

"I won't move this until I graduate," she said out loud. "Just run the engine for five minutes every other day to keep the battery charged." She quickly reviewed the numbers. "Six minutes just to be sure."

She made sure the headlights were off, opened the door and pushed the skinny lock knob down with a snap. She got out, checked the back seat. Nothing there, of course. She felt the key in her pocket and slammed the door shut. The seal was so good the interior air pressure would bounce the door back unless she pushed extra hard so she leaned into it. The door closed with a satisfying thump. She walked around to the sidewalk and checked. Positioned well, she figured. She tested the passenger door. Locked.

"All right." She walked across the street and away from the little park with its dry grass and solitary bench covered in peeling paint. She was thankful the streetlights were the bright, new amber types. She looked at her humble yet wonderful red Volkswagen. She hated being out of visual range.

"I won't move it until I graduate." She began walking back to the house, several long blocks away. "Or until I have to go to the grocery store again, which is now almost the same thing," she said, smiling.

Going down the shadowy, quiet sidewalk, she thought about Catherine. Was this all a game? Does Catherine really like me or is she just playing a part? Was it all an act? And how should I act? What's my part?

Still, she thought, whatever this all is, I do like her. And I got a kitchen full of food and other things.

She walked faster. The cold air stung her cheeks. The sky was lowering. There would be no stars this night.

"This is a surprise," she said to the gathering darkness. "This is definitely a surprise."

When she got to her house and entered the cheerily lit kitchen, she smelled coffee and cooking hamburgers. Catherine was slicing a russet potato with the new chef's knife on the new plastic cutting board. Catherine looked up and said, "What?"

"What?"

"What is it? What's wrong?"

146

"Nothing."

"Is it your car?"

"No, the car's fine. Everything's fine."

"You don't look fine." Catherine finished slicing the potato into thin strips and then faced her. "Is it about me staying here? Because I can leave."

"No, of course not."

"You sure?"

"I want you to stay."

"I don't know now."

"Please don't leave."

Catherine set the knife down and gathered the potato slices into the new glass bowl. She washed her hands at the sink. "All right, I'll stay. On one condition. Tell me what's wrong."

"Catherine."

"I'm serious. Level with me or I'm gone."

Gabrielle wiped her face with the dish towel. "Okay. I was walking back here from parking the car and I was thinking about how you would be here. Waiting for me."

"And that made you upset?"

"No. Just the opposite."

"What's the opposite?"

"I," Gabrielle said, "thought it felt good."

"Good?" Catherine's skeptical look was replaced by puzzlement.

"It felt wonderful. I'm so glad you're here. No one's ever done this before." Gabrielle was almost whispering.

"Oh."

"Nothing's wrong."

"All you had to do was tell me that," Catherine said just as softly. "I can't read minds."

"I'll try."

Catherine shrugged "You'll try. Well, at least that's honest, I guess."

Gabrielle looked at her. "You are so mysterious."

Catherine grinned. "It's great, isn't it?"

Gabrielle could only nod. She went into the bathroom and heard Catherine walk into the front room. "Elliot. Wake up. You want a hamburger? Is that yes? You're drooling. Go back to sleep, I'll let you know."

As Gabrielle washed her hands, a thought crossed her mind and this thought at first gave her a twinge of fear.

I have no idea what I'm doing, she thought, and I have no idea what's going to happen next. I have no idea. I really have no idea at all.

She smiled at herself and her thoughts and went out to dinner.

Elliot's reaction to the hamburger, fried potatoes, and sautéed green beans was, "Gabrielle, Cathy can come over any time she wants."

"Catherine."

"Right. She's good."

"Why thank you."

"She goes by Catherine."

"Ah." He nodded and pointed his finger at her. "Check."

"And she's making dinner tomorrow for everyone. Probably six or six-thirty. Don't forget."

"Don't worry. Finally, someone who really knows how to cook."

"I can cook."

"Oh, I know."

"I cook all the time."

"Sure."

They all watched tv until eleven. *Chips* and a *Rockford Files* rerun. They all agreed James Garner was cool. Catherine and Elliot sat on far ends of the sofa while Gabrielle sat in the recliner with her homework. Catherine glanced at it.

"You can do that and watch tv at the same time?"

"It's pretty easy. Just my math class."

Elliot laughed. "You're something, Gabrielle."

"What? It *is* easy. It's my philosophy class that's hard."

"How could anything be hard for you?" Elliot said, then to Catherine, "She's a genius."

"She does seem fairly smart."

"Uh, huh. Watch." He leaned out and said, "What are you working on these days besides math, Gabrielle?"

She put down her pencil. "My real interest is light. I've always been obsessed with light and so of course now lasers so I'm really getting into the quantum mechanics of photons and I think it might be possible to create a kind of optical electronics except you couldn't really call it that because it wouldn't be using electrons so maybe photonics. But anyway, imagine... what?"

Elliot nodded. "See?"

Catherine stared at Gabrielle. "God, that's hot."

Gabrielle stared back for a moment, closed her textbook and notebook and set them on the coffee table. "Well, I'm going to bed."

Catherine stood up. "Yes, it is late. I believe I will also turn in as well. Don't stay up all night, Elliot."

"Uh, I won't I don't know how you stand it in that basement, Gabrielle. Isn't it freezing? There's no heat."

"There's heat," Gabrielle said.

"There is?"

"Sure." They passed through the dark kitchen and reached the door to the stairs.

"Good."

"Yes, it is," Catherine said with a giggle. She closed the door behind them and turned the lock.

The second night was different, Gabrielle thought later in the darkness. Better in some ways. Not quite as exciting. More expectations. More relaxed, maybe even comfortable. Well, she could see a pathway to comfortable. In the meantime, the exploration was good. The journey she visualized herself as now embarked upon would last, she speculated, the rest of her life. But how long would *this* last. This, now. How long will I be with her. And who is she?

"Hey."

"Um."

"You're thinking pretty hard there."

"Sorry. I guess I do that."

"Remember me telling you I don't read minds?"

"I know."

"I promise I will answer all your questions."

"When? Sorry, that's a question."

"Very soon. It's almost time. Just not yet."

"Okay."

And then Gabrielle discovered with familiarity came an increase in intensity and she made a mental note to definitely, most definitely, investigate that further.

Morning came too soon. Breakfast, a big bowl of Cocoa Krispies and coffee from the new plug-in percolator, passed without much conversation. Gabrielle could tell Catherine, preoccupied, had made plans. And she didn't think it was about the big Sunday dinner. There was something else looming.

Catherine sat next to her, sunlight on her face. "I'll need to start dinner at two."

"Two o'clock?"

"To get it on the table at six."

"What are we having? Oops, sorry."

"It's all right. I forgive you. What do you want to do until then?"

"Well, I found the perfect parking spot so I don't want to move the car."

"Okay, something that doesn't involve driving."

"Normally, I would do homework or maybe walk up to downtown."

"What would you do up there?"

"Just look around."

"Do you, you know, go in the stores?"

"Sometimes. It doesn't feel right."

"Because you can't afford anything. Well, this is not your normal Sunday."

Sure isn't, Gabrielle thought.

"And I like the idea of not driving," Catherine said.

They sat in the kitchen talking until it was nine-thirty hypothesizing that the stores would open by ten. Gabrielle spent some time examining her new food supply which filled half the refrigerator and all of the freezer as well as five of the six upper cabinets. Catherine watched her with a satisfied smile except once when once when Gabrielle caught her reflection in the kitchen window and she looked worried, almost frightened.

She closed the door on a neatly stacked array of canned peas, green beans, creamed corn, and artichoke hearts. She had no idea what hearts of artichokes were but the picture on the label looked pretty unappetizing. "Okay, let's go," she said.

Catherine seemed happy to get moving. She zipped up her yellow windbreaker and they left the still sleeping house. The morning sky was clear and the air was cool.

"Nice and quiet around here." She stuffed her hands into her pockets.

"Not much to do on Sundays. May as well sleep in."

"Later there'll be something."

"Later?"

"After dinner. You'll see."

They walked west on Gabrielle's street and then north. The old houses seemed to be a bit larger the closer they got to the downtown while the few businesses – a dusty paint shop, a single bay radiator repair place – had a neglected look. The sidewalk was cracked and lined with weeds even in front of the big, remodeled Victorian-style houses with their trimmed trees and grass yards, the sort of house Gabrielle thought of as a mansion.

Catherine didn't talk much but did not seem uncomfortable. Gabrielle watched her carefully. She's my lover, she thought. I'm walking down the street with my lover, the woman I slept with last night.

She could feel the familiar image of her mind, the towering data structure she was so used to imagining, suddenly begin to lean and tip over, the base buckling as the entire foundation crumbled. She stubbed her toe and shook her head. Maybe it's time for a new mental structure, she thought, and had no idea what that might be.

Catherine noticed the thoughts crossing her face and grinned. She kept her hands in her windbreaker pockets and they both walked a little faster.

On the main street they walked west again with the sun in the corner of their eyes. Gabrielle noticed Catherine was watching the sparse traffic closely, looking intently at each car and truck as they approached on the one-way, three lane street. A block from the French pastry shop, they crossed the wide street and found themselves in a small lane of clothing stores and cafes. Away from the main thoroughfare, Catherine visibly relaxed. The small stores were all still closed but a large department store had just opened. Catherine rushed in and Gabrielle followed her to the men's clothing area. It was good to be out of the sun, she thought. The atmosphere was hushed. It smelled like clean, pressed cotton and perfume. She had no idea which perfume.

Among rows of dark suits, Gabrielle caught up with her as she asked a saleslady wearing heavy glasses on a chain, "Do you have a young man's department?" and with a dismissive point they were directed deeper into the store.

Catherine said, "Thank you," graciously and when they were well away muttered, "Bitch."

The air was heavy with new clothes smell. Gabrielle calculated it had been over a year since she had last bought an item of clothing. It was the zip-up sweatshirt she was now wearing, complete with hood, six dollars and ninety-five cents from the campus bookstore.

"This is perfect," Catherine said as she looked around the racks of plaid shirts and shelves of jeans, most of which were stiff, dark blue Levi's. "I need to get a bunch of stuff and I nearly forgot. See?" She pulled a lightweight, navy blue jacket from a stand. "London Fog. A golf jacket that doesn't look too golfy. More outdoorsy." She checked the size and got two more, black and light gray. "For acquaintances of mine. Now." With her free hand she brushed off Gabrielle's shoulders. "Medium. Young man's medium. Oo. I never thought of it like that before."

"Catherine."

"Not saying it's hot, just never thought of it that way before. Also, it's hot."

"You don't have to buy clothes for me."

"But you're my friend."

"I know. But."

"It's not charity. I like buying you things."

"How isn't that charity?"

"Your whole face lights up. You have no idea. You lit up that whole supermarket yesterday."

"Well."

"I'll make you a deal."

"I guess I did need a few things. But."

"Wait," Catherine said. "I'll make you a deal. I need some things, too. And if I buy two of something, you can borrow one of them. So I'm not really buying it for you. And you never have to give it back even though you're technically borrowing it because it's a new category called non-reciprocal bi-level exchange which I just made up."

"Wow."

"Pretty cool, huh?"

"That almost makes sense."

"Being around you has made me more technically minded. I think my IQ's gone up."

"I'm sure it was already pretty high."

Catherine thought for a second. "No, not really."

She picked out a fourth jacket, a black one, and gave them all to

Gabrielle to carry. Catherine set off for the other side of the store and quickly found the young ladies department. She picked out two wool sweaters, charcoal black, with a loose semi-turtleneck kind of collar. Then, to Gabrielle's embarrassment, a collection of white silk underwear including very sheer panties and undershirts. "For protection from the wool. Otherwise you'll do nothing but scratch."

"I've never seen silk before."

They went to a cashier in the men's department so they wouldn't encounter the same rude saleslady. Instead, it was a young woman with bloodshot eyes who nodded in appreciation of the sweaters. "These don't suck," she said in a tired voice. The total came to $218.81 and Gabrielle stepped back from the register as if it were a rattlesnake.

"Thanks," Catherine said and pulled neatly folded money from the pocket of her shorts, three hundreds and a twenty. She put one of the hundreds back in her pocket and gave the rest to the woman who blinked rapidly. The sweaters were folded perfectly and placed into flat boxes, the jackets folded into a large heavy plastic bag with handles. The silk underthings were placed into another smaller bag inside. Catherine carried the sweater boxes out of the store while Gabrielle had the big bag under one arm. It was too heavy to carry by the handles.

"Do you want to get coffee?"

"I've really had too much."

"Well, I could use some."

"Then let's get coffee."

"But you don't want any."

"I'll have a little."

"So you really want some?"

"If you're having coffee I'll have some, too."

"Okay. Good."

There was a coffee shop across from the department store and they sat in a booth with red vinyl benches and a battered Formica table. The blonde waitress, name tag 'Rebecca', barely spoke to them. But Catherine knows her, Gabrielle thought.

Catherine watched the people walking by their window. She studied the young women in their cool weather going shopping clothes and grown-up hairstyles.

"I was always interested in beauty," she said. "I studied beauty. I mean, I like to look at beautiful things and pictures and people. I wanted to figure out why I felt the way I did when I looked at a beautiful face. I analyzed it. This was when I was in the eighth grade. I worked on it for almost two years. Then I had to stop. But I came up with a system."

Gabrielle saw her focus on someone walking on the other side of the street.

"See her? Let me tell you how I look at this."

The woman had on a black leather jacket and black jeans. Her black hair was tied in a ponytail. She went quickly into the department store.

"It just takes a glance," Catherine said. "Personality is written in your face. In fact if you really study this almost everything about you is right there. So."

"She looked nice."

"Exactly. See, you can tell. She had large eyes and the end of her nose had a kind of rounded off look. That's someone who almost never gets angry. If you were to talk to her she would be a crack up. She could be a really good friend."

The store door opened and a young woman came out carrying several large bags. Gabrielle guessed mid-twenties. Gray wool skirt, gray sweater with a thin black scarf. Loafers without socks.

"Okay, what about her?"

"Ah good," Catherine said. "There's a feature that all by itself is a good indicator. Do you think she's attractive?"

"Yes."

"I'll bet I can tell exactly why. But first I would say in general sharp features, sharp mind. And also high self-regard."

"Oh?"

"Yeah. They're always a bit disappointed in people. Doesn't she look like that?"

"She looks angry."

"In a sexy way."

"True. What's that one feature?"

"Her lips."

The woman paused on the sidewalk and rearranged her bags. She looked at the sign for the coffee shop and seemed to consider it.

"Most people, and by people I mean women, have normal lips. This is type one. Average. Thin. Not well-defined. Not interesting. Then there's type two. For example."

The young woman's gaze snapped down from the sign and picked them both out. Gabrielle looked away. Catherine started right back.

"Full. Perfectly defined, and that's really the key characteristic. Sculpted."

The young woman frowned and turned her head away with a haughty snap. She hefted her parcels and walked away. Her scarf waved in the breeze.

"Girl watching is fun," Catherine said.

"I'm type one." Gabrielle sipped her coffee.

"Oh I'd say not. You're a combination. My categories are broad."

And you're type two, Gabrielle thought.

"You're a lumper," she said.

"A what?" Catherine's eyes flashed.

"As opposed to a splitter," Gabrielle said quickly. "It's from biology. It just means you categorize broadly."

"Oh. Okay then. A lumper. So what are you?"

"I really don't know."

"You think you'll ever find out?"

"I don't know."

Catherine finished her coffee.

"You and your honesty. You need lessons."

"Lessons in not being honest?"

"Think of it as creative perceptualizing."

"Did you just make that up?"

Catherine smiled.

"You're learning already."

Catherine grabbed the $1.65 bill and slipped a twenty under the sugar dispenser.

Out on the sidewalk, Gabrielle said, "Big tip."

"She needed it," was all Catherine would say.

They got back to the house close to one o'clock. None of the guys were home. They took the new clothes in their big rustling bags down to Gabrielle's room and set everything out on the washer and dryer.

"Do you want to try them on?" Gabrielle asked. She opened one of the sweater boxes and ran her hand over the fabric. "This is so beautiful. Thank you."

"Let's take a nap."

"I'm not all that sleepy."

"Who said anything about sleeping?"

It was close to three when they heard the kitchen door slam. Probably Brian, Gabrielle thought, from the way he tromped to the upstairs bathroom.

"Lost track of time," Catherine said as she put on one of Gabrielle's university t-shirts. "Better get cracking."

Gabrielle's stomach growled as she sat up.

"Someone worked up an appetite," Catherine said and laughed.

"It was all that walking."

"Yeah, that was probably it," Catherine said. "Massive amounts of walking. Incredible non-stop walking."

They both giggled as they climbed the stairs but stopped when Gabrielle opened the door. Catherine walked quickly to the kitchen and opened the fridge.

"Dinner will be fried chicken, mashed potatoes and gravy, sweet peas, and biscuits. Biscuits made from scratch, of course. Haven't decided on dessert. Have you ever made fried chicken before?"

"No, it always seemed like too big a risk."

"Risk? I'll show you how. Just a few tips. See?" She held up a carton. "Buttermilk?"

"First step, we marinate the chicken in buttermilk."

"Uh. You put chicken in milk?"

"Hour, hour and a half." She shook the half-gallon milk carton and opened it.

"Are you serious?"

"Yes. I need a big bowl."

There was no bowl large enough so Catherine used the Brian's spaghetti pot. She unwrapped the chicken from the butcher paper, washed each piece in running water and positioned them carefully in the big stainless steel pot. She's done this many times, Gabrielle thought. Catherine then poured in the buttermilk, making sure every bit of the chicken was covered.

"There. This will make the chicken taste great. And the rest of the buttermilk is for the biscuits. You're not taking notes?"

"Oh, sure. I just like watching you."

"Why thank you." She put the pot in the fridge, pushing back other cartons of milk and orange juice.

"You're making biscuits, too?"

"We are making biscuits."

"I'll write this down."

"Don't you need your notebook?"

"I'll do it later."

Catherine looked confused. "You'll take notes. Only later."

"I'll remember."

"You can remember everything?"

"Everything."

"Then why take notes?"

"Professors expect you to take notes, so I do. I have noticed, though, as I get older I am losing this ability."

"Older? Yes, you are just aging terribly, Gabrielle. What are you, twenty?"

"I'll be twenty-one in July."

"So at the old age of twenty, you're losing it."

"Just a little."

"All downhill from now on."

"In some ways."

"Wow."

"It's still mostly there."

"Can you show me?"

Gabrielle laughed.

"It's not that I don't believe you."

"Oh, that's okay. It took me forever to realize not everyone can do it. Let me think."

"I feel like a jerk asking this. But it's exciting."

"No, it's fun." Gabrielle let her mind's eye roam back to the morning, the walk, the department store. "Okay. When you paid for the clothes, you took some money out."

"Right."

"You paid the cashier and then put the rest of your money back in your pocket. There was a hundred dollar bill. The last five digits of the serial number are nine nine four seven and then the letter A. Your thumb was covering part of it."

Catherine wiped her hands on the dishtowel and pulled the neatly folded money from her front pocket. The top bill was a hundred. Her eyes widened.

"Month of Sundays."

Gabrielle, who had been freaking out teachers her entire life, said, "That's nothing."

"But how can you do that?"

"I focus on something, pay attention to it, and I can't help remembering. I hardly ever see a hundred dollar bill so it caught my attention."

"Holy."

"It took me until just a few years ago to kind of get it under control. I keep my attention on a leash. My dad taught me to do that."

"So it's something you have to control."

"I remember when I was very little just being swamped by the world. I had no way to handle it. You have to categorize, organize. Signs, labels, people talking, the radio always playing. I could read when I was one and a half."

"*Wow.*"

"That whole time is still all disjointed. I think in order to escape I retreated into my own mind. Just to get away from it all. When it gets to be too much I get this vinegary taste in my mouth and I start daydreaming. Flying through the clouds. Being in a field of flowers with the sun shining. It gets to be a habit."

"Alone."

"What?"

"You are alone in your daydreaming world with no one talking to you. All peaceful."

"Yes. And I'd probably still be there if it hadn't been for my dad. And then there's *counting*. I have to tell you about *counting*."

Catherine stepped forward and hugged her, tucking Gabrielle head under her chin. "You never told this to anyone before, have you?" she finally said.

"There was no one to tell."

"Sometimes things change." She rubbed Gabrielle's back. "God, I wish I could see the world the way you do."

"I could try to show you. If you want."

"I don't want you to feel alone."

"Even though I am alone."

"No, you're not."

"Okay. If you say so."

"Gabrielle."

"Show me how to make biscuits."

Catherine, without another word, showed Gabrielle how to make buttermilk biscuits and then fried chicken, perfectly golden brown, and mashed potatoes and gravy and peas. The peas came out of a can but she counted them anyway. Two hundred and twenty-one. Elliot and Brian came in around six, as requested, and Mark came out of his room after Elliot yelled at him. Catherine opened two bottles of wine, one white and one red, both with unpronounceable names, and Gabrielle was surprised to find she really liked wine. Well, the white wine. The red wine was a bit much. The chicken with its salty, crispy skin was impossible to stop eating and at one point Catherine had to reach over with a napkin and wipe Gabrielle's chin, which got a big laugh. Catherine ate modestly, making sure everyone was happy, and when they were all close to being finished they all looked at each other and gave her a round of applause. Catherine blushed and her hand went up to her face, Gabrielle saw, unconsciously trying to cover her scar. When Catherine smiled the scar was hardly noticeable.

They all cleaned up. Catherine wasn't permitted to help so she retired to the basement. With four people it only took a few minutes to wash dishes and put everything away. The leftover chicken was stashed in the fridge along with bowls of mashed potatoes and biscuits and gravy. There was the problem of what do with all the used cooking oil. Actually it was shortening as Gabrielle pointed out. No one knew what shortening was. It was full of tiny crispy bits and smelled really good but there was no way of keeping it. After some consideration, they poured it down the kitchen sink while running hot water. The guys went into the front room to watch tv and Gabrielle washed her hands in the bathroom and went downstairs.

At the top of her stairs, she stopped. "Whoa." She swayed and held on to the bare wood railing. The basement seemed to spin. "This is interesting." She descended carefully, one step at a time.

Catherine was waiting for her.

She wearing her new black sweater. "Hurry. Get dressed. There's something I want to show you." She had Gabrielle take off her t-shirt and slip on the new silk top followed by the sweater.

"This smells nice. And it doesn't really itch. Uh."

"Dizzy?"

"I think it's the wine," Gabrielle said seriously. "It's affecting me."

"It can do that." She brought out a tiny glass bottle and removed the top. The air was instantly scented. She put a drop of perfume on her fingertip and touched Gabrielle's neck, on the pulse points.

"Oh."

Catherine smiled and applied perfume to her own neck. "You look great." She adjusted the collar of Gabrielle's sweater. "All you need is a little something right there. Like a silver chain. Something simple."

"I got something right here," Gabrielle said and she pushed up her breasts with both hands.

"Yes, you do. Come on."

"My best feature. All the boys say so."

"I'll bet. Up the stairs." She got behind Gabrielle. "Up."

"And now all the girls say so." She got to the first step. Her right foot did not want to behave. It wavered and with an effort of will she got it onto the board. "It was unexpected. You know what, Catherine?" She took two more interestingly difficult steps with Catherine's hands on her back.

"What? Keep going. You're almost to the top."

"This is surprisingly hard to do."

"What do you mean? Girls?"

"No, you mysterious sexy person who can cook. I mean the stairs. I keep missing."

"Okay. Stop talking. One more step." They squeezed onto the landing.

"Now it itches a little."

"Around your neck?"

"Actually I mean my whatchamacallit." Gabrielle bounced on her heels twice. "There. You may open the door."

"Oh, my God. You're a crazy drunk. All it takes is two point four glasses of chardonnay and you become crazy. This is going to be insane. Now we're going through the kitchen so keep quiet."

"Two point four. Wow. You are very technical."

"Plus half a glass of *pinot noir.*"

"Say that again."

"Not now."

They crossed the dark, fried chicken smelling kitchen. Gabrielle could hear the tv. Voices were yelling. *All in the Family.* The guys did not hear them at all. They went outside and Catherine closed the door softly.

"I'm sorry. I'm being silly," Gabrielle said. It was like her tongue was thicker but the part of her brain that did speech was in overdrive. "It's so cool out here. It's always foggy."

They walked side by side down the sidewalk, lost in shadows. Gabrielle wasn't sure of their direction until she saw her car sitting at the apex of the tiny park. The streetlights were smudges of warm light in the mist. She managed to step off the curb without tripping.

"It's hardly ever so cool and foggy in Covina. It's usually just smoggy."

"Same as Pasadena."

"Pasadena. Oh, right. Your big house." She covered her mouth. "I forgot."

"The house? What about it?"

"Nothing. Where are we going?"

Catherine watched her intently. "We're just going somewhere I like to go sometimes. It's a place."

Gabrielle adjusted her glasses.

"You're not using language very precisely but I don't mind. I'm really more of a numbers person myself."

Catherine laughed. "Even drunk you're scary smart."

"Thank you," Gabrielle said and took Catherine's hand. "We're both wearing the same clothes. And the same perfume."

"That's true."

Then a car came by and Catherine let her hand go.

"Sorry," she whispered.

"No one can see us out here."

"Yes they can."

Gabrielle took her hand again and when another car passed she held tight. Catherine sighed and looked straight ahead.

They went down the street which became another street where the streetlights were not working and the houses were dark and silent. Gabrielle couldn't make out the street signs. A short ways in, Catherine stopped. She pointed between two small cottages. Behind them was an old garage with two big doors that looked like they hadn't been opened in decades. A garage for a Model-T, she thought. It was covered with chalky white paint that gave it a gray, muddy appearance.

It was so dark, Gabrielle had to feel where to step with her toes. There was just enough space for a small car to pass between the houses but the place for a driveway was overgrown with gardenias. Long branches clogged with flowers, powerfully fragrant in the night.

"That's it. Come on."

"We're going into somebody's backyard?"

"That old building."

They went zig-zag through the gardenias. Gabrielle began to hear music. It sounded like the Bee Gees.

They stopped in the midst of the dark flowers. Gabrielle felt her face being cupped in Catherine's hands and she closed her eyes. Catherine kissed her intensely and when she pulled away said, "All right."

"I," Gabrielle said, "Never been so much kissing. Before."

They stepped out of the gardenias and the branches tugged at their sweaters and deposited petals in the folds.

"Welcome to the Carriage House," Catherine said. "Isn't that a great name?"

"Just so great." Gabrielle could just make out a door. Catherine knocked twice and then three times. The door opened an inch and was stopped by a heavy chain. There was light inside. The music was slightly louder then cut off. Gabrielle saw someone standing just inside with their face turned away.

"Catherine and Gabrielle," Catherine said, leaning forward.

The door closed and there was silence. Then there was a thump as the chain was unhooked. The music came back on. The door opened just enough to slip in sideways.

"Come on. Quick!" Catherine pulled Gabrielle in with her.

"Oh," Gabrielle said, "it's big."

The chain was put back. It was Rebecca. The walls and the forest of rafters of the old garage had been painted flat black and there were tiny colored lights strung everywhere. There was a dance floor – a plywood platform also painted black – with a mirror ball hanging above. The mirror ball was long razor-edged shards of glass glued to a cardboard box with their sharp edges pointing down like icicles. It dangled just out of reach. The high, round tables clustered in the back of the room also looked homemade. There was a stereo on a table against one wall. The dial glowed soft blue and the tape deck was playing a Bee-Gees song softly. The air was heavy with cigarette smoke.

Catherine silently hugged Rebecca. She listened to something Catherine whispered in her ear and then nodded, unsmiling. Catherine held Rebecca's hand for a moment and then took Gabrielle to a table in the furthest corner of the room, against a layer of black curtains. There were several unlit candles on the table. Black wax. They sat on wooden stools. Gabrielle's jeans snagged plywood splinters.

"You'd never guess this was here, would you? You can't hear anything from the street."

"I can't breathe."

"Oh, you'll get used to it. It's just Debbie. She wants to open a night club and is using this to experiment."

"Good thinking."

Debbie, Gabrielle thought. That Debbie? Rebecca seemed the only other person in the place.

"I know, huh? They're still working on stuff. Like the floor. It's pretty basic."

"It's all right. It's fine."

"It's great. You can relax and be yourself."

Rebecca appeared from the inner darkness with a tray. The garage had been added on to, Gabrielle saw. It was all obscured by the curtains, black-dyed, wrinkled bed sheets. There was no telling how far back it went. Rebecca placed two glasses in front of them on small napkins.

"You're the only customers all day so this is on the house."

"Oh, thank you," Catherine said.

"Thanks, Rebecca."

She looked at Gabrielle. "You're welcome. You know my name?"

"Sure. I saw you at the coffee shop."

"Oh, right, right. Well, nice meeting you." She smiled slightly and went to the stereo. She put a new tape in the player and it began to play *Moondance*.

"That was great," Catherine said. "What you did."

"I just remembered her name." Gabrielle sniffed her glass. Oh I probably shouldn't, she thought.

"I'll tell you about her later."

Catherine sipped from her glass and set it down. She took both of Gabrielle's hands in hers and gripped intensely.

She said, "This is our world. It's only for us. It's private. It could be this place or your car or your room. No one else can be in our world. No one can know or even suspect it exists. It just has to be this way."

"Okay. I'm sorry."

"You didn't know. Do you trust me?"

"Yes," Gabrielle said. "I trust you."

There was a loud voice deep behind the curtains, then the sound of something breaking. The curtains billowed and Gabrielle felt Catherine's grip on her hands suddenly tighten almost painfully.

"There are worlds within worlds," Catherine said. "It's dangerous. I'm ninety-nine percent sure. But I need to be a hundred percent." She looked at Gabrielle's glass and released her hands. "You know, that was on the house. It would be rude not to drink it."

"It's really strong."

Someone muttering with rage, a female voice, came close to the curtains next to their table and stopped, unseen. Gabrielle sensed them listening.

"Just drink. Quick. The whole thing."

The stereo began playing *Deacon Blues*.

Catherine stood up. "For God's sake, drink it."

Gabrielle took a big gulp and choked. It was fruit juice mixed with a lot of alcohol and a good bit went up her nose. She started coughing and her eyes burned. Catherine pulled her up by her hand. Gabrielle sniffed loudly and swallowed. Her snot tasted like booze.

"You're doing *great!*"

She took two deep breaths as if she were about to go underwater and drank the rest of it. It burned all the way down. She looked at the glass. Empty, she thought. I actually drank it. She suddenly noticed that Catherine's glass was still full.

"Oh, here. Drink this too." Catherine gave her the glass.

Gabrielle concentrated on talking. "It's just too much."

"This is barely sufficient. Believe me."

"Okay, I'm not sure I believe you but I trust you." She sipped. The little glass almost slipped out of her grip. "Man, this really tastes awful. Don't they have hot cocoa?"

"Huh. That would have been better. In the meantime, keep drinking."

Out of the corner of her eyes, Gabrielle saw the curtains part. A woman in black was standing there.

"Hurry," Catherine said and pulled Gabrielle away from their table. "Hurry, hurry."

"All right, all right." She took another gulp. "Ahh. That's half. Can I just save the rest?"

Catherine took the glass from her and set it on one of the stereo speakers. "Let's dance." She pulled Gabrielle by the arm to the plywood dance floor.

"What? Oh, I can't dance."

"Sure you can. I love this song. I love Steely Dan, don't you? It's so much better than disco."

"Is that someone's name?"

In the center of the dance floor, Catherine put her arms around Gabrielle's waist and began to rock her hips to the music. Gabrielle, not knowing what to do, simply copied her. She interlaced her fingers in the small of Catherine's back and started rocking her hips also.

"See? You're good."

Gabrielle tried to get her hips in sync. "Really, I can't dance."

"Does it feel good?"

"Yes. I mean, yes." Gabrielle rested her head on Catherine's shoulder. There was a click and a light shined on the jagged mirror box. The box began to turn slowly. She said, "Wow," at the moving wedges of light.

"Look at that! Almost makes the place beautiful. Okay."

"Ah," Gabrielle said. Catherine's hands pinched her back. She looked up and saw that Catherine's scar was suddenly very prominent. She twisted head around to see what Catherine was looking at.

There were now four women, all dressed in black, standing by the curtains watching them. None of them were smiling. The one on the end, the tallest, looked very unhappy. Gabrielle thought she seemed familiar but for some reason it was difficult to keep her eyes focused.

"You trust me, right?" Catherine whispered fiercely in her ear from behind. "I have to be a hundred percent sure."

She let go of Gabrielle's waist.

Gabrielle turned, staggered.

Catherine was gone.

She stood alone on the dance floor. The music stopped. The light on the dangerous mirror box went out. In the candlelight, the four women watched her in silence.

She cleared her throat.

"Thank you for the drink. It didn't taste very good but I drank it anyway because I didn't want to be rude."

She took a step towards her table and felt everything in the world slide to the right and surge back, like a bathtub sloshing. "Interesting effect," she said. She couldn't stop swaying. "I guess Catherine left."

The tall woman came up to her. "Yeah. Hope she doesn't get hit by a car."

"Oh, hi, you're one of the ladies in MacDonald's. You gave me the cheeseburger and fries. Thank you so much. I was so hungry that day."

"Right. You and what's her face."

"Yes. Did you hear what happened to her?"

The woman made a face that was almost a smile but crooked. "We heard."

"God, it was so horrible."

The woman said nothing.

"My name is."

"Gabrielle. I know."

"Oh, good. Are you Debbie? You look like Debbie now that I look."

"You remember."

"I remember everything. It's a great responsibility. Mrs. Havacheck in fourth grade told me that once and I never forgot. Because I can't forget." She giggled. "That's funny if you're like me."

Debbie nodded. "I've heard of you. You're supposed to be some sort of genius. Geniuses usually die insane, don't they. Do you think you'll go insane?"

"If I was insane I wouldn't know it. Everything would be normal to me. So I can't answer your question. I might be insane right now."

"Yeah, that's right."

"No, it's not. I made a logical error but I can't think straight. I'll figure it out. Unless I'm insane. Why did Catherine leave? Are you having a fight?" Gabrielle realized one of the other women was now somehow standing behind her. It was the skinny one with very short black hair.

"A fight," Debbie said with a laugh. "With... what did you say her name was?"

"Um." Gabrielle felt her heart begin to pound. "Catherine."

The woman behind her got very close. She pressed her upper body against Gabrielle's back and reached around with her right leg. She placed her bare foot on top of Gabrielle's right shoe. She started rocking her foot front to back, massaging. Her breath was hot on the back of Gabrielle's neck. Gabrielle heard her start to make slurping sounds.

"Are you talking about that idiotic, repulsive bitch that ran out of here as soon as she saw us? Who showed up here uninvited? Oh, and the dummy who let you both in, already forgot her name, I fired her. And now you're standing in front of me drunk on my booze."

"I'll pay for it. I didn't know."

"We can talk about that. This is Susan, by the way. She thinks you're cute. Don't you, Susan?"

Susan hugged Gabrielle's waist from behind. "Oh, perhaps," she said.

She had an accent, Gabrielle thought. English accent. No, not quite.

Susan cupped Gabrielle's breasts and squeezed.

Gabrielle stepped backwards and bent her knees. She snapped back her right arm and with her elbow hit Susan in the hip. Susan let go and Gabrielle turned to face her. Different looking, she thought, she is different.

"Hi, Susan," she said and looked Susan in her wide set eyes. "I would grab your tits too but you don't have any."

Debbie burst out laughing.

Catherine was right, Gabrielle thought. I am a crazy drunk. Also, I really like this. Also, I can't feel my feet.

Susan put her hands on her hips and almost smiled. Gabrielle did not understand her expression. She filed it away for later analysis. Just as she was thinking that, Debbie turned her away.

"Let's go sit down. Don't mind Susan. She was just testing you."

"Testing?"

"Yeah. The official California bra safety test."

"But I'm not wearing a bra."

"Then you're safe."

"Oh good. Thanks." Gabrielle carefully let herself down onto the swaying, dipping, spinning tall chair.

Debbie sat opposite and picked up Catherine's glass. "She couldn't even be bothered to drink it all." She set it on the table behind her. "Unless you want it."

"Oh, no thanks, I've had way too much. And I'll pay for it. Them."

"Two mixed drinks. Nine-fifty."

"Oh, gosh, okay." Gabrielle kept her tiny wallet in her front pocket and she had to slip off the chair and stand up to get a grip on it. Inside was all the paper money she possessed. She took out a five and three ones. Coins she kept in a green rubber pouch which opened when squeezed on its long axis. She had a bunch of quarters. "That's eight and here's..."

"Don't worry about it."

Gabrielle hesitated only a second. "Okay. Thanks, Debbie." She stuffed her money back into her pocket as far as it would go.

"Don't have a purse, huh?"

"No. Never got one."

"Ah."

"I have a backpack. It's kind of the same thing. A purse is too girly." Gabrielle realized she had never thought of it that way. But yes.

"It wasn't your fault. I don't want to lose you as a customer. If anyone should pay it should be what's her face."

"I'll tell her."

"If you ever see her again."

Gabrielle looked at Debbie in surprise.

"Let me guess. She just appeared one day. You spend a few days together, mostly screwing. She cooked dinner for you and then poof."

"Well." If I were sober, Gabrielle thought, this would be embarrassing.

"I know she's kind of hot. And she is a good cook. So it's fun. That's fine. But that's all it is. Do you even know her last name?" Debbie leaned back and took out a pack of cigarettes. She took one out and held out the rest. "Don't smoke?"

"God, no."

"Yeah, it's supposed to be bad for you. I started when I was ten. I figure I'm already good as dead. So why not." She lit up with a green plastic lighter and blew smoke out into the room, most of which drifted back. "Oh, sorry."

The annoyance caused Gabrielle's head to clear. It was true she knew very little about Catherine but wasn't that part of the game? A game she had consciously agreed to. She remembered the revelation she had in the bathroom. What was going to happen? No idea, and that was the exciting part of it. Of course it was. She shook her head. How could I forget all that? Alcohol. Bad for thinking. Very bad. And Catherine. I like her. Debbie knows her. I could ask Debbie all kinds of questions. Not sure if I could believe the answers, however, so I think I'll keep my mouth shut.

She thought, I'm thinking really fast but it's all really stupid.

Someone came up behind her again and put their hand gently on her shoulders. They began to softly knead. "Your neck stiff?"

"A little I guess."

"I can tell." She bent over and put her face very to Gabrielle's. "Hi." She had a hairstyle similar to Debbie's. Blonde, severely razor cut. Despite that, she's definitely cute, Gabrielle thought. She was beautiful in the low light. Her sculpted lips were perfect. Type. Um, what type? There's this type I know.

"Nice to meet you," she said, massaging deeper. "I'm Susan. Does this feel good?"

"Gabrielle says yes," Debbie said, standing up. She quickly disappeared behind the curtains.

The second Susan continued to massage Gabrielle's shoulders. "Looks like everybody split." Her hands slipped around to the front. "Let's go over there where it's really dark. If you want. Do you want?"

"Yes," Gabrielle had to admit.

"Then come *on*," she said excitedly and tugged Gabrielle up by the armpits. They went around the tables to the far back corner where almost no light reached. Susan pushed her against the unfinished wall of spider web covered two-by-fours and pressed her body close, not forcing, but trying to fit herself as well as she could.

Susan exhaled into her left ear and then she felt the tip of Susan's tongue explore the area of her neck where it curved out to her shoulder. Gabrielle pulled down the front of her new sweater. Susan made a throaty chuckle and began kissing her collarbone. Gabrielle heard footsteps outside and then a muffled laugh. The black curtains billowed and two women appeared by the tables, silhouetted by the multicolored Christmas lights. Over Susan's head, she saw them conferring. They separated and came up on both sides. A flanking maneuver. One was the tall, black-haired Susan she met on the dance floor. Gabrielle thought, how long ago was that? What time is it? How long have I been here? Oh, this is bad. Susan made a sigh and went back to kissing her neck.

The new girl, who was wearing a loose – what was it called – tank top tucked herself in on Gabrielle's right. "Hi," she whispered. "Are we having a four way? My name's Susan. Nice to meet you."

The Susan who was kissing her, Pretty Susan, Gabrielle thought, put her hands on the wall behind cradling Gabrielle's head in her arms.

"I've never had a four way," The new Susan said. New Susan.

"Yes you did," said Tall Susan in her odd accent.

"That wasn't four."

"No, it was five."

"Well, see?"

Pretty Susan let out an exasperated snort under Gabrielle's chin and whispered in her ear, "You want to get out of here?"

"Um."

New Susan put hands around Pretty Susan's waist and said, "Come on." Pretty Susan took her hand off the wall, shook off the dust, and snapped her left elbow back smartly making a solid hit on New Susan's upper arm. New Susan gasped and stepped back, rubbing the spot.

"I told you not to touch me," Pretty Susan growled.

"I thought that was just for yesterday," she whined. Gabrielle saw she was also cute and had long blonde hair. Her breath was bad, though. Not into brushing her teeth.

"Why do you have to be so dumb?" Then to Gabrielle, "There's a place we can go. It's right back there. It's private."

"I don't know. I'm kind of seeing someone right now."

"Her? Huh. Yeah. She might come back. Maybe you're lucky."

Tall Susan said, "She's hot."

Pretty Susan glared at her.

"She didn't know till just now," Tall Susan said. "She had no clue. I can tell."

"God." Pretty Susan shook her head.

Gabrielle stopped leaning against the wall. "I have classes tomorrow." And then she found herself saying, "Maybe we, um, later. If you want."

Pretty Susan sighed and took Gabrielle's hand. Gabrielle almost winced. Her palm felt like sandpaper. "Sunday's are good."

"Okay."

"We're usually here."

"Maybe I'll drop by."

Pretty Susan took Gabrielle's face in her hands and kissed her. She moaned and thrust her tongue into Gabrielle's mouth as far as she could. Gabrielle found the kiss to be surprisingly unarousing. Pretty Susan tasted like the sour fruit juice from the drink. She noticed Gabrielle's lack of response and pulled back.

"So, I'll see you."

"Sure." Gabrielle slipped through them and found the door.

"Are you actually leaving?" Tall Susan said plaintively.

Gabrielle just smiled at her, opened the door and broke into fresh air. She walked as fast as she could through the maze of gardenias. She coughed at the overpowering scent and tried to shake it out of her clothes. On the dark sidewalk, fog condensed on her overheated forehead and itched. She wiped it away. Somewhere behind her, a blackbird began to sing.

On the sidewalk, she crossed her arms against the chill, hugging herself, and was a quarter of the way home – she knew by counting steps – before she allowed herself to think.

It's completely crazy, she thought. Maybe I should be flattered. It's not that I don't like it. I definitely like it. Tall Susan was really cute. They were all cute. All these cute girls keep kissing me. Catherine was right. It has to be private. Secret. It's safer that way. It's more fun that way.

It's more powerful that way.

The wet streets passed by silently. She guessed it was no later than nine. Already the town was asleep. Halfway home, she had seen only a few cars go by. An old pickup. A black Jeep. She reached the tiny park and walked up to the point. She wanted to double check her car's doors. Sometimes they only partially locked. She knew she was being obsessive and she considered it a good thing.

She went up the sidewalk to the apex and stopped. Her heart began racing again. Her car was gone. The perfect parking spot was empty. She ran to the place and stood there. *How*, she thought. I know I locked it. She felt her pockets. Where are the keys? I don't have the keys.

She checked her pockets again. There was only her wallet and coin purse. No keys. She thought furiously. How can I not have the keys? I left the house without the keys? I actually did that? Or did Catherine take them?

Her memories were disjointed, unsteady, like movie film with torn sprocket holes.

God *damn* it, she thought. Why would she steal my car? She's *rich*. Oh, this is bad. To hell with drinking. Oh, this is bad, bad, bad.

She ran.

I have no idea who Catherine is, she thought. I don't even know her last name.

She ran down the middle of the street. She scanned all the parked cars and tried to look down all the intersecting streets.

How did she get the key? Did she pick my pocket?

The keys were still not in her pocket.

She ran.

She reached her street. Sweat made her glasses slide off her nose so she took them off. She kept running, blurry-eyed.

I'm never drinking again, she thought. Never. It's not that great anyway. Damn it. Damn it.

She got close to her house and slowed to a walk, winded. The large trees in the neighbor's yards and the masses of parked vehicles made it hard to see but there was a familiar shape at the head of her driveway. She stood in the center of the street, breathing heavily, and put her glasses back on.

It was real. Her Volkswagen was sitting beside the kitchen door, the bright light shining on the beautiful weathered red paint.

She wiped her face. She went to it, dizzy, and patted the engine cover. It was warm. The doors were properly locked. "Okay," she said, "Okay." She said she doesn't drive, Gabrielle thought. She *said* that.

She turned the kitchen doorknob and went in slowly, reluctant to lose sight of her car again. She closed the door behind her after a final peek.

Her keys were sitting on a placemat on the dining table. She picked them up. The sound of a television commercial began to blare about deodorant and Elliot came in from the living room.

"Good, you found them. Cathy, I mean, Catherine brought them by. She said you dropped them outside."

"I guess I did. I kind of panicked."

"Well, that would be a good reason. Did you see her?"

"No, there's no one out there."

"You just missed her."

"I didn't see anyone walking."

"No, someone picked her up."

"Who was it?"

"I just saw the car. Brand new Jeep with a hard top. Nice."

"Oh, yeah. Sure. Well, good," she said. And then, "Was it a black Jeep?"

"Yes, it was." Elliot backed away in the direction of the boy's bathroom. "What were you doing out there? Jogging?"

"No. Why?"

He shrugged and went up the stairs.

Gabrielle stuffed the keys as far into her pocket as she could and went quickly to her bathroom, made sure the door was closed tightly, turned on the hot water in the shower, got on her knees and vomited into the toilet. She flipped the lever without looking up and puked again into swirling water.

She felt better. She got out of her sweatshirt and sat on the floor with the shower running. The room filled with steam and she closed her eyes. She felt much better.

In the basement, Catherine's pile of jackets was gone. But her filmy blue top was lying on the bed. Gabrielle felt it with the back of her fingers. She's still wearing one of my t-shirts, she thought. Is this silk? The fabric snagged on the rough skin of her hands.

She took off her glasses, set them on the nightstand box, and then took off her shirt and smelled it – perfectly good. She set it on top of her clothes pile for the next day.

She picked up the blue top. She held it out. Yes, those were her shoulders. She bunched it up and brought it to her face and inhaled. Her perfume. Her shampoo. And her.

"Oh," Gabrielle said, "oh my goodness." There was suddenly no strength in her legs. She dropped to her knees. It lasted a long time.

Of course I'll see her again, she thought. Of course I will. She turned off the lamp and curled up on the bed. She pulled the blanket up and went to sleep with the blue top beside her on the pillow.

That night, she dreamed of being immersed in an empty void, the blue sky all around in every direction. She felt physically perfect. She saw the entire arc of her life, the life she was now beginning. She saw everything all the way to the end. And end it would. That's me, she dream-thought. That's all of me. I have to remember. I have to. There were many faces, all unknown and yet amazingly familiar. Faces she loved.

She awoke in total darkness to the blaring horn of the midnight train passing the house. The blue top was tucked under her face, and the entire dream hung vividly before her eyes for a moment. She blinked and the vision collapsed into a bright blue line, the thread of her life. Then the thread was gone. It had all been so clear. She could feel the hole in her memory.

All right, she thought, on her tiny bed. She wanted to get going. She wanted things to start happening. They have plans for me? I might have plans myself. She wanted to get on that thread and ride it. With this flush of excitement she relaxed and fell asleep easily.

She bounced out of bed.

Monday morning, five thirty. She had a breakfast of coffee from the new coffee maker and Cocoa Krispies. As she walked the two miles to the campus, she kept watch on the lines of traffic passing her. There was no black Jeep. In the science building, she studied the crowds of students filling the hallways, escaping the cold weather. She did not see a yellow windbreaker. It would have stood out like the sun breaking through the clouds. No one wore bright colors the first week of February. It was all earth tones and flannels. There was one girl wearing a pink coat but from the crowd she was with Gabrielle concluded she was wearing it ironically. The coat was filthy dirty, smeared with grease. Her companions were wearing frayed scarves and old-fashioned hats and all the guys had patchy wanna-beards. Art majors, she thought, shaking her head.

Gabrielle took out her Shakespeare book, which included all the plays and sonnets. The book was heavy, with a plain blue cover, and the pages were thin to the point of being translucent. Her professor was always imploring the class to read other plays than the one they were going over in class, which was *Macbeth*, begging them to just read anything independently. Gabrielle had started reading the sonnets with an eye to using them, somehow, for her term paper. Since they would not be covering the sonnets in the class, it would be a way to show a little initiative if she could figure out how to do it. There were one hundred fifty-four sonnets. That was a lot but they were fairly short and she liked to read them while waiting for other classes to start.

The writing of the sonnets was *concentrated*. There was just so much in each small poem. She was beginning to get an idea of writing about the structure of them. Maybe she could graph them out in some manner. Graph out the emotions, she thought. Not very romantic. She shrugged and wondered if anyone had ever done that. It seemed like a graduate student sort of exercise and was probably old hat but still.

The next sonnet was number 138. She began to read it and on the very first line started blushing. Then she started laughing. Oh, *this one*, she thought.

She folded the corner of the page down.

In the echoing hallway of the Science building, on the old linoleum, Gabrielle pulled her sweatshirt hood over her head and kept reading.

When she got home, every piece of the leftover chicken was gone but there was a bowl of gravy and five biscuits in the back of the fridge. She grabbed it all and took it to her room and ate everything cold leaning against the dryer while it rumbled and shook.

Tuesday in Rimmler's class there was no flash of yellow in the doorway. She tried to concentrate on the equations and upcoming second mid-term. Her fellow students displayed a conspicuous lack of high spirits as the middle of the quarter approached. No more chanting the professor's name. The problem was simple. Too much reality.

Physics of the Transistor was a sobering experience for everyone with the exceptions of the back row guys, who were all gone after the first mid-term, and Gabrielle, who usually loved every minute of it. She looked at her notes and could not remember writing them. Yeah, *that's* a good sign, she thought. She sighed so loudly Rimmler gave her a look.

Wednesday morning, she discovered the milk was almost gone. Elliot, she knew. She had cereal anyway with the remaining two tablespoons. It wasn't bad. Slightly damp, the Cocoa Krispies were extra chocolaty. She checked all her stuff in the fridge and the cabinets. At least they weren't stealing everything, but no more milk, and she had no interest in going to the grocery store. Well, Cocoa Krispies would keep. She hid the box of cereal in an upper cabinet behind a bag of flour. It'd be safe there. No one in the house was going to touch flour.

Friday afternoon. Introduction to Philosophy for Non-humanities Majors.

Nine minutes to go. The cloudy and windy world outside beckoned, cool and gray and free, through the line of fluorescent glaring windows.

It's been a whole week, she thought.

Since her.

Professor Townsend, now forever Professor Tingles, possibly trying to compensate for letting the class out early the previous Friday, moved in front of his desk and looked at each student in turn. There were now eight students left of the thirty-five who had started the quarter. Townsend put his hands on his hips and frowned. Gabrielle knew he was trying to look stern but she thought he resembled a bearded, overweight child attempting to blow up a balloon. One of those long skinny balloons you can twist into different shapes like a puppy or a bunny.

"You're all asleep!" he said loudly.

Gabrielle started. The big guy in front of her muttered, "Not anymore." He tugged on the collar of his plaid shirt-jacket. Annie glanced at him in a silent warning. Gabrielle wrote *asleep.* Then *bunny.*

"I had the pleasure, last night, of driving past that monstrosity of a power plant which the fools put right on the bay thus blighting the view forever. Well, we need electricity. I guess they had to put it the ugly thing somewhere. But now I realize it's very good we can see it. Because we need to keep an eye on it. We need to pay attention to what they're doing. Last night, you would not have believed how much crap they were dumping into the atmosphere from those awful smokestacks. Gigantic clouds of pollution."

Gabrielle scribbled, *this guy's an idiot.*

Andrea, alone in the front row, nodded in grim humorless agreement.

"And, the thing is, it's only at night that they dump that crap."

"*Wow,*" Andrea said.

"Like they think no one will notice in the dark. Are they that stupid?"

Andrea gave him a huge smile. Blank looks from everyone else. Gabrielle dared to look at her watch. Four minutes to go.

Annie raised her hand and, getting a nod, said, "Professor Ting– Townsend, don't you think the fact that it's cold at night might have something to do with the visibility of the output? You know, like how you can see your breath when it's cold."

Townsend stared at her hard. Gabrielle cringed. He *had* to have heard that.

But he continued. "They switch the fuel. They burn the dirty stuff at night. It's obvious."

"It takes a long time to switch the fuel. It's natural gas this time of year."

"Natural gas," Townsend said flatly.

"My boyfriend's father works there. He's always complaining about how much work it is."

Boyfriend. Oh, well.

Townsend went around to his desk, black tie swinging, and opened the grade book. He looked over the class, and began making marks.

"But doesn't that make more sense?" Annie said.

"Sense?" Townsend sneered.

One minute to go. Gabrielle closed her notebook. Townsend looked up at the motion, squinted at her, and made a mark in the grade book. The other students held perfectly still.

Townsend closed the grade book and placed it in his briefcase. He stood up. "All right," he said. "Remember, your papers or presentations are due in the week before the final. You had better be working on them. The second mid-term is a week from next Monday. If you have any questions or need guidance, I will not be in my office." He left the room.

Andrea followed, her books tucked under her arm. The classroom echoed her fast little steps. The door closed.

"Wait," the big guy said.

Annie laughed softly.

They all heard the heavy door at the end of the hall. Everyone exhaled.

"Damn," the big guy said and turned around. "What did you do?"

"I closed my notebook. Guess he didn't like that."

"Tingles has it in for you. One week until the drop deadline."

"Nope. No dropping."

"Yeah? Good luck, then."

"Thanks."

He and Annie left together, holding hands. Well, Gabrielle thought.

They all evacuated the classroom as efficiently as they could. Friday afternoon, Gabrielle loitered in the hall. She decided she did not like the silence. She left the deserted English building and walked out under the last of the February sunlight. She found herself going in the direction of the library, even though she did not want to go there. The beige structure loomed in the twilight. It looked timeless, unchanging, almost ancient in the cold light. May as well go in, she thought.

The lobby was empty. As usual there was no one at the check-out counter. The door to the Stacks hung open. Gabrielle relaxed. Her favorite place. And, as she went up the metal steps, she saw she had it all to herself. No footsteps or whispers intruded as she climbed to the fourth level. The sound of her shoes on the concrete floor was swallowed up by floor to ceiling shelves of books. There was no one sleeping at her corner desk. She sat there, her backpack on hcr lap.

She got up quickly. She felt a mixture of impatience and sadness. She walked away and went to the stairs. She exited the library and left the Stacks behind.

On the inner campus street, she put her backpack on, both shoulders. Long distance walking configuration. She adjusted the straps and walked south. She passed the old gym with its clock tower. *4:25*. She went down the service road between the Graphic Arts building and Computer Science and entered the transition zone where the university dissolved into suburban streets. They were lined with newer ranch-style houses and she felt almost at home but the streets curved around in a most unCovina-like manner. She sussed out the way. She got to the main street and went west. She crossed the big north-south highway and passed the bank, the modular looking building was dark and empty.

She really did not want to see the place again. She felt she should. She had to. She went into the deserted strip mall. Her grocery store was at the end of the sidewalk. She came to the storm drain. Why am I doing this, she thought. But she knew.

She had been alone. She had died alone lying on a dirty asphalt parking lot. The last thing she had seen was the ugly tangle of power lines. She had died alone and Gabrielle did not want her to be alone.

There was no indication anything had happened. The gray, patched asphalt, the rusty grill over the drain were completely clear of – she didn't want to even think the word.

Gabrielle was startled by her reflection in the clothing store window. But there was nothing there. And no reason to be standing there. It was already getting dark. She wiped her face and adjusted her glasses. She put her hands in her pockets and walked away.

Her house was on the far side of town. She decided to try a new route, the only other path through the north-south barrier of the freeway. She went back out of the strip mall and pushed the walk button at the complicated intersection just to the west. She crossed the busy street and the headlights of the cars, glaring silently, watched her. She looked only straight ahead.

She went south, past another little shopping center, and the street curved and dipped. The sounds of traffic faded behind her. The houses were small and huddled together behind trees and hedges and banks of flowers, all gray in the twilight. She had driven this way once before and knew all she to do was go straight, straight through the downtown, and then bear east towards her neighborhood. There were many other streets she had never been on.

She flipped up the hood of the sweatshirt and tugged it down over her ears. Warm and snug. Now I'm protected, she figured.

She was suddenly curious.

Just pick a street, she thought. You can't get lost. The town isn't big enough to get lost in. Maybe there'll be something interesting.

The bulk of the roaring freeway overpass loomed before her, a blocky concrete edifice.

Her legs felt strong. She walked effortlessly. The light left the sky with each step. She walked under the freeway. The overpass was flanked by drooping palm trees and the concrete was covered with vines. The sound of the vehicles above faded rapidly as she walked under. She could just see the tops of trucks going by at high speed. They made a cottony rumble. Under the overpass, her footsteps crunched loudly and, self-conscious, she walked softly.

Then, on the other side, she turned and looked behind her. The fog was there. The fog had caught her. Gray chill mist draped over her shoulders and hood. Enveloped, she was a phantom. Yes. She relaxed fully now. All the stiffness in her neck vanished and she breathed more deeply, more freely.

The traffic noise from the freeway was completely gone. The cold night air tickled the back of her neck. Over her shoulder, she could no longer see the overpass. Twelve steps and the 101 was invisible.

She walked down the wet sidewalk. She liked the fog. It smelled clean.

A side street appeared. She got up close to the sign. *Miranda St.* She decided it was as good as any. The sidewalk stretched before her.

The windows of the small houses glowed with inviting warmth. One house had open curtains and she could see the television set in the front room, black and white. Cartoons were playing. As she passed, she saw an old woman on a sofa, motionless and stiffly upright in the bluish light of the screen. Gabrielle looked away, embarrassed.

The sky directly above was the color of a moth's wing. The color of wet ashes. The windows of the houses became blurry even just across their front yards from the sidewalk. The houses on the other side of the street were vague shapes. The streetlights, old yellow incandescent fixtures on cast iron poles, shone on only a small circle around their bases. They were, at least, markers in the fog. Between streetlights, it was very dark.

She stood still. It made no sense, where she was.

She had counted her steps as always. She knew she should be past the main north-south avenue. She should be getting run over by a real estate agent in a Buick. Even accounting for deviations from a regular grid pattern, she should have crossed the main street and encountered heavy traffic and the new, garish amber streetlights.

She walked a little farther.

Her mind was suddenly full of the subliminal buzz of new panic. There had been no breaks in the curb, no intersecting streets. One long continuous sidewalk without end. This was not possible. There were other streets, she knew, the area north of downtown was a nice, organized grid. How could I have missed all of the streets?

The fog blew around her, the wind was freezing. She could see the line of antique streetlights going off into the distance. The line of glowing dots curved up steeply up before vanishing.

She thought of the mountains to the east of the campus, with the freeway cut into it, a decent hill to climb. It had challenged her car many times.

That is impossible, she thought. An illusion of some sort. It just can't be real. Go back. Get out of here. Just go straight back. Go. Now.

Something moved under the streetlight before her. A bulky shape close to the ground. Gabrielle blinked behind her fog dappled glasses.

It was a bear, a black bear. It poked its head up, sniffing the air. Looking for trash cans to tip over. Looking for something to eat. The bear's pointy snout scanned in her direction. It can smell me, she thought. It's lost like I am and it's very hungry.

The hairy bear, nose close to the ground, walked with a powerful saunter across the street away from her.

Gabrielle ran past it. She grabbed her backpack straps and ran. She angled away from the sidewalk and on to the asphalt and noticed for the first time there were no parked cars. Empty curbs left and right.

She crossed the street, now on the side away from the streetlights. Have to remember you can park anywhere you want on Miranda.

She was in the dark zone between streetlights and all the houses were dark. She stopped and turned. The fog had filled in the area behind her. There was no movement. The bear was not following her that she could tell. And it had definitely been a bear, a real huge black bear.

She decided that jogging briskly was a good idea and she ran exactly a hundred steps when she saw a man standing at the edge of the circle of light two streetlights up.

She dropped to a walk, breathing heavily, mucus dripping from her nose.

The man was naked, she saw, his back to her. Don't lose sight of him, the impossible naked man, she thought for no reason, heart pounding, throat tightening. Keep track of him. She continued to walk quickly.

She drew abreast of him. She could see him clearly. His skin was the same shade of gray as the sidewalk. He was waving his arms and running his hands over his face, anguished or confused. He snapped his head from side to side. His bare feet twitched.

He might hear me, she thought. And I don't want him to hear me. I really don't want that. Quiet. Be quiet. Be absolutely quiet.

Look, she told herself, he's afraid to move. But you don't know. He's so agitated. Keep going and don't make a sound. Not one sound.

She passed him, moving down the opposite sidewalk, no cars or trees to hide behind, walking heel to toe, and then she looked back and finally saw his face clearly in the weak light. Her heart began pounding. Her pulse rate shot up to absolute maximum.

The left side of the naked man's face from his cheek area to his forehead was a black hole. There were sharp looking white ridges in the void there. Probably shards of shattered bone, she thought. She was seeing the demolished remains of the inside of the man's skull. She felt confident she was actually seeing this. She tried to breathe and accidentally made a coughing sound. The naked man's single remaining eye found her in the dark. His mouth opened. He took a step in her direction. Then he sprang into high speed.

Gabrielle ran. One shoe caught a cracked slab of the sidewalk and she tumbled forward, scraping her chin. She did not pause. She scrambled up and ran headlong into the darkness, her face stinging. The air was freezing. She pumped her legs as fast as she could and tried to breathe. It was *hard* to breathe. Her throat burned. She ran on her toes. I feel light, she thought, I can go so fast but I'm going to pass out. Then she heard it. The slap of bare feet on asphalt, on concrete. The sound got louder. Faster than she was, much faster. Catching up. How was that possible, she thought furiously. Something like crying came out of her.

The slapping of bare feet was right behind her. She knew any moment she would feel his fingers snag the straps of her backpack and bring her down. And then what? What would happen? He was right behind her. She heard herself scream, a terrified, strangled mewling.

She sloughed off her backpack. She dumped it. Left arm out, right arm, it slipped off her shoulders and she heard it hit the ground. A heavy nylon slump. She ran, not daring to look. Breathe, dumbass, breathe.

She lost count of her steps but it was eight streetlights before she looked behind her. There was no movement on the sidewalk or the street.

She came to a stumbling stop. Her legs felt like rubber. Her face and body were covered with sweat, hair wet against her head. She gasped for air. She felt her chin. Pretty good cut. The blood on her hand was black.

She could only see one streetlight back. That was it. Farther away was total darkness. It didn't look like fog anymore. It looked like nothing. The darkness was unmarred by movement. The naked man, if he was back there, she thought, he can't find me now.

She considered going back for her backpack. God, she wanted to. She needed it. But she did not want to walk in that direction. If I go into that darkness I will get lost, she thought. Possibly forever.

Just keep going.

All the houses lining the street were small and silent and no light came from them. It crossed her mind to knock on a door. And who would answer, she thought. Who's in there, in these nothing little dark houses? Ahead of her the line of streetlights was visible, straight at ground level and curving up and up.

Into the mountains? she thought, perplexed.

She couldn't quite see the sidewalk she was on but it felt solid. She got her wind back. She rubbed her shoulders where the straps had been. It was so dark.

Just keep going, she thought again. The air was still and cold. Chilled now, she walked and her footsteps were the only sound.

She walked sixty-four steps. There was someone in front of her. Someone on the sidewalk walking the same direction she was. She saw the slender figure of a young woman. Gabrielle realized she was gaining on her. The person was about her height and she got the impression of a mass of bouncing black hair. The figure seemed to be in a bit of a hurry and made a sharp turn to the right, away from the street, into the line of dark houses, houses that were now hard to discern. Gabrielle moved faster. She started jogging again. She had the strong feeling that she must follow her. Her heart began pounding again and she gasped.

Dark silhouetted shapes arrayed themselves around her, impeding her, but not quite solid. Miranda Street, she suddenly saw, was full of people. The dim streetlights–they were barely putting out any light now– shone on the tops of their heads, dozens of people, their faces hard to see but all looking where the lights arced up and vanished.

She paused. Dozens? No, there were hundreds of people. What in the world were they doing? All so quiet and patient.

Well, this was fascinating. She was strongly tempted to join them. It was pretty hard to tell but no one seemed to be wearing clothes. That was kind of funny, she suddenly thought. Heck, this might be fun.

Beyond understanding, she stood at the edge of the street. The mass of people were joined by still more, coming out of the wall of blackness to her left, all naked. It was a river of people and they all began to move up the street to the right, heading for the place where it met the lightless sky.

Then a cold feeling came over her, a surge of profound sadness.

I don't belong with them, she thought. They don't want me here. They want me to leave.

There was a scuffling sound. The cute figure, which had been waiting a short distance away, scooted between two houses.

Gabrielle, with difficulty, tore herself away from the river of people.

She got to the spot where the figure had turned and a brilliant white cold light hit her, smeared with colors in the background. Warm air blew through her hair. Car exhaust. She saw the figure in the center of the light, waiting, arms at her sides. Gabrielle's eyes teared and when she blinked the figure was gone. She was alone in the glare. She tried to clear her vision and half removed her glasses and rubbed her eyes. Her face was numb with cold.

She was looking at the floodlights in a corner clothing store display window. The lights were shining on stylishly dressed manikins, one of which was a petite female shape. It was wearing a dark blue sweater and black jeans and was smiling enigmatically, its plastic face framed by a wig of curly black hair. The traffic lights of the busy intersection reflected in the store window.

Gabrielle's skin tingled. There was a hollow ringing in her ears. She felt utterly drained. It took effort to raise her feet. She saw one of her shoes had come untied and she did not have the energy to crouch down and tie it.

She looked behind her. It was a residential street lined with parked cars. New amber streetlights. There was no fog. No crowds of silent people. The houses had normal lights on inside. She walked a few steps towards it but her backpack was not visible anywhere. She quickly returned to the bright light of the store window. She closed her eyes and just let the light shine on her face for a minute.

She recognized the busy street she was on. She knew where she was, near the center of town, and knew the path she would take to get to her house. No detours. She would observe her surroundings carefully and watch where she stepped.

She touched the window and looked up at the black-haired manikin. She said, "Thank you," in a clear voice. It seemed like the right thing to do. She waited for a moment but the manikin made no response. Then she went to the curb and pushed the walk button.

She still felt a vague sadness. All those people. But they weren't alone, she realized. No, they had each other. This was something she just knew.

She was pretty sure she wanted to lie down.

Saturday morning she woke up clear headed. She was alone in the house. She made a breakfast of scrambled eggs and three pieces of toast with butter and orange marmalade, which she wasn't at all sure she liked, sweet and orange and also bitter and fibrous. But she thought, as Barbara would say, what the fuck ever.

She made a pot of coffee and took it into the front room. She wasn't interested in watching cartoons on the one tv channel but there was nothing else to do. She thought of reviewing her physics notes, or maybe work on her project, and had to remind herself: everything was gone. All her notes. Her big project notebook, companion of many years, gone. She checked her car to see if maybe. Nope. No backpack.

So she sat on the sofa in front of tv with the sound off and thought about the events of the previous day. Her legs were stiff and there was definitely a cut on her chin.

She noticed the sadness had faded, but the feeling of rejection had not.

What she had seen, and, she thought, I *really did* see what I saw, hung before her mind's eye like the shattered end of a nightmare. The memories did not seem to be fading in the manner of dreams. Bringing up the image of the naked man caused her pulse rate to spike. She stared at the tv screen and drank coffee.

It had been quite real.

She wasn't overly concerned about losing the notes to her classes and her Shakespeare book. She could remember everything. She was pretty sure she could remember everything. Then she thought, if I'm not remembering something, how would I know? I've never forgotten anything that I know of.

On the other hand, Miranda Street.

It seemed real but it couldn't be real. It simply could not be. This demonstrates I cannot tell real from hallucination. Or dream. Maybe I forget stuff all the time and don't know it. Because I have no memory of it. It's just gone.

This line of thought made her feel very vulnerable. This line of thought led to the ragged edge of everything she was and beyond that was a great nothing. The unknown and unknowable. The boundaries of the self. The physical limits of the mind.

She put the coffee back in the kitchen. Stupid coffee just wasn't helping at all.

She turned off the tv in the middle of Bugs Bunny and made sure all the doors were shut, used the bathroom, and went to her room. She curled up on the narrow bed and pulled the thin blanket over her. She loved her room and decided to stay in all day. It was no use worrying about the test on Tuesday. She either knew it or she didn't. She wanted to think about the previous day, she wanted to go over everything.

But the bed was very comfortable.

She slept until three-thirty and woke up with a nasty, eyeball pinching headache that got immeasurably worse when Elliot came in and turned the tv on loud. *B.J. and the Bear.* How could he watch that? She wondered if the station ever put on *The Avengers.* Probably not, she thought, because only people like me like it. And how many of us are there?

At least, thinking about Mrs. Peel seemed to help her headache. She went into the front room and watched the show with Elliot, who just smiled at her.

When *B.J. and the Bear* was ending, he asked, "Is Catherine coming over?"

"I don't think so."

"You don't know?"

Getting annoyed, Gabrielle said, "She shows up when she wants to. I guess she doesn't want to."

"You can't call her?"

"I don't think she has a phone."

"How can she not have a phone?"

"Elliot, not everyone has a phone."

Elliot seemed to find this almost incomprehensible and said, "Well, I was just wondering if she was going to make dinner tomorrow and what we were having, you know, so I could look forward to it."

Gabrielle sighed. "Right. Sunday dinner."

"That's tomorrow."

Gabrielle closed her eyes. "I know."

"So is she coming?"

"I don't know. I guess we'll have to wait and see."

"What if she doesn't come?"

"I don't know."

"You'll have to make dinner then."

"Me?"

"You don't want to? That's okay."

"No, I want to."

"You do?"

"Sure."

"Are you going to?"

"Um. Well, I want to."

"What are we having?"

"Well." Gabrielle pushed herself from the recliner. "Let's see what we have."

"That fried chicken was so good!"

"I know we don't have chicken."

"Oh."

"We ate it all."

"Oh."

"Let me look, okay." She pushed the button on the old wall switch and the single bulb in the ceiling came on weakly. Gabrielle opened the fridge.

"Thanks, Gabrielle!"

"Don't thank me yet. I'm not sure I can actually do it."

"But you want to?"

"Yes, yes. I want to." She checked the freezer.

"Hot dogs!" Elliot cried.

"That would be fine."

"And potato chips."

"Everyone would love that." Gabrielle didn't want to use up the supply of small steaks, all labeled with a big 'G.' There was also a package of hamburger in white paper. Dinner for four, she thought. There you go. Frozen but a week old now. May as well use it. She took the hamburger out and wrote 'Sunday' and placed it on her shelf in the fridge to defrost. Also on her shelf was a bunch of celery, a head of iceberg lettuce, a bag of tortillas, two sticks of butter, and that weird jar of orange marmalade.

In the supermarket they had gone to, on the first aisle with all the well-dressed ladies and the classical music playing, Catherine had asked her what her favorite jam or jelly was and Gabrielle knew that professing not to have a favorite, which was the reality, would simply not do. She knew how it would have gone:

G: I don't care. Pick anything.

C: No. Tell me your favorite.

G: I don't have a favorite.

C: Everyone has a favorite.

G: I don't. Really.

C: Tell me.

G: I not crazy about any of them.

C: What? Why not?

G: I don't know. They're all, like, sticky.

C: Well, jam is supposed to be, you know, sticky.

G: Yeah. Not crazy about that.

C: Uh. How about strawberries? Do you like strawberries?

G: I guess.

C: Don't guess. Yes or no.

G: No. All those little seeds.

C: That's impossible! Everyone in the world likes strawberries!

So, to avoid all that, Gabrielle simply pointed at the nearest jar, a glistening orange substance. Who knew what the heck marmalade was, anyway. It was chunky.

She remembered Catherine's face. Surprise, and a clever squint of her blue eyes. *She had no idea I was so sophisticated.*

Gabrielle closed the fridge. "Okay. We're having hamburgers. And baked potatoes."

"That's not very good."

"You don't get to vote."

"We're not having a vegetable?"

"A what? No."

"You sure Catherine can't come over?"

Gabrielle raised her voice. "She's probably never coming back. So stop asking."

"Okay. Sorry." Elliot went back to staring at the tv.

Gabrielle stood at the top of the basement stairs. She swallowed. "I'm sorry I yelled at you."

As she closed her door, she heard him say, "You weren't yelling. Just being forceful."

Her room in the basement, her compact, half-underground refuge from the outside world, lay cold and silent at her feet. She stopped on the last step. *Different,* she thought. *Has it always been like this? What am I doing here?*

The room smelled of detergent and musty socks. She sat on the edge of her bed and smoothed out the blanket. *This is the way it's going to be,* she thought. *I just have to get used to it. Why did you think it would be otherwise?*

She saw the blue top peeking out from under the pillow. *Don't,* she thought. Don't touch it.

She pulled it out.

Well, you idiot, at least don't smell it.

She held it up to her face and inhaled deeply. She tried to distract herself by studying the material. Nylon or something. Who knows. Not that much stretch to it. She thought of Catherine wearing it. She thought of Catherine taking it off.

"Not doing this."

She stuffed the filmy thing into the bottom of her stack of t-shirts. There was a blonde hair clinging to the fabric. She grasped it and held it up. Ten inches long.

She looked around the room. She didn't have so much as a piece of paper. With her free hand, she tipped over her pile of t-shirts. Nothing. She upended her pants. She scattered her underwear and all of her four socks. Huh. Yep.

She picked up a sock, gray and low cut with a dirty hole where her big toe went. It would have to do. Can't wear it, anyway. She blew into the sock and it puffed open. It had a rank smell. She carefully guided the hair in it, letting it coil up. Then she folded both ends closed. She found the matching sock, equally dirty and holed, and rolled it over the first, making a tight bundle. Satisfied, she searched through her tiny closet area. Her old green jacket with the uncomfortable collar had a vest pocket with a brass snap. Without taking it off the rusty steel water pipe, she unsnapped the pocket and tucked the sock bundle into it, positioning it so it wasn't too tight, and snapped it shut. Safe and snug. She then put her clothes back in their neat piles. All right, she thought.

It was barely dark outside. She wasn't hungry. She didn't want to go for a walk. *Hell* no. She didn't want to use up the gas in her car. She didn't want to watch tv. She had no notes to look at.

She sat on her plywood slat of a bed. She had no idea how she was going to get through the night.

Much later, the blackbirds sang to her again and her dreams were filled with voices. A great wind carried her bodily across the sky towards a field of brilliant swirling colors. Red, gold, orange, green, all in motion. She held out her hands. She wanted to gather it all in and keep it forever.

She awoke very early. She got out of bed effortlessly and went into the bathroom. Stepping into the shower, she saw herself in the mirror. Well, she thought. Now what? Considering that question she used up all the hot water.

Everything went well for Sunday dinner. It was fine. It wasn't an applause getter like Catherine's but it was okay. No one expected it to be like Catherine's. Everyone was silent.

"So does everyone like their hamburgers?"

"Fine," said Brian.

"Fine," said Mark.

"Really good, Gabrielle," said Elliot.

"I might have burned yours a little. Sorry."

"That was the best part."

"Really?"

"Oh, yeah. The burned part tastes the best." The others all nodded.

"Okay. That's crazy."

This led to a discussion about cooking and grilling versus barbecuing. Gabrielle found it all interesting because it was new to her. They all agreed cooking was tricky and expensive but potentially fun especially if you were hungry.

Gabrielle was cleaning up – the guys only helped a little – when she reminded them that next Sunday was their responsibility and also that she couldn't afford to keep feeding them in general. So stop stealing the milk unless they wanted to make small recurring cash donations.

This perfectly reasonable idea caused all of them to exit the kitchen instantly. And that's why Gabrielle was alone when she found it.

She was putting away the bottle of vegetable oil she had used to fry the hamburgers, because Catherine had used oil on seemingly everything and that automatically made it part of the standard food preparation protocol no matter what was being cooked, and she bumped the bag of sugar on the top shelf. There was a clinking sound. There was a bottle of some kind behind the sugar. Like it had been hidden there. Gabrielle, on tip-toe, wiggled it out. It was a tall, dark bottle with a dark label. She had to hold it under the light. *Pinot Noir.*

"Uh, oh," she said. She looked around her. They had all left. And had they helped with the dishes?

"Then they can't have any," she said. She found the rusty corkscrew, rinsed out a large glass, the one with the fewest hard water deposits, and went to her room.

The cork came out in pieces and bits ended up floating in the glass. The label said 1974. It was very different from the white wine. Deep, deep red. Thick. Strong smell, almost unpleasant.

She paused. No, it's definitely unpleasant.

And the taste was complex. Yes, that was the word, she thought. It's what you say when you don't want to admit you don't like it. She sipped some more. The effect on the inside of her mouth was different, too. There was the acidic stinging as well as a strong tightening sensation. There was a word for that and after pouring a little more into the glass she gave trying to remember it.

It's Sunday evening and I really should be studying for that test, but I have no notes to study, she thought. "So I'm in trouble," she found herself saying. "I guess Catherine doesn't like me. I guess she doesn't."

The glass needed more wine again.

"No, she likes me. There's something else going on. That's what it is."

The bottle had plenty left. She poured a bit more. Someone walked across the kitchen floor. The open rafters creaked. She could tell they were headed for the fridge.

"Those guys. They're going to eat everything I have. Everything she gave to me. I wonder what I'm supposed to do? Because that's the way it looks. I'm supposed to do something. She has to be a hundred percent sure."

She noticed the bottle was now less than half full.

"Oh, no, that's too much. If only I hadn't broken the cork. But I did. And that cannot be undone." She giggled. "And I am absolutely certain that I am. I am definitely good looking. Enough. I am cute. I may not be a fox or whatever they call it but I am cute. I think. I am cute enough to." She allowed herself to think the thought. "I could have whomever I want."

She grabbed her sweatshirt.

"I could have her. Whoever. Whomever. I could *have* her. I could." She started up the stairs and kept a firm grip on the railing. "So the question is." She crossed the kitchen. "Who do I want?"

"What?" Elliot was behind her, going to the fridge.

"Catherine was right." Gabrielle opened the kitchen door.

"She was?"

"Yes. I should not shift for myself anymore."

"What?"

"No more shifting. Self-shifting. *You* know."

"Of course I know. Your Beetle has a stick."

"Oh, *no*. Boys don't get it," Gabrielle said intensely. She patted Elliot on the shoulder. "Poor, poor boys."

She closed the door on his confused face and set off down the sidewalk.

"I mean, honestly, boys are dumb."

The fog was back but she didn't think she would see the black bear or the other things. It felt different. I'm heading for the center, she thought. That street was leading me further away. Now I'm going deeper.

It's just hard to go in a straight line.

The previous Sunday, she neglected to note the names of the streets along the way, however she was confident she could find the place again. She always counted her steps. She couldn't help it. Hands buried in her pockets, she turned right at nine one seven. The side street, more of an alley she now saw, appeared on schedule at one two one four. And then the gardenias, amazingly fragrant in the fog, tugged at her clothes.

And there was the Carriage House, ghostly in the half light of the backyard. She stopped. The old nineteen-twenties era garage was completely dark. She went to the corner door and listened. No music came from between the boards.

"Maybe I'm late." Her watch said 9:25. She stared at it in astonishment. No idea it was so late, she thought. How did I do that?

"Oh well. Susan did say they *might* be here. Or was that Susan?" She knocked softly. There were no murmurous voices or rattle of a padlock. She went back to the gardenias. Damn. Her feet were sore. So have I been walking everywhere..

The door opened with a snap. She jumped. No light spilled out. She saw a face peer out.

Don't be an idiot, she thought, and said, "Gabrielle."

Someone stepped all the way out. They beckoned her to come in.

Gabrielle stepped into the doorway and voices whispered her name. She smelled perfume and bad breath and sweat. The thin door was closed and a match was struck. It was Tall Susan and she lit a tall candle.

"I thought for a second you were closed," Gabrielle said.

"Shhh!"

"Sorry," she whispered.

"We're having problems with the neighbors," said another Susan. Pretty Susan, but she looked different.

"Yeah. We have to keep quiet so the assholes don't call the cops."

"Turns out it's against some law to serve alcohol without a license. Just like Nazi Germany."

"Then they cut the electricity off."

"But that was her fault."

"Yeah, totally her fault."

Gabrielle lost track of which Susan was talking. Pretty Susan lit another candle from the first and Gabrielle got a better look at her. She had a black eye. Her left eye and cheek were a purple mass with green edges. She set her candle on a table near the hanging dyed sheets.

"Oh, wow. Are you all right?"

Pretty Susan's face twisted. "Am I what?"

"She'll be fine," Tall Susan said with her odd accent. From behind, she put both hands on Gabrielle's shoulders and massaged. "I can't tell you how nice it is to see you again."

"Thanks, me too. Did you know this is mid-winter's day? It's the exact middle of winter and we are heading for spring now. Isn't that great?"

"Hm. Doesn't feel like spring."

"I am not a winter person," Gabrielle said. "Fall, maybe. Fall is nice."

The third Susan – what *was* my made-up name for her, Gabrielle thought. Little Susan? Baby Susan? New! New Susan – came close. She reached around with both hands, grabbed Tall Susan by the waist and pulled. Gabrielle was sandwiched between them. Pretty Susan looked away, hurt and then angry.

"You look like you could use a drink," New Susan said, moving her body up and down. She was wearing a black, skin-tight leotard. "Doesn't she?"

"I'm okay."

"Here." Tall Susan said behind her and handed New Susan a full paper cup, who took a sip. Gabrielle then felt Tall Susan begin to smell her hair and left ear and neck. Her breath was slow and hot. New Susan handed Gabrielle the cup.

"Drink this."

"What is it?" It looked like water. Didn't smell like water.

"Who cares? Drink it."

Gabrielle sipped and her mouth burned.

"Fucking drink it!"

Gabrielle swallowed the whole thing in one gulp. It burned all the way down and her stomach lurched.

"Holy shit."

"Did you see that?"

"God."

New Susan turned her head sideways and kissed her. Then she licked Gabrielle's mouth and chin. The tip of her tongue tickled. "Can't let that drop get away." New Susan encountered Tall Susan under Gabrielle's left ear and they kissed, both making tiny moans which seemed quite loud. Gabrielle tried to catch her breath. Suddenly New Susan was trying to pull her zipper down.

"We're the only ones here," Tall Susan said. "We could go in the house."

Pretty Susan leaned towards them "We're not supposed to go in the house."

"It's all right," Tall Susan said.

"No it isn't."

New Susan stopped kissing Gabrielle's neck and stopped fondling her zipper. She let go of Tall Susan, pulled away, and pushed Pretty Susan hard in the center of her chest and she stumbled back one step then straightened up defiantly. New Susan pushed her again with both hands. Pretty Susan didn't stumble. She made a growling sound.

Tall Susan pulled Gabrielle away by the shoulders. "Come on." Gabrielle took a step towards the hanging sheets. She tripped. It was hard to tell where the ground was. Tall Susan walked her to the back door. Gabrielle heard one of the others snarl, "Bitch!" and saw Pretty Susan take a wide swing. Her fist caught New Susan at the tip of her jaw and her head snapped to the side.

Wrong way to do it, Gabrielle thought. Dad at least taught me how to throw a punch the right way. I mean, get *inside* their defenses.

Oh, It's funny. My thoughts are so detached.

Pretty Susan swung her fist again. New Susan blocked it easily with her forearm.

See? Gabrielle thought. Tall Susan tugged Gabrielle through the back door.

Suddenly out in the cold darkness between the old houses, Gabrielle said, "I was thinking about my thoughts being detached. But then I thought if I'm thinking that, I'm not detached. Right?"

She heard more blows landing accompanied by short, sharp screams. Who was hitting who, she could not see. There was a loud thump and the sound of breaking glass. A table was knocked over.

"God damn it," Tall Susan muttered. "Hey!" she shouted back behind them.

The two Susans were rolling around on the dirty floor. They rolled into another table and it tipped over along with a chair and burning candle.

"I don't think they're listening," Gabrielle said. Tall Susan was now pushing her from behind. She concentrated on where her feet went. They got away from the garage and Gabrielle saw an orange light fill the doorway.

Then she was along a white picket fence and then a sidewalk. Well, I am clear on the other side of the whole place, she thought. The house was another Craftsman style bungalow. Tall Susan stopped her at the gate and then slid her hands around Gabrielle's waist and kissed the side of her neck.

"Go ahead and go in. It's not locked. I have to go take care of those halfwits."

Gabrielle swayed and grabbed hold of Tall Susan's arm.

More glass broke in the old garage. It sounded like a large bottle shattering.

"Damn it," Tall Susan said. She brought Gabrielle's hand up to her mouth. Gabrielle felt the tip of Tall Susan's tongue press into her palm and roll around. They stayed like that for a moment, Tall Susan's breath so hot again.

"Oh," Gabrielle said.

"I'll be right back. Go ahead and go in." Tall Susan released her and ran to the back of the house. There was some sort of light flickering back there.

Gabrielle looked at the gate in front of her. It was double-sided, like an old-time saloon door, and the white paint was marred where something had been scraped off. Probably their name, Gabrielle thought, still detached. Only the first letter remained of eight spaces, a square, black stick-on 'L.'

She put her hand on the gate and the wood was rough and cold.

The train horn pierced the misty night across the town. Gabrielle listened as the sound echoed off the low clouds. She took her hand off the gate and stepped back.

Don't go in there, she thought. Don't go in there.

Her head cleared some. She wanted to go home. Back to her room. Just get out of there.

Get out of there.

But she didn't want to go past the Carriage House and didn't want the Susans to see her. The path through the gardenias was the only way she knew, however. She looked up and down the new street she was on, another quiet, leafy corner in the great maze of her college town. Maybe all I have to do is head east, she thought. What is this street anyway? She looked for a sign. She saw an antique streetlight with a cast iron base putting out weak, yellowish light.

"Nope. Nope." Gabrielle walked quickly away from the gate and the streetlight. "Go *this* way. Just go fast."

She jogged along the picket fence and past the open door of the garage, filled with ominous bright orange light. There was crackling and popping.

In the center of the Carriage House, Tall Susan was waving her arms. The hanging sheets were exploding into flames and tongues of fire were tickling the rafters above. Smoke filled the room to the top of her head. Bathed in firelight, the two Susans were on the floor, one on top of the other, both blondes wearing black leotards so Gabrielle couldn't tell which was which. The Susan on top had Susan's arms pinned and was forcefully thrusting herself into Susan's lower body. As she did so, she was rhythmically making a sound which was a cross between and moan and a grunt.

Gabrielle hurried past the building. The firelight cast bright orange and yellow spots. She waded into the midst of the fragrant gardenias, and stood still. "Well. There's just no stopping it," she said and sank to her knees. It was a full minute before she could breathe normally.

"Okay. Get out of here," she whispered.

She got to the connecting street and on step one fifty-eight, sirens screamed to life behind her. A fire engine came out of a cross street, all whirling red lights, and roared back the way she had come. A fireman in his helmet, coat still undone, waved from the back platform. Gabrielle waved back.

Above the rooftops and between the eucalyptus trees a huge column of smoke was boiling up, illuminated from below by bright orange and yellow flames.

Gabrielle gaped. "Wow," she whispered and kept walking. I hope they got out, she thought and almost laughed. I wonder if they even noticed.

By the time she got close to her house, she was feeling almost back to normal. She patted the roof of her car, still safely parked at the top of the driveway. The house looked friendly, even inviting, with its old fashioned woodwork and low wattage lighting. In the kitchen, it smelled of overcooked something. Maybe hamburgers. Those guys, she thought, at least they're trying.

At her bathroom door, she stopped. "Oh, right. That was me."

In the shower, she considered her forgetfulness. "That was just earlier this evening. Today," she whispered into the running water.

In her room, propped against her pillow, was the third-full bottle of wine. The heavy smell of it made her stomach lurch. She took it to her bathroom and began to pour it down the sink and stopped. She had a better idea. She left it on the kitchen counter and turned out the light. They could have it.

"That's enough of that," she muttered and went to bed.

It was going to be a busy week and she was anxious to get to it. Three midterms, calculus (not worried), Advanced Topics(not worried) and Introduction to Philosophy on Wednesday (worried.).

Professor Tingles promised the test would be multiple choice.

This made everyone nervous because they all assumed he was lying. So, not multiple choice, right? No. God damned essay questions. Well, all she wanted from that class was a C. It would knock her GPA down from 3.97 to about 3.90. So she would end up with straight A's in her core engineering classes, mathematics, and science. B+'s or better in the few required English classes and all the other general education crap, which she breezed through barely paying attention, and a C in some completely forgettable humanities course. When she applied for a job and they checked her transcripts it would be good for a laugh.

It felt weird to walk around without her backpack. She kept rubbing her shoulders. She went to the bookstore behind the student union and looked at the array of new backpacks on display. They were really cool. The shoulder straps all had padding now. And nifty zipper pockets on the sides. Nice.

She sighed. She really didn't want a new one. She shook her head.

No, she wanted one. But they were more expensive than ever and she was so close to graduation. She decided to get by as simply as possible. She bought a 5-subject spiral bound notebook, blue cover, along with three yellow pencils.

She would have to start her Shakespeare paper over. The textbook she knew she would miss but there was always the library if necessary. She knew the sonnets, at any rate. She hadn't even started the paper for Intro to Tingles, so that was good. Maybe not even do a paper in that one, maybe a presentation. It would be less work.

Her notes for all the other classes could be retrieved by memory, she hoped. So nothing critical for her current schedule. But the other losses were more important. Her project binder. A high quality mechanical pencil, a present from Linda two Christmases before.

She walked out of the busy bookstore into the winter sunlight. Judy Collins was playing in the background, singing about clouds.

It was all almost over anyway, she thought in the warm winter wind. Just move on. The pencils wouldn't fit in her jeans pocket so she carried them in her hand.

The rest of Monday passed weightlessly.

Tuesday morning she skipped breakfast and left the house an hour early. Walking eased her nervousness. When she got to the campus, it came back full force.

Her pencils sweaty in her hand, her heart thudding, at seven a.m. she walked into the calculus test cold. The professor, Watkins, was a short, elderly woman who never smiled except when dispensing bad news. She passed out the test sheets grinning from ear to ear.

Gabrielle smiled back and this caused the professor's face to snap back to its normal dour configuration. No one spoke. No one ever spoke. Gabrielle placed her notebook on the floor and all three pencils on her desk. She brought one pencil to attention. As usual, Gabrielle's nervousness drained away as soon as she started working. And as usual, the professor hovered over her, watching, still unable to believe Gabrielle did not need or even own a calculator.

Not that she disliked calculators but the good ones were incredibly expensive. The HP-65 was something like seven hundred dollars. She couldn't imagine spending that much money for such a thing. She could imagine *creating* such a thing. For other people to use. People who needed help.

Gabrielle finished before everyone else, again, as usual. Twenty minutes to go. The back of the last sheet was extra credit, which she didn't need, but what the heck. She turned it over and scanned the problems.

And froze.

She felt her face burning.

Extra credit consisted of three simple arithmetic problems.

This was at the top of the page:

a = 597141862293

b = 749465118187

Then the instructions: *Perform the following operations. Limit response to first 100 places.*

1. *a+ b*

2. *a * b*

3. *b / a*

Gabrielle heard a surprised gasp from the back of the room as someone got to the same place. "What the hell?" they said. Twelve digit numbers were far beyond the capacity of pretty much all the 'scientific' calculators the students had. The super expensive jobs might be able to do it, Gabrielle thought, but that was beside the point. Maybe the professor was playing a little trick on a bunch of advanced students. Maybe the professor just liked to revisit the basics from time to time.

But Gabrielle knew exactly what this was. She knew she had a reputation. She was a genius. A savant. And she knew there were some on the faculty – *not* engineering faculty – who thought that was all nonsense and she was just a nasty little cheater. They didn't know how she was cheating but she most assuredly was. Cheating big time.

Her embarrassment turned to anger. First, addition: a + b. Miniscule energy required. She wrote:

1) *134660698480*, and circled it. That was easy.

She took a deep breath. Multiplication. She would have to read each number, be fully conscious of it, and then let her talent take over. Her *wild* talent, as Mr. Weber, her high school guidance counselor, had once called it.

Multiplication took a lot of power, a lot of *current*. She visualized electricity moving in a wire. The amount of current varied but the wire – her brain – always remained the same size. If the current was too great for the wire a red light would come on in her mind's eye as a warning. She had started thinking about it in terms of current in the third grade when she read a simple description of how a light bulb worked. Being able to visualize it helped her control her talent and also fueled her budding interest in all things electrical.

The red light idea was suggested years later by Mr. Weber. One day in his office, as they were talking about college plans – she was in the ninth grade – without warning, he had pulled out a set of flash cards. "If it looks like it'll be too much, just stop, Gabby!"

No one else ever called her Gabby.

She nodded, surprised and scared. Mr. Weber held up a big square card with a blocky symbol and number : $\sqrt{2}$.

"Red light! Do you see it? Do you see the red light?"

She had automatically begun to calculate and the numbers piled up in her 'outbox,' another conceptual invention of Mr. Weber's: *1.4142135623730...*

"Close your eyes, Gabby! Close your eyes!"

She had closed her eyes and the calculating stopped. The square root of 2 has no exact solution. The numbers would have gone on forever without stopping, leaving Gabrielle in a seizure-like state, helpless, until she lost consciousness.

"You know how you feel right now, Gabby? That's the red light. Okay? Let's try another one." And after a few sessions, she had seen it. Like a big, red traffic light in front of her face. She had learned to close her eyes. She learned to cut it off. And then subdue and *control.* Control was critical.

Extra credit, she thought, the hell I need this.

But here you go: a times b.

The red light awakened. Low. Steady. It was okay. She shuddered, swallowed, and wrote down the answer:

2) *4475369963978828523822791*, and circled it.

There was another gasp. It came from the professor.

Now the fun one. Division, a hundred places.

Here you go, asshole: b/a.

The red light exploded in her face. She heard Mr. Weber's voice. *"Stop, Gabby! STOP!"*

Sorry, Mr. Weber.

She began to write.

3) *1.2550872171465001818...*

Her temples throbbed. She *counted* as she wrote down the numbers piling up in the outbox. There were voices around her, very far away.

54735628493857730663169759342...

The red light was so bright, she imagined the heat of it on her cheeks. She wrote out another line, her pencil arcing across the paper. It was slowing down.

19674673006990290003...

She realized she might not get to a hundred places. From somewhere in the farthest reaches of her mind she heard herself say, "You're getting old," and that was funny. Her hand cramped.

756538679747...

Her head was really hurting now. The red light hung there. Maybe I don't need the red light anymore, she thought, because I'm

"Burned out," she said out loud. More voices around her.

Oh, just keep going, she thought. Almost there. You got it.

The red light went away.

3163367569033...

Okay stop, she thought. Don't go past a hundred.

593063.

Stop, she thought.

She set down her pencil. Her head still throbbed. I haven't done that in a long time. Wasn't that bad.

She started to fold her test papers lengthwise but the bottom had something wet on it. She wiped it off. It was on her shirt, too, all down the front. Wet and sticky. She had drooled all over herself.

For God's sake, she thought. Mortified, she wiped her chin as quickly as possible and covered up the wet spot on her shirt by zipping up her sweatshirt. She folded her test, name on the outside, and stood. She went to the front and dropped the test on the professor's desk without looking at her. She went back to her spot to get her notebook and pencils. All the students were staring at her, wide-eyed. She got her stuff and walked out.

The halls were empty and the silence oppressive. Outside in the crystal clear air of the inner campus, she wiped her chin again. The sunlight reflected around the edges of her glasses. Her eyes weren't quite focusing or looking in exactly the same direction. But her head no longer hurt.

"Don't react," she said. "That's what they want. Don't do anything. Just let it go."

She headed east, notebook and pencils in hand. The campus sloped down before her, the street lined with overhanging trees and pre-war buildings of modest size and aspect. They all had big front steps leading up to massive doors. The windows were heavy, hinged, and multi-pane frosted glass. Everything painted the same beige, the timeless color of the library. The street opened out into a quad of grass and benches. Beyond that was the old gym with its clock tower.

"It doesn't matter," she said. "I'm almost out of here. Then I will never see them again."

Her next class was Jogging, the only P.E. class she had ever liked, followed immediately at ten o'clock by Advanced Topics. It was always a race to change clothes afterwards and get all the way back up campus to the science building. She decided to go running in her street t-shirt instead of her athletic t-shirt. That way it was just her shorts and running shoes she had to change. That would save a lot of time. And skip the shower, too. No one's going to smell me, she thought.

Not anymore.

Amid the laughter and shrieks of the other girls, she tossed her new notebook and pencils into her locker and took out her athletic clothes, a pair of black short pants and her running shoes. She took off her deck shoes and jeans and pulled on her shorts.

She had to be careful tying the running shoes. She had owned them from her second year at Northview High School when she was fifteen and they looked it. As objects, they could no longer in any objective way be functionally called shoes. In an artistic sense, however, they created an impressionistic interpretation of shoes, each one a decrepit webbing of blue cotton semi-glued to a foot-shaped slab of white rubber, eroded along the outside edges as if by a belt sander. She tended to run on the sides of her feet. The eyelets for the shoelaces were long gone. Gabrielle threaded the laces through the old fabric and, at several spots on the left shoe, through holes in the rubber sole itself. Her toes poked out of the front. There was no other material remaining.

All they had to do was hold together until the end of Winter quarter, she thought. That was it. No more Physical Education ever again forever. Finished for all time.

She folded her jeans and set them on the notebook along with her deck shoes. She closed the locker door softly and clicked shut the three dollar padlock. She jogged out of the double doors of the clock tower building. Her feet slipped two and fro in the ragged shoes. They did not fall off. It was a little after nine.

The structure of the curriculum of Jogging 101 was beautifully simple. The instructor, Dr. Swanson, left her notebook on a chair by the door. There was a piece of paper with a hand drawn map and instructions.

It said, *"Start at the clock tower, go up along the library, then across the street and up the trail to the Swine Unit, and touch the black door knob. Don't worry, you'll see it. And then back. As soon as you get back you are dismissed."*

Each student would put a check mark next to their name with the instructor's pen and they were off. No one ever cheated as far as she knew.

Gabrielle checked her name with the pen and took a look at the map. Swine Unit trail? The top of a hill, it looked like. She had never been in that part of the campus. She took a series of deep breaths and started running.

Under the swift clouds and bright blue sky, she jogged past the library dumpsters and then up and across the new street, which now linked the upper parking lots with the highway. Then into the vastness of the Agriculture Department. Stands of oak trees dotted the green rolling hills. There were goats and sheep behind wooden fences and horses and cows behind barbed wire. Small fields of crops in rows. Farm equipment was parked everywhere. There were buildings full of machinery and areas for trucks to pull in and out.

Gabrielle felt completely unqualified to deal with animals, to say nothing of growing plants. Still, it was all fascinating. The Swine Unit was a barn with a corrugated steel roof and one of the other students, a girl with a blonde ponytail, already heading back, waved her hands at Gabrielle. "Oh, my God it reeks!" she said, out of breath. Gabrielle thought it hardly smelled at all. She couldn't see any of the little piggies. There was a big red wooden door with a shiny black door knob and she ran up to it, came to a clomping stop, tapped it and made a quick reverse. Then the wind shifted and she really smelled it.

"Nice piggies," she coughed. She ran downhill, breathing hoarsely. Hurry, she thought, laughing, just enough time to make Advanced Topics.

She ran back behind the library and across the big lawn. She was sweaty and her side hurt some, but not nearly as badly as the beginning of the quarter. So it was working, she thought, I'm getting in shape. Well, yeah. She brushed her hair back from her face.

Gabrielle liked the old gym. The school had outgrown it long before and there was a new, modern gym on the other side of the campus but the old place was preferable. More comfortable. And she liked the clock in the tower, also, and loved the way it rang the hours. The rumor was, it was rigged to ring thirteen at midnight on Halloween. She had never actually heard this but she believed it. Of course, it wasn't as restful as a train horn but it was okay.

She looked up. About nine forty-five. Early. Her classmates were still spread out all over the trail and she was alone in the place. She just enough time to change and get to the science building. She went past a group of female students having an intense conversation at the double doors. They were wearing black shirts. She had to turn sideways to get through them. One of them made a sharp laugh as she went by.

The locker room was mostly empty. Gabrielle went to the back aisle and turned left past the windows of the offices. She went to the center row of lockers. Right in front of her locker, there was a woman in street clothes sitting on the bench, fiddling with her socks. She had dark hair and was wearing a black sweater and a pair of those new jeans supposedly made especially for women and really expensive. Those were black, too. Shiny, black leather shoes. And those socks. What was the word? Argyle?

The woman looked up at her and smiled. "Hi, Gabrielle."

Gabrielle had never seen the woman before. The hair on the back of her neck stood up.

The woman's smile got bigger. She shook her head slightly. Then a sharp nod.

Someone behind Gabrielle grabbed her left arm above the elbow with two hands and squeezed hard. Fingernails dug into her bare skin. Her arm was jerked up sending her off balance She was yanked around and another pair of hands got hold of her damp hair, bunched it up tightly. Her face was slammed squarely into the locker doors. Gabrielle's chin and nose took most of the impact. Blood squirted out of her nose and dribbled onto her shirt. Her arm and hair were let go. There was a metallic taste in her mouth and gasped for breath. She put her hand over her nose and turned around.

It was Pretty Susan and New Susan. They both looked angry.

"That felt good, didn't it, Susan?" New Susan said.

"Better than sex, Susan," Pretty Susan replied. She still had a shiner. She plucked Gabrielle's glasses from her face.

"God, I want to do it again. Don't you?"

"She *is* still standing," Pretty Susan said. "Therefore."

"Our work is not yet done."

New Susan made a lunge but pulled it. Gabrielle forced herself not to flinch. Her nose started to throb and she had to stifle a sneeze. The Susans were drenched in perfume.

The woman with the argyle socks stood. She was tall and Gabrielle noticed the black sweater she was wearing was the same kind as the ones Catherine had bought. The two Susans took positions on either side and pushed her back against the lockers. Her head bounced on the tinny metal. They held her tightly by the shoulders. New Susan started sniffing her hair and neck.

"Susan, is she ready?" the tall woman asked.

"She smells all hot and sweaty," New Susan said.

Pretty Susan smelled the other side of Gabrielle's neck and said, "Moist," and giggled. She put Gabrielle's glasses back on her face and carefully adjusted them on the bridge of her nose. "She can see you now."

"My name's Patricia." She came close. "We're going to be friends."

The blood had almost stopped flowing. Gabrielle resisted the urge to wipe it off and let her hands drop to her sides. She looked closely at Patricia. She had a shiny something on her face, on her nose. It took a couple blinks to figure out what it was. Patricia had a nose ring. It was a tiny silver ring of the type normally seen in ear lobes and the little straight part was poking through her left nostril.

She had had a hole drilled through the side of her nose, Gabrielle thought. On purpose. The skin was a bit red around the entrance hole. It must hurt, she figured. Otherwise, she thought Patricia was very good looking. She had silky brown hair and hazel eyes. There were freckles on her cheeks. But a nose ring? Gabrielle focused on it. Patricia was smiling at her.

"The poor thing doesn't get it. She is only now learning how the world works. Susan, listen carefully."

The Susans looked at each other. Pretty Susan raised her eyebrows.

"I want you to take pleasure from Gabrielle."

New Susan nodded and turned her head sideways and put her mouth on Gabrielle's mouth. Gabrielle decided to go along with it. She held as still as she could.

When New Susan took her mouth away there was a spot of blood on her cheek. She grabbed Gabrielle's hair again and tugged a little, making Gabrielle's head tip back, then let go.

"Pleasure is something you *take*," Patricia said. "It cannot be given, only taken. Susan was taking pleasure from you. Don't you want to take pleasure from her now?"

Gabrielle put her hand back over her nose. "No."

"Oh," Patricia pressed her body against Gabrielle's, keeping her arms at her sides. The Susans continued to hold her shoulders. "Well, how about me? Don't you want to?" Patricia took a deep breath and Gabrielle felt her shudder. "Take it, Gabrielle. Take pleasure from me."

Gabrielle became aware of a sudden silence in the locker room. She could hear muffled voices and laughter. Girls peeked around the corner and watched for a second then disappeared. They were taking turns. One row over, someone yelled in a piercing voice, "Oh my God, stop *fucking*!"

Patricia stepped back in annoyance and looked in the direction of the voice, to her left. Gabrielle figured this was about as good an opening as she was going to get. She made a fist with her right hand, and keeping her knuckles parallel to the ground like her father taught her, straightened out her arm as fast as she could and punched Patricia in the face. Upper left cheek. She felt the cold silver ring scrape her middle finger.

Patricia made a sound like, "Alp," and staggered back. Both Susans instantly let go and went to Patricia's side.

"Oh my God, Patricia!" New Susan said.

"Are you okay?" Pretty Susan said.

Free to move, Gabrielle made her fist as hard as she could, wound up and hit Patricia again, straight and level, same spot, putting her upper body into it. There was a wet snap that reverberated back up to her shoulder. The nose ring made an excellent aiming point.

Patricia fell to her knees on the concrete floor. Both Susans lost their grip on her. They both looked at Gabrielle.

"You can't do that," Pretty Susan said. Her face was composed and serious.

"You are so in trouble," New Susan said. She had a slight smile.

Patricia, wide-eyed with pain, held one hand on her face and the other on the cold floor.

Gabrielle shook her hand and flexed her fingers. The snapping sound had come from one of her knuckles. She touched her nose. No more blood.

"If any of you ever touches me again, I will fucking kill you."

She left the old gym. All the other students had fled. The professor, wearing a white golf jacket, was standing at her desk staring down at a pile of papers. Gabrielle saw no indication of being noticed.

She made herself walk at a normal pace. She tried not to breathe hard. No one saw her wipe the blood from her chin. The clock in the tower said nine-fifty. She would be on time. No need to hurry. So don't hurry.

At the halfway point, by the postage stamp vending kiosk, she remembered the notebook and pencils in her locker. But there was no going back now. No one in the fast flowing throngs of students paid much attention to her. A few glanced at the large blood stain on her shirt and tipped their heads in curiosity.

It was cool and windy and the shadows of the clouds marched past. Gabrielle felt almost electrically charged. Only the crowds of students prevented her from running the whole way.

Dr. Rimmler was waiting in the familiar classroom. He was holding the stack of test sheets and smiling. His smile turned to open-mouthed shock when Gabrielle took her front corner seat. He managed to close his mouth and studied her hard. Her swollen face and sweat matted hair. The blood on her shirt. His expression cycled from concern to worry to the reluctant realization it was none of his business. He made himself look away. "No talking," he said.

Gabrielle held up her hand.

Rimmler found this fascinating. "Yes, Gabrielle?"

"I don't have anything to write with. Could I borrow a pencil from somebody?" Her voice was stuffy. Dried blood was still caked around her nose.

"Gabrielle needs a pencil," Rimmler snapped. "Daniel, give her one."

"I'll give it back."

"Tell her she can keep the pencil."

"You can keep that, Gabrielle."

"Thank you!"

"No talking. All right. Ready for the second mid-term? Of course not. Here we go."

Halfway through, Gabrielle's hand cramped up. When she made a fist, one of her fingers made a loud crack. She couldn't help giggling. She finished well before anyone else, as usual, turned in her test and smiled at Dr. Rimmler who smiled back, amused.

She bounded happily into the quiet hallway. Knocked it, she thought, out of the park.

Back at the gym, she did a quick scan. No sign of the three girls in black and she was grateful none of her fellow students from the jogging class were there either. It was quiet and her footsteps echoed off the tinny locker doors. The place smelled of perfume and armpits. She made a detour into the restroom to wash her face and quickly retrieved her notebook and pencils. She was doubly grateful for her good shoes and especially her heavy sweatshirt.

She walked back out under the clouds. The tower said eleven forty-nine. She no longer felt energized. She was suddenly cold and her feet dragged. For the first time in weeks, she decided to have lunch.

She decided to have a cheddar burger.

Tucked into a window-lined niche in the student union, just outside the big room with the bowling alley and the pool tables, was the Burger Bar. It was a sliver of a space with a flat top griddle and attached grill, a counter for the register, and that was it. No room for eating. You took your burger outside. The banner in the window overlooking the central plaza said, 'Build a Burger and Much, Much More!' You could build a bacon burger, an avocado burger (although no one ever did), a diet burger which had a two pieces of lettuce in place of the bun, or various kinds of cheeseburgers. Swiss, Monterrey Jack, pimento (whatever that was), or cheddar.

Just thinking about the cheddar burger made Gabrielle's mouth water.

When she saw that there was no line at the Burger Bar, she walked faster through the union lobby, almost skipping. On the ceiling speakers Carole King sang about a jazz man. The aroma of sizzling burgers greeted her when she opened the door. Good, I can still smell, she thought. Why don't my hamburgers smell like that?

The guy tending the griddle, toothpick in the corner of his mouth, turned as she came in. He gaped at her. The toothpick fell onto the counter.

"Whoa! Let me guess. Softball, right?"

"Volleyball."

"Man!" He shook his head. "Did you at least win?"

"Yeah. I won."

"Right on."

"Yeah, it was good." Gabrielle was grinning. "Could I have a cheddar burger, please."

"Oh course you may. Fries?"

"No thanks. Not today."

He nodded. "Because who needs the calories?"

"Too much fried stuff lately," Gabrielle said.

"Yeah, everything's kind of fried, isn't it?"

"That's a good way of putting it."

He shrugged and grinned. He had very blue eyes. "Every now and then I come up with a good one. It'll just be a minute."

He got a new toothpick, stuck it the corner of his mouth, and slapped a fresh patty on the grill. It sizzled lustily and sent up a cloud of smoke. Gabrielle tried to breathe it all in. The guy seemed to Gabrielle to count mentally and then flipped it. More excellent sizzling. He took a bun, opened it and put the halves face down on the grill to toast.

Then came Gabrielle's favorite part. He set a slice of cheddar cheese on the grilled meat with some care. The cheese was a good quarter of an inch thick but wasn't wide enough to cover the patty completely. So he put on a second slice, overlapping the first one. The cheese began to melt at the edges and he let it flow down to the grill for just a moment and Gabrielle saw him nod to himself. The cheddar burger was done.

Other students came in, two guys and a young woman, burdened with bulging backpacks. One of the guys stared at Gabrielle's bare legs.

The cook wrapped the burger up so fast Gabrielle couldn't follow it. As she paid, all she could think was, I got two slices of cheese. I got *double cheese.* And it was only $3.15 so she even got change back from her only five.

He smiled at her and said, "Enjoy!"

"Thank you," she said sincerely. She pushed the door open with her shoulder.

The plaza, under the chill early February sun, had an array of cast concrete planters. The trees in them had been planted the previous summer and the bare, spindly branches danced in the wind. Gabrielle sat on the one with the fewest students.

She set her cheddar burger on her folded jeans and contemplated it. The melted cheese was oozing through the white paper. My reward, she thought. It's been quite a day and it's only noon. She sniffed. Her nose wasn't bad but her chin still hurt.

She peeled away the paper slowly not wanting to expose too much too quickly. When a small part of the burger was visible, she smelled it and closed her eyes. Toasted bun, grilled meat, and cheddar cheese, crispy on the edge. Incredibly, the cheese was thicker than the meat. She took a bite. Juices squirted into her mouth and she swirled the luscious bits around. She chewed the bun first with its toasted side and then she couldn't help it she chewed the meat and cheese. She held it all in her mouth and swallowed.

Someone sat down next to her. Their clothes rustled stiffly. She smelled a familiar perfume.

"That's not bad for only three ingredients. Your nose okay?"

Gabrielle opened her eyes. Bright yellow. Catherine was not smiling. Her scar caught the cold sunlight. Her hair was pinned back in the chill wind.

"A few blocks from your house there is a small park. You know this park? There is a bench there. This Friday, I will wait on that bench from five to six in the evening. If you come by, I will take you out to my place. Everything will be revealed. If you don't come by, at six o'clock I will leave.

And you will never see me again."

Catherine stopped talking and got up. She looked away, seemed to think of something else but hesitated. She stood with her left leg pressed against Gabrielle's right knee. "Remember. This Friday. Five to six."

She bent over and kissed Gabrielle firmly. A lock of her hair fell across her face. She made the kiss last a long time and stopped only reluctantly. Still not smiling, she walked away and disappeared into the student union.

There was a row of students on the planter opposite, three guys and one young woman. Two of the guys had puzzled looks on their faces and the third looked embarrassed. The young woman, who had very short black hair and lots of eye makeup, was smiling with raised eyebrows. She avoided eye contact and nodded to herself.

Gabrielle picked up her stuff and her burger with one bite taken and got out of there.

She went to the Stacks, fourth floor. She sat in the corner study desk under the sign that read 'No Food or Drink' and ate her cheddar burger in the dim light, licking her fingers. No one could see her. The cheese seemed stronger. Sharper.

She thought about Catherine. Patricia and the Susans. And M. Her elation about doing well on her mid-term had vanished.

They weren't going to stop. As much as she wanted to see Catherine again, she did not want any more contact with the others. It was going out of control, she thought. Catherine knew about the fight already. It wasn't even two hours ago. New Susan saying I was in trouble suddenly didn't seem so silly. I *am* in trouble. They'll retaliate for what I did to Patricia. And if there's another fight in the locker room at some point Swanson will see it. They expel you for that.

She shifted uncomfortably on the hard bench.

Expelled from college for fighting. How could I possibly explain to Mom? And even if I get back in, I'll be set back *years*.

I need to let this go. All of it. I can't get sucked in any further. I can't see Catherine again. I can't go to the park on Friday.

That's that.

She finished the burger and licked the melted cheese off the paper. She left the stacks.

At the front doors of the library, she stopped suddenly. She studied groups of students passing to and fro across the lawn, looking for any wearing black. Or bright yellow. Students sat on benches or walked by carrying books or backpacks. It was all peaceful. She stepped into the sunlight feeling chill, feeling it was already too late.

She spent Wednesday morning hanging out in one of the electronics labs. She knew all the instructors and they tended to view her as a great assistant teacher, available at no cost. She just wanted to be somewhere inside.

She watched crowded hallways carefully, moved through doorways swiftly. She checked dark corners and empty rooms, shadowy clumps of bushes. She started to relax a little.

The Introduction to Philosophy mid-term was indeed a multiple-choice test, just like high school. She answered one question wrong on purpose so Townsend wouldn't also think she was a cheating little smart ass.

Get perfect scores in an engineering class and they want to give you a parade. Get perfect scores in a philosophy class and they think you're cheating. Because philosophy is ever so much harder than silly, childish engineering and no one could possibly be *that* smart.

Semiotics is the study of a) Celestial bodies, b) Signs and signals, c) Semi trucks and trailers, d) All of the above. She checked a) and felt like an idiot.

She changed the route she walked to school. She tried to stay off all busy streets.

For a moment, she considered moving. She shook her head. Not feasible. Housing was becoming extremely expensive and scarce. Gabrielle was pretty sure the only reason her basement room was still cheap was that Mrs. Rosenberg simply wasn't paying attention. Another deal like this? Nope, she had to stay.

Wednesday evening, she felt better. Nothing had happened. Her nose and chin no longer hurt. For dinner, she made waffles in her new toaster and ate them the way her dad used to, with Log Cabin syrup and ketchup. Three ingredients, she thought, and went to bed in perfect peace.

Thursday morning, under a dark overcast sky, she walked to the school a different way, on the street with the futuristic dorms. The instant she got to the campus she knew she was being watched. For a minute, she stood in the shelter of the theater lobby and watched the flow of students, all bulked up with parkas and sweaters.

No, this is a waste of time, she thought. Of course I'm not going to see them.

Her calculus class had a substitute teacher, a graduate student named Javier, who wore glasses about an inch thick and who announced the professor would taking the remainder of the quarter off.

She got an A on her test but didn't receive extra credit for the incredible division problem because she had forgotten to circle her answer. She crumpled up the paper and threw it into the overflowing trash can beside the steps.

Heading for jogging class on the inner campus street, she kept her eyes straight ahead. The wind cut. She could feel spring in it but she kept her hands in her pockets and her notebook clamped under her elbow.

Great jogging weather, she thought, if it doesn't start raining. And even then.

The clock tower came into view. They won't be in the locker room again, she thought. They wouldn't risk going back there. Too many witnesses. She crossed the lawn and walked unconcerned in to the women's locker room. The tinny slamming of sheet metal doors greeted her. She saw several members of her class already running towards the upper parking lot. Same basic direction as Tuesday but they couldn't be going to the Swine Unit again. She knew there was a landing strip up there and a bunch of old aircraft, even a retired Titan II missile. Aeronautical Engineering Department. Man, they had a blast in that major. That would be a really interesting jogging target, she thought, and it would certainly smell better.

She dashed to her locker. The smell of old socks made her start to relax but there was something wrong. The row was full of girls changing into gym clothes, hurriedly tying the laces on expensive new shoes. No one was talking.

A tall student with dark blonde hair was opening the locker right next to Gabrielle's. She twirled the dial of the padlock and yanked on it. It did not open. She yanked on it again with a metallic crash. She pulled on the lock until the tendons in her neck popped. Her face became distorted with rage. Deep furrows formed on her forehead and her lips stretched back over her teeth. She was breathing erratically as if she were in pain and silently screaming.

Gabrielle recognized her. Her hair had been brown then.

The other students were looking, saying nothing, not even whispering, and changing clothes as fast as they could. Gabrielle opened her locker quickly and sat on the bench to take off her shoes.

The tall student seemed to force herself to calm down. While Gabrielle watched, she tried the combination again and this time the lock popped open. She looked at Gabrielle and said, "Ahh! That felt good!" and she swung her arms in a wide cartwheel, coming close to Gabrielle's face.

She opened the locker and Gabrielle saw there were no clothes inside. No wrinkled t-shirts or wadded up socks or worn out shoes. There was a flat box. Metal. It looked like aluminum, maybe, and was the size and shape of a large hardcover book. The girl gave the box a pat and started taking her clothes off. She slipped off her leather jacket and hung it up in the locker. She pulled off her shiny black shoes and tossed them in. Black socks. Jordache jeans, yes, that was the brand. She stripped them off and folded them carefully. Black stockings underneath. Gabrielle saw out of the corner of her eye as she unbuttoned her white men's dress shirt, it was a black leotard.

Gabrielle gave up trying to tie her shoes. She stood up, shoelaces on the floor, and faced her directly.

"Holly," Gabrielle said.

Holly was six inches taller than her with wide shoulders and a long, narrow waist. Her legs were muscular and sleek. Her thighs are twice as big as mine, circumference-wise, Gabrielle calculated. She estimated Holly outweighed her by thirty-five pounds. The leather jacket had disguised that.

All the other students had fled.

"Gabrielle. You remember me." Her voice was throaty with a lilt as if she were about to start laughing. She had huge dark eyes and a pointy chin. Her cheeks were concave and taut.

"It's my thing. Remembering."

"Oh, I see." Arms at her sides, she took a step closer.

Gabrielle decided not to move. "Thanks for the cheeseburgers."

Holly's eyebrows arched down in irritation as this attempt to distract her. She took another step and when Gabrielle failed to back up, her right cheek twitched.

Gabrielle knew it would be a mistake to take her eyes off of Holly's face. When Holly's breasts, clad only in the thin black material, brushed the loose red cotton of her t-shirt, Gabrielle could only blink. Throwing a punch at this one would not work. Nope. She briefly considered bringing her fists up under that chin but she doubted she was fast enough. Besides, there was no space between them now. Her hands would just bounce off the undersides of Holly's tits.

"You think this is funny?" Holly said softly. "Look. Am I touching you?"

"No." Gabrielle's next idea was to slam her forehead into Holly's face. That would make her back up, maybe, and she could then just walk out. She doubted Holly would attack her inside in the locker room. Too many people would see.

Holly seemed to sense changes in Gabrielle's muscle tension and got even closer. She tipped her head forward to the tip of her nose was less than an inch from Gabrielle's nose. "If I'm not touching you, you have no reason to get upset, right? Isn't that your rule?" She spoke very slowly. "If I touch you, you'll fucking kill me."

Gabrielle started to feel floaty. She's inside my defenses, she thought with growing panic. I screwed up. I screwed up.

The instant she thought that, she got another idea. It wouldn't be easy and she had to act fast before Holly said anything else. But Gabrielle felt angry now. She wanted to turn the tables on her. She wanted to get inside *her* defenses. She swallowed. Can I pull it off?

Holly was very close. Her hair smelled of strawberries and perfume, kind of an industrial smell. Her dark eyes bored into Gabrielle's. Her smile had gotten bigger and she let her tongue run out over her lower lip.

Gabrielle knew she had to act.

"Holly," she said. She glanced quickly to either side. No one visible. This was crazy. She stared straight into Holly's eyes. She took a deep breath, tipped her head to the right and kissed Holly as lightly as she could.

Holly moved back in surprise and her gaze flashed from one of

Gabrielle's eyes to the other. Gabrielle took the opening.

"The restroom is good. Trust me," she said and giggled. She tried to make it a throaty giggle. "The back stall."

Holly squinted. "No. You…"

"Someone's going to see us," Gabrielle said. She rubbed Holly shoulders copying the way Catherine had done it in the clothing store. As she did this she closed her eyes in anticipation of Holly slugging her in the face. "You want to, don't you?" She opened her eyes. "I just keep thinking about you."

Holly stepped back. Her whole expression changed. She smiled again, to herself, and shook her head. Gabrielle pinched the black material between Holly's breasts and tugged.

"The last stall. We can't go in together." She looked at the end of the row of lockers with what she hoped appeared as urgency. "Swanson's going to come by any second."

Holly ran her fingers through her hair and her eyebrows moved unevenly. She knows she's being bamboozled, Gabrielle thought. On some level, Holly's eyes said, you're lying. But on another level she looked Gabrielle up and down and her smile got kind of crooked. Why not? She slid one hand between Gabrielle's legs and brought it up quickly. Gabrielle tried not to gasp. She made herself smile back.

"I'll count to ten," Gabrielle whispered, and closed her locker. The room was very quiet. She gripped Holly's shoulders again and this time let one hand wander to the front. She gave Holly's left nipple a little squeeze. She tried not to show it, but she felt something odd when she did that. There was a hard object right there under the fabric.

Holly stepped back. She closed her locker, snapped the lock shut, and walked away. She disappeared around the corner.

Gabrielle took two deep breaths and said, "Ten." She ran to the end of the lockers and listened. She heard the creak of an old door and swoosh of the closer. She peeked. Holly was in the women's restroom.

She went to other way, towards the main entrance. She went past the office, enclosed in windows, and saw Dr. Swanson at her desk. When Swanson saw Gabrielle, she frowned, got up quickly, and came to the Dutch door.

"Running a little late?" she asked sternly.

"Yes. I'm sorry, Dr. Swanson. There was this girl bothering me."

"Bothering you?" The web of wrinkles around the corners of her eyes grew deep and angry.

"I think she went in the restroom. She's really weird. She kept touching me."

Swanson opened her mouth in surprise and looked hard at Gabrielle. "Ah. And she's in there now?"

"Yes, I think so."

"All right. You go and catch up. I'll take care of it."

"Okay. Thank you Dr. Swanson."

The professor nodded vigorously. Her short white hair flipped over her forehead. "You go on. Up to the Swine Unit again."

Gabrielle gave a final nod and jogged to the doors and pushed them open. The air outside was freezing on her skin. She had to shield her eyes from the bright overcast sky. She was startled to realize she was covered with sweat. The gym doors closed with a thump and she sat on a bench to finally tie her shoes. She wiped her mouth several times.

She heard Dr. Swanson's voice, penetrating, very loud. She couldn't make out the words. Commands. And then what sounded like "Stop! *Stop!*"

Gabrielle looked at the doors in terror.

"She got past Swanson! She got past Swanson!"

Shoes still not tied, she jumped up and ran. North, in the general direction of the Swine Unit but she didn't care. She willed her shoes to stay on. The tips of the laces whipped her ankles. She made it to the edge of the lawn and dodged two architecture students with long T-squares protruding from their backpacks. She heard the gym doors bang open, Swanson's distant yell.

She found herself in the alley between the library and the ultra-modern, cast-concrete architecture building. She ducked behind one of the green library dumpsters. It didn't smell too bad. She heard running feet.

"Dang," she muttered and held still, hunched over. There was a big steel hook sticking out of the bottom of the dumpster for hauling the thing around and she stepped up on it. There was room for one foot. She balanced herself on it, quietly as she could, and kept bent over double as a shadow went by. The shadow paused, then retraced its steps.

She stayed in the position, straining, until her leg was shivering. When she couldn't stand it anymore, she stepped off, and got to her knees. She looked out from under the dumpster. There was no one in the alley. She stayed like that, catching her breath, and tied her shoes. She stood up.

Don't stand there like an idiot, she thought, be a moving target. She broke cover and ran out of the alley and up and across the parking lot. She found the trail and encountered a group of her classmates already coming back down. Step it up, she thought. They passed her without a sign of recognition. Maybe they didn't see, she thought. Maybe they'll forget. At least no one laughed.

She settled into a rhythm of synchronized breathing, as recommended by Dr. Swanson, where she inhaled and exhaled only when her left foot hit the ground. A raindrop hit her between the eyes. The Swine Unit made its presence known.

Breathing the heavy cold air as deeply as she could, she gave in to the odor. Her mind cleansed of fear, she had several thoughts. One, there was no question now. She was definitely in trouble. There was no doubt about it. However, going forward they would probably stay away from the locker room. Swanson would be on the lookout. So, two, the women's locker room was no longer dangerous. It was the entire world outside the women's locker room that was dangerous. And three, Dr. Swanson was a *sister*. She didn't know how she knew, but she knew.

By the time she got back to the gym, she was soaked. She barely noticed. She knew what she had to do.

She got an A on Rimmler's mid-term. To her relief, the class did not chant her name. She walked home in the rain, fearlessly, not bothering to watch for Jeeps or women in skimpy black clothes. She warmed up a can of mini-ravioli for dinner. She wanted to make hot cocoa but of course there was no milk so she used water instead. It was delicious. She fell asleep to the sound of her clothes tumbling in the dryer.

A quickly darkening sky of slate gray overcast.

Friday evening. Gabrielle stood perfectly still in the blowing mist on the sidewalk of a street that happened to have an excellent view of the tiny park. She calculated and concluded if she held still in this light the chances of her being observed would be near zero. If people looked out of their windows they would not even notice a solitary dark form, sweatshirt hood firmly over her head.

It had been a rainy day. No one was outside. The people in the houses did not look out their windows. Curtains did not move. The soft light inside was not disturbed.

Gabrielle did not have to look at her watch to know it was almost five o'clock. There was no one sitting on the bench. Full darkness was fifteen minutes away. Eleven vehicles had passed since she took her position. Three full sized sedans, two old pickups, one new pickup, and seven cars that, judging from the dents and patches of primer, were student vehicles. None of them so much as slowed down.

The palm fronds creaked above her. The air was heavy with wet smells. Droplets of rain dotted her forehead. They tickled. She made no move to wipe them off. At the moment she knew to be one minute before five, a small compact car appeared from a side street. Dark blue Toyota. It rolled through the stop sign and braked. Just sticking their nose out, checking the place. The car turned left and the headlight beams swept over her. She saw no indication she had been observed.

The Toyota stopped in the middle of the street and the passenger door opened. A bright flash of yellow in the gray. Catherine in her windbreaker, cut-off jeans, and a dark beret, got out and walked into the park. The Toyota lingered. When Catherine got to the bench, she waved back. The car moved away slowly and made a sharp right. Gabrielle held her breath. It did not reappear.

Gabrielle saw Catherine take something from her jacket pocket. It was a small white towel which she unfolded and carefully positioned on the bench scat. She sat down on it without leaning back. She perched herself on the edge. She adjusted her beret and stopped moving.

Nervous, Gabrielle thought. Now, she did look at her watch. Five oh five. "Hm." she said. "That's long enough."

She left her spot between the trees and crossed the short street. She entered the park. The wind in the eucalyptus branches masked the sound of her footsteps and Catherine didn't see her until she was within a few feet. Her eyes widened under the beret at the sight of the hooded figure. She stood up, hands becoming fists. Her scar deepened and, in the bad light, seemed to cover half her face. Gabrielle flipped off the hood.

Catherine closed her eyes and put a hand over her chest. "*God.* We... I never know what you're going to do."

"I know," Gabrielle said.

This made Catherine grin and she pushed a strand of bedraggled hair from Gabrielle's cheek. "You're very confident."

Gabrielle took both of Catherine's hands in hers and held them. "I'm getting better."

Catherine nodded and they walked out of the park, hand in hand. When the headlights of passing cars played over them, Catherine, instead of letting go, squeezed more firmly. They reached the house and Gabrielle got out her car keys. She opened Catherine's door for her and then got in the driver's seat. They both closed their doors simultaneously. They were both silent for a moment.

"Here we go," Catherine said.

"Yes." Gabrielle found she was breathing fast. Her heart thudded.

"I'll give you directions. I'll tell you exactly what to do."

"All right," Gabrielle said.

Catherine settled back in the seat. "Activate the vehicle."

They made their way up the east side of town and then went west, skirting the edge of the campus. They left the expensive houses and student apartment buildings behind and rolled out onto a dark valley.

The highway opened up, curving towards the sea. They sped past tidy square fields behind barbed wire fences. There was a thin glowing line on the horizon before them. The remains of the sunset over the ocean.

"Never been this way before," Gabrielle said. Catherine stared straight ahead.

Immense eucalyptus trees, so tall their tops were lost in the clouds, swayed on both sides of the road. Sentinels guarding another world. They passed through an area of streetlights and stores and tightly spaced houses and then they were quickly out. The soft darkness overtook them.

The road dipped and became narrow and the wet asphalt patched and uneven. The weak headlights shone on dense chaparral. Gabrielle ran the wipers intermittently. She couldn't see anything away from the road, but

the sea was close. The salt smell, she thought. It was exciting. She slowed
the car to twenty. It had been some time since there had been any other
traffic.

Deeper still, plunging through a forest of eucalyptus. Strips of ash-
colored bark were peeling off the tree trunks like streamers. The trees were
so close their branches tapped the roof of the car. The narrow, crowned road
dipped for a final time and rose up to an open plain of rolling dunes. Wind
buffeted them full force. The road was bounded by drifts of sand. A tiny
mouse with a long tufted tail darted in front of them and then sped back.
Gabrielle snapped the wheel to miss it.

Catherine breathed a laugh. "Just a little farther. On the right."

An opening in the wind whipped sage and chemise appeared and
Gabrielle stopped the car. There was a trail in the sand. She moved the
car a little closer and saw two tire ruts with a high hump between them.
She could tell the car would fit but if the tires sank even a little and high-
sided she knew she'd really be stuck. The engine ticked and wind whistled
through the wing windows.

"Here?"

"Uh huh."

"Maybe we should walk."

"Don't worry, you'll be okay."

"It's just that it looks really soft."

"That's just right here. It's in better shape once you get a few feet in.
Nice and solid. It keeps out the riff-raff."

Gabrielle took a deep breath and put the car in first. She knew she
couldn't chicken out at this late date. The stubby branches of the sage
danced and shimmied in the headlights.

"All right." She needed to hit it square. In first, she gave it almost
maximum throttle. The front suspension bottomed out with a bang, she
heard her tire jack bounce out of its spot under the hood, and the car
mushed nose down and slowed. The engine lugged.

"Come on, come on."

The front tires found firmer ground. The back of the Volkswagen
drifted left a few inches and Gabrielle's door was scraped by sage. Then she
was out of the soft part and she steered to keep in the middle of the path.
The headlights showed nothing beyond the precisely cut walls of coastal
chaparral.

"Okay," she said, and decided to keep it in first. Catherine still said
nothing but was smiling slightly.

Wind driven rain started pelting Gabrielle's window. She could smell
sage and the salt tang. The sand road turned right and up an eroded hill.
There were no lights ahead, no buildings. They reached the top of the hill
and Gabrielle slowed even more. The headlights swept across a closed gate.
She pulled up to it.

The gate was a rectangular frame of pine boards, blackened by sun and salt air, with a single diagonal cross piece. The top board had a word chiseled into it, gouged into it. The letters, weather softened, were perfectly readable. *PERSEPHONE.*

She put it in neutral and yanked up on the parking brake. On the right end of the gate, she could see a simple latch of hammered iron.

Next to her, Catherine held still.

Gabrielle popped her door, shouldered it open against the steady wind, and got out. Her unzipped sweatshirt whipped around her waist. Rain stung her forehead like needles and made streaks in the headlight beams. She went to the gate and lifted up on the latch. She pushed the gate open. She saw a loop of wire dangling from the bottom corner. It clearly was meant to go over the end of a rusty steel pipe which had been driven into the sand next to a small shrub heavy with yellow flowers. She secured the gate and went back to the car. Her hair blew across her face. In the seat, she wiped off her glasses on her sweatshirt. Then she drove in.

Catherine immediately opened her door and said cheerfully, "I got it!" She jumped out and closed the gate behind them. As she got back in, she gave her windbreaker a shake. "Sorry. Didn't mean to get your car wet." She slammed the door. "Fa-reezing! It's just a bit farther. We go around this hill thing and it'll be on the right."

Gabrielle drove forward and the hill, a barely visible ridge of sand covered with dense vegetation, pulled back. A light was there, a bare bulb in the vast rainy landscape of sand dunes.

"That's our porch light. The house is like tucked into this little pocket and you can't see it at all from the main road. I mean, it's perfect."

Gabrielle noted the 'our' again

"Sure is dark."

"The beach is just out of sight on the other side of those sand dunes. The dunes you also can't really see. And the beach, it's totally deserted. It goes on for miles. You can do anything you want. There's so much I want to show you! Park anywhere in here."

There was an empty gravel area in front of the house. Gabrielle stopped close to the light. She didn't see a Jeep or a Toyota. They both got out. Gabrielle followed Catherine up the front steps.

The house gave the impression of squareness. The porch was square, with its steps and peaked roof, and so were the windows on either side. The wooden siding looked like it was in good shape even though the white paint was flaking off in spots.

"It's bigger than it looks," Catherine said. She pulled open the wood framed screen door and then the front door. Chalky white paint lined with cracks, small brass doorknob.

"Not locked?"

"I never lock it."

Gabrielle stepped through the front door into the dark room.

"I smell books."

"Now that you mention it," Catherine said as she flicked the wall switch, "I think there might be a *few* books."

The front room of the old ranch house had built-in bookshelves on three walls, floor to ceiling. There was even a shelf of books over the door leading to the next room, something Gabrielle had never seen before. Books everywhere. There were two small sofas under each window, love seats, she thought they were called, and each sofa had its own chrome floor lamp. There was a stone fireplace with a wide hearth and a pile of bean bag pillows, blue and black, on the polished hardwood floor beside it.

"This is the library, and this," she stepped through the next door, "is the middle room."

"Two thousand eleven."

"What?"

"Nothing. Just something I do."

"But what was it?"

"I counted the books. I can't help it."

"You counted them? You mean books? Just now?"

"Yep."

"Oh, okay. Good." Catherine looked at her. "Thank you."

"Sure."

Catherine pointed. "The small bathroom. Just in case."

The middle room had a continuous bench seat around the walls, a low, round table pushed to one side, and a fireplace made of brick. All the walls above the bench seats were smooth matte green. Chalkboards, Gabrielle saw. Perfectly clean but she could smell the chalk. The room had the aspect of a multi-modal classroom. Another door, closed, led deeper into the building.

"This was all the original house." Catherine stood with her back to the next door. "This *was* the door to the outside. To the barnyard, you know, where they had horses and chickens. There was a barn but it fell down. Someone bought the place and probably had the idea of turning it into a bed and breakfast and added a lot of rooms. It was subsequently modified further, as I will now show you. Hm. Did I use subsequently correctly?"

"I think so. But I never do all that great on those tests."

"So you don't get good grades in English classes?

"I do okay. I always get an A."

"Yes, that *would* be okay."

"But I have to work at it. I really don't have to work at math. It's easy."

Catherine shook her head and said, "Because you're a numbers person."

"I'm a numbers person if I'm anything at all."

"You..." Catherine, with a frown, started to say, then changed her mind. "Close your eyes."

"All right." Gabrielle heard the door open.

"Do not open your eyes until I say so. We're going to walk straight forward. Here." She held Gabrielle's shoulders from behind. "Take a step. One more." Catherine's hands left her shoulders and she walked around.

The room smelled like baking bread or maybe cookies. There was a click and music started playing, a loud, brassy tv show theme song from the sixties. British. Gabrielle recognized it immediately. *The Avengers.*

"Open your eyes!"

Catherine hit a switch and lights set in the ceiling undimmed. Halogens. Tiny spotlights gleamed on the largest, most expensive looking kitchen Gabrielle had ever seen. Spotless stainless steel appliances. Counter tops made of some unknown material. It looked like polished rock. Cabinets of deep red wood. Some of the cabinet doors had glass windows with more lights glowing inside. There was a long, curved island with two sinks.

The kitchen opened up to a wide dining area cupped in a semi-circular wall of windows. Catherine pulled back vertical blinds in time with the music and spread her arms. "Welcome!"

She turned down the cassette deck set in niche next to yet another fireplace, this one surrounded by weathered steel panels.

"This is the main room of the house, in my opinion. Let me show you. Refrigerator."

The tv theme song finished in the background.

"It's huge. Wow."

The fridge had double doors and a massive freezer drawer.

"Barely big enough, believe me. And there's a real freezer out back, too." Catherine ran her hand affectionately over the controls of a six burner cook top. "Proper cooking equipment. Specially modified to handle propane, which I don't like. It's always leaking. But I'm stuck with it."

To the left of the large cook top were two stainless steel ovens built-in on top of each other.

"My ovens, custom built for me."

"You can do that?" Gabrielle said and came close to panicking. Crap, I just asked a question, she thought.

"You can do anything."

Gabrielle relaxed slightly.

"If you can pay for it."

Gabrielle pointed to an appliance on the back counter. "You have a microwave."

"Yeah. That thing."

"I've never seen one before."

"Overrated."

"Oh?"

"For real cooking, I mean. For reheating coffee, it's perfect." Catherine picked up a towel and cleaned a spot on the island counter. "This is the prep area. Two sinks, because I need two."

"What's that little spout?"

"Instant hot water. Real hot. For tea or whatever. You see them all over Europe."

"Oh. And is this marble?"

"Granite. And cherry cabinets. Watch this." Catherine hit a switch and the main lights faded out and lights under the cabinets came on. The effect was soft, intimate. "I like it this way."

"This is all really something."

"Feel free to use anything you want. Help yourself. There's plenty to eat." She waved at a long rack of skillets and pots and implements Gabrielle couldn't identify.

"I'd be afraid to."

Catherine laughed. "Why?"

"I'd burn the place down."

"Hmm." She considered this. "You'd be fine. Shall we continue our tour?"

"Very well. So far, I have found the facilities to be acceptable."

Laughing, Catherine went to the end of the room, past the large dining table, to a door bracketed by leather reclining chairs and more bean bags, two red and one that was a kind of blue-green. Gabrielle pointed at it.

"That's a nice color."

"Teal."

"Oh, that's good. I knew it was different. Vertical blinds. Microwave oven. So many new things."

"It's just stuff."

"But nice stuff."

"It could all disappear tomorrow and I'd be just fine. Can't get too attached to things."

Gabrielle just said. "That's true."

Catherine pulled open the door. "Through here, are the bedrooms and the big bathroom. They're all connected. It's a big suite."

They entered a carpeted hall with several closed doors. There were sconce lights on the walls with dark blue covers. Catherine opened the bathroom door and the lights came on gently. White counters with three sinks and a tub with two shower nozzles. The faucets and towel racks were all stainless steel.

"I love the lighting system you have."

"Isn't it cool? Now in here." Catherine slid a mirrored cabinet open to reveal a series of brightly colored containers. "Just so you know, are things like shampoo and conditioner. And body wash. About six kinds of hand lotion. You know, girly stuff. Sometimes you need it."

"Girly stuff," Gabrielle said, thinking, what's body wash?

"Oh, and here's my perfume, *Fracas*." A tiny glass bottle. "If you like it."

"Thanks."

"Okay, now I'm going to show you something you'll really like. Right through here." She opened the door next to the tub. "I hope you can see it. If it's not too foggy."

They entered an unlit, carpeted bedroom. A small bed, with a single nightstand, sat just to the right of a wide, plain window. No blinds or curtains. And no other furniture. Like the other house, Gabrielle thought. It's not quite finished. She went to the window and Catherine came up beside her in the quiet gloom.

"This looks to the north. And there. See it? Right in a notch in those sand dunes. You can see it, right?"

Three red lights pulsed slowly on the horizon, miles away across the bay.

"Oh, that's beautiful!"

"Your favorite building. That awful power plant."

"Now I know where I am, in a way."

In the warm darkness of the bedroom, Catherine said, "You just have to analyze everything, don't you?"

"No." Gabrielle looked down.

Catherine left the room.

Gabrielle stood there in the dark for a moment. Did I make her mad, she thought. I don't see how I did that.

Gabrielle followed her back to the kitchen. All the lights were back on. Catherine had taken out a wooden cutting board and a large knife. She set both on the island and pulled open the refrigerator.

Gabrielle sat on the single stool. She knew she wasn't seeing anything like the complete picture. There were other variables, currently being kept off the counter, so to speak. She realized it was like her earlier insight. I'm following someone's plan for me, she thought. All these schemes.

She watched Catherine as she began to cut up something on the board. Her perfect blue eyes were serious. Pensive. Her blonde hair danced around the sides of her face. The scar was quite prominent in the halogen light. She did not look up and Gabrielle leaned over the counter.

"What is that?"

Catherine blinked. "This is an eight inch chef's knife."

"No, I mean that," Gabrielle said, looking at the item Catherine had been slicing. It was lozenge-shaped, about two by one centimeters in size. Pale white. Cream colored.

Catherine squinted at her. She set down the knife and picked up a sliver of the item. "Here."

"What?" Gabrielle pinched the slippery thing between her thumb and forefinger.

"Eat it."

"Really?"

"Yes."

"I can just eat it?"

Catherine laughed and Gabrielle noticed the scar had all but vanished. "It's okay."

Gabrielle put the bit in her mouth. It had a strong smell she did not recognize.

"Chew it. Go ahead."

"Oh." Gabrielle chewed it and almost spit it out. It had a piercing, hot flavor which spread to the back of her throat and instantly suffused up into her sinuses. She sniffed.

"Good, huh?"

"It's really strong."

"It's called garlic."

"Oh." Gabrielle swallowed it. "*That's* garlic."

Catherine looked at her in amazement. "They don't have garlic in Covina?"

Gabrielle thought. "I don't think so."

"Wow."

"I mean, I've never seen it."

"That's terrible. Where do you go shopping there?"

"Center Market on Citrus."

"Huh."

"It's a great store."

"No supermarkets?"

"No. Nothing close anyway."

"Huh." She picked up another piece. "Do you like it? Have some more. There's all kinds of garlic around this place."

"My eyes are watering."

"Garlic is one of the best things in the world."

"Thank you. For showing me."

Catherine smiled. "That's just crazy that you've never seen it before."

"I know a lot about some things but not cooking so much, I guess."

Catherine resumed slicing the garlic. "So what do know the most about?"

Gabrielle was happy to see that Catherine's dark mood had lifted for the time being.

"My major is electronics. I would say I know something about transistors."

"No kidding? So you're an expert in transistors?"

"I would never say I'm an expert."

"Even though you are one?"

"Other people would take it as a challenge. Like I'm trying to one-up them. They almost see it as an insult."

"Just avoid those people. They're awful."

"They're usually the professors."

"Oh. Never mind."

Gabrielle laughed. "Or the grad students. It's not all of them. Most of the professors are really pretty cool. Just never say you know something if you don't know it."

Catherine popped a piece of garlic into her mouth and chewed thoughtfully. "Hm. I would say this is local stuff. I am very sure I know this. I was thinking of having broiled salmon with *pom Catherine* for dinner. How's that sound?"

Gabrielle saw some of the distracted, frowning state of mind return to Catherine's face. "That's sounds good," she said. Catherine did not look up.

She slipped off the stool. She saw a way to detach from Catherine's complicated mood swings. "While you are working I'm going to go browse around your library."

Catherine just nodded.

Gabrielle went to the silent front room and switched on one of the floor lamps. She opened the front door a few inches and peeked out. Her car was fine beside the scraggly Manzanita. The night was all rain and salty wind. She closed the door and let herself down onto the bean bags.

The game isn't over, she thought. It's just beginning.

"I'm right in the middle of it," she said and shifted uncomfortably. There was a big lump under the blue bean bag. She put her hand underneath. It was something with sharp edges, cold and metallic. Lying prone, she pulled back the lip of the rubbery fabric. On the hardwood floor was a flat box the size of a hardcover book. The box was featureless. She tried to pick it up but could not get her fingers under an edge. Is it bolted to the floor? she thought, and gave it a shove. It moved a few millimeters. Huh. Super heavy. And that wasn't aluminum. She scratched it with a fingernail. She knew what the material was. There was no edge line of a lid. No latches. No switches. No keyholes. At least on the sides she could see – maybe it was face down. I would need a screwdriver to lift up one edge and then something to hold it up, she thought. She tapped it. Hollow. Machined from a solid block. Pretty high end stuff. But so *heavy*. Interesting.

She pushed herself up to a sitting position. She heard Catherine walking from kitchen. She covered the box back up. Just like the one in Holly's locker.

Catherine appeared at the door. "It'll be just a few minutes. As soon as the potatoes are done, I'll start the salmon."

"Sounds really good."

"We don't have a tv set."

"I noticed." Gabrielle also noticed Catherine was now saying 'we' without hesitation.

"There's no signal out here, anyway."

"You're pretty isolated."

"No tv, no phone. Plenty of books, however," Catherine said, rolling her eyes. "Exciting."

Gabrielle shrugged. "Depends on the book." She took *I'm Ok, You're Ok* from a shelf.

Catherine shook her head slowly. "I know! Want a glass of wine?"

"Sure." She set the book down on the bean bag.

"Good. Me too! Come on."

Back in the kitchen, after Catherine poured them both a glass of something called Riesling, Gabrielle leaned on the granite counter and watched Catherine prepare two salmon fillets. She used a pair of needle-nose pliers to yank out wicked sharp bones from the fish.

"You don't want to eat these." She held one up.

"Yikes."

"You always want to check salmon for pin bones. They come right out."

"There are so many," Gabrielle said. The Riesling was very sweet. She pushed her empty glass away. "Oh. Drank too fast."

"You like it?"

"I love it. Too much."

Catherine filled her glass back up. "Just sip. I believe it will complement the potatoes nicely and yet play well with the subtle flavors of the salmon."

"Wow."

"And if we drink it all, there's more somewhere."

"You said *pom Catherine*? Pom means potato? It smells so good."

"It's just my little idea. Every chef has their own version. Kind of a trademark thing."

"Are we going to have a vegetable?"

"Um, no." She looked at Gabrielle. "What?"

"That's what Elliot asked me on Sunday when I was making dinner for them all. I made hamburgers and baked potatoes."

"Elliot? Oh, really. A vegetable. What a smart ass. I woulda smacked him."

"I almost did."

"Those roommates of yours. I'll bet they're eating all your groceries."

"Just all the milk and bread. And cereal. They haven't touched anything in the freezer."

"Yes. Food in the freezer is safe from people who have no actual cooking ability. Can you imagine Mark trying to cook a frozen steak? He would spend half an hour unwrapping it and put it in a skillet and..."

"And stare at it. He doesn't know how to light the stove."

"Right. Cooking is supposed to happen all by itself. So he would go watch tv. And when *The Dating Game* is over he'd go back to the kitchen."

"And he'd stare at it some more."

Catherine was laughing. "Why aren't you cooked? Gabrielle, the steak is broken!"

"He would go running to Mrs. Rosenberg. She'd take one look and turn the hose on him."

"His first shower in a week."

They laughed about this and then Catherine fell silent.

She's not going to tell me anything, Gabrielle thought. Not a thing. She's not going to give me the slightest clue. I just have to wait it out.

Gabrielle watched Catherine prepare their meal and they sat on opposite sides of the table and ate. They talked about the weather. Rain, off and on. *Pom Catherine* was thin sliced potatoes with a light cheese sauce and once Gabrielle started eating it she could not stop. She finished it off with the salmon, also delicious. She had two more glasses of wine. They cleaned up together and put the plates and glasses and utensils into a dishwasher, the first dishwasher Gabrielle had ever seen. There was kind of a system for loading it, it turned out.

Gabrielle went back to the library and found a whole shelf of electronics books and sat crossed-legged on one of the small sofas reading *The Active Filter Cookbook*. She thumbed through it, unable to concentrate. Catherine came in and curled up on the other sofa, her hands in her lap. After a while, Gabrielle looked up from a schematic of a third order filter and found Catherine gazing at her. She set the book down and uncrossed her legs.

It was time for bed.

They walked through the house checking doors and turning off lights and ended up in the dark corner bedroom with the wide window. They took turns using the bathroom. Catherine had a fast shower and came out with damp hair and wearing white silk pajamas.

"There are some pj's like these, if you want them, in that front cabinet."

Gabrielle found them. The fabric was so light as to be practically nonexistent and yet seemed fairly tough. It shimmered. She held the pj's up to her nose. They had no smell at all, not even soap. Relieved, she took off her sweatshirt and other clothes.

A scary thought crawled into her consciousness. You were afraid, she thought. You were afraid you'd detect someone else on the pajamas. Their scent. What if I smelled Patricia? Or Holly? That awful perfume of hers.

She fumbled with the tiny buttons on the top. "What do you care?" she said softly. "It's all a game. She doesn't really like me anyway. That's obvious. I just want to see what this is all about. That's why I'm here."

She looked at herself in the mirror. "I'm kind of cute in silk pajamas," she said and took off her glasses. "And blurrier is even cuter."

She put her glasses back on and turned off the bathroom light. Back in the bedroom, Catherine was standing at the wide window. The night had become crystal clear. The distant lights across the bay sparkled. The milky way wheeled above the black shape of the huge rock formation at the bay's entrance, hundreds of feet tall, an ancient eroded volcanic core.

"This is the first place I've ever lived where I can see the stars,"

Catherine said.

"I've never seen anything like this place," Gabrielle said. She saw with more relief that this was a good thing to say.

"Just wait until tomorrow. I'm going to take you to a place that's magical."

"Okay."

Catherine looked at Gabrielle's face.

"I can't wait," Gabrielle said.

"Good," Catherine said. "Well, it's late. This is your room. Feel free to raid the kitchen if you get hungry."

All Gabrielle could do was nod.

"And I'll see you in the morning. Night."

Gabrielle got out, "Good night," as Catherine walked out of the bedroom without a backwards look. One of the other bedroom doors opened and closed.

Gabrielle sat on the bed. The house was dark and silent. No footsteps, no whispers. The night wind off the ocean was picking up. The window rumbled. The room smelled of salt and Catherine's perfume. She resisted the urge to check her watch. The bedspread was amazingly light. Another comforter, she figured.

Maybe I'll just sit here, she thought. I'll sit here all night. Certainly not sleepy. And I'll leave the door open. She fell asleep curled up on top of the down-filled comforter.

She awoke to the sound of kitchen cabinets slamming. Still awaiting the sun, the low dunes outside her window were clear and sharp edged under the cold blue sky. That'll change, she thought. The wind will pivot to the other side of the horizon and another storm will come in. And not a sprinkly warm front, either. She saw black clouds where the sky turned a glassy jade green, their movement visible to her naked eyes.

Catherine peeked in the still open door. She held out an over-sized coffee cup. "Good morning. You wake up early."

"Not always. But I'm glad I did."

"Yeah?"

"I could stay here all day by this window and just watch."

"I'm glad you like it."

"It must be wonderful to live here." She sipped the coffee and it was just like the little pastry shop only twice as strong. "This is so good."

"Child's play. See what you think of my crêpes."

"Okay. What's a crêpe?"

Catherine just smiled.

Gabrielle hit the bathroom first, saying, "Wait." And when she got to the kitchen, still in her white pajamas, the cool air smelled of pancakes and cinnamon and strawberries. She got more coffee from a countertop coffee makcr with a digital readout. The room, with its curved wall of glass and Catherine at its center was electric with activity and promise. Gabrielle allowed herself to think, people live like this in real life. And I'm here, too.

She caught herself.

I'm here to see it. I'm just an observer. I don't belong here. I'm not one of them. Mysterious rich girls. She's just trying to impress me for reasons unknown. It's all part of the game and therefore not real.

Although, Gabrielle thought, it *is* really fun.

"Hey! I see what you're doing. I can read you like a book, dollface."

"What am I doing? Was I doing?"

"You were thinking."

"Well. Yeah."

"Knock it off. No thinking. Got it?"

"Got it."

"Here. This is a strawberry crêpe. There are also chocolate."

A crêpe, Gabrielle discovered, was like a thin floppy pancake. But it was the actual tastiest part of a pancake all concentrated into a thin, golden brown, crispy layer and rolled up into a cone shape. And then it was filled with a delicious, thick strawberry filling. She ate the whole thing without taking a breath.

"Like it?"

"Hmm."

"What?"

"Hmm hm."

"In that case, try a chocolate one."

Gabrielle ate the chocolate crêpe almost as quickly.

"I can make as many as you want. You'll need the energy later."

"Understood."

"There is a bit of hiking involved. So you like them?"

"This is one of the best things I've ever eaten."

"Thank you!"

"I could never cook anything like this." Gabrielle could smell vanilla and butter and another spice she could not identify which had aspects of honey, orange blossoms, lavender.

"Oh, I could teach you a few things," Catherine said and once again looked away. "Have one more and I'll go get ready. And then we can take off as soon as you want."

When Catherine was in the bathroom, Gabrielle decided she wasn't hungry anymore. She wrapped up the half-eaten crêpe in a paper towel. Can't let her think I don't like it, she thought. I can have it later.

She pulled the vertical blinds open. The sun had come up and filtered by high clouds, the light was flat on the brown dunes. Small birds streaked through the brush. The feeling had returned. Anticipation. Uncomfortable, but interesting. Something was imminent.

She went to Catherine's spice rack, a wooden frame with many small glass containers. The labels were handwritten with a fountain pen. Coriander. Star anise. Allspice.

"Nutmeg," she said. "That's what that was."

She heard the shower running. I have a minute, at least, she thought. She went to the stereo with its big chrome knobs, a turntable with a plate glass bottom, a cassette deck bigger than the amp, and a shelf of records. Were these her records? She had to see.

There were several albums by The Seekers with covers showing clean-cut musicians, the men in black suits and ties, a smiling lady in a nice dress. There was an album called *A Tramp Shining*. The intelligent looking man on the cover had old-fashioned side burns. A couple of Moody Blues. Then there were multiple Steely Dan and Fleetwood Mac albums, newer, but she thought they belonged to someone else. The sleeves on them were worn. They were well traveled records, she thought. The toilet flushed. She put them all back the way they were.

Catherine came out in her standard attire. Cut-off jeans. Sneakers, no socks. And the oversized bright yellow windbreaker.

Gabrielle got ready as quickly as she could. She carefully folded the pajamas and put on her clothes from the day before. If you didn't actually try to smell them, they weren't that bad. When she came out, Catherine gave her t-shirt a hard look.

"I completely forgot to do the laundry. Damn it," she said. "I'm glad we're moving out early. It's a ways away. By the time we get there it'll be lunchtime. So." She lifted a picnic basket onto the counter. The basket had a clever multi-compartment lid and several small drawers, all made of wicker. And there was a system of straps attached to it, wide straps that looked like a harness.

"Oh, that is nice."

"It's a real picnic basket."

"It *is*."

They left the house. The front door remained unlocked. The morning, much cloudier, was almost warm. Seagulls circled. Gabrielle could see the gray line of the ocean through gaps in the dunes. Catherine placed the picnic basket on the back seat. She set the seat back and sat, feet together, hands folded.

"I'll show you exactly where to go."

Gabrielle closed her door. She saw Catherine's mood was suddenly much brighter.

"Activate the vehicle."

Gabrielle pulled out the choke and turned the key.

"Starts easy."

"Yeah."

"Because it's *your* car."

"Right," Gabrielle said.

"Right. And what is the fuel level?"

"Still on full."

"Okay. We can go straight there. Go out to the tarmac and head inland. Mind the sand trap."

She did. They drove back through the small community with its tightly packed houses and turned north. They went alongside an estuary and then found the main highway. A sign said Big Sur: 65 miles.

"We should be able to make that," Gabrielle said. Tarmac?

"We're not going that far."

"Ah."

Catherine shook her head. "Very clever."

"Not every day." Gabrielle grinned.

"Most days, I bet."

Gabrielle kept driving. They left the beach cities behind and came to an area of green pastures dotted with oaks trees and cattle. The light became grayer. They passed another town where the highway was lined with more gigantic eucalyptus trees, these draped with tendrils of moss. The road broke free and hugged the coastline, low and ragged. Waves broke over black rocks. The western horizon was light and cloud swept, the hills to the east, dark green. Gabrielle took it all in, wide-eyed. She had never been so far north.

At one point on a long, straight stretch, Catherine pointed at the hills and said, "See?"

Gabrielle saw grass and rough wood fence posts. "What?"

"Up there."

"I don't see anything."

"Higher."

Gabrielle ducked her head almost to the steering wheel. "Oh." It took a moment to perceive the scale of what she was seeing. "Wow."

"Incredible, isn't it?"

"Is that real?"

"Yes it is."

"It's huge. I mean those towers."

"It would be so wonderful to live in a place like that. You could have all your friends stay over. For their entire lives."

"No one would ever want to leave."

"It would be like a village."

"Castles were really like that."

Then they lost sight of it. Most of the time, they were the only car on the highway. The road became narrow and at one point ran just a few feet from the foaming water and tide pools. The landscape became wilder. No more structures were visible. The road dipped low through a sandy cove and then started up a steep grade chiseled out of the sage and pines. Gabrielle had to drop to second. A sharp hairpin turn with no guardrails, then up, still higher. Gabrielle caught a glimpse of boulder-strewn surf, almost straight down, and felt her stomach do a flip. The car strained but second was handling it. She whipped around another turn.

"This is nuts," she managed to say.

"You're doing great," Catherine said happily.

"It's beautiful, but I don't think my car was designed for this."

"Not much farther."

They came up on a slow moving pickup truck which had an elaborate wooden camper shell on the back. White smoke chugged from the exhaust pipe. They were stuck behind it, choking, until it drifted onto a narrow shoulder and slowed.

When Gabrielle passed, Catherine rolled down her window, put her whole arm out and waved. "Thanks, hippies!"

Gabrielle saw the shadowy form of the driver wave back.

Catherine pulled back in shock. "God, did you see that guy? He looked like Charles Manson. Go faster."

Gabrielle gave it some gas and they quickly lost sight of him.. "He's pretty slow."

"Good. He's probably already on his C.B. radio telling all the other hippies about the two chicks in the red Volkswagen. Faster!" Her whole body shivered. "Ew!"

"I didn't see an antenna. You know, for the radio."

"Oh, my God! You don't need an antenna!"

"Oh."

"Faster!"

She tried to go faster. They went around another sharp, dizzying point, the ocean breaking directly below, and then back to an equally sharp turn amidst cypress and pine trees. Water cascaded from cliffs overgrown with Manzanita and sage. On one such reverse turn where there was a gravel shoulder, Catherine suddenly said, "Here, here! Pull in just to the right of that big tall pointy thing!"

"That tree?" Gabrielle said as she hit the brakes.

"Yeah, yeah, right. Sorry. Just to the right, see? There's a road there."

There was a rutted trail on the other side of a low berm, Gabrielle saw, not easily visible from the highway. The berm scraped the undercarriage as she went over. The road was really more of a foot trail.

"Hurry before anybody sees us. If anyone sees where we're going the trip is canceled. They *must not* see us."

"All right."

Four car lengths in, they were at least partially hidden behind a mass of thorny vines which had grown over sections of a chain-link fence stacked against a shelf of rock.

"Stop, stop, stop!" Catherine jumped out of the still moving car, ran back to the entrance and started pulling hard on the edge of the fence. "God damn it!" The fence would not move.

Gabrielle shut off the engine, pulled the parking brake, and got out.

The section of fence Catherine was pulling on had a rubber wheel on the bottom corner.

"Wait. I forgot." Catherine reached down near the wheel and drew out a steel rod. "Hurry, hurry! Now pull!" The section of chain-link rolled easily and reached across the trail. Catherine slid the rod back in and jammed it into a gap between two boulders.

"Thank God. Okay. Hold still."

They stood hidden by the vines with their long, white thorns. Camouflage, Gabrielle thought. I'm learning a lot about camouflage.

"Did anyone go by?"

"No. No, I don't think so. Wait."

They both heard a vehicle approaching from the north. It was a truck with a built-in toolbox and rack of ladders. The sign on the door was for an electrical contractor. It did not slow.

"Good. We might be okay." Catherine listened. A black Cadillac cruised past, all seats full. "Real estate agents." Then a station wagon going north. "Tourists."

"In February?"

"I know. Crazy, huh?"

"Well, they have the whole coast to themselves."

"Oh, this is the best time of the year. It's just usually..." Catherine frowned. Her scar suddenly deepened.

This was the closest Gabrielle had been to her when that happened. The effect was disturbing.

"Here we go," Catherine said. "Don't make a move."

The old pickup with the wooden camper shell chugged around the curve to the south, trailing white smoke.

How on earth could she hear that over the wind? Gabrielle thought.

"Keep moving," Catherine muttered to herself. "Don't slow down."

The old truck coasted downhill to the turn a few feet from them. Gabrielle heard the whine of the synchros as the driver jammed it into first then feathered the throttle. There was a noisy clatter. He revved it right past them and began to climb to the next point. Catherine didn't move until the old vehicle was out of sight. She waved away the fumes.

"Hold position. It might be a trick. Hippies can smell fear."

They stood still for a full minute. No other cars passed. A large bird launched itself from the pointy tree. It was a barn owl. It made a circle, observing them with its heart shaped face, and was gone. The truck did not come back.

"That's a blown head gasket," Gabrielle said. "He's trashing his engine."

"It's what hippies do. Okay. We're here. Gosh, that was close." She hugged Gabrielle tightly for a long moment and the wind tickled her hair.

"And no one knows we're here."

"No one in the entire world."

"I kind of like it."

Catherine nodded. "This is for us. Just us."

"Okay."

"We go up that trail a ways. It's not bad. Are you hungry yet?"

"Starving."

"*Told* you."

Catherine pulled out the picnic basket. As she swung it onto her back, Gabrielle made sure the car was locked.

"That's not too heavy? Do you want me to carry something?"

"Oh, this is nothing. It's not far, now. You can carry the blanket."

They walked away from the car and the highway. It became very quiet. The trail went up steeply into a jumble of Torrey pines. Catherine led the way, her strong legs effortlessly propelling her. Gabrielle soon began to sweat. The trail leveled off and the chaparral thickened. At the densest point where there was no visible break in the vegetation, Catherine stopped and slipped off the basket.

"Can you hear it? We're almost there."

Gabrielle figured they were only a hundred fifty yards from the car. She held still, listened, and heard running water.

"One day last fall, I was walking through here and I heard that stream and, well, you can't see it now, but there was a tree with autumn leaves. The sun caught it perfectly. I saw it right through here." She pointed to the left where the hill dropped off under the sagebrush. "It was so beautiful. Bright orange and red and colors I don't know the names for. I just wanted to see it. I *had* to see it."

She got on her knees in the dirt and pointed at the shadow under a massive black sage. She put her hands under the bottom branches and lifted. There was a notch on the soft cliff face.

Gabrielle couldn't see anything but an empty hole.

"Look what *I* found!" Catherine exclaimed. She turned around on her knees, her back to the sagebrush, and put one foot into the opening. She started letting herself down, blind. The sage branches slid off her windbreaker. "Trust me. Do it like this." She got her other leg in and was waist deep. She grabbed the picnic basket. "Come on, I'll show you." And she dropped out of sight.

Gabrielle got on her hands and knees and stuck her head into the dark space. It went down sharply. Catherine had been standing on something but she couldn't see what. She pulled back and flipped the sweatshirt hood over her head.

"Can't chicken out now," she said again. She rolled onto her stomach and inched backwards over the cliff holding the blanket under her chin. The sage clawed up her sweatshirt and t-shirt and scratched her bare back. "Uh, Catherine."

"Keep going." Her voice was far below.

"But." Gabrielle stretched out her foot and when she was balancing on her belly button, the toe of her shoe tapped something. She risked putting some weight on it.

There was a nice flat spot.

"Oh." The hillside was so clogged with vegetation she couldn't see what she was standing on. She tugged her shirt back down in the tangle of branches and tried to peer into the shadows. At least the sage smelled fairly good. There was another ledge to the left, farther down. She stepped sideways onto it and her head was below the level of the trail.

"They're like steps," she said. "Kind of."

Catherine's voice was faint. "Yes they are. Keep going."

Gabrielle tried to go faster, still hugging the hillside. The foothold turned into a set of stairs, neatly cut into the dirt and rock. The Manzanita and dry grass pulled away.

She was twenty feet above a fast flowing creek. The water had carved out a wide spot in the canyon and where it leveled off, this area was covered with green grass and flowers. The tree Catherine had mentioned was at the end of the flat area, scraggly winter branches gray and gnarled. Upstream, the canyon floor rose to another open, grassy glade. She could see an old, broken chimney protruding from the encroaching sagebrush, the bricks blackened and crooked.

There was a flat rock, knee high, in the center of the lower glade. Catherine was using it as a table. She had opened the top of the picnic basket and several cloth bundles were sitting on a small tablecloth. She pulled open one of the tiny drawers and removed two sets of silverware bundled up with napkins.

"One of the advantages to doing this in the middle of winter that I didn't quite realize," she said. "No bugs."

"It's a perfect day," Gabrielle said. She sat on the edge of the rock table.

"It's freezing and it's going to start raining any minute and then overnight the real storm will come in. So you're right. That's pretty much perfect." From the basket Catherine produced full sized plates and smaller saucers, She placed thin slices of light brown cheese on each saucer and handed one to Gabrielle. "This is my favorite. It's called *brunost.*"

Gabrielle took a big bite. It tasted like roasted, tangy chocolate. "I had no idea cheese could taste like this."

"It's different, huh? You like it?"

"I love it. I could live on this."

"I know. It's about a hundred dollars a pound."

"Uh."

"Hard to find, too. Finland. So what do you think? All this?"

"I think it's wonderful."

"Yes."

"And it's hidden. No one hiking that trail would have any idea this was here. I found it by accident last October. I was hitchhiking. Here."

She pulled a bottle of white wine and two napkin-wrapped glasses from the basket. Catherine opened it with a clever ratcheting corkscrew and filled the glasses. She held a glass out for Gabrielle, holding it by the stem. As soon as Gabrielle took it, she picked up hers. "Wait," she said. She leaned over and clinked he glass on Gabrielle's.

"Just a custom. Which I observe." She sipped her wine and took her cheese plate in her other hand. "I'll give you a tour. Welcome to the Glades of Arcady. This is the Western Meadow with the famous Communion Rock, the social focal point of our community. Up here," she said as she stepped on an exposed boulder, "is the Upper Meadow, which some still call the Eastern Meadow." The wet grass danced at her feet in the wind.

They walked into the upstream area which, Gabrielle saw, much larger than the Western Meadow. The rock foundation of a vanished house was barely visible, half filled in by leaf litter. The rest had collapsed and partially washed away, the mortar long ago eroded. The canyons flood in rainy years, Gabrielle thought, and in dry years it burns.

Catherine went to the remains of the fireplace. The bottom part of the fire-blackened chimney was mostly intact, the red bricks at the base dislocated by grass and tiny purple flowers which seemed to glow in the gray light.

"This was their living room," Catherine said. "This is where they sat before the fire on cold, foggy nights and read Mark Twain to each other. And I think this was the kitchen." She went to the far corner of the broken square room. "This is where she would bake bread and for breakfast make scrambled eggs in a cast iron skillet."

Gabrielle walked carefully to the spot, overhung with swaying pine boughs. "It feels like we're trespassing."

"I bet they wouldn't mind. I bet they would welcome visitors. And here is the bedroom." Her voice trailed off. Catherine looked at the spot of ground for a moment, holding her plate and glass close to her chest. She walked purposefully to the far end of the foundation, stepped up and over the low wall, and went to a notch on the canyon wall. She stopped.

"See? I'm sure it's all right that we're here. As long as we're respectful."

There were two graves at their feet, side by side, with markers comprised of plain wood boards. The letters and numbers carved into the silvery redwood were weathered and illegible, except for a partial date on one of them.

"That looks like born nineteen something and died nineteen-thirty," Gabrielle said. "Definitely a three and zero. So they couldn't have been older than thirty."

"I didn't see that before. You're right. They were young," Catherine said. "I wonder what happened. They had their whole lives ahead of them." She walked away quickly and went back to the flat rock.

Gabrielle cleared leaves and twigs from the graves and then wandered over to the stream and the bare tree, which seemed out of place. The fallen leaves from the previous autumn had collected in a drift at the base of a rock shelf. She studied the leaves in surprise. She searched through the flattened pile and found a perfect one, still bright red and orange, like a frozen flame. She cradled the delicate object in her hands and slipped it onto the saucer. She tucked the piece of cheese remaining into her sweatshirt pocket. She carried it to Catherine.

"Look. That's a liquid amber tree," she said and set the bright, soggy leaf on a napkin. Gabrielle saw Catherine had tears in her eyes.

"It's beautiful," she said. "You should save it. Wrap it up in that." She looked at Gabrielle carefully. "You really like it, don't you?"

"It's just like the one in my front yard at home. They're not found in this area. They had to have planted it. One of earliest memories is my father holding me up to the leaves in the fall. It was like being in a spaceship. All this incredible color. I think it was my first autumn. I would've been about six months old."

"And you can remember that?"

"I can remember having my diaper changed. I was lying on my back on my mother's knees while she watched the tv. Everything was fuzzy. I couldn't focus my eyes, but I could hear. There was a commercial for Ford on the tv set. I remember hearing the word Ford. And when she put a clean diaper on me and tugged it and it got all snug."

Catherine looked at her with a smile then handed her a plate and refilled her wine glass. Lunch was a sandwich on a baguette bursting with red onion and lettuce and slices of tomato all sprinkled with a vinegary dressing. Gabrielle crunched the red onion slices.

"Thank you for making all this."

"Oh, it's no problem at all," Catherine said. "I make food. It's what I do." She took a bite of her sandwich. "One of the things."

As Catherine ate, Gabrielle watched the scar gradually withdraw. It was as if Catherine were forcing it to heal by an act of will. As she talked about the wonderful food she had made with their unpronounceable names, Gabrielle kept quiet, happy for the opportunity to just look at her.

They finished their sandwiches quickly, and wine glasses in hand, went to look at the creek gushing between rock walls. They marveled at how the creek seemed to vanish after it flowed from the Glades, gurgling through the roots of a huge cypress tree.

"It goes underground?" Gabrielle said.

"A secret underground river only you and I know about," Catherine said.

"The River Arcady," Gabrielle said.

Catherine took Gabrielle's now empty glass from her and carried it back to the flat rock. She packed it and all the plates and silverware into the basket and picked up the green blanket. She took Gabrielle by the hand and they went together to the liquid amber tree. They sat on the damp leaves and she draped the blanket around them. It was scratchy and smelled of moth balls. A rain drop tickled Gabrielle's cheek. Catherine's hands found her. Gabrielle started to say something.

"No more talking," Catherine whispered.

The remainder of the day they passed in silent communication, like a long, complicated dream with many passages and chapters, adventures and expeditions. Under the gray sky, time itself ground to a stop and the axle of the Earth shuddered in space. The wind turned cold. They did not notice.

Now I have secrets, Gabrielle thought with a part of her mind as the world swayed. My secrets. She made sure they were tucked away and safe.

Finally, in the chill mist, with a quick look in each other's eyes, they knew it was time to leave. They picked their way down the canyon, ducking under heavy branches and slipping on moss covered rocks. The trusty car was waiting for them. As Gabrielle pulled out onto the highway the light was going fast. The long trip back passed wordlessly and it was full raining dark when they reached the house. She stopped near the square porch.

It was here that Catherine broke the silence. She got out of the car and said, "Go to your place and get the rest of your clothes. I'll wait here."

Gabrielle turned the car around and headed for town.

At her house, she was able to park in the driveway. This usually meant no one was home and, as expected, all the lights were out save the bluish tv glow in the front room. Gabrielle was surprised to find the kitchen door locked, such attention to detail not being standard operating protocol for her roommates. She knew how to defeat it. She used both hands and just twisted the knob as hard as she could. It gave way with a dull snap and she yanked the door open. She flipped on the kitchen light and checked the freezer. All her frozen food was still there. No, wait, one package was missing. She remembered it being a small New York strip steak. Oh, well, she thought. Elliot was probably pretty hungry. I know what that's like. She turned off the tv in the empty room.

In her basement, her dusty, cold, silent room, she stopped to think. How long will I be staying out there? A day? A week? Forever?

"I'll play it by ear," she said. "I know what that means."

She picked up her pile of t-shirts and the spare pair of jeans. Also, the silk underthings and the black sweater.

There was the thin blanket. The pillow. The uncomfortable coat. The old box of electronics projects. No need for those right now, she thought.

Up the stairs, she made a final glance of the room. Her finger on the light switch, she paused as a cluster of vague feelings assembled themselves into a coherent thought.

"I may never live here again," she said.

Setting things on the table, it was then she saw the envelope with her name on it under the salt shaker. The illegible scrawl identified the writer as Mrs. Rosenberg. She had paid the rent through March. What could Rosie want? She snatched it up and tucked it between two t-shirts.

Then she got everything out of the bathroom. She got her toothbrush and dental floss and the tiny bottle of Catherine's perfume, *Fracas*. Everything fit into one of her sweatshirt pockets. The silver chain she started to stuff into her jeans and then thought, well, why not.

She flipped her hair back and put the chain on. The effect in the mirror was interesting, she noticed. Gabrielle was not in the habit of studying herself in mirrors and trying to figure out if this or that effect was working and she had little patience with people who did. She usually just brushed her hair, made sure nothing was stuck to her face from breakfast, and left it at that. But now, this evening, she looked at herself squarely.

"It doesn't make sense," she said. "I'm not like her. Not anything. A plain girl with a silver chain is still plain."

For a moment, she considered putting everything back and forgetting the whole thing. Have Cocoa Krispies for dinner (after going to the store for milk). Watch tv for a while. Finish classes and get ready for spring quarter. The last quarter. The enormity of graduation overwhelmed her for a second. And then the transition to graduate school. So different. So much more difficult. So much more at stake.

She hesitated. Then she gathered her things from the table in a big bundle, turned off the light with her elbow and left the darkened house. She dumped everything in the back seat. She turned the car towards the beach.

By the time she reached the long valley, her mood had lightened. She had another new thought. Out in the night there is a house with the lights on and someone is there waiting for me. For me. And I will belong there with her.

Then she thought, with a sudden tight feeling in her chest, no, it's just this one time. This might never happen again. So I'd better pay attention to everything because I want to remember. Because it won't last. It's a game. But.

With her mind churning, Gabrielle drove through the small community with its streetlights and houses. She drove through the eucalyptus forest.

The house was where she left it amid the sand dunes. There was a light on in the front room. When she stopped the car, the door opened and Catherine was standing there.

Gabrielle got out and walked up the porch steps.

"Did you get your clothes?" Catherine asked.

"I got everything. It's all in the back seat."

"Good. Let's deal with it later." She gently enfolded Gabrielle in her arms. "No more talking."

Eventually Catherine made dinner. Nothing fancy this time, just spaghetti. They were both famished. Lots of garlic, Gabrielle noted. Then in the middle room, Catherine put rough-split oak in the fireplace. Using pieces of cardboard as kindling and an antique leather bellows, she efficiently got the fire going. She got a book from the dark library. They both lay on bean bags by the fire, the only light on a tiny study lamp. Catherine opened the book and quickly found her page.

"This is my favorite poem," she said. "I'll show you. It's called *Ode on a Grecian Urn.*"

She read Keats to her in a soft voice. Gabrielle was so nervous she had trouble following.

The fire had burned low. Catherine looked up as if checking the time. There was no clock in the room.

"Well, it's getting late," she said, unsmiling. She closed the book. "I've laid out your pajamas on your bed." She pushed herself up.

"All right," Gabrielle said.

"And I'll be in my room." She hugged the book of poetry to her chest. "The kitchen is, you know, always open. If you want anything."

Gabrielle stood up, too. "Thanks."

Catherine stepped back from her. "So, good night." And then she was gone.

Gabrielle waited by the dying fire until she heard a bedroom door close. She walked through the kitchen. A solitary under-counter bulb was on and the room was filled with shadows. All the bedroom doors were closed. She did not know which room Catherine was in.

Her room was as before, with its big bare window a field of blackness, but there was a new lamp on the night stand. Another tiny study lamp, pointed at the floor. The bed was perfectly made up and the silk pajamas unfolded by the pillow. The bathroom, apparently still only for her, was clean and fresh-smelling, lit by a nightlight under the mirror cabinet. She decided against taking a shower and just washed her face. She put on the pajamas, closed the bathroom door and made sure the bedroom door was closed but not locked. Just turn the knob and come in. She pulled back the bed covers and slipped inside, trying not to untuck the sheets.

As comfortable as she had ever been in her life, she set her glasses on the night stand, remembered her watch was way over in the pocket of her jeans, and switched off the tiny lamp. This house is quiet, she thought, but not empty. It's watching me.

The thought didn't bother her. It made her curious. She could feel the waves breaking on the sand as she fell asleep.

A door slammed.

Gabrielle awoke suddenly to find the room filled roseate light. Through the window, she could see ragged clouds racing northwest.

Her heart began pounding. There was someone standing at the window, their back to her. She started to reach for her glasses.

"Catherine?"

Her expression was grim in the blood red storm light.

"It's you," Catherine said. "You are the goddess. You are Persephone."

Both of the doors burst open and people dressed in white hooded robes rushed in. One of them flung off the bed covers and another took the blanket and threw it over Gabrielle's head. She felt herself being picked up. "Ah! Hey!" was all she had time to say.

"Take her," Catherine said.

The silent hooded people, with firm hands, carried Gabrielle out of the room.

The Fall Meeting

It is one of the simple constants of life here in Grimpen, Oklahoma. Something that goes without saying. No explanation necessary. If during the middle of a cold, wet day one takes off one's shoes and sits in a comfortable chair before a pleasant fire, *something* will happen that will force one to go outside in one's bare feet.

I do not get upset when this happens because it means the universe is operating normally.

I got the fire going just right (oak, for once, not that lousy pine), and I kicked off my hiking boots, noting holes in both of them. I rolled off my socks and let myself slump back into the recliner. The handle which would make the recliner recline was broken off, so I stayed sitting upright. The recliner chair had come with the house. Everything had come with the house.

The headache which had been forming at my temples was just beginning to fade when someone started honking their horn out front. Kind of a *beep.* Please shut up.

They kept beeping.

"Very well."

I nodded politely to inevitability and peeked through the pink curtains. The little blue post office Jeep was sitting at my mailbox and I could see the mailman struggling with something in the back.

I opened the front door and walked out in my bare feet, glad I had gotten around to sweeping the walkway. It was cold and clear and damp. Nice for early fall but not barefoot weather. And there are cultural norms to consider. After Labor Day, one simply does not go around barefoot in central Oklahoma lest one encounter disapproval.

The mailman turned at the sound of the door and then stared at my feet. He was a she. Kind of familiar. I'd seen her somewhere. It's a small town. Short black hair [*no nonsense*], blue eyes [*quick thinking*], nicely shaped lips [*high self-regard – no time for dummies*], and a turned up nose. A certain acquaintance of mine might have described her face as *friendly* overall, but otherwise be on your game around her, pilgrim. She stood there, shoulders back, head held high. Feet held apart a couple inches more than standard, kind of a *stance*. Sexy. Sexy as all get out.

Totally out of my league.

So... now that we've broached the subject, what might be her current target phenotype?

I thought all that while I took three steps.

Oh, PG, you have really messed me up.

"Hey," I said.

She had hold of a big cardboard box on the tailgate. An old Prestone box reinforced with lots of duct tape.

"Hey," she said. "I'm sorry to bother you but this thing is kinda heavy."

"Well then don't you lift it. I'll get it."

"No, I got it. Here."

She took a step and the box popped out of her hands and fell on the edge of the curb. It broke open along the top seam.

"No, no! I'm sorry."

"Told you not to lift it. I'm sure it's fine."

"We don't usually get heavy items like this."

"Don't worry about it." The name stitched into her uniform shirt was *Carissa*. "I think I know what's in it. Nothing all that fragile." I knelt down and turned the box onto the top of the curb causing it to split the rest of the way.

The Prestone box probably dated back to the seventies and only lots of tape had been holding it together. The contents spilled out onto the soggy grass.

Notebooks. Spiral-bound notebooks, some with brightly colored covers, some with the logo of a university in California. There were bulky 5-subject jobs and slender single subject types, suitable for classes in the humanities, I believe. The edges of all the pages were darkened with sweat, and – I looked closely at one – was that blood? Different ages, none very new. And many others. Composition books with marbled covers. A bundle of yellow legal pads held together with cracked and dried rubber bands.

My first instinct was to preserve the order of them. Might be important. I tried to push them back into the box but that poor thing was history.

"Are you all right?"

"Careful with this all. Research material."

"*Research?*"

"For a book I'm working on."

"A *book?*"

I looked up at her amused face. "I'm writing a book."

Carissa let her mouth hang open in surprise and seemed to take me all in, especially my feet. "Oh. *That's* what you do."

"Yep." Checking me out? You don't say. "Not much money in it. Obviously. My aunt left me this house. Makes a good base of operations."

"You're from around here?"

"Oh, yeah. The house I grew up in was just a couple streets over. It burned down when I was a kid."

"That's too bad. What happened?"

"I set fire to it."

"Ah." She made a little shrug. "Well, sometimes you have to do stuff like that."

"Guess so."

She nodded.

I pushed the spiral notebooks into a pile but the slippery composition books would not stay corralled.

"Hang on." Carissa grabbed a plastic mail tray from the back of the Jeep. She knelt on the other side of the box and lifted the legal pads out. She looked at the top page closely. "So what have you done? Anything I've read?"

"Thanks. That's real nice of you. Well, so far two novels. *I Will Never Leave You* and *The Blue Sky Machine*. They've done," I shrugged, "not too bad."

"*Blue Sky Machine* sounds familiar."

"It got a bit of interest. You know, reviews and all. It pretty much got me my current job."

"Wow."

"I'm all out of spare copies or I'd give you one."

"Oh, don't worry. I'll get ahold of it at some point. So what is your new book about?"

"It's different." Close up, Carissa was stunning. Perfect skin. And those eyes would not quit. "Uh, it's a biography of a well-known person."

"Okay. *Who's* it about?"

"Someone on the west coast. An intellect far greater than my own whom I struggle to understand. They would prefer I not talk about it."

"I see," Carissa said. "Hey."

Sticking out from the stack of legal pads was a white piece of paper. Didn't see it before. It had a familiar, computer printed look to it. An airline ticket. Carissa snatched it up before I could react.

"Oh my God. Look where you're going." She held it out of reach for a moment and then let me have it. "First class, too."

I saw my destination. "Oh, no."

"What?"

"Damn it. Well, there is an uncomfortable phone call in my near future."

"You don't like planes or, uh," she took my ticket hand and pulled me closer, "Shanghai?" She kept hold of my hand for about three beats too long.

"I don't have a passport."

"Oh."

"Yeah."

"Why not?"

"Born and raised around here, who has a passport?"

"I have one."

"Really."

"Born and raised in Wewoka."

"Oh, well, sure, Wewoka. But here?"

She nodded and rolled her eyes at the empty streets.

"So you travel a lot?" I had almost everything out of the old box.

"Just to Canada. Got family there."

"How long did it take to get yours?"

"Gosh. Months."

"Yeah. I'm screwed."

I picked up the entire stack of spiral-bounds and placed them in the tray. The one on top, with a water damaged cover, slid onto the grass.

"These things just have a mind of their own, don't they," I said with too much annoyance in my voice. A flat, black object which had been stuck in the pages popped halfway out. It was a small booklet with an official looking seal stamped on the cover. I pulled it out.

"Hey," Carissa said.

"Oh, come on," I whispered. I opened it My picture was right there. Good lord. I handed it to Carissa. "I don't think I've ever seen a passport before, but you have. Does this look like the real deal?"

Carissa turned serious. "It does. Hm. I'll get mine and we can compare them. But it does look real. That's ...you." She squinted at me. "From a ways back."

"I've never applied for anything like this. I've never had my portrait done."

"I bet I know." Carissa flipped through the pages. She saw something interesting because she smiled in a crooked way. "So what's Russia really like?"

"Russia?"

"You've been there twice. See that? The Russian Federation." She pointed at a purple blotch on one of the pages.

"Nope. Never been to Russia." What the living hell was PG up to? My left temple started throbbing.

"Australia. Thailand."

"Never even been to the east coast. Although I did just get back from Hawaii. And I have been spending time in California lately."

"Ah. So just Colorado and now California. Really? I'm sorry to hear that. Were you being punished?" Carissa said, continuing to scan the pages.

"It's not like that at all." I shrugged. "California surprised me."

"South Korea. Vietnam, I think." She held the thing out for me to take. It was making her nervous. "Don't worry. I won't tell anyone."

"Hey, I don't care. Who'd believe it?" I dropped it into the tray next to

the plane ticket to China and got all the notebooks centered. I turned back
the cover of the pink one, which had held the passport. The writing started
on the second page. *The Book of Audra*, it said at the top, *A recollection.*

"Audra?" I whispered in surprise.

"Who's that?"

"Someone who died a long time ago. Decades." The notebook was two
hundred pages, this was printed in the corner, and the writing – pencil –
filled both sides of the pages.

"What happened to her?"

"She got run over by a truck in a grocery store parking lot."

"God, that's horrible." She nodded. "Sounds like California. But that's
not who you're writing the book about?"

"No, it's not."

"Then what does she have to do with it?"

I smiled despite my mild irritation. "I don't know yet."

"I'm sorry."

"It's all right."

"I can't help it."

My knee made a crack as I lifted the tray. "That is *blamed* heavy."

Carissa leaned over to help lever up the tray. Something fell out of her
uniform skirt pocket, a slim metallic object, and it landed on the dry grass
by her knee. I scooped it up with my right hand and held it against the tray.
She did not notice.

"Thanks for the help."

"You can keep that tray thing. We have lots of them. Will you tell me?
When you find out?"

"About Audra? All right." The hidden metallic object was cold in my
hand.

"Her and everything else."

"Sure." I cradled the heavy tray on my knee.

"Sometimes on Fridays all of us from work get together. You know that
place in the old hotel? In the basement? Stan's?"

"I have seen the sign." The five story Altamont Hotel, the biggest
building in town by far, had closed up in 1969 but they somehow managed
to keep the bar open, off and on, under series of different names. Operating
licenses optional. It was at least an ongoing source of amusement to a town
where the main subject of debate was whether to fix the one and only traffic
light or just go back to stop signs.

The only other action the Altamont had seen in recent years was a
series of ghost hunting television crews. I had never seen the shows they
produced from the old place. It would have required cable and I don't need
that kind of monthly expense. Have to say I was curious though, I mean,
ghosts? Don't doubt it.

"If you were to wander in there about four-thirty or five I might be there," Carissa said. "I'll bring my passport if I can find it."

One thing I was certain of.

If PG had gone to the trouble to create – fabricate – *forge* – a passport for me, you could bet your left-handed mother-in-law it would be perfect in every way. Flawless. I felt no need to check PG's work.

"All right," I said. "That sounds like a plan. Next week, maybe. This Friday I'm going to be stuck in some airport somewhere."

"All right." Carissa smiled and hopped back into the Jeep. Then she leaned out and said, "Stan's is pretty high class, you know. I'm afraid shoes are required."

"Oh, I see. Well, I probably have a pair of shoes around here somewhere."

"Glad to hear it."

"Don't quite remember how to tie shoelaces, though."

"You'll figure it out." She winked and drove off. I knew I messed up her schedule by talking to her for so long, but she didn't seem to be in a hurry. Huh.

I took the heavy plastic tray inside, along with the broken up box, and set it all on the kitchen table. The metallic object was a cell phone of course.

I went to college in Colorado. At no point in the conversation did I ever mention being in Colorado.

Yeah, I'll be keeping the cell phone.

Looked like decent brand, too. Apricot? Pomegranate? What was the name of that little fruit company? I stuck it under my aunt's copper flour bin. I'd fool with it later.

I made sure the front door was locked and closed all the pink lace curtains. I wiped my face and strongly considered having a stiff drink. There was an unopened bottle of Maker's Mark in the pantry. Came with the house.

I decided to stay clear headed for now.

Why did I do that? I asked myself.

"I get to go to China," I said and stuck the ticket firmly into the fake passport and set them both aside. It was unnerving. Almost terrifying.

Go to Shanghai. The one in China. By myself. Where? How do I even do that? And after I get there, then what?

I shook my head. I was being ridiculous. This was PG. All I had to do was show up. I would be met at the airport. Everything would be arranged. Every detail. First class.

"What a story," I said to the empty house.

I had that drink. I got the fire going again. I had another drink. Outside, the light had changed. Thin clouds covered the sky. I listened to the mockingbird in the backyard whose insistent song was clearly a warning.

With only a slight hesitation, I poured the remainder of the glass down the kitchen sink.

Standing at the kitchen table, I began to examine my treasures. There was a thick spiral-bound notebook, black cover, which looked like it had been submerged in water at some point long ago. The paper was stiff and crinkly, the blue and red lines had dissolved and run. The writing was in pencil and still legible. I turned to the title page. *The Book of Holly, Her Dreams, Her Passions.*

"What the hell is this?"

The mockingbird did not answer.

I set *The Book of Holly* in its own place at one corner of the table. *The Book of Audra* went into another corner.

There was a group of three notebooks with red covers and university logos. I opened the one on top. The title page, which like the others was the second sheet of paper, never the very first page, said *The Book of Samantha.*

I was sure PG wanted me to start with Audra. That's why the fake passport had been placed there. Every PG interaction pertaining to me was done in a calculated way. It was her way of communicating without getting too close. Have to keep me at a safe distance. Intimate, sometimes, but never unguarded.

Yeah. I was being ridiculous again. She didn't mean it that way. I suddenly saw it for what it was. This was her way of giving me notes. That's all.

Janice was right. I was jealous. But not the way she thought.

I quickly learned to read this person's handwriting. They had a fast, printed, shorthand scrawl. Always in pencil. For corrections, they crossed out instead of erasing. Faster, eh? I read the first page and stopped. The writing was that of someone in a hurry, someone sloppy. Someone just doing a job they didn't like.

I stood back. What?

It was in this hyper-skeptical frame of mind that I began reading *The Book of Samantha.* Then *The Book of Holly.* The sun disappeared unnoticed behind the heavy clouds on the horizon. The night passed. As the light returned, I finished and turned to *Audra.* Then scanned a couple of the others. The legal pads I just flipped through.

In a sleep deprived fog, I made my decision.

I made myself some scrambled eggs in a cast iron skillet and crashed for about twelve hours. The next day, Thursday, I did laundry and packed.

I made sure the red Volkswagen in the garage was as secure as I could make it. The padlock was new, the hasp was as old as the house and might deter Mrs. Findley next door who was seventy-nine and had to drag around a heavy, green oxygen tank on a two-wheel cart. But no one else.

So I spent an hour nailing lengths of two-by-fours inside across the door and frame. They would have to cut their way in. Or pry open the back kitchen door and get into the garage that way and cut their way out. If they really wanted it they would eventually get it. But no harm in making it as difficult as possible for the assholes, right?

Oh, and the gas tank was empty and the battery I removed from under the back seat and buried under the apple tree by the corner fence. I thought about taking the tires off. Put the car on blocks and stick the wheels in the attic. Yeah, nice. But there just wasn't time.

Did solve one mystery. While crawling on the garage floor looking for the oil drain plug - I wanted to sabotage the whole thig - I saw the name, engraved in the side of the block. *Porsche*. She had put a Porsche engine in her old VW. I sat on the cold concrete.

I own a Porsche. I felt seemingly permanent mental constructs begin to totter and tip.

"Well now."

At five that evening, I made ready to leave and stood in the front room, the *parlor*, running down my mental checklist. All fuses pulled save the one for the fridge. Water turned off at the southwest corner where the pipe comes out of the ground. Freezes there every February, she told me once.

"And her accent," I suddenly said to the dusty kitchen, "was all wrong."

People in Oklahoma don't have an accent as much as a subtle drawl, if I do say so. Carissa, I realized, had been doing a fake Alabama accent right out of *Forest Gump*. Raised in Wewoka? Hollywood's never gotten Oklahoma right.

Boy, two blue eyes and I'm completely befuddled. And legs. And *Mademoiselle*, I think. Pixie hair. And she touched my hand.

Yeah, I knew I was being played. But, you know, I had to agree with PG from way back in 1979. This was *fun*. By all means, whoever you people are, send me all the Carissas you want.

Smiling to myself and mainlining adrenaline I locked the front door and tossed my backpack onto the back seat of my Subaru. I wanted to spend the night at a motel by the airport. The flight was at 5:05 the next morning out of Will Rogers and I was way too nervous to do time management.

I left my street, turned onto Main, and drove through town, right past the Altamont. The sign was there above the basement door a few steps down from the sidewalk. *Stan's* in stick-on letters. It was Friday. Perhaps even now there was a quiet group of Post Office employees there, at a table in a corner, having a beer after a long week and all of them as authentic as Carissa.

I waved as I went by.

The rest of the town was all empty windows in brick buildings and deserted sidewalks. The only active places were the real estate office ('Buy Sooner! Not Later!') and the nail salon, which still had no name. The Foodmart, the shoe repair shop, the auto parts store, the gas station, the antiques/junk seller, were gone for good. The three churches faded away long ago, about the time I left for college. Came back for a visit one weekend and found them all boarded up. All three, just like that. Not long after, someone stole the fancy Church of Christ sign, which had real copper letters. Just backed a truck up and dragged it off. They said the truck had Alaska plates.

If the post office ever closed, an event rumored for years, then you could stick a fork in Grimpen. Our three-person police department, two-man fire department, and the city hall people, all still hanging on somehow, would have to send their resumes out into the cold, cruel world. Or maybe just go fishing. The whole place already looked haunted. A collection of faded dreams in the old sunlight, waiting for the prairie to return.

Keep moving. Do not stop. That's the ticket. Life is movement.

I left my dying town behind and accelerated across rolling hills of grass towards I-40. The feeling of freedom briefly returned, muted I'll admit, but still the same feeling I had when I first got my license and wanted nothing more than to barrel down the four lane concrete freeway, east or west, I didn't care, and go somewhere, anywhere with the wind blasting me in the face.

I downshifted up the on-ramp. The Interstate stretched before me, all the way to the Pacific if I wanted. I tried to keep up with the trucks. My car can't quite do seventy.

Under it all, my stomach was churning.

"What was she thinking?" I said as the car bounced. The retreating sun was an orange ball sinking into the dust. I would get to see what fall in China was like. Probably beautiful. Shame I wouldn't get to enjoy it. I had to go because there was no other way to contact PG. She didn't have a phone and all her email addresses had been canceled. No digital footprint that I had any knowledge of. So I had to go physically. There was no other way for me to tell her I was quitting the project. I would give her everything I had done to that point, it would all be her's free of charge, like she would care, and then I would walk away. Probably have to pay my way home.

Those notebooks.

Let's just say I was disappointed. Shocked.

Written by a friend of her's, a literary genius, she liked to say. Someone she knew back in the time of having friends. She had never read them, she told me.

This, I believe.

If she had, I doubt I ever would have learned of their existence. The writing itself was atrocious. No descriptions to speak of. Dialogue that was completely perfunctory and hackneyed. People I was already familiar with, characters like PG herself, were barely recognizable. Flat, boring, featureless.

But forget the style and look at the story.

Audra, the entire notebook, was primarily an account of PG's encounter in McDonald's with Holly and Debbie. Audra is seen as a nasty, foul-mouthed little creep who attacks Holly, unprovoked, leading to Holly being dragged out of the place weeping. There is no mention of the parking lot accident. Audra's face is repeatedly described as 'twisted'. Holly, on the other hand, is always 'beautiful', 'loving', and 'saintly'.

In the notebook titled *Holly* the second locker room incident, to give one example, was to say the least a bit different. PG aggressively drags shy, innocent, beautiful Holly into the restroom and shoves her into a stall. She is just about to start tearing a terrified Holly's clothes off when she is interrupted by Dr. Swanson. PG swears at her professor, laughs, and walks off.

The rendezvous with Catherine never happens. In fact, Catherine fails to make an appearance in either notebook.

That was enough. I never cracked any of the others. Guess I'll have to ship everything back.

By the time I pulled off at Will Rogers, it was full on dark. Traffic wasn't bad. Or maybe it only seemed that way because I was still acclimated to the frantic, caffeine-addicted drivers on the California coast. By contrast, Oklahoma traffic operated in slow motion.

I picked a motel at random and the clerk, name tag 'Henry' – with the quotation marks – gave me a big smile even as his eyes bored into me through thick wire-rimmed glasses.

"Smoking or non?"

I rested on my elbows and asked myself if this still felt like a mistake.

"Yes, it does," I said.

"So, yes smoking? Really?"

"No."

"No, really?"

"Yes. No, really. I mean non."

'Henry' digested this fact. "Non it is, then."

"Thank you. Whatever you have that is cheapest, please."

"Nothing is cheap."

"Of course not."

"There is expensive and extremely expensive. Driver's license and credit card."

"Then expensive, please."

"Credit card," he repeated, without looking up from his screen.

"See if this one works." I set the worn out Discover card on the counter and pinched my license from its slot in my wallet.

"Oh. That's the picture."

"Picture? Sign here."

"Sorry. Just talking to myself."

"Ah. My uncle talked to himself all the time. Then he passed away from a brain tumor."

"Henry, I'm real sorry to hear that."

"Yes. Yes. You are room three fourteen." He handed me everything back along with a blank, white key card and a receipt for $119.70.

"You know, that's not expensive. Not really anymore."

He shrugged. "Enjoy your stay."

The room smelled of industrial disinfectant and grilling steak from the restaurant at the end of the building. I was the least hungry I had ever been in my life. I tossed my backpack on the bed, took off my shoes, and stood still on the thin carpet. Every two or three minutes, the sound of a jet taking off rattled the place. Outside in the parking lot, a group of drunk businessmen just exiting the steak house were laughing and yelling. Fortunately, they departed quickly in plus-sized SUVs.

I turned on the small tv. Only local stations.

Sleeping was out of the question. I was too nervous to so much as sit down. I paced back and forth beside the bed. The clock radio on the nightstand said *7:15*. I stared at the tv. I mentally blessed the inventor of the mute button. The clock said *10:59*. There were several programs featuring men and women with handguns. Guns were waved around and pointed at people. Not much actual shooting, I noticed. They were using guns like a fashion accessory or a class signifier. The Gun People. I was glad to be only an observer of the society so featured.

It really wasn't so bad in my sleepy little town.

2:46.

I blinked suddenly. Must have dozed off standing up, which isn't possible. Take a shower? Change clothes? 'Henry' maybe has coffee in the lobby. All vetoed.

I used the bathroom and put my shoes back on. I picked up my backpack and opened the door. The heavy early morning air was cool and smelled of jet exhaust and cow flop.

It was good. It was all right. I felt good.

I locked the key card in the room. *4:25.*

Outside, I was the only visible thing moving. My car started loudly in the darkness and I went around the deserted ring of pavement to the long term lot. The guard leaned out of his booth on the other side of the place. It was the same guy from my other trips. Steve. His face lit up when he saw me.

"Marnin'! You have a nice trip, now," he called.

"Thanks. I really don't want to go this time."

"Oh? Where you headed?"

"China."

"Wow!"

"Nah. Not looking forward to it."

"That's way over there, ain't it? Bet you're gonna see some interesting things."

"Yeah. Crazy things." A wave of dizziness broke over me. "Anything's possible."

Steve made a final wave. "Aw right, then," he said, suddenly perspicacious.

The dizziness did not go away and as I entered the brightly lit terminal my ears started ringing. I struggled to get both eyes focused at the same time. My right foot snagged on the threshold of the door and I nearly pitched onto my face. The only person in the place was the guy behind the airline counter where I had to go, and he never looked up from his computer.

Completely submerged in mental cotton batting, pieces of paper were exchanged, my driver's license scanned, and I was checked in. I went over to the security area and handed over my backpack to a conveyor belt. I stepped through the metal detector. At the next stage up, I saw the whole body scanner.

The uniformed TSA lady (pockmarked cheeks, brown eyes) at the other end grabbed my backpack out of the x-ray machine and without looking at me opened it, rummaged about, and removed my passport. She passed it to another woman who had just come out of a door behind her.

Not TSA. Blonde, athletic, late fifties maybe. Black skirt. Tailored jacket. No name tag. Another agent from an agency. She opened the passport, looked inside, then stared at me hard. A cop stare. Her face had an expression somewhere between amusement and hunger. My heart began pounding. It did not help my eyes focus.

"Come with me please," she said. "Bring your belongings."

I tried to shrug and picked up my still unzipped backpack. The woman opened the door she had just come out of. Steel, solid, soundproof.

I went in. Small room with beige walls and glaring fluorescent lights under thick plastic covers. The room had a table in the center and a second door just opposite. No chairs. It smelled of sweat. The blonde agent entered behind me, closed the door with an ear popping wump, and the predawn murmur of the airport was cut off.

"Place your bag on the table and step back, please."

I did so. I tried to smile.

"May I see your driver's license?"

I didn't move. "Sure. Could you identify yourself, please?"

She sighed and pulled out her id. She held it out so I could see it.

"Special Agent. FBI? Ok, good. The FBI I get. Those Homeland people, I mean, who knows about them." Buttering her up did not soften her expression. I got out my wallet again and took out the license. I handed it over. She opened my passport and held the license next to it. She studied them.

"Are you aware that the photographs in your passport and on your driver's license are identical?"

"No. Did not know that."

"And are you aware that your passport contains biometric and other data on an embedded RFID system?"

"Bio. Metric?"

"Among other things." She squinted at me.

"Well, of course it does. This is America." This almost made her smile.

"Your name is. Let's see – " She read my name and address off the license.

"Yes, ma'am. That's me."

"And this is your passport?"

Heart rate kicked up to warp speed. She could probably hear it. "Yes, it is."

"Are you sure?"

"As far as I know, it is."

"Uh huh."

"Well, that is my name on the thing. Is there a problem?"

"Yes, your name is printed in it. However, the embedded data tells a different story. It says you are Arvil Pridowchek, a known Chechen arms dealer. He is the go-to guy for chemical weapons in Yemen and Syria. He likes to supply all sides. He has an office in Moscow and a nice set up in Pyongyang." She flipped a page. "You were recently in the Russian Federation, is that right?"

Answering that question in any way would quickly get me thrown in jail.

Telling the truth about the whole deal would get me thrown in jail.

Shit.

Jail it is.

But one Hail Mary, for the heck of it. I mean, am I writer or ain't I?

"They hacked it. The Russians hacked it somehow. It's what they do. It's their thing. We invent, they hack. Or they made a duplicate and switched it somewhere. It was a scheme to steal my identity and they botched it. I mean, who am I? Trying to come up with a new identity for the arms dealer, what's his name, Kevin? A nobody like me would be perfect. Get him into the country. He had my data system thing and all he had to do was switch photos. And for some reason they didn't finish and it's all fouled up. Oh, this is crazy." I waved my arms. "Right now, somewhere in Yemen is a serious bad guy with my embedded data system popping up on scanners all over the place."

"Sir."

"Cancel it. Cancel the passport and driver's license and everything. You guys can do that right? I'll start over. I can prove who I am. Hell, man." My voice sounded hollow. My ears were suddenly stopped up.

"Sir."

"I don't know how but I'll do it. Start over from the beginning." I took a deep breath and swallowed. "So when you scanned this all kinds of alarms went off?"

"No."

"Oh, well, that's something at least."

"Just doing a favor for an old friend. That was good, though. Plausible."

"It's more than plausible, ma'am. It had to have happened that way. When did you scan that evil thing, anyway? It's been in my bag the whole time."

"We didn't."

"You didn't scan it?"

"That equipment is currently not deployed at this location." The agent went to the second door and inserted a key and snapped open the deadbolt. "I just made up that stuff about the arms dealer."

She opened the door and Janice entered. Her face was luminous. She was wearing a black jacket and skirt and fluorescent orange running shoes. And a barely concealed smile. I gaped. My heart rate slowed but my face was burning.

"You were right. He's good," the agent said.

"He's a professional liar," Janice said levelly. "Don't believe anything he says."

"Oh, don't worry." She held out my license. I plucked it out of her hand. She held up the fake passport. She was not smiling at all. "This I'm keeping."

I nodded. "You're pretty good yourself, ma'am."

"Thanks. Get out of here."

Janice grabbed my sleeve and pulled me to the door. "*Stop* talking. Thanks, Rebecca."

"I know when to shut up."

"The hell you do."

We stepped into a long echoing corridor. Institutional lighting and many unmarked doors. Many doors. The far end was open, a dark rectangle. A vehicle was waiting down there in the amber floodlights. Janice kept hold of my arm.

"You are so fucking, *fucking* lucky it's not even remotely funny," she said. Janice had a new short haircut and a new set of lines on her face. Her voice was light and humorous as always and her eyes glinted. Dark. Not humorous.

"Where are we going?"

"Hush. Keep walking. Do not speak. There are microphones every eighteen inches."

We went quickly down the chill corridor and stepped into a dark echoing corner of the main parking garage. Engine sounds reverberated and the air was heavy with diesel exhaust. A huge black Expedition was sitting at the curb. The windows were opaque.

"What is this, Janice?"

She did a fast scan of the area and grabbed the rear door handle.

"Just get in."

"I'd rather take my car."

"No. You need to come with me."

"Why?"

"It's not my place to say."

"You may as well tell me anyway because I'm not getting in that thing until you do."

Tires screeched beyond rows of concrete pillars and Janice froze for a second. Her right hand reached under her jacket and then withdrew.

"Okay. Fine. You're as stubborn as. We think they're watching your car. It would be better if they think you got on the plane. At least as far as Los Angeles. We might get a little more time that way."

She pulled open the door. On the back seat was an old Prestone box, patched up with duct tape. The seat belt was fastened around it.

Janice grinned. "That's the real one."

I looked at the box. I looked at her. I got in.

"And don't worry, she's around here somewhere. She'll catch up." She slammed my door with a massive thump and got in the driver's seat. The scale of the damn thing, she looked like a child sitting there. She had to use both hands to pull her door shut.

"This baby's bulletproof, EM proof, and gets four miles to the gallon. It's seventy miles to your place so we'll have to stop for gas a few times."

I laughed. "Okay."

"Don't worry. I know exactly where you live."

"You astonish me, Janice."

She smiled at me in the mirror. "So who else is at your house? Just so I know."

"I operate from a position of solitude."

"Of course."

"You said this thing is soundproof. So who are you? Not FBI. But you're an agent, right?"

"Oh, you goofball."

"Treasury?"

She barked a laugh.

I thought for a moment while she watched me in the mirror.

"No, wait. *DARPA.*"

She gaped in surprise. "What a clever boy you are."

"Yeah. That's me. Are you armed?"

She stared ahead, motionless, expressionless.

"Right. Were you armed in Hawaii?"

She took a deep breath and adjusted her seat belt. "Well, what do you mean? The whole time?" Her eyes darted up to meet mine in the mirror.

It was my turn to remain expressionless.

"Don't be silly," Janice said. "Where would I have hidden a weapon? I mean, you searched *everywhere.*"

She winked. Her grin was, shall we say, electric.

The massive vehicle began to move. It had been idling silently all along. We exited the dark garage. The diesel fumes cleared. Out in the open air, the sky was brightening.

I tried to shift the weathered Prestone box and could not budge it. The tape looked as old as the box itself. Unopened for decades.

"Heck with it."

I cut the tape with my fingernail leaving a thin trail of blood. I opened the flaps. Inside, spiral-bound notebooks were tightly packed. I removed the top one.

"Janice," I said.

She looked at me in the mirror. She had put on sunglasses and looked every bit the young, professional, well-compensated agent in the current, all-powerful Federal style.

I placed the notebook in my lap. Plain dark blue cover. The first page was blank. The writing started on the second page. Ink, looked like fountain pen. In clear, open cursive it stated, *The Book of Samantha, being an honest recollection of her life and of her time with us. As told to Gislaine.*

"Janice."

I slipped the notebook delicately back into the old box. My hands were shaking.

"Who's they?"

"She'll have to be the one to tell you. That's how she wants it," Janice said. She hit the turn signal and was abruptly serious. "It's the next part of the story."

"Then let's get going."

Janice tromped on the gas.

Under a sharp blue autumn sky the big vehicle powered onto the interstate and I braced myself as we turned to face the newly risen sun, finally clear of dust and shadows.

The Cult of Persephone Gabrielle

The hooded, silk-rustling figures were silent as they carried Gabrielle through the kitchen and then into the middle room. Her head still covered by the blanket, their bare feet on carpeting, then tile, and carpeting again. A chair was moved. There was no whispering or giggling. One of them was breathing heavily. The two who had her by the armpits lifted and she was brought to almost standing position. Her legs were kept straight and horizontal. She felt a chair get pulled under her and she was lowered very slowly onto it. All the hands let go at the same moment. The blanket was peeled away with care.

She was in the center of the multipurpose room. A study lamp was pointed at the floor. The robed figures, faces still covered, were illuminated from below. Huge shadows leapt to the ceiling. Three were sitting, still hooded, on the bench seat in front of her. On the right, one was in a chair angled in. The one who had removed the blanket was standing next to her, turned away.

They dropped the blanket on the floor and then held out Gabrielle's glasses. She grabbed them and put them on as the person pulled back their hood.

It was Audra, eyes twinkling.

Gabrielle gasped in surprise and without thinking reached out and touched Audra on the cheek. Audra leaned over and kissed her on the forehead. She went to the bench and sat on the left end.

All the others removed their hoods. It was Catherine in the center chair. Seeing her, Gabrielle felt alarmed. Catherine looked worried, almost terrified.

In the weird light, it took Gabrielle a moment to recognize the other women. They were the two from the grocery store where Audra had her accident, who had led her away. The one with long blonde hair was Rushel. The other had dark, curly hair and she remembered her name. Gislaine. She had a notebook in her lap and was writing in it with a large pen.

The last, closest to Catherine, several inches taller than the others, had long, straight, black hair and was staring at her with cold fascination. Large

248

brown eyes, skeptical and intelligent.

The gazebo.

Gabrielle's heart slowed was they watched her, motionless, ghostly shapes. She made a conscious effort not to count the beats but was unsuccessful. At beat 65, Audra coughed and the tension withdrew. They all shifted slightly.

Rushel smiled at Gabrielle appraisingly and then said to Catherine, "State your reasons."

Catherine cleared her throat and wiped her mouth quickly. "At no point did she ask a single question."

Audra nodded as she listened.

"She rejected evil twice. Twice. The first time was when I left her at the Carriage House. The second time was when she went back there by herself. She actually stood before the door, the very door, and turned away. Then she fought back without being asked, without having the slightest idea what was going on. She slugged Patricia."

"Pow! Right in the nose ring!" Audra said in a loud whisper, getting an exasperated look from Rushel.

"She outmaneuvered Holly," Catherine said. This drew an appreciative nod from all of them. Then Catherine said something that Gabrielle found shocking. "At the very beginning, that first night, the blackbirds sang to her. They sang to her even when she was asleep. She dreamed them. They welcomed her and told her the secrets. I was witness."

The one with the long black hair looked at Catherine in surprise. Her expression maybe softened a bit. Audra and Gislaine glanced at each other and placed their hands in their laps.

They all held still. Gabrielle could feel the waves hitting the sand and rocks just beyond the dunes.

Catherine wiped her eyes. "And, finally, as you all know, she opened the gate."

Rushel said, "Thank you." She regarded Gabrielle, head tilted, her eyes unfocused, as if lost in thought. The others watched her. Gabrielle heard Catherine swallow.

A gust of wind rattled the windows in the dark library. At this sign, Rushel stood.

Catherine covered her mouth. Audra held her hands over her chest. Gislaine wrote furiously. The one with the long, black hair remained motionless.

"It would appear," Rushel said, "that, as before, one of us has managed to seduce the goddess Persephone while she was temporarily in human form."

Rushel smiled at Catherine, who nodded, still covering her mouth. Gabrielle could see tears in her eyes.

Rushel went to Gabrielle's side and said, "From time to time, one of the Immortals will lose their way, stumble through one of the many doorways and wander into our realm. They are always extraordinary people."

Gabrielle thought Rushel's voice was like her hair, almost weightless, flowing without effort. Rushel knelt next to Gabrielle so her face would be at the same level.

"We are a family. There are six of us. We have been together many years and we love each other very much."

Gislaine wrote swiftly in her notebook and Audra took a deep breath. Gabrielle saw that Catherine and the black-haired one were holding hands.

Rushel spoke close to her ear.

"All your life, you knew you were different. You never really fit in. And your friends always had a way, a subtle way, of letting you know you were not one of them. And now, even those friends have faded away, leaving you with nothing. As far as you can see into the future, nothing. You stand outside in the dark and watch the life within, unable to enter, unable to belong.

"We will give you a chance, if you wish."

All of them were watching Rushel now.

"Audra, do you love Gabrielle?"

Audra looked down at the floor. "No," she said.

"Catherine, do you love Gabrielle?"

Catherine swallowed again and looked Gabrielle in the eyes. "No." She turned away quickly.

Gabrielle managed to breathe normally and held her head up.

Rushel seemed to read her expression and said, her face close, "Love is a gift from the Creator to us, the human beings. Love is the coin which will ferry you across the river and into the land of the living. It must be earned. If you can earn the love of one of us, you may join us. If you fail to do so within the allotted time, you will be cast out." She said the last few words as a whisper.

Rushel stood up and then retook her seat between Audra and Gislaine.

"If that were to happen, you would never return here. You would simply go on as before. You would think of us, if you thought of us at all, as not quite real. You would continue to wander the Earth, not quite alive, feeling little, until you dissolve back into your realm. And the dream would end."

Rushel smoothed out her robe and took a deep breath.

"If you do wish to join us, I have one final caution. Listen to me carefully. As a human being you will face certain inescapable conditions. You are today young and beautiful and will live a long and successful life. You will know fame and fortune. The amazing products of your mind will enrich the lives of millions of people."

Gabrielle felt her cheeks burning.

Rushel continued. "There will come the fall. When the generous fulfillment of your rich life is at its pinnacle, at the peak of your happiness, on that very day, everyone you love will be taken from you. You will know devastation and ruin, emptiness and loss, from which you will never recover. In this state, utterly bereft, you will yet live because you must.

"Much time will pass. Your youth and beauty will become a thing of the past. Your health will fade. Weak and ill, you will struggle to remember even the faces of those you once loved. Your incredible gifts will be completely forgotten. And, many years from now, on a day of vast hollowness, you will find yourself alone beneath a cold, cloudless sky. You will see someone approaching. She will seem familiar. She will smile and take you by the hand. And for an instant all of your memories will flood back into your mind. You will hold them there, in crystalline perfection, cherished, for a heartbeat.

"Then you will let them go. And you will be led away from this realm forever.

"The world will go on without you. In time, everyone who ever knew you, ever heard your voice or seen your face, will themselves pass away. Your wonderful contributions to humanity will be surpassed and made obsolete, forevermore unknown. And it will be as if you never existed."

The house thrummed under the heavy surf.

"I tell you, Gabrielle, if you follow our path, if you are accepted as a human being, this will be your fate."

Rushel tilted her head.

"Do you accept these conditions?"

Gabrielle saw them all turn to look at her. She kept her voice steady.

"Yes," she said.

Rushel nodded and stood up. These was a gasp. Audra, Gabrielle thought. Catherine wiped her eyes again.

"The Goddess is here," Rushel said strong and clear. All the others stood at once. "Persephone Gabrielle, for the allotted time, we are at your service. We are your priestesses."

Rushel grinned.

"Command us."

They all regarded her with anticipation. Gabrielle looked at each of them in turn and when she got to Catherine and saw her smile, her mind seemed to unclench. She cleared her throat. The sound of the wind deepened outside.

"Please sit down," she said.

"Yes, Goddess," they all said in almost perfect unison and sat.

"Okay," Gabrielle said. "Um. Thank you."

"You don't have to thank us," Audra said. "You're the Goddess."

"I will anyway."

"Yes, Goddess."

This made Gabrielle laugh and when she saw no one else was laughing she choked it off. She tried to compose herself. "Well. I think. I think this is the most interesting thing that has ever happened to me." She saw this made

Rushel smile.

"Yes, Goddess," Rushel said. "And I remembered something I should do. Audra, you know. I am Rushel." She pronounced it Ru-shell. "This is Gislaine." Gee-slain. "Samantha." The dark-haired one nodded. "And Catherine."

"Nice to finally meet you all." She saw that Samantha was at least smiling a little. And she was also holding Catherine's hand again.

Gabrielle thought for a moment. "I have a few questions."

"Ask away, Goddess," Audra said, grinning.

Gabrielle couldn't help laughing at almost everything Audra said. "Who is Patricia?"

"Patricia was cast out," Rushel said abruptly. "So was Holly."

"Pathological Patricia. Debbie Darkness. Homicidal Holly. And the four Susans," Audra said.

They all nodded.

"All right. So who is L?"

Rushel and Audra looked at each other in astonishment. Samantha squinted at her again.

"I told you," Catherine said with a triumphant smile.

"L is the one who hates us," Rushel said bitterly. "Hate is her only reason to live. She is the enemy of M. She wants to destroy us."

"Literally destroy us, if possible," Samantha said.

Gabrielle was surprised by her voice. Higher up. Not girlish. Musical, she thought, and I know nothing about music.

"But we're safe here, we think," Rushel said "Here and at our place down south. Where you visited us." She smiled.

Gabrielle was startled. Good God, she thought.

"What?" Catherine said suddenly. "What is it?"

"Catherine," Audra said.

"I'm sorry. Goddess," she said softly. "What is it?"

They all looked at Catherine and then at Gabrielle.

"There is something I have to tell you," Gabrielle said. She wiped her eyes under her glasses. This is too fast, she thought. I have to think. She got an idea. "Catherine, would you make breakfast for everyone? After breakfast, we'll have a meeting."

Catherine locked eyes on her. "But..." Looking vexed, she finally said, "Yes, all right. Goddess." She and Samantha got up and went hand in hand into the kitchen. There was the sound of cabinet doors being slammed.

Now she's really mad at me, Gabrielle thought. Not that it matters, I guess. Samantha close up is sexy as hell. It's her posture. Poise. That's the word. And the way she moves. Her hair. And her looks. And everything else.

"Goddess, this thing you're going to tell us," Audra said. "Is it bad?" Rushel and Gislaine looked concerned.

"I want to tell everyone at once. So, after breakfast, okay?"

"Yes, Goddess." They all glanced at each other.

Gabrielle stood up and went through the door and into the library, dark with the mini blinds drawn, and pulled open the front door. Fresh air.

So what am I doing, she thought.

The surprise had worn off and she was left with the problem. What do I do next. What do they want?

The world outside was gray, oddly warm, and alive with movement. Fast clouds passed over the house, heading west, revealing patches of blue sky which were swiftly swallowed up.

Beams of sunlight split the gray and were gone. Sand scattered over the porch. The sagebrush danced before her. She held out her hand. She could almost feel the electricity.

"Do you like storms?" It was Rushel, Audra beside her, both still in their white robes.

Rushel is perfect, Gabrielle thought. Perfect face. Gorgeous hair. Tall and slender. Long legs, long waist. She considered. Samantha: short legs but long waist. Relatively, she thought. I'm better at putting words to all this now.

"I love storms. It's so different here," Gabrielle said. "It hardly even rains at home."

"We're getting more than our share of rain now that the drought is over."

"If you really want to experience storms," Audra said, "We should go up Highway One. The stretch just before Big Sur where the storms just slam into the cliffs. You can feel the ground shake. It's fantastic."

"I've never been up that far," Gabrielle said.

"Oh, we have to go. Before spring comes. Yuk. I hate spring."

"It's beautiful," Rushel countered. "Flowers as far as the eye can see."

"Bleh. Foggy." Audra shivered. She pointed at the busy winter sky. "Cool. Exciting. Wonderful."

Rushel sighed and stared at Audra. She raised her eyebrows. Audra locked eyes with her and made a funny nervous smile. Gabrielle couldn't tell if Rushel was signaling *hurry up*, or *for God's sake, not now*. Audra turned her head towards Gabrielle, keeping her eyes on Rushel for a moment.

"Um," Audra said. "There was something I wanted to ask you. We want to ask you."

Rushel kept her eyes on Audra.

"Okay."

"Well." Audra tilted her head with a shrug. "It'll take Catherine a little while to make breakfast. She's such a perfectionist, as I'm sure you know."

"Uh huh."

"Well." She cleared her throat. "Since we have some free time, we were wondering if the Goddess would like to retire to one of the bedrooms and use our naked bodies for pleasure." On the last word, she stared hard at Gabrielle.

Rushel coughed and then giggled. She turned away and giggled again. She covered her mouth and walked quickly away into the back of the house.

Audra watched her go. She shook her head.

"Chicks."

Gabrielle said, "Maybe later?" It seemed like the safe thing to say.

As if reading her mind, Audra said, "You're a free agent. Free as a bird." She stood close in the open door. "That was her idea, actually. Not that there's anything wrong with it, if you'd like my opinion."

Gabrielle decided to tell her. "I like the idea." I *am* a free agent, she thought. I guess. That's a pretty good term. "So Catherine and Samantha are together?"

"Not that way."

"Really? It seemed like it."

"They gravitate towards each other. Because of their injuries. But I'll get in trouble for talking about it. It's just not my place."

"I absolutely won't tell a soul."

Audra relaxed but came closer. She let her upper arm bump into Gabrielle's elbow. "Catherine, well, you've seen. She's all right now, pretty much, although I don't how she survived her childhood. Samantha, much worse. Devastating."

"She looks fine."

"Yeah. She's incredibly strong."

"I can't imagine her being hurt by anything."

"I know." Audra pulled away. "She'll have to be the one to tell you. All right? It's up to her."

"All right."

Audra's robe blew across her feet. Gabrielle saw something shiny on her right foot. She was wearing a gold ring on her second toe.

"That's to remind me," she said. "To remind me I'm not perfect. That I fuck up."

"Everybody fucks up."

"Not like I did. You met Holly."

Gabrielle smiled. "I seem to remember her."

"We used to be together. For over a year. A whole year. An entire year of my mortal existence bringing me that much closer to dying alone under a cloudless sky. It took me that long to realize she's insane. Please don't tell her I said that. It would not go over well."

"I'll bet." Gabrielle laughed. "She's kind of scary."

"A couple gears short of a transmission. A speeding car without a steering wheel." She held up a finger. "A speeding car without a steering wheel going over a cliff and exploding in a ball of fire. That's Homicidal

Holly."

Gabrielle laughed and Audra smiled again. She likes being funny, Gabrielle thought, kind of like Barbara.

"And I'm sorry about this." She put her hand on her throat. "We... It was just a theory we had."

"It was very realistic. You scared the hell out of me."

"The real trick was Rushel and Gislaine blocking your view and getting you to leave. A couple more seconds and you would've seen through it. The theory part, that was my fault."

"You had a theory about faking your own death?"

"Well, it was something I noticed. Seeing death makes you horny. You know, after the shock wears off. And if the person wasn't too close to you. I noticed this after I went to this funeral."

Horny? Gabrielle didn't remember feeling like that after the funeral of her father. That and the whole time after – months – had a sealed off quality in her memory. That's just my mind trying to protect itself, she thought, and still the memories came bursting forth as she stood there. The smell of the hospital waiting rooms. Her father's face as he tried to smile for her. The look of pain. Life ending pain. Her mother's voice unable to say the words. After my mom passes away, she thought, it will just be me who remembers. And when I'm gone...

"It was this uncle of mine I think I met only once, and after the funeral I just wanted to do it. Crazy. Out of the blue. So I went to this weird bar. I was only eighteen, but... Are you all right?"

"No," Gabrielle snapped. "Never do that again."

Audra fell back, shocked. "I'm..." she managed to say.

"It wasn't funny. At all."

Audra nodded, suddenly pale, near tears. She left Gabrielle at the open door.

Gabrielle watched the light rain blowing sideways across the porch. A door slammed at the far end of the house. She shook her head. Come on, they didn't know, she thought. How could they have known? You have to.

She closed the door. "Audra?" she called. There was no answer.

She started for the kitchen. In the middle room, the door ahead was flung open and in a blizzard of white robes Rushel, Gislaine, and Samantha rushed in. They all looked angry.

Rushel took a deep breath. "We are not sure what Audra did to upset you but if she ever does it again she will be cast out." The other two nodded. "She is in her room. What would you like to do?"

Get a God damned grip, Gabrielle thought. I have to be more careful. This is really happening.

"Stay here. I'm going to go talk to her." She walked between them and into the kitchen. She smelled bacon cooking and saw biscuits ready to go in the oven. Catherine was leaning against the refrigerator, glass of wine in hand. She caught Gabrielle's eye.

"It's always like this," she said. "Not even breakfast yet."

Gabrielle just nodded. When she got to the hallway door, she said, "Rushel, would you come with me, please."

Rushel turned with a start. Her angry expression gone, she said, "Yes?" in a worried voice. They entered the hallway. Rushel pointed to the last door on the left.

Gabrielle knocked. "Audra, it's me."

The door opened. Audra, downcast, started to say something and stopped when she saw Rushel.

"Both of you, sit on the bed."

Audra sat on the end. Rushel, looking even more worried, sat on the side. They did not look at each other.

"Look, I'm..." Rushel started but Gabrielle held up her hand.

"I'm not really mad at either of you. You could not have known. My dad died three years ago. Three years in March. Your little trick really got to me."

Audra was open mouthed with surprise. "Oh, my God, Gabrielle, I'm so sorry!"

Rushel started at the floor in embarrassment.

"Never do anything like that again."

Both of them said, "Yes, Goddess," simultaneously.

"We're really sorry," Audra said.

Rushel glared at her. "No, *I'm* sorry. Don't tell her how I feel. I'll tell her. There is no we."

"Perish the thought."

Rushel shook her head. "I'm sorry, Gabrielle. There. Audra's on her own."

"Oh my *God.*"

That really made Rushel smile. She dared to look up at Gabrielle. "When you left in the middle of the night, we thought we had completely blown it. All our plans went out the window. Since we... Audra and I are both students here we were going to see if one of us could hitch a ride with you in the morning. That was our idea. We'd flip a coin and one of us..."

"Or maybe both of us," Audra said with a shy smile.

"One or the other."

"Or both."

"Whatever. And then we'd use the trip to get to know you. And maybe that would work."

"Work," Gabrielle said. "To seduce me."

"Yes," Audra said quickly.

"Well," Rushel said.

"Seduce. That's the correct word," Audra said, grinning.

"To get me into bed," Gabrielle said.

"I wouldn't..." Rushel said.

"*I* would," Audra said.

"Okay, okay. That's flattering, I guess."

"I'm really good at flattery," Audra said. "I'm an expert."

Rushel turned halfway around. "Good grief."

"Well, I am."

"Um."

"Gislaine put it in her notebook once. That makes it official."

"Gislaine gets carried away sometimes," Rushel said, and then to Gabrielle, "She has a degree in literature."

"From Stanford," Audra said. "So she could teach high school or get a great job at McDonald's."

Rushel nodded. "Pretty much."

"Okay," Gabrielle said, backing up.

"There's nothing wrong with McDonald's."

Gabrielle opened the bedroom door and stepped out. She heard Rushel say, "Then why don't you get a job there?"

"How do you know I haven't?"

She closed the door behind her. In the darkness, she almost laughed. Kind of impossible to stay mad at them.

When she went in the kitchen, Catherine was pulling back the vertical blinds. The rain had begun. Samantha was kneeling on the floor and lighting a pile of sticks in the fireplace next to the dining table, her hair draped over her shoulders and down to the back of her bare ankles sticking out of her robe. Catherine went behind the counter and brought out a large glass.

"Here, especially for goddesses." She pushed it forward. "You're gonna need it." This made Samantha laugh.

"What was that all about, anyway? On second thought, don't tell me."

Gabrielle could smell it over the bacon. "Wine?"

"It's all right. It's six-fifteen."

"In that case." She sipped. "Oh, it's that real sweet one. Riesling?"

"Whoa," Samantha said.

"Yes, a seventy-eight Amador Ridge Riesling is the perfect Sunday breakfast wine, in my opinion. How many eggs would you like? Two?"

"Three." Gabrielle took a big gulp.

"Three? Really?"

"Make it four. You're cooking bacon in the oven?"

"One of my tricks. It cooks perfectly evenly. And you don't get bacon grease all over the place."

"Yes, the dead animal's decomposing bodily fluids are nicely contained," Samantha said as she poked at the burning kindling. She placed a dark chunk of wood on top and jabbed it with the poker.

"Samantha's a vegetarian," Catherine said.

"I know it's inconvenient."

"It is *not* inconvenient."

"Yes, it is."

"No," Catherine said. "It's just the way I was trained was pretty traditional."

"She went to school in Paris," Samantha said.

"Wow, Paris." Gabrielle took another gulp.

"It was a lot of work. Especially if you don't speak French."

"Hardly any vegetarians in France," Samantha said.

"No. But lots of butter, eggs, cheese, and piles of adorable creatures with their throats slit. Blood, internal organs, buckets of little severed heads…"

"Oh, my." Gabrielle felt her stomach lurch.

"You're drinking that way too fast," Catherine said. "Only sip."

Gabrielle just nodded.

"You handled those two pretty well." Catherine took a small drink from her glass, still nearly full. "Oh, here, have some more." She refilled Gabrielle's glass.

"Do you have brothers?" Samantha asked as she sat at the table. "Like younger brothers?"

"No, I'm an only child."

Catherine and Samantha exchanged a look.

"A while back I had a job as a lab assistant. Paid thirty-two dollars a month. It was an introductory electronics class, circuit analysis, and it was nothing but freshman. All boys. I had no trouble handling them."

"Some people just have the knack," Catherine said.

"So you're saying you simply treated Audra and Rushel as if they were teenage boys?"

Gabrielle hadn't thought of it that way. "I guess."

Catherine set down her glass and turned to the oven. "Appropriate."

"Yes," Samantha said so seriously that Gabrielle couldn't help giggling.

Catherine opened and closed the oven doors. Gabrielle smelled biscuits along with the bacon. "A few minutes. Okay." She topped off Gabrielle's glass again. "So what's the secret?"

Gabrielle knew she was drunk – wine worked really fast! – and she knew what she wanted to say but it was as if a different part of her mind was in charge of her voice. "I have to wait for the meeting. I have to tell everyone at the same time."

"You can tell me. No one will know."

"Except me," Samantha said.

"And her."

"It would be wrong."

"No it wouldn't."

"It would create an imbalance in the group. The dynamic group. Group dynamic."

"Okay," Catherine said. She leaned very close. "But is it good or bad? Just tell me that."

"Pretty bad."

"How bad?"

"Bad."

"Damn it! Tell me."

"I can't. Even though I really like you." Wine, Gabrielle suddenly thought with an interestingly detached part of her mind, is going to be nothing but trouble. And it doesn't really taste that good. But I like it anyway.

"Well, thank you," Catherine said. "I like you, too."

"And I liked sleeping with you. I never slept with anyone before although I certainly thought about it a lot. But I don't know what's going to happen now." Gabrielle turned to Samantha. "I like you, also. You're very sexy."

"Thanks." Samantha grinned. "I am, aren't I?"

"Yes. I like your shoulders," Gabrielle said, suddenly feeling flush. "I'm not sure why. I want to touch your shoulders. They're the sexiest part of you. Besides your hair, I mean. And your hands. You have beautiful hands."

"Thanks, Goddess. Touch me any time you want."

"Okay, I will," Gabrielle said, nodding. "You know, just a couple weeks ago, I would not have had the ability to say things like this because I never thought about it very much and I never thought anyone liked me anyway so why worry about it, right?"

"Right," Catherine said, trying to cover her smile.

"I mean, I'm just average looking. You are all much prettier than me. On the other hand, I'm smart. I am God damned smart."

"I never noticed," Catherine said.

"I am. I figure things out really fast. So I know you got me drunk so I would tell you the secret and, well, it's not going to work. Sorry."

"Darn. It was worth a shot."

"It isn't a secret, anyway. It's just something I know and you don't. I don't think."

"Something bad," Catherine said. "About our place down south. I saw your reaction when Rushel said that."

"I'll tell you all about your house at the meeting."

"Our..." Catherine said and stared at Samantha. She turned and raised her voice. "You two get in here!"

Audra and Rushel came out of the hallway door still talking.

"But no one knows what it really is," Rushel said. "It clearly isn't chicken."

"It tastes like chicken. I don't think they can fake that."

When they saw Catherine's face they became silent and sat at the table next to each other.

Catherine yelled at the door to the middle room. "Come on!"

The door opened and Gislaine came out with her notebook. "Sorry.

Bathroom."

"This whole time?"

"Yes," she said, sounding embarrassed. She sat between Rushel and Samantha.

"Okay, this is the meeting," Catherine said. "I changed the schedule, Goddess. Is that all right?"

"I guess it's okay," Gabrielle said. Get it over with, she thought.

They all sat at the table and looked at Gabrielle.

"I kind of wanted more time to think about it. But you all deserve to know."

They all held rigidly still. Catherine squinted at her.

"The Wednesday after Christmas, I took my friend Linda up to see your house. She's a friend of mine from high school. She works as a waitress at *Winkies.* I had to show her this mysterious place where I was going to help M set up the laser disc player. And we went up the same road to the same spot and the house was gone."

Samantha pushed back from the table and stood. Her eyes were wide and empty as if she had been punched in the stomach.

"The two pillars were pushed over and overgrown. There was no driveway and just an empty lot where the house had been."

"*Fuck,*" Audra said forcefully.

"God damn it," Rushel muttered.

"This was right after Christmas?" Gislaine asked.

"And it wasn't just torn down. It was made to look as if there had never been anything there. There were weeds all over."

"Yeah," Rushel said.

"That's it, then," Audra said and looked at the others. No one met her gaze. "That's it."

"No," Catherine said.

"Yes, just face it."

Catherine sat in one of the dining chairs. She stared at the floor.

"I have no idea how you could even do that," Gabrielle said. "Or why."

"I know why," Samantha said. "We're losing."

"No," Catherine said, looking up.

"Or we've already lost."

"Don't say that."

"That's what's going on. That's why she's been gone so long."

Catherine said nothing.

Samantha stared out the window at the rainy sky. "We still have this place."

"For how long?"

"We don't know anything," Samantha said gently. "We have to wait."

Gabrielle stood at the island and watched them, feeling sick to her stomach. Two big glasses of wine before breakfast, she thought. Just brilliant. She wanted to say she was sorry for bringing bad news but that seemed trite. She felt dizzy and put her hands on the counter for support.

And right then the part of her mind which handled low level processing jobs wrapped up its calculations and sent them up to the head office. Gabrielle felt it almost physically.

"Oh, right. It has to be," she whispered.

They all looked at her.

"Who is she, really?" Rushel said softly.

"She's one of us now," Samantha said.

Catherine raised her eyebrows. "Yes, Goddess?"

"Two things," Gabrielle said. "First, your biscuits are burning."

Catherine jumped up in white silk flurry.

"Second, I'm pretty sure I know what's in that heavy box you have hidden under the bean bags. And I'll bet I know how to open it."

Catherine banged a sheet pan onto the counter and covered the slightly darkened biscuits with a towel. She turned off both ovens with the twist of a knob and the displays went to zero.

"You really are a goddess, aren't you?" Audra said.

In the library, Rushel cranked open the blinds and switched on both floor lamps. The room filled with cold light. Gabrielle pulled away the red and black bean bags. They were surprisingly substantial and she had to use both hands. The gray box was where she left it on the oak floor.

"Why do you have this lying in the middle of the floor like this?"

"It was too heavy," Rushel said. "We dropped it on the bean bags."

"We panicked," Audra said and laughed.

Gabrielle didn't see how what made sense. "Why'd you panic?"

"We thought we were dead," Audra said. She looked at Rushel and they both shook their heads, remembering.

"It was scary," Audra said.

"Yes," Rushel said.

"Okay," Gabrielle said, still puzzled.

"We have to explain," Gislaine said.

"Yes, teacher," Audra said. "According to what we have heard, inside that box is a vial of nerve gas, a super fragile glass vial which will break if you tamper with it."

"Nerve gas."

"Yes. So don't smash it with a sledgehammer. Or try to pry it open."

"Or drop it," Rushel said.

"Instant death," Audra said.

"Nerve gas," Gabrielle said, forcing herself to keep a straight face.

"*Yes,*" Audra said, almost angrily.

"So." Gabrielle noted that Gislaine was grinning. "So it's booby trapped."

"According to what we have heard. And we believe it."

"Why?"

"It was L herself who told us," Audra said. "And she is absolutely evil and crazy. In her house there's a room full of these things."

"We just don't know what's inside it," Rushel said. "It's like a safe."

"A portable safe," Audra said.

"Not all that portable."

"Yeah, you need a crane to lift it."

"So this belongs to L?" Gabrielle said.

"No, it's ours."

"She gave it to you?"

"We borrowed it," Audra said.

"Permanently borrowed it," Rushel said. "I just grabbed it and almost killed myself taking it to the car."

"We think she thinks one of the Susans took it because one of the Susans was cast out right after and they got a new one."

Gabrielle said. "I know who you mean."

"We assign them numbers."

"Oh, numbers are good. I made up names. There's Tall Susan, then Pretty Susan, and New."

"Right, that makes sense. Tall. Right," Audra said. "Which one's Pretty?"

"Just the one that seemed prettiest while they were beating me up." Gabrielle thought for a second. "It's hard to tell them apart."

"There's still one you haven't met," Samantha said from the doorway. She sat in the chair next to Gislaine. "You probably won't think of her as pretty. She's the oldest."

"Okay. She can be First Susan."

"That's good," Rushel said. "First."

"First in *evil*," Audra said.

"You said you knew what was in it." Rushel brushed dust from the box. "And how to open it. Isn't this some kind of aluminum?"

"Titanium. Do you have a scale?"

"A bathroom scale?" Samantha got up. "Titanium?"

"And a flat screwdriver."

"No, no, you can't try to pry the lid off," Rushel said.

"I'm not. Don't worry. Nerve gas."

"Yes, really. It's real."

"Do you have any electrical wire? Sixteen or eighteen gauge would be best. And electrical tape. And scissors."

"Gauge?" Rushel looked at Audra.

"We have Scotch tape somewhere," Audra said and headed for the kitchen.

"Never seen any wire. Oh. There's wire on those lamps."

"That might work."

"You need wire to open it?"

"Yep. Here I'll show you." Gabrielle crouched down and put her face level with the top of the box. "This is just something I noticed yesterday. When the light shines on it just right. See?"

Rushel pushed the bean bags back a bit and got on her knees. She tipped her head down and her blonde hair fell across the box and Gabrielle's hands. It smelled of her shampoo. Coconut. "Oh, sorry."

"That's okay. Now…"

Samantha came in with a bright red bathroom scale and set it next to the box. "Wait." She got between them and let her black hair drape over Gabrielle's shoulders. "What are we looking at?"

"Well," Gabrielle said. She brushed the mingled blonde and black hair from the box. She cleared her throat. "See this circular pattern on the surface? From something rubbing on the metal."

"I see it," Samantha said.

"Kind of," Rushel said.

"I think that's from an induction coil. That's how they power the locking mechanism inside. I might be able to make one." Gabrielle put both hands on the floor. The room almost stopped spinning around her. She gripped the box by the sharp machined edges and pulled it on the wooden floor until it bumped her knee. Then she heaved and tipped it up. She slid the scale under it and let it back down. The scale dial spun and vibrated. "Just under twenty three pounds. Yep," she said.

"I understood the word 'coil'. How about you, Sammie?"

"Uh huh. I know that word. Still don't see how it's supposed to work." Samantha let her shoulder rub against Gabrielle's.

Audra came in, saw them all on the floor together, and made a loud, "Tsk." Gabrielle saw on her face a flicker of surprise and pain, then sarcastic anger. Audra dropped a pair of scissors and a tape dispenser in front of them. "There," she said. She slumped into the big chair next to Gislaine.

"Thanks," Gabrielle said.

"Oh you're welcome."

Samantha made a barely audible sigh and got up gracefully. She went to Audra and bent over and kissed her on the cheek, whispered something in her ear, and kissed her on the mouth. She crouched beside the chair and took Audra's hand. "Please proceed with your plan, Goddess." She locked eyes with Audra. "This will be good, huh?"

Audra nodded, slightly softening her angry look.

"What do we do now?" Rushel said.

Gabrielle had Rushel cut the wires from both floor lamps, after unplugging them, and the room became gray. Samantha, Audra, and Gislaine watched intently.

On one lamp cord, Gabrielle pulled the two lamp wires apart, unzipping them, and cut off the wall plug. The other cord she only partially unzipped and kept the cord attached. With the scissors, she carefully striped the black insulation from the ends of the two unzipped pieces, exposing the bright copper, and spliced them together. She wrapped the splice with tape. She then stripped the insulation from one of the ends and made a sharp bend. It looked like a hook.

"Okay. We have to be neat and tidy. That's what Mr. Weber always said. Keep everything under control."

"Doing what?"

"We're going to make a flat coil of wire. Just the right size."

She pulled the long wire to the box and in the near darkness made a small loop, the hook end sticking up, and taped it so it wouldn't unbend. She put this on the surface of the box and pushed it flat and made it round.

"Now we just roll it up and tape it every so often."

Gabrielle turned the wire loop with both hands, keeping it flat. When the flat, black coil was as wide as the box she started coiling inwards. This went a little faster. After two layers of coiling, the long wire was almost used up. She used the last of the tape to stick the coil to the box, the short bare copper poking up in the center. She sat up, shoulders sore and stiff.

"How did you know how to do that?" It was Gislaine.

"I saw it in a book. It's nothing new." The coffee was strong and only lukewarm. "It won't be very efficient. Probably less than forty percent. In the box there's a coil like this one, or so I think, and when we apply power to mine, the alternating current is coupled to the one inside. If we're lucky."

"You're good at making things. I was waiting for everyone to come back for breakfast but that's okay."

"You plug it in and then touch the wire from the plug to that center piece, right?" Rushel said. "What do you think will happen?"

"Blow a fuse. We have to put one of the lamps back in the circuit." She walked on her knees to the closest floor lamp and dragged it to the box. Gabrielle unzipped the remaining wire and stripped the ends. One was connected to the plug wire, the other just bare copper. She twisted the shiny strands to make them neat.

Gabrielle nodded to Rushel waiting by the wall socket.

"It's plugged in," she said. "You know what's in there, you said."

"Oh, she knows," Catherine said.

"I don't want to say. It would sound crazy. But this is so heavy, it could only be one thing."

"Oh my God. Look at her," Catherine said. "She is absolutely loving this."

"Yes, she is," Samantha said, grinning in the dark room.

"Well, let's see how good my ideas are." Gabrielle touched the two bare copper wires together. The floor lamp came on, then dimmed. Rushel knelt close to the box.

"It made a sound! I heard it!"

The flat top of the box popped open and rose up half an inch. Rushel jumped back and ran to the front door. Samantha and Audra both exclaimed and leaned forward. Gislaine squinted intently, saying, "Whoa."

Catherine stood, arms crossed. "Huh," she said with a proud smile.

Gabrielle carefully unplugged the lamps, disconnected the wires and tucked them away. She got on her knees and examined the box. She could see machined latches on all four corners. She pulled up on the lid. It was riding on a central rod. It came smoothly off and she turned it over. She could see a circuit board and intricate, tightly fitted actuators. "Oh, this is *nice.*"

She turned her attention to what was inside. There were rows of shiny metal disks, six groups of them. They were tightly packed. Gabrielle thought it wasn't nearly as shiny as she imagined it would be. Still, pretty shiny.

"See? It had to be," she said. "Gold."

"What?" Rushel said.

"Oh, come on," Catherine said.

Audra jumped out of the chair and dropped down. "Can I touch it?"

"You're kidding, right?" Samantha stood up but didn't come closer.

Gislaine craned her neck from where she sat.

"Sure, you can touch it." Gabrielle tried to pull one of the coins out. "Something's holding them in." She took off her glasses and examined the interior. "Need a flashlight. Yeah, there's a little clip. Like a spring."

"That does look like gold," Catherine said weakly. "Not that I've ever seen gold before."

Gabrielle put her glasses back on. No one was smiling. They were all acting scared. She picked up the screwdriver.

"No," Rushel said quickly.

"I don't see any vials of nerve gas."

"I know. But." Rushel pushed herself back. "Be careful."

"I will."

Gabrielle put the tip of the screwdriver in the spot where the spring was pressing on a bar. She carefully twisted it and the spring flew off with a loud ping and hit the glass shade of the floor lamp. They all jumped back.

Audra clamped her hands on the side of her face. "Give me a heart attack."

Gabrielle tried to pick out one of the now slightly loose coins but her fingers slipped off. "Boy, they're heavy. Okay." The coins were set in a machined recess and too close together for her to get a grip. "I don't suppose we have a pair of Channel Locks?"

"Channel," Rushel said, "locks?"

"We do have pliers in that drawer," Audra said. "At least we did."

She went into the kitchen and Gabrielle heard a drawer yanked open hard.

Audra came back, saying, "Just these." She handed Gabrielle a small pair of pliers, decades old, cheaply stamped out.

At least she didn't throw them at me, she thought.

"Those are way too small," Rushel said. "You need way bigger ones."

"These are okay. Like this." Gabrielle turned the pliers upside down and used the handles to grip one of the packed row of coins.

"Oh," Rushel said. "You're smart."

Gabrielle squeezed with both hands, it was a difficult angle, and pushed up. The bottom of the roll of coins moved a fraction of an inch. She pulled down and out and the coins came out of their socket. They spilled onto the floor with a heavy metallic wooden sound.

They were all gathered close. The gold coins gleamed in the shadows. Gabrielle set one on the tinny scale. She thought if she touched it, it would feel warm. She felt it with the back of her middle finger. The gold was freezing cold. There were dents in the metal from the pliers.

Catherine touched it, tipped it up to test its weight.

"God," she said.

Samantha turned the coin around on the scale. "Pretty obvious. Krugerrands."

"One ounce each," Gabrielle said. "Times three hundred sixty. About twenty-two and a half pounds."

"Shit," Audra said, "that explains my back." She showed no inclination to touch them.

"Okay, just estimating then," Gabrielle said, "because I happened to see the price of gold on the news a few weeks back. About two hundred thirty dollars an ounce."

"I'm gonna puke," Catherine said.

Audra stood with her eyes closed.

Gabrielle said, "Eighty-two thousand, eight hundred dollars altogether."

Catherine slumped into one of the chairs. "Well, I guess we can afford new lamps."

"It's L," Audra said. "That paranoid psycho. We all wondered where she was hiding the money."

"She must have converted everything to gold after last year," Samantha said. "In Europe. Then she could bring it back into the country undetected."

"That's why she didn't go to the police after we, you know, borrowed this." Audra rubbed her temples. "So it's ours. There's nothing she can do about it."

"Steal it back," Samantha said, still kneeling by the box.

"If they find out we have it," Catherine said. "Which they won't."

Gabrielle picked up the lid and peeled off her induction coil. The tape stuck to her hand and she lost her grip. The titanium lid fell. Samantha lunged forward, stretched out, and caught it an inch from the hardwood floor. Gabrielle flinched back in surprise. So *fast*, she thought.

Samantha, lying across the box and a bean bag, got on one elbow, the gray titanium lid in the other hand. "Sorry," she said. "I thought I saw something."

Gabrielle took it from her. "Are you all right? You saw something?" She carried the lid to the window and took off her glasses again.

The locking mechanism was extremely compact, a system of finely made gears in a rose petal design, very thin and flat, all of the same gray metal. Half a centimeter thick, total, she thought. The whole thing was part sensor, part actuator. There was the corner of a printed circuit board that she saw before. It seemed digital, traces much smaller than anything she had ever worked with, but also had a section that looked like an RF circuit. A radio receiver or transmitter. She couldn't see how it was all fastened together. No screws or welds. No wires or motors were visible. But there was something bright in the center of the main gear, something shiny.

"See? Right there." Samantha pointed from a couple feet back.

She doesn't want to get close to it, Gabrielle thought.

"What?" Rushel said. "For God's sake, be careful."

Gabrielle tilted the thing to the light. The shiny part was glass. She felt the hair on the back of her neck stand up straight.

"Could someone drag that bean bag over here," she said. "I don't want to move."

Samantha pulled the red bag over with one hand and flattened it out. Gabrielle knelt, holding the lid steady and level, and set it down on the soft vinyl. She took her hands away slowly and backed away from it.

Samantha came up behind her and whispered, "It's a glass vial, isn't it."

"Yep." Gabrielle turned to the others, all standing in a tight group. "It would be a good idea if you all left the room. Now that I've energized it there's no telling what it's going to do."

"I told you it was real!" Rushel exclaimed.

"Samantha and I will get rid of it."

Samantha stared at her.

Gabrielle made herself nod. "It's safer this way. You should all go wait in the kitchen."

No one budged.

"Bullshit," Audra said. "Whatever it is, we face it together."

"It might actually be dangerous."

"Then you'd better get moving," Catherine said.

Gabrielle picked up the titanium plate and held it level. The mechanism made a very audible click.

Samantha moved quickly. She opened the front door. Cold, wet air flowed into the room. She pushed open the screen door and held it, stepping out onto the sand sprayed porch.

"We go straight over the dunes and throw it into the ocean," Samantha said. She pointed at the sagebrush.

Gabrielle walked to the door holding the lid out in front of her. Audra, behind her, said, "Are you scared?"

Gabrielle did not slow down. She crossed the porch, sand sticking to her bare feet. "Don't think I've ever been less scared," she said softly. Her silk pajamas rippled in the wind and tiny rain drops pelted her face. Her glasses became speckled.

They all followed her, Samantha at her right hand. They left the door hanging open and walked single file into the rainy chaparral, their blowing white robes luminous in the morning storm light. A seagull wheeled at the base of the fast moving clouds and cried in alarm.

Gabrielle held the lid before her like an offering. She was surprised how soft and yielding the coarse sand was. Her feet kept twisting sideways while Samantha guided her through the sage. No one spoke. The land fell away and they entered a notch in the convoluted dunes, a secret pass. She started to sweat and a piece of shell cut her right foot. Samantha never left her side but made no move to take the lid from her.

That's because you're the leader, she suddenly thought. They are looking to you.

She walked a bit faster. Samantha kept up, the others fell behind.

She completely forgot to count her steps. Some unknown distance later, the vague trail ended at a flat spot between towering dunes. There was a steep slope down to the narrow beach of dark sand. The angry sea, dark gray, stretched to the horizon. Waves thundered onto the sand, foaming and furious, leaving long strands of kelp. There was driftwood and white lines of broken shell.

Gabrielle hesitated at the verge. It would be easy to slide down the dune. Climbing back up would be another matter. Samantha came very close. She smelled of cinnamon and perspiration. Their hair blew into tangles together.

"I'm have an idea what's in that thing," she said, her voice clear in the constant wind.

"In the glass?"

"It's ink. Indelible ink. It's a theft detection system."

Gabrielle felt great relief. "Right. That makes perfect sense." She wiggled her toes in the sand. It wasn't quite as cold underneath.

Samantha scanned the beach and sky. "I can get it from here."

"Thank you."

She passed the lid into Samantha's hands. She had long fingers and perfect nails.

"You don't have to thank me." She held the sharp-edged thing in one hand and flexed her arm like she was holding a Frisbee. The long sleeve bunched up at her elbow. She slipped the robe from her left shoulder, then her right, switching the lid from hand to hand. She caught the robe and held it up to Gabrielle who took it after a second, quite nearly frozen with surprise.

Naked, Samantha turned sideways to the sea, her hair streaming away, and took the measure of the wind.

Gabrielle thought, oh, I mustn't look. Blowing, Samantha's hair reached up and tickled her cheek. She looked.

Samantha's olive tan skin was covered with goosebumps from her muscular shoulders down to her calves. She had small breasts and brown nipples. Her abdomen was concave and her thighs, set apart, were smooth and taut. She had small feet, with perfect toenails, and she pushed them into the sand. Her skin was covered with fine, light hair which caught droplets of rain. Gabrielle risked a glance out of the corner of her eye. No pubic hair.

Samantha brought the lid up in her right hand, the wind fluctuated and she held still, eyes calm and unblinking, all the muscles in her arms and shoulders tense. Then she threw it. Her body unfolded in a single fluid motion, giving no indication of effort or strain, and the titanium lid sailed spinning over the beach, over the breakers, buoyed by gusts, until it finally tipped over and disappeared into the churning water.

Samantha brushed back her hair with both hands and smiled.

Gabrielle opened the robe to the wind and Samantha put her left arm into the sleeve, then her right. She tugged it up over her shoulders and Samantha turned and wrapped her arms around her and squeezed. For a moment, Gabrielle couldn't think. She put her hands on Samantha's waist. Samantha held her for two deep breaths and just as quickly let go.

"That was good," she said.

Gabrielle cleared her throat and turned around.

On the trail, Rushel and Gislaine stood arm in arm. Rushel looked worried, Gislaine seemed fascinated. Catherine had an astonished grin on her face.

Audra, arms crossed, was not smiling. Her black hair danced around her bright, sharp eyes. She turned and began walking back to the house, taking long steps.

"Well." Catherine pressed her hand onto her cheek. "I'll bet everyone's hungry *now*."

The coins were gone.

Gabrielle noticed that no one so much as glanced at the strange empty metal box on the porch. Catherine had used it to prop the screen door open.

Her bare feet tingled and she tried not to track in any sand. She wiped her glasses with the sleeve of her pajamas as she walked through the middle room. At the kitchen door, she stopped in surprise. She put her glasses back on.

All five were standing at attention around the dining table, their arms at their sides. They all looked straight ahead, faces composed. Someone's stomach growled and Rushel glanced at Audra in exasperation. Plates and silverware had been set out and there were several serving dishes on the table along with a silver coffee pot.

Catherine pulled out the high-backed chair from the end of the table closest to the fireplace, where a cheerful fire burned.

"This is your seat," she said.

Gabrielle nervously stepped to the table. Catherine pushed the chair under her and she sat. The fire warmed her back. Catherine went to the opposite end of the oval table, placed her hands on the back of her chair and said,

"The Goddess is here. Please be seated."

They all pulled their chairs back and sat, fluffing their robes, in almost perfect synchronization. They placed their hands in their laps. Gabrielle carefully did the same. No one reached for the scrambled eggs, bacon, waffles and strawberries.

"I forget whose turn it is," Catherine said, "It's been such a long time."

"Me," Samantha said.

"Are you ready?"

"Yes."

Samantha closed her eyes and held both her hands over the table. Gislaine took her right hand. Gabrielle pushed up her long sleeve and took her left. Samantha's hand was warm and smooth and she gripped Gabrielle's hand hard enough to make her gasp. Audra reached out and clasped Gabrielle's left hand. She closed her eyes. Then Rushel and Catherine and Gislaine linked. Rushel made a sound like a sigh.

Gabrielle closed her eyes also and thought, is Rushel crying? The wind gusted and something skittered across the roof. She felt Audra's hand clench in surprise.

"After so long," Samantha said, "we are now complete. Everyone can feel it. We who were lost have now been found. The loneliness and wandering of the human beings has finally come to an end here in the world we have created. We know as long as our circle remains unbroken we will be protected from evil. We give thanks for the wonderful bounty we are about to receive. May we be ever mindful of your love for us, our Creator, and may our hearts and arms always be open to each other. So shall it be until the end of our days."

Gabrielle heard Audra whisper, "So shall it be." Then the others murmured it.

"So shall it be," Gabrielle said clearly and opened her eyes.

They were all looking at her and smiling. Gabrielle thought Samantha looked particularly happy.

"Thank you, Goddess," Rushel said softly and sniffed.

There was a long silence. Finally, Catherine said, "Food's getting cold."

Still no one moved.

Hmm, Gabrielle thought. She took two biscuits from under the white towel covered dish. "These look so good, Catherine, thank you."

They dug in. Audra took the silver spoon from the scrambled eggs before Rushel could and Gislaine snagged a waffle with her fork. It was the biggest waffle Gabrielle had ever seen. There were purple splotches.

Gislaine put three pieces of bacon on the waffle, which filled her plate, and covered the whole thing with syrup from a tall porcelain cup.

Samantha got a waffle and a biscuit, with her bare hands, and then spooned strawberries onto it. She poured out only a small amount of syrup, avoiding the strawberries, and saturated the biscuit. She drank her orange juice in one gulp and moved the butter next to Gabrielle plate.

"Would you care for raspberry jam?" she asked.

"No seeds," Catherine said.

"Yes, thank you." Gabrielle split one of her biscuits and buttered it. She took a big bite. The biscuit was crispy and had a soft steamy inside. And the butter. Gabrielle licked her lips and had a sip of coffee.

"That's real butter," Catherine said. "Surprising, huh?"

"Um hum," Audra and Rushel both said with full mouths. They had plates full of scrambled eggs and bacon. Audra was putting more pepper on her eggs.

Gabrielle laughed. "I've never tasted anything like it. I just used way too much." She spread raspberry jam on one half of a biscuit.

"You're fine," Catherine said. "What else would you like?"

Gabrielle saw Catherine had nothing on her plate. She started to formulate a sentence about how Catherine should eat something first but she knew there was no arguing with her.

"I'd like one of those waffles."

Samantha put down her fork and passed the serving dish. The dish was a piece of white ceramic, surprisingly light, and not really cookware at all. More like an industrial artifact, Gabrielle thought. There was a square piece of wood glued to the bottom as a base. She slid a waffle onto her plate and passed the fascinating dish back, feeling edge with her fingernail. Not glass, she thought. She saw Catherine and Gislaine exchange a glance. She didn't care. Her mouth was watering.

Samantha passed the bowl of strawberries. Two spoonfuls were perfect. And then just a little syrup, a light amber substance. With her fork (which was heavy, maybe real silver?) she cut off a piece with a purple spot and put it in her mouth. The purple part was tangy and sweet in a way that was brighter than the syrup, which had its own flavor. The inside of her mouth puckered.

"This is delicious, Catherine."

"Thank you."

"Yes," Samantha said. "Thank you for breakfast."

All of the others said thank you, mumbling around their food.

"You are all more than welcome. When everyone's talking with their mouth full, I know I did a good job. Goddess, do you like the syrup?" She scooped out a helping of scrambled eggs and got two pieces of bacon. Audra passed her the salt and pepper.

"Real maple syrup?"

"You've had it before?"

"No, just guessed. Oh, and those are blueberries, aren't they?"

"Yes indeedy."

Gabrielle drank half her cup of coffee. "This is all so good." She drank the whole glass of orange juice, more tangy than sweet. Then she finished the waffle and sopped up the syrup with a biscuit.

Samantha, only halfway through her waffle, passed Gabrielle the coffee percolator and then the large bowl of scrambled eggs. "There's some bacon left," she said.

"Thanks." Gabrielle refilled her coffee cup and then got scrambled eggs and two strips of bacon, and another biscuit.

"The Goddess was hungry," Catherine said as she sipped her juice. "I guess dinner was kind of light last night."

Gabrielle ate the scrambled eggs in two large mouthfuls and then a piece of bacon almost without tasting it. "Don't know why I'm so hungry. I hardly ever eat breakfast."

"From what I've seen you hardly eat anything."

"We'll fix you up," Audra said. "Lots of times there's not much to do around here except eat. And, well, you know."

"For pity's sake," Rushel blurted. "Is that all you think about?"

"Your unsolicited question invades my privacy."

"It does what?"

"You heard me."

Gabrielle swallowed the last of her bacon. "No fighting at the table."

Audra stared at her and Rushel frowned. Catherine glared at them both.

"I'm serious. This is a new rule. Also." She thought for a second. "There will be no mention of bodily functions while eating."

"Ah," Samantha said. "Good one."

Audra said, "Yes, Goddess," then she smiled smugly at Rushel who looked straight at her.

"Yes," Rushel said. "Goddess." She tried to smile but wound up making a face at Audra.

"Ah, ah!" Audra said. "Don't!"

Rushel pushed back in her chair. "May I be excused?"

Gabrielle made sure to keep a straight face. "You may."

Rushel plopped her napkin beside her plate, stood, and went to the middle room. Gabrielle heard the bathroom door slam.

Audra turned to her. "Oh my ..." she got out before Gabrielle held up a finger.

"And no talking about people behind their backs."

Audra sighed. "Well, hell."

"No," Gabrielle said. "None of us. Outsiders, okay."

Audra nodded.

"See," Samantha said. "She's good."

Audra squinted at her. "Of course she's good." Then to Gabrielle, "I'm pre-law. My advisor Dr. Athanasayu says I'm a pistol. I do get carried away sometimes. Would you like my last piece of bacon?"

Gislaine set down her fork and got up. "Be right back." She followed Rushel into the middle bathroom.

"Thanks," Gabrielle said. The bacon was crispy and salty and melted in her mouth. While she was chewing, Audra started talking.

"Rushel and I have been best friends since second grade. Rushel is a genius. One day, back then, they gave her an IQ test. They couldn't believe it. One ninety-one." She nodded at Gabrielle widened eyes. "They made her take it again. One ninety-one. Her parents were devastated. I know, crazy, but they saw being smart as a handicap for a girl. Smart girls don't have boyfriends. They stay home on prom night. They don't have weddings or make grandchildren. Interestingly, these stupid ideas of theirs have proven useful, but that's another story. They took little Rushel to a psychologist all the way over in Tacoma and gave her a different type of IQ test. One ninety-six. The story was, her mother punched out the doctor. Might be true.

"Rushel gets interested in something and just tears into it. Then she gets bored and drops it. Her grandmother is from Poland so she taught herself Polish. Gislaine's grandmother is from Japan so Rushel taught herself Japanese. God knows what else. I don't think she's ever gotten interested in technical stuff or math to any extent. Your field. But she might. She could. She always surprising me."

Gabrielle could only nod and sip her coffee.

"This is all her invention," Audra said. "Our culture, you could say. I'm breaking your rule here."

"That's about backbiting. I hate that."

Audra looked at Samantha and they both nodded.

"Agreed," Audra said. "M." She stopped.

"We've said next to nothing about M," Catherine said. "Or L." She looked at Samantha and Audra with uncertainty. "Gabrielle, I mean Goddess."

Gabrielle raised her eyebrows.

"How would you like to proceed?"

"How do you mean?"

"I promised you that all would be revealed. Would you like that now?"

Gabrielle set down her cup. "Well, Audra's little trick almost put me in the hospital. I've been beaten up twice in my jogging class. And in the front room you have a titanium box that once contained eighty thousand dollars' worth of gold coins." She had to pause because Samantha was laughing. "Now being used as a doorstop. If I'm going to be Goddess, I would like to know as much as possible."

"All right." Catherine turned and yelled, "You two get out here!" She stood up and gathered her dishes. She said to Gabrielle, "I want everyone to know what's being said. I don't want anyone to feel excluded. Slighted. Insulted." She gulped the last of her coffee. "Etcetera."

Samantha reached over and gathered Gabrielle's plate and silverware. She stacked them on top of her own and did the same with Gislaine's. Audra piled her dishes on Rushel's and said to Gabrielle, "The Goddess doesn't lift a finger."

Within sixty seconds they had the breakfast table cleared off leaving only the silver coffee pot. They placed everything in the corner sink and quietly retook their seats. Catherine walked around to refill Gabrielle's cup with the last of the coffee.

"Hey, you two," she said not quite as loudly. "We're doing it now."

Gabrielle heard the toilet flush and giggling as the bathroom door opened. Gislaine, carrying her notebook, slid back into her seat and folded her hands on the table. Rushel pulled back her chair with a thump. She cleared her throat.

"I would like to apologize," she said, "to Gabrielle, for my bad behavior. It was very immature of me."

Audra, elbows on her placemat, covered her mouth with both hands while Samantha squinted at her.

Gabrielle nodded and said, "Apology accepted."

"Good," Catherine said. "First thing, we need to tell her about the names."

"Yes," Rushel said. "Before there's an accident."

Gabrielle thought, did I hear that right? Names?

Samantha began. "We all have secret names. Your secret name is known to everyone but you. You must never hear your own secret name."

"Never," Rushel said.

"At some point," Audra said, "we will all come up to you and tell you one of the other's secret name. This way, you will learn them all."

"But not yours," Samantha said.

"You must *never* hear your own secret name," Audra said.

"If you do," Rushel said. "The world will end."

"End?" Gabrielle blinked. "Okay."

"We already have your name figured out," Audra said. "And it's perfect."

"It's the best one," Rushel said.

"It took us forever," Gislaine said.

"It kind of gave us goosebumps," Catherine said.

Gabrielle began to say, "But, can..."

"No," Audra said.

"Forget it," Samantha said.

"The world would end instantly," Rushel said. "Ka-blooey."

"All right. You really know how to make life intriguing."

"It's kind of our main thing, huh?" Audra said.

Gabrielle nodded vigorously.

"Good," Catherine said. "I think that the one who has been with M the longest should begin."

Gislaine folded her hands on her notebook. "That would be me."

"Gislaine and her notebooks," Catherine said.

"Sylvan historian," Rushel said.

Gislaine's dark eyes flashed. "Our way of life is coming to an end. You all know it. Maybe someone will want to read about us one day."

No one spoke for a long moment. Gabrielle sensed they all agreed with her.

"I'll try to keep it simple," Gislaine said. "M was born in nineteen thirty-six in the area of Los Angeles known as Hollywood. Her father was an executive at a movie studio and her mother worked in an office there. As a child M was, as she herself put it, holy hell. She ran away so many times she lost count. She said she came to know the cops better than her parents. She went to Hollywood High School and when it was time to graduate – with a G.P.A. of three point nine seven – her mom and dad gave her an ultimatum. Enroll at UCLA as an art or home economics major, meet a nice young man and get married. Or get a job at the studio, meet a nice young man and get married.

"So naturally, the day before her graduation, she ran away. But not before she slugged her father in the face and knocked out one of his teeth. It was a famous incident at the time. They even made a movie based on it. *The Tornado*, starring William Holden, nineteen fifty-six. I've never seen it.

"She disappeared quite professionally. She managed to elude all the private investigators sent after her until nineteen fifty-eight. She was living in New York City, in SoHo, and had just turned twenty-one and there was absolutely nothing they could force her to do. So, since it was now of her own free will, she came back home with several of her New York friends, and started college. UCLA. She lived on her own and paid her own way. She majored in," she smiled at Gabrielle, "Physics."

"What?" Gabrielle said.

"Surprising, huh?" Audra said.

"Well, I wondered about all the technical books."

"Yes, it get crazier."

Gabrielle sipped her cold coffee and Gislaine continued.

"M at twenty-one was very attractive. Extremely attractive. And she had other qualities. 'Ineffable', as Hitchcock put it once. Big time producers and directors sought her out and she told them all to get stuffed. She absolutely avoided cameras and wanted no part of the movie business. The climax came in nineteen sixty, when she was talked into going to a party in the Hollywood hills. A producer of certain, shall we say, adult entertainment offered her a huge sum of money to be in one of his pictures. A very special picture, he told her, something fairly new. All female. According to people who were there, M listened to this guy describe the excellent career and marketing possibilities. She nodded and smiled the whole time, then took a lighter out of her pocket, flicked it, and lit his tie on fire. Polyester. The flames tickled his nose before he realized what was happening.

"There were repercussions. M's friends handled them. And show business never bothered her again.

"Bachelor's in physics, nineteen sixty-one. Master's in nineteen sixty-three. And finally, nineteen sixty-five, PhD in Astrophysics, UCLA. Space was the happening thing. She walked right into a job with a large aerospace company that had very lucrative high profile contracts with the federal government. I'm not sure what she did there. M had never talked about that period at the company except for two times."

"Hang on," Audra said. "Are you okay, Goddess?"

"She's a little glassy-eyed," Samantha said.

Gabrielle shook her head. "I'm trying to get used to the idea of M having a PhD in Physics."

"Piled higher and deeper," Audra said.

"Anything is possible," Rushel said.

Gislaine said, "One day, M and I were watching a special on tv about the Apollo program. This was in Long Beach."

The others all nodded.

"M watched that show with an intensity I had never seen before. When the program got to the part about Apollo 8 orbiting the moon for the first time, M turned to me and said, 'You're welcome,' and left the room.

"That was one time. The only other time, M was on a company retreat and she met the only other woman in the science division, a biologist we shall call L. One week later, they moved in together. It was that apartment in Laguna." She turned to her left. "I showed you once."

Samantha smiled.

"They fell in love. I guess. And not long after that, in the spring of nineteen-sixty-nine, they got married." She paused.

"Wow," Gabrielle said in surprise. "I wouldn't have expected that. Who'd they get married to?"

Gislaine said, "They married each other."

Gabrielle thought she wasn't understanding it. "M married L?"

"Yes."

She continued to think about it. "Two women can marry each other?"

"You can do anything you want," Samantha said.

"Okay, but I didn't know you could do that. Officially."

"You can't," Audra said. "It was a private thing."

"Yes," Rushel said.

"A private agreement between two people is just a contract," Audra said. "A contract can be anything, even marriage. Assuming whoever wrote the contract is good."

Gabrielle found the whole idea mind boggling and a little scary. "So, was there a wedding?"

"Oh, yes," Gislaine said. "They pretty much went by the book. All the planning. Invitations. Flowers. Cake with two brides on top."

"Wow."

"There was someone they knew in Laguna who could perform the ceremony. Over a hundred people came. They wore identical wedding dresses. Navy blue. It took place on Aliso Beach on a Monday because that's the first day of the week. Symbolically, the first day of their new lives. And when the ceremony was complete, they both signed the contract."

"Their fates were sealed," Rushel said.

"They had the reception at this big house owned by a friend of L's, a mansion on the edge of a cliff. It's still there, I think."

"I've seen it," Samantha said.

"You've *seen* it?" Gislaine said in alarm.

"Don't worry, I didn't knock."

Gislaine shook her head. "That was dangerous."

"Danger is Samantha's middle name," Catherine said. "It's not her secret name, however."

"No, it's not," Gislaine said with a grin to Samantha's eye rolling. "The reception lasted all night and then all the next day and looked to just keep going. Then on the second night, other people started to show up. Strangers. Scary people. The impression was, these were people L knew. And then what happened, happened."

Gabrielle set down her coffee. Gislaine looked suddenly uncomfortable.

"This was the spring of sixty-nine. No one knew anything. It was pretty much the peak of the sixties. No one could have guessed." She took a deep breath. "There was an incident. Four people died. All women. One was M's friend from New York. They were found at the bottom of the cliff, on the rocks, on the morning of the third day. The police called it an accident. This was impossible. There was no way to simply fall. The cliff isn't that steep. They had to have been dragged down a trail, invisible from above, and thrown over. No motive. No reason at all."

"God, that's sickening," Gabrielle said.

"And, of course, the scary strangers were nowhere to be found. No one knew their names, where they were from, nothing. They vanished completely. No arrests ever made.

"L seemed to pretty much take it all in stride."

"Huh," Audra said. "That so."

"But the effect on M was huge. It was too much. There was no getting over it. So the Sunday after the wedding she ran away. Gone. No one knew where she was for an entire year. She has never talked about it. Not to anyone."

Gislaine looked almost resentful, Gabrielle thought.

"Then she reappeared, reconnected with L. Then they broke up.

Reconnected. Broke up. This phase lasted through nineteen seventy-two, when M seemed to want to settle down. So she got married again. This time, officially, to a man we refer to as T. He was a big wheel at a gigantic aerospace company. Lots of government deals. He was very well off."

"You left out the best part," Audra said.

"I didn't leave it out. I'm just getting to it."

"Good."

Gislaine sighed. "When M married T, there was one condition M insisted on. The marriage had to include L."

"He married *both* of them?" Gabrielle said in surprise.

"The original contract was still in force," Audra said.

"Pretty complicated," Catherine said.

"So L was included in a contractual way. Privately."

"I doubt M had to talk him into it. T knew what he wanted. And he got it, good and hard."

Catherine and Rushel almost laughed.

"That's Mencken."

"Wanting and having," Samantha said.

"A permanent three-way," Audra said. "You will not be surprised to learn that T is no longer alive."

"Oh, that's awful," Gabrielle said. "Poor M."

"No," Rushel, Catherine, Gislaine, and Samantha all said together.

"I shouldn't laugh," Gabrielle said, choking.

"No, you can laugh," Audra said.

"You're right. That's complicated." Physics is easy compared to this, Gabrielle thought. This is way beyond me.

"So M gets married for the second time in seventy-two and T passed away in early seventy-four."

"Heart attack," Audra said, looking sideways at Gabrielle. "In bed."

"Awful."

Gislaine continued. "So what happened was, in his will T left the entire estate to M. Thirty million. L got ten thousand dollars. That's it. A kick in the face. L contested the will but got nowhere. The court did not recognize her contract as being valid."

"The judge refused to even look at the actual contract," Audra said. "He said such a thing is plainly illegal. She was completely shut out."

"I'll bet she was upset," Gabrielle said.

"Little bit," Catherine said.

"M felt terrible and offered her a million dollars cash," Gislaine said. "L would not take it. M offered her half of the estate. Fifty-fifty. L said no. So M offered her everything, all of it, thirty million, retaining just a small amount to live on. That's all. I think the figure was twelve thousand bucks. She could relocate. Start over."

"L said, 'Fuck you,'" Audra said.

"So M said,"

"'*Fuck you*,'" Rushel whispered.

"L disappeared. Vanished. M said the suspense was like waiting for the thunderbolt which didn't come. And didn't come. And then."

"It came," Rushel said.

"On a Wednesday morning in the summer of seventy-five," Samantha said, "all of M's bank and brokerage accounts were emptied. This accounted for about twenty-five percent of the total assets. The rest of the money was held in three trust funds in separate institutions in Switzerland. Ten million each. She was to have the first fund distributed to her at age forty, the second at fifty, and the last at age sixty."

"Set for life," Audra said.

"Samantha's an accountant," Catherine said. "Much better than her previous profession."

"Yes, it is," Samantha said. "The money had somehow been transferred. Those old gentlemen managing the trusts were blindsided. They never had a chance. One of them died soon after."

"L killed that guy," Audra said. "Sure as shit."

"So on Thursday," Samantha said, "M was left with the following. There was a half-built house above Pasadena. The money to build it had been placed in an escrow account that L did not know about. We don't know what happened there yet, but M must have lost control of it somehow. I'm not well versed in real estate. It was new construction. L maybe subverted the title company. She could do that. I'm guessing M destroyed the house to keep it out of her hands."

Gabrielle looked at Samantha, wide-eyed. "M did it?"

"Probably. Then there's this house where we now live, purchased with cash which T gave to M for her birthday, the first after their marriage. Twenty-five thousand. L got the same amount on her birthday. She spent it on jewelry. M was thinking about teaching and I know at least talked to people here about an assistant professorship. It hasn't worked out yet, but she fell in love with this area."

"M believes in real estate," Gislaine said.

"M squirreled away all she could when she started to get nervous about her second marriage. She accumulated five thousand, give or take. And she had her own checking account."

"M does not believe in joint accounts," Audra said.

"The trusts weren't completely emptied," Samantha said. "L, in her pycho-ness, left her ten thousand dollars in each. M received the first distribution in seventy-six. And that's it. L got all the money and all the power."

"And we got the brains," Catherine said.

They all looked at Gabrielle.

"Which got back some of her money," Audra said.

Catherine started laughing. She knocked over her coffee cup.

Gislaine looked at her. "What?"

Catherine had to wipe her eyes. She coughed and pointed at Gabrielle.

Gabrielle felt her cheeks burning but she almost laughed, too. "I know where there is another of those little safes. And I know exactly how to get it. It would be easy."

"Goddess," Audra and Rushel said.

"Two of them," Gislaine said.

"Over a hundred thousand," Samantha said. "In gold."

"It's in a locker in the old gym."

"The clock tower building? What's it doing in there?" Rushel said.

"Don't know. It's just where she had it."

"Who?"

"Holly."

"*What?*"

"It's in Holly's locker."

"Oh my God."

"And you know how to open Holly's locker, Audra said thoughtfully," Audra said.

"Her locker is right next to mine. I saw her open it on the day she beat me up. So I know the combination."

"Um, I feel like I'm missing some information," Audra said.

"She can do that," Catherine said. "If she saw whorebitch open the thing."

"I play it back in my mind."

"No shit," Audra said skeptically.

"It's true," Catherine said. "I've seen her do it."

"Okay, I believe you."

"Good. You should always believe me."

"I do."

Rushel sighed. "So you know where it is?"

Gabrielle nodded. "It's Sunday morning. We'd be the only ones in the place."

"Yeah," Rushel said as she thought. "I doubt the building's locked. We're going, right? We have to be at work at ten."

"Tennis," Audra said. "Perfect for a nice Sunday morning."

"I love tennis," Rushel said.

Rushel got two tennis racquets from Audra's closet and a can of green tennis balls.

"I'll come with you," Samantha said. "I think I should."

"Okay. Good," Gabrielle said. "I don't how to play tennis."

"Gosh, I don't think anyone does," Rushel said.

"We just make up games," Audra said. "Rushel is really good at that."

"Or we just play," Rushel said.

Gabrielle couldn't help smiling. "Then this will be fun." It might actually be, she thought.

They all changed clothes. Gabrielle took off her now somewhat smelly silk pajamas, threw on her t-shirt and wiggled into her jeans. She really wanted to wash her underwear, the silk panties, but there wasn't time.

She decided not to wear socks and slipped her deck shoes over her bare feet. She rinsed her glasses in the bathroom sink and brushed her hair with a brush with a wooden handle she found in a drawer. The name *Fuller* was printed on it. She checked her watch. 7:15. She found her sweatshirt under the bed.

In the kitchen, Catherine and Gislaine were sitting at the table, sipping coffee.

"Are you really going?" Catherine said. "You really need to be careful."

"At the first sign," Gislaine said, "the very first sign of trouble, just get out of there."

"We're not trying to tell the Goddess what to do," Catherine said.

"That gym is enemy territory."

"I got that impression," Gabrielle said.

Catherine stood up, something in her hand. "Close your eyes and open your mouth."

Gabrielle did so and smelled something hot and sugary. A crispy flaky éclair was in her mouth and she bit down reflexively. Coffee and chocolate. "Thum mie," she said and opened her eyes.

"I don't know how to spell that," Gislaine said over her pen.

Gabrielle locked eyes with Catherine as she ate the éclair. Then she zipped up her sweatshirt and went to the library where the others were waiting at the wide open front door. The wind gusted outside. There was sand all over the hardwood floor. Rushel and Audra were both wearing jeans and white athletic shoes and both had on the new jackets acquired by Catherine at the rude department store. What Samantha was wearing surprised her. It was a two piece tunic, beautiful dove gray, the sleeves long and loose, the bottoms belted at her waist with what looked like a length of cotton rope. Her hair reached straight to her ankles. She had on sandals seemingly fashioned from interleaved strips of leather which spiraled up her calves. She looked at Gabrielle with a smile.

"How are you feeling, Goddess?"

Rushel looked worried. Audra was serious.

Gabrielle felt strong and energized and turned on. "This makes me uneasy."

"Yes."

"There's no rhyme or reason for Holly to have that box in her locker," Gabrielle said.

"Yes, there is."

Gabrielle thought. "She wanted me to see it."

"Right."

"Then it's probably empty," Rushel said. "If it's even still there."

"Or maybe that how L pays her," Audra said. "Untraceable."

Gabrielle thought for a moment. "We have to check. We go straight in and open the locker. If it's empty or gone or anything looks wrong we get the hell out."

Rushel and Audra nodded. Samantha stared out the door.

"If it's there but empty we take it anyway," she said.

"Then they'll know we know," Audra said.

"Would that be bad?"

"Let's think about it," Gabrielle said. She went through the door and pulled her keys out. She scratched sand on the porch with her shoes.

"We can take my car, if you want," Audra said.

The sky above was gray, the western horizon glowed. Samantha's tunic rippled and dark strands of her hair swung out. Gabrielle's hair whipped around her face. Rushel kept a hand on the back of her neck but her blonde hair flew out of control.

"Okay," Gabrielle said. Raindrops stung her cheeks.

"Wait," Samantha said. "Gabrielle's car might get a better reaction if they see it."

"I'm sure they know her car," Audra said.

"But Gabrielle is still kind of neutral. She wouldn't inspire the reaction your car would from certain people."

"And what reaction would that be?" Audra said, hands on hips.

"Instantaneous out of control rage."

Audra grinned. "Yeah."

Rushel pushed past them. "It's already almost eight. I'm freezing. Come on."

They went to Gabrielle's VW. Samantha insisted on driving and after hesitating Gabrielle handed her the keys and climbed into the back seat beside Audra. Samantha started the engine, using the choke correctly, and shifted into reverse without problem. They backed up alongside the walled in patio, then rolled forward. On the narrow sandy road through the chaparral, Samantha smiled at Gabrielle in the mirror. She held it in first.

"Don't worry. I'm good at this." She rolled the window all the way down, something Gabrielle never did.

"You're the first person I've ever let drive my car. After my dad."

Samantha nodded. At the gate, Rushel got out and walked it open. She closed it behind them and hopped back in. "I can drive, too."

"Yes you can," Audra said, shaking her head.

"All you need is a car." Samantha wound up the engine and powered through the sand trap. On the pavement, she shifted to second. Gabrielle got between the two front seats to see better.

"Speed limit's twenty-five."

"I know." Samantha slipped it into third.

"The part through the old trees drop back to second and go to third when you pass the new houses."

"Okay. Runs real smooth."

"I adjust the valves every four thousand miles."

"You do it?" Audra asked.

"Sure. I taught myself."

"Wow."

"It's pretty easy."

"If you're mechanical, I guess."

"A mechanical Goddess," Rushel said.

"Could you show me how to adjust the things on my car?"

"Sure. We just need to get the book. There's probably one for your Toyota."

"That would be so *cool*. I can't afford to take it anywhere."

"We could give it a tune up."

The road of cracked asphalt, faded to gray, dipped through the groove of eucalyptus. They drove over strips of chalk-white bark peeled from the trees by the wind.

They encountered no other cars until they came out of the trees. A huge silver Eldorado, so wide Samantha had to jog the Volkswagen to avoid the big side mirrors, careened past them and powered back into the grove. The driver was a middle-aged woman wearing an elaborate necklace. She frowned at them as she flew past.

"Hm," Audra said. "Looked full."

"Real estate people," Rushel said.

"They all looked kind of young," Samantha said. "The people in the back."

"Buying up everything," Audra said, "and putting up big no trespassing signs."

"The lady driving seemed a little upset," Rushel said.

"There's no real estate back there where they're going. Just the state park. Probably looking for a place to make a u-turn," Samantha said.

"And there isn't one until you get all the way to the beach," Audra said. "How many miles is that?"

"Poor things. We mustn't laugh at them," Rushel said.

"No, we mustn't. However, did you see the way she looked at us?"

Rushel nodded. "Bitch."

"Bitch."

Samantha shifted to third, laughing, and they passed houses clinging to nearly vertical hillsides above and below them.

"Would you build a house stuck on a cliff like that?" Audra said.

"Great view," Rushel said.

"I like the beach."

"Our house is wonderful," Gabrielle said.

Both Rushel and Audra cocked their heads minutely. Our house.

Gabrielle sat back. Samantha obviously wasn't going to wreck her car. She was even managing the windshield wipers correctly, switching them off when the rain let up instead of just letting them run on dry glass. Gabrielle realized she was beginning to trust her.

That makes two, she thought.

Gabrielle studied the world outside. She was hardly ever a passenger in a car.

The road ran out of the hills and onto the valley floor, flanked by volcanic ridges and rolling grassland, green and wet. The sky was alive with clouds, swift gray on gray. The wind from the open driver's window tousled her hair and tickled her eyelashes. She tried to keep her hands still. They're doing it again, she thought. They're looking to me.

She watched the winter landscape of the central California coast pass by and attempted to calm the flutters in her stomach. The cool air helped. She breathed deeply. There were flowers somewhere.

The density of the houses gradually increased. They passed the borders of the town. They made the turns into the university. Gabrielle noticed the tension in the others.

"Go slow," Audra said. "If we see one of them, duck down, Goddess."

"Okay."

"Put your head in my lap. You'll be safe."

"No she won't," Rushel said.

"Perfectly safe. You want to test it?"

Gabrielle could tell Audra was nervous.

"Yeah, let's test it."

This made Audra open her mouth in surprise. Gabrielle turned around in the seat.

"We're here," Samantha said.

"Well, hell."

The upper parking lot was completely empty. Samantha pulled into a space a row back from the south end, which overlooked the library and the old gym, the grass plaza and walkways. There were no people visible. The west side of the campus was swept by broken clouds. The rain had not started.

"This is good," Samantha said. "No one can see us up here."

They all got out and Samantha gave the key back to Gabrielle. She made sure the car was locked. There was a large oak tree and a thick hedge in the corner of the lot, close to the concrete stairs which led down to the library level.

"Would've been a good idea to do a scan of the other parking lots," Samantha remarked.

"It'll be all right. We're here now," Gabrielle said

"If you want, I can go down first. See if anyone pops up."

"We should stick together. Let's go straight there, fast as possible. Get in, get out."

"Goddess," Samantha said. She looked hard at the other buildings, her long black hair blowing. English building. Engineering West. The cast-concrete edifice of Architecture. Gabrielle tried to follow her gaze. The campus was full of shadows.

They started down the steps. Gabrielle kept her eyes forward. Audra carried the case in her arms. They reached the bottom and went past the dumpsters. They crossed the windswept plaza. No one appeared. The clock on the tower above stood at *8:44.*

The gym doors were propped open, black openings where nothing moved. Gabrielle felt the others hesitate, even Samantha. She strode to the doors without pausing and entered the old gym.

Inside it was quiet. No voices, no slamming lockers. Their footsteps echoed. The air was scented with Pine Sol and dirty socks. The fishbowl office, directly ahead, was dark and empty. She went around the partition wall and then down the aisle along the rows of forest green lockers. All the fluorescents were off but there was plenty of light coming from the milky windows high up at the edge of the ceiling. At the third row, she turned left and went almost to the end. They were just a few feet from the wall of white tile that surrounded the showers. Samantha went past her and looked over the wall. She turned back and nodded. No one there.

They all came close behind. Gabrielle's locker was on top, second to the end, Holly's next door on the left. She grabbed Holly's lock, a chrome Master with a black dial. She spun the dial to the right several times around and stopped on eight.

Samantha appeared at her right elbow, glanced at the lock, then faced out, still scanning. She let her arms hang at her sides, her hands hidden in the long sleeves. Audra stood at the other end of the row, also scanning. Gabrielle felt Rushel looking over her shoulder as she turned the dial left one turn and stopped at twenty-five. Then carefully right to eleven.

She pulled on it. No good. The rattling echoed in the high ceiling.

"Try it again," Rushel whispered.

"No." Gabrielle spun the dial again to the right. "Twenty-six next."

"You said you knew it!"

"Her thumb got in the way." *Eight.* "Twenty-five to thirty-one for the second number." *Twenty-six.* "Okay." *Eleven.*

No good.

"Oh my God," Rushel muttered.

"People coming!" Audra whispered fiercely.

Gabrielle heard female laughter outside the main doors. She started over. "Twenty-seven now."

"It would be good if you hurried," Samantha said calmly.

Gabrielle yanked on the lock. It held firm.

"You messed that one up," Rushel said. "Try that one over."

"Negative." *Twenty-eight.*

"Oh, shit," Audra said. "Don't you smell it? *Subterfuge.*"

Music started playing. A pretty good portable cassette player, Gabrielle thought absently. It was a disco song, the volume was suddenly cranked up to maximum, and the speakers sounded like they were ripping themselves to shreds.

"Disco Tex and the Sexolettes," Audra said flatly. "*Get Dancin'.*"

Gabrielle, hands shaking, got the dial to eleven again and pulled. Nothing. Female voices were at the doors. She heard hard shoes scuffing the concrete floor. She spun the dial and overshot eight. Start over.

"We're dead," Audra said.

The music moved closer. It was inside, bouncing off the ceiling and the hanging lights. It moved up the aisle towards them.

Gabrielle held her breath. She could smell that perfume, stronger than the sweaty socks. It was instantly familiar.

Twenty-nine, then eleven. The lock fell open.

Gabrielle took the lock off, lifted the latch up with a loud clank not quite masked by the blaring music, opened the locker door, and looked inside. She closed it, trying to be quieter, and put the lock back on.

"What?" Rushel whispered in a panic.

"Nothing there. Nothing. Let's go."

The music was right around the corner in the showers. The tile walls made competing echoes. Samantha backed up and bumped into her. She heard Audra sigh loudly. Someone giggled. She could just see over Samantha's shoulder.

Three people, back-lit by the high windows, came around the corner. The one in the lead was wearing a black wool sweater and a black skirt. Black running shoes. She was holding one of the titanium safes in her hands like a book. Behind her was a woman in an identical sweater and skirt and beside her, a woman in black jeans and a black leather jacket. Gabrielle saw that this one was wearing boots with sharply pointed toes. She felt her stomach lurch.

The woman with the safe had a red, swollen nose. The tiny silver ring was still there. She held her hand up languidly and the music was cut off.

"Oh, hi, Patricia," Gabrielle said quickly, a deflection maneuver. She kept her voice low in an attempt to mask the fear she was feeling. "Hi Debbie. Hi Holly." She knew at least one of the Susans was directly behind her, with another around the corner with a – what was it called – a boombox. Audra was right about the smell. *Subterfuge*, about a gallon, and lots of cigarette smoke. Samantha was holding perfectly still, half blocking Patricia's view of her and almost completely blocking Holly's.

"What's up?" The perfume was about to make her sneeze.

"You creeps looking for this?" Patricia held up the metal box.

"What are you talking about? What is that?"

"Oh, Little Miss Genius, I think you know what it is."

"I was looking for my socks. We were going to play tennis."

Gabrielle saw Patricia's eyes dart to her feet. One for me, she thought. She also saw Holly's expression flash from sneering triumph to angry and bored and she sensed an advantage. "Sorry I hit you but you started it."

"You almost broke my nose."

"You slammed my head against the locker."

The Susan behind her giggled and Patricia sighed in annoyance.

Holly suddenly smiled. "I have an idea, Patricia. Would you like me to almost break Gabrielle's nose?"

Gabrielle perceived all of Samantha's muscles tense up and then just as quickly relax. Samantha's head turned towards Holly.

Holly's smile faltered, regrouped, grew intense.

Samantha flexed her fingers and her hands became fists. She moved to the right placing herself in front of Holly, who looked away from her. Indifferent, Gabrielle thought. But then she pushed her hair back with both hands and waved. The music started up again, very loud.

Holly took a deep breath and raised her left hand. She extended her middle finger to Samantha. Samantha took a small step forward and tipped her head to the side to clear her hair from her shoulders. Her right arm cocked back, her fist just visible poking out of the gray sleeve.

Those speaker are going to *melt*, Gabrielle thought. She fought the urge to run. Someone yelled and she gasped.

"Oh my God!" It was Audra.

Holly's smile vanished and she turned away and looked down. The music stopped again.

Audra came past Gabrielle and got in front of Samantha.

"Holly! Look at me. Who the hell do you think you are?"

Holly could not raise her eyes.

"Do you have any idea how embarrassing this is? How dare you threaten to hit Gabrielle?"

Holly managed to say, "I..."

"I don't care. You understand? There is no excuse."

Holly turned her head from side to side, refusing to look at Audra straight on. Her eyes were wide. Audra put her hands on her hips and stared at her.

Gabrielle saw that Patricia seemed angry and shook her head.

"Do you think this is a game?" Audra said with a bit more volume. "Listen. Listen to me."

Holly dropped her hands to her sides. Gabrielle saw her jaw twitch. She seemed to be looking at Audra's shoes.

"Good," Audra said. "We are not getting back together. It's over. We are never getting back together. Holly, I don't love you. Are you listening? I do not love you."

Holly took another deep breath and Gabrielle could hear a shudder. She started to say something and stopped.

Patricia, also looking down, uttered a word.

Debbie and Susan watched, frozen.

Audra said, "I admit."

Gabrielle could see her trying to psych herself up.

"I admit there was a time when I loved you. It was a long time ago. I moved on and I no longer love you. It's like disco, right? Disco was everything and now disco is over. Completely over. Our relationship is *over*. You should move on also, okay?"

Gabrielle was astonished to see tears in Holly's eyes. She said, clear and low, "I will always love you."

"No," Audra said firmly.

"Always." Holly raised her head fully. "Always."

"I want you to get out of here. Stop bothering my friends. Go on."

Holly turned away, hesitated, then walked quickly down the shower wall. Gabrielle heard her sniffle. Her footsteps faded.

Patricia shook her head slowly. Debbie, eyes red, left to follow Holly. Susan came around Audra to take her place.

Samantha said, "We should be going," and with her arm gestured to Gabrielle, ushering her back. Patricia simply watched them until they got to the other end of the lockers. The clock on the tower somewhere above began counting eight.

"I know you took it," she said.

Gabrielle did not blink. "Still don't know what you're talking about."

No one spoke until they reached the car out in the fresh air.

Rushel said, "Wow, Audra," and rubbed her eyes.

"You all owe me a million dollars."

"No problem," Gabrielle said and unlocked the doors. Samantha's knees bumped the button on the glove compartment. The little door popped open and papers slid out.

"Sorry." She gathered everything in her lap, a collection of maps and a receipt for tires and an unopened envelope.

"Wait," Gabrielle said. "That's the note from my landlady. Forgot all about it."

"This?"

"Never mind. Just stick it back in there. Not in the mood for Mrs. Rosenberg."

Gabrielle glanced in the mirror. Audra was sitting up straight, looking out her window. Her face was calm and happy. Tears were running down

288

her cheeks. Gabrielle started the car and drove back to the house.

Catherine had coffee for them. Samantha and Rushel sat at the dining table and told Gislaine what happened. Audra went to her room. They all heard the bedroom door lock. Gabrielle took her coffee to the curved window and watched the clouds scudding over the dunes.

"They were waiting for you?" Gislaine asked incredulously.

"They were all in the boy's side."

"How could they possibly know you were coming?"

"We have to give it back." Rushel shrugged. "That stuff."

"It belongs to M," Catherine said. "I hid it all, by the way, and no one will ever find it if they break in."

"What if they have guns?"

"I'll run away down the beach. They would have to shoot me in the back."

"They'd like that."

"They'd still never find it."

"If we give it back," Samantha said, "they might leave us alone. But they weren't exactly leaving us alone before. L bought that house of hers just to be close to us. She's completely obsessed."

"Then we take all of it," Gabrielle said suddenly, still looking out the window.

They all looked at her.

"Put them out of business."

Samantha thought about it. "That might not be impossible. But."

"How?" Rushel said.

"If she's obsessed as you say, there's no way out. We have to fight." Gabrielle thought about how Holly wanted to hit her.

"Well." Rushel sipped her coffee.

"We have to fight," Samantha said with an uncertain tone. "But they have all the power."

"They won't expect it." Gabrielle set her cup on the table and stood there.

"True."

"We would surprise them."

"Surprise them with what? Our ability to lose?" Rushel said.

"Speak for yourself," Catherine snapped. "There is a way."

"Sure."

"We need to think of a plan." Catherine got up and put her cup in the sink.

"Okay." Rushel rolled her eyes.

"Even assuming L converted all the assets to gold, we have no idea where it is," Samantha said. "Could be in multiple locations."

"She wouldn't trust banks. Not after what she did," Gislaine said.

"What's the inside of her house like?" Gabrielle sat in her chair.

"Audra would know. She stayed with them."

"I was only in there for a minute once," Rushel said, and wrinkled her nose. "It smelled awful. Like someone peed on the carpet and just left it. And all the windows were covered with really thick curtains like blankets. And they had houseplants everywhere. There must have been fifty of them, on all the shelves and counters. The leaves were all dusty." She shivered.

"This was when you borrowed that thing?"

"Audra wanted to get her favorite sweater back. Holly wanted to keep it. It was green. Matched her eyes. So we parked down the street and watched the house until we saw Holly leave. She has this little Mercedes."

"Really."

"They like spending M's money. Anyway, Holly takes off like a bat out of hell."

"She *is* a bat out of hell," Catherine breathed.

"We zip in there and Audra doesn't even knock, just opens the front door and goes in. Only one there besides L was Susan Four. And L was just leaving."

She wanted to ask about L but said, "Which Susan was that?"

"She's gone now. She's the one they cast out. She just said hi to Audra and went in the bathroom. She didn't look good. I think she was throwing up."

"Drunk," Catherine said.

"Didn't act drunk."

"Pregnant," Gislaine said, writing.

"That's possible."

"No kidding," Gabrielle said. "Pregnant?"

"With them, anything is possible," Rushel said.

"What a mess, huh?" Gislaine said.

Gabrielle just shook her head.

"Maybe that's why they cast her out," Catherine said. "Can't have a pregnant girl hanging around."

"It means she saw a boy naked," Gislaine said. "After that, she would have been ideologically impure."

"Contaminated," Catherine said.

"Audra went straight into Holly's room and started ransacking the place," Rushel said. "She threw Holly's clothes all over the place. Into the hallway. All over the kitchen with all the filthy dishes in the sink. Threw them out the window. And there was this little room off the kitchen. A little narrow room."

"The pantry," Catherine said.

"Right. Pantry. Audra whips open the door and I could see this metal box on a shelf. More than one. They caught my attention. They looked like boxes of cereal made of metal. We went back to the living room and there was one of them on the coffee table. L was just going out the door, she told us about the nerve gas like it was a joke. When she was gone I just grabbed it and almost dropped it. It was super heavy. Audra had to help me. The edges of that thing were so sharp it cut my hand." She pointed to red marks on her right palm. "I had no idea what it was. I just took it. I don't think Susan even noticed. Not one of the swifter Susans. Patricia came into the store one day a week later and told us how dangerous the box was. Repeating what L said. Just checking my reaction. They're incredibly sneaky."

"They're always thinking a couple steps ahead," Gislaine said. "At least Patricia seems to."

"Patricia's the leader?"

"Yeah, her and Debbie together. Debbie's the weird one."

Gabrielle tried to think of what would constitute weird.

"She's actually kind of normal."

"Huh. That *is* weird."

"This was all last year," Rushel said. "The morning after Thanksgiving. Then, that afternoon we went down south."

South to your new house, Gabrielle thought, that is no longer there.

"They've been on red alert ever since. There's no way in hell we're getting back in there."

"We'll think of something."

The hallway door opened and Audra came into the kitchen. She had changed into a black sweater and black jeans. Gabrielle looked and got a flash of anger from her.

"You'll think of what?" she asked.

"How to get into L's house."

"Oh, easy. First, go insane then just knock on the door. Since I know you're not insane, why would you want to do that?"

"We're going to steal back the rest of those safes," Gabrielle said. "We're going to get M's property back and shut them down."

Audra's eyes widened and then she smiled, a crooked smile. Gabrielle looked at the others. Samantha and Catherine were grinning. Gislaine looked uncertain. Rushel looked worried.

Audra clasped her hands together and gazed out the window for a moment. "There's a way. Let me think about it," she said. "Come on, you don't want to be late for work."

Rushel and Gislaine got up and followed Audra out of the kitchen.

"Don't worry," Rushel called back. "I have the list."

Catherine refilled Gabrielle's and Samantha's coffee. They heard Audra's Corona start up after a couple tries. The sound disappeared around the dunes. Rough popping. A tune up and a muffler, Gabrielle thought. Maybe an exhaust gasket.

Samantha seemed lost in thought. Catherine smiled warmly.

They're comfortable just sitting together, Gabrielle thought. They don't have to be constantly talking.

Catherine nodded at her, reading her mind as usual.

"Audra didn't seem too interested," Gabrielle said.

"Hard to tell sometimes," Catherine said. "It would reopen old wounds with Holly. But she might not care."

Samantha set down her cup. "If we were only partially successful it would be all out war. We would have to take them down completely."

"They're wearing us down day by day," Catherine said. "I say we at least strike back for the house."

Samantha looked grim.

"I really liked that kitchen."

"I know."

"And you liked the library."

"It was beautiful. Should have known something was wrong when we got all those boxes of books. M didn't say a word."

"Almost got the UPS truck stuck in the sand. Remember?"

"Almost killed poor Disco," Samantha said and they both laughed.

"Killed who?"

"Disco Lifestyle. The only UPS driver who's ever been able to find the house and also get his truck down our road."

"Wait. That's his name?"

"He's really hard to understand," Samantha said, smiling.

"Impossible."

"He slurs his words like you wouldn't believe. Plus the music. Can't even hear him."

"We asked him his name once and what he said sounded like Dismo Lindblan."

"Dankin Lindbloom."

"So Disco Lifestyle made sense. Because of the music."

"Oh my God."

"Good old Disco. Nice guy," Samantha said, grinning.

"You'll meet him at some point. We're always getting deliveries."

"Yeah," Samantha said. "Always blasting out the Bee Gees. The Sound of Philadelphia."

"Donna Summer. KC and the Sunshine Band."

"It did something to his brain."

"Or perhaps it cured him!"

"Yes," Samantha said. "His reality is not our reality."

"Perhaps his reality is higher than ours," Catherine said. "Because the music *never stops!*" Catherine set down her cup. "I think I'll go lie down."

"And I need to do my exercises," Samantha said.

"A nap sounds good," Gabrielle said. "Don't usually get up so early in the morning."

"Rest while you can," Catherine said.

Gabrielle went to her room.

She took off her shoes and lay down on the soft bed, which had been neatly made, She started to go over the events of the day but found herself listening to sounds from other parts of the house. A window rattled in the wind. The roof creaked. A door opened and closed. Catherine's door, she thought, but she wasn't really sure. The sliding glass door to the patio made a penetrating squeak. That would Samantha's room.

The pillow was very comfortable.

There was the wind again and she came awake to silence. The rain had fled and the light was low outside her window. She stretched and sat up. She rubbed her eyes under her glasses. She had forgotten to take them off.

She opened her door and poked her head out. The hall door was open to the dark and quiet kitchen. Down the hall to the right, Samantha's door was ajar. Gabrielle left her doorway and walked past. She saw that the sliding door to the patio was closed, the bed unslept in. Catherine's room was directly opposite.

Feeling she was doing something terribly wrong but unable to stop, Gabrielle stood before Catherine's closed door and listened. Her heart thudded in her chest and there was a pressure in her head as if her scalp had suddenly tightened. She put her ear close. There was a sound. A creaking bedframe. A whisper.

Gabrielle stepped back. She made herself turn away and went back to her room, to her window. The dunes stretched to the horizon in the slashing light. She felt dizzy and her face was hot. She could make out a trail through the sagebrush and ice plant.

She decided to go for a walk.

There was a black raincoat hanging by the front door in the library. She put it on over her sweatshirt and made sure she had everything. Keys. Wristwatch. The clothes on her back. That was it.

The sand skittered. She closed the front door and screen behind her and walked away, to the north. She refrained from thinking. She found the trail. There were tiny purple flowers and big yellow ones. The sand was fluid with broken shell and she had to work for each step. A wide gap in the dunes appeared and she turned towards it. Red sunlight refracted in her glasses. Wind pressed on her forehead and sweat ran off the tip of her nose. The air was salt and seaweedy and contained a tingle of energy. She glanced back. The house was invisible.

She entered the gap, making sure not to step on any flowers, and followed the path up and then down to the beach.

Ahead was the sky and the gray, surging line of the winter sea. She slid down the weather side of the dunes and the wind again found her. She flipped the hood of the raincoat over her head. She walked towards the surf down terraces of sand and past fascinating piles of driftwood. There were piles of seashells and green strands of kelp. A wave rushed up and soaked her shoes. She wiggled her toes. Not all that cold.

Gabrielle stood at the edge of the continent and looked west. She calculated azimuth. There is nothing between me and Japan, she thought. There is nothing between me and Australia.

The sun hid behind a reef of clouds. The horizon beneath was bright with moving points of golden light. Chaotic and orderly. Currents collided and joined, split, and swirled.

"I can actually see it," she said and for a moment forgot everything. The orange ball of the sun reappeared, the light attenuated, almost gentle.

She turned north again and walked at the edge of the surf where the sand was compacted. She became absorbed studying the debris that had washed up. Shells and bleached wood, eroded and ancient looking. The sand was far from uniform and there were chunks of sandstone sculpted into complex shapes.

She thought the shells were interesting. She picked up one with a scalloped shape and softened edges. There were dark growth rings on the convex side. She ran her thumb over them and turned it over. There, it was smooth and opalescent, a flattened funnel with a small dark spot at the focus.

This is where it lived, she thought. A being incomprehensible to me. And the rings and ridges were a record of its existence. A map of its life from birth to death. She studied the complex patterns. Some of the ridges were thick, others pretty thin. Good years and bad years. She bent her knees to put it back on the sand and stopped. Instead she tucked it in her pocket and said, "You're safe with me."

She kept walking. She lifted her eyes. Low fingers of fog reached in from the sea. The sky directly above was blue fading to gray. The beach ahead ran to infinity. She kept walking. The sun appeared for a final moment in the gap where the fog met the sea and a brilliant golden light suffused the world. Then it was gone. She felt she could walk forever. Night was coming. Stars then and the wind steady at her back. What wonders will I see, she thought.

There was a flash of yellow at the top of the dunes. She saw someone work their way down, past tussocks of tall grass, and stand still on the beach before her.

Gabrielle paused and then kept walking. The figure in yellow began to walk also. When they were twenty feet apart, they stopped.

Catherine's face was red. "If you're running away," she said, panting, "I'm going with you." He windbreaker billowed around her shoulders. There was sand stuck to her bare knees.

Gabrielle went to where she stood. Catherine's hair was soaked with sweat and Gabrielle wiped her forehead. She leaned in and kissed her on the corner of her mouth.

"What are you doing?" Catherine reached out, opened Gabrielle's raincoat, and put her hands into the pockets of her sweatshirt. Gabrielle allowed herself to be pulled close. Catherine was shivering and her pulse raced at her throat.

"I know Samantha was in your room."

Catherine showed surprise by blinking.

"I just felt like getting out of there."

Catherine looked into Gabrielle's eyes. "You're misunderstanding. It's not like that."

Gabrielle shook her head. "I don't know what anything is like. It's not my place to say what anything is like."

"Don't talk like that. This is your place. This will always be your place."

Gabrielle felt the heat from Catherine's body as she was pulled closer. Their foreheads touched, a spot of warmth. Wind rushed around Gabrielle's fluttering hood.

"With Samantha, it's complicated. She saved my life. She saved my life. And." Catherine swallowed hard. "There's more. It's the most private thing about her. It's what makes her who she is."

"Okay," Gabrielle said.

Catherine rested her head on Gabrielle's shoulder. Gabrielle liked the feel of her breath. Hot and urgent.

"I need to rest a minute."

"Okay."

"It's really hard to run on that sand." She snuggled in. "You like this?"

"Uh huh."

"Good." Catherine's voice was muffled by Gabrielle's collar.

Gabrielle clasped her hands together around Catherine's waist. She made a long sigh, her lips on Gabrielle's ear.

"I suppose we should head back to the house," Catherine whispered.

Gabrielle answered by grasping her more tightly.

"Before it gets dark."

Gabrielle ran her hands up Catherine's back.

"Before it gets too dark, I mean, because it's already pretty dark."

Gabrielle giggled and Catherine took her head off her shoulder and kissed her. She kissed her again.

"I'm sorry I made you upset."

"It's all right."

"I'll make it up to you. I promise."

They walked back down the beach, into the wind. Catherine gripped Gabrielle hand so tightly it almost hurt. When they reached the gap in the dunes, barely visible, Catherine led the way and easily pulled Gabrielle up to the trail. An unseen bird scolded them from the scrub Manzanita. When they reached the turn in the trail and saw the house, Catherine said, "Oh!"

The windows of the house were brightly lit. Two floodlights mounted on the patio wall spilled light up the hill, casting swarms of shadows in the sage. Catherine's hand squeezed even tighter. There was a new car parked by the front door. A black Jeep.

Catherine began to walk a little faster. Gabrielle let herself be pulled again.

A figure appeared on the porch. Gabrielle recognized Samantha as her hair blew about her. She waved and jogged towards them in the gloom.

Catherine waited until she was close to ask, "How is it?"

Gabrielle saw that Samantha's attention was fixed on her. Samantha gripped her by the upper arms and kissed her on both cheeks, firmly. Samantha's skin smelled faintly of coconut shampoo. The knot that had been in her stomach relaxed.

"I was worried," Samantha said, then to Catherine, "Not too bad. But not the greatest."

"Did you."

"No."

"Tell her about."

"No."

Catherine sighed. "Don't know."

"What to do. Yeah."

Gabrielle said, "Why are all the lights on?"

"She just likes to see," Catherine said. "Make sure we're talking care of the place. She say anything?"

"She has to go back. Tuesday, probably."

"Did she notice we're out of everything?"

"Rushel got the list."

"Hope so."

Catherine took one of Gabrielle's hands again and Samantha took the other. Together they walked to the house.

"I'm glad I took a nap," Gabrielle said.

"Long day," Catherine said.

"This is *nothing*," Samantha said.

The screen door opened and M came out on the dark porch. Light from the library shone on her blonde hair and white jacket. She saw them and Gabrielle thought, did she smile? Then her expression turned to impatience.

"There you all are," she called.

Catherine let go of Gabrielle's hand and went quickly to the porch.

"There's nothing in the refrigerator," M said scoldingly.

"I know."

"You're not having supper? Did you forget to plan, maybe?"

"We just have to go to the store."

"Oh, that's all."

"Rushel took the list."

"I'll go," Gabrielle said. She flexed her hands, suddenly cold.

M nodded to herself. "In your little hippie car?"

"Sure. You can fit a lot in there." Gabrielle felt Samantha begin to rub her back.

"Nonsense. We'll take my Jeep, a proper vehicle. Come on."

"Okay." Gabrielle noticed the return of M's playful tone.

M now focused on Samantha. "There's a pile of stuff for you to look at."

"I will." She gave Gabrielle a final pat on the arm and then headed for the front door. Gabrielle walked towards the Jeep. The library was full of light. She saw that both floor lamps were on, shining through the miniblinds. Samantha smiled at her. Seagulls cried above.

M was already in the Jeep. Gabrielle went to the passenger side and got in. There was no dome light. The seat was cold and hard. The top was black fabric supported by black tubing and it all smelled of soap. M started the engine and wiggled the stick shift.

"So you're the reason everything's screwed up." She put it in reverse.

"I guess so."

M was wearing *Fracas* which Gabrielle thought kind of went well with the soap smell. Her jacket was perfectly fitted white leather glowing in the dashboard lights, and had a bit of extra material in the shoulders. Her hair fell around the sides of her face, feathered and breezy.

Gabrielle finger-combed her damp, sticky hair away from her smudgy glasses.

They bumped slowly along through the open gate. Gabrielle got out and closed it behind them and engaged the latch. When she got back in, M was smiling at her.

"I wondered if I would see you again."

M skillfully drove through the sand trap in first gear. On pavement, she revved it up and went directly to third. They rolled through the eucalyptus grove.

Gabrielle dug into her pocket. "Before I forget," she said. She found her folding money and unwrapped a five dollar bill and held it out to M, who made no move to take it.

"What's this?" She took her eyes from the dark road for an instant.

A long-tailed kangaroo mouse the color of spring rain clouds dashed in front of them and was gone.

"Your change." They were passing the eucalyptus trees.

"My what?"

"The deal was for seventy-five dollars. You left me four twenties."

"Yeah, but." M squinted at the money.

"I owe you five bucks."

M's look of suspicion turned to uncertainty. She took the five and tucked it into the jacket pocket. "All right. Thank you."

Gabrielle nodded. She turned sideways in the uncomfortable seat and rested her back against the small door. She watched M drive. Never figured her for a Jeep person, she thought. More like Mercedes. But maybe this is just how she wants to be. Maybe she's trying to engineer herself.

Gabrielle watched the road. They passed through the small town with its streetlights and then they entered the long dark valley.

M smiled at her in the bluish speedometer light. "You're thinking pretty hard there."

Gabrielle watched her carefully and said, "Why me?"

M didn't take her eyes off the road. "You mean you don't know?"

Gabrielle shook her head impatiently. "It doesn't make sense. I'm not beautiful like Rushel. I'm not funny like Audra. I'm not strong like Samantha. I hate writing, so Gislaine is much better at that. And according to Catherine I can't even boil water."

M said firmly, "Gabrielle, you are the key. You are all of those things. You are beautiful. Writing and cooking are things you could easily learn. If you want to be funny, well, you could learn that too, but God knows why you would want to. And Samantha, yes, she is certainly strong." M looked at her. "You don't think you're strong? You have amazing strength. It's why the others are drawn to you, our little family and everyone else. You radiate strength. It's all about you, even now. In time, your awareness will grow and you'll see I'm right." She took a deep breath. "How old do you think I am?"

"Actually, that's something else I'm not very good at."

"Just guess."

"I don't know, M."

"Guess."

"All right. Forty-nine."

M burst out laughing and the Jeep swerved halfway into the opposite lane.

"I knew you were smart," she finally said. "I suppose I asked for it."

"What?"

"That's wonderful. So you're learning to be funny, huh?"

"I don't know what you mean."

M made herself stop laughing. "Oh."

"I'm sorry. I really don't know."

"It's okay."

"I'm sorry."

"It's *okay*. Listen."

Gabrielle thought, *good grief,* Gislaine told you what year she was born in. Nineteen thirty-six. At most she's forty three. What's the matter with you?

"I am forty-two," M said. "My birthday's in September."

"I wasn't trying to be a smartass."

"Of course not. Forget I asked. Although it was pretty funny. Look, my point is, I am now middle-aged. A middle-aged woman driving a Jeep. Soon to be old. I remember what it was like to be your age. I remember perfectly. I was living in Greenwich Village. I had friends. It was... It was as good as it could be. I know that now, looking back. And that's how I'll always think of that time of my life."

M slowed and stopped in the left turn lane, aiming for town. She hit the blinker.

"That's all in the past," she said. "If you think I'm completely out of line, I'll understand. If you disappear and never come back, I'll understand. You tend to live in your head. That makes sense. There's a lot of room in there. But this is the springtime of your life, Gabrielle. Don't you feel that? I want you to be able to look back and think, I was young and alive. That's all."

She checked the sparse traffic around them. The light turned green and M shifted through the turn. They traveled up the highway towards the town and the store.

"So what do you think?"

M drove into the empty parking lot of College Costs Less and stopped in front of the automatic doors. The lights inside were bright and cold. Gabrielle could see several people in the check-out line. Gislaine was running items across the new laser scanner and making conversation. M shut off the engine and headlights. She sat back and did not look up.

"M," Gabrielle said. "I'm absolutely exhausted. I have a real bad headache coming on. I'm trying to put everything that's happened into some sort of order. But, you know, today has been the most fun I've ever had. Right now, that's all I can say."

M made a curt nod and got out.

She's afraid she said too much, Gabrielle thought. She got out also.

M turned back and said, "That headache is caused by hunger. We need to get something for supper."

"All right." The door opened for them with a bad grinding sound.

No purse, Gabrielle realized. In fact, none of them carry purses. I never noticed that before. Good.

Gislaine in her blue smock barely looked up. M yanked a shopping cart out of the chrome rack and set off down the closest aisle. Canned vegetables. Pasta. Spaghetti sauce. M got six boxes of spaghetti and about a dozen boxes of other pasta with unpronounceable names. Gabrielle grabbed a jar of spaghetti sauce, the kind Audra liked.

"Oh, no," M said. "You-know-who would have a cow. Pasta, she'll compromise on. Otherwise, it's only fresh, homemade from scratch tomato sauce for her. *This* way."

Gabrielle put the jar back and jogged to keep up. At the end of the aisle she turned right and rolled to the bakery department. There was no line at the meat counter. Gabrielle caught a glimpse of Rushel in the back of the butcher area. She was mopping the floor.

"Store bought bread is all right for some things." She swept five loaves of the good sliced bread into the cart. $1.19 each. "I had to put my foot down. I mean, we're not in the bakery business."

Gabrielle saw the stuff she usually bought was on sale for twenty-nine cents.

"This is cheaper."

"Too cheap, She'd throw it to the seagulls."

She pushed on to the end of the store, the produce department. "Here we go. You can help. It'll be faster if we split up." She handed Gabrielle a slip of paper.

"Is that the list?"

"This is about half the produce. Rushel has the big list. Just bag it up as best you can and pile it in here. Can you read her writing?"

The writing was an elegant cursive in ink, but not a ball point. The first item was *Russet 15kg*.

"She prefers the metric system.

"No problem."

"It's easier, isn't it?"

"I use it all the time."

"It's best if we go fast," M said and headed for the tomatoes. "Beefsteak tomatoes, two for ten cents. What a rip off." She began filling a plastic bag.

Gabrielle went to the neatly stacked Russets. About thirty-three pounds, she thought. I'll round up. Go fast.

It took seven of the little plastic bags. Then came five kilos each of the red and white rose potatoes. Spanish onions. Red onions. Green beans. Then turnips, broccoli, Brussels sprouts (just one bag). Then oranges and lemons (which didn't look very good but she found a couple good ones). Limes and pears (*Pears, any type*, it read. They only had Bartlett). And finally, apples. One kilogram each of five different varieties of which the store had two, Red Delicious and Granny Smith. She consulted M, who was picking out bell peppers.

"Oh, she always does this. She forgets this isn't Paris, or even L.A." The missing types were Gala, Fuji, and Pippin. "Just get an extra two kilos or so of those. She'll have to make do."

The shopping cart was completely full to the top rails when they came to the end of the list. Five loaves of bread perched on top of a mass of plastic bags. M strained to push it. She turned up the aisle to the checkout stand.

"Hamburger's on sale for thirty-nine cents a pound."

"We don't want that."

"Hot dogs are on sale, too. Look, only forty-nine cents."

"Who in the world would eat hot dogs?"

"I like hot dogs."

They were on the snack foods aisle.

"How about potato chips?"

"No."

"I really like Tingles."

M gave her a squinty stare.

Then Gabrielle saw something. "Oh, wow!" She took a small can off the top shelf. "Look, it comes in like a spray can. I love this cheese. I've never seen this before."

M snatched the can of Fun-Cheese away from her. "My God, Gabrielle. You can't possibly be serious." She tossed the little can onto the shelf and knocked over all the others like metallic clattering bowling pins. "It's not even real cheese."

"I'm pretty sure it is."

"No."

Gislaine was ringing up two girls who were getting cans of Dr. Pepper and a big bag of M&Ms. They seemed very young to Gabrielle. Both were wearing identical navy blue hooded sweatshirts. They giggled as they chatted with Gislaine. As they stood at the cash register, they let their hands bump. Then one of them extended their index finger and the other did the same and without either of them looking down they let their fingers hook up. It lasted no more than a second, as they talked and laughed, and then the one doing the money got her change and they walked quickly out into the night.

M scanned the area. "Do you see anyone else?"

Gabrielle shook her head. A fluorescent tube over the register began flickering and making a buzzing sound.

Gislaine waved to them. "Whoa, feeding an army, huh?"

Gabrielle put the bread on the conveyor belt. Gislaine ran the first one over the scanner window and it made a beep. The other four loaves she tossed into the bagging area without scanning.

"An army of baby birds."

"Oh, that sounds cute."

She weighed a bag of tomatoes and punched the code. After it beeped, she slid all the other tomatoes past the scale. First bag of Russets she scanned, the rest she slid past. Green beans, tossed. Onions, tossed. The bagging area was getting full. The register display showed a subtotal of $2.25.

Gabrielle started looking around nervously. "Maybe I should," she began and got a paper grocery sack and stated unfolding it.

"You don't have to do that," Gislaine said. She picked up the phone and hit a button.

Her voice boomed through the store. "All available service personnel to the front, please. Bagging assistance required."

Gabrielle heard running footsteps and Rushel came around the corner by the photo-processing counter, her hair flowing out behind her. She wiped her hands on her smock, grabbed a paper bag and whipped it open with one snap of her hand. She smiled and began selecting heavier items to go on the bottom. These she threw into the bag, keeping her other hand inside to catch. In seconds, she had two brown paper sacks full. "So how has your Sunday evening been so far?" she asked cheerfully.

"Eventful," M sighed.

"Really?"

"Then I realized I was just out of *everything*."

"Eating you out of house and home, huh?" Bag three was full. "That reminds me, ma'am. Your order came in."

"Oh, good."

"You can pick it up at our loading area."

"Thank you so much."

"You're more than welcome." Rushel pulled the shopping cart past Gabrielle and efficiently loaded it with the heavy bags. "This should keep you for a while."

"Eh. Maybe two weeks' worth."

"Well," Rushel said with sincerity, "I hope we see you on your next visit. Thank you for shopping with College Costs Less. Do you need any help out to your car?"

"Oh, thank you, but Gabrielle can handle it. Go ahead, honey, while I pay the nice lady."

Gabrielle nodded. "Okay," she said slowly, trying to keep a straight face. The total on the register was $8.15.

M took money from her jacket. She had a five and several ones. That's the five I just gave her, she thought. Last November she was spending eighteen hundred dollars on that silly movie player.

M dug in her pocket. She found a dime and several pennies. "One cent short," she muttered. Gislaine slapped the register keys and the drawer popped open.

"Good enough."

Gabrielle looked away and pushed the cart. Her shoes slipped on the linoleum floor. She put her shoulder into it and the cart started moving.

"The back is unlocked," M said behind her.

"Right."

Under the flickering fluorescent lights the automatic doors opened with the sound of grinding metal. In the parking lot, Gabrielle pushed the cart past the spot where Audra had lain. M rushed out behind her and caught up.

"Quick, quick," she said. She pulled down the small back gate. "Put everything on the left as much as possible."

Gabrielle began to put the heavier bags in first.

"Just toss it in. If something gets smashed, tough toenails."

"Okay."

M slammed the gate shut and hopped in.

The Jeep was moving before Gabrielle could sit down. She stayed on one knee in the open door and M drove to the side of the store, headlights off.

The emergency door opened. Rushel was standing there. M positioned back of the Jeep close to the door. She left the engine running and got out.

"Here's your order, ma'am," Rushel said. "All this." There were four large cardboard boxes in the doorway. "That's the heavy one."

Gabrielle dragged the top box off the stack. It was labeled *Premium Meat Service*. She slid it into the back, pushing aside a bag of bell peppers. M got the next one, making a sound like "Urp." The third box was a bit heavier. Then she tried to lift the last box.

"Careful," Rushel said.

Gabrielle got her fingers under the bottom edge. "You weren't kidding." She could barely move it.

"Hurry," M said, looking at the parking lot. A small car pulled up. Two students got out.

"I have to close the door." Rushel got on her knees and pushed the box over the metal threshold. She closed the door quietly, holding down the panic bar.

In the back of the store darkness, M got on the other side of the box. "Can't see a damn thing. Ow! Dang." She shook her hand. "Watch out for broken glass."

"Are you all right?"

"Do I sound all right? Okay, on three, we lift. Ready?"

"Wait."

"Hurry. We lift and you swing your end to the gate."

"I can't get... Okay."

"On three. Ready? Three!" M managed to lift her side a couple inches and dropped it.

"You're just saying three?"

"Of course. You need me to count?"

"I wasn't ready."

"Fine. I'll do a countdown."

"That's what I was expecting."

"Okay. One. Ready now?"

"Yes, M."

"Two. *Three.*"

They both lifted and groaned and Gabrielle, shoes slipping on gravel, got her box corner on the gate. She pushed up with her knee and the box moved a bit. M bore down, an onion rolled out, and the big heavy thing slid in.

"There. Good God." M got out her keys. She was breathing hard. "At least unloading won't be so bad. Let's get *out* of here."

The both got in and M had the car moving before Gabrielle closed her door.

She took the back way out. On the main street, M made a right without slowing for the red light and hit the gas.

"That's so much better. Always better to be moving. And I'm really hungry." She looked at Gabrielle. "Is there a problem?"

Gabrielle didn't see any police cars after them.

"No. No problem."

"Good."

M kept it at sixty on the residential street. Gabrielle noticed she sped up a bit between streetlights.

"So what are you working on these days? Anything interesting?"

Gabrielle settled into the seat. M was passing all the other vehicles. The Jeep had a much stiffer suspension than her VW. She could feel every little bump. M swooped around a Chevy Vega that was belching smoke.

Gabrielle held onto the straps bolted to the top of the door frame. "My focus right now is on understanding the transistor. The physics of the transistor."

"And how's that going?"

"I'm keeping up."

"I'll bet. Rimmler, right?"

"Uh, yeah. How did you know?"

"We've met."

"Dr. Rimmler?"

"Oh, sure. He's quite charming. So besides that, what else are you working on? Any projects?"

Gabrielle made a mental note to look up the definition of 'charming'.

"I did have one big project. Something I worked on for years. Since I was fifteen."

M seemed to notice the past tense. "So what happened? What was it?"

"I wanted to create a transistor using only light. Coherent light. Nothing else. And I'm pretty sure I got that to work." She saw M's reaction. "Then I started working on logic gates and I got to the point of using a series of interference pattern standing waves."

"As memory," M said excitedly.

"Right. Not sure if that was the correct path to take. I had other ideas but I did a lot of work on it."

"I would love to see this."

"Well, everything was in my backpack when it." She paused. "Disappeared. I always carried it with me thinking it was safer."

"Disappeared? You lost your backpack? You don't have copies?"

"No. No copies. It was all in my project binder which I had since the seventh grade. So I'm going to try to recreate it all."

"You're talking about an optical computer."

"I would need an shortwave laser. Ultraviolet. But there might be other ways in terms of prototypes. Clock speeds would be terahertz range."

M stared at the road. She made a little shrug. "Thousands of gigahertz. No heat generation. There might be potential for something like that."

She turned onto the dark valley highway.

"You're going to keep working on this, of course."

They drove past warmly lit houses tucked behind rows of trees.

"It's nice to be able to talk about all this," Gabrielle said. "With someone who's knowledgeable."

"Yeah?"

"Very knowledgeable."

M smiled.

"You stood there in that store and let me explain analog and digital to you. And you have a PhD. For all I know, you invented digital."

"Well, once you got going I couldn't very well stop you. You did an excellent job."

"Thanks."

"This is all working out so well," M said cheerfully.

Gabrielle leaned back in the seat. She took off her glasses and covered her face with her hands. She rubbed her eyes and took a deep breath. The headrest cradled her as the blurry night passed by.

"We'll have a nice supper and everything will make sense. You'll feel much better."

They went through the small town with its traffic lights. They reached the eucalyptus grove, mysterious in the dark. M slowed the Jeep.

"Gabrielle, this is the reality. Everyone knew about you. There's us, there's L, and there are many more you know nothing about. You were the perfect apple hanging from a high branch, almost unreachable. All by yourself, all unaware. Someone was going to pick you." Her voice grew intense. "We won because we wanted you the most. The others are greedy. Cruel. Wasteful. Powerful. It was close. But we knew you belonged with us." She grinned. "We're the smart girls."

She propelled the Jeep over the sand trap and around the hill. The porch light greeted them on the sandy, windswept clearing. M stopped next to Audra's car.

Gabrielle put her glasses back on and cleared her throat. M looked up at her with a quick, shy glance.

"M," she said. "Yes."

M seemed surprised but only for a second. "What do you want for supper? We have everything now. How's your headache?"

"It's much better. I'm starving, though."

They both popped their doors open at the same instant.

"There was one other thing," Gabrielle said. "Please don't call me honey."

"What do you think about rib-eye?"

Gabrielle stared at her.

"I mean for supper."

"Oh. I don't think I know what that is."

"Then this is going to be so much fun." M leaned into the car and gave the horn a short beep. Samantha appeared at the front door.

Gabrielle tried to help but it was not allowed. The boxes were opened and the contents transferred to the kitchen. Catherine worked at high speed. Happily, Gabrielle thought. The heavy box turned out to be full of steak and chicken, all packaged in styrofoam trays and free of any price stickers. There were frozen hamburger patties in wholesale-type wrappers. There was fresh fish. Pink salmon, she recognized and unlabeled white fish she did not. Catherine called it ti-la-pia, which didn't seem like a word. It took Audra three trips to bring in all the potatoes. The island counter was covered with grocery bags and Gabrielle watched them systematically restock the refrigerator and freezer, the pantry shelves, and in a small space under the back counter, built-in wire bins that moved on nylon tracks.

"Okay," Audra said. "I'll be back." She went to her car.

Gabrielle watched Catherine prepare dinner – supper – for everyone. She was impressed that Catherine's first move was to open a card file. She laid out a 3x5 card for everyone. Seven cards now, including one for 'Catherine'.

"You have a card for yourself?" Gabrielle couldn't help asking.

"Oh, yes. My menu must be in harmony with the others. There must be balance." She took the card labeled 'Gabrielle', which was blank, and got a pen. "Okay. Potato chips." She started writing. "Cocoa Krispies. Frozen waffles. Hot dogs. That's you." She picked up her own card. "Baguettes, extra virgin olive oil, garlic, strawberries with clotted cream. That's me." She dropped the pen. "Fucking harmonious."

Gabrielle laughed. "I know what garlic is."

"As of now."

"Yes. Don't know those other things."

"You might like them. Dinner will be served when those two get back from work. The store closes at eight, they usually get away at eight-thirty, so about nine or whenever. We always eat together whenever possible."

"Of course."

Catherine brought out a tray. There was a plate with a piece of cheese and a glass of white wine.

"Gruyere. It's delicious."

Gabrielle took the tray as Samantha came in with the last box. Bottles of cooking oil and several bottles of red wine.

"Did you tell her anything?" Catherine asked.

Gabrielle spoke softly. "No, I didn't."

"At some point, we will have to."

Gabrielle started to reply but the door to the middle bathroom opened and M emerged. She smiled at Gabrielle and sat at the dining table. "What are you two talking about?"

"Menus," Catherine said, holding up Gabrielle's card. "Gabrielle wants peanut butter and jelly sandwiches for dinner. What do you think?"

"Hm. What kind of jelly?" M asked, concerned.

Catherine checked the card. "Grape."

"Grape? Yuk!" Gabrielle said.

"You poor child," M said. "Catherine, you must help her."

"Might be too late, M. Look what I found."

She held up a can of Tingles.

"Oh," M said tearfully and wiped her eyes. "How did *that* get in there?"

"Hobbits," Samantha said. "Man, those guys."

"Oh good grief. I'm going to go read," Gabrielle said to their laughter and went to the library with the tray.

She set the tray on the floor beside the bean bags, which had a nice vinyl smell to them. She made a quick check of the floor lamps. Her induction coil had been undone and the wires spliced back together with lots of clear tape. Samantha knew how to do it. Samantha knows a lot.

Gabrielle thumbed through a textbook on optics and got caught up in the dramatic story of polarization and birefringence. She tried sipping the wine instead of gulping it and only ate half the cheese so her appetite wouldn't be ruined.

It doesn't take much to fill me up these days, she thought.

At last, Audra came home.

Rushel and Gislaine, both still in their blue smocks, hit the bathroom.

While they all waited for supper, Gabrielle went outside with a flashlight and looked over Audra's car. Audra popped the hood and they checked out the engine. Pretty clean. Plugs easy to get to. One wire looked burned. The wind was calm and there were stars. Audra wiped the engine compartment with a rag while they talked about cars and shared the last of the wine.

When they went back in, the house smelled of grilling steak and the stereo was playing the soundtrack album from *Romeo and Juliet*. They all took turns washing their hands. Catherine tapped a wine glass with a spoon and they all gathered in the dining room. Samantha turned the music down.

Gabrielle watched as Catherine, with professional efficiency, assembled everyone's individual plates on the island. She made a final check, stepped back and gave a nod. Rushel and Gislaine got theirs first, then Audra and Samantha. M picked up two plates and carried them to the table, laid out with silverware and napkins and glasses. There were daisies in a crystal vase. M set one of the plates in Gabrielle's spot and then with her free hand pulled back the tall chair. The others went to their places and stood behind their chairs, plates in hand.

Gabrielle went to her place and M pushed the chair under her. Gabrielle sat and folded her hands in her lap.

M went to her spot next to Catherine and held her hands over her chest. "The Goddess is here," she said.

Without speaking, everyone set down their plates and sat. No one touched their silverware or napkins. Catherine brought her own plate over, checked everyone, and finally sat down. "Audra," she said.

They all reached and clasped hands. M closed her eyes and they all followed this signal, Gabrielle being the last.

Audra said, "For the blessings we are about to receive this day, for wonderful food and wonderful friends, for the gifts of love and joy and laughter and peace for our family which is now complete, we thank you, our Creator, the source of our being and our happiness. So shall it be."

They all murmured, "So shall it be," and Gabrielle opened her eyes. Gislaine and Samantha were looking at Audra in surprise.

"That was very nice, Audra," M said softly.

"Thank you," Audra said and raised her eyebrows at Samantha, who nodded and shrugged.

"I helped," Rushel whispered.

"Yes you did. A little."

Gabrielle finally looked at her plate. Catherine had given her a small round steak. It had something cooked and crispy wrapped around its outer edge. She couldn't tell what that was. There were thin sliced potatoes in a thick cheese sauce and broccoli, also with a cheese sauce. There was a wicker basket of rolls covered with a white towel being passed around. And everyone had water to drink.

"That's bacon-wrapped filet mignon," Catherine said.

M and Gislaine said, "Oh!" and Audra said, "Decadent!"

"Bacon?" Gabrielle began cutting into the steak with a wooden handled knife.

"We don't have filet mignon every day," Catherine said.

"Gabrielle needs all the food you can give her," M said.

"Thank you, this looks so good. I've never heard of bacon wrapped around steak before." She got a small piece of both steak and bacon on her fork and put it all in her mouth. The aroma and crunchiness of the bacon mingled perfectly with the savory steak, which was almost as soft as butter. "Oh my goodness."

They all fell to eating. Rushel and Catherine had fish. Audra and Gislaine had the same steak as Gabrielle. M had a larger one. Maybe rib-eye, Gabrielle thought, and Samantha's meal looked very interesting. Grilled baby carrots, broccoli without the sauce, and golden brown potato slices. The last item on Samantha's plate Gabrielle did not recognize. It was similar in shape to the fish fillets but had a much lighter color under the grill marks. She knew it couldn't be fish.

Before she could ask, Samantha noticed her curiosity, sliced off a piece, and held the interesting morsel out on the end of her fork. Gabrielle leaned to her right and let Samantha put it in her mouth. She pulled it off with her lips as Samantha withdrew the fork gently. Someone dropped their silverware with a loud clatter. Without looking, Gabrielle knew it was Audra.

"Gabrielle," M said, smiling, "Work it around with your tongue. Have you ever tasted anything like that before?"

"It's delicious. I have no idea what it is."

"One of my favorite things," Samantha said.

"Oh, it's my favorite, too," Rushel said, biting off a piece of fish. "It just tastes so good."

The flavor was hard to define.

"Tangy," Gabrielle said.

"Safe to say we all like it a lot," Gislaine said.

Audra grabbed her glass and began gulping water.

M grinned. "Well, I've had it for a lot longer than any of you and believe me, you never get tired of it."

"And just the way it feels in your mouth," Gabrielle exclaimed. "It's so *juicy.*"

Audra began coughing. Rushel patted her on the back.

"You're going too fast, dear," M said. "Just go slow."

Audra tried to clear her throat and kept coughing. She got up, covering her mouth, and headed for the back bathroom. They heard water running and Audra coughing into a towel.

When Audra sat back down, Gislaine said, "Some things just go down the wrong way."

"Yes. So let's make sure we all have things go down the correct way. Right, girls?"

They all agreed. Audra just stared at her plate.

"You're all so smart," M beamed.

"It's called tofu," Catherine said.

"Tofu?"

"You just have to know how to work it."

"Well, you know what you're doing, working wise," Gabrielle said.

Catherine smiled. "I *am* an expert."

"You certainly are," M said. "And we all appreciate it." She turned to Rushel. "Sweetie, I was less than happy with your last report card."

"Uh oh," Gislaine whispered.

"I know. Fall quarter sucked."

"I don't want you to suck, dear. I want you to get ahead."

"This quarter's much better. I love my symbolic logic class."

"Good."

"No science classes." She glanced at Gabrielle. "So I am getting ahead."

Audra closed her eyes.

"We all want to get ahead," Gislaine said.

Gabrielle raised her glass of water. "To getting ahead."

"To getting ahead," they all said, except Audra. She raised her glass to clink with the others, however.

Gabrielle leaned closer to her. "Are you all right?"

Audra looked at her squarely. "No."

"You look a little flushed."

"I just need to go lie down."

"It's getting late," Gabrielle said and was puzzled by Audra's blank look.

"Um, well," Audra started.

Gabrielle leaned closer. "Come again?"

Audra exhaled. "Hoo kay."

They finished eating. Gabrielle leaned against the wall by the fireplace and watched them clean up, feeling growing anxiety about the next fast approaching crisis point of the evening. Sleeping arrangements.

Seven women. Four bedrooms. I guess I still get my room, she thought, but other than that.

When the dishes were almost done, when Catherine had the drying rack full, Rushel and M ducked into the middle room and came out wearing their white robes. Gabrielle felt mild alarm. Samantha turned off the stereo.

"Goddess, there's one more lesson for today," M said, and held out her hand.

Gabrielle walked across the room. "Okay."

"This is the big one," Rushel said. She gave her a robe.

Gabrielle unfolded it and pulled it on over her t-shirt and jeans. Rushel straightened out her glasses for her.

"Don't be nervous."

"You do realize saying that makes me extremely nervous."

She took M's hand. As she was led into the middle room, Audra caught her eye.

"Gabrielle," she said. "We live the examined life."

Wondering what that meant, she went through the door. The room was set up with the study lamp, as before, pointing at the floor, casting shadows up the walls. And there was something new. A large easel with a big pad of paper was propped up in front of the bench seats.

"You sit here." M directed Gabrielle directly in front of the easel and then sat beside her. "We'll wait for the others to join us. This is kind of a touchy subject. And I'd like you to keep an open mind."

"Of course."

"We're going to talk about sex."

"Relationships," Rushel said. She sat on the other side of M.

"Like they're not the same thing."

"We talk about emotions," Rushel said. "Not body parts."

"Yes, sweetie," M said, and then to Gabrielle, "I hope you won't find it too embarrassing."

"Kind of think I'm beyond embarrassment at this point."

M took her hand. "We all find this confusing at first."

"Maybe we should," Rushel said.

"I don't know," M replied. "I mean."

"Yeah. But it would be perfect."

"Well."

"It would."

"All right."

Gislaine, Catherine, Audra, and Samantha came in, all wearing their white robes. Gabrielle settled into her seat. This was going to be something.

"We should go to class dressed like this," Audra said. "The entire university would lose bladder control."

"Audra," Rushel said.

Audra cocked her head under her hood. "Yes, Charlie. Charlie, is that *you*?"

M laughed and coughed.

"You're not funny," Catherine said.

"I know I'm not funny. I'm *Lynette*. But you can call me *Squeaky*."

Samantha and Gabrielle began laughing. Rushel cleared her throat loudly.

"Audra, we want you to do yours after me."

"What? Now?"

"It would be perfect."

Audra looked wide-eyed for a moment. "I can see that. Okay." She left the room quickly.

M patted Gabrielle's hand and said to Rushel, "Hit it, sweetie."

Rushel got up and stood next to the easel. She held her hands over her chest. "A while back, I decided I needed to figure out my life. You know how it is when your feelings start to take over. You feel like you're going out of control. I don't like that. I can't live like that."

She pulled back the cover sheet on the big pad on the easel.

"So I sat down and tried to figure out how relationships work. I tried to put everything into some kind of rational framework. I did all this when I was starting junior college. I was a little older than you are now, Goddess, and a boy fell in love with me."

Gislaine made a 'tsk' sound.

Her first page read across the top: *The Seven Stages of Love.*

"I tried to understand what he was feeling. I tried to see things through *his* eyes. His name was…"

"Uh," M said.

"Yes. We'll call him A. Because he was the first." She flipped over the next page. *Stage One*, it read. *Elutheria or Freedom.*

"This is our state between relationships. We are single. We are free. And then this happens…" She pulled the paper back.

The next page read *Stage Two: Ekplexi or Surprise.*

"Someone catches your attention. You see them or hear them. You find them interesting. The surprise is that someone like that *exists* in the world. It seems new and wonderful. I felt that was about A, a little. He didn't look at me the way all the other boys did. Maybe I was reading too much into it."

"Yes," Gislaine muttered.

Rushel shrugged and tugged at her robe. Her hair was bunched up at the collar. "If you can't over-analyze yourself, what can you over over-analyze?"

The door opened and Audra came in with a similar large pad of paper.

"Good, you're only on Two. Can't wait for Four."

"Yes, we know, dear," M said. "You're hooked on Four."

"I wish."

Rushel continued. "That's Stage Two." She flipped the paper over. *Stage Three: Afi or Touch.*

"Ah fee?" Gabrielle asked.

"Yeah. I was learning Greek at the time. I almost used archaic but finally went with contemporary."

"Your junior college taught Greek? That's unusual."

"Oh, God no. They barely had Spanish. I just got interested in Greek so I taught myself."

M patted Gabrielle's hand again.

"Stage Three. After you see, you want to touch. Test the waters. If there's the slightest hitch, the relationship may not go any further. The way I think of it, relationships are fundamentally an ongoing economic transaction and emotions are the currency."

"Ooh," Audra whispered as she sat back down with a large folder.

Rushel said, "What that means, you want your feelings, the currency, returned. And that leads to more feelings. This is the actual beginning of the relationship. You're both nervous and extra attentive. If touching continues at the correct speed, if there are no negative signals, like an inappropriate joke, or not listening, disinterest, then we may proceed to the next stage."

"Finally," Audra said.

"No, not finally."

"It is for me."

Rushel rolled her eyes. "Stage Four." She flipped the page. *Vida or Breathe each other's breath.*

Audra raised her hand.

Rushel ignored her. "With A, one day he just came and sat down next to me in the library. North Bay Community College. I was at Stage One. I never noticed him staring at me the way most boys do. He just started talking. I thought he was funny. And it was definitely surprising. Most boys were incapable of speech around me. The librarian kept shushing him but he didn't care. I liked that."

"Wow. Kind of a bad boy, then," Audra said. "Talking in the library."

"Yeah, actually. That was Stage Two. We spent a lot of time talking. I liked talking to him. He liked it more than I did. Then at lunch one day, he asked me out on a date."

"And you said yes," Gislaine said.

"I thought I was supposed to."

"You need to have an excuse ready at all times," Gislaine said. "So you don't have to think about it."

"He was a *nice* boy," M said.

"He seemed nice. These days I'm much better at avoiding awkward situations. On our date, he picked me up in his dad's car. He was wearing a new shirt. You'll never guess where we went. A bookstore. We went to Main Street Books and browsed around for an hour. He bought me a really nice edition of *Metamorphosis.* I got the impression he actually knew what it was. I still have it. Then we went to Carl's Jr. and had dinner."

"Doesn't sound so bad," Gabrielle said.

"No, it wasn't. That was my first date ever. And he didn't try to kiss me or anything."

They all nodded approvingly.

"Then he asked me out again."

"Uh oh," Audra said.

"I didn't have an excuse ready. I said yes. And really, I didn't know what I wanted. I guess I was a late bloomer. I didn't know what desire was. When I looked at someone, what did I feel? I would have... feelings, every now and then, but it was all so confused.

"One day, I sat in a different seat in the college library where it was crowded so A couldn't find me right off and I looked at my fellow students and tried to figure out what I felt. I looked at all of them systematically. I'll never forget it."

"So smart," M said softly.

"My theory is, we don't know what we want until we see it. And then we're surprised. *Ekplexi*, right? And the more we look at what we like, the more we like it. I decided that I would, right then and there in the library, determine what I liked. What I wanted. What I desired."

Rushel threw back the hood of her robe and unleashed her hair, pulling it up past the collar. She had to use both hands. Then she tossed her head back. Her thick, silky, golden hair tumbled over her shoulders and draped her body all the way to her waist. The perfect planes of her face were put into relief by the low light.

Gabrielle thought she was the most beautiful woman she had ever seen. She heard someone gasp. Couldn't tell who, but not Gislaine.

"The library was always full. There was no other place to sit down out of the rain, and this was Falkirk, Washington. It was pretty much always raining. The students self-organized by tables. From where I was sitting,

I could see most of them. Some were groups of friends, some were school clubs. There were the guys who were always working on cars. There were the girls who liked celebrity magazines and did things to their hair. The whole chess club was in there. All three guys. They always looked scared. There was the jock table. All guys except for one cheerleader."

"Which one?" Audra asked quickly.

"I told you before."

"But tell who it was again."

"Edwina."

"Oh, God."

"Audra, you have to give it to her."

"Because she was born with tits?"

"Yeah. Plus her ass."

Audra shrugged. "Her ass was excellent."

"She's going to wind up fat."

"Oh, so fat."

"Anyway, I looked at all the boys in turn. I knew I was supposed to like boys. And they were all kind of cute, I thought. One had nice eyes. Another I thought had a really good profile. You know, chin, nose. Another boy, I thought, well, his mouth was sexy. I felt something then. I looked at his mouth and thought about it on me. I considered what I was feeling. I felt, really, I was on to something. And *then* I thought about the rest of him. Huh. All of it. The smell. Dandruff. I mean, boys with oily dandruff? And his grabby hands. And, you know. *That.*" Rushel held out her hands, "*Sayonara!*"

They all laughed.

"But I *was* on to something. There was a kind of thread I could follow. And the thread was, someone's mouth on me. I knew suddenly, sitting there with my books, that I desired a mouth to kiss me. I knew it. And it all fell into place. I thought of my body. I had actually never thought about my body all that much. I was having my period and I handled that like you're supposed to. I looked up everything in the library. They had a medical encyclopedia way in the back. It was just a bodily function. Like wiping. My mom told me what to do. Very undramatic.

"However, no one ever told me about this feeling. This other feeling. And, God, I suddenly thought about someone kissing me. I had to put my head down. And my mind was just spinning around, I thought, *hell's bells,* if it wasn't boys I desired then what? What else *was* there?

"And now every time I get a good grade on a test and I start to think, wow, I'm smart, I'm so smart. Super smart. But I didn't know that I wanted was right in front of me. Literally. I wanted Edwina's mouth on me. I focused on her lips from across the room. It was noisy. People in coats were walking between us. I stared at her lips as she talked.

"I felt really embarrassed. I left my books and went to the girl's restroom. Thank God no one was in there. I went in the one stall. They only had the one. It was just the beginnings of desire. In hindsight, it was nothing. And then the door banged open and Melissa and Terry came in, laughing. I fake flushed and pulled up my jeans and got out.

"I thought they would know. I expected them to stare at me. But no. Terry ducked in to pee. Melissa kind of gave me a look. That was all.

"I went back to my seat. There was a girl sitting right next to me. A senior. Didn't know her name at that point. Fluffy blonde hair. I wanted her. On the next table, the one with long brown hair who always wore her glasses way down on the end of her nose. I wanted to kiss her. Hard. The one in a chair by herself who always looked half angry. The way she frowned. I wanted to go over and put my mouth on hers. I had never kissed anyone. Never. I could not stop thinking about kissing."

"Uh huh," Gabrielle said and swallowed.

"That was pretty much the extent of my imagination, for the most part. At least that day in the college library. I thought about lips. Kissing girl's lips. Lips kissing me all over. Funny, never thought about tongues until much later. The whole tongue thing.

"Then, in shock, I remembered I had a date with a boy. I was gripped with panic. I had heard from a friend of one of his friends that he was going to take me to a drive-in movie. Even I knew what that meant. But I got my panic under control. I did not lock myself in my room. I realized I had a secret weapon. The greatest secret weapon poor, unworldly, late-blooming Rushel could ever have. And her name was Audra."

Gabrielle gasped. Audra jumped up and waved her hand over her head. Samantha and Gislaine clapped.

Rushel pulled over the next page of her pad. *Gnosis, or knowledge*, it said.

"Date night arrived. A pulled up in his dad's car. He didn't come to the door and my parents didn't try to invite him in. They were so happy I finally had a boyfriend they didn't want to scare him away.

"I came out the front door and waved. A reached over and opened the passenger door. I got to the car and just at that instant, Audra jumped up from behind the neighbor's hedge, dashed over and jumped into the front seat. I got in and slammed the door. And Audra said."

"Whoa! Nice car! Thanks for inviting me! What movie are we gonna see?" Audra said.

"Oh, and the car was a Le Baron which had bucket seats. So Audra sat half on the transmission and half on my lap, all the while leaning on A with her arm on his shoulders.

"He handled it pretty well.

Audra: "He said, oh hi, Audra. You can sit in the back if you want. And I said, no I'm fine."

"He acted like it was funny and he looked at me and instantly knew exactly what I was doing. *Gnosis*. Knowledge. Deep, unspoken understanding. Which you see is followed by *Chorista*, which means *asunder*. Break up. This is inevitable. Sometimes it happens in months or years. Sometimes it's till death do you part. But you always part. In my case, it was about twenty seconds. From knowledge to asunder."

"Wow, Rushel," Gabrielle said.

"And then we went to the movie," Audra said. "*The Return of the Pink Panther*."

"I've never seen that."

"That movie, the main thing I remember," Audra said, "is the actress in it kind of looked like Rushel. We thought that was cool."

"And he didn't get mad?"

"No. I knew he liked Audra."

"Everybody likes me. I'm a scream."

"Yes you are," Gabrielle said, laughing. "But poor A."

"He was a smart young man," M said.

Rushel made a tiny shrug. "I guess he was okay."

"He was okay," Audra said.

"Yeah. But."

"But."

"No."

"God, no."

"So we never went out again. I didn't exactly tell my parents and for the longest time they thought I had a boyfriend. I didn't want to disappoint them. It was what they wanted. I was going out, you know, but not with boys. When I thought about it at the time, I realized this was a pretty important episode for me. My first boyfriend, even though all we did was hold hands for about one second in the bookstore. And I also realized he was probably my last boyfriend because *now* I knew what I wanted." She turned over the next page. "And that brings us to Stage Seven. *Vathys,* or *Profound.* You can't go back to a state of unknowing. You are forever changed." She turned over the final page.

It read *Elutheria or Freedom.*

"There. The cycle is complete. You are free once more."

Gabrielle felt M hand tighten on hers.

Finally Audra spoke into the silence. "And what did you do then? After A?"

Rushel gave her a look that said, yes, I'm getting to it.

"Now I knew what I liked. What I *desired.* And I knew I was good looking enough to get it. So I did. I thought all this the next week while I was sitting in the library again. I looked at that girl sitting next to me, she was back, the one with the feathered hair, and she smiled. So I leaned over and kissed her. She seemed surprised but not very much so I kissed her again. I asked her if she wanted to go out sometime and she said, sure, like it was an obvious question. Her name was Helen. She had a car. She told

316

me later she'd had a crush on me for a while. So it was no mystery why she
ended up sitting next to me. And the crazy part, when I kissed her, no one
noticed."

"Oh, they noticed," Audra said.

"Didn't look like it. No one said a thing."

"Paralyzed with incandescent lust."

Rushel nodded. "Yeah. I guess we've all been *there*."

"And after Helen, then what?" Audra asked.

"Maria."

"Uh huh."

"Tina. Cynthia. Jessica. Diane. The other Diane. Um." Rushel paused,
remembering.

"Gosh," Gabrielle whispered.

"Yep," M said.

"Toni. Jill. Katie. Carrie. Glenda. Delilah."

"Oh, I forgot about Delilah. Yum," Audra said. "What was she like?"

"She wouldn't stop giggling."

"Oh. Ew."

"I know. Barbara. Marisa. Nora. And, um, Edwina."

"You saved her for last?"

"Not on purpose. Then, it all changed."

"How so, Rushel?" Audra asked gently. "Used 'em all up?"

"Good grief, Audra. Over that summer, I realized I liked women who
were older than me. Adults. It got a little crazy."

"How crazy?

"Pretty crazy."

"Was there anything specific you could tell us? Just an example."

"Fine, Audra. You're going to be a pretty good lawyer." She wiped her
eyes. "I'll give you an example. One night my friends got in a big fight in
the parking lot."

"This was at the junior college?"

"Yes."

"And who were these friends?"

Rushel sighed. "Two P.E. instructors, a biology professor, and the Dean
of Women. It started out as just yelling, and then the professor and the
Dean pulled guns."

Gabrielle gasped.

"No one got hurt. They were terrible shots. Just a few windshields and a
window in the admin building."

"So what was the fight about, Rushel?"

"They were fighting over me."

"Doing it for extra credit, huh?"

"No. But I could've," she said with a smile. "In hindsight."

"Hindsight's a good word for it," Samantha said.

"I decided to leave the area because of that. And other events. I applied for college out of state. I looked over Audra's shoulder one day. This place seemed nice."

"Not very Washingtonian," Audra said.

"Totally not. It's kind of subtropical."

"Tropical? Here?" Gabrielle said.

"Sure. This is more than halfway to Mexico. I'm getting used to it." She tossed her hair. "I'm a California girl now."

"Okay, Rushel," Audra said. "Let's get to the heart of this. Why were the women fighting over you with guns? Someone could have died, including you."

Rushel folded over all the pages of her pad and took it off the easel.

"It is the evolution of desire. An extension of my idea of relationships as economic transactions. This is the actual mechanism by which the human race reproduces. Throughout history, all civilizations as far as I can see, are based on this." She spoke directly to Gabrielle. "And now Audra will give you *her* explanation."

Audra got up with her big pad. Gabrielle saw she also had a yellow yardstick in her hand.

"Audra, adorable one," M said. "It's getting late so I need you to get to the point."

"Acknowledged." She put her pad on the easel. "And may I say I appreciate the way you put that."

She dramatically whipped back the heavy cover sheet to reveal the first page.

Samantha, Rushel, Catherine all exclaimed, "Ah!" and turned away. Gabrielle covered her eyes. M made a hissing sound and gripped Gabrielle's hand so hard it hurt.

Gabrielle took her hand away from her face and looked.

On Audra's first page was a drawing in felt pen, a line drawing of a male torso from chest to knees, with a fully deployed and erect penis.

"Wait," Gabrielle said. "Is that real? I mean."

"Oh yeah," Audra said grimly. "All too real."

"But is it really like that?" Gabrielle said. She thought her voice had a panicked tone to it.

Audra stood before the drawing, yardstick in hand. "I understand your reaction. To *this*," she said and whacked the picture with the yardstick, "The male pleasure weapon. How many of you have seen one of these in the flesh?" *Whack.*

Gabrielle felt M start at the sound.

Audra raised her free hand. "I admit, I have."

Samantha turned her arm up at the elbow. "Me."

Audra hit the picture again, much harder. "That." *Whack.* "Is two too many." *Whack.* The yardstick broke into multiple pieces. One fragment flew across the room and hit the tiny lamp. She dropped the small piece she had left and quickly folded back the picture. There was a blank page underneath. Everyone exhaled.

"Thanks for the nightmares," Catherine growled.

"A necessary reminder. Two points." She winked at M. Gabrielle could almost feel M's eyes rolling. "*That* body part is what controls the males. It's not their brains. No, their brains are weak in comparison. Servicing that organ, giving that thing what it wants, is the explanation for most male behavior. Violence. Rape. War on a planetary scale.

"Point two. *We* don't have to deal with that. This is our world. It's just for us. I am so glad I was born a woman. We have it good here. I just wanted to say that."

She turned over the next page. It read in large letters: *The Irrational Heart*, and below was a drawing of a Valentine heart broken in two.

Audra took out a sheet of paper. It was looked like it had been ripped from a spiral-bound notebook and looked like it had been folded and refolded many times.

"I want to read you something that pertains to our world," she said. "It is a poem. The title is *Broken.*

"A crack?

"The egg is toothy

"As a shredded window

"Screen in a green

"Tornado.

"Where is each piece?

"An arm. Ankle. Ear.

"My table is out of room.

"My blueprint is torn and

"Missing. Only. Fragments.

"Slippery parts wet and

"Drying in the sun. Not

"Sure about that socket all

"Smooth glistening rejection.

"If you see any dreams

"Hiding in the dead grass like

"Rainbow snakes feel

"Free to adopt."

She cleared her throat. "Care to guess who wrote that?"

Gabrielle looked at Audra in amazement.

"Holly."

"Yes. This came a week after we broke up. Holly is an honors student. English major."

Gabrielle shook her head. "English."

"I could see her becoming a professor. She could do it if she doesn't self-destruct."

"My God," Gabrielle said. "Professor Holly."

"This is where relationships become dangerous. Those women Rushel named. At first, they wanted her body. Well, *that's* simple. They saw her and they could just taste her. And she let them because she wanted them as well. But in some cases, there was more going on. They weren't really your friends, were they, Rushel?"

"Most of them, no."

"How did you think of them?"

"Horny chicks that needed to get their rocks off. Same as me."

Catherine covered her mouth to stifle a laugh.

"So you got as far as *vida*, correct?"

"Most were like that. There was a *gnosis* in there."

"Did you know that the Greek word *vida* doesn't mean 'breathe each other's breath'? It means 'screw.'"

"I prefer my translation."

"Okay. So you screw and walk way and that's that. If you want to do it, just do it. Rushel was in control of her emotions, I'm guessing. I'm also guessing some of those women were not. I don't mean to judge them but I'm judging them. They were not in control because on some level they did not want to be. Lack of awareness causes this. Lack of self-knowledge. This is how lives are lost. It's possible for feelings to be so strong you are swept away. If you feel it happening, assert control. Keep your eyes open.

"So Rushel, tell us what A did after our movie date."

"He wouldn't talk to me. He wouldn't look at me. I walked right up to him in the lunch line and said hi and he ignored me. I thought, fine, and left him alone. Then a few nights later, I spotted his car driving by my house. He would go real slow and then take off. He'd go around the block ten times doing this. It was an every night thing for a couple weeks. Once, he caught me getting picked up for one of my other dates. He had no idea it was Helen, of course. He followed us but Helen managed to lose him. We drove into a bank parking lot behind a big tree and turned out the lights and ducked down. Helen loved it. She was really turned on. We just stayed there and made out.

"But, you know, I couldn't stand it. So one night I waited for him to come by for the first lap and then I stood in the middle of the street in the rain. He came around the corner, five houses down, and slammed on the brakes. I put my hands on my hips and didn't move. He sat there for a like three minutes and then he put it in reverse and floored it and tried to go back around the corner. My house is up on a hill, so he misjudged it and ran over someone's mailbox. It ripped his back bumper half off. He didn't drive by anymore after that.

"He started up something new. He started sneaking around my house at night. This was weird. I think he came up to my window once. His footprints were in the mud by my ferns. Then it all stopped."

"Just stopped?" Audra asked.

"I didn't see him in school anymore. It took a while to find out what happened because I didn't want to just ask because then everyone would've thought I had a thing for him and I definitely didn't. But I heard a couple teachers talking. Teachers would talk around me. They liked to try to impress me. It was their way of flirting. One night, A went into a Seven-Eleven and got a case of Budweiser and just walked out the door with it. The next thing anyone knew, A drove his dad's car backward down the highway and veered into the harbor. Had to have been going fast. It's all huge rocks. Then I think he went in the navy."

"Well, so much for A," Audra said, exhaling. "Now Helen."

"When Helen found out I was going out with Maria, she locked herself in her car and drank a whole bottle of whisky. She was all right, eventually."

"God!" Gabrielle said.

"And Maria."

"She didn't care. We just did it."

"Uh huh."

"Tina and Cynthia, just screwing. Jessica cried for days. Diane threw rocks at my house. The other Diane, we did it in the library, in the science fiction section. You remember that place?"

"That was a great spot," Audra agreed.

"Toni, Jill, Katie," Rushel continued. "No drama at all. Carrie disappeared for a week. Everyone was worried. I hardly noticed. She came back and tried to get my attention but I was with Glenda by then."

"Glenda," Audra said. "That one."

"She actually dumped *me*." Rushel shrugged. "It was mutual."

"But, *Glenda*," Audra said. "That mole? And her nose?"

"What? She got together with Jill."

"Poor Jill."

"Pretty much. And Delilah." She sighed. "Yeah."

"Giggles." Audra turned to Gabrielle. "Nonstop."

"Sadly," Rushel said.

"And then you discovered the college faculty."

"One of the P.E. instructors was fired. The Assistant Dean was promoted to Dean."

"So that wasn't so bad."

"Then I met Diane's sister Deanna this one Saturday at their house."

"You went to their house?"

"Sure. Her dad liked me. Dads always liked me. Anyway, Deanna. She was having problems in school." Rushel turned in her seat to face Gabrielle. "What happens is, people look at me. Everyone looks at me. I've determined that there are three basic categories of looking. There is the look of admiration. This is usually older men and a few older women. They look at me openly and kind of nod. Then, there is the look of competition. This is most women in my age range and a few men. They're hostile and never open about it. Then, lastly, there is the look of lust. This is almost all males in my age range and a few women. It's very simple. The males I avoid. The women, if I like them, I just go up and introduce myself. We'd get together and do it."

"Crude."

"That's how I looked at it in those days. Simple as could be."

"All right. About Deanna."

Rushel turned back and was silent.

"Do you want me to tell it?"

"No, Audra."

Audra crossed her arms. They all waited. Gabrielle saw Rushel thinking hard and struggling. Finally, her face blank, she pushed her shoulders back.

"Deanna was having problems in school in Seattle," Rushel said. "That's all I knew. What I didn't know was the reason she had come home from college was because she had tried to kill herself. She had taken a bunch of pain pills and passed out in her Medieval History class. She told everyone it was an accident. The school counselors just sent her home for the semester. They covered it up. They all just hoped it would go away, that she would get better.

"And then I showed up.

"This was right after the shootout. No more junior college, I mean, get me out of there. I was looking around. I thought she was interesting. Older, right? Honey blonde, brown eyes. Cute. I liked her. She looked at me. We got together. She kind of latched herself onto me. She called me on the phone constantly. Not the sort of relationship I wanted. I finally had to." Rushel stopped.

Gabrielle saw powerful emotions fighting across her face.

"I went to her house. She came to the door. I told her I couldn't see her anymore. I told her I no longer liked her. And her reaction. She just smiled and said okay. And I left. That evening she told her mom she was going out for a walk. She went down her street, then up to the railroad crossing. She walked up the tracks. No lights at all there. She went all the way to the bridge and waited. Around nine, the Northern Pacific came through as usual. Not fast. They can't go fast. She lay down on the tracks in front of a slow train. No one saw her."

"It wasn't your fault," Audra said insistently.

Rushel gazed at her steadily. "We've been over this many times, Audra. My position is not going to change. I was complicit in Deanna's death."

"That's not what complicit means."

"Fine. I... My behavior was a contributing factor." Rushel turned to Gabrielle again. "I decided to change my life. The way I lived my life. I stopped doing what I was doing. I didn't have sex for two years. I started reading a lot more. Ancient philosophers. The Bible. Things became more clear after a while. By that time, I was here in school with Audra. It was better. And one day I met M and I began my new life."

Gabrielle heard M exhale with a shudder.

"I love you so much, Rushel," M said.

"I love you, M."

Audra wiped her eyes and said, "Catherine."

Catherine tensed. "Yes."

"I don't mean to be cold, but could you tell us about your friend, Rebecca."

Catherine cleared her throat. "I met Rebecca when I was applying for a job at a restaurant over on the south side of town. She was a waitress there. Didn't get the job. They went out of business anyway. Rebecca was going to school part time and living with her girlfriend Amanda in this tiny trailer by the beach. They were having problems. They were beginning to want different things. One day, last fall, Rebecca told Amanda she wanted to live alone. I guess they had a fight."

"What happened after the fight?"

"Well, not long after, Amanda passed away."

"Say what really happened."

"That is what happened."

"Amanda did not *pass away*. She slit her wrists and lay down on their bed in that little trailer and bled to death. She killed herself."

Catherine said, "Yes."

Samantha and Gislaine both embraced her. Gabrielle could feel a breaking of a certain tension, as if they had all been waiting for Audra to mention this.

"We honor the memory of those who have died," Audra said. "by being honest. The irrational heart has its own rules. But instead of learning by trial and error, we try to understand ourselves from first causes. We are living things. Our animal nature underlies our emotions and behavior. Some women, when they learn this, *really* learn, choose to opt out. They never have physical relationships. They even deny their physical selves to a degree. They become hermits. If you were to go that way we wouldn't stop you, Goddess. Do you want to go that way, Gabrielle?"

Gabrielle, startled, said, "No."

"Sure?"

Gabrielle smiled mildly. It had been a momentous day filled with life changing moments. As far as decisions went she thought this one was easy. "I'm sure."

"Goddess," they all murmured in the close and warm room.

Gabrielle, feeling herself close to tears, saw a crooked smile cross Audra's face.

"Know yourself. You will master your animal nature and make it work for you." She flipped over the next page of her big pad. In authoritative letters, it said: *Human Sexual Response.*

"Oh, you expanded it," Rushel said.

"Been doing research. It was getting a little obsolete."

"Yeah, that class was a year ago."

"Wait." Gabrielle couldn't help it. "You did this for a class?"

"*Sex and Civilization.* It's the only class Rushel and I have ever taken together. When you're applying to law school they like to see stuff like this on your transcript."

"Interesting."

"It's supposed to indicate what a well-rounded young person you are. Turned out to be a great class."

"Because of the professor," Rushel said slyly.

"Donna was cool," Audra said, grinning.

"As you found out first hand."

"Yeah. For once." Audra couldn't stop grinning. "Everyone in the class wanted a copy of my project. The professor wanted a private demonstration."

"You got a better grade than me."

Audra sighed. "First time for that too. Anyway."

"A *lot* better grade." Rushel turned to Gabrielle. "Classic Stage Four."

"When you know what's what," Audra said, "relationships like that can be fun instead of traumatic. It helped that Donna wasn't a rookie."

"By a long shot."

"*Girls,*" M said. "Shall we."

"Sorry." Audra brushed her hair back and straightened her robe. "Let us now consider human sexual response, in particular, that phenomenon known as the orgasm." She turned over the next page of her pad, revealing, *The Male Orgasm.*

She tore the page off the pad with a loud rip.

"Nobody cares." She crumpled it into a ball and threw in the corner. Samantha laughed out loud.

The page underneath was blank. Audra lifted it partially and looked at them all.

"Let's cut to the fucking chase, shall we?" She turned the paper over. The next page read, in authoritative letters, *The Female Orgasm: Command and Control.*

"This is new," Gislaine said, writing. "Go slow."

"You could argue that the male orgasm is necessary for human reproduction. For now. But the female orgasm is in a class all its own. As far as we know, the female orgasm exists for the sole purpose of pleasure. Where the inferior male version is constrained by physiology, the female orgasm is liberated. First, some basic terms and concepts."

The next page was a graph.

"Have you seen this before, Goddess?"

"No, I haven't. *T* is time, of course. What's E sub *x*?"

"Ecstasy."

"Oh," Gabrielle said slowly.

Audra put her finger on point *Ac.* "Activation. You are watching tv and that show with Blondie Whatshername comes on. You turn the sound down but keep watching. You notice that in this particular episode she's not wearing a bra under her thin shirt. Perhaps you begin to feel desire. We call this activation. Then Blondie starts doing jumping jacks. The feelings of arousal begins to increase. This is the excitation level. Don't worry about the exact blood circulation and neurological events for now. The line starts going up. If Blondie keeps at it, the excitation reaches a leveling off point, a plateau. You can stay here for a while. And with *Ex* at 0.5, it feels good. But if stimulation continues, for example, your girlfriend comes home and catches you watching Blondie and starts cuddling and kissing your neck, you may break away from the plateau and shoot upwards. *Ec* levels will surge to a peak and *Ex* will hit 1.0 and your girlfriend will scream because you are pulling her hair. Then *Ex* will drop back to *Pt.*

"Now, for the poor males, that's it. They'll have to wait half an hour to hit 1.0 again, if they even can. But females, with their superior ecstatic systems, just keep right on rolling. See here."

She pointed to the right side of the graph where the line was spiky.

"From *Pt* to 1.0, again and again. And again. The multigasm."

Gislaine paused in her rapid writing. "Did you make that up?"

"Yeah. Pretty good, huh?"

"It's all right."

"Just all right? What would you call it?"

"Fantasmagasm. Sequential wondergasm."

Audra said, "I was trying to be descriptive. I'm not doing porn. Anyway, I'm trying to be a service to the Goddess. Maybe this graph will help her in some way."

Gabrielle cleared her throat. "Yes, thank you, Audra."

"You've never seen this before? This?" She indicated the multi part.

"Never knew it existed."

"I got all this from a book. This graph. Turns out, this is only the beginning."

Rushel and Gislaine exchanged a look. Gabrielle saw Catherine roll her eyes again and shake her head slightly.

Audra lifted the paper with the graph and unfolded an extension from underneath. The graph continued. It was now twice as long.

"Research of mine, if not actual experience, had indicated that the following may be true."

"Audra, dear," M said.

Rushel suddenly leaned forward and pointed. "What is *that,* superchick?"

"With proper stimulation, as the line indicates, we can achieve what
I call metaplateau 1, where the plateau level is actually the 1.0 orgasm
level. *Yes*, one long continuous 1.0 orgasm becomes the floor from which
we push higher to a mind boggling 2.0 orgasm. Indescribable ecstasy
capable of obliterating the barriers between conscious minds allowing
us to achieve true union with our loved one. Now, as far as I know, there
is no physiological basis for this, no higher level of muscle tension and
release which is the basis of 1.0. I believe a 2.0 orgasm may be achieved via
neurological ecstatic pathways alone. That's what I think is going on."

Gabrielle saw Audra give an interrogatory look to Samantha, who
remained impassive and motionless. She was also aware that Catherine,
tight with anger, was glaring at Audra without blinking.

Gislaine tapped her notebook with her pen. "Are you saying you've
done this?"

"You mean 2.0?"

Gislaine looked at Rushel, who was studying the extended graph
intensely. They snuggled a bit closer. "Or is this like a research project?"

"I've read accounts of it," Audra said. "I have no reason to doubt that 2.0
is possible."

"Okay, but those other pathways," Rushel said. "What are those?"

"Well."

"I mean, how do you get there?"

"There are many reports of metaplateau."

"That's the continuous orgasm."

"Yes, the 1.0. And I think the conventional approach would be to get to
the meta and try to stay there and build up energy. But, the other pathways
are fuzzy. I'm still trying to figure out what heck they're talking about in
some cases but there are definitely other modes of stimulation besides the…
you know. I promised no body parts."

"Thank you, dear," M said.

"And that, I'm still studying."

"Okay." Rushel sat back. "Thanks, Audra. That's interesting."

Gislaine kept writing. "Let us know what you come up with."

Audra smiled.

Gabrielle saw Catherine glare at Rushel and Gislaine and then look
down. Samantha caught her eye and tipped her head with a nod that
seemed to say, it's all right. Gabrielle, still not wanting to ask questions,
simply nodded back. She knew it was something very private. She would
find out when she found out.

M released her hand and Gabrielle said, not wanting to appear too
enthusiastic in front of Catherine, "Yes, thank you Audra. And Rushel,
thank you, also."

Rushel just said, "The Goddess should be fully informed." Her face was tired and her shoulders slumped.

"Catherine, I'm so sorry about Amanda," Gabrielle said.

Catherine nodded, still angry.

Gabrielle suddenly realized she really didn't need to say anything else. "I feel overwhelmed," Gabrielle said. "I'm going to take a shower and go to bed." She stood up and her knees cracked.

"Goddess." They all stood and were silent as she left the room.

Going into the flower scented bathroom, she heard angry voices behind her. Catherine and someone else. She could pick out Samantha's voice, a calm and even tone. Then they were all talking. Gabrielle closed the bathroom door. She felt like an intruder. They'll be fine, she thought. They're all old friends. I'm the newcomer.

She took a quick shower thinking others would want to use the bathroom but no one came in after her as she went into her bedroom. She clicked on the tiny lamp. Her silk pajamas were on the bed where she had tossed them, unlaundered by hobbits. No more voices. She thought fleetingly of getting dressed and sneaking out and going back to her basement. Rent's paid through March, everything's still in the car, she thought. It would be just like what I did before. Except of course they would cast me out.

She put on her pajamas. They still smelled of perfume. Catherine's.

She sat on the bed. Her watch on the nightstand said *12:18*. She sighed. I'm still a college student, she thought. I still have to get up in the morning. Driving, parking. Required now. And gas. A fairly long commute.

"I already made the decision," she said. She was not in the habit of second guessing herself or running away. If someone gets mad, just handle it. She sighed again and realized she had, after all that, still not figured out the sleeping arrangements. She giggled. Rushel's scheme was going to stick in her head, she just knew it. And so was Audra's.

She quietly turned off the lamp and opened the bedroom door. There was no light or sound in the hall or the living room and kitchen area. And no one had used the bathroom after her. Of course, there was the small bathroom off the middle room but it didn't have a shower.

Maybe they all took showers in the morning, she thought. A traffic jam when you're getting ready to go is annoying. Brian and Mark were always getting pissed off at each other about hogging the bathroom. Naturally, Elliot had the right idea: never take showers.

She giggled again in the darkness. She supposed Catherine and Samantha were in one of the bedrooms. The thought did not create a surge of jealousy. She knew she was now thinking differently about them both, especially Samantha. Rushel and Gislaine were undoubtedly together. Good for them. That left M and Audra.

She shook her head. "I'll have to think about that," she whispered.

The smell of the steaks was still strong in the silent house. Hm, she thought, where exactly did Catherine put the Tingles? She got out of bed and padded across the hall onto the tile floor of the dining area. She found the switch for the under-cabinet lights.

Illuminated this way, the white tile and stainless steel kitchen seemed almost cozy. The cabinets with their glass windows were full of cereal and cake mix, dishes and cups and glasses. Tingles might be wherever the canned food is, she thought. There was a tall, narrow door beside the refrigerator. It was a shelf unit on tracks, loaded with glass containers of flour, sugar, and rice. She opened the fridge.

Maybe there's leftover tofu, she thought. Yes, there was a small plate covered with aluminum foil tucked behind the cartons of milk and cream and golden bottle of apple juice and yellow, pulpy orange juice. She set the plate on the counter under one of the tiny bulbs and peeled the foil from one edge. It was cream-colored slab with grill marks.

"Ah, good," she said and got a butter knife from the drawer. She sliced off a very thin piece. "I hope Samantha doesn't mind. This is so good." She chewed it slowly. Savory with just the right texture. "What a funny name. Tofu."

Someone spoke from the darkness of the living room. "Oh, God, not tofu again."

Gabrielle froze in mid-chew. It was Audra. She was in one of the reclining chairs and covered with a dark blanket. Gabrielle quickly covered the plate back up.

"Sorry, I didn't mean to wake you up."

Audra looked very comfortable curled up in the big chair.

"Wasn't asleep. Just thinking. You know, you can have all that. If it's in the fridge, it's fair game."

"I just wanted a taste. I was really looking for the Tingles."

"No idea where she'd put Tingles." Audra sat up. "On the other hand, I do know where she keeps the wine." She threw off the blanket. And got up, a ghostly figure in her white robe. "Want some?"

"All right. Half a glass, maybe."

Audra came around to the back of the island where Gabrielle was standing and dropped to her knees in front of her. "Always the bottom cabinet." She opened a door. "Hm. She does move it around." She opened the next one, under the sink. Gabrielle moved back. "Ahh. Behind the Ivory. Sneaky." She brought out a dark bottle and stood. It was about half full. "Merlot. Perfect for a night like this."

"She won't miss it?"

"Oh, she'll know." Audra got two small water glasses from an upped cabinet. "But we have all kinds of wine. Oodles. We have an actual wine cellar. I don't think you've seen it."

"Haven't explored the house that much yet."

Audra put an inch of the dark red wine in each glass and gave one to

Gabrielle. She took her glass and clinked it. "To the two point oh."

Gabrielle grinned. "The two point oh." She took small sip. This was the strong stuff. It made her mouth pucker.

"I assure you it's real."

"Okay. Well, maybe I'll encounter it one day."

"Yes." Audra clinked her glass on Gabrielle's again. "And I hope I'm there when it happens." She gave Gabrielle a quick look, turned away and went back to her chair and picked up the blanket. "It's an embarrassing subject."

Gabrielle sat in the other chair. The soft leather fit her shoulders like the palm of a hand. She relaxed and settled back. "I'm not embarrassed, really. It's interesting. I just don't know what to say. The same with Rushel. I feel stupid."

"No one in their right mind would know what to say. Rushel is unique."

"You're all so much more experienced than I am."

Audra took a large sip. "You're the most mature of all of us. I would rate you higher than M. And believe me, Rushel is a little girl compared to you."

The fireplace next to the dining table made a ticking sound as it cooled. The roof creaked as the wind picked up.

"I didn't feel that way. And Catherine. God, I had no idea."

"Amanda? I only met her once. Brown hair. Brown eyes. I used her as an illustration of how your emotions can kill you. Because I'm an asshole. And now Catherine is doubly mad at me." She gulped the rest of her wine and got up. She dumped the rest of the bottle into her glass. She stood at the island and stared at the hallway door. Then she sat back down on the edge of the chair. "You are the least vulnerable person I've ever met. That won't be your reaction." Audra eyes bored into her. "When it happens to you."

Gabrielle held still.

Audra let herself slip back onto the cushion, holding her glass out and level.

"You're kind of like me in that way. But you have more of an even keel. I'm not like that. I'm mercurial."

This made Gabrielle laugh. "I like talking to you."

Audra shrugged and sipped. "I can be pleasant. That's not my goal in life, however."

Gabrielle sipped also. "What is your goal?"

Audra's eyes lit up. "When L stole M's inheritance, she told me it felt as if she had been violated. And since I've known her, I've seen L do shit you wouldn't believe. The house in Pasadena. We all thought that was our safe place. Safer than here." She shook her head. "God, I never want to feel helpless like that again. My goal is to have power, I guess. Power to protect. Power to fight back. I like your idea of stealing M's stuff back. I'm still thinking about it." She took another drink and looked at her glass. "So my plan is to go to law school. Stanford, maybe. Wherever."

Gabrielle let thoughts form for a moment. "I want to create computers. That would be power. Power to understand the universe. Power to cure diseases like cancer."

Audra sat up and leaned forward out of her chair. She got very close and held her glass up. "Power over *evil*," she said fiercely.

Gabrielle touched her glass to Audra's. "Power over evil."

They both drank the rest of their wine. Gabrielle put the glasses in the sink. Audra in her chair pulled the blanket up to her chin.

"How come you're sleeping in here?"

"M is in my room." She cocked her head. "At least I think she is."

"Well, you know, you could sleep in my room if you want. You know, with me."

Audra smiled just a little. "Thanks, but these days I sleep alone. It's for the best." She curled up her legs. "I know myself." She pulled up the blanket.

"Okay. Well, sleep tight." Gabrielle turned out the under cabinet lights.

"I might fall asleep eventually. We'll have to see." She nestled her head against the chair.

Gabrielle walked across the dark room to the hallway and heard the thump of a closing door. Couldn't tell which one.

"Gabrielle," Audra whispered behind her.

"Yes."

"We will become powerful. You and I."

"All right."

"I know. I can tell." Her voice trailed off.

Gabrielle waited for a moment. Audra was quiet.

She went into her room and closed the door behind her. She made sure it wasn't locked.

The wind gusted outside and rain pelted the big window. She could feel the waves on the beach and the pounding of her heart. She turned in her bed and watched the door.

That night in the beach house, her first night as Goddess, Gabrielle was awakened twice. There was a slamming door from the far end of the hall. She could sense the anger in it and she lay on her back, listening, and drifted back to sleep.

Then she dreamed of walking down a street, searching. She was searching for a house in the early morning, just before dawn. The street was sharply curved and the houses were hard to see behind hedges and fences and trees. There were no lights on, the people inside were all asleep, she knew. The houses were like dark caves.

She felt triumphant. She was returning from a long journey. The air was warm. Behind her, the sun was about to come up. The sky was clear and glowed electric blue and red and green. She felt it was vital she find the correct house before the sun came up. She knew she would recognize it by the windows and the front steps. She knew she belonged there. The people inside would welcome her and would greet her warmly and she would tell them the amazing things she had seen and learned.

She walked and walked and then opened her eyes again in total darkness. She had to think where she was, thrashing under the perfumed sheets. In a bed, not on the twilight street. She wanted to go back. She had to. She wasn't done searching. Here, the sun was still far away. I'll never find the street again, she thought in dismay.

Then a sound, a different sound. She breathed and waited and the sound returned. Weeping, muffled but close. She sat up. In the hall, wait, the bathroom. The sound of someone crying was coming from under the bathroom door. It lasted a minute and then there was no other sound at all.

Gabrielle lay awake.

Gradually gray light overtook the darkness outside her window. The rain had returned. She swung her legs out and put her feet on the floor. She stood up slowly. Her whole body was tired. She quietly went into the bathroom and left the lights off. There was the smell of perfume and shampoo. Who was it, she thought. Is there any way I can tell? Is there any evidence? There was a towel on the floor beside the toilet. She picked it up. Do tears have a smell?

Maybe they do, she thought. But it is beyond me.

She dropped the towel in the hamper and went out into the hall. She wiggled her toes in the carpeting and smelled coffee.

Audra was standing at the curved window holding a coffee cup in both hands. "They all left," She said.

Gabrielle stopped.

"They took off really early. Rushel and Geegee are still in bed."

Her hand on the warm coffee pot handle, Gabrielle said, "Geegee?"

"No one can pronounce her name. I'm sorry, it's ridiculous."

"She doesn't seem like a Geegee, though."

"That's why it's funny."

Gabrielle drank half her cup in one gulp. "So M left? Is she coming back?"

"It's because of me," Audra said. "I made Catherine and Samantha upset. Well, Catherine, mostly. Sammie usually doesn't get upset at anything. If the past is any guide, M has taken them somewhere to make them feel better. And you know what that means."

"A trip to a fancy store?"

"Shopping. You have learned much, Goddess, of the strange ways of us humans."

"Thank you." Gabrielle got a bowl and spoon. She opened one of the upper cabinets and took out the box of Cocoa Krispies. "I now realize how limited my knowledge was."

"We are complex. And yet simple."

Gabrielle got the carton of milk and peeled it open.

"Pretty complex."

"If it's Santa Barbara, they'll be back this evening. If it's San Francisco, they'll stay overnight. Maybe more than one night. And this feels like Frisco level upsetness." Audra watched Gabrielle pour sugar on the Cocoa Krispies and then douse everything with milk. "So, Goddesses live primarily on sugar?"

"And chocolate. And caffeine."

Audra looked at her coffee. "I knew it. This is *literally* the food of the gods."

Gabrielle was anxious to get going but Rushel was late getting up and riding in Gabrielle's car, bundled against the rain and cold, they got to the upper parking lot a few minutes before seven-thirty, the start of math class. The lot was packed and Gabrielle, squinting through the rain smeared windshield, drove in circles down the rows of Toyotas and Fords and Chevys. Finally, she saw a green Pinto back out of a space one row over and floored it, beating out a Datsun coming from the other direction.

The Datsun stopped, the door opened, and the driver got out. He was pudgy and was wearing black framed glasses. He put his hands on his hips and glared at them.

"Hey, asshole, that was my spot! Hey!"

As she turned off the engine, Gabrielle said, "Oops. Didn't see him."

Audra, in the back seat, snorted and said, "Who gives a shit?"

Rushel in her black sweater got out and stood at the open door. She tipped her head and tossed her hair. Under the dark overcast, the blonde strands all but fluoresced. The guy stared at her.

"Oh, hi, gosh, I didn't see you. I'm sorry." She put her hand to her mouth. "Um," she said, making it sound like a sob. "Do you want me to move?"

"Well," the guy said in a normal tone.

"I didn't want to be late and I saw this spot. Is this your spot?"

In the car, Audra quietly said, "Keep your head down."

Gabrielle pretended to study her notebook.

The guy looked away from her.

"Please. I really didn't see you," Rushel said with an extra girlish pleading tone and smiled. She walked over to him and put her hand on his shoulder briefly. She took her hand away with another hair toss, as if embarrassed. "I'm sorry," she said in her breathy voice and went back to the VW.

The guy kept staring at her. His expression softened. "Sure. Go ahead. Don't worry about it." He dropped back into the Datsun and put it in gear. "I hope you're not late," he yelled as he drove past them.

They watched him leave the lot entirely and go down the campus road.

"Heading for the big lot," Gabrielle said.

"That'll be full, too," Audra said and laughed.

"Thanks, Rushel," Gabrielle said. "That was pretty good."

"Well, I *am* the reason we're so late." She carried her things in a black satchel bag with a shoulder strap. "Always feels weird to do that."

They locked up the car. I'll just make it, Gabrielle thought.

"Another few minutes and that guy would've probably given you his car and all his money," Audra said. She had a gray backpack with padded straps, a nice new one.

"I've never actually done that," Rushel said.

"You should some time."

They headed for the stairs.

"I don't think I should employ my talents in that way."

"When that guy is ninety years old and lying in a hospital about to pack it in he will still remember the blonde girl in the parking lot."

Rushel made a half shrug.

"Well, yeah."

"You turned it around so he was all of a sudden doing you a favor," Gabrielle said. "So you made him happy."

"I want everyone to be happy."

They went down the wet concrete steps.

"You touched a boy," Audra said.

"It'll wash off."

That afternoon when they got back to the car, Gabrielle discovered someone had scratched the paint, probably with a key, a long deep scratch across the driver's door, all the way down to the metal. Standing in the drizzle, they all looked at it silently and knew it wasn't the guy in the Datsun.

They drove home without talking, agreeing silently it had been, despite everything, a pretty good Monday.

That evening in the quiet house, when Catherine, Samantha, and M didn't return, Gabrielle started to make herself dinner but she remembered and stopped. Gislaine and Rushel – they both had Mondays off – came out of their room and they made Campbell's tomato soup from two large cans along with small, delicious grilled cheese sandwiches. They all sat together at the table and this time it was Gislaine's turn. It was short and, Gabrielle thought, very nice.

"We thank you, our Creator, for our evening meal and for this refuge from the storm. May we be ever mindful of your love."

"So shall it be," they all said.

"Dinner last night was fairly big," Gislaine said. "So soup seemed appropriate."

"This is my favorite," Gabrielle said. With only four of them present,

Gabrielle could feel the emptiness of the house and room. A silence lay over the table but they talked, in subdued voices, about school. How the fees were now over two hundred dollars a quarter, upcoming tests, and how many students were dropping classes.

"My Advanced Topics class is down to seven and philosophy has eight. Shakespeare's still pretty full."

"People like Shakespeare, maybe," Gislaine said.

"It's a required class. My math class is like that. Everyone's still there. You have to take it and suffer. They don't give you a choice."

"What's your philosophy class?" Rushel asked. "I love philosophy."

"Another class I should've gotten out of the way years ago. Introduction to Philosophy for Non-Humanities Majors."

Rushel laughed. "Oh my God. Who's the teacher?"

"Townsend."

"I think he's new."

"He's impossible to understand sometimes. Wait, I gotta show you something." Gabrielle got up and fetched her notebook. "This is what he said today. It was like a speech." She found her notes and read: "'As we navigate blindly through our entrapped awarenesses, reading and being read, we must keep in our fragmented consciousnesses the wisdom of Lacan, who said, something in French, then let the subliminal be prioritized in the hierarchy. Let the real and the anti-real be one.' And then everyone applauded. All eight of us."

"Oh, wow. He's a postmodern deconstructionist."

"A what?" Gislaine laughed.

"They try to dissect everything. Books, movies, shopping lists, everything. They pick it apart until there's nothing left. And they think the goal is to be hard to understand. They love that. It's a game to them. I've gotten in big fights with some of those guys."

"Yes, you have," Audra said.

"I have to write a paper. Or a presentation. Haven't even started."

"Oh. Well, I could help you."

"That would be great, Rushel."

"What's it about? Did he give you a topic?"

"No. It can be about anything in philosophy."

"You know what would be funny? Let's deconstruct something!"

Gabrielle laughed. "That, I'm pretty sure, would go over well with Townsend. What do we deconstruct?"

"Don't know. We'll just look around."

"Right. There has to be something. This is gonna be great."

"Yeah. It's pretty easy. What's that other class you have? Advanced something?"

"Advanced Topics. Graduate level."

"Cool. So what's the big topic there?"

"Physics of the Transistor."

Gislaine held up her hand. "What exactly is a transistor, anyway?"

"Yes," Rushel said. "We can finally find out."

"She knows everything about transistors," Audra said.

They all looked at Gabrielle. She set her spoon down on the folded napkin.

"Okay, they're pretty simple. It's a device which allows you to control a large amount of electrical current with a small amount of voltage."

"I see." Gislaine took a tiny bite of her sandwich. "What exactly is current?"

"It's the term for the flow of electric charges. The volume of it. Think of water flowing in a pipe. There's the pressure of the water, that's voltage, and the diameter of the pipe tells you the volume. That's current. So a transistor is like a valve where a tiny flow can control a big flow. It can act like a switch and just turn a line on or off. Computers use transistors like that. Or it can amplify a tiny signal, like from a radio antenna, so you can hear it."

"So," Rushel said, "radio waves are electricity?"

"That's what I always thought," Gislaine said.

"Radio waves are the same as light. Electromagnetic radiation."

"So not electricity."

"Nope. The waves travel through space and encounter the metal in an antenna and cause electrons in there to move. Put that tiny movement of electrons at the gate of a transistor and you can amplify it. Or on the other hand make electrons move in a wire in the right pattern and you will get radio waves."

Audra cleared her throat. "Electrons?"

"Outer part of atoms. Orbiting the nucleus. They have a negative charge. The inside part, the nucleus, has protons in it. Those are positive. So they balance out usually. In metals, the outermost electrons can move to other atoms of the metal. They're loose. So you make wire out of metal. In fact, that's pretty much the definition of a metal."

"So they're actually real?" Audra said skeptically. "Electrons?"

"Well, yeah. That's what electricity is."

"It's just that I kind of thought they were making it all up. Atoms and stuff."

"Really," Rushel said.

"No, it's not made up," Gabrielle said. "I mean this is all theory."

"A *theory*?" Audra said.

"A pretty well established theory. The atomic structure of matter. It's actually fairly new, the way we use it. Quantum electrodynamics just since the forties."

"But it's just a theory?"

"You can't actually see what's going on so you create a hypothesis to explain it. Then you do experiments to test your hypothesis. So, yeah, just a theory. If someone came up with a better theory we'd all use it."

"Okay, wait. Back to transistors. And electrons, right? What are those?" Rushel asked, and dipped her spoon into her soup.

"We're not bugging you too much, are we?" Gislaine said.

"She absolutely loves this," Audra said into her sandwich.

"No, this is fun. It's good to go over the basics."

"This is what we do instead of watch tv," Audra said. "We pummel each other with questions."

"I haven't watched tv in years."

"Me neither."

"An electron is an elementary particle that has a negative electric charge. The charge we call negative one. And the proton is positive one. Simple. Electrons can move around in metals like copper. Set up a coil of copper wire in the right way and move a magnet inside it and you have a generator. The magnetic field pulls the electrons along the wire. The electric charges were already there, you just made them move. Spin the magnet fast and you get voltage and you can send the electrons a long way. They make a loop. They go out of the generator or battery and come back along another wire. That's a *circuit*. Electrons are real physical things. They have mass. The electron shell around atoms are all we experience of matter in the world. When you look at something you are seeing photons of light reflected from that electron shell. Some light is absorbed, some bounces off, in complicated ways. So the light can tell you about those atoms and their electrons."

"Okay," Rushel said. "Electrons are particles. I get that. And they have an electric charge. So what are electrons made of and what is this electric charge?"

"An electron is one of the fundamental particles of the universe and no one has ever been able to split one. So no one knows what it's comprised of. On the other hand, the proton has been split and we know it's made of three other particles called quarks. So are neutrons."

"Quark. I've heard that word. So that's real, too?" Audra said.

"A quark is a fundamental particle like the electron. But you never see quarks by themselves, only as parts of other bigger particles."

"How many different particles are there, anyway?"

"A lot. I don't know. Particle physics isn't really my field. I mean, it's interesting."

"So no one knows what an electron is made of, right?" Rushel said.

"Right. And electric charge is similar. It's a fundamental property of certain particles. I mean, we know, in a way, where it originates but that explanation won't make sense. When the universe was young and hot..."

"Now you're talking," Audra said.

"Finally getting some action," Gislaine said.

"I mean, temperature-wise."

"Oh, so do I," Audra whispered.

"Like ten to the fourteenth degrees."

"That would do it for me," Rushel said.

"At that point in the universe, all four forces were bound up together," Gabrielle said, trying to continue.

"Bound. Oh, my God," Audra said. "It's like she's reading my mind."

"And then the universe cooled and the forces separated and one of them was electromagnetic radiation," Gabrielle said quickly.

Rushel looked at her blankly. "Huh? Oh, I'm sorry. I got distracted."

Gabrielle drank her water.

"So electric charge is another mystery," Gislaine said. "It just *is*."

"Okay, you still haven't explained how transistors work," Rushel said impatiently. "I mean, I just don't see how they do that switching amplifying deal."

"Well, they're complicated. Kind of messy. Basically what happens..."

"I want to know the details," Rushel said.

"Okay."

"I want to know what really happens inside one of those things. If it's technical, well, let's see anyway. You never know. Maybe I'll understand."

"All right. There's more than one theory about them. I'm halfway through my class, I really like it, and I learn new things every day. I doubt I'll ever know it all."

"Tell me how *you* understand them."

Gabrielle took a deep breath. "I see things in terms of particles and electric charge. The Feynman method. So you have an atom, any atom, and the nucleus is positively charged and the electrons in orbit around it are negative. And normally the charges want to balance out so the atom overall is neutral. Opposite charges attract, and like charges repel. If there are too many electrons, the atom would have a negative charge. The electron would probably just zip away. If a neutral atom loses an electron it would suddenly be positively charged and any electron wandering along would really want to fill the empty spot. An atom like that with a missing electron is called a *hole* because an electron would want to fall into it."

"I kind of see it," Rushel said.

"Huh," Audra said. "Yeah, not really."

Gabrielle thought for a moment. "In copper," she said, "there are huge numbers of negative charges and they all move pretty freely. So copper is a great conductor. But in the plastic that's coating the wire, the charges are fixed in position. That's the way it is in organic compounds, non-metallic compounds. The electrons are locked in. So that's an insulator. Electrons can't move very much. Plastic and glass are like that. The main ingredient of glass is silica, which we are surrounded by here."

"That's sand," Audra said. "That, I know."

"And silica is silicon and oxygen. Melt it and drive off the oxygen and you can grow a crystal of silicon. It's a great insulator. None of the charges can move. But what if, when you made the silicon crystal, you added something to it. Contaminated it on purpose. Just a tiny bit of something that has somewhat moveable charges. Phosphorus is good. You dope the silicon with phosphorus. That's what we call it. Just add a little. Then you don't have an insulator or a conductor. You have a *semi*conductor."

"Doped?" Audra said.

"Doped." Rushel said.

"It conducts electricity but only with a little resistance. With the right voltage you can get the electrons to vacate the phosphorus atoms."

"Which gives you holes," Rushel said.

"Right. With phosphorus, your semiconductor has an overall positive charge. We could call it P-type. Or make it with something like boron and you have a negatively charged semiconductor. N-type."

"Okay. So what does that do? It that a battery?"

"Kind of," Gabrielle said thinking, damn, she's fast. "If you stick these semiconductors together very interesting things happen. It's called a PN junction and it's the basis of diodes and transistors and pretty much all of solid state electronics."

"Well," Rushel said excitedly, "wouldn't all the electrons in the N-type be pulled into the P-type? But then that would leave all the holes empty so the electrons would want to go back." She thought for a second. "Something like that would have to happen." Her eyes seemed to lose focus.

"That's exactly what happens."

"Wait," Rushel said. "The P and N. That's a transistor? Doesn't look like enough."

"Right, it's not. That makes a diode. There needs to be one more part."

"Okay." Rushel stood up. "I think I'm getting it. Let's make a transistor. Right here."

Gabrielle stood up also.

She saw Audra grinning at her. "Now you've done it."

"This helps me learn," Rushel said. "I'm very physical."

Audra and Gislaine got up also.

"Let's say the table is the transistor," Rushel said, waving a hand. "So what are all the parts?"

Gabrielle came around to her side. "This end, the whole left end, is the emitter."

"Emitter. The whole left side?"

"And it's N-type."

"Negative charge. Too many electrons."

"Right. And the whole right end here is called the collector. Also N-type."

"Collector. N-type."

"And right here in the middle." Gabrielle picked up all the spoons and forks and laid then end to end across the width of the table. "This strip is the base. A little layer in between. And it is P-type."

"P for positive. Base. Emitter. Collector."

Gabrielle nodded. "So that makes this an NPN bipolar junction transistor. A BJT."

"Bi what?" Gislaine said.

"Bipolar."

"Ah," Audra said. "A BJ."

Gabrielle looked at them, puzzled, knowing there was some joke she wasn't getting.

"Makes it easier to remember, doesn't it, Gislaine?"

"Yes, Audra, it certainly does."

"Okay, okay," Rushel said. "This is cool. There are two PN junctions, aren't there? Connected together. You said something interesting happens at the junctions."

"Electrons from the N-type migrate just a little ways into the P-type and fill the holes."

"So if I'm an atom of phosphorus in the base." Rushel stood with her back to the line of silverware. "Right on the edge, right? My hole is getting filled." She looked at Gislaine and smiled.

"Oh my *God*," Audra said.

"You're now a neutral atom. No more naked charge."

Rushel put her hands on her hips. "Huh."

"So wait." Gabrielle said. "It's easier to see if we make a circuit." She looked around the living room. "Pretend the chair is a nine volt battery. There's a wire coming from the negative terminal to the emitter. And a wire is going from the positive terminal, passing through a light bulb, and attaching to the collector."

Gislaine went to the floor lamp beside the recliner. "Is the light on or off?"

"Off."

"Why off?" Rushel asked as Gislaine turned the switch.

"Because of you. You have no movable charges."

"Right." She held up a finger. "My hole is filled."

Audra made a tsk.

"Yep. Your movable charges are depleted. You are in what is called the depletion zone. So an electron from the negative terminal of the battery can't get through to complete the circuit. They are blocked."

"Depletion zone."

"In this state, the transistor is off."

"How do we turn it on? Wait, I know, Audra, you be the electron."

"I really don't want to be the electron."

"You're the perfect electron," Gislaine said.

"You're the electron in the circuit," Rushel said. "Come on."

Audra came around to the emitter side of the table. "Fine."

"You're an absolutely adorable electron," Gislaine said.

"I'm so learning to hate that word," Audra said.

"The electrons from the N layer have drifted into the P layer, the holes on the other side of the junction. There is now a region of the semiconductor without mobile charges. We need to make those charges mobile again. We need to knock those electrons loose, open up holes, and let the battery electrons through to the other PN junction at the collector."

Rushel nodded. "The emitter emits electrons and the collector collects them."

"Right."

"So we do something with the base now, I'll bet."

"This is how you turn on the transistor. Pretend I have another battery here. A very small one. I connect the positive wire to the base. What does positive do? The positive charge attracts electrons out of the depletion zone."

"Wait," Rushel said. "I'm an atom in the zone. You have a positive charge. This positive charge pulls my electron loose." She took off her paisley shirt with a cross arm pull and stood topless before Gabrielle. "Here. Take my electron." She handed over her shirt.

Gabrielle took it, trying not to look shocked.

"Now I'm a naked charge, as you so provocatively put it."

Gabrielle stared at her breasts. "This would be an example of a base current, I guess," she said, and smelled the shirt. No perfume, just sweat.

Rushel turned to Audra.

"I'll bet that little electron over there is attracted to me now."

Audra squinted at her.

"It's one of the fundamental forces of the universe," Rushel said. "There's no denying it."

Audra, standing at the end of the table, made an audible gasp as Gislaine also removed her shirt.

"Hi," Gislaine said. "I'm also a positive charge. From the battery."

Gabrielle, again, couldn't help staring. Gislaine had small, perfect breasts. There was a mole beside her right nipple.

Well, Gabrielle thought, here goes.

"So I'm a positive base voltage," she said. She took off her glasses and pulled off her t-shirt.

Audra covered her mouth and closed her eyes.

"There. Now I'm positive. Slightly." She put her glasses back on.

Topless Rushel, standing calmly, looked topless Gabrielle up and down. "Gosh," she said. "There's a lot going on in a transistor."

"They're rather festive," Gislaine said.

"So the transistor is now *on* and the current can," Gabrielle waved her hand, "flow from the battery to the light bulb. There is now a circuit."

"The light should be on. But it's not on," Rushel said. "Doesn't our little electron find me attractive?"

Audra shrugged at Gabrielle. "Well, of course I do."

Rushel opened her arms. "Then, come on, you cute little movable charge. It's a law of the universe, descended from the well-known weak hypercharge and isospin way back in the time of the Big Bang."

Gabrielle looked at her in surprise.

"M gets *Scientific American*," Rushel said.

Audra went to Rushel, eyes held high, and they hugged.

"But you can't stop there because the battery charge is too strong," Gabrielle said.

"Oh, no," Rushel said. "I'm losing you."

"Her attraction is strong enough to pull you out of that hole in the depletion zone," Gabrielle said.

"Did you just call me a hole?" Rushel said. She tightened her arms around Audra.

"Technically, yes."

"That's so hot I may pass out. Farewell, my electron." Rushel spread her arms and Audra pulled away. She stopped at Gabrielle.

"Definitely feel attraction," Audra said. "Maybe I'll get stuck here."

"Well," Gabrielle said, "I'm only point seven volts."

"I love decimals." Audra, arms at her sides, faced Gabrielle straight on and bumped into her. Gabrielle's breasts rubbed against Audra's soft sweater.

"Oh," Rushel said. "There's that look. Now I'm jealous."

"So now what happens?" Audra said, smiling.

"You, I mean, the electrons are more attracted to the collector than the base, so..."

"Nine whole volts," Gislaine said. "*Nine*."

Audra sighed. "Okay."

"She's only point seven."

"Right."

"So you continue in the circuit," Gabrielle said.

Audra stepped back, turned, and went to Gislaine. She bounced on her heels. "Yee ha. I'm on the circuit."

"Well, hello there. Welcome to my highly charged current flow."

"That's very nice of the you," Audra said and hugged her. "I guess I go to the battery now?"

"Yes."

"All right." She released Gislaine and went to the chair.

"And that makes the light turn on."

Audra reached under the shade and the lamp came on with a click. "Turned on. Obviously."

"And then back through the transistor."

She went to Rushel. "Whee!" Rushel hugged her and she went to

Gabrielle and bumped her, saying, "My base." Then she got a hug from Gislaine and stopped at the chair.

"No, you keep going," Gabrielle said.

"Really? All right." Audra went past the lamp to the emitter end of the table.

"Uh oh," Gabrielle said and quickly put on her t-shirt without removing her glasses. "The base voltage just dropped to zero."

"Wow," Rushel said "That means..."

Gabrielle handed her the paisley shirt. Rushel put it on and pulled her hair from the collar.

"I'm neutral again. Holes filled. My beautiful charge only a memory."

"The transistor is now off." Gabrielle clicked the lamp and it went dark. "The electrons in the emitter can't get past..."

"The depletion zone," Rushel said. "And what a cold and lonely place it is."

Audra pointed. "At least the collector's still hot."

"Yes I am," topless Gislaine said. "All nine volts of hotness."

Gabrielle made a snipping motion. "There. The wire to the battery is cut."

"Golly. What a letdown."

"Neutralized," Rushel said, smiling, as Gislaine put her shirt back on. "And that's a bipolar junction transistor."

"Yes. You see how complicated it all is. I want to simplify it."

"This is something you're working on?" Rushel said.

"I want to make a transistor using only light. Like lasers. No electrons but it would perform the same function in terms of switching. Much faster. Very small power requirements. No heat generation."

"Would that work?"

"I think so. I haven't actually built anything."

"Why not?" Gislaine said. "I would love to see that."

"I can't afford to do anything. Like buy a computer."

"You never know," Audra said and exchanged a glance with Rushel, who raised her eyebrows in a question.

"So you could make a computer out of light," Gislaine said.

"Maybe."

"That's fantastic," she said. "What would that even look like?"

"I would show you but I lost all my work. I have to start over."

"You lost everything?"

"It was all in my backpack when I lost it."

"Oh, I was wondering why you were just using that little notebook," Rushel said.

"One more quarter till I graduate. I didn't feel like spending the money. I can get by."

"It was stolen?" Audra said. "Like, when you were in the Union? Those restrooms make me nervous."

"No, I lost it," Gabrielle said and instantly regretted it.

"How could you just lose it?"

"I," Gabrielle said. They were all watching her. "I'll tell you what happened but not now."

"You can't tell us?"

"I'm still trying to think about it."

"Wow," Gislaine said. "Can you tell us anything?"

"Whatever you say we'll believe you, Goddess," Rushel said. Audra and Gislaine both nodded.

Gabrielle, looking at Rushel's serious, searching face, had to struggle for words. "It was a very strange event. I have to think about it some more."

"Okay," Rushel said softly.

They stood around the table in silence.

Audra said, "Wanna play Monopoly?"

"Sure."

"Okay."

Gabrielle, relieved, watched them clean up the table and wash the dishes. Then Audra got out the Monopoly box from a drawer under the bench seat in the middle room. Gislaine got a fire going in the brick fireplace and they put the board on the hearth. Gabrielle got to be the top hat. Audra had fun creating a running commentary about everyone's holdings and Gislaine laughed the whole time. Rushel played intensely.

She's really serious about play, Gabrielle thought as she lost.

They all went to bed early. Rushel and Gislaine vanished into their room. Gabrielle got another book by Seneca from the library, thinking she should read something philosophical. She passed Audra curling up with her blanket in the recliner again.

"I just like this chair," she said. "And I have the whole kitchen to myself."

"Okay, but if your back gets sore, my door will be unlocked."

"Thanks. I'll be fine. I'm just like you. I don't mind being alone." She pulled the blanket up under her chin. "I meant what I said earlier, you know." Her voice was sharp and clear in the darkened room. "You're my base, Gabrielle. You'll always be my base." She tucked her head into the cushion. "It's just something I know. Good night."

Gabrielle stood still. "Good night."

In her bed, the book forgotten, Gabrielle's thoughts raced and she tossed and turned. I don't mind being alone. Haven't I always been alone? Of course. What's the big deal?

She got up, went to the window and put on her glasses. She found the red lights of the distant power plant smokestacks. She watched them until she became drowsy and lay back down. She took off her glasses and firmly closed her eyes. It was after midnight before sleep came and she dreamt of the predawn houses again. The sense of immanence was strong. In the dream, she stood in the middle of the street and looked all around her, looked at all the quiet houses nestled behind trees and hedges, and felt the presence of great compassion and love just out of sight. Yes, it was her friend, she sensed. Of course it was. She felt silly, it was so obvious. She knew she'd recognize the house when she saw it. She started walking. The clear sky was lightening. Suddenly, there wasn't much time. The warm air caressed her face.

Seagulls woke her up. In her pajamas, bleary eyed, she padded into the kitchen. Audra was on the front porch throwing bits of bread into the morning chaparral. A raucous gaggle of gulls was snatching them out of midair.

"It was all moldy," she said amid the noise.

Gabrielle nodded. There was coffee.

That morning on the drive to school, Audra told her the secret names of Catherine and Samantha. She thought Catherine's was amusingly appropriate but Samantha's just didn't make sense. Audra said, "Just give it time. You'll see."

They dropped Rushel off at College Costs Less. Rushel had no classes on Tuesdays and Thursdays and could almost work full time. Gislaine only worked weekends.

Gabrielle went to her classes in a state of serious distraction. The clear sunlight made her wince. My thoughts are unresolved, she thought, as she walked down the inner campus road amid throngs of dark-coated students. She shook her head at herself for thinking so much about thinking. But it was true. She knew there was something she had to work out.

After Advanced Topics – at one point, Dr. Rimmler had used the phrase 'moveable charge' and this caused her to giggle – she went to the Burger Bar. There was a different guy at the grill. No toothpick, no funny jokes. Acne. She ordered fries and scooped up a big handful of ketchup packets.

She took her fries out to the same small quad and sat on the edge of her favorite planter, the one with the Manzanita bush. She tucked her notebook under her thigh and tore the corner off one of the ketchup packets. She tried to focus her thoughts and pulled a single French fry from the holder. She carefully applied ketchup to the length of it, without dripping, the beautiful red sauce in a line atop the crispy, golden slice of potato. She popped the whole thing into her mouth and chewed it up. She did the same with the next fry. Marshall thoughts. Ketchup deployment sequence. Eat.

When she was down to five, a familiar voice said, "At least they know how to make *pom frites* here."

Catherine sat down beside her, her yellow windbreaker crinkling as their shoulders bumped.

"Golden brown on the outside, light and fluffy on the inside. Not all oily and soggy." She smiled. "Did you miss me? What'cha doin'?"

"Yes. And thinking."

Catherine had a new haircut. Bangs, and her hair just touching her collar. And the bangs were clever. Sculpted, she thought was the word. Also, sexy. That word, too.

"Makes me look younger, doesn't it?" she said with a brilliant smile. She fiddled with the hair on her forehead.

"Yes," Gabrielle said. "But you'll always look young."

Catherine bumped her shoulder for the compliment. She scanned the crowd of students having lunch of just sitting outside protected from the wind.

"So what are you thinking about?" she said as Gabrielle ate another French fry.

Gabrielle said, "Um," as she chewed.

"Are you thinking about her?" Catherine pointed with her eyes. There was a young woman sitting on the planter in front of them, facing away at ninety degrees. She had sat down, Gabrielle now realized, right after she started eating the fries. Brown hair, straight and clean-looking, parted in the middle. Small nose, strong chin. Full lips. Eyes dark and quick and wide-set. Gabrielle looked away just as those eyes turned in her direction.

"She's not sitting there by accident, you know," Catherine said.

Gabrielle set her French fries on her lap and took Catherine's left hand, generating a worried look.

"Forget her," Gabrielle said.

"Forget who?"

Gabrielle laughed.

"Are you going to tell me what you're thinking about?"

"Yes."

"All right," Catherine whispered. Gabrielle felt her hand tighten.

Gabrielle cleared her throat and she saw Catherine smile for an instant then raise her eyebrows.

"The river," Gabrielle said. "The River Arcady." Catherine's gaze did not waver so she continued. "I want to live that way."

Catherine looked away for a second and then back, deeply into Gabrielle's eyes.

"It's a complex thing," she said.

Gabrielle felt her chest tighten.

"But, yes." Catherine let go of Gabrielle's hand and stroked her arm. "Yes."

"All right," Gabrielle said, and began to breathe again.

"All right."

Gabrielle watched Catherine's face. Her eyes, blue and gold, were steady and untroubled. Her mouth was relaxed, her lips parted. She could barely see the scar line along her cheekbone. Her whole expression was one of anticipation.

"When we get back to the house," Catherine said, "there will be a surprise for you."

"Oh, okay. I can hardly wait."

"I have an idea. If you're finished with lunch."

"Yes, I'm full."

"Oh, good. So you don't want these?"

"No, go ahead."

Catherine took the remaining four French fries. She pulled out one and bit off half. "Mm. Not too shabby," she said and swallowed. "Probably an accident. They'll never be this good again."

"Then it's lucky I got them."

"I suppose. If you believe in luck." She blinked inquisitively. "Do you?"

"No."

"Me neither. Want to go to the library?"

Gabrielle looked at her in surprise. Then she got it.

"Yeah, let's go."

They both got up. Gabrielle kept her eyes down, finally risking a glance at the other planter. The young woman with the dark eyes was gone.

Catherine sat in the front seat on the way home, keeping her left hand firmly in Gabrielle's lap. Audra sat in the back, shaking her head and almost, but not quite, rolling her eyes. Rushel, in her blue smock, just looked out the window.

On their sandy road, Catherine got out and opened the gate and after she closed it she set the latch. When she got back in, she said, "We need to be more careful about the gate."

"Is there a problem?" Gabrielle guided the car around the hill. The house appeared in the low light. One of the lamps was on in the library.

"No. I was just thinking we were getting a little lax around here. The gate bugs me. And the propane. I swear I keep smelling propane."

"They fixed that," Audra said.

"Well then it's broken again."

"We'll try to find the leak," Gabrielle said. "Hopefully it's just a loose fitting." She stopped the car at the front door.

"You think you can fix it?" Catherine opened her door. Rushel pushed the seat forward and got out quickly.

"Sure. It's probably just a brass fitting. Sometimes they're not very well made. You're supposed to use Teflon tape on the joints."

"So those guys ripped us off," Audra said.

Rushel was fast into the house and Gabrielle heard the bathroom door slam.

"We'll make a trip to the hardware store," Gabrielle said. She got out and pulled the seat forward for Audra, who was dragging her oversized backpack.

"And then we'll go to the auto parts store."

"Cool." Audra looked to the west, to the setting sun. There was a large accumulation of seagulls in the sky above the dunes at the ocean's edge, a wheeling swarm of black specks. "Huh. Look at that," she said. "Hitchcock making a sequel?"

"Who?"

Rushel burst back out of the front door with a screen door clatter, her hair flying. She waved her hands frantically. "Oh my God! Oh my God!"

They all froze.

"Oh shit," Audra said darkly and dropped her backpack onto the sand.

Catherine gasped and stepped back.

Gabrielle started to speak but Rushel exclaimed, "No, no! Come on! Oh my God you have to see it!"

Audra ran up the steps, past Rushel, who pointed left. Audra stopped and her voice echoed in the book-lined room. "Whoa! *Whoa!*" She came back to the door and stared, wild-eyed, at Gabrielle through the doorway, hands over her mouth. She shook her head. "Completely *insane*," she said hoarsely and then vanished inside.

"Oh *right*," Catherine said softly, smiling. "Yeah, there was this thing."

"What?" Gabrielle said.

She got to the porch and Rushel grabbed her by the shoulders and jumped up and down on her heels creating a big wave in her hair. She made a squealing sound and pulled Gabrielle inside.

Audra was kneeling on the floor in front of a small wooden table, which was new, with her arm resting on the dark blue fabric seat of a rolling office chair, also new. She was looking at what was on the table. There was a low-profile plastic box with a keyboard built into the angled front face. The box was beige, and the neat, functional-looking keyboard was dark gray.

The word *TESS* was embossed on the top in colorful letters. There was another box, square and bulky, sitting to the side. A disc drive. Perched on the rear edge of the table was a tv set. A compact color tv set with a black plastic case.

There was a small unopened box with a big Sony label, five and a quarter inches, it said, as well as a flip-top case with more discs. They had felt-pen scribbled labels. Resting on top of the beige box was a collection of electrical cables fitted with interesting connectors of a type Gabrielle had never seen before. There was also a thick paperback book. A manual.

Gabrielle adjusted her glasses. She brushed back her hair. She looked at Rushel and Audra.

She said, "Wow!"

Rushel began bouncing up and down again.

"We have a computer! We have a computer!"

Audra reached out to the keyboard and gingerly touched the A key. She took her finger away. Then she touched it again and pushed. There was a faint clicking sound. Audra inhaled sharply. "It seems to be real."

Rushel bent over her. "Let's turn it on. Can we turn it on?"

Gabrielle picked up the manual and thumbed the pages. "That's a floppy disc drive. I've only seen pictures of them before."

"What do they do?"

"They record data on the discs. The floppies."

Audra laughed. "Floppies."

"These things?" Rushel opened the storage case and took out a disc labeled *Word Processor.* "They actually call them floppies? What's a word processor?" She stuck her finger through the center hole and wiggled the disc in its paper sleeve.

"It's like magnetic tape. It records computer data like a cassette tape records music. It's pretty much the same process."

"I have no idea what computer data is," Rushel said with a note of impatience. "What is computer data?"

Audra tipped her head back and smiled at Gabrielle.

"Well, I want to know."

"Actually, I haven't used computers very much. Just the data processing class."

"Right. I have to take that," Rushel said.

"Punch cards," Audra said. "Lots and lots of punch cards."

Gabrielle sat back. "Yep. Those things. I got a tour of the computer the university has. An IBM 360. It wouldn't fit in this room. This is *much* more what I want to work on."

"Wait, wait." Rushel waved her hands. "Just tell me what computer data is. Please. Right now."

"Ones and zeros. That's all there is. A wire has a voltage, which would be a one, or it's off, which is zero."

"Like the transistor."

"Exactly like that." Gabrielle tried to organize her thoughts. "Computers are just lots of transistors. You can put millions of transistors on a single integrated circuit. You put them on a silicon wafer like a photograph. Photo lithography. Then hook up wires to them." Gabrielle shrugged. "My idea's better."

"Millions? In *there*?" Rushel stared at the beige box.

"Oh yeah. In the central processing unit."

"Oh my God."

"Millions of transistors in complicated patterns."

"I like patterns."

Gabrielle began to explain what computer data was and was well into an exposition of bits and bytes – "That's with a y." "Oh, that's just too *cute*." – when a voice behind them interrupted her. Samantha and Gislaine were standing in the doorway to the middle room, coffee cups in hand.

"The young people seem to have found it," Gislaine said.

"This is fantastic!" Rushel said.

"Before you tear into it," Samantha said, "I have to explain."

Catherine sat in one of the easy chairs. "Ah. Tell them about whatshisname."

"Okay. We visited a big computer company. In Palo Alto, I think."

"Cupertino," Catherine said. "It all looks the same."

"It does. This computer was loaned to us by someone high up in the company. Steve something."

Gabrielle blinked. "Steve?"

"Really interesting guy," Catherine said. "Intense. He was all over M."

"Yeah," Samantha said, grinning.

"But *Steve*?" Gabrielle said.

"This is an advanced research computer, incredibly expensive. That case is just camouflage. There are spies everywhere, he said."

"He's absolutely right," Audra said.

"M told him that she was mentoring a group of young female students. That's how we got it. We're supposed to give it back at some point."

"Unspecified," Catherine said.

"Right. And feedback is requested."

"Sure," Rushel said.

"I suppose I could do that," Audra said.

"A few more things." Samantha took out a slip of paper. "This computer employs something called a graphical user interface."

Gabrielle looked at Rushel and Audra. They both shrugged.

"It has five hundred and twelve K of ram. Whatever that is."

Gabrielle raised her eyebrows.

"There is a very advanced and experimental," she read from the paper, "graphics display card and a ten megabyte hard drive."

"What?" Gabrielle exclaimed. In the computer room of the university there was a ten megabyte hard drive. It was the size of a washing machine. "How is that possible?"

"It's what he said. There are no operating instructions because they haven't been written yet. That book, don't use it, it's part of the deception. He said it should be obvious how the cables hook up. Just plug it all in and turn it on. The tv set, too. It's not a regular tv set. It's made to look like one, that's why the case is so bulky, but it's something called a monitor."

"Monitor," Gabrielle said.

"Oh," Samantha turned and dragged a large cardboard box from behind the door. Heavy, the cardboard flap ripped off as she pulled. "Well, in here, if I could move it, is more stuff that goes with it."

Audra jumped up and was the first to reach the box. This made Rushel grin.

"Oh my God, is that a printer? It's huge!" She reached in and pulled out a long beige wire. There was a small flat plastic box attached to one end. "What's this?" The box had a button on one side that clicked when she pushed it and on the other side was a hole through which a plastic ball partially protruded. It was puzzling.

"Right, that thing. He didn't say what it was but he said it's the most secret part of the whole computer."

"This?" The plastic ball was heavy and clunked back and forth as she turned the box.

"Yeah. We mustn't let anyone see it."

They all stood around the cardboard box. The printer was indeed large, wide enough to handle any kind of paper.

"Can we use the printer?" Rushel said.

"Yes."

"Okay." Rushel paused. "How do you use the printer?"

"Maybe we should wait for M to get back," Gislaine said.

"We don't know when that'll be. Don't know where she went," Catherine said. "Aren't you going to set it up?"

"Sure," Gabrielle said.

"You all act like you're afraid to touch it."

"We are," Audra said. "It's probably worth more than the house."

"He did say just plug everything in and turn it on," Samantha said.

Catherine pushed herself up. "While you are working on that." She and Samantha headed for the kitchen. "Dinner will be at six-thirty."

Gislaine took Catherine's place in the chair. "I'm just going to watch."

Gabrielle stood with Rushel and Audra. "Well, first of all," she said. "Bathroom."

"Yeah," Audra said. "This is exciting."

Rushel wiped her forehead. "I really have to go again."

When they were all back in the library, they settled on a plan. They laid out all the cables and took a look at the complicated connectors, some of which had metal flanges complete with tiny machine screws for secure attachment. They decided to save the printer for a later date. It took two of them to even lift that thing. The monitor, the floppy drive, and the little roller-ball-box all had their own individualized cables. The two power cables seemed interchangeable.

"That's simple," Gabrielle said. "That's really good. One for each. You can't mix them up."

"So we plug everything in, then," Rushel said.

"Yeah, lets pull the table over to the plug."

"The wall receptacles," Audra.

"Right. I always just call it the plug," Gabrielle said. She carefully pulled the square table close to a floor lamp and rotated it so all the connection spots faced the center of the room.

"Audra said to Rushel, "Are you surprised I knew that? Receptacles?"

"Nothing you do surprises me anymore." Rushel put her hands on her hips. "We're way past that point."

"Are you feigning annoyance?"

"Feigning? *Feigning?*"

"That's a good word," Audra said. "I plan on using it every day. Another good one is cajole. I like cajole. What shall we plug in first, Audra cajoled the beautiful women in the beach house."

They all crouched around the back of the monitor.

"It looks like you're supposed to set the monitor on top of the computer," Rushel said. "But I don't know."

"Better not." Gabrielle stood and picked up the monitor and set it on the floor. "Power cables last," she said. "Let's see. That one first."

With great care, they put the computer together. The strange connectors had many intricate pins and they were terrified of bending them. Audra found a tiny screwdriver and they tightened all the screws to the flanges. The funny little box they set on the top of the computer case, roller ball facing up. The power cords were inserted, the floor lamp removed, and in the darkness, both plugged into the wall. Gabrielle set the monitor back in its spot. They came around to the front of the table and paused.

"Um," Audra said. "I have to."

"Me, too," Rushel said.

They all hit the bathroom again.

"So we just switch it on," Rushel said.

Audra raised a finger. "We should switch on the monitor first so it can warm up."

"Makes sense," Gabrielle said. "Go ahead."

"Okay." She did not move.

"I'll do it." Rushel reached over the table.

"I'm getting it."

"Then do it."

"I am. Do not cajole me." Audra pushed the button slowly. There was a click from inside the housing. "All right. I heard something." The screen remained dark. "Uh oh."

"It might need a signal," Gabrielle said.

"Signal?"

"From the graphics circuit. Go ahead and push that big button."

"You mean push it?"

"Yeah."

"All right."

Gabrielle was impressed by Audra's nervousness. Audra reached behind the computer, seemed to count to three, and with an effort depressed the button. It clicked loudly in the shadowy room and Rushel gave a start. From inside the beige case came a muffled beep and the sound of an electric motor spinning up, very fast, amazingly fast.

"Oh my God." Rushel hugged herself.

The flickered. A modulated whirring sound came from the computer, a pulsing whisper. The floppy drive emitted a series of clicks and then a brief buzz.

Then in a flash, words appeared in large, sharp-edged letters of ashy white. They were the color of the wing tip of a snowy plover that Gabrielle saw perched on the patio wall that morning, the color of a brush rabbit's chin, the color of silk robes in a rain storm.

This TESS computer belongs to the Goddess Persephone. Use by other individuals only by express permission. And then at the bottom. *Press any key to continue.*

Audra stepped away from it. They stood in a tight group. The computer waited.

Gabrielle knew what to do. "Okay." She gave the space bar a tap. The words vanished and a moment later the screen came to life. It was a bright rectangle. They all leaned closer.

There were tiny pictures in rows, some like little file folders, one looked like a gear with square teeth, and another was a tiny picture of telephone poles with wires. Several were just blank squares. They all had labels which Gabrielle was too excited to read. In the center of the screen was a small arrow. It pointed up and left.

"I may pass out," Rushel said.

"We're supposed to do something," Audra said.

Suddenly Gabrielle saw it. She went to the beige case. "Wait. Look. It has to be." She picked up the little roller ball box and turned it sideways. The little ball clunked inside. The arrow on the screen moved a sixteenth of an inch.

Rushel gasped. Audra peered closer.

Gabrielle turned the box over, button side up, and set it on the case. She felt the roller ball move. Yeah, like that. The arrow twitched again. Then Gabrielle pushed the box forward and the arrow moved up the screen in tandem. She wiggled it from side to side and the arrow followed the motion.

"Is that *real?*" Rushel's voice was hoarse. "It really does that? That's the most amazing thing I've ever seen in my life!"

Audra rolled up the blue office chair for Gabrielle and she sat without taking her eyes from the screen. She moved the box with both hands while Rushel knelt at her elbow and Audra looked over her shoulder. Gislaine leaned as far as she could out of her chair.

"It's a selector," Audra said. "You select the symbols. Those pictures."

"You move the arrow to the picture," Gabrielle said, "and then click the button."

"And then it does something," Rushel said. "What?"

"Let's see."

Still using both hands, Gabrielle moved the arrow to one of the file folder shapes lined up on the left edge of the glowing screen. It was labeled *filestr*. She centered the arrow in the folder outline, took her hands off the box, and pushed the button with her index finger. It clicked and the folder changed from a dark outline to light. They all held their breath. Nothing else happened.

"We're not doing something," Gabrielle said. "Maybe."

"Push the button again?" Audra said.

"Or the keyboard?" Rushel's nose was almost touching the little screen.

Gabrielle clicked the button again. There was no change. "Maybe." She scanned the keyboard. One of the larger keys was labeled *Enter*. She tapped it. Nothing. She clicked the button again, then in frustration clicked it multiple times. The machine whispered.

"Oh!" Rushel backed up. "Did you break it?"

The folder shape made a flicker and a box appeared in the screen, an outlined rectangle. The rectangle filled itself in. There were partitions across the top of it, *filestr* was there as well as the words *File, Edit, Tools, Housekeeping*. Inside the rectangle, several paragraphs of text appeared. Everything was sharp and clear.

"This is absolutely beyond fantastic," Audra said. "I can't believe I'm seeing this."

"This is incredibly advanced," Gabrielle said soberly. She sat back.

"You ever see anything like this at all before?" Rushel said.

"No. This is all new."

"And we have it." Rushel stood up straight. "We have a *computer*." She read the text in the rectangle. "This is telling us about something called the file structure. All information is in files. There are different file types. Ok, hang on. Click the pointer in that." She took out a ballpoint pen.

Gabrielle moved the selector box gingerly, the arrow overshot, she backtracked and zeroed in on the spot and pushed the button. In a blink, the text scrolled up.

Audra started laughing. "I'm serious. I am going to faint."

Gabrielle saw Rushel's gray eyes move rapidly back and forth.

"Okay. Got it. Move it down some more."

Gabrielle clicked the spot again and pushed back in the chair. "Here. Go ahead and sit down."

"Really? You sure?"

"I'm sure."

"All right. I mean, it is your computer." She sat in the office chair and scooted up to the table.

Gabrielle watched Rushel take control of *Tess*. She rapidly learned to use the selector box, one-handed, and began activating the other screen symbols. Clicking the telephone pole symbol brought up a numeric pad.

"Huh. I guess you could use this to dial the phone," Rushel said.

"You could store all your phone numbers on it." Audra was now kneeling beside Rushel.

"Seems a little cumbersome."

"That's probably a modem," Gabrielle said.

"Modem." Rushel nodded, saying, "Well, of course it is."

Gabrielle laughed. "It's for communicating with other computers. It converts digital data into tones that can travel over phone lines."

"Oh, that would be fun. You mean, what I type here would appear on someone else's screen?"

"Yep. If only we knew someone else with a computer."

"Right."

Gabrielle noticed Audra looking at her closely.

"What's wrong," she said. "Don't you like it?"

Gabrielle sighed. "I love it. It's just that, I realize now how far behind I am."

"Behind?" Audra sounded incredulous.

"I'm years behind."

Rushel turned to look at her.

"I mean, I had no idea this even existed. We had this little Altair computer in the lab which didn't do much." She pointed at the colorful logo on the case. "Some of these. But they don't let the students use them. Or even touch them. And now this?"

"Well, no one's seen it before. It's top secret," Audra said.

"Right." Rushel sat up. "This is a prototype. Even I know that. I would bet." She grinned. "I'll bet even your professors have never seen anything like this."

"Maybe, when they finish it and get it into the stores, in a few years, they might let a professor buy one." Audra scrunched up her face. "Maybe."

"So you are actually years ahead of them." Rushel patted the logo. "You should get a job there."

Gabrielle felt the surge of anxiety begin to fade. She patted the logo, too. "We'll see."

"And the more you learn about it the more ahead you'll be." Audra reached over and patted the case, also. "I already love *Tess*."

"Ohh," Rushel said.

"And this is true love. The real thing."

Rushel wiped pretend tears from her eyes. "I feel similarly."

Gabrielle laughed.

"All of a sudden computers are hot."

"Way hot."

Audra got a faraway look. "Tonight, I will be dreaming of a little arrow. And a button."

Rushel rolled her eyes. "Too much."

"I always do that."

"Always."

"You never know. It might catch on one day."

"Literally, in your dreams."

Gabrielle sat on the hearth by the dining table and let the fire warm her back. She watched the evening world outside the curved windows and listened to the voices of the two in the front room exclaiming and laughing at new things. Catherine, preparing dinner, exchanged a look with Samantha who was reading through a stack of papers from a manila envelope.

When dinner was finished, everybody got fish except Samantha who got what looked like a hamburger somehow made of, Catherine explained, rice and chickpeas.

Audra said, "Did UPS come?"

"No, sorry." Gislaine fastidiously cut off a perfectly square piece of the white fish.

"Was the gate open?"

"He knows how to open the gate."

"Who knows what he knows."

"No, he knows."

"I hope so."

"What did you order this time?" Rushel sipped her water.

"Two shirts. I really need them."

"Flannel?"

"Of course. And a pair of socks."

"You're getting clothes mail order?" Gabrielle wiped her plate with a piece of French bread.

"Yeah, it's really good stuff. L.L. Bean."

"I've heard of that."

"I'll get you the catalog. Should be here any day. They'll probably fit you if you want to borrow them."

Audra took all the dishes and silverware to the sink and when she was finished and everything was in the drying rack, stood next to Rushel with her hands clasped.

"Can Rushel and I play with *Tess*?"

Gabrielle couldn't help grinning. "Yes, but be nice."

"Oh we will be. Won't we." She nudged Rushel.

"I'm always nice," Rushel said. Audra nudged her again. "We'll be very nice."

"All right then."

Audra clapped her hands and ran to the front room. Rushel ran after her.

"Don't stay up too late. You both have school tomorrow."

"We won't!" they both called back.

In the silence, wide-eyed, Gislaine said to Samantha. "This is great."

Samantha nodded. "It takes a Goddess."

"Apparently so."

Catherine took down four small porcelain cups and filled them with coffee. Then she produced a small glass bottle of liquor and put a shot in each cup. She showed the bottle to Gabrielle. "Brandy. Coffee for adults."

"Oh thank you."

Catherine and Gislaine and Samantha talked about the weather – it was warming up – the proper way to cook fish, which olive oil was the best, and the complicated accounting and tax problems of M.

Gabrielle sipped her coffee, studied the changing colors of the oak table as the sky outside turned to night, and thought about light. She thought, since the project binder is gone and I have to start over anyway, why not come up with an architecture for a CPU. An optical CPU. She knew she was making lots of assumptions but she wanted to work out the topology of such a thing. And was there a method of storing a program in a purely optical way? Using no electrons at all? *Maybe.* No electrons – she liked the concept – of course, you'd have to generate light somehow. Solid state lasers powered by a small battery. Or, even better, use sunlight. All the required wavelengths right there.

A rainbow as a computer. That would be quite a demo.

I could breadboard it, she thought, it would be kind of big, use fiber for interconnections. Definitely big, table-size. But just get it to work. Small scale, so to speak. Thing would be *fast*. No heat. Micropower. Immune to radiation.

She thought about applications. Spacecraft floating in sunlight. Mainframe size setups. Could I make it small enough to fit on a desk, in a box? Don't know. What would I need, how much would it cost? Start writing it down.

Then, unexpectedly, in her mind's eye the flat, table-size optical CPU broke into sections, like the neighborhoods of a miniature city. One section collapsed in accordion fashion and nestled against the largest central part, all of which curled up into a cylinder. The other large section also became a cylinder and fitted inside the first, telescoping. Smaller. She tried to maintain the vision. The CPU was now the diameter of a pencil. She imagined vibrant red light then intense blue fading into ultraviolet. Awash in a vibrant spectrum of coherent imaginary photons, she looked up, startled. They were all smiling at her.

"Where on Earth were you just now?" In the low sun, Catherine was putting another splash of brandy in her cup.

Gabrielle felt herself blush. "Just thinking."

"That's always dangerous," Catherine said.

"What about?" Samantha knocked back her coffee.

"How to make a computer processor using only light. The idea is, no electrons."

"Ah. So no bipolar junction transistors." Gislaine said. Catherine and Samantha looked at her quizzically.

"Nope. What I'm thinking of would be about twenty thousand times faster than *Tess*. It would be as big as your pen and you could run it on a nine volt battery."

"Wow. Could I put my recipes on it?" Catherine said.

"Anything."

"I doubt computers will really catch on until you can fit them in your pocket," Gislaine said.

"But what would you do with a pocket computer?" Samantha frowned. "It would be like carrying around a typewriter."

"It would be perfect for recipes. I have a *lot* of recipes."

Gislaine leaned forward. "You gonna build it?"

"Thinking about it."

"Like I said before." Catherine set her cup down.

"I know, I know." Gabrielle got up. "Homework." Catherine did not meet her gaze.

Gislaine blinked. "Right. I keep forgetting you're a student," she said. "You seem so beyond it."

Gabrielle only said, "Yeah." Damn right I'm beyond it, she thought.

She went to her room and read Seneca under the tiny study lamp. Out in the early night the surf was up and the bed pulsed and vibrated. She found the old Roman easy to follow and she scanned most of the book, a collection of his essays and letters with the creased cover coming loose from the spine. She considered his warning to avoid *engrossments* – trivial concerns that do nothing but steal time and detract from life, and how important it was to keep death in view. She began to hear Rushel in the words, and an echo of Audra's 'examined life'. She knew that was another philosophical reference. She had no idea where it was from.

Maybe electronics is an engrossment, she thought. A time-stealing sideshow to real life.

"It's fun, though," she said.

At ten o'clock, she heard doors opening and closing. Taking showers and getting ready for bed. She noted the page number and set the book on the nightstand.

She peeked out her door. The house was dark. She heard a cough. Audra in the living room, bedding down in her recliner. She closed the door as quietly as she could. So who was in who's room tonight?

Just as she sat down on the end of the bed, there was soft tapping at the door. Just a fingertip. For a second, she considered ignoring it. She shook her head and got up.

She opened the door and Catherine slipped in sideways and made a half spin. "How did you like your surprise?" She had on cut-off jeans and a university t-shirt.

"It was wonderful. Just amazing."

Catherine looked puzzled. She scanned the room.

"I don't see it."

Now Gabrielle was puzzled. "Well, it's still in the library."

Catherine's eyes widened and she grinned. "That isn't the surprise, you goofball."

"It's not?"

"Uh uh." Catherine stepped closer. She put one hand on Gabrielle's shoulder.

Gabrielle felt a warm electric shiver run down her back. "So," she said.

"Hm?"

"It's not?"

"No, it's not the fancy computer machine."

Gabrielle couldn't look away from Catherine's mischievous eyes. Catherine now had both hands on her shoulders.

"But I'll tell you."

Catherine begin to massage the area above her collar bone.

"It's somewhere in this room."

"Okay."

"But I wonder where?"

Catherine began nudging her backwards. Gabrielle felt the back of her legs contact the foot of the bed.

"Where could it be?" Catherine said.

Gabrielle started giggling. Catherine gently pushed her onto the bed. Gabrielle sat and then lay straight down on her back, legs still hanging over the end. She gasped as Catherine straddled her and then leaned forward, reaching towards the pillow. They were face to face.

"Maybe it's over here. Ah. Wait a second."

Gabrielle tried to tip her head back. She heard Catherine's hand slip under the pillow.

"Oh my great goodness, I found it! I have my hand on it right now. Oh, *yeah.*" She hitched up her hips. Her cut-off jeans were pressing Gabrielle's belly button. She made a final stretch, she breathed into Gabrielle's left ear, she then she pushed herself up onto one elbow. Gabrielle saw her grin again as she sat up.

She had a shiny white object in her right hand. It was a can of Fun Cheese, Cheddar, *Sharp.* She tore off the orange plastic cap. Gabrielle laughed in astonishment.

"You want some of this, baby?" Catherine's voice was low and throaty. "You like this, I bet, huh? Cheddar, baby. I have my finger on the nozzle and all I have to do is *press* it." She pointed the can straight down over Gabrielle's face. "Tell me you want it."

Gabrielle swallowed. "I want it."

"I'm sorry. What was that?"

"I want it."

"You want me to give it to you, baby?"

"Yes, give it to me." Gabrielle could barely stand it.

Catherine adjusted her legs and lay fully down on Gabrielle, lowering the nozzle of the can almost to her lips.

"I'm gonna give it to you now, oh God, here it comes... oh!" She pushed on the nozzle and a tiny string of yellow cheese appeared and stopped. She pushed harder. Her fingertip mashed it until it hit the rim of the can.

Gabrielle, through squinting eyes, saw a look of extreme consternation on her face.

Catherine sighed loudly, "Oh *come on.*" She pushed on the nozzle with her thumb. The can made a wet pop and a high speed extrusion of cheddar cheese exploded from the tip and covered Gabrielle's face in yellow curlicues, forehead to chin. The can popped again and the cheese stopped.

Catherine let the can drop. "Oh my good lord."

Gabrielle, eyes clenched shut, cried out as Catherine pinched her shoulder.

"I'm so sorry. It's all over. Keep your eyes closed. Om." She wiped a glob of cheese that was in the corner of Gabrielle's left eye. Gabrielle heard her suck it off her finger. "Yum. I forgot how good this stuff is. Sticky, though."

"You actually like it?" Gabrielle said, and Catherine's finger was immediately in her mouth. She wrapped her tongue around it. "Um." The cheese was tangy and salty.

"You bet I like it. I like all cheese. I don't care if it came out of a can. I ain't no snob." She started licking Gabrielle's face. She sucked on her cheekbone.

"May I have some more, please?"

"Of course you may. Keep your eyes closed."

The next thing Gabrielle felt was Catherine's mouth on hers. The little can held quite a bit and they used it all up. Somehow the lamp was knocked to the floor and went out.

Gabrielle woke up alone in darkness amid the sound of towhees in the sage outside the window. She stretched her legs and arched her back. Perfect, warm, complete. Morning light would be soon. There was a noise from the kitchen. She put on her glasses and left the dark bedroom.

Catherine, in white pajamas, was making coffee in the glow of the under-counter lights. She stopped and Gabrielle saw her look nervously into the still dark living room. Gabrielle kissed her uncomfortable face.

Catherine looked at her. "This is between us," she whispered.

"All right," Gabrielle whispered back, not quite understanding.

"Only us." Catherine looked at the silent form in the chair. "It's just the way I am."

Gabrielle said softly, "Then that's the way I am, too."

Catherine nodded slowly, still worried. "Maybe you get it, but I'm not sure. You want to hold hands in public."

Gabrielle said nothing.

"It can never be that way. Never."

"Like I said, I'm that way now, too."

Catherine sighed. "Okay. But you still don't know. I can tell. You just don't." She put her hands around Gabrielle's waist. Gabrielle felt her hands clasp in the small of her back. She saw that Catherine's breathing was unsteady. "Just for the record, Goddess, I want you so much right at this moment I may pass out." Her clasped hands pushed down on Gabrielle's hips. She exhaled into the curve of Gabrielle's neck. Gabrielle tightened her arms around Catherine's body and held her up and she trembled and her knees buckled.

At that moment, they both heard the sound of the toilet in the big bathroom. Catherine, head down, released Gabrielle and cleared her throat.

Samantha came out of the hallway door wearing a long blue robe. She saw them and smiled. Gabrielle immediately felt uneasy.

"Everybody's up early," Samantha said.

Gabrielle saw Audra on the chair under the blanket. Audra remained motionless. She stood at the kitchen counter and drank coffee but Catherine didn't speak to her again.

Gabrielle walked with Audra up the inner campus road, threading their way through the morning's heavy first wave of students. Audra's first class, *The Law and Your Body*, was held in the big Architecture building by the library, but she needed stamps and was accompanying Gabrielle as far as the Post Office vending machine kiosk in a niche of big leafy trees. She waited as Audra put quarters into a machine and got a small book of first class stamps.

"I have to send my parents a postcard at least once a quarter to let them know I'm still alive. I forgot once and my mom called the FBI. Did you know there are female FBI agents? So *cute*."

"Were you in trouble?"

"Kind of. But we had a nice date."

"You went out with an FBI agent?"

"We just went for coffee. Stephanie. She was actually pretty weird. But she paid."

"Oh. Well."

"I know." Audra looked at the passing students. Navy blue nylon coats and backpacks, down vests, dark flannel and bright sweaters. "So the usual rendezvous point?"

"Sure."

"Watches synchronized?"

"Could be."

This made Audra laugh. Gabrielle knew Audra wanted to say something else.

"Hope it's a non-eventful day," Gabrielle said. She walked across the street through a gap in the moving crowd feeling Audra watching her.

"You're nuts," Audra called across the river of streaming students.

On the far sidewalk, Gabrielle turned and said firmly through the passing crowd, "No, I'm not."

Audra shook her head. "I know it seems like that. It seems like the right thing to do, doesn't it?"

A guy with long hair wearing an unbuttoned red plaid shirt abruptly stopped as Audra spoke, not wanting to block her. Audra glared at him. He just nodded, tossing his hair. A young woman in a threadbare green Army jacket, startled, stopped beside him. Her dark hair was streaked with gray. They both watched Gabrielle.

Gabrielle said, "It *is* the right thing to do."

The two students now looked from her back to Audra. Another guy, coming the other way, saw them and paused, looking unsure. He let his backpack slip off his shoulder and followed the gaze of the first two. The sun broke out of the overcast.

"That's proof that you're nuts. You can't tell you're nuts from the inside. It takes an objective observer."

The two guys seemed to agree. The young woman in the Army jacket made a face. All three now swung their gaze to Gabrielle.

That was the signal.

All the students on the tree-lined street now stopped with a shuffling of backpacks, both directions, leaving an open channel between Audra and Gabrielle. Five. Eight. Fourteen. They quickly became synchronized and watched Gabrielle.

Gabrielle found all the concentrated attention energizing. She held her chin up.

"Look, I understand you had problems," she said. "But does that mean I don't get a chance?"

The swelling crowd turned their faces to Audra.

"You need to control your feelings. You can't let your feelings blank out your mind," Audra said.

There was widespread murmuring. Gabrielle didn't detect a clear yes or no.

"How do you know my mind is blanked out? Maybe I *am* controlling my feelings."

One student applauded. A scrub jay squawked from a Torrey pine.

Audra looked exasperated. "You can't tell."

"You don't know me well enough to say that."

"Fine. If your mind is in control, give me a reason you're doing this."

"I want it."

"That's not a reason."

A couple people laughed. The rest listened.

"How about *this* for a reason. I'm twenty years old and I'm in love for the very first time."

Many of the students gasped and there was more whispering. Gabrielle, standing on the curb, now counted twenty-four.

Audra shook her head. "That's what I'm saying. You're nuts."

All the faces turned back to Gabrielle.

"I'm going through with it. I now know what love feels like. I'm not going to give up before I even begin."

Numerous people applauded. A young woman in a white sweater sobbed and covered her face with both hands.

"Audra, I want to be alive and know I'm alive and I'm going to fight for what I want. Isn't that the examined life?"

A guy with black rimmed glasses said flatly, "Whoa. Checkmate."

Audra gave him an angry look and swung her backpack over her shoulder. "Super. When the Piper Cub slams into the mountainside let me know and I'll start a search for survivors. *Nuts.*"

Several of the guys nodded at this and the young women scowled at them.

After a beat, all the students continued swiftly on their way, avoiding eye contact with each other. Gabrielle stood on the curb for a moment. Audra had deftly vanished.

This is the right thing to do, she thought. I am in love. I know it.

Then as she walked up the hill, she thought, dang, Audra really hates to lose an argument. I better not do that again. It might be dangerous.

And she found the idea of Audra being dangerous not funny at all.

That evening, Audra refused to talk to her.

Instead of using the computer with her and Rushel, Gabrielle joined Samantha and Gislaine outside to play catch with a Frisbee.

The only rule was if the catcher failed to catch it the thrower had to retrieve it and hand it to the recipient. Gislaine was an expert and when she tossed it to Gabrielle, the candy-apple red disk flew flat and level, perfectly angled into the stiff breeze. And every time Gabrielle tried to throw it back, the Frisbee veered off at sixty degrees and landed in the chaparral. Running over and over to pick it up, with the sun always in her eyes, she was getting as winded as she got in her jogging class. And she had several scratches on her arms.

"The trick is to let go an instant before you think you should," Gislaine said and fired it back to her, the stupid thing fast and level. "You know how when you're driving and come to a curve you start to turn the wheel a bit before you reach it. Same idea."

"Okay." Gabrielle curled her sweaty fingers around the Frisbee's cleverly shaped outer edge and tried to open her eyes fully into the low orange sunlight. Every chip and scratch on her eyeglasses was highlighted. "I'll throw it to you," she said to Samantha. "It'll be into the wind so I don't have the chase it so far."

"Really hard," Samantha said. She clapped her hands. She was standing in front of a row of large sagebrush. Very prickly sagebrush. "Right here."

"Hard. Okay." The wind whipped. "Here we go."

She wound up and spun the Frisbee away. It went high and curved to the left. Samantha lunged just as the wind gusted. The disc sailed up into azure sky and disappeared behind the house. Gabrielle heard it skip on the roof. Several seagulls began crying.

"Whoa," Gislaine said.

Gabrielle sighed. "Might need a ladder." She walked past Audra's car. When she got to the cinderblock patio wall she called back, "Do we even have a ladder?"

"Actually no," Samantha said, "but we can jury rig something. We've done it before. We can make a ramp from the hillside."

"All right. Swell. Well, let me see where it is."

The wind followed her around the corner of the wall and sand pattered her shoes. Samantha and Gislaine's voices were cut off by the high patio wall. The back side of the roof canted east and the sandy hill, crowded with Manzanita scrub and more sage, was too close to allow a viewing angle. She craned her neck but couldn't see the edge of the Frisbee on the shingles.

She walked the back of the house with interest. Past the end of the brick patio wall, there was a door. It was half the height of a regular door, painted dark green, with a tarnished brass knob. The top of the door was at her chin. The wine cellar, she guessed.

Sheets of gray plywood had been leaned against the house there. There was movement in the shadow.

A brush rabbit, small enough to fit in the palm of her hand, ambled slowly out and with its single dark eye regarded her calmly. Its brown fur rippled and then it darted along the back of the house and stopped at the far corner where sage made an arch.

Gabrielle thought the rabbit was just about the cutest creature she had ever seen. Cutest mammal definitely. The snowy plovers were the cutest bird. She saw the Frisbee then. It had come to rest propped against the house just behind the stacked plywood.

"Why thank you, Miss Brush Rabbit," she said. "How neighborly of you to show me where it was."

She walked around the dirty, peeling plywood. In her hands, the red disc was luminous in the half light. She looked under the plywood where the rabbit had been sitting.

There was shiny black plastic tubing coming out of the sand. It made a ninety degree bend and went through a rough hole in the wood siding.

There was white caulking around the hole. The caulking looked new. The brush rabbit had probably been nibbling on it, she thought.

The old plywood had been hiding the shiny tubing.

She looked for the rabbit in the sagebrush but it was gone. There was something else in the same spot. It was a small cat. Kitten, really. Tortoise shell or calico.

"Hey, kitty. Kitty, kitty."

The cat glared at her and sped away around the house.

"Oh, well, bye."

She took the Frisbee out front to the cheers of Samantha and Gislaine and they continued the game. She said nothing about what she had seen. She wanted to think about it. Then it was time for dinner.

Rushel said grace in the sunlit dining area. Gabrielle picked up a phrase of Seneca's which she thought was older, possibly Greek instead of Roman.

Gabrielle sat in her high-backed chair and checked the corners of the living room ceiling and the tops of the door frames. There were those glass light covers over the kitchen area. They looked too sealed up. In the cabinets? Kind of noisy. The dining table? The big chandelier over the table. All the little light bulbs with their thin tubular steel support. Oh, that would be perfect.

Catherine, shaking her head at her, served chicken strips with a very crispy breading, baked not fried. Chicken strips were new to Gabrielle and she ate three without taking a breath. There was mashed sweet potatoes and a vegetable dish called collard greens, strewn with garlic, also unfamiliar. It was all delicious.

Samantha, she noticed, had another interesting tofu dish. Catherine caught her looking. She seemed about to say something when Audra spoke.

"Thank you, Catherine."

Everyone nodded and said thank you with full mouths.

"I couldn't help but notice," Audra continued, "that this seems to be a rather low calorie meal. No wine, no bread and butter. Are we on a diet?"

Catherine folded her hands.

"*I* couldn't help but notice you let out your belt a notch when you put on your jeans this morning.

Rushel started laughing.

"Water retention," Audra said.

"Oh. And you," Catherine said to Rushel.

Rushel stopped laughing.

"You're getting jowls."

"Huh?" Rushel dropped her fork and felt under her chin.

Audra stared at her, open-mouthed. "Oh my goodness."

Rushel used the back of her hand to feel along her jawline. "No."

"But."

"No."

"Of everyone here," Catherine said, "only the Goddess can eat whatever she wants without worrying and that's only because she was so undernourished to begin with. Oh, Goddess, I was meaning to ask you."

Gabrielle raised her eyebrows, her mouth full of mashed sweet potato.

"Is there something wrong with the chandelier? You were checking it pretty good there."

Gabrielle, alarmed, waved her hands and swallowed as fast as she could. She held a finger to her lips.

"First letter!" Audra said.

Gabrielle shook her head and cleared her throat.

"Something go down wrong?" Catherine was smiling in a concerned way.

"Not that again." Audra held her head.

Gabrielle said, "Um." She thought frantically. "Outside. In the front."

"Outside?" Samantha said.

"There's something I have to show you. Everyone. It's the house. There's a problem."

"What?" Samantha put her fork down.

"I have to show you." Gabrielle pushed her chair back and stood up.

No one moved.

"I never know what she's up to," Catherine said to Gislaine.

"Can it wait til after dinner?" Rushel took another chicken strip.

"No. I have to show you. We have to go outside."

Samantha and Catherine looked at each other. They both stood up. Gislaine and Rushel did the same.

"Come on," Rushel said to Audra.

Audra pushed her chair back.

"Thank you," Gabrielle said. "Follow me, please." She went through the middle room and across the library and opened the front door. It was just turning dark outside. The wind was steady. They followed her single-file.

"Outside?" Catherine said. "Really?"

"Just the porch." She opened the screen door and they all walked out, Audra last.

Gabrielle turned the door knob to make sure they wouldn't be locked out then closed the door firmly. She came around the screen and closed it too.

"Okay. Sorry I had to do that. I was trying to figure out a way to tell you but then you mentioned the chandelier."

"Right." Catherine hugged herself. It was getting cold.

Gabrielle turned to Audra. "You told me this place has no telephone. Right?"

Audra looked at Gabrielle in uneasy confusion. "Phone?"

"You have no phone here. That's what you said."

Catherine and Samantha looked curiously at Audra, who said, "Right.

There is no phone. There's never been a phone."

"You're positive?"

"Yeah. As far as I know."

Gislaine raised her hand. "M told us. The real estate agent selling the house said the old rancher who built the place hated phones and refused to pay for one. And the people setting up the bed and breakfast ran out of money. They had to dump the place. That's why M got such a great deal."

"And the place was a mess," Catherine said. "I mean, we could not live here, really. We had to finish it. And there was never a phone."

"Okay. Let me show you what I found. We have to go around to the back."

Gabrielle led them off the porch, down the side of the old original house and around the patio wall. When they reached the tiny door, Samantha cried, "Hey, what's all that crap?"

She went to the pile of plywood and grabbed the top which made Rushel and Catherine cringe. She tipped the heavy splintery sheets over onto the sand.

"You don't put rotten old wood against the siding. You'll get termites and dry rot."

"We didn't do it," Audra said. "That stuff looks like it came from the old barn."

"Good. This all fits," Gabrielle said.

"Good?" Samantha pushed the top sheet of plywood into the sage with her foot.

"Right. See that?"

Audra leaned over. "Plastic tubing." She picked at the caulking with her fingernail.

"That's an underground phone line. It's pretty new. And where's your power pole? Where the transformer is. I see the wires right over the fuse panel."

"It's over the top of the hill there," Samantha said. "Just out of sight."

"Transformer?" Rushel said the word slowly.

"Oh come on," Catherine said. "Even I know what a transformer is. What on Earth do you do in that college?"

"She's a liberal arts major," Audra said.

"Right. It's great. We talk about things. Sometimes we draw pictures. It's pretty good."

Audra looked like she was about to say something but she shook her head. "What about the transformer?"

"That's where you'll probably find the other end of this line."

"Like we would know what it was even if we saw it," Gislaine said.

Rushel looked confused. "Why put a phone line in but no phone?"

"It was last summer. Shit," Audra said. "August."

"Whoa." Samantha crossed her arms. "Yeah."

Gislaine saw it. "They could have just moved in. Who would have known? Contact the phone company and set it up how they wanted."

"No neighbors," Audra said.

"And the bill goes to them. We don't even get mail here," Samantha said. "Not bad. But."

"What are they doing with it?" Gislaine said.

"This is why I had to get you all out of the house. Away from the dining table. There's a device, I've read about it, it's very simple. It's a circuit, a little thing, a phone that answers itself and just listens. All they do it dial the number, this thing picks up, and they sit there and listen. And the microphone could be as sensitive as they want. They're tiny. I've seen them in the lab. They're the size of a grain of rice."

"They had weeks to install it," Gislaine said. "And cover their tracks."

"The microphone is in the chandelier," Catherine stated. "Is that what you think? Perfect spot for it. And the wire goes through my wine cellar." She gave the tubing a kick. "We got a hacksaw?"

"Sure do," Samantha said.

"Bugged for months. What bizarre assholes they are," Audra said.

"No, don't cut it." Gabrielle knelt in the sand. "I want to find the device and see if I can do anything with it."

"Like what?" Rushel was smiling.

"Well, at the very least we now have a phone. I'm absolutely certain I could hook up a regular telephone to this line. And they are paying for it. And I have another idea."

"I'll bet it involves bipolar junction transistors," Gislaine said.

Catherine shook her head. "Okay, what *is* that?"

"They're hot," Rushel said with a giggle.

"Really?"

"The phone system hasn't changed much since the nineteen thirties."

"So they can dial us up and eavesdrop any time they want," Audra said angrily.

"We'll have to be careful around that chandelier," Samantha said.

"We can't live that way."

"If my idea works we won't have to."

Catherine grinned. "Look at her."

Gabrielle grinned back. "Do we have a flashlight?"

"Yes. Maybe," Gislaine said. "I mean, I'm not sure it works." She headed back up the path and around the patio.

"Careful what you say in there," Catherine said, and then to Gabrielle, "You're really sneaky these days."

"I've always been kind of sneaky."

"Oh. Good."

"You're letting it all out now," Samantha said.

"When she comes up with schemes her voice changes and she gets this funny light in her eyes."

"I noticed."

"We should teach her how to play poker."

"Ooo."

"I'm not very good at games."

"We'll teach you," Rushel said. "Poker comes in handy."

"A card game?"

"Oh, it's great. It teaches you how to read people. It's a good way to learn about human nature."

"And then there's strip poker," Audra said. "The best game of all."

"Oh my God."

"Strip poker *really* teaches you about people. Like, you know, who wears a padded bra."

"Eww."

"Or who doesn't shave. Where they're supposed to."

"Shave?" Gabrielle said laughing.

"You know. In sensitive areas. Hint. Her name starts with a H."

"Oh no."

"I mean, it's like a jungle down there."

"Please don't talk about this. I'm still eating," Rushel said.

"Do not want to hear this," Catherine said.

"Everything about Holly is just so interesting," Samantha said.

"And then there are the piercings," Audra continued.

Catherine covered her ears. "No."

"Oh, yes. With bangles."

"I said no!"

Gabrielle, feeling squoogy, remembered feeling something hard under Holly's sweater. And lower down? She held up her hands.

"I'm not sure I want to hear about this either."

"It's really not that bad."

"That's okay."

"There's hardly ever any blood."

"Stop!" Catherine commanded.

Audra shrugged and with a satisfied smile put her hands in her pockets.

Gislaine came around the corner in a fast walk and stopped suddenly, flashlight in hand.

"What happened?"

Catherine pointed at Audra.

"Oh," Gislaine said, laughing.

The flashlight was a rusty Eveready. There was a crack across the lens. Gabrielle pushed up the crooked switch.

"Nice and bright. Let's get in there."

"I'll go first." Catherine crouched and turned the old door knob. "There are two steps. You have to duck way down." She pushed the door open. A hinge popped. Inside was total darkness. Their voices started echoing, a hollow sense.

"It opens in because whoever installed it didn't know anything about doors. But they did like wine. See?" Catherine bent at the waist and stepped through. "Might need that."

Gabrielle switched the flashlight on and handed to her. Catherine pointed the light at the steps, worn slabs of sandstone. Gabrielle climbed down. She saw wooden racks lining both sides of the small room. She smelled salt and damp wool. There was just enough room to stand up under the dry splintery joists. The floor was covered with a heavy wool rug and sandstone walls imperfectly held back the encroaching sand. She turned her attention to the substantial wine racks. Sticks of wood, painted black, formed a dense grid from floor to eye level. Seven hundred slots of which four hundred sixty-one were occupied by black, sand sprinkled bottles, their necks pointed down.

"Whoever the old rancher was he was probably a hoot. Most of this was here when we moved in. We've only added a few cases. The bed and breakfast people didn't seem to care for it. Look at this." She pulled a bottle out of a bottom slot. The label was very faded. "Domaine Romanee Conti, nineteen fifty-one. That's at least two hundred dollars. This whole lower section is French and the middle is Italian and look at this." She carefully took a bottle from the upper left corner. "Look at that label. I mean, what is that? Is that Russian?"

The label looked like it had been made on a very well used typewriter: хорошее вино с 1972.

"Looks like it."

"They make wine in Russia? I'm telling you, this old rancher guy got around." She gave Gabrielle the light and put the mysterious bottle back. She pulled two from the middle. "For later. Now find that evil thing you talked about."

Gabrielle shone the flashlight into the lower corner where the phone line penetrated the wall. "There's always a junction box of some kind. Usually on the outside so the technicians can get to it. But not always." She could see a black wire wrapped with lots of electrical tape, coming out of the wall at shoulder level. It was out of reach behind the rack fully loaded with bottles. The wire went up along the wall studs to the floor joists where there was a dark shape.

"That might be it. I don't see how they got back there. There's no way to move this rack. Is there another way back there?"

"Don't think so."

"The rack is right against the rocks."

"God damn it." Catherine made fists. "They moved it."

"This thing?" Gabrielle figured it was half a ton total.

"Last summer. When we got back at the end of August I noticed this whole room seemed cleaner. Everything was where it had been but less dust."

"So they took all the bottles out?"

"They unloaded the whole rack, moved it, did that." She pointed at the wire. "Then put everything back. Yes, I wondered about that because they got a row backwards. The California Zinfandel switched with the Merlots. So I didn't imagine it." She sighed and suddenly looked very tired. "What a bunch of creeps."

Gabrielle removed one of the top bottles and set it on the rug. She stood on tip toe and could just reach the edge of the floor joist where the box was. She strained and pushed against the rack.

"Don't worry. There aren't any spiders."

"Huh? The wire's right there. I can feel it."

A shadow appeared in the open door. Samantha was leaning in. She held out a steel bucket.

"You can stand on this," she said.

"That's great." Gabrielle said gratefully.

She turned the bucket upside down and stood on it with one foot. She reached through the slot and found the wire. It was hanging on a nail. She flicked it off and the dark object came with it. There was just enough slack to get it to the front of the rack.

"Here we go," she said. "They weren't very neat."

"Sounds like them."

The phone line, a flat molded wire, was plugged into the box with a small plastic connector. It came out when she clicked on the catch with her thumbnail. "This is the phone and this." She looked at the other end. "Is the microphone."

There was a small three-wire plug with a brass retainer ring, both nicely machined. It wasn't very tight. She unscrewed it and the round connector came free. She examined the box in the beam of the flashlight. Pretty expensive, she thought. There were tiny screws in the corners on one side.

"All I need is a screwdriver this time."

"It's not going to blow up, is it?"

"We'll find out."

"Don't talk like that."

"I really doubt it." Gabrielle shrugged.

"But you don't know."

"Yes I do."

"Just admit you don't know."

Gabrielle saw that Catherine was very nervous. "I don't know."

"Was that so hard?"

"Um."

"Was that so hard?"

Gabrielle stood up straight in the dark room. "No."

"Right." Catherine brushed her bangs away from her forehead. "Please continue."

Gabrielle saw Catherine's eyelids flicker unevenly. "Are you all right?" she said.

"Fine. This wind always gives me a headache."

Samantha was crouching at the door. "Did you find something?"

Gabrielle ducked her head and climbed the steps, Catherine close behind with the wine.

In the twilight, she showed them all the metal box.

"It was hanging on a nail just out of sight."

"They weren't expecting anyone to look for it," Audra said. "See, no one could possibly be a smart as they are."

"What do we do with it?" Rushel sounded nervous, too, Gabrielle thought.

"Evil can be neither created nor destroyed," Audra said. "It merely changes form and seeks a new host." She held up a large rock. "I say we release the evil with this."

Gabrielle laughed. "How about we turn the evil back upon them. This thing is ours now."

Audra hefted the rock. "I'm willing to listen. What's your plan?"

Rushel rolled her eyes. "Audra, this is a cult, not a democracy."

She dropped the rock. "Yeah. Kind of a wimpy cult, you know."

"We're not a mind control cult. Those are horrible. We are a cult of sensuality and spirituality."

"I have to admit that sounds nice. But aren't we really just a bunch of girls playing games in a funky beach house?"

"No."

"Just checking."

Gabrielle went to her car. Her toolbox was an old fishing tackle box made of rattling, dented steel her father had given her when she was in the eighth grade. Along the way, she told Audra her plan. She had a soldering iron and a set of small screwdrivers and nut drivers, all from Radio Shack, along with a nearly worn out wire cutter, wire striper, and rusty needle-nosed pliers. In the upper compartments, she had a fairly complete collection of resistors and capacitors. And several transistors.

They took everything into the house.

She laid out the metal box on the dining table and arrayed the soldering iron and short bit of solder around it.

"Pardon me." Catherine slipped a plastic placemat under the soldering iron. It was a laminated tourist map of California adorned with pictures of oranges and avocados. Gabrielle set the flashlight reflector and bulb on a drawing of a palm tree. She sorted through the toolbox.

"Well, I was afraid of this. I don't have enough wire."

"Wire. Like phone line?" Samantha said.

"That would work. But anything with two conductors in it. Like the lamp cord."

Samantha looked around. "About how much?"

"It has to go from the wine cellar into here. Kind of a lot."

"Just go over the patio wall," Samantha calculated. "Out the little door, diagonally over the wall then over to my room. Then around to here. I'll just have to not close my sliding glass door all the way. Where does it have to go?"

"That table," Audra said. "This is great."

"Would this wire work?" Samantha turned around one of the stereo speakers. There was a roll of gold and silver wire hanging on the back. "About twenty-five feet and." She turned around the other speaker. "Another twenty-five feet."

"We were going to hang the speakers way up on the wall," Rushel said. "But then we realized we didn't know how to hang things on walls."

"And of course no ladder," Gislaine said. She was writing quickly in her notebook.

"This wire would work perfectly," Gabrielle said. "If I could use it."

"You can use anything." Samantha began unfastening one of the rolls.

"Hold on for just a minute. Let me make sure it's even possible."

Gabrielle put the small metal box front and center. More titanium. The screws in the cover weren't exactly Phillips, they had five points instead of four, but she tried her tiniest flat screwdriver and it semi-fit. The screws came out easily.

"This is the same material as that safe," she said. "Bet it came from the same place."

She picked at the corner of the cover plate with her fingernail.

"We know L spent a lot of time in Europe," Gislaine said. "Switzerland. Holland. And according to M lots of trips behind the Iron Curtain. Mostly East Germany but also Czechoslovakia. Prague."

"Are so absolutely certain it's not going to blow up?" Catherine said loudly.

"It's going to blow up?" Rushel said.

"No," Audra said.

"Why--" Samantha said.

The cover plate popped of the box and ricocheted off the chandelier with a loud pang and fell to the floor. Rushel and Audra jumped back. Catherine stood frozen, her face in her hands, eyes shut.

"--would it blow up?" Samantha said.

Gislaine put down her notebook. "Well, I don't have to pee anymore. Excuse me." She walked to the bathroom, keeping her legs together.

Gabrielle looked at Catherine. "Sorry."

Catherine glared at her.

Gabrielle examined the interior of the box. Machined from a solid block of metal, she thought and took off her glasses. There was a circuit board, painted flat white, she saw with relief.

"Well, that's something, anyway," she said. "I was afraid it would be potted with epoxy."

"What would you then?" Rushel said.

"Nothing. There would be no way to access it. But this is easy to figure out."

There was a reed relay where the phone line came in, she saw. Covered in paint, she would have to guess at some of the components, but the copper traces were still discernable. The key was the connection to the microphone. Three wires. No getting around it. Ground, positive, and signal. She picked out the positive solder point. Right there.

"I need to plug this in." She picked up the soldering iron and Samantha got an extension cord. Gabrielle used the tiny screwdriver to scrape the paint off the solder points. The soldering iron began to emit a thin stream of white smoke and she melted a bit of solder on the tip.

Samantha looked over her shoulder. "Are you going to take it apart?"

"I'm going at attach a couple wires to the board." She fished a piece of wire from the toolbox and cut it in two and striped the insulation from the ends. She blew the smoke away and with her face inches away from the box soldered wires to the microphone's ground and power connections. She straightened up and rubbed neck. "There. Finished."

Gislaine, who had returned from the bathroom wearing different pants, looked at Samantha and Catherine. "I'm guessing this is where the transistor comes in."

"Whoa." Rushel leaned over the table, holding back her hair. "I've never seen a transistor before. Even though I am rather familiar with their operation."

"As am I," Audra said. "Is it the thingie with three wires sticking out?"

"Yes, it is," Gabrielle said. She took a small black component from the toolbox and laid it on the placemat. There were tiny numbers printed on it. *2222.*

"Emitter, base collector. Right there." Rushel touched it with her finger. Catherine said, "What the hell?"

"You're making some sort of alarm, right?" Audra said.

"Yes. When they activate this device power is sent from the phone line. I think it's forty-five volts. It goes to the microphone amplifier. Guessing twelve volts at that point which is perfect. Very low current. I going to steal some of that power to turn on the flashlight."

"Oh! We'll know when they're listening." Rushel grinned. "This could be fun."

"Lots of fun," Audra said.

"So," Rushel said, "the positive voltage goes to the base of the transistor, right? And then you have the flashlight circuit running through the emitter and collector. Good. I get it. That's simple."

Audra nodded.

Gislaine said to a bemused Catherine, in a serious voice, "We had an excellent class in basic electronics. Electrons, electric charge, PN junctions, transistors. It was memorable. There was nudity."

"There was what?" Samantha said.

"It was done metaphorically," Rushel said.

"We got naked for science," Audra said.

Catherine said to Samantha, "We better not leave them alone again."

Samantha said, "I would like to learn more about the metaphorical nudity. Is it from ancient Greece?"

"It's my invention, actually."

"Sounds festive."

Gislaine slapped her pen down. "That's what *I* said!"

"Can we just finish this thing, please?" Audra began uncoiling the speaker wire.

Gabrielle used black electrical tape to secure the soldered wires, and taped the lid over them. Then they all went back outside to the wine cellar. In the darkness, she plugged in the phone line and microphone, screwing down the brass ring. She laid the box on the top row of bottles.

"Okay," she called to the others all waiting outside, "Unroll the wire. Just don't pull on it very much."

Samantha played out the silver and gold speaker wire on the sand, tugged it over rocks and grasping sage bushes, and tossed the coil over the patio wall just above her head level. She took out the slack. "Is that too tight?"

"No, it's good." Gabrielle climbed out of the cellar and taped the bright wire to the upper left corner of the short door. She pulled it shut leaving a half inch gap. As long as it's not being pinched, she thought.

Samantha was waiting for her in the freshening breeze.

When they got back to the kitchen, Audra was already on the patio unrolling the other coil of wire.

"It made it just to the door. Probably need about half of this. I need your wire strippers."

"Perfect. That thing is plugged in so it could go live at any moment."

Audra nodded grimly and they connected the second roll to the end of the first. Gabrielle used lots of tape. It would be on the ground in the rain. They ran the wire to the opening of the sliding glass door and secured it with a brick.

Gabrielle had never been in Samantha's room before. The walls were bare, painted white. There was a short floor lamp at the head of the small bed. No night stand. A bookcase set against the wall was piled with books. Samantha uses the Vertical Hierarchy method, she thought. The books she read the most were on top of the several piles, the rest in descending order.

She was intensely curious but didn't want to seem to be prying. Religious books, she saw.

They draped the wire from the brick along the bedroom wall to the hallway door, tucked it into the edge of the carpeting so the door would go over it, then down the hall and around the corner into the living room. The last six feet Gabrielle set on the reading table.

"Just enough left for the stereo," Audra said.

Rushel pulled Gabrielle's chair back and put the soldering iron in position. "This is your workstation."

"Thanks."

"Workstation. I like that," Audra said.

Gabrielle sat back down and picked up the transistor.

"I want to see this." Rushel pulled up her chair next to her. "Anyone want the last chicken strip?" She ate it in two bites.

Gabrielle took her glasses off again as Audra sat on the other side.

"The one in the middle is the base. And this the collector and this the emitter. So we solder wires to them to make it easier to hook up. Then I get the flashlight and solder wires to the battery and light bulb. Couldn't be simpler, although a light emitting diode would be easier on the batteries."

Gabrielle began soldering. In a moment the kitchen was full of fumes.

"I like the smell," Rushel said.

"It smells like victory over evil," Audra said.

"What," Rushel said dragging her chair closer, "*exactly*, is a light emitting diode?"

"Here we go," Audra said.

Outside in the encroaching evening seagulls caroused and the surf made the kitchen cabinets rattle. Catherine poured coffee.

"You already know," Gabrielle said, concentrating on the short wires of the transistor. "Remember the PN junction?"

"Sure. Interesting things happen at the PN junction."

"If the transistor is on, the current is flowing through the junction. Forward biased. That means positive to negative. If it were uncovered, not molded into plastic, every time an electron went through you could see it. It has to give up some of its energy going from one material to the other and it releases a photon of light. A PN junction by itself is a diode. So if you isolated that PN junction, just had that, and hooked it up to a battery it would glow. A light emitting diode. That's basically it."

"That's simple."

"Well, I'm simplifying it a lot. Quite a lot. They have to experiment with all kinds of materials to get the right light emission. It's really expensive."

"You could do that. Get a job like that. Experimenting."

"That would be *great*." Gabrielle put the bulb back into the reflector. She soldered the light bulb tip wire to the positive tip of the battery. It took her a couple tries. She roughed up the chrome of the D cell with a nail file and the solder stuck. She leaned back in her chair. "Do you remember where everything goes?"

"Maybe."

Gabrielle unplugged the soldering iron. She moved the flashlight assembly and transistor to the reading table. They all gathered around her.

"I remember. Because I was the electron," Audra said.

"No, I know," Rushel said.

"Go ahead."

"Connect the emitter to the negative side of the battery. That's the one on the reflector. Then the wire from the light bulb to the collector. No."

Rushel stood back. Audra watched her, smiling.

"There's the light bulb circuit. You break the circuit and that's where the transistor goes. It becomes a switch. So then it's all about polarity."

"Right," Gabrielle said.

"Let me think. The emitter emits the electrons so that wire goes to the negative end of the battery. That I'm sure of. So the collector goes to the other wire for the light bulb, on the reflector. Yeah. So the circuit is complete with the transistor being the switch."

"Keep going."

"Now the base. Oh, I see! The wires from the cellar, one is positive and the other negative. The positive goes to the base. There. Does that work?"

Gabrielle twisted the wires together.

"But that last one. Okay. I don't know that."

"Think of negative as ground. It's just a way of visualizing it."

"The negative wire from the cellar goes to, what? Can't be the battery."

"It's the battery."

"That works? Totally different negatives connected together?"

"That's how you do it."

"Huh."

"No, it is."

"All right."

"There has to be a ground to the signal otherwise you can't know what the signal is."

"I kind of see it."

Catherine and Samantha shook hands.

"Well done," Catherine said.

"We trained them well," Samantha said.

"At this point," Gislaine said, "you need to take your shirts off."

Rushel grinned. "Maybe later."

"So," Audra said, "a positive voltage from the evil box goes all the way around the house, through Samantha's bedroom, to the base of the teensy little transistor and causes a change in a PN junction and allows electricity to flow through the light bulb. And it lights up."

"You get an A," Gabrielle said.

"Are you changing your major?" Samantha said, sipping coffee.

"No."

"Yes," Rushel said.

Audra stared at her.

"I'm starting the process tomorrow."

Audra continued to stare at her. "This is monumental."

"Pretty much. I've been thinking about it. Time to do it."

The flashlight came on. Catherine gasped. The yellowish beam shone onto Gabrielle's hand. She snatched it away.

"Holy," Audra said.

They all held perfectly still. The flashlight went out.

The fire crackled.

"Good God," Catherine breathed. "What in the world do we do now?"

"I'm thinking," Audra said.

Gabrielle stood up. "We want then to think they're winning. So we don't change anything. We can play the stereo when we're eating, that'll help. Or we just go into another room."

"I'm afraid to talk now." Samantha covered her mouth.

"Me too," Gabrielle said.

They all watched the flashlight.

"This is awful. I'm going to the library." Rushel left the room in a fast walk. Gislaine followed her.

"Let's just wait for a few minutes," Audra said. "Remember, I know how they think." She sat in her recliner next to the reading table and checked her watch.

Gabrielle sat in the other big chair. Catherine got everyone more coffee. Samantha cleared the table and then sat in her place, hands folded.

Audra kept checking her watch.

The flashlight came on. Catherine inhaled sharply. After thirty seconds the light went out.

"Got 'em." Audra clapped her hands. "They have one of the low level Susans assigned to spy duty and she's calling to check us during commercials." She tapped her watch. "About every fifteen minutes. All they do in that house is watch tv. That's all. For hours and hours. Even on weekends."

"So we pay attention to the light and when it comes on we talk about boring things and avoid certain words," Gabrielle said. "Like gold."

"Or L. Or any of their names."

"Ok." Gabrielle got out of the recliner. "We're going to need batteries. Maybe I should get a battery holder."

Audra got up and bounced on her feet. "This is going to be great."

Catherine sat her cup down with a thump. "What are you going to do?"

"You'll see."

"Tell me."

"Nope. Uh-uh."

"You better tell me."

Audra smiled crookedly. "Probably the time of greatest danger is dinner time, like now. First thing in the morning they're disorganized and scatterbrained. Hungover. And late at night they're drunk or stoned, or screwing like the animals that they are. Last Sunday, mid-morning, that was probably just sheer luck. They're not smart enough to really use this." Audra's smile vanished. "They're vicious and ruthless. They broke into our house. They violated us. We must strike back."

"Do you have a plan yet?"

"No," she said tiredly "Maybe. Pieces."

"It'll come to you."

"Great. You really know how the scare the crap out of a girl."

That night, they all sat in the living room, reading. The bean bags had been dragged in. The flashlight did not come on. Reading Epictetus, Gabrielle felt herself nodding off and turned in at nine.

"I feel like I've always known you."

"It was just a dream you had. You can't know me."

"I could try."

"Like you'll protect me from evil."

"So no one knows you."

"No."

"Not even Samantha."

"No."

"I'm just fighting for what I want."

"I know. So am I."

Thursday evening, Audra came into the carrying the old galvanized pail and stopped in the middle bathroom where she picked up a towel. In the kitchen she spread the towel on the dining table centered under the chandelier and set the pail on it. She walked around a skeptical Catherine to get three large glasses from the cabinet and filled them with water. She set the full glasses on the towel and checked her watch. *5:31.* She stood at attention and watched the flashlight. It had not come on all day. Gislaine and Samantha came into the room. Gabrielle and Rushel came in from the library. Rushel saw the set up and giggled.

Catherine shook her head. "You better not break anything."

"Shh!"

"And you're gonna clean up any mess you make."

"*Hush!*" Audra whispered.

Gabrielle looked at her watch. *5:44.*

Samantha said, "Oh!" The flashlight was glowing.

Audra looked straight at Catherine and grinned. She picked up a glass of water.

"Oh my God!" Audra said. "Why didn't you tell me!?"

"Tell you what?"

"I actually *ate* them. They're oysters!"

"Oysters?"

"I ate raw oysters! Oh God. Oh God!" Audra made a loud burping sound.

Catherine was now smiling. "But oysters are supposed to be eaten raw."

"I'm gonna die. I'm gonna u*rrrp!*" She poured the glass of water into the pail and it made a splashing sound, focused upwards.

"Oh Audra!" Catherine said.

"Urrrp! *Bleahhh!*"

She poured the second glass into the bucket. Slowly this time. The sound was *thicker.*

Audra made a crying sound, breathing heavily.

"Oh, heck! There's puke everywhere!" Catherine held her face in her hands. "Look at the chunks!"

Audra let out a moan followed by another, "Bleahhh!" and poured the final glass into the pail. She stepped back, covering her mouth, trying not to laugh.

"Audra! Audra!" Catherine said. "Open your eyes! Please, sweetie, oh God, look at the blood! There's so much blood! Help! Somebody help me!"

Samantha raised her hand. "It's out."

"Ah ha!" Audra shouted.

"It went off on the third vomiting."

"Then I know who it was."

Gabrielle found this fascinating. "You can tell?"

"Susan number three. That would be New Susan using our updated nomenclature."

Gabrielle laughed. "Nomenclature."

"She hates puking. She runs out of the house. And there's always puking in that house."

"It's a house of upchucking?" Catherine said.

"God, all the time."

"Yeesh," Gabrielle said.

"Someone's always got the cramps or the flu. Or they had too much vodka for breakfast. Morning sickness." Audra tapped the side of her head. "New Susan. Very good."

"What's next?" Rushel said.

"You'll see."

"Huh. This is fun," Catherine said. Still skeptical, she took away the bucket. "Dinner will be at seven."

Later, they gathered around *Tess*.

When dinner (cheeseburgers and veggie burgers) was finished, Gabrielle went back to the computer with Rushel. Audra came in and watched. Then Samantha crouched between them, silent and poised, in the icy electronic glow.

Rushel turned to her. "We're trying to figure what all the little squiggles mean. Like this." She pointed to a rectangular area covered with a crosshatch pattern. "This is the text moving zone."

"Scroll bar."

"Oh! Thanks. Scrolling!"

Gabrielle pointed at the area in the corner, a mottled pattern. "That looks like that cat." She noticed Audra come to attention.

"What cat?"

"Behind the house. When I found the conduit. There was a brush rabbit."

"Oh they are adorable!" Rushel said.

"Yep. The cutest creature ever. And it ran to the corner of the house. And then when I looked there was a cat there. A kitten."

"What did it look like?" Audra said, keeping her eyes on Samantha.

"Calico. Or, you know, tortoise shell. Anyway, it ran off."

Audra and Rushel exchanged a look.

Gabrielle clicked on the symbol labeled 'Draw'. There was a column of simple pictures on the left edge. A square, a circle, a pencil shape.

"Pictographs," Samantha said. "They meant something to the people who created this."

"We have to experiment to see what they do."

"But you know they mean something."

"Of course," Gabrielle said.

Samantha nodded. "What if when you activated it there were random letters on the top. Seemingly random. And the pictographs were jumbled and disordered."

"Seemingly disordered," Rushel said.

Gabrielle felt Audra tug on her sleeve. Audra gave her a smile and raised eyebrows. *Watch this.*

Gabrielle pushed back from the screen and Samantha took her chair beside Rushel. "Why do you agree with my characterization of the disorder as 'seemingly'?"

"Whoever created the program intended for there to be meaning," Rushel said.

"The random letters and images must have meaning," Samantha said. "Because someone created it and you are *assuming* imbued then with meaning?"

"Yes. And we can discern the meaning by experimentation and observation."

"Because it must have meaning. Couldn't be a trick, right?"

"I would operate under the assumption that it is not a trick," Rushel said.

Audra watched them intently and kept hold of Gabrielle's arm.

Samantha looked out the window. Gabrielle could see creases form on her forehead.

"Do you think the universe has a creator?"

A tiny smile crossed Rushel's face.

"No, I don't believe that it does."

Samantha said, "My grandfather died when I was eleven. He was in the Army and died in some city called Berlin. We lived in his house in Colorado. The night they told me, I ran outside, crying. The wind was so cold. It was darkness all around me but then I saw a star. There was a tiny hole in the clouds and a bright star, all by itself, was shining down at me. I was the only person in the whole world who saw. It was only for me, that star. My grandfather was saying goodbye. He was journeying to someplace fantastic. A far journey. Perhaps I would meet him again, I remember thinking, and I dried my tears. The sky, the world, seemed so amazing to me at that moment. I could suddenly see a great distance. I was happy, beyond my sadness, to be alive in such an amazing place."

Rushel said firmly, "That occurrence had no objective meaning. Seeing the star was a coincidence. Your grandfather was not saying goodbye. He was dead. And after death there is nothing."

Samantha stared at Rushel. Their knees were touching.

"One morning," Samantha said, "when I lived in New Mexico, I got up early and went out into the desert. I stood on a hill and watched. First, the sky was all was gray like ashes. Then a line of clouds on the horizon came alive with light. Deep red then orange, exactly the color of fire. The sky above was a glassy blue green. The air got warmer. The clouds turned white hot. I took off my shoes and stood on the sand. It was very quiet. I spread my arms and the sun appeared. I could not look at it. It entered me. I stood there for a long time, surrounded by the sagebrush and the birds, drifting in the midst of beauty so intense I almost forgot to breathe."

Rushel sighed. "You saw light from the sun being refracted by the atmosphere. Chaotic energy and random matter have no beauty. Nor is there beauty in plants or other living things."

"I tell you it was beautiful beyond my ability to describe."

"Beauty is a cultural construct created by societal conventions. In reality there is no such quality as beauty."

"You find the idea of beauty offensive."

"What does not exist cannot be offensive."

"And yet you are offended. Are you also offended by the idea of meaning?"

"As an objective quality? There is no meaning to be found outside of human interaction. Languages, verbal and visual, possess meaning. That does not offend me. Any meaning outside of that realm is an illusion."

"I find meaning everywhere in the world. If I could perceive the universe I would find meaning in that vastness as well."

Rushel shook her head. "An illusion. It would be like saying there is a hidden meaning in the Periodic Table. Without a creator there can be no meaning in the universe."

"You perceive the same things I do yet you find no meaning in them."

"I'm trying to help you. I see everything clearly. You find meaning and beauty where none exists."

"You use the power of your mind to destroy meaning."

"I see clearly. That's all."

"No, you expend a great deal of energy to destroy meaning and beauty. They offend you."

"I am above such petty feelings."

Samantha took a deep breath. "One day, when I was living in New Mexico, I was walking to school through the desert on a path only I knew about. I came upon a dove. It was standing on a rock right at my feet and as I got close it held still. At the base of the rock was another dove lying motionless on the sand. This was its mate. I tried to shoo away the dove from the rock, fearing for coyotes. It fluttered to a high branch of a scrub oak. As I walked away through the wildflowers it flew back down to the rock. I was late for school so I had to leave. When I got out of school I ran back down the secret path as fast as I could. The sun was in my eyes. I came to the rock. Both doves lay motionless on the sand, side by side. I buried them right there because that was where their lives had brought them. I buried them as deep as I could and the sun set as I finished. That spot must have had meaning to them, I thought, and I knew I had to respect that. What do think the meaning of that event was?"

"You saw instinct," Rushel said. "Genetically programmed behavior. There is no meaning."

"Those two doves were living things possessing consciousness. They were not mechanisms. They felt love for each other. Love kept them together. The dove on the rock died of a broken heart. Do you really think the entire universe and the Earth and life came into existence billions of years ago, all that time, just so that little creature could suffer and die in such terrible loneliness? Does that make sense?"

"Random matter happens to combine in a random pattern that takes up energy from the sun. Life is born. More energy, more life, all random. There is no sense for it to make."

"You mean stochastic not random."

"You're probably right, Miss Smartypants."

"That's a little detail that's going to trip you up."

"No, it won't," Rushel said.

"Random is not the same as stochastic. Mathematical randomness does not exist in nature. Order increases over time. Complexity increases. Life is inevitable. The little dove was *meant* to exist and its love for its mate will transcend death. Order extends far beyond the range of human perception."

"You saw that poor bird and are now trying to come with a system to handle the pain."

"You handle the pain by denying the existence of pain. Is love real?"

"That has nothing to do with it."

"Is love real?"

Rushel stared over Samantha's shoulder, eyes unfocused.

"Damn you."

Gabrielle felt Audra release her arm.

"I like the computer programming angle," Rushel said.

"It just came to me. Never saw a computer before this one."

"They're something new, aren't they?"

"Devices immersed in meaning. Symbol processors."

"I have an idea for our continuing discussion. Does the human mind exist? And what is consciousness?"

"I have some ideas, " Samantha said.

"Then we will continue our debate."

"Of course."

Rushel leaned forward and they kissed.

Audra spoke into Gabrielle's ear. "It's like watching Chrissie and Martina. And I don't mean tennis."

Gabrielle whispered back. "Who?"

Audra just nodded to herself.

They spent the rest of the evening playing with the drawing program. Audra loved the text functions and all the stair-step jagged edges of the letters when she made them really big. They giggled over the fake signs they made. *Today Only! All Textbooks Free!!* For the Burger Bar: *New Item! Dog Burgers! Ground Up Puppies and Much Much More!*

When they finally looked up from the screen, the house was dark and silent. Audra pushed the power button and the computer deactivated itself, a feature Gabrielle found amazing. In the living room, the flashlight was on, casting long shadows up the wall.

Audra froze.

"It's her," she whispered. "I know it's her."

"This is a lot creepier than I ever thought it would be," Gabrielle said.

"No, it's all right" Audra went to the edge of the dining table. "This way I know where she is. I can track her. How sensitive is this microphone?"

"Fairly."

Audra stood at the empty table and spoke in a tiny child's voice. "Mommy? Where are you, mommy? It's so dark. Mommy? I'm lost. I'm lost, mommy."

The flashlight went out.

Audra laughed. "If they think the house is haunted maybe they won't call as much." She stopped. "Don't worry, the house isn't really haunted."

Gabrielle felt a chill run down her back. "Of course not."

Audra said, "I think I'll sleep in Samantha's room. Good night." She walked quickly to the hall door.

Gabrielle stood alone in the dark living room. The flashlight came on. The shadows jumped. She held her breath. Say something, she thought. No, don't.

It went out. The house creaked in the night wind.

"You're shivering."

"It's silly."

"What is?"

"Audra can be kind of scary."

"You're just now noticing? Oh, goosebumps."

"I know. All over."

"Well, come here. I have a cure for that."

Friday after school Gabrielle joined Audra and Rushel at the computer again. Rushel clicked on the symbol which looked like a tiny telephone. A numeric keypad appeared.

"This is," Audra said. "This is just absolutely mind boggling. It is just amazing. I cannot even begin to imagine all the possibilities."

"Who do we call?" Grinning, Rushel began punching numbers.

"Anyone, I guess," Gabrielle said. "Not sure what would happen."

"We need more wire. We could hook it up to the phone line!"

"Hmm," Gabrielle said.

"Does Radio Shack have wire?" Audra said, smiling.

"I think so."

"You actually go in Radio Shack?"

"I love Radio Shack."

"I would think you'd need more pimples."

Rushel laughed.

"Don't those guys freak out when a girl walks in?"

Gabrielle sat cross-legged on the bean bag.

"Yep, they do."

"I'll bet you could get free stuff."

"Doubt it would go that far."

"I get free stuff," Rushel said. She clicked the button labeled 'Dial' and a tiny hourglass symbol appeared.

"You get free everything," Audra said.

"Now that's just goofy. No, I don't."

Rushel suddenly stopped, listening.

Outside there was the sound of a truck engine.

Rushel's eyes widened. She put her hands to her face. Audra gasped and they both turned in the direction of the sound. Then they faced each other and waved their arms as if they were on fire.

"It's *Disco!*" they shrieked in unison and ran to the front door and flung it open.

Gabrielle, shaking her head, could hear music blaring from a completely overpowered speaker. A big brown truck was coming to a stop in front of the house. She heard squealing and Rushel yelling. "Whoo-hoo!"

She pushed herself up and stood in the open door.

Audra and Rushel were dancing in the sand. Audra tossed her curly hair over alternating shoulders, clapping and lifting her knees. Rushel was doing a chugging motion with her arms and fanning her hair out in the cold sunlight.

The truck's door slid back, the music got even louder, and a tall guy in a brown uniform stepped out. He had a small cardboard box in one hand and a clipboard in the other. Shoulder length blonde hair. Gabrielle thought he was good looking but not in an arrogant way. He smiled and said something. Both Audra and Rushel stopped dancing and cupped their ears.

"An artu-dees, ay?"

Audra only paused a half second for translation. "We're great, Disco, how are you?"

Disco shrugged. "Ant-cup cin."

Rushel quickly said, "We can't complain either!"

Audra winked.

Disco gave her the box and held out the clipboard. He pointed at a line. Audra scribbled her name.

"Awe nye." He took and clipboard back and smiled shyly. "Ewe dies ik-see," he said and turned back to the truck.

"Oh we will!"

"Disco," Rushel said in her girly voice. "Are we ever going to go dancing?"

"Yes! We want to go dancing!" Audra hopped and clapped.

Gabrielle saw him blush.

"Uh, yeah," he said clearly. *Staying Alive* ended and *Last Dance* started up.

"Well," Audra said, also trying to sound girly. "How do we get a hold of you?"

"Yeah, what's your phone number?"

Disco dug a scrap of paper out of his pocket and wrote something on it and gave it to Rushel, not looking directly at her. "There you go."

Audra, startled, said, "All right. Thanks."

Disco stepped up into his truck and started the engine, He gave a final wave and jammed it into reverse.

They waved as he backed up and went around the hill. The roaring engine and music faded.

"Wow," Rushel said.

"Oh my God," Audra said.

"*Wow!*"

"I *know!*"

"What did we do?"

"This is."

"Serious. I hope he's okay."

"Poor Disco."

"Look. It's his number and address, too."

"Wow."

The sun disappeared behind the gray fog bank over the dunes. They all went back inside and Audra opened her box from L.L. Bean. She insisted Gabrielle try on the blue flannel shirt and bulky wool socks and joined by the others (Catherine stayed in the kitchen) and fortified by mugs of coffee with vanilla cream they discussed fashions in front of the fire in the library. After dinner, Gabrielle put on the shirt and the stiff cotton was snug and warm against her bare skin.

The flashlight did not come on that night. A soft night, it seemed to her, as she turned in.

Gabrielle awoke in the darkness to Catherine turning and turning. In her area of the bed, untrespassed that evening, Gabrielle could only be silent. She couldn't tell if Catherine was awake or asleep and dreaming. Maybe it was just a dream she's having, she thought. Catherine's breath came in gulps. Gabrielle thought it sounded like sobbing.

Saturday morning, Gabrielle found herself alone. She had missed breakfast and everyone was gone. She stood in the kitchen of polished granite and stainless steel and sipped lukewarm coffee.

She's with Samantha, she thought. So that's all right.

What do I have to do today? My second Saturday here.

The sun was brilliant outside the curved windows and the sky was a deep blue. Small birds darted in the wiry branches of sagebrush.

Nothing, she thought. Although I am kind of hungry.

Gabrielle looked around the kitchen. The tall refrigerator hummed. The coffee maker gurgled. The microwave oven, with its white door, sat silent.

"Oh, right," she said. "And what could I do with high energy photons?"

She put her coffee cup into the oven, right on the sheet metal, and snapped the door shut. She turned the timer dial to 30. Hm. Make it a whole minute. The window in the oven door had a metal screen with fine perforations. Gabrielle found the size of the tiny holes fascinating. They are smaller than the electromagnetic radiation, she thought. I can actually see it.

She pushed the start button. A fan came on and there was a buzzing.

The timer counted down and a bell rang. She took out the cup and nearly dropped it. Burning hot. Way too hot to drink. She set it on the counter.

"This is *great*."

She opened the fridge and got the package of hot dogs from the plastic drawer labeled 'meat, etc'. The drawer was crammed styrofoam trays packed with small steaks of many kinds. She only recognized rib-eye. She slit open the hot dog package and plucked out a wiener. It dripped on the floor. She tore off a paper towel with her free hand and put it and the hot dog onto the oven floor. Thirty seconds this time. She hit the button.

She watched through the screen. The hot dog shivered and stretched out as if it were alive. There was a wet pop and it split open and rolled off the towel.

"Whoa!"

She pulled open and the door and stopped herself but a micro-switch shut off the power. She let the hot dog cool – the paper towel wasn't even warm – and then ate it with ketchup over the sink. She stuck another one in the oven, this time with a thin slice of cheese from a sandwich pack, folded in two. She turned the timer to forty-five seconds.

She hit the button and watched intently. At twenty seconds the rubbery cheese slumped and flowed onto the paper towel. The edges bubbled and then started to burn. She waited for the bell and then pulled the whole mess out and set it on the counter. A lot of the cheese was stuck to the paper but there was plenty on the hot dog. She ate it with ketchup.

She got another paper towel and a third hot dog. Forty-five seconds too long, she thought. But that sure was cool.

Just as she pushed the button again, Catherine and Samantha came in the front door and bell rang as they got to the kitchen. Gabrielle stood behind the counter, embarrassed.

Catherine slipped out of her yellow windbreaker and cocked her head. Samantha sniffed.

"You look so guilty," Catherine said with a crooked smile. "What have you been up to?"

"Nothing."

"Hot dogs." Samantha crossed her arms over her black sweater.

"*Goddess*," Catherine said.

"How can you eat those?"

"They're really good."

Catherine peeked into the microwave and grabbed a pair of tongs from the hanger. She opened an upper cabinet and got a small plate. Then she slid open the wooden door of the bread box and took out a sandwich roll. She carefully slit the roll lengthwise. About seventy percent through, Gabrielle thought. Like a pocket.

With the tongs, she picked up the still warm hot dog and tucked it into the roll.

She picked up the ketchup bottle. "Nope." And put it back in the fridge. She got a butter knife and went to the main pantry shelves and got a jar of something. Samantha saw what it was and laughed.

"Uh," Gabrielle said. "Peanut butter?"

"Trust me." Catherine spread a carefully gauged layer of peanut butter along the hot dog in its bun.

"Okay," Gabrielle said easily.

Catherine opened the fridge and got another jar. It was orange.

"That's." Gabrielle leaned in.

"Apricot preserves."

"Yum." Samantha leaned in also. "Not the hot dog."

Catherine daubed preserves on the peanut butter. From another cabinet she got a small red bottle. She took off the tiny red cap and with expert control placed drops of hot sauce down the length of the hot dog. She put the bottle away and eyed the plate and gave it a spin.

"There. Try that."

"Peanut butter and jelly and hot sauce on a hot dog?"

"Just try it."

Gabrielle's mouth watered. She took a small bite, trying to get a bit of each ingredient. The hot dog itself was still warm and juicy. Well, greasy. And it mingled surprisingly well with the salty peanut butter. The cold preserves were enhanced by the hot sauce which made the cold sweetness into something else, much stronger. The apricot flavor came through and it set off the taste of the hot dog, an edge of bitterness. The whole thing reminded her of the way she made frozen waffles with ketchup.

"We're going sunbathing," Catherine said. "Out on the patio.

She and Samantha went hand in hand into the hallway.

"Come on!"

She took another bite of the hot dog and set it back on the plate. Sunbathing? But I don't have a swimsuit, she thought.

She heard laughter and hesitated.

She went to the hallway door. She saw the flashlight had come on and shook her head. She went into Samantha's room, minding the speaker wire snaking across the carpeting, and froze.

Samantha was standing with her back to the glass door. She was wearing only bikini bottoms. Her hair fell straight down past her shoulders, shoulders which were broad and filled out with taut muscles.

Looking at her shoulders, Gabrielle thought, does things to me. This is getting complicated.

Samantha turned and saw her.

"Goddess, won't you please join us on the lanai?"

Gabrielle went through the open door. Catherine was on one of the rattling aluminum lounge chairs. Also topless.

"Lanai is what we'd call it if we were in Hawaii. So we just pretend."

Catherine lay back in the weak sunlight. "Never been there."

"Me neither."

"Samantha's been to Hawaii."

"Wow." Gabrielle unfolded her towel. It had bright blue and red seashells printed on it.

"Yes. I was working at the time so I don't remember much." Samantha sat on her chair and it made a scrabbling noise on the concrete. "Didn't get outside a lot."

"Doing accounting?" Gabrielle sat down slowly on the middle chair. It was just low enough for the cinder block wall to deflect the cold wind. She found if she held still it was almost warm. She took a deep breath and pulled her shirt off over her glasses. Sure, she thought, warm.

"No, this was my previous life. One of them." Samantha lay back on the dark blue towel. "I was a prostitute."

"An escort," Catherine said.

Gabrielle felt herself blush.

"I suppose escort does sound nicer."

"Most of those ladies never even touched you."

Samantha shrugged and closed her eyes.

Gabrielle could sense the sadness in her. "I'm glad you're not doing that anymore."

"Yeah. Paid well, though." She kept her eyes closed. "It's over. I'm here now."

They all lay back in the spindly nylon webbed chairs. The chill wind gusted over them.

"Ahh, feel that warm tropical breeze," Catherine said. "I can smell the flowers. And pineapples."

"The trade winds," Samantha said. "They give me goosebumps."

A seagull cried far above.

"I wonder what exotic tropical bird that is making a comment about my tan." Catherine rubbed her eyes and sat up. "Persephone Gabrielle, I'm sure you remember I said everything would be revealed. This probably isn't the last secret but it is the biggest. We were waiting for the exact right moment, weren't we, Sammie?"

Samantha swung both her feet to the concrete and stood up. She shook back her hair. "I hope this doesn't upset you too much, Goddess." She untied the strap of her bikini bottom and let it fall to the ground. She stood naked. "This is my scar."

Gabrielle, heart pounding, stood up.

"It's all right. You can look."

Feeling very uncomfortable, Gabrielle couched down.

"Right here, see?"

After a moment, Gabrielle saw it. A delicate ridge of skin and then a long indentation up and to the left. It was two hand-widths long.

"What," Gabrielle said. "What caused that?" She saw the thoughts play out silently across Samantha's face. Her forehead winkled.

"It was a knife. My knife. I was aiming for something else. And I got it, too. I was a little upset at the time. I almost severed the nerve. I did sever my urethra. And opened up my bladder." She shrugged. "Sliced a bunch of muscles and the bone there, whatever it is. Missed the artery so I didn't die. A lot of what happened that day I still can't explain. Anyway, it's a long story, the result of which is I am unable to experience what you call orgasm or any meaningful sexual arousal as one doctor put it. He was an asshole but not wrong, unfortunately. Although I must say I think I have a pretty good idea how it all works."

Gabrielle stood up and gently hugged her. She had no idea what to say so she didn't say anything. Catherine joined them.

"A different doctor," Samantha's voice was muffled. "told me if ten years go by and there's no improvement at all, that's that. He said stay healthy and let nature work. So that's what I'm doing. He was an older guy. Much better doctor."

Gabrielle could feel Catherine sobbing. Samantha whispered something she couldn't understand and Gabrielle felt a surge of guilt for trying to eavesdrop. Somehow Samantha sensed this and kissed her cheek.

"But you have had improvement," Catherine said into Gabrielle's shoulder.

"Maybe. Hard to tell."

Catherine broke away and wiped her face. She turned into the wind.

Gabrielle could hear a distant thumping sound.

Catherine put her hands on her hips. "There he is again."

"Your boyfriend," Samantha said and they all laughed.

A small helicopter with a plastic bubble cockpit flew slowly by in the cloudy sky, well offshore. It hovered then began to move closer. It pivoted in the wind. Gabrielle could hear the engine straining.

"He came by the same time yesterday while you were at school."

"We figured he was watching us sunbathing." Samantha laughed. "Now he's got three of us."

Gabrielle grabbed her shirt and put it on.

Catherine laughed too. "Oh I'm sure it's too late. What is it with guys and tits?"

Gabrielle, mind still spinning from Samantha's revelation, tried to think. She said. "A couple days ago there was a huge flock of seagulls right about there."

Samantha looked at her sharply. "And that's roughly where."

"Those dunes."

"We need to go look."

"Soon as that thing leaves."

The helicopter seemed to pull away farther out to sea. Then it moved south. He can't stay too long, Gabrielle thought. Hovering must use a lot of gas.

There was another sound. Audra's blue Toyota, its windshield reflecting the bright hazy sky, came around the hill, engine chugging.

"That's terrible," Gabrielle said. "Running on three cylinders. Let me look at her car first."

"All right," Samantha said. "Didn't she go to the auto parts store?"

"Yeah, I think so," Catherine said. "If it's the store I'm thinking of the guys there really like her."

"If they want her to like them they should just fix her car."

"They probably tried." Catherine smiled at Gabrielle. "but she wants someone else to fix it."

The small helicopter reversed course and headed north and they lost sight of it against the thin clouds. When Gabrielle got to the front door Audra had already popped the hood and was staring at the engine, a black and red box in her hand.

"Are these the right ones?" She pulled the bundle of spark plug wires from the box.

Gabrielle took a quick look at the wire ends and the distributor cap.

"They look okay. This is pretty easy. Just do one at a time and match the length."

Audra began to untangle the rubbery black wires. She got one free and laid it over the engine. "I'll do it," she said. "I want to learn how. You just supervise. Next weekend is Washington's birthday. A three day weekend. You want to go on a trip? We could stay overnight."

"Yeah, okay. Where do you want to go?" Three day weekend, Gabrielle thought. Completely forgot. Stay overnight?

"I have an idea." She held her hand over the engine.

"The engine's pretty hot. As supervisor I say wait a few minutes."

"You got it. Break time."

"Sometimes they're really hard to pull off the plugs. You can burn your hand."

"Thanks, boss. What do you think." Audra stared around the open hood. "What the *hell.*"

Gabrielle looked up. Two figures were walking around the hill coming up the driveway. She thought furiously, confused. In a landscape of sagebrush and flowers and drifting sand they were human shaped silver white metallic suits that sparkled in the diffuse light. Hooded, their faces were black rectangular windows. They stopped and seemed to take in the Toyota and house.

Audra dropped the plug wires. Gabrielle was surprised how angry she looked.

"Hey! This is private property!" Audra walked up to them and blocked their way. "Did you see a gate? Huh? What did you do, break it down?"

The silver suited figures stopped and glanced at each other. The one on the left put gloved hands on its helmet and lifted. It was a young guy with short black hair.

"Oh, hi." He smiled.

"Well? Did you notice the gate?"

"Yeah, we just walked around it."

The other figure took off their headgear. It was an older man with a cowboy mustache.

"We had no idea this all was here," he said.

"This is your house? Wow!" the young guy said.

"Wait a minute. Don't tell me." Audra crossed her arms. "You work for my government, don't you."

"We are from the County health department. We had no intention of trespassing," the older man said.

"You don't have a mailbox."

"No we don't. So what does my government want?"

"We're just checking on something," the older man said. "On the beach right over there." He looked in the direction of the path through the dunes and nodded.

"We just need samples," the young guy said. There was a bundle of plastic bags hooked to his silver belt.

"Okay. Samples of what?"

The two looked at each other again. The older man gave the young guy a warning raise of eyebrows.

"Nothing you have to worry about. Do you ever go swimming or surfing?"

"These things happen from time to time," the older man said. "Toxins from shellfish or other organisms cause fish to die off."

"Die off? Here?"

"Yeah, it's pretty routine. A week from now there won't be anything much left. And we're just curious what's going on. Just be a few minutes and we'll be out of your hair."

Both men hefted their helmets.

"With your permission we'll proceed over yonder and do our little job."

Audra uncrossed her arms. "Fine."

"Thank you, ma'am."

"Are you looking for roommates?" the young guy said. "I mean, wow."

"Actually, I already have five roommates. It's kind of crowded."

"Oh. Yeah."

Audra took a step back. "Go ahead."

"Thanks."

Both men put their helmets back on and started down the beach trail. Gabrielle saw that Audra suddenly looked worried. They watched the two walking spacesuits until they went out of view around a shelf of ice plant.

"All right," Audra said, distracted.

They finished putting in the new plug wires in her car. The old ones came off the spark plugs easily. They were loose, Gabrielle noticed. Probably the whole problem right there. How'd it ever run at all? Who would do that?

Audra turned the key and the engine caught and ran perfectly smooth except for a loud tapping sound that faded after a few seconds.

"Okay that's really good," Audra said, not smiling.

"Let's go inside."

Audra turned her car off and locked the doors.

"Thank you so much for helping me."

"I like helping you."

Gabrielle saw this made her smile a tiny bit.

They all gathered in the library stood at the windows. Audra told them what the men had said and, tensely, they all watched the beach path. Fog invaded and withdrew. The wind picked up. After almost an hour the two silver suited County men appeared trudging heavily through the sand. They were both carrying bulging transparent plastic bags in each hand. When they passed Audra's car, Gabrielle could clearly see the contents. Small shiny fish in one, larger dark fish in another. A mass of white matted feathers she thought were several seagulls. And in one bag a black wet mess. The mess had flippers.

"Oh my God!" Rushel breathed. "It's a baby seal!"

Audra watched stonily.

Catherine covered her mouth and looked nauseated. Samantha put a hand on her shoulder.

When the two had disappeared around the hill, the older one with a weary trudge, Gabrielle opened the front door. Cold air rushed in.

"I have to go see."

"Goddess," Rushel said.

Samantha joined her and they walked off the porch. Gabrielle gave a wary look down the driveway and they walked quickly into the chaparral then began jogging. Sweat ran chill on Gabrielle's forehead and they found the secret notch in the dunes. Not so secret, Gabrielle thought.

"That smell," Samantha said. "It wasn't like that. I mean the beach always smells. The first time I went to a beach I remember thinking why do people want to live here. Stinks to high heaven."

"I guess you get used to it. But this is different."

"So different."

There was a small sign on a stick stuck crookedly into a mass of ice plant. *Beach Closed.* They went past it and got to the overlook point.

"Oh," Samantha said.

"Holy shit," Gabrielle said and her stomach lurched.

The salt air was saturated with the stench of dead fish and birds.

Feathers lay in large drifts on sand stained black with decaying smelt and striped bass. A crab ran from behind a pile of mangled seagulls dragging a feather. The waves were gray and sluggish around the partially submerged rocks.

The piles of dead fish and seagulls extended south as far as Gabrielle could see. Clear to the north, though, she thought. Sea currents?

"Samantha, when I dropped that thing."

"Yeah."

"If you hadn't caught it."

"Yeah."

"It really was."

Gabrielle wiped her forehead. She took off her glasses and rubbed the bridge of her nose.

"What are we doing? I mean, we can't."

"Let's just think about this." Samantha flipped her hair back.

They walked back from the point. The smell faded. Thank you, wind, Gabrielle thought. She kept stumbling. Her legs felt rubbery.

"Fifty yards back and you can't smell it. The tide," Samantha said as they walked. "Those guys were right. In a week it will all be gone."

"Yeah. Good. I wonder how far it goes."

"What's south of here? Not much."

"I really don't know."

When they emerged from the trail and saw the worried faces in the windows, Samantha laughed.

"You know the worst part of all this?" she said.

"My God, what?"

"We know have no choice but to believe everything Audra and Rushel say."

Dinner was spaghetti and meatballs after an emergency request of 'no fish'. Audra seemed lost in thought. When the flashlight came on they all stopped talking.

Audra took a deep breath and said into the chandelier, "Yum, Catherine." She held up a meatball on her fork. "These braised eyeballs are delicious."

"Those are testicles."

Gislaine dropped her fork.

"They have a nice crunch to them." Audra bit off half the meatball and chewed loudly.

"Thank you," Catherine said. "The trick is freshness. Testicles must be as fresh as possible."

"I see. Tell me more."

"Ideally, they should be removed from the animal before it's killed."

"But the screams."

"The slaughterhouse is always filled with screams."

"Um." Audra swallowed.

Catherine smiled at her.

"The extra effort is worth it."

"That's my philosophy."

"Then we're on the same page."

"In many ways," Catherine said.

"Why thank you. I hope I wasn't out of line."

"Don't worry about it. Eat your balls."

They all looked at the flashlight. It refused to go out. Audra rolled her eyes.

"You know I only have so much material."

"You'll think of something," Catherine said.

"Yes. Everything depends on it."

Audra slowly twirled spaghetti on her fork and they finished dinner in silence.

Catherine spoke softly in the darkness.

"Now that you know about Samantha there's something I want to ask you."

Gabrielle said yes by running her fingers through Catherine's hair.

"You handled that very well, by the way."

"Her scar."

"Yes. She trusts you now."

Gabrielle nestled her head under Catherine's chin. "I trust her, too."

"What I wanted to ask was, I don't like her to be alone, it's not good for her to be alone, and would you mind if she joined us?"

Gabrielle felt Catherine hold her breath.

"No, of course I wouldn't mind."

Catherine exhaled and kissed her and slid out of bed. A minute later she returned with Samantha, tall and quiet. Nervous and excited, Gabrielle settled in between the two women.

Another night with no sleep, Gabrielle thought, as she once again lost track of time. At such moments in her basement room she had felt as if she was connected to the Earth itself and all the creatures on it. A god-like feeling. Here, she felt as if she were treading on the edge of space and the world was far below. She felt a faint anxiety she might drift away. She sighed.

I need to get it together, she thought. Get down to business. I love one of them. The other I think I could love, perhaps I love her already. So I will love them both. I make the rules.

Invisible in the darkness, Catherine and Samantha silently agreed with this arrangement and in the middle of it all Gabrielle felt something new, a new feeling from her commanding position in space. Exultation.

Sunday afternoon, Rushel and Audra took Gabrielle to the movies to celebrate one whole week as Goddess. Rushel didn't have to be at the store until three. The theater in the middle of town had been mostly empty and the movie kind of depressing, Gabrielle thought.

She didn't say that. Instead she said, "That actor, what was his name?"

"Warren Beatty." Rushel rolled the passenger window down.

The day was sunny and warm.

"He was certainly cute."

Audra, stretched out on the back seat, said "I'd do him."

Rushel laughed. "And I'm sure he'd do you."

She sat up. "Well of course he would. I'm adorable."

Gabrielle turned off the big three lane street and started up a hill lined with multi-story houses, the kind with lots of fancy woodwork falling into disrepair.

"Why are you going this way?" Rushel rested her arm on the open window.

Gabrielle didn't want to tell them she was looking for a certain street she was afraid did not exist. She downshifted and gave it gas. They approached a group of guys standing on the sloped sidewalk in front of one of the bigger houses. They all looked too old to be students. Heavy flannel shirts and jackets.

"Next time," Audra said, "*Animal House.*"

"Ew." Rushel shook her head.

"It's going to be great. Oh, hey, look who it is."

"Who? Oh my goodness! Slow down!" Rushel stuck her head out the window and let her hair blow alongside the car. Gabrielle pulled to the curb.

"Hi! I almost didn't recognize you without your uniform!"

A tall blonde man in a green flannel shirt looked at her in puzzlement. All the other guys stared at her, open-mouthed.

"Disco, it's me! The girl at the beach!"

He smiled and waved. "Sa thin oh, hi!"

Gabrielle smiled. "Uh."

Audra leaned between the seats. "Just pretend you understand."

"Right."

Audra called out the window. "This is where you live? That house is huge!"

Disco shrugged and nodded. "E es-tint sug. Eight?"

The guys laughed.

Gabrielle said, "I almost got that one."

Rushel pulled her hair back in. "Okay, well it was great to see you." She made a little wave. "Bye." Audra also waved.

Disco gave her a thumbs up. "O ah uh you!"

Gabrielle let out the clutch and moved back into the street. "Okay."

"That house is gigantic," Rushel said. "Probably has ten roommates."

Gabrielle shifted to second and said, "Wow. Ten."

Audra still tucked between the front seats said, "Fuck me."

Rushel laughed and Gabrielle looked at her in the mirror. Audra was staring wide-eyed at the floor.

"I know how to do it. I know how to *do it*. It would work. Wait." She held up he hand. "Yeah. Yeah. Oh my God. Um! Um! Turn around!"

Gabrielle took her foot off the gas and the Volkswagen shuddered.

"Go. Go around the block. Go back to Disco's house!"

Gabrielle made a right and then another right and sped down to the main street. She had to wait for a clutch of nervous looking boys in the crosswalk. They were all wearing expensive distressed blue jeans and oversized untucked shirts.

"Gah, freshmen," Audra said. "Get out of the way!"

One of them caught sight of Rushel and tripped over his new Nike's. Gabrielle saw no change in Rushel's expression.

They finally turned and Gabrielle got to third gear by the time they reached Disco's street and turned at the old gas station. It was being converted to a drive-thru coffee place she now saw. She dropped to second and powered around the corner and pulled up to Disco's. Only two of the guys were still there. Gabrielle did not see Disco.

Audra pushed on Rushel's seat.

"Okay, okay."

Rushel got out and Audra, head down, dove out of the back seat and ran up the concrete walkway to the front door. She yelled, "Hi!" to the two scraggly haired guys standing there and pulled the door open. She took a quick glance and went inside. Through the plain window in the door Gabrielle could see her waving her arms.

"She didn't knock."

"She can do stuff like that," Rushel said, standing at the passenger door. The two guys were staring at her. "Hi," she said.

Hey," the shorter of the two said. "So you're friends of —"

Down the hill a truck going through the main intersection laid on its air horn. A small black and white dog ran to safety.

Rushel, startled, said, "Sort of."

"Why's you call him Disco?"

"It was the best we could do. He's a little hard to understand, sometimes."

The taller guy laughed. "Sometimes?"

"No, that makes sense. He's always playing that music."

"Non-stop."

"His whole family's like that. Kind of a different wavelength."

"We call him Disco Lifestyle."

They both laughed.

Audra burst out of the house.

"Well," the tall one said. "His actual last name is —"

"Okay! Great!" Audra stepped into the back seat. "See you guys! This is going to be great!"

The short guy gave a thumb's up. "Great!"

Audra spoke into Gabrielle's ear. "We need to get back to *Tess*."

Gabrielle pulled away from the curb as Rushel closed her door and waved at the two guys. They did not wave. They nodded.

"We have to get that printer working."

Rushel turned around in her seat. "We're going to print something?"

"Oh God yes."

They worked on the computer for the rest of the afternoon. It was a whole new world full of things like 'fonts' which none of them had ever heard of. Gabrielle was surprised how quickly the day passed into night. Catherine had to drag them away at dinnertime. What they had created on the little screen made them giggle.

Disco's Last Blast was at the top in giant jagged letters that gave it futuristic look, they all thought. Then Disco's street address and the date, Saturday after next. Dance Contest! Major Prizes! The Last Dance of Its Kind! And the funniest line, *Period Attire Requested*.

They all laughed as they washed their hands.

"Platform shoes," Audra said.

"Pink silk shirts. Bell bottoms," Rushel said.

Audra looked at Gabrielle. "You'll need a dress to wear."

"Me? I don't think I own one."

"Do you dance?"

"No."

"But if you had to," Rushel said, "could you?"

Gabrielle felt a sharp surge of panic. "Why? I have to dance?"

"It would help."

Audra dried her hands. "You didn't go to the prom?"

"I got a job at a shoe store when I turned sixteen and then made sure I had to work weekends just so I could say I couldn't go to the prom. Turned out I didn't have to worry. I graduated a semester early and missed it all."

"That's too bad." Rushel sounded genuinely sad.

"It was a relief."

"Well, it would be better if you knew a little. Just in case."

Gabrielle felt her stomach clench. "I don't know."

"We'll teach you."

Gabrielle made herself nod.

They discussed the printer. They had to get paper with registration holes on the sides – maybe the bookstore had it. Audra wanted to do a picture like the poster from that movie with a guy doing a dance move. She wanted to draw it on the computer.

"You can do that? Draw pictures?" Rushel said. "That thing's incredible."

At dinner, keeping a sharp eye on the flashlight, Audra told them her plan. They all thought it might work except for Catherine who said, "This is nuts. There."

The flashlight came on. Audra put a record on the stereo, disco music, Gabrielle had no idea who the band was, and they finished their roast chicken speaking in subdued voices about the weather, looked like rain was coming again. Samantha picked at her vegetables and cheesy potatoes. The flashlight stayed on.

Audra put another record on the turntable. "*Telly*," she whispered to Gabrielle. "For punishment."

The flashlight did not go out until the record was almost over.

Audra relocated to Samantha's room. Gabrielle noticed she hadn't said a word about the new sleeping arrangements, not even a sarcastic look. Gabrielle also noticed this seeming lack of interest made her uneasy.

As they piled into the Volkswagen the next morning Rushel insisted on sitting in the back seat, which Gabrielle knew she hated because her legs were too long, and Audra did not turn on the radio, which she always did because she loved listening to music and also Captain Buffoon. Gabrielle began to get nervous.

When they reached the long cold valley, Rushel suddenly leaned between the seats and began speaking directly into Gabrielle's ear.

"Now that you are in the land of the living, you must be careful. From this exact point, time moves only in one direction. There is no going back."

Gabrielle struggled to keep the car centered in the lane. The sun just rising over the hills was blinding. She jerked it back from the shoulder and went across the double yellow. A Ford van with more primer than paint honked at her.

"Decisions made cannot be unmade," Rushel said. "Words spoken cannot be retrieved. Treat this as a game and the coin could be lost forever. You have been successful in the first stage of the test. You have earned the love of one of us. You must think and act with the utmost deliberation and seriousness."

Gabrielle didn't move her hands on the wheel. She didn't blink or turn her head. She could feel Rushel's gaze burning into the side of her face.

"If you fail here, if you lose the coin, you will be cast out. And you will never see any of us again in this life. I hope I've made myself clear."

Gabrielle made a quick nod. She heard Rushel sit back. They drove the rest of the way to school in complete silence.

That afternoon while walking down a crowded hallway in the English building she heard music playing in a closed office. Other students were hearing it and laughing. She recognized the song, *Laughter in the Rain*, and she pulled out of the flow of students and listened to the words.

I've never done that, what the song describes, she thought, but I could now. I'm now part of the world the song is talking about.

This idea caught her by surprise.

She wanted Catherine more than ever at that moment and it was impossible to concentrate on classes. She scribbled notes in the silly philosophy class and watched the clock.

When she finally got home with Audra and went quickly to the kitchen, Catherine looked at her with glassy eyes and did not smile.

"What's wrong?" Gabrielle felt a familiar fear and an equally familiar feeling of utter helplessness.

"Nothing."

"Okay."

"It's just a headache. It comes and goes."

"Okay."

Catherine turned and staggered. She spoke to the space over the stove. "You can hug me if you want."

That night they all slept without touching. Samantha was totally silent and Gabrielle thought, didn't sleep at all.

In the morning as she poured coffee Catherine smiled, not quite bright eyed, with a look that said, don't worry about it. But Gabrielle did.

That afternoon, Gabrielle rummaged around the electronics lab, her realm from years past, and in a cardboard box labeled *El Junk* found an old telephone. She pulled it out of the mass of tangled power cords and printed circuit boards. Shiny, black and heavy. She checked the thick wires. Frayed but intact. The dial spun smoothly.

She looked around the darkened room. Well, it was the junk box so it should be okay. She wrapped the wires around it and went to the door.

She had taken several classes here. The lab stations were a dwarf forest of gray shelves crowded with simple test equipment and power supplies. It all seemed so long ago and distant, as if it had happened to someone else.

Have I changed that much? she thought.

Just outside the door of the Science building, under the blowing whispering pine trees, she heard a laugh.

"What are you going to do with that old thing?" It was Daniel in a black sweater. Terrence was right behind him.

"What?" Terrence said.

"Look what she has."

Terrence stared and seemed to think hard. He pointed at the phone. "That makes no sense."

"I know. But it's Gabrielle."

"So it has to make sense."

"It certainly does."

They both waited.

"Frequencies," Gabrielle said.

They looked at each other.

"Of course," Daniel said.

"I see what she's doing," Terrence said.

"Information theory."

"Fourier."

"Which you love."

"Hate."

"But that whole thing, you know, there must be something happening."

"She won't tell us."

Gabrielle just smiled.

"And after all the classes we've had together," Terrence said.

A grand total of one, Gabrielle thought.

Daniel shook his head. "If you have to ask, you lose."

"Affirmative."

"She'll lose all respect for you."

"She'll give you the look."

"And we don't want that."

"Nope."

They nodded to each other.

"You have a nice evening, Gabrielle," Daniel said.

"I, as well, would like to wish my fellow student a pleasant evening," Terrence said.

Gabrielle hefted the heavy telephone. "Thanks, guys. Bye." She turned on her heels and walked quickly away. Don't laugh, she thought. Don't do it. When she was clear on the other side of the Graphic Arts building, she giggled.

At home, Gabrielle ascertained that Catherine was better and then went back to the wine cellar with the old phone and the leftover speaker wire and her tool pouch. It took her only a few minutes to clip the phone into the metal box. She lifted the receiver and a loud dial tone filled the tiny room. She dialed *959* and the prerecorded voice read off a phone number. She hung up quickly. What would they think if they got a busy signal? She set the phone on the top row of bottles and ducked out the door with her tools.

Audra, in her dark blue sweater, was waiting at the front door. She smiled in the sharp cold light.

"Uh oh. She has tools."

"We now have a phone."

"A phone phone?"

"A real phone. In the wine cellar."

"Wow! Can we put it in here?"

Audra backed into the library. Rushel sat at the computer. She barely glanced up. Gabrielle knocked the sand from her shoes and stepped in. The fireplace crackled.

"Anywhere you want. Just need wire." Gabrielle stopped. Audra was looking at her, head tipped, arms crossed over her chest.

"Come with me, Goddess."

Gabrielle followed her into the living room. Catherine, Samantha, and Gislaine were sitting at the dining table, glasses of wine before them. The reclining chairs had been pushed up against the walls leaving an open space on the hardwood floor. She saw that the stereo was on. The long timer dial glowed blue white and the turntable was spinning a record. The tone arm rested on its post.

"Oh. Um," Gabrielle said self-consciously.

"That's right. Drop the soldering iron, baby, and just watch me."

Audra set the needle gingerly onto the record.

"*If I Can't Have You*," she said. "This is so beautiful."

Audra kicked off her shoes and in her new L.L. Bean socks went to the open area and stood with her head down, her soft curly black hair covering her face. When the singing started she looked at Gabrielle and opened her arms invitingly then spun away, her hair making a wide fan.

Rushel came in from the library. She looked very unhappy. She made a loud "Tsk," and went into the back bathroom, giving Gabrielle a grim, sideways look.

"See," Audra said over the music. "You just move to the beat. And this song is perfect."

Audra brought her hands up to one shoulder, then the other, as if hugging.

Gabrielle stood behind one of the recliners and tried to analyze *dancing*. She knew what the beat was and could see it might be possible to simply copy some of Audra's moves. Keep feet on the floor and move your upper body. Turn from side to side no more than forty-five degrees from partner. Do something with hair; shake head to toss hair. Bob chin up and down. Nod in sync with arms, elbows bent, hands closed. Don't stick fingers out.

She tried to see the song the way Audra did. Try to *hear* the song. There was the beat and rhythm. There was the changing tone of the music. Orchestral then just one instrument. Quiet instantly followed by a kind of restart. It *was* beautiful. The lyrics, especially the line about dreams, were sad. It was a song about loss.

She tried to synthesize her observations. Beautiful music about loss. The end of dreams. And you dance to it. You dance to your sadness.

Catherine was at her side with a glass of wine.

"You seemed thirsty."

Gabrielle just nodded. She was surprised by tears in her eyes. The glowing flashlight sparkled blurrily. She drank the wine in two gulps.

The next song she was not familiar with. It was about Beethoven and kind of short. Audra danced easily to it.

When it finished she put on another record and held out her hand. "Come on."

Gabrielle swallowed and looked for a place to set the glass down. Samantha was suddenly there and gently took it.

"Shoes," she said.

Gabrielle took off her Top Siders. Both of her big toes poked through the old socks. She sighed.

This was a song Gabrielle only vaguely remembered. My memory doesn't work for music, she thought with a shock. How could I not know that?

Audra pulled her right arm around her waist.

"Hold me like this. Nice and tight."

"All right."

Audra's face was resting on her chest. Her right hand found Gabrielle's left and grasped it. She looked up and smiled.

"Just follow my lead."

The beat of *Night Fever* was similar to the first song but it wasn't sad. It was, she didn't know, she found it hard to think because Audra was yanking her arms around.

"Can you see my feet? Watch my feet. See? One two three."

Gabrielle copied the stepping movements and found herself moving in a slow turn.

"Okay, can you hear the song?"

"Huh? Well, yeah."

"I want to try something, okay?"

They turned around the living room twice more. Audra took her arm from around Gabrielle's waist. The song reached a crescendo.

"Now!"

"What?"

Audra lifted Gabrielle's hand and passed it over her head, making a spin. Audra's hair brushed her arm. Someone clapped and Gabrielle, startled, saw that all the lights were off except the reading lamp. Audra smiled in the darkness.

"Oh."

"Isn't that great? Do it again!"

The song was ending but they did the twirl again and again, faster each time. Gabrielle laughed.

"You just need a good partner."

"I see that."

Rushel flipped the record over. She was now wearing a shimmering silver blouse.

"Could the band play this one next?"

She indicated a track with her fingernail.

Audra squinted and then said softly to Gabrielle, "Here we go."

Rushel went to Samantha, who had changed into a long green dress, and said in a breathy voice, "Hi. Would you like to dance?"

Samantha flipped her hair from her shoulders.

"Yeah, okay."

"I'm Rushel." She held out her hand and leaned forward tilting her head sharply.

"I'm Samantha." They shook hands. She pulled Rushel close and looked her up and down. "That's a beautiful name."

"Thanks. Do you come here often?"

"Actually I live here."

"Oh, that explains why I always see you."

They laughed as Audra shook her head.

"Hi," Catherine said loudly. "I'm Catherine." She held out her hand to Gislaine.

"Hi. I'm Gislaine."

"Your name is beautiful and really hard to pronounce even for someone like me who spent months in Paris."

"Thanks. I like it."

"You want to make out?" Catherine said in a breathy voice.

"Yeah, sure."

Rushel made an amused gasp.

Catherine stood up. "Maybe later, dollface."

"Anytime."

Gabrielle felt dizzy. Rushel and Samantha walked by her both running their fingers through her hair. They both had on a lot of *Fracas*.

Rushel tilted her head sharply again making her lips hover over Gabrielle's. "You're next." Then to Samantha, "Right?"

"I can hardly wait." Samantha also tilted her head. "Get ready, baby."

Gabrielle tried to swallow but couldn't. "Okay," she managed. She felt sweat on her forehead.

"This is the real lesson." Rushel put her hands on her hips. "As soon as the band gets it act together."

Audra exhaled. Gabrielle blinked her blurry eyes and saw her turn the volume all the way up. Then she lifted the needle and set it down. There was a hiss and a thump Gabrielle felt in her chest. Music began pounding from the speakers. Several books fell off the shelf above. *You Should Be Dancing.* Gabrielle, transfixed, watched Rushel and Samantha.

Rushel was making her chest pulsate to the Bee Gees and her shimmering blouse bounced when she tipped her head back, mouth open, her blonde hair surging in silky waves. Samantha's dress was slit up the side from her ankles to her armpits. Gabrielle could not see any strap holding things together. She danced in a kind of counterpoint to Rushel. She held her arms out as if in invitation and still moved to the beat, except a different beat, like there was more than one. Gabrielle, standing there, could not see how she was doing it. They danced so close there was no space visible between them.

"No *way*," Gabrielle said.

Catherine came up on either side of her. Catherine gave her a large full glass. Gabrielle sipped. More wine. She wrinkled her nose. Extra stuff. She felt them lean back and talk behind her head.

"What is that?"

"Half a bottle of chardonnay and two shots of vodka."

Gabrielle sipped again. Really should go slow, she thought and then she forgot what she was thinking about.

"You are an object of desire," Audra whispered in her ear.

"You are object of lust," Catherine whispered in her other ear, her breath hot.

"Don't you want to be with them?"

"Can you feel the music inside you?"

Someone's hands gripped her jeans at the belt loops and started working her hips from side to side.

"They want you to join them."

"Go on up there."

Gabrielle took an unsteady step. Samantha turned and, dancing, held out her hand. She snatched Gabrielle's arm and pulled her in.

Gabrielle was between the two taller woman dancing in the soft light. They pressed against her. Samantha's hair flew across her face. She tried to copy their moves. She lifted her arms and rocked to the rhythm and shook her head. She snapped her head from side to side and Rushel said, "*Wow*," and so she did it again. The room spun. She thought, where did I put that glass? She looked around, still dancing, and saw it under the lamp. It was empty. Oh no no, how long have I been doing this?

She felt herself falling backwards and strong hands caught her.

"Hi," she said and the music seemed to go down her throat. She burped loudly. The strong hands were joined by others and she watched from far away as she floated over the living room floor into the hall then into the big bright bathroom. A voice said, "Bathtub. Quick." Samantha has a sweet voice, she thought.

"But I don't *want* to take a bath."

Then the edge of the tub was before her. She held on to it. She gripped it hard.

"Okay. This feels good."

She puked up wine and vodka.

"Well," she said, breathing heavily, "that's not." She saw the stuff in the tub. She vomited several more times and Catherine was at her side with a towel. The music was no longer playing.

"You'll feel better if you take a shower."

"I don't want to take a bath. I can't. Look." The tub spun in tight circles around her.

"No, a shower. In the shower."

"Well." She vomited twice more and the nausea subsided. She felt for her glasses. She felt all around her face. She looked in the tub thankful she couldn't quite see it and Catherine tugged her arm.

"I have your glasses. See?"

"Very funny."

"Here. Come on."

Gabrielle raised her arms as Catherine pulled off her shirt. She slowly straightened out her knees and was somehow standing.

"Now get in the shower. No, leave the curtain open."

Gabrielle watched the walls of the shower sway to her pulse and then Catherine opened the valve. Freezing water hit her head and shoulders.

"Oh! Ah!"

"I know." Catherine's voice displayed no satisfaction.

Gabrielle felt Catherine holding her. Catherine was getting wet also. Gabrielle, her jeans soaked, covered her chest with her crossed arms.

"I'm sorry, that was stupid," Catherine said. ""It's my fault. You'll feel better in a second."

Gabrielle let the water hit the top of her head. The cold water was starting to feel warm as Catherine turned it off.

"There's a towel. Don't look at the tub."

Gabrielle stepped out. Her jeans and socks squished. No, it's my fault, she thought. I'm the one who drank it. She started to say something but Catherine began to towel off her hair and shoulders.

"You don't have to dance. Whoever heard of a dancing goddess anyway."

"Okay."

"What, you want to?"

"Not really, but."

"You don't want to, but. You don't like to fail."

"I guess."

"You can learn later."

"Okay."

"I'll teach you."

Gabrielle took back her glasses. "I didn't know you liked to dance."

"Sure. Hardly ever do it anymore. There, do you feel better?"

"Much better. Never had a cold shower before." She stared shedding her wet pants.

"Yeah, you'll get used to them."

Gabrielle thought, well then I'll get used to them.

"Thank you for taking care of me."

"It's what lovers do."

Gabrielle, her jeans at her ankles, looked at Catherine in surprise.

"I love you," she said.

Catherine's eyes widened.

"We can discuss this."

"Okay."

"For a crazy drunk you are very romantically minded."

"I suppose so."

"You're talking about love standing naked next to a bathtub full of vomit. I know so."

Gabrielle stepped out of her pants and faced her directly. "I don't."

"Ah ah." Catherine held up her hand. "Not here. I want you to lie down and rest. Come on, get those socks off."

Gabrielle thought, I've never said that to anyone before. And now I have.

In her bedroom, she stood at her window. It was just becoming night.

No one's ever said that to me, of course. But I don't care. I don't see how it matters. I know what I feel. And Rushel said.

She tried to think. What exactly did Rushel say? Damn it. No more wine.

The room was no longer spinning. She watched the night. There were stars and her distant red lights. A silence came over her mind.

I feel strong, she thought. I feel strong.

Wednesday evening, Gabrielle was in the library with another book of philosophy. Derrida this time. It was rough going. She kept reading paragraphs multiple times to try to figure out what the author was going on about. The style of writing, she thought, seemed designed to make things less clear.

She shook her head. Why do it that way? She was about to conclude the author was kind of incompetent when loud yelling broke her concentration.

Audra and Rushel were standing on opposite sides of the dining table shouting at each other. They were both holding sheets of paper covered with dense, single-spaced typing.

"It's all your fault, Rushel. Just admit it!"

"How was I supposed to know."

Audra held up her paper and pointed at a line. Rushel studied her paper, annoyed.

"She was like that."

Audra covered her face.

Rushel took a deep breath and said, very seriously, "How was I supposed to know she was like that?"

"Fine. But it was your silly ancient Greek mystical cult thing."

"It's not silly."

"Goofy."

"I worked really hard on it." Rushel glanced at the shining flashlight and rolled her eyes.

"Anyway, Audra, you recruited her."

"We all recruited her."

Audra smiled. Gabrielle saw her shrug.

"Okay, quiet. Here she comes."

"God, I hate her," Rushel read.

"Oh, hi!" Audra said loudly. "Gabrielle."

"Hi," Gabrielle said flatly.

Audra gave her a sheet and hurriedly indicated her line. Gabrielle saw what she was supposed to say and shook her head, shocked.

Audra mouthed, *You have to!* Rushel nodded.

Gabrielle sighed. Fine.

"What are you two bitches doing in here? Get your fat asses outside and start washing my car. I'm the fucking Goddess! Get moving!"

She closed her eyes on the f-word.

Audra and Rushel both said, "Yes, Goddess." Audra walked to the front door, clomping her feet. She opened the door, slammed it shut, and came back into the kitchen. They all looked pensively at the glowing flashlight. Rushel pointed at scattered papers on the table. Audra picked up a sheet and gave it to Gabrielle. She put her finger on a spot halfway down the page. Gabrielle saw her line.

"Boy," she said, "did I screw up. Patricia and Holly were right. I should have gone with L. What a mess this place is. I suppose it's too late now. They probably hate me. If they only knew how much I want to change sides."

Gabrielle saw the next part. She shook her head. Audra nodded vigorously.

"What am I going to do?" Gabrielle read. She made a sobbing sound. "This is all screwed up." She tried to put a hitch in her voice.

The flashlight went out.

Gabrielle dropped the paper on the table. "Oh my God."

"Great! That was great! Susan's probably peeing her pants!"

"This is kind of fun," Rushel wasn't smiling. "In a way. But I don't like it."

"Yeah. I don't think either of you have fat asses."

Catherine walked in from the hallway. "Don't be too sure. Lasagna, seven o'clock."

Audra and Rushel both said, "Ohh." Gabrielle said, "Do you need any help with anything?"

Catherine looked at her, glassy eyed again. "No, I don't need help."

"All right."

Catherine swallowed. "But thank you for asking."

Gabrielle said, "Lasagna sounds wonderful. Well, homework."

She went back to the library and sat in the midst of the beanbags and stared out the window as evening swept in, feeling helpless. Feeling there was something she was supposed to be doing. And having no idea what that was.

Thursday, Samantha got dragged into the act.

"Gabrielle. She's just awful," she said to the chandelier.

Gabrielle was sitting with Catherine at the the table with a cup of coffee. No lines today. Samantha masked laughter by making her voice deep and sultry.

"Maybe we should cast her out."

Gabrielle thought she sounded very sexy.

"Then they'd know we messed up," Audra said gruffly. "Can't have that."

"So we're stuck with her, the little four-eyed freak." Samantha had to turn away from the table, covering her mouth.

"I'm afraid so. Now let's get to work on the dance. It's going to be a blast. We're going to have a DJ and a contest and everything. And an open bar."

"Wow!"

Catherine also had to cover her mouth.

"But I can't put anything about the bar on the poster or the cops will show up. So just remember to tell everyone."

"Right. Open bar. And what."

The flashlight went dark.

"That's kind of rude." Samantha dropped her page on the table.

"They're idiots. Oh my God this is working so perfect. Susan is right now telling all the other Susans about the open bar. They will absolutely *have* to be there. Yes! Okay, I gonna be late for class."

"Don't you have to organize the whole thing? That's a lot of work." Catherine drank the last of her coffee.

"Sid will do it all. That's the beauty of it. He does dances almost every weekend. He makes a fortune, too. He'll have everything set up, no problem. You select items from a menu. Type of music. Contest. Prizes. He's a total pro."

"This is a guy?" Catherine grinned.

"My best friend in pre-law. He's up in Stanford now. He wants to be a judge. He's gonna be really good."

"I'm kind of getting interested in this dance. I can come, right?"

"Of course. You have to come."

Catherine stood up. "We'll see." She turned to the sink and Gabrielle saw her pause abruptly. Her knees buckled and she dropped her cup into the sink where it shattered. Samantha was there before Gabrielle could move from her chair.

Samantha put her arm around Catherine's shoulders and whispered in her ear. Gabrielle heard Catherine say, "I just felt funny. I'm fine. I just felt funny." Samantha lifted her from the edge of the sink and Gabrielle got on Catherine's other side. She looked at Samantha gratefully. Samantha acknowledged by rubbing her arm. Then they all went into the bedroom.

The flashlight came on four times that evening but no one paid any attention to it.

Friday afternoon.

Gabrielle did her homework to the sound of thunder. *Vector fields and line integrals: Find the circulation of F = (x - y)i + (y - x)k along the curve C around the square bounded by...*

She was kneeling at the hearth in the middle room. Windows were too much of a distraction and she liked to tend the fire. She could see they'd need firewood soon. As she wrote swiftly she wondered how you got firewood. Was it something you buy? And what kind of wood was it anyway?

She finished the problem and let go of the pencil. Her knuckles popped and she rubbed her fingers. There was a nice red callus on the joint of her little finger, on the verge of bleeding. How many miles of paper have I scraped that spot over, she thought, I should put something on it.

"I know," she said and laughed. "Girly stuff."

Thunder boomed again. Close now. One of the windows by the dining table made an ominous rattle. The chaparral was brightly illuminated by lightning. Thunder followed instantly and rain swept the dunes.

That was right next door, she thought, and headed for the big bathroom and the cabinet full of hand lotion. The kitchen was dark. She wasn't sure where everyone was. Catherine, who had looked the same that morning, was resting in her room. Audra and Rushel wanted to go shopping, she knew. Maybe Samantha and Gislaine went with them. There were a couple department stores on the south side of town. No doubt they were all scouring the clothing racks for bargains. Gabrielle did not feel left out. She had never succumbed to the rapture of shopping. But it's fun for them. You needed that sometimes, she thought as she walked into the hallway.

To her right, the sound of rain. Through Samantha's shadowy room she saw that the sliding glass door was wide open. The curtains billowed in the sudden wind, warm and humid. More lightning and immediate thunder. The storm was going to head out to sea. The sky outside was charcoal black and ash gray. Bands of clouds, shreds of clouds, crossed in front of her. She went into the room and grabbed the handle of the door. The floor was getting wet. There was a flash of light far away on the western horizon.

She stepped out onto the patio.

The sun appeared in the gap between the edge of the storm and the distant churning surface of the sea. Brilliant golden light flooded the landscape before her. Cold and pure, the light seemed to bounce inside her eyes. Wind gusted then turned into a roar. The roar increased until it sounded like a jet engine, a freight train.

Her ears popped painfully. She suddenly found it hard to breathe. She felt the air being pulled from her lungs. At the other end of the patio the lounge chairs impossibly rose into the air and spun around.

The tornado passed directly over her, swift yet unhurried, just above the roofline and paused at the verge of the sagebrush. She could see into the heart of it and it was ablaze with blue white lightning and the undulating vortex walls, moving at fantastic speed, refracted the sharp horizontal sunlight and threw it back.

Ice, she thought, it's made of ice.

Her shirt whipped up and hit her face and she felt as if she were rising up, leaving the ground. Lightning streaked and arced across the vacuum of the tornado's interior in a *pattern*. It's alive, she thought, it's alive and aware. Looking up, she realized she could move her feet freely because she was no longer standing on the concrete.

It knows I'm here, she thought and thumped back to the ground. The lounge chairs crashed straight down, one of them balanced atop the patio wall. She held perfectly still.

The funnel began to destabilize. The undulations became a convulsive wave of disassociation and the blue white lightning vanished. Then the vortex abruptly spun apart into a wrack of clouds, black against the gray. No structure remained.

Hail struck her head. With shaking hands she felt blood at her hairline.

"*God*," she said.

Then a voice directly in front of her.

"Father."

Gabrielle looked down in total surprise. There was someone kneeling inches from her feet in the darkness of the walled patio. Ice continued to fall. The sun touched the horizon.

"Father, this is your faithful servant Samantha." Her raven black hair draped over her in a protective shroud.

Gabrielle moved back as quietly as she could. But she listened.

"Please, Father. The power of your love has lifted me up and sustained me so many times. Please, Father, don't take her from me. I'm so frightened. She's the only one I've ever loved. Please don't take her. I love her so much."

There was surge in the stinging hail. Gabrielle winced and put her hands up. The hail was the size of golf balls.

"I have always been and always will be your faithful servant. Thank you, Father. Amen."

It began to rain, heavy hot drops mixed with ice. Gabrielle backed up to the doorway, embarrassed yet also feeling privileged. She crossed

Samantha's floor and stood in the hallway. Her hair dripped water mixed with blood onto the carpet. In the kitchen, she leaned on the dining table.

The flashlight came on and shone up the wall in a weak fan of light. She spoke softly, angrily to the chandelier.

"You stay out. You don't come in here."

The flashlight went off. Behind her, she heard the patio door close and then Samantha's bedroom door.

Gabrielle sat in her chair and wiped the blood off her forehead.

"Now what's going to happen?" she whispered.

Saturday morning.

Samantha and Audra were in the recliners, reading. Audra was halfway through *Time Enough for Love*, Samantha was just starting a book called *The Gnostic Gospels*. Rushel and Gislaine were cross-legged on the floor, leaning against Audra's chair. Rushel had a magazine, *Vogue*, and Gislaine was intently reading *Time*.

Gabrielle watched Catherine going over a French cookbook. Catherine had gotten up early and made coffee and chocolate crêpes. Gabrielle thought she seemed much better. She caught Gabrielle studying her and turned aside in annoyance. So definitely better. The cookbook looked prettily heavily used. Many pages were turned down and there were dozens of scraps of paper bookmarks. The torn book cover had a picture of a friendly looking French lady named Julia Child.

Gabrielle was sitting at the counter. She opened her book reluctantly. Lacan. She hated it. Every sentence, every paragraph. But she refused to give up. She thumbed the remaining pages...

Something hit the front door hard.

Rushel yelped. They all heard the creak of the screen door hinges. It had been knocked loose. Before the sound had faded, Samantha was on her feet, Audra right behind her. Audra went to the curved sliding glass door and pushed it open. Gabrielle saw them exchange a glance. *Go.*

Audra ran out onto the sand in her bare feet, acing away from the house. Gabrielle lost sight of her. Samantha went to the front door and without hesitation yanked it open.

Gabrielle, standing at the kitchen counter, saw Samantha look down, then step outside. It looked to her like she stepped over something.

"Well." Catherine closed Julia Child. "I hope it's not another seagull."

"Sounded too big." Rushel was standing. She dropped her magazine on the floor.

"Sounded like it broke the screen," Gislaine said.

Gabrielle went to the curved windows. Audra was coming back past the dune path, passing the parking area, peering up into the sage and Manzanita behind the house. Gabrielle thought she had run down the driveway at least as far as the first curve. Audra in the parking area held

412

very still and shielded her eyes. Finally, Gabrielle saw her put her hands on her hips. She shook her head and came back to the sliding glass doors.

"Nothing," she said. She knocked sand from her feet. "Man. Winded. No one there. No one on the drive. Almost got to the gate. No sound, no car. No footprints."

Gabrielle heard Samantha come back in the front door.

"Could someone run fast enough?"

"No way." Audra coughed. "In that sand."

In the corner of her eyes, Gabrielle saw Samantha was carrying something.

"Anything?" Audra took a deep breath.

"The sand all the way past the cars was undisturbed," Samantha said. "There was just this."

She swung a heavy object onto the dining table.

Gabrielle stared at it. Her heart began pounding. It was her backpack.

"Really?" Audra said. "That?"

"Holy shit!" Catherine exclaimed. "Look at her! Gabrielle, what? What is it?"

Samantha reached for the zippers.

"Don't touch it!" Gabrielle yelled. "Get away! Get back!"

Samantha backed up instantly to the recliners.

"Oh, fuck," Rushel muttered.

"Please." Gabrielle could hear her voice crack. Her mind went into overdrive.

Catherine came around the table and got behind Samantha and peeked over her shoulder.

Gabrielle, trying to breathe, stood at the table and bent close to the thing. No question. Blue nylon with a black abrasion resistant bottom. Frayed sharp-edged straps with no padding. She got as close as she could and kept her hands under the edge of the table. The blue fabric looked different. There were threadbare spots where one of the shoulder straps was sown on. She didn't remember that. She knew she would have noticed wear like that.

It looked older, she realized. Years of wear and tear. And the tab was missing from one of the large zippers of the main compartment. She was absolutely certain the zipper had not been broken before.

But it was her backpack. Purchased in the campus bookstore in nineteen seventy-six.

She reached out and turned the back of her hand to it. It was not radiating heat. No, it was cold. She touched it. Cold as ice.

"Goddess," came a whisper.

"Sorry," Audra said. "What's going on?"

"Oh my God, Gabrielle." Catherine was near tears.

Gabrielle stood straight. "It's mine. It's my backpack. But it can't be

here. This is impossible." She faced them all. "It couldn't. This is impossible."
She felt sick to her stomach.

"You said you lost it," Gislaine said.

"Yes. Yes, I lost it. But."

Samantha touched her arm.

They all walked into the middle room. Samantha closed the door.

"There. Now you can't see it."

Gabrielle sat on the padded bench, Catherine and Samantha on either
side. Rushel and Gislaine sat close together next to them. Audra stood in the
center of the room.

"Start at the beginning," Audra said firmly.

Gabrielle told them about that night. She found it mortifying at first
then she saw how seriously they were all taking it, especially Samantha
and Rushel. She told them about the fog and quiet freeway. Miranda Street.
The bear and the man with half a face. Running and tripping and losing the
backpack. The cold and dark. The street which climbed into the sky. And the
river of people, silent and naked, and the feelings she got from them. And
finally, the guide who led her out. The figure with curly hair.

"I kind of thought that was you."

Now Audra looked embarrassed.

Rushel leaned toward Samantha. "I'm thinking the freeway."

"Yeah."

Rushel said to Gabrielle, "When you got home what time was it?"

Gabrielle found she had no memory of that. "I didn't look."

"But it was late, right? At the underpass, the sun was just going down.
That spot is less than two miles from your place. So maybe an hour to walk
it. On that date, the sun set at five twenty-one. So you got home about six
thirty. Did it seem later than that?"

Gabrielle looked at Rushel in astonishment. Audra was grinning. At that
traffic light, she thought. It wasn't early evening traffic at all. It was calm
and relaxed.

"Now that I think about it, yes. Everyone was in bed and the tv was off."

"And has this ever happened to you before? This time thing."

"Yes." The memory was sharp. "The night I walked to the Carriage
House. It was six forty-five when I left the house. I remember looking at the
clock over the sink. And when I got there it was almost ten. But. I was kind
of drunk."

"That probably had nothing to do with it," Rushel said. "Did you notice
anything out of the ordinary as you walked?"

Gabrielle shrugged. "No, I wasn't noticing much. I wasn't even *counting*.
It was Sunday night. I think maybe three or four cars went past."

Rushel sat back. "We might be able to figure that one out. But Miranda
Street."

"We have no choice," Samantha said.

"Agreed."

"Oh, sorry to interrupt," Audra said, "but aren't we driving up the coast this weekend?"

"Could we go tomorrow?" Rushel said after a moment of thought.

Audra rolled her eyes. "Sure."

"And just stay one night?"

"Of course, Rushel. And what a nice safe adventure we will have. What a crazy bunch we are, huh?"

"It might *get* crazy," Samantha said. "Who knows what it's like up there."

"You optimist."

"Why thank you."

"We need to discuss this," Rushel said. "This is serious."

"Wait." Gabrielle stood up. She opened the door and went to the table. She grabbed the strap of the backpack and set it upright.

"It seems heavier than it used to be. All right."

She unzipped one side of the main compartment, then the other side. She stepped back. Nothing flew out. She looked inside. There was her bulging project binder with its blue vinyl cover. She took it out. The cover was sticky. Then she remembered the plastic had always been sticky. She set it down. There was her little humanities notebook and the two big five-subject notebooks with her real notes. She arranged them all on the table.

"That's it. Everything's here."

She opened the small top pouch. Her pens were there and Linda's pencil was tucked into its sleeve.

She looked at the bottom of the main compartment. There was a quarter and a dime, 1977 and 1976, and a resistor, 10K, she remembered dropping. And sand. She checked all three notebooks – all as she remembered. She opened up the project binder and paged through it. All the material for the optical computer seemed different. She would have to go through it. Some of the writing.

She wiped her hands on her pants.

"There's dust on everything."

"Looks like it's been lying out in the desert," Samantha said.

"Yes." Gabrielle examined the new worn spots on the straps. "How do you lose a backpack on a street that doesn't exist. And how does it come out of thin air and hit the front door."

"If someone was good," Audra said, "they could have stood by the cars, flung that thing then run fifteen feet and dropped down in the sage. Drop and freeze. You'd never see them. Then just run off when we turn our backs."

"Hm," Samantha said.

"If someone were good."

"And you know someone like that?" Catherine said.

"You bet I do. The only real question is why. And, well, just assume they're insane and like messing with people. And." Audra crossed her arms. "And as far as Miranda Street goes. You said you fell and hit your chin."

Gabrielle touched the spot, still sore.

"Being cold and confused are symptoms of shock. Getting hit on the chin is a good way to get knocked out. You could have been going in and out of consciousness without knowing it. Running hard would've made it a lot worse."

"It felt completely real. And it all sort of made sense. What I saw."

"Okay."

"And the night she walked to the Carriage House?" Rushel said.

"Don't drink multiple glasses of wine and wander out into a winter night and expect your wristwatch to make sense."

This made Gabrielle laugh. The knot in her stomach relaxed some.

Audra said to Rushel, "You said you wanted to investigate?"

Rushel nodded.

Audra put her hands on her hips again. "One day, when I'm a high-powered attorney, you could be my leg man."

"Really?" Rushel grinned.

"Sure, everyone just falls over for you. And you too," she said to Samantha.

Samantha nodded seriously. "We *are* good."

"Wait," Catherine said. "You could have this gorgeous legal headquarters with a huge desk and lots of houseplants. And they would never see you."

"They wouldn't?"

"No, they'd talk to you over a speakerphone. That would be amazing."

"Well, yeah," Audra said. "Oh God damn it."

"Hi there, Angel," Catherine said in a breathy voice. "Come here often?"

"Actually," Samantha said, "I live here."

Rushel laughed so hard Gabrielle thought she would pull a muscle. Catherine bumped her arm and smiled.

"Are we still driving up the coast tomorrow?" Gabrielle said.

"Yes."

"Yes!" Audra bounced on her toes.

"I think I'll stay here," Rushel said.

"We'll both stay here," Gislaine said.

"I just don't feel like driving."

"You're going to miss everything."

"You always say that."

"It's always true."

Gabrielle saw Audra's eye flash.

"Well, tell us all about it when you get back." Rushel brushed the hair from her face.

Gabrielle took the backpack and her notebooks into her bedroom. She tossed the rumpled thing on her bed and stepped to the window. Sylvan blue sky. Birds darted through the brush and a lizard ran onto the path and then back under cover.

Samantha and Catherine came into the room quietly. Samantha cleared her throat.

"Goddess, I want you to know I believe you. I think you saw something the living were never meant to see. It was incredibly dangerous."

"I think I barely escaped," Gabrielle said.

"I also want you to know I believe in science. My grandfather taught me, long ago. He was definitely not mystically minded. We may never figure this out."

"We shouldn't," Catherine said.

"There is very little of the universe we can actually perceive. It's endless," Samantha said. "You can get lost out there. And there are powers."

Gabrielle had the sudden urge to tell her about the tornado. The look of something close to fear on Samantha's face stopped her.

"Rushel wants to investigate. Like, right now. I think I can talk her out of it."

"Good."

"That's someone who is mystically minded. Until she learns," Samantha said. "So that." She pointed at the backpack. "Any clues?"

"Yes. I'm glad you're both here. I noticed it a minute ago."

Gabrielle took out her heavy blue project binder. She opened it to the last section, the optical computer.

"That's a serious notebook," Samantha said. "It needs wheels."

Gabrielle laughed. "I bought the backpack just to carry it around." She popped open the rings. "These are my notes for the computer I want to build." Going back how many years, she thought. The carefully drawn circuits and notations seemed almost alien to her. That was me back then, she thought. I was someone else.

"The computer made of light," Samantha said.

Gabrielle took out the pages of graph paper and spread them on the bed. "Look. At an angle."

They bent down and the soft light from the window showed it. There were indentations in the paper as if someone had scribbled on them hard through another piece of paper.

"Look right here. This is my old idea for the accumulator. This is where the processor gets its instructions. It's a register. It stores a binary number so it can be read."

The sheet of graph paper had large X pressed across it and over her precisely written description, *a sapphire, Al2O3, waveguide etched to 300 nm,* a very clear *NO*.

"That wasn't there before."

"Someone didn't like it," Samantha said.

"So in the other world people are assholes just like here? What's the use?" Catherine said.

"And look."

Gabrielle spread out all the sheets. There were lines and scribbles all over them.

"I'm beginning to see a pattern. I'll have to study this."

She stuffed the binder into the backpack and put the papers into pile on the nightstand.

"Audra's probably right. Someone found it in the street, maybe one of the Susans, and they're just messing with us."

"Audra has her views," Samantha said. "Wait." She left and went to her room.

"Let's not worry about it right now," Catherine said. "Fool with it when you get back."

Gabrielle felt a surge of excitement. "We're going?"

"Sure. First thing in the morning."

"All right. So. I don't know what to do."

"You've never done this before?"

"I've never gone on a trip with my friends before. Overnight."

"We'll get you used to it," she said and Catherine giggled.

Samantha came back in with something in her hands. Gabrielle felt a chill as she stood behind her.

"You need this," Samantha said and held out a necklace for her to see. It was a leather string, like shoelaces, she thought, knotted together. Samantha tied the final knot at the back of her neck.

"There. That shouldn't come loose."

"What's this for?"

"This is your link back to us. When you find yourself on the other side and you're afraid, just touch it and you can never get lost."

Gabrielle touched it. "Thank you."

"It will cancel fear and become a conduit of our love for you. Like a beacon."

Gabrielle touched it again. Samantha kissed her on the forehead then went into the bathroom.

The backpack went on the floor of her closet. She didn't want to take it. She had to pack but had no other luggage. She didn't care. This was too much fun.

"I can't wait," she said as Catherine giggled again.

"That's the trunk?"

"I usually just put tools and spare parts up here." Gabrielle pulled the hood down. The red sheet metal flexed from side to side and the pushed the pin into the latch.

"My car has a real trunk. Doesn't gas slosh over everything?"

"No," Gabrielle laughed. "All our stuff will fit behind the seat."

"That little space?"

"I want to take my car. I want to drive. If I'm just a passenger my attention is divided. I want to remember everything. You've driven up north lots of times. I've never done this before." Well, almost, she thought.

They all had a light breakfast of toast and jam and coffee.

"Having to pee along the side of the road is one thing," Catherine said. "Taking a shit is a whole other level of exposure."

"Shit," Samantha said seriously.

"Shit. It's real," Catherine said.

"Real shit."

Gabrielle laughed so hard she spit her coffee all over the carpeting.

They all brought their things out to the VW. Catherine had her wicker picnic basket, Samantha a beautiful calf skin duffel bag, Audra her backpack with its wide, padded shoulder straps. Gabrielle tucked a clean blue t-shirt, socks, panties (silk), all folded, and a small white towel into a corner of the back-of-the-seat space.

"A Goddess travels light," Audra said.

Gabrielle went to the back of the car and opened the engine cover. She checked the dipstick. Oil level was good and still fairly clear. She thought she could hold off changing it until the quarter break. And the gas tank was full. She closed the cover and turned the latch. She tried to wipe the rust from the chrome bumper but the stuff seemed permanent.

The tires were good and the clutch only had five thousand miles on it. Replacing the clutch was the biggest job she had ever attempted on her car and it had almost been too much. Unbolting the engine from the transaxle had been really hard. She had done it all by herself over a summer weekend and it had taken two weeks to get the grease out of her fingernails. But it had been necessary and she had not flinched.

Catherine was grinning at her. "Look at the sexy car mechanic."

She smiled back. "Who wants to sit where?"

"Shotgun!" Audra said.

"I'm shotgun. I'm always shotgun," Catherine said.

Samantha raised her hand. "It kind of hurts my knees to sit in the back."

"Then you're shotgun," Catherine said. "Whenever you're in this car you're automatically shotgun."

"Oceanside!" Audra called.

Catherine looked sideways at her. "Really."

"Take turns." Gabrielle opened her door.

"And guess who's turn it is."

"Just get in."

Catherine looked surprised when Audra went around the car and got in the back seat on the passenger side. Catherine got in beside her and unzipped her windbreaker.

"Thought you wanted ocean side."

"On the way back this will be ocean side." Audra began to roll up the sleeves of her new flannel shirt.

Samantha sat on the passenger seat, tucked her knees together, and pulled her legs inside. She was wearing white sneakers.

"Tight fit," Catherine said.

"Yep. That's why I wore this." She tugged down her gray skirt over her thighs.

More silk, Gabrielle thought as slid into the driver's seat. Her jeans were still comfortable even though they fit a bit tighter than they did a couple weeks before. She closed her door. Samantha rolled her window down an inch and pulled her door shut. Gabrielle noted this with approval. She turned the key. The engine fired up instantly.

As her left foot moved on the clutch, the front door of the house opened. Rushel appeared and waved and ran off the porch. Samantha rolled down her window.

"I changed my mind. I want to go."

Samantha popped her door open and got out. Audra pushed the seat forward and got out also.

"I thought I had to work today but I have the day off. Gislaine has to go in at ten to open."

"I thought you both had weekends off," Audra said.

"Gislaine decided she wanted the money. You know Mick?"

"The tattoo guy."

"His latest tattoo made him sick and he's out for a week. She's filling in for him."

"All right. Don't you have any stuff?"

"No, I'm fine." Rushel ducked down and got in the back seat.

Audra looked at Samantha. They both shrugged. Audra squeezed in and pulled the seat back. Samantha folded herself into the front.

"How will Gislaine get to the store?"

"Oh she still has your keys."

Gabrielle looked at all her friends with a growing sense of excitement and started down the driveway. She glanced back at the house.

"Gislaine didn't come out."

"She's doing a lot of extra writing. Plus she has to get going in half an hour.

Gabrielle looked at her watch as they reached the gate. *8:35.* She got out. "It's later than I thought."

"The Goddess said, ominously," Audra said.

Gabrielle opened the gate, got back in and moved the car past it.

Rushel said, "Gislaine will close it."

Samantha nodded.

"She'd never leave it open."

Gabrielle closed her door. "Okay."

"So it's all right," Rushel said. "Off we go."

"Off we go," Catherine said.

Samantha laughed. "Off we go!"

Gabrielle felt Catherine's warm hand on her shoulder and she guided her car down the well-known bumpy, sandy path in the chaparral and powered through the sand trap. The paved road was shrouded in mist. She shifted into second.

She drove out into the young day with her friends. Under the long gesturing branches of the eucalyptus trees and over the gaps in the pavement, the car felt light and agile. The old road dipped and curved.

How many times have I gone this way, she thought.

She knew the answer and avoided contemplating it. She knew the count would end one day. It would be fixed forever in the past and she would pass this way no more. But not yet. Catherine rubbed her shoulders.

"I like sitting in the middle like this," Rushel said. "You get a nice perspective. I'm not blocking the mirror, am I?"

Rushel's smiling face filled the rear view mirror completely.

"No, of course not, you're fine," Gabrielle said.

Samantha adjusted her knees and Audra pressed her face against her window.

"Be on the lookout," Audra said.

"For what?" Catherine turned her head sharply.

"Anything."

"Anything?"

"Anything can happen."

"You're so young."

"Damn right. And I will always be this way."

Samantha laughed. "Me too."

"Yeah," Audra said.

Gabrielle guided them north. The highway was almost empty. Soft gray clouds clung to the tops of the green hills. Above, the sky was bright blue. They left the small port city, with its trio of smoke stacks and tangle of power lines looming over tightly packed houses, and passed through the beach town pressed down against the cold sand, dotted with foam. The long pier stood empty. Driving fast, Gabrielle glanced up. Hills backed by more hills with many paths.

The highway turned away from the winter sea. Deep green mountains now surrounded them, rocky and steep. There were broad pastures with oak trees and cattle.

"This is the season of Demeter, goddess of the harvest," Rushel said. "This is the time when she returns to the land of the living after searching the underworld for her daughter, Persephone, who was kidnapped by

Hades. He saw her picking flowers one day and decided to make her his wife. When Demeter goes back down to search for her again, as she does every year, all life departs with her and the world becomes dry and dusty and nothing will grow. In our case I think Persephone was probably just the old rancher's favorite horse."

"Did Persephone marry Hades?" Gabrielle saw the huge, spectacular house on the hilltop to their right. There were palm trees framing it. Incongruous, she thought.

"Yes, she did. She ate a pomegranate seed and had no choice but to stay. She became queen of the underworld."

"So no picking flowers," Catherine said. "Someone might be watching."

"Okay."

"We wouldn't want Holly kidnapping you and dragging you down to the underworld," Audra said.

Rushel laughed. "She is from somewhere close to hell, isn't she."

"Let's not talk about them," Catherine said. "Let's talk about where we're going."

"Yes. What's up there?" Gabrielle said.

The highway snaked down a boulder strewn beach. A wave broke over the pavement with a thump they could feel in their seats and the car splashed through the heavy spray. The churning sea was translucent green and gray.

"We go up along cliffs about a thousand feet high where the slightest mistake means plunging to a watery death," Audra said.

"Wow," Gabrielle said.

"Then there are huge sea lions that weigh as much as two cars and they'll come out of the ocean at thirty miles an hour and chase you and, man, you gotta be fast to get away."

"Incredible," Catherine said.

"But they can't turn very well. That's their weakness. They *skid*."

"I'll remember that."

"And there are seagulls and pelicans and great big herons. And there is a place where the forest comes right down to the ocean and the trees are all these weird shapes from the wind. It's really beautiful but also really scary. And there's this place, I forget the name, and there's this secret tunnel that leads to this hidden cove. Holly liked it. Oops, I talked about them."

"Is that where we're going?"

The highway narrowed and passed through a notch cut laterally through a series of ravines. On the other side, they were surrounded by flowers and dense chaparral behind old fence posts. A perching hawk calmly turned its head to watch them.

"Past there," Catherine said.

"We go over these bridges," Audra said, "that are about the most amazing things ever built by humanity."

"That's right. There's this place."

Gabrielle shifted as they skirted a rocky cove. The highway climbed steeply. There was a sharp curve coming up, she remembered.

"We should stay up there," Catherine said.

"By the sea."

"Is it really by the sea?"

"Oh my God." Rushel covered her eyes.

Gabrielle whipped the car around the curve. She caught a glimpse of furious surf far below. Wind buffeted the car and her hands slipped on the wheel.

"Yep. That looks like a thousand feet," Catherine said, eyes closed. "Straight down."

"I cannot look," Rushel said.

They went through a series of sharp switchbacks. Each time they rounded the curve overlooking the ocean, inches from the sheer drop off it seemed, they all went, "Whoa!" and "Oh my God!"

Behind them the sun broke through the low clouds and and the highway and hills were suddenly brightly lit against the dark northern sky. The light was so different, Gabrielle thought and almost missed the hidden turn off and the tall pointy thing. Catherine massaged her left arm from around the seat back. Then they were past it and Gabrielle tried to take everything in.

The world was moving shadows and sun, green brush, and wet crumbling rock. Golden poppies grew everywhere on the roadside. They dipped their heads in the cool wind. The only other vehicles she had seen were a couple of work trucks loaded with ladders and a big Continental she figured was full of real estate people. No sign of the pickup with the bad head gasket.

"Ow," Rushel said. "Move over a little, Squirt. My ass is getting numb."

"I'm not a squirt."

Of course not," Catherine said.

"I'm never a squirt."

"Fine. Move over, Pocket Mouse."

"That's better."

"Really? Good."

"Pocket Mouse. That's my secret name, isn't it?"

They all shook their heads.

"It's not?"

"Not even close," Samantha said.

"I'll figure it out one day."

"On that day, the world will end," Catherine said.

"Oh, right, that's true. Never mind then."

Past a wide beach, Gabrielle saw the perfect spot to stop and guided the car into a circular turn out bordered by granite boulders. There was a drinking fountain set into an old rock wall, a stainless steel bowl.

"Potty break," Gabrielle said.

There were worn stone steps leading up and behind a huge tree.

"Ah, good." Samantha popped her door open and unfolded her legs. They all got out and her and Catherine sat on the rock wall.

Audra got a drink from the fountain. "This place is cool. Bet it was built in the thirties."

"We're about the only people for miles," Catherine said.

A Highway Patrol car rounded the curve from the north and passed them. Gabrielle could hear the officer take his foot off the gas. He gave them a long look as he went by. Catherine smiled and waved. They all saw the officer wave back.

"Friendly," Audra said. She zipped up her flannel coat.

"He was just checking to see if we were broken down," Samantha said.

"Yep," Rushel said. "A car full of girls. That spells trouble."

"We do look like a bunch of troublemakers," Catherine said. "That sweatshirt with the hood makes the Goddess look like a juvenile delinquent."

"Juvvies usually don't wear glasses," Audra said.

"A smart juvvie might."

Gabrielle went to the stone steps. "If nobody else has to go then I will."

"Aren't you worried about snakes back there?" Rushel said.

"Poison oak," Catherine said. "All up in Yolanda."

"Ohh, Yolanda would be displeased," Audra said.

"Thanks. Now I won't be able to go."

The steps led to a dark notch between two huge boulders and then to a nearly lightless depression in the dirt behind the tree. The heavy branches shrouded the spot. At least it doesn't smell too bad, Gabrielle thought. Smells like mud.

There were several wads of toilet paper on the edge of the depression. They looked like they'd been there for months. Gabrielle turned towards the tree and unzipped her jeans. She pushed them down to her knees and that's when she saw it. There was a piece of notebook paper stuck to the tree bark with a red push pin. She bent over at the waist, not wanting to touch anything. The paper was covered with blocky writing. She felt her heart begin to pound . It quickly went back to normal. I'm getting better at this, she thought. She lifted up her glasses to read in the low light.

Good Morning Goddess! We hope your having a nice trip. Too bad the beautiful scenery is being ruined by such lousy company. We sympathize but we tried to warn you about them. Perhaps your more willing to listen now. Don't worry we are keeping a close watch on you.

We'll be in touch, Goddess.

Patricia and Holly

Gabrielle immediately had two thoughts. Audra's plan was working.

And two, there had to be a second microphone. There could be many microphones. Damn it, she thought, I should've traced the wires. It's in the library. Or outside. The porch. It can't be in my bedroom. God, if it's in there.

She yanked out the red pin and took the paper. She stuck the pin back into the tree. Maybe someone else could use it.

There could be microphones everywhere, she thought. Did I underestimate evil?

"I can't do that again," she said.

When she walked out from behind the tree and down the steps, she held out the paper.

"You were right. There were snakes."

Audra read it and snorted. "'Your'. Illiterate as always."

They drove north in relative silence and carefully checked the sparse traffic. They crossed bridges – wonderfully engineered, Gabrielle thought – over yawning canyons of primeval wilderness. The fog lifted. The highway went inland and they entered a small town.

There were rustic looking motels and art galleries tucked behind towering trees along narrow wandering roads. Beautiful, Gabrielle thought, but not inviting. They don't want just anyone to visit. There was a general store and a gas station, both done up in unpainted pine clapboards.

Gabrielle hurriedly used the rest room in the back of the gas station. The women's room had a creaky floor of wide boards and an old fashioned toilet with a pull chain.

Maybe this is real, she thought. Not fake rustic, real rustic.

But she was in no mood to trust appearances.

Rushel and Audra, both laughing and shaking their heads, caught her as she came out of the restroom into the hazy sunlight.

"You have to see this," Rushel said.

"You know, we should move up here," Audra said. "We'll be running the place in a month."

They went to the front of the little gas station. It had one pump island, where a woman wearing a powder blue pantsuit was filling up a blue Volvo. The station had no repair bays, just a small cashier's office, slightly expanded to include a convenience store. Gabrielle saw overpriced bags of chips and candy bars and a big rack of cigarettes. The cashier was sitting on a folding chair just outside the door in the shade of a tattered awning. She thought he looked to be around fifty. White flop-flops, Levi's with worn out knees, flannel shirt, sleeves rolled up. He was smoking a funny little cigarette. He held it pinched in his left hand. Gabrielle wrinkled her nose at the smell. What is it with guys in gas stations? She thought. The cashier rocked from side to side in the spindly chair.

"You know what that is?" Rushel whispered.

"No, but I've smelled it before."

"That's pot."

"What? That?"

"Yep."

"He's doing that in plain sight?"

"They probably don't care around here."

"But don't they put you in jail?"

Audra broke away and stepped towards him as if she were going into the store.

"Hey, Mike," she said.

He slowly turned his head in her direction. His face was deeply wrinkled and his long hair was tied into a neat pony tail. Someone had to have done that for him, Gabrielle thought. Like, his girlfriend.

The man smiled at Audra.

"Mike, it's me."

The man nodded.

"I can't believe this. Look at you. Gosh darn it, Mike, you said you were going to get yourself clean. What happened?"

He shrugged. "Don't remember saying that," he said with a drawl.

"But you don't even remember me."

"No, I remember you just fine."

"Sure you do."

"I *do*."

"Then what's my name?"

A car door slammed. The blue Volvo tore away from the pump and headed south.

"She didn't pay," Audra said. "She took off without paying." Her tone was incredulous.

"All right," the man said.

"What are you going to do? Is she a friend of yours or something? You gonna call the cops?"

"Nah."

"No? What? Which one?"

"Your name is Clarinda." He pointed at her. "Yes, ma'am. I remember you perfectly." He took a long drag from his joint.

Audra held up her hand. "Stop. I'm not Clarinda." She turned to Rushel. "Clarinda. Can you believe it?"

Rushel loosened her jacket and with both hands pulled her hair out. It flowed over her shoulders and down to her knees. The man froze and achieved immediate visual lock.

"Mike, we're through."

"*No*," he said emphatically.

"I can't take this anymore. It's just too much."

"Oh, don't say that."

Rushel unzipped her jacket and pulled it completely open.

"This body will never be yours again. Take a long last look."

"Well, all right."

"That's enough!" She crossed her arms. "Come on, Clarinda. We're wasting our time." She headed back to the car.

"Hang on, Lucille," Audra said. "I'll be right there."

In the back seat, Catherine was doubled over with her face in a towel, shaking with laughter.

Audra faced the man again.

"I'm going to give you one last chance, Mike. This is the very last time. Cut out the drugs and come clean or you will never see either of us again. You understand me?"

He nodded.

"You *understand* me?"

He nodded vigorously.

"I understand you."

"All right then. Do not disappoint me again."

She walked back to the car. Samantha was standing there with the door open.

The man cleared his throat. "My name's Stanley."

Audra stopped instantly and turned back.

"Not the Stanley thing again, Mike. I mean don't start that."

"No really."

"Don't. Just don't."

The man's shoulder's slumped and Gabrielle heard him say, "I guess Mike ain't so bad."

Audra jogged to the car and slipped into the back seat. When Samantha had gotten in and closed the door, Catherine said, "Clarinda, you were so nice to help that poor man."

Gabrielle started the engine to cover the sound of laughter. Stanley waved as they made a left onto the highway.

"Well hell," Audra said. "I could've shoplifted something to eat. He never would've noticed. Now I'm hungry. "

Still laughing, they headed north, leaving the forest behind. There were hills that sloped up to near vertical crested with oaks.

"That was funny at first and then it turned creepy," Rushel said.

"It turned creepy when you started to take your clothes off."

"I did that for comedic effect. It worked, too."

"That guy was just plain creepy," Catherine said. "So there was no avoiding it."

"He seemed really old," Gabrielle said.

"Forty, tops," Audra said.

"Really?"

"He's been sitting in the sun for years getting baked," Samantha said and Rushel laughed until she started coughing.

As happy as she had ever been, Gabrielle drove a bit slower between the deep blue crashing waves and the green fields lined with flowers with the low sun over her shoulder.

They crossed a final bridge, the biggest and most impressive of them all, and the landscape turned borderline sagebrush. There were large houses with gated driveways and shopping centers with undersized signs. Audra pointed out a small motel next to a convenience store.

"We should seriously consider that one. It looks really tacky," she said.

They stopped at a red light and cross traffic roared past them.

"They're all in a big hurry," Samantha said.

Gabrielle followed Catherine's directions and made a left turn, finally leaving the highway. The place had a familiar feel. Palm and eucalyptus trees mingled. The street was lined with small houses and every conceivable parking place had a vehicle in it. Mostly smaller imports, she noticed. She saw four Mercedes convertibles in a row.

Then through the knarled trees she saw the ocean and she turned onto a narrow street running along a wide sandy beach. Here there were many parking places, all angled diagonally. Just like downtown Covina, she thought, no problem. She pulled into one.

"How's this?"

"Perfect." Samantha opened her door.

"Welcome to heaven by the sea," Catherine said.

"Heaven?"

"In heaven there's always a place to park."

Gabrielle switched off the engine. The beach was an expanse of golden sand under a blue sky dotted with soft clouds. There were no other people visible. Catherine turned around in the seat and pulled out the picnic basket while Audra and Rushel untangled their legs and ran out onto the sand. Samantha got out and stretched, tipping her head from side to side, her hair blowing across her sunlit face.

The air was cool and scented with salt and flowers. Gardenias again. Gabrielle helped Catherine with the basket. The thing was heavy and she heard glass tinkle.

"To that table," Catherine said. She pointed at a concrete picnic table resting on the sand, slightly listing. Gabrielle carried the basket to it. She sat on the bench and took off her shoes. Sand was pouring through all the tears in the fabric. She tugged her socks off and stood up. The tops of her feet were cool and soles warm. She wiggled her toes. Samantha sat beside her.

"This is just a snack," Catherine said. She opened the basket and took out a paper plate wrapped in clear plastic film. "I mean part of the fun of going on a trip is finding new places to eat. There's a great sandwich shop right over that way, I think. It's been a while. We could go see if it's still there. And we keep a look out for a place to have dinner."

"And we'll stay in that motel?" Gabrielle said.

"Looked kind of small."

"Looked funky," Samantha said.

"Do we want funky?"

"Funky usually mean bugs." Catherine unwrapped the plate.

"Well, anything would be fine." Gabrielle took one of the hors d'oeuvres. It was a cracker topped with a slice of cheese and half an olive. "I never stayed in a motel before." Gabrielle wasn't sure she liked olives but its flavor seemed to go well with the cheese.

"Don't worry. You haven't exactly missed much," Samantha said. "Of course, I'm thinking of places in New Mexico and Texas. There're always kind of an adventure." She laughed.

"A terrific adventure," Catherine said. "To hell and back."

"Who knows what California motels are like."

"Doubt they're any better." Catherine pulled a bottle of white wine from the basket. "Hmm. Maybe later."

"Wine for lunch?" Gabrielle took another cracker cheese thing. She waved at Audra and Rushel standing at the water's edge. They both started in.

"Yeah." Catherine slipped the bottle back. "Getting plastered in a motel room is actually much more fun."

"It's what motels are actually for, I think," Samantha said.

"Also, lots of sex."

"Naturally."

Gabrielle felt herself blush as Audra and Rushel ran up.

"This beach is so *clean*," Rushel said.

"And it even smells good," Audra said. "I mean it smells like the ocean. No piles of seaweed or dead things. I love where we live but sometimes."

"Fecund," Catherine said.

"Yeah. Really fecund."

"Good word," Rushel said with her mouth full. "Fecund."

"Far out," Samantha said.

They discussed various f-words and washed the cracker olive things down with Perrier which came in tiny green bottles. Gabrielle had never seen such a thing before.

"Water in bottles?"

"It even comes in six-packs." Catherine held it up. "One left."

"It's really good."

"Much better than pop," Audra said.

"You mean soda?" Catherine said.

They discussed how soft drink nomenclature varied by geographical region. Gabrielle, Rushel, and Audra: pop. Catherine: soda. Samantha: coke.

"Everything's coke," Samantha said.

"What if it's Dr. Pepper?" Catherine said.

"Still coke, generally. Just slightly different."

"So, Dr. Pepper-flavored coke?"

"Yep."

"Coca-Cola has such a good thing going."

They all agreed with this assessment.

"Okay, I have to ask." Audra sipped her mineral water. "Who made the Goddess blush? You can't blame me this time."

"She was almost ultraviolet," Rushel said.

Gabrielle tried not to smile.

"I simply mentioned the traditional connection between motels and sex," Catherine said.

"Especially the showers," Samantha said.

Audra stood with her mouth open.

Rushel said, "Motel showers are great. At home it doesn't work that way."

"Not what it sounds like," Samantha said.

"Really?"

"Not that we're eavesdropping."

"Well I always end up with my face pressed against the tile and there I am looking at the grout and thinking, I need to clean that. And the hot water always runs out."

"Uh huh," Gabrielle said. She drank the rest of her water and almost dropped the bottle.

"It's distracting. In a motel you're not thinking about stuff like that. And you never run out of hot water."

Catherine said, "In France, every bathroom has its own water heater. It heats the water up instantly as you need it. There's no big tank. It's much more efficient."

"Ohh, we need to get that!" Rushel said.

"We do."

"I'll research it," Samantha said.

"That place on the highway, do you think it would be all right?" Catherine said to Audra.

"It looked cheap. The sign said eight ninety-five."

"I guess that's cheap."

"Even Motel Six is more than that now."

"They'll have to change their name," Rushel said. "Okay now I'm getting hungry." She set down her Perrier and looked around the periphery of the beach. "Not the greatest area for restaurants. Just big houses with fancy landscaping."

"Yeah, they're okay," Catherine said.

"I like our house," Gabrielle said. "I like the way sand comes right up to the door. And the flowers. And the brush rabbits and way the snowy plovers sit on the patio wall." She slipped her empty bottle back into the six-pack. "And no one can see us. That might be the best part. Along with the food."

"Thank you," Catherine raised her Perrier.

"I'm starving. Let's go find that sandwich place."

"Goddess," they all said.

Everyone put their shoes back on. The picnic basket was locked back up and they set off down the empty beach sidewalk. South, per Catherine's directions.

"I might be wrong," she said.

"That's all right."

"It might be the other way."

"Let's look."

"Might be closed until summer."

"We'll find something."

They walked as a group close together with Samantha and Rushel first, behind them Gabrielle, and behind her, Catherine and Audra. Gabrielle felt a bit uncomfortable but she didn't say anything. She saw they took this formation automatically. And she did feel safe. Incredibly safe, she admitted to herself.

They walked beneath rows of palm trees and near the end of the curving beach sidewalk they saw it. On a side street was s small restaurant built into an old house. There were planters made of sawed off wine barrels overflowing with daisies. There was a hand painted sign above the covered front porch. *Melinda's*. A small card in the window said *open*.

"Yeah," Catherine said. "And a new owner. Cool."

"That looks good," Rushel said.

Samantha nodded. "Hm."

"What?"

"Just hm."

Gabrielle looked closely at the repurposed house to try to see what Samantha was picking up on. Single story Craftsman style like many houses in her old neighborhood. Blue siding, white trim. Two old wooden rocking chairs on the porch. There were antique items hung on the porch posts and framing. Gewgaws was the word, she thought. A rusty kerosene lantern, an iron fireplace grate, a big metal spoon. Kitchen gear from the previous century, she thought. As they climbed the porch steps, she studied the rocking chair closest to her. The wooden back had an elaborate carving of flowers and in the center, in a small flat space, someone had recently scratched a symbol, two deep lines, bright against the darkened old wood. It looked like a fish lying on its side.

The bell tied to the doorknob tinkled when Rushel turned it and they all filed into the front room. Gabrielle smelled baking bread. There was a guy with long hair and a scraggly beard standing behind a long glass cabinet. There were round pedestal tables with spindly legged chairs.

Two women sat at the table closet to the front window. Gabrielle thought, middle-aged. Well, older than me. They both had very short hair,

one dark the other bleached white. The dark one looked up and raised
her eyebrows when Rushel took off her jacket and let her hair out. Audra
stepped up and blocked her view. Gabrielle saw Rushel smile, almost a
secret smile.

"Hey, good morning," the guy said. Gabrielle picked up the now familiar
burnt cloth smell. "This is our menu." He gave Catherine a photocopied
sheet from a stack next to an adding machine. Samantha looked over her
shoulder to read.

"We don't have our board yet."

"Because you haven't done it like you were supposed to!" a woman
yelled from the kitchen.

The guy shrugged. "My sister."

Catherine grinned but Gabrielle saw Samantha, brows furrowed, did not
look happy. It was a look that said, *anticipation of annoyance.*

"Our special today is thin sliced, slow roasted turkey breast on wheat
with all the fixin's you want. Lettuce, red onion, bean sprouts." He gestured
at a row of stainless bins behind the glass. "Our bacon, lettuce, tomato is
also good today."

"Ah," Audra said then looked at Rushel. Rushel and Catherine were
looking at Samantha. Catherine shook her head almost imperceptibly.

Samantha looked at the guy.

"Do you have any vegetarian selections?"

His eyes flickered around her face.

"Um, vegetarian?"

Samantha stared at him and nodded. Gabrielle felt Catherine grip her
arm.

"Well, I suppose we could make you a grilled cheese. How about that?"

"Oh. Anything else?"

"That's really it."

Through the open kitchen door they heard a plate slam onto a steel
counter.

"Kyle!"

Kyle rolled his eyes.

"We're still working on vegetarian."

"Oh," Samantha said.

"It's kind of tricky."

"It's easy," Catherine said. "Focaccia maybe, toasted with garlic infused
olive oil. Then."

Kyle frowned.

"Slices of tomato and maybe grilled eggplant or butternut squash.
Sprinkled with bean sprouts and Feta cheese. That's a great sandwich. Omit
the cheese and it's officially vegan."

"Vegan?" Kyle looked annoyed. "You know."

"Or just have it open-faced and add slices of Mozzarella and stick it under the broiler for a minute. Like a mini pizza!"

"Now I'm really hungry," Audra said.

"Yeah, me too," Samantha said.

"You know." Kyle took a step back from the counter. "I'm just saying, in the beginning we were given dominion over the Earth and all the creatures in it. All the birds and fish..."

"Kyle!" A woman came through the kitchen door. She had golden blonde hair in a tight net. Blue eyes. Gabrielle heard Rushel inhale sharply.

"It's nature's way," Kyle said.

"Your sandwich idea sounds pretty good," the woman said quickly over Kyle's shoulder. "I don't have butternut squash but there's something I just found out about."

"Or Portobello mushrooms, grilled of course," Catherine said.

"Yes! I might be able to get that."

"Hard to find sometimes."

"Yes. But I do have this new stuff, it's definitely different. You marinate it and then grill it. It's called tofu."

"I love tofu," Samantha said.

"I love it too," Gabrielle said softly.

"You could say we're tofu oriented," Audra said.

"We would all like that," Catherine said. "Tofu however you want to do it."

"Great! It'll be a few minutes. This will be interesting."

Rushel said to Gabrielle, "Tofu is never not interesting."

"Never."

Melinda came back out and whispered in Kyle's ear. He made notes on an order pad.

"Fine," he said. "Tofu special. Would you like chips? Anything to drink?"

"Three bags of chips and five ice teas."

Kyle tapped his adding machine.

"Eleven ninety-one with tax."

Samantha gave him a twenty. Gabrielle could smell the tofu cooking, smelling almost like hamburgers.

As Kyle handed Samantha her change he said, "You're Native American?"

"No. Apache," she said without looking up.

Gabrielle saw Kyle's expression go from startled to confused and then determined.

"Wouldn't you agree," he said, "that eating meat is nature's way?"

Samantha looked at him without blinking. "And let them have dominion over the fish of the sea and over the birds of the heavens and over the livestock and over the Earth and over every creeping thing that creeps on the Earth. Right?" she said.

Gabrielle heard Audra whisper, "*Yeah.*"

Kyle nodded.

"It's not really a religious thing with me, it's a diet I follow, but since you brought it up."

Gabrielle winced as Catherine's grip on her arm became painful.

"We have dominion over the Earth and all living things on the Earth, correct?"

Kyle recovered. "Yes, that's right."

Samantha leaned forward.

"Did you ever stop to think it might be a test?"

"A test."

"Kyle, from now on I want you to stick with the New Testament, okay? Just that." Samantha spoke softly. "Nature is suffering. Nature is innocent creatures dying in pain and fear. That's nature's way. Nature is *fallen*. In the kingdom of God this will no longer be the case. The lion shall lie down with the lamb. You've heard of that, right? I think you should work towards that. Reject your animal nature, Kyle. Work towards recovering the grace of God."

She turned away curtly.

They all stood silently at the counter and watched Kyle who pointedly looked out the front windows. When Melinda brought out the sandwiches wrapped in white paper on a bamboo tray she nervously looked at them, then at Kyle, then rolled her eyes and went back into the kitchen.

Catherine picked up the tray.

"Shall we luncheon on the semi-enclosed deck?"

"Yes, let's." Rushel picked up the tray with the iced tea and chips. "The view is lovely."

"It's quite charming."

Audra, watching the two staring women, said loudly, "I *can't* believe Daddy's going to give you the Porsche. It's obviously *my* car."

"Probably, dear sister, because you no longer have a driver's license," Rushel said without hesitation.

"Oh, that."

"Well, you can't just run over kindergartners."

"They were in my way."

Gabrielle opened the door for them. The two women continued to stare, wide-eyed.

"You still get the helicopter, after all," Rushel said.

"I suppose. But we can't fly it until Gunther gets his immigration problems sorted out. If he ever does."

"He's still in detention?"

"No, they deported him."

"Poor guy."

"Lithuania."

"Right. Where is that?"

"Beats me. I'm going to miss him."

"*Him?*"

"Well, you know. Just that one part."

"Honestly, my dear sister, you worry me sometimes."

Catherine and Rushel set the trays on one of the square tables and Audra pushed a second table next to it. They all unfolded their chairs and sat. Gabrielle was between Audra and Samantha. She heard Audra's stomach rumble. A seagull called overhead.

Rushel said, "Hang on, Pocket Mouse," and they all took hands. Gabrielle closed her eyes.

"I would address the creator of all things," Rushel said. "The transcendent intelligence at the heart of our existence. Thank you for the gift of our loving family and the wonderful meal before us. And thank you for your protection and guidance no matter what dark and lonely street we find ourselves on. So shall it be."

They all said, "So shall it be." Gabrielle opened her eyes. Rushel was smiling at her. Faces were in the window were gaping at them.

Catherine stood up in a scuffle of stiff yellow nylon and said, "Transcendent. I like that word. Who wants chips?"

They poured all the potato chips onto a paper plate and unwrapped their sandwiches.

"This is so good," Catherine said, chewing. "She really knows how to do the onion."

"Delicious," Samantha said.

Gabrielle thought her tofu sandwich tasted almost exactly like a hamburger although the texture was different. She took a gulp of the sweet iced tea. "It's all great."

A full minute passed as they ate in silence.

"We were all hungrier than we thought," Catherine said. "And I'm going to steal this sandwich idea. The tea's good, too."

Rushel was already half finished. She picked up a potato chip.

"Speaking of delicious, my dear make-believe sister, why don't you go see if Melinda is doing anything tonight?"

"Hm." Audra nodded. "Well, I mean yeah, but I would have to interact with the creep who creepeth upon the Earth."

"Not necessarily."

Audra ate one of the chips. "Hm."

Rushel pushed back her chair.

"I have to go to the little girl's room. Come on, we will discuss this further."

Audra shrugged and got up. As they opened the door, Rushel said loudly, "Just sell the helicopter."

"It would break Aunt's heart. I'm supposed to be a pilot and then the first female astronaut, remember?"

"Oh. Aunt."

"Right."

"Aunt lives in a fantasy world, my dear sister."

Gabrielle watched them through the window as they walked past the two women. The white-haired one looked up as Rushel passed. She's staring at her ass, Gabrielle thought, Audra couldn't block the view this time. And the way she's looking I feel like punching her.

Gabrielle started as Samantha placed her hands over her's and squeezed, firm and gentle. Gabrielle found her expression hard to read, her forehead wrinkled, her dark eyes concerned, no, amused. Over Samantha's shoulder she saw the restroom door open and Audra and Rushel emerge.

Way too fast, she thought, and Audra looked angry.

Catherine sighed. "Now what."

Rushel pushed open the front door and Audra said, "Goddess, you better see this."

Gabrielle felt the familiar thudding of her heart. She swallowed and stood.

"All right."

Inside, she walked past the two women. They both smirked at her. Melinda and her brother were in the kitchen arguing loudly about the bakery bill. The restroom had a narrow door. It's an old closet, she thought.

She turned sideways and slipped through. The tiny bulb over the sink was bluish. She looked at the floor and the toilet. All normal and fairly clean. She adjusted her glasses and looked back at the sink. There was something on the mirror. Smudges across the top.

No, she thought, that's writing.

There were words scratched into the glass. The letters were distorted. The writer had to bear down hard, Gabrielle thought. A carbide awl or a diamond tipped glass cutter.

Holly Loves Audra! Holly is going to Love Gabrielle! Her name trailed off to the chrome frame.

Gabrielle backed out of the tiny restroom. She whispered to Samantha, "How much money do you have?"

Samantha shrugged. "I hardly ever count it."

Gabrielle walked up the Kyle who was tapping his adding machine.

"Can I talk to Melinda?"

"I don't know, can you?" He did not look up.

Without hesitation, Gabrielle walked around the end of the counter and brushed by Kyle, deliberately bumping him with her elbow, and stepped through the kitchen door. The kitchen was small, maybe the original of the old house, with just a few additions. A rack of pots and skillets on hangers. A stainless steel sink. The back door was propped open and cars on the next street over roared past in bright sunlight. Melinda, her back to her, was slicing tomatoes.

Gabrielle felt a touch on her arm. Audra was beside her. Samantha stood in the kitchen door blocking Kyle's view.

"Hi," Gabrielle said.

Melinda turned and smiled. She wiped her forehead with the back of her hand. Her eyes went to Audra and Samantha.

"We didn't mean to barge in but it's your restroom."

Melinda's eyes widened. "The bathroom?"

"Well, the mirror."

"Oh, that." She looked at them all, uncertain.

"We know who did it."

"It's not a big deal. I thought it was funny. I mean, better than the usual graffiti, right? I mean, those names. Audra. Who names their kid Audra?"

"I'm Audra," Audra said with a sigh.

"Oh. Oh wow. Look."

"We'd like to pay for the mirror."

"Look, I'm sorry. Audra is a beautiful name."

"It's all right."

"Like I said, we know who did it and you'll never get any money out of them."

Audra cleared her throat and smiled.

"We'd still like to pay you."

"Actually we got that for free. Kyle found it lying around somewhere. Came out of the trash, really."

"How much to replace it?"

Melinda shrugged. "Twenty-five bucks?"

"Hm. That sounds low," Audra said.

Samantha stepped into the kitchen and dug into the pocket of her jeans. "It's a commercial item, They always overcharge."

"Yeah, I know."

"Here's a hundred." Samantha held out twenties, tightly folded.

"That's too much."

"It's gonna be more than you think," Audra said.

"Oh, no..."

"How about eighty?" Samantha peeled off a twenty.

Melinda's eyes went went from Samantha's hand to her face. She seemed shy, Gabrielle thought.

"Okay, sure. Thank you."

Blue eyes flashing, she took the money and tucked it into her back pocket without looking at it.

"Good," Gabrielle said.

"We're from down south. And we have to go back in the morning." Audra stepped forward, smiling. "We were wondering if you could recommend a restaurant for dinner. And, you know, if you weren't busy this evening you could come with us. I could tell you all about Holly."

"Holly. Oh my God."

"It's fairly insane."

"I can imagine. Gosh." Melinda wiped her hands on her polka-dot apron. "First of all, I've always liked, well, were you thinking a really nice restaurant?"

"Not super nice," Samantha said.

"Just nice nice." Catherine was standing at the open back door. Rushel was behind her. "We don't want a dress code."

"Oh, God no. Italian? Mexican? Indian?"

"Indian?" Samantha cocked her head.

"Punjabi, I think."

"Ah."

"Then there's a great Japanese place right across from the Thai place. Then there's a Vietnamese place right across from the French place. Everyone thought that was funny when they opened."

"French?" Catherine came in the door.

"They're kind of going downhill.

"But it's French?"

"Yeah, but the last time I was there they weren't exactly casual. *Henri's.*"

"Ooh."

"It's over on Tidewater where it crosses Driftwood."

Gabrielle immediately visualized the spot. Yield sign. Two palm trees against the sky. Buildings with large windows set back from the street and obscured by immaculately trimmed bushes fulsome with flowers.

"I know where that is," she said.

"Really?" Catherine said. "Wait. What am I saying."

Samantha laughed.

"I'm curious about *Henri's,*" Melinda said. "Haven't been there in like a year."

"Great! You should definitely come with us," Audra said. "We really could use a guide in this town.

"I'd love to but it's just not a good time." Melinda face dropped. "It's my boyfriend." She shook her head. "Like I said, it's stupid."

Audra and Samantha nodded.

"Bring him along," Catherine said. "It would be educational."

Melinda, Gabrielle saw, seemed to become angry. "He never wants to do anything. I go home, I make him dinner. That's it."

Gabrielle saw Audra struggle to remain silent.

Catherine said, "Well, we should find a phone and call *Henri's* for a reservation."

"They don't take reservations," Melinda said. "You just show up and try to get in."

"Ah, yes. One of those."

"Yeah, but they're hurting for business."

"Huh."

438

"Otherwise, back on the highway there's this great burger place."

"I might have seen it."

"They're good. Burgers, fries, and shakes. It's pretty tricky."

"Tricky?"

"Getting the fries right."

"It's an art." Catherine nodded.

"It really is."

"Order!" Kyle's voice blurted into the kitchen.

Gabrielle, still watching Audra, said, "Well, Melinda, we're sorry you can't come."

"Yeah, me too. If you ever come back up."

"Definitely," Audra said. "We're just going to walk around town and then get a room somewhere. We were thinking about that place by the liquor store. Sun something."

"Sunrise Inn. Yeah."

"Think it's okay?"

"It's cheap."

"You've stayed there?"

"Once. While back."

Gabrielle was surprised to see Melinda blush slightly.

"It was fine. No bugs."

Audra shrugged.

"We'll try them first, then."

She went through the street side door without looking back. Gabrielle thanked Melinda and then she and Samantha followed. The sun was out and they both squinted. Melinda called after them.

"Thanks again. For the mirror."

"Sure," Samantha said.

"So this Holly person. Should I look out for her?"

They all stopped. Gabrielle said, "I wouldn't worry about her at this point."

"All right. Great. Still, she must be something."

"Eh." Audra returned to the door. "I'll be back and tell you all about her."

Gabrielle pulled back a few steps. Catherine and Samantha took position behind her. Rushel stood, hands on hips, directly behind Audra.

"Good. I'm very curious now." Melinda took an order pad from her apron and quickly wrote something with a pen. She tore off the sheet and handed it to Audra. "My home phone. When you get back up."

"Okay, sure."

"Just call me."

"I will."

They all heard Kyle's voice again.

"I gotta go." Melinda waved and went back in.

Rushel put her arm around Audra's shoulders and turned her away. They all walked up the sidewalk in a tight group.

"You clicked," Rushel said into the bright, windy air.

"I guess so."

"You did. There was clickage."

"There's clicking and then there's clicking."

Gabrielle felt Catherine squeeze her arm.

"You gonna call her?"

"We'll see."

"We do have a phone now," Samantha said.

"Outgoing calls?" Rushel said. "Right?"

Gabrielle nodded.

"And someone else is paying for it," Catherine said.

"That's right." Rushel rubbed Audra's shoulders. "Fifty-nine hour rule."

Audra held her thumb up. "Fifty-nine."

"Okay," Gabrielle said.

"Audra will call Melinda no later than fifty-nine hours from now," Rushel said. "Tuesday evening, I think."

"Tuesday," Audra said.

"We will prepare the wine cellar," Catherine said.

"Why, thank you."

The sidewalk was weathered and uneven and perfectly clean. Gabrielle looked down at Catherine's hand still on her arm as they walked.

"It's okay here," Catherine said softly. "So what do you think?"

"It's all so new."

"After you graduate you could move up here. I'm sure you could get a job in your field."

"It might be possible."

"Uh huh. You could start work at Super Advanced Stuff Incorporated and get into management and when you get home every day dinner would waiting for you."

"Really?"

"Along with other things."

"Okay."

"Special things. How does that sound?"

"It sounds fine." Gabrielle thought it sounded wonderful.

"Good."

"Let's go in here!" Audra said.

They all went down steps into a small store. Gabrielle could not tell what kind of store it was. Set back and slightly below sidewalk level, the windows were obscured by masses of yellow and purple flowers. She looked from side to side as she went thought the door, which all the other stores and restaurants, had the same type of multi-pane windows in the top half. She had no idea of the proper name of such a window but she knew it was associated with a certain old fashioned style, probably from England, and was a signal to observers. It was supposed the send a message. She was pretty sure the message was: *You can't afford to buy anything in here.*

She stopped next to Catherine, who also seemed puzzled. Samantha, Audra, and Rushel dashed to the back of the place. There were tall cabinets made of dark wood. The lights were low. The air was scented with brewing coffee and cinnamon and the same kind of soap they used on the floor in the chemistry department stock room. There was a wooden counter. No cash register visible, no employees. No desks with ringing phones, so probably not a real estate office. No racks of skimpy, expensive clothes. Just big cabinets topped with flowers in vases and in every corner a plant in a clay pot hanging in an elaborate woven holder, that rough rope stuff. A flower shop, she thought, no wait, one of those places that sells stuff to freshmen for their dorm rooms. No, those cabinets, they had shelves.

Catherine spoke softly. "Furniture store?"

"Maybe."

"Pretty blamed expensive looking."

Gabrielle took a step. "Ah, I see. Look."

"Oh. Books." Catherine put her hands on her hips. "Like it would kill them to put up a sign."

Audra came around a cabinet carrying a magazine. "There you two are." *Road and Track.* "What are you doing?"

"We couldn't tell what kind of store this was."

"I know."

"Or even if it was a store."

"Yeah. Neither could I."

"They don't have a sign."

"I know. I just barged in. I like to do that sometimes."

"I usually don't," Catherine said.

"Don't you get in trouble?"

"Oh, gosh, all the time. I did it once in Hollywood. There was a door in a big blank wall. No markings of any kind. But people were going in and out."

"People?"

"Mostly men but a few women. Grownups. And nicely dressed, like business people."

"Or lawyers," Catherine said.

"Yep. So I just went up and turned the doorknob and walked in like I owned the place. Know what it was? A porn shop. Books and magazines and all sorts of rubber things. It all smelled like plastic."

"Ew."

"The funny part was, it was really brightly lit. Like floodlights all over, you know, so no shadows. Because they don't want."

"Right," Catherine said. "The weirdos would never leave."

"And this guy comes out with a broom and like sweeps at my feet."

"Oh my God."

"'You cannot be in here! You must get out! You are not old enough!'" Audra made a sweeping motion. "Which was true. And I'm still not old enough. I'm just so very very young."

"I've never seen that stuff," Gabrielle said.

"Huh. Never?" Catherine said. "Porn's not big in Covina?"

"No. We have a lot of churches. Don't know about West Covina."

Catherine began to laugh. "There's a *West* Covina?" She doubled over, laughing. "West! Oh my God!" She had to turn away.

"It's actually more to the south," Gabrielle said.

"South Covina!" Catherine covered her mouth and bumped into the counter. "Where's the garlic, y'all?"

With Catherine still laughing, Audra led them to the back of the store. Magazines covered an entire wall. There were benches where people were reading. An elderly lady with white hair wearing a pink jogging suit was reading *Home Firearms*. Next to her a women in an expensive looking jacket was looking at *Architectural Digest*.

Samantha had *Newsweek* under her arm and was scanning *Life*. Rushel had *Vogue* and something else underneath. It seemed to Gabrielle that Rushel was hiding whatever it was. She noticed Audra had picked up a magazine she thought had something to do with the music industry. *Punk Now!* The woman on the cover had a very painful-looking hairstyle, all brushed over to one side.

Gabrielle picked up *Modern Electronics* then put it back and got *Scientific American*. She turned to her favorite part, *The Amateur Scientist*. It was a cool telescope driver project that used a cheap calculator as a controller. She sat beside Catherine, *Bon Appétit* on her lap, open to a pastry recipe, and they all read in silence.

The elderly pink jogger made a snorting sound and dropped her magazine on the floor. She stood and said, "They don't know the difference between Kimber and Glock! Bah!" She gave the magazine a kick and it slid across the hardwood floor and bumped into Samantha's foot.

"Oh." Samantha picked it up. There was a shiny handgun on the cover. "Neat."

"Sorry," the woman said.

"Oh, don't worry. So this isn't very good, huh?"

"They don't know shit about nine millimeters."

"In that case."

Samantha slipped it back into the rack, covering up an issue of *Throbbing*, a black and white magazine printed on newsprint. The cover showed a frowning bikini-clad girl on a large motorcycle. Final Issue! it said across the top. Next to it were similar publications. *Streaker* and *Burn!*

The lady in pink looked at Samantha with interest. "You own guns?"

"These days I prefer more silent means." Samantha said and grinned.

"Uh." She snorted again and put away her glasses. "Well good luck." She adjusted her headband as she left the store.

"I wasn't too sure," Samantha said, "but I kind of like it here."

"So do I," Rushel said.

"We could fit in," Catherine said.

"We need to." Samantha put *Life* back.

"Look around more," Catherine said.

"All right," Gabrielle said. "I like it here, too. Seems a bit expensive."

"So all we need is money," Audra said.

"Ahem," Rushel said.

Gabrielle felt herself blush. "I can't believe I forgot."

"Me, too," Samantha said. "Funny."

"You never said where you hid it."

"Somewhere very safe," Catherine said.

"Well, good," Samantha said.

"Okay." Gabrielle put *Scientific American* back on the rack. "Let's get out of here."

Rushel held up her two magazines. "Can I get these?"

"Of course."

They all went to the plain front counter. Audra laughed. There was a handwritten notice taped to the Formica. *We Eschew Obviousness.*

Rushel giggled. "Sums up this town."

"Cutesy pseudointellectual flapdoodle," Audra said.

"Do they eschew getting paid?" Catherine said.

There was rustle from the tiny back room and a young woman came out. She had blonde hair done in a big curl over her forehead and was wearing a bright white turtleneck sweater. Her nametag said *Darlene!* She gave them a big smile.

"Hi! Are you ready?"

Rushel shyly put her magazines down. "Yes. I just didn't want to seem obvious."

Darlene tsk'd. "Don't worry. You can't."

"Ah."

"This is the Non-Obvious Bookstore."

"We were wondering what it was," Catherine said.

"Because it really isn't clear," Audra said.

"At the Non-Obvious Bookstore, nothing is taken for granted." Darlene used a pocket calculator and wrote on a pad. "We eschew, in addition to obviousness, complacency, preconceptions, arrogance, and all known assumptions. Our goal is the individual mind unbound."

"That's a tall order," Audra said.

Darlene nodded seriously. The curl on her forehead bounced. "Yes it is. Five twenty-nine." She tore off the slip.

Rushel gave her a ten. Darlene gave her change from a hidden drawer.

"I hope you enjoy the rest of your day."

"Thank you, Darlene."

"Thank *you.*"

When they were all back on the sun drenched sidewalk, Rushel said, "That was kind of cool." The breeze sent her hair flying.

Audra scoffed. "Nope."

"You never know."

"Girly girl."

"She seemed nice," Samantha said.

"Yes," Audra said. "That's true."

"That sweater," Rushel said.

"Liked the sweater."

"I noticed you liked the sweater."

"It was a nice sweater."

They made their way back to the car and Gabrielle drove through the town to the highway. They left the city limits and came to the motel and liquor store, two old single story stucco buildings crouched under drooping power lines, hemmed in by weeds and dead brush.

"It's cheap," Audra said from the back seat.

"Well." Gabrielle adjusted her glasses.

"Eh," Rushel said.

"Think of it as an adventure," Samantha said and that decided it.

Gabrielle steered off the highway into the spot closest to the half-open office door. They all got out into the noisy parking lot.

"We're a bit early for check in," Samantha said.

"Can't hurt to ask." Audra went into the office.

Gabrielle got out. The air was gritty and tasted metallic. There were no palm trees on this side of the highway. She got to the office door and saw Audra speaking to a man behind a counter. He looked a lot like Stanley.

Well, she thought, kind of the same class as Stanley, so *class:Stanley*, as they would put it in the programming course she had taken. Software made Gabrielle impatient. She didn't like being required to memorize arbitrary rules someone made up. She had not enjoyed that class. She shrugged. At least I got an A in the silly thing, she thought. But I don't like *class*. The idea of it. No, I will eschew *class*.

The liquor store next to the motel looked like a bunker. The walls were concrete blocks and the one window had steel bars welded over it. The door was riveted steel plates. A small sign hung from the doorknob. *Come In!* The bare wall beside the door had an array of advertising banners for beer and cigarettes. At eye level a stenciled sign said Tatoos and Piercings. An arrow pointed to the back. There didn't seem to be any customers. But, Gabrielle thought, it's pretty early.

Catherine, Samantha, and Rushel pushed her through the office door just as Audra said, "Room for one, please."

The man looked at them all without a change of expression. The office had plywood paneling and a worn vinyl floor. At least it didn't have that burning rope pot smell, Gabrielle thought. It smelled like cigarettes and chlorine.

"Aw right," the man said in a gravelly voice. He slid a slip of paper and a pencil across the counter. "If you wouldn't mind, Miss." He scratched his eyebrows.

Audra shook back her hair. "Not at all." She filled in the form and slid it back to him.

He put the paper under the counter without a glance.

"Very good. Thank you for choosing Sunrise Inn." There was a brass key in his hand. Gabrielle saw his gaze move to all of them in turn, starting with Rushel.

"That'll be eight ninety-five. We only take cash."

"Sure."

Audra pulled a bundle of ones from her pocket. The man watched as she counted off nine dollars. He traded her the key for them and produced a nickel from his own pocket. He dropped it into her hand.

"Hope you enjoy your stay."

"Sure. Thanks."

"Now, ah, ladies."

Before Gabrielle could speak, Catherine said, "We're with her."

The man stood up straighter. "Oh, well, you see."

Rushel turned sharply around, sending her hair out in a brilliant fan and said, "*I nie dostać tego. Możemy iśá czy nie?*"

Samantha said, "She vants to know if there is problem."

Gabrielle forced herself not to smile at Samantha's accent.

Audra shrugged. "I suppose we could go somewhere…"

"No, no, there's no problem," the man said, smiling at Rushel.

Rushel went out the door. "*Czy dlatego ze to dziewczynki?*" she muttered.

"*Nie dziewczynki,*" Samantha said sympathetically and followed her out.

"I don't know," Audra said.

"Everything's fine." He clutched the dollars tightly.

Audra stepped back. "All right. Thanks."

"You ladies enjoy your stay. Continental breakfast is at six," he said.

In the parking lot, they all got away from the office door and walked down the row of rooms. Audra looked at the key. They went to the end and around the corner. The building extended to a gravel lot.

"All the way down," Audra said. "Number one oh two."

It was the room at the very end. The door was painted orange and had a layer of powdery oxidation. My first motel room, Gabrielle thought. She stood behind Audra.

"At least we're away from the highway," Audra said.

She put the key into the brass doorknob and turned. The door opened with a pop. Gabrielle saw orange shag carpeting and then a square bed with an orange and black striped bedspread. Light leaked around the edges of the heavy orange curtains.

"This is great!" Audra went to the foot of the bed and flopped backwards. "Ahhh!" The bed rattled.

"Thanks for paying for the room," Gabrielle said. Her shoe snagged the carpeting. She stumbled and sneezed.

There was a square table, painted black, with a single black chair. There was a fold up luggage stand set against the wall. A door, painted white stood half open. She could see the edge of a toilet. There was another door next to the head of the bed. Sunlight was visible at the bottom.

Rushel came in with Catherine.

"Okay," Rushel said. "Good. I'm not breaking out in hives. Can we all fit in that bed?"

"Of course." Audra lay flat with her eyes closed.

"I accept your judgment."

"As well you should."

"Pretty darn cozy." Catherine headed for the bathroom.

"Cozy is not actually festive."

"Don't say festive."

Samantha stood in the door. "Now this is more like it."

"As long as the toilet flushes." Catherine closed the bathroom door. Gabrielle heard water running.

"Toilets don't have to flush, you know," Audra said.

Gabrielle saw Samantha smiling. "They don't?"

"As long as they don't overflow you're good. Ah, this brings back memories."

Catherine in the bathroom let out a sharp laugh.

Samantha pointed at the second door.

"What the heck is that?"

Audra rolled over. "The back door?"

"Motel rooms don't have back doors."

Catherine came out of the bathroom and slammed the door into the wall. There was a preexisting dent for the knob to fit into.

"You *have* to see this," she said.

"Really?" Samantha grinned at Gabrielle. "I bet I know."

"Now don't get upset," Catherine said.

Gabrielle didn't move. "All right."

Audra bounced off the bed onto her feet. "No way!"

Catherine stepped aside to let Gabrielle go in first.

Gabrielle sighed. They were all smiling at her. She went through the small bathroom doorway, stepping around the front of the toilet. The paint on the wall was cracked and chalky. There was a bright little window of prismatic glass with a mirror and sink screwed to the wall beneath. Then a metal box with a chrome knob and a coin slot. The box had pictures on it, gaudy color drawing of things. The things were not tampons or pads. It took her a second to decipher them.

"Oh."

She looked more closely. They were labeled 'Health Aides, Large and Extra-Large'. And there was something labeled 'Tickler Ring'.

"Oh my goodness."

Audra laughed and Catherine came up behind. Rushel and Samantha crowded in.

Gabrielle knew she was blushing and couldn't help it.

"I had no idea. I mean."

She tried to peer into the dispensers output slot.

"How big are these things?"

"You mean, *how* big?" Samantha held both her index fingers up a few inches apart. "From like this to about like this."

Gabrielle considered her feelings. Maybe seven inches maximum. She found she was curious and profoundly embarrassed at the same time, as if she accidentally got a glimpse of a stranger undressing. She examined the shapes of the condoms.

"Is the Goddess feeling anything," Catherine said. She was holding up her hand to shield her eyes from the pictures.

Gabrielle had to clear her throat. "Feeling?"

"Feeling feeling."

"Oh."

"I'll say it," Rushel said. "Does the thought of having one of those inside you cause any reaction. Like."

"Hm," Samantha said. "Feeling feeling."

Rushel put her hands on Gabrielle's shoulders. "Like, you lie naked on the bed and your boyfriend climbs on top of you with his thing sticking out and you spread your legs..."

"Oh my God!" Audra said. "*Boy*friend? When did you become a *pervert?*"

"Yeah, this is a little, shall we say." Samantha said.

"Freaky!"

"Disturbing."

"I saw it in a movie," Rushel said. "In San Francisco." She let go of Gabrielle's shoulders. "It was kind of, I don't know."

Catherine was still protecting her eyes with one hand and now covered her mouth with the other. "Do we have to talk about this? I just ate tofu."

Gabrielle turned away from the metal box. "Look, I don't feel anything. I was just curious. I mean, it's weird. This thing. It just appears? I can't even imagine that."

"I think it's funny," Rushel said.

"We can use it against them." Audra nodded.

"I used to hate them but now I just feel sorry for them," Samantha said.

"I'm not that evolved," Audra said.

"Older guys are a little better," Rushel said.

"Because their things don't work anymore." Audra laughed.

"Maybe. Probably."

"Definitely."

"I think after they get old enough they figure it out," Samantha said. "In some cases."

"If they manage to live that long."

"If you don't mind my saying so, I know," Gabrielle said, "I know it took a while to realize this. But I'm just so glad I was born a woman."

"Yes," Catherine said.

"And I never thought there would be a place for me but now I know there is. And I have all of you to thank for that."

Catherine hugged her tightly and buried her face in the sweatshirt. Rushel and Samantha joined in with one arm each. Gabrielle saw Audra step back, a distant look on her face.

"Let's rest up and then walk around the town some more," Rushel said. She glanced at the dispenser. "Poor boys."

"Poor sad boys," Samantha said.

Gabrielle felt Catherine laugh against her chest.

They made sure the lock worked and brought in all their things, except Samantha. She left her leather satchel in the rear compartment of the VW. The motel room's back door had a very basic lock and opened out so there was no way to jam it with the chair. Samantha did not like that at all.

They opened the back door and peeked out. There was a dirt courtyard behind the L-shaped building. Audra thought it looked like someone had started to put in a swimming pool and gave up. They all thought this was plausible.

Back in town, Gabrielle parked in a small lot with parking meters and Samantha put in a dime, enough for two hours. They walked up the busy street in the chilly wind. The fog was returning. Audra led the way. She kicked a eucalyptus branch out of the way. The sidewalk was thronged with people that looked like tourists. A couple directly in front of them walked slowly. The man was wearing short pants, a polo shirt, and a gold jacket. The woman a knee length skirt and cardigan sweater. Her sandals scuffed.

Gabrielle thought they were by far the youngest group visible. Rushel kept her hair tucked under her jacket collar.

They went into a store Catherine called a 'boutique'. The air was scented with vanilla and there were many hanging plants. Audra couldn't stop sneezing. They all got sunglasses even though Gabrielle couldn't exactly wear them over her regular glasses. When she put them on, Audra said they made her look 'dangerous'. Samantha wouldn't let her see how much it all was as she paid.

They window shopped at a leather goods store and picked out their favorite handbags. "Technically not purses," Rushel remarked.

"So they're okay?" Gabrielle really liked one with a wide padded shoulder strap. "That one costs more than my car." The leather looked amazingly soft. Wouldn't need a backpack, she thought, maybe it's time I graduated from those things.

The proprietor waved and smiled at them from inside.

"Do we want to go in?" Gabrielle said.

"Let's just keep walking." Samantha pointed. Next door was a jewelry store.

They waved back at the leather man and moved on to the diamond man.

"You know," Audra said, staring at silver necklaces draped over black velvet, "I'm not really into shiny things, but." There was another stand under a floodlight showing off small diamond earrings. "Gosh."

"You're allowed one shiny thing," Rushel said. "It's in the handbook."

Audra turned in surprise and said, "Oh, right, I forgot," so seriously that Gabrielle couldn't help laughing.

"One? Decisions," Catherine said. "Like I said, a simple silver necklace with that sweater."

"Uh huh."

"All you need."

Across the street there was a gallery of some kind. Art? Gabrielle thought. The building had diagonal wooden beams on the plaster walls. A German style maybe. She didn't know. The roof was elaborately shingled giving it a fairy tale look.

She thought this beach town was an interesting place.

"Hey," Audra said and pointed at a small handwritten sign on the jewelry store door.

'*We buy Gold!*'

She hooked her new sunglasses over the top button of her flannel shirt.

"My dear sister, there is something I need to investigate."

Rushel lifted up her sunglasses.

"And what is the nature of this investigation?"

"Financial."

They looked at each other for a second.

Rushel took off her sunglasses and placed them on top of her head. Very stylish, Gabrielle thought. I might be able to do that. She brushed back her hair.

Catherine took her own sunglasses and positioned them on Gabrielle's head. "You look like a movie star trying to be inconspicuous."

Rushel turned. "Ohh! Have I seen you in anything?"

Audra paused, hand on the doorknob.

"Well," Gabrielle said.

"She doesn't like to brag." Samantha put her arm around Gabrielle's shoulders. "That little project with Truffaut. The disastrous Hitchcock thing. The whole James Bond business."

"A Bond girl! Right, I know you! What's Roger Moore really like?"

"He's um." Roger who? Samantha knows movies?

Samantha whispered in her ear. "He's very debonair."

"He's a gentleman," Gabrielle said. "Very debonair."

"Wow!"

Audra pointed her chin up.

"*We* are the Von Stilts sisters. We rarely notice the motion pictures. We love shopping, travel in the south of France on a whim, possibly London in the proper season, and boys. In that order."

"If it requires more than a moment's thought, we are not interested," Rushel said.

"Sitting through an entire movie? Unthinkable."

"What a horrid bore. Surrounded by strangers from the lower orders."

"Come along, Victoria."

"Oh, very well, Regina."

Gabrielle winced. Reg-eye-na?

As Audra pulled the door open, she said loudly into the store, "But that's the Penrose clan. We should no longer be surprised by their tiresome antics."

"Surprised is not the word I was thinking of," Rushel said irritably.

Gabrielle stood in the doorway and watched.

The man behind the counter and wearing a dark suit and black tie. He had a wispy gray beard. He squinted at them without smiling.

Rushel walked quickly to the end of the counter while Audra looked the man in the eyes. Gabrielle could see him struggle to pay attention to both of them. Catherine tugged her arm.

"Not too close," she whispered.

They both pretended to admire a glass case full of diamond rings. Samantha came around and stood to her right, obscuring the man's view of her.

"Hello," the man said to Audra, trying to keep Rushel in his peripheral vision.

"Good afternoon. I was looking – ."

"Is *this* all you have," Rushel said. The main case was full of necklaces and bracelets covered with diamonds with a smattering of rubies and emeralds.

"Your sign," Audra said.

The man head snapped back and forth.

"About gold."

The man steadied himself. "Gold?"

"I don't know," Rushel said.

"You buy gold."

"We." His dark-clad shoulders twitched. "Yes."

"You do?"

Audra held out something. Gabrielle heard Catherine gasp. It was one of the gold coins.

"Would you be able to tell me the value of this item?"

She set the coin on the velvet mat.

Still a bit rattled, the man looked hard at it, slipped on a pair of glasses. The right lens had a fold down magnifier. He kept his hands behind the counter and bent over the coin. After a moment he pulled back and Audra flipped it over.

"Ah," he said. He took of the magnifier and from a lower shelf brought out a heavy instrument. It had a thick base with a keypad and a top comprised of four glass sides. He pushed a button on the device and then produced a set of calipers.

Gabrielle was impressed. She recognized the laboratory grade scale, capable of measuring down to a ten-thousandth of a gram.

The man carefully measured the diameter of the coin, still resting on the velvet. He set the calipers down and put on white cotton gloves.

"May I?"

"Certainly," Audra said.

Rushel was halfway down the counter watching everything from the man's blind side.

He picked up the coin and guided it on the center of his left palm. With his right hand he opened one of the glass panels and gingerly pushed the coin onto the scale's platform. He shut the panel and pressed a button. Audra watched from inches away.

He opened the panel, pushed the coin back onto his palm and tipped it back onto the velvet. He took off the gloves and put the heavy scale back in its secret place. He stepped back from the counter, arms once again at his sides. He raised his eyebrows, confident once again, Gabrielle thought, of having the upper hand.

"Could you tell me your opinion of this item," Audra said. She silently gestured for Rushel's judgment. Rushel nodded.

The man saw Rushel and his eyes widened with surprise. He looked at Samantha. Then he kind of shrugged to himself. Distracted by gold, as always.

Samantha was staring hard at him and not smiling.

Gabrielle thought the game Audra and Rushel were playing was funny but it went way beyond that. And she could see another purpose. The town seemed friendly but was it? Why take chances if you don't have to? Divert attention, create confusion, try to arrange things to your advantage. This seemed smart to her. She wished she could do what Audra did. She sighed.

And there was no competing with Rushel at all. But they're on my side, she thought.

Gabrielle took Catherine's hand. Yeah, I get it, she thought. It's scary but I get it. She cleared her throat.

Audra and Rushel both looked at her.

The man glanced at Gabrielle, stared for a long moment, and said, "Were you thinking of selling this item?"

"Perhaps. In your professional opinion what exactly is it?"

"It is eight point three percent copper and ninety-one point seven percent fine gold. Total weight thirty-three point nine three grams with a diameter of thirty-two point seven millimeters. That is a genuine Krugerrand."

"So it's real gold?"

"Oh yes. One Troy ounce."

"This is the sort of things you buy?"

The man nodded.

"What would you give me for it?"

"Today." He checked a piece of paper taped to the countertop. "Two hundred twenty, even."

"Two twenty?"

"Yes, that's as of today. Come back tomorrow and it could be different. The market for gold is of course very volatile."

"Would you say the trend is up or down?"

He shrugged.

Rushel came to Audra's side.

"That's fascinating. Thank you so much for your time."

She plucked the gold coin from the counter and stuffed it into her pocket.

"Not at all. Any time you wish to transact it would be my pleasure to be at your service."

"Thank you."

The instant Audra said that Gabrielle felt Catherine tug on her arm and Samantha backed up into her. Together they guided her out the door and into the sunlight and cool wind. Gabrielle took the sunglasses off her head and Catherine put them on.

Audra and Rushel came out.

"Rip," Audra said.

"Off," Rushel said.

Samantha put her sun glasses on also. "Gold is about two forty-five."

"So it is gone up," Gabrielle said. She looked at Audra. She held out her hand. "May I?"

Audra dug the coin out and dropped it onto her palm. It was surprisingly heavy. She liked the graceful antelope, or whatever it was, that was on one side. She clasped her hands over her chest. "I think I'll keep this."

Audra started walking. They all had to work to keep up.

No one wanted to window shop anymore.

They drove back to the motel. Catherine, Samantha, and Rushel lay on the bed. Audra got an extra pillow from the office and lay on the floor in the space between the bed and the wall. Gabrielle sat in the black chair and watched her car. The parking lot was beginning to fill up. There were dusty pick-ups and a mud-streaked silver Mercedes. A huge Cadillac, spotless and gleaming, came and went multiple times. Its massive doors slammed solidly. Seemed to be dropping people off and then picking them back up. Through the small window she could not see directly who was coming and going. She kept detecting waves of perfume wafting through the screen. It made her pulse race but it wasn't Holly's. She could at least tell that much. She tried to breathe normally.

The sun dipped behind the tress on the other side of the highway. She could hear room doors slamming and toilets flushing.

"At least we have the end unit," Catherine said, her face pressed into the orange and black bedspread.

Audra sat up. "Place is a dump. They don't even have a tv. There's still time to go somewhere else."

"Too tired," Rushel said.

"Might be hard to sleep," Samantha said. "You know what's going on here, right?"

"Let's just put up with it," Gabrielle heard herself say. "I'm sleepy."

"Goddess," Audra said.

"Well, we have to have dinner," Catherine said.

"I saw a Denny's." Rushel was sitting up.

"Love Denny's," Audra said.

"You don't want to go to the place Melinda talked about?"

"Henri's?" Now Catherine was sitting up.

"I don't know." Audra got up and headed for the bathroom.

"I am getting hungry again," Samantha said. "That sandwich wasn't very big."

Gabrielle turned the switch on the table lamp. The bulb was very dim. "We could go to Henri's and if it seems too snotty, someplace else."

Audra emerged from the bathroom.

"We have to go somewhere."

"Maybe we'll see Melinda."

"She's probably right now cooking Carl his favorite dinner," Audra said. "I can just visualize it. Fried baloney on soggy white bread with mustard and pickles."

Catherine held her hands over her ears.

"And a healthy salad of wilted lettuce sprinkled with boiled potato skins. And Carl likes ketchup on his salad."

"I will not puke. I will not puke." Catherine stood up and bounced on her heels.

Samantha crossed her arms. "We must not judge Carl too harshly."

"Oh, we won't," Rushel said.

"Perish the thought," Audra said. "Grotesque and meaningless yet oddly memorable."

Samantha nodded. "That's not too harsh at all.

Gabrielle laughing put her shoes back on. "Okay. Bring everything." She shoved the window shut. Catherine grinned. "Let's go to Henri's."

They rolled past the restaurant in the gathering twilight. The sign was tiny, *Henri's* on a small plaque beside the door. There was no line.

"There's someone just in inside the door," Samantha said.

"The maître d," Catherine said.

Gabrielle could only see dark wood and low light. Very serious, she thought. Not the sort of place she would ever consider going to. Very expensive. But Catherine was excited and that was all she really cared about. She was worried they'd be turned away at the door.

Well, we have to try, she thought

A block to the west she found a parking spot in front of a flower shop and they all got out. The streets were nearly empty. A white Jaguar cruised past and the woman in the passenger seat stared at them unsmiling.

Samantha zipped up her jacket and glared back.

They walked up the sidewalk and admired the huge overgrown roots of the trees along the street and the way the sidewalk flowed around them.

"Everything is so clean," Gabrielle said.

They passed an art gallery and a row of dark offices. When they were close to Henri's Samantha held up her hand and they all stopped to watch two people approach the entrance. It was a middle-aged man in a black suit and tie and a young woman with feathered blonde hair. She had on a blue dress that hugged her hips and a fur stole around her shoulders. They spoke to the maître d, and entered.

"Hm," Samantha said. "Ermine, I think."

Rushel sighed. "No way."

Samantha shook her head. "We'd be lucky if if the guy even talks to us."

Catherine looked down.

Audra cocked her head. "I can't believe you two."

"It's hopeless. Did you see them?"

"Yes but you forget."

Rushel thought for a moment. "Oh come on."

"Audra."

"I hereby invoke," Audra said, "the Prague Protocol."

Samantha closed her eyes. "Oh, no, no."

"It," Rushel said. "We're."

"We have everything we need and if we don't, we improvise."

"Gee, I haven't seen the Prague Protocol in I don't know how long." Catherine said. She grinned at Gabrielle.

"Well, the last time we tried it we almost got arrested," Rushel said.

"That was just bad luck. They have actual security at the Academy Awards. This is merely a restaurant."

Gabrielle looked at them in astonishment.

"I actually saw Dustin Hoffman," Audra said. "You know who that is?"

Gabrielle said, "That's not James Bond?"

Rushel took a deep breath. Samantha looked at her questioningly.

They all watched the entrance as another couple approached. Leather jacket and blue jeans. Bright flowery dress and high heels and sparkling handbag. They talked with the maître d. And talked.

"Oh, I'm zo zorry," Catherine said with a French accent, "but you are looking at a minimum of two hours, pozzibly three. Or even four. I'm so zorry. It is a holiday weekend. May I suggest Zack In The Box out on ze highway, eh?"

The couple stepped back. The woman dropped her arms to her sides in disappointment. Her bag swung by the strap. They retreated.

"Challenging," Rushel said.

"Probably didn't like that dress."

Samantha turned abruptly. "Okay. Fine."

They followed her back to the car. She got her satchel and folded back the soft leather and rummaged inside. She looked at Rushel and nodded, then looked around.

There was the flower shop, set a step below the sidewalk level like so many of the stores. Next to it, the small office complex. Gabrielle saw understated signs for an accountant and a dentist. Angling away from the streetlights, there was a walkway lined with thick hedges and more flowers. There were no lights.

"Should be fine," Samantha said. She put the satchel over her shoulder and took Rushel by the hand. Heads down they walked into the darkness.

Gabrielle spoke softly. "Prague? What's in Prague?"

"It's a game," Catherine said. "Rushel's idea."

"She loves this stuff," Audra said.

"Yes she does."

And, Gabrielle thought, I'm living in one of her games already. And then another thought surfaced in her mind along with a twinge of disloyalty: Why don't I come up with my own game?

She felt a chill.

At some point, I'll have to.

Samantha came quickly up the walkway. She grabbed Catherine by the sleeve of her windbreaker. "Come on."

"What?"

"Hurry. We need you."

"Oh, no, I couldn't."

Samantha pulled her into the shadows.

Gabrielle thought Catherine looked flattered and excited.

She leaned back on her car. Audra leaned beside her. Their shoulders touched. At the edge of night, the sky was dark overcast. The street behind them was quiet.

"You can ask questions if you want."

Gabrielle clasped her hands. "It's better if I don't."

"Better?"

"It's more fun this way."

Audra grinned. "That shirt fits you pretty well."

"I know, thanks. It's nice and warm, too."

Audra straightened out Gabrielle's collar. "You can keep it."

"Wow, Audra, but."

"No, you should have it. I have all kinds of shirts."

Gabrielle adjusted her glasses and brushed Audra's wrist. Their fingers tangled together. Gabrielle looked at her. Audra looked straight ahead. Gabrielle took a firm hold of Audra's hand.

"The other day I should not have said what I said. I thought. I'm an idiot."

She moved a few inches away. Gabrielle felt Audra's hand relax so she gripped a bit harder. She looked down the empty street.

"I thought I had a chance. Then. This is a mistake. You don't know. You can't do what I'm doing now. You just can't."

Gabrielle slid over to touch Audra's shoulder again.

"Certainly are a lot of rules," she said. "Make new ones."

"It's not that easy."

"Easy is boring." Gabrielle was glad this made Audra smile. She heard laughter from the dark office walkway.

"Here we go," Audra said.

Catherine came up first. Gabrielle stared in amazement. She was wearing the black silk sweater. The yellow windbreaker was nowhere to be seen. Her sneakers had been replaced by high heels. Her hair had been brushed onto her forehead and Gabrielle thought it had been trimmed. Her blonde bangs were dead straight. In the dim light it took a moment to realize what was different about her face. Catherine was wearing makeup. Eye shadow, she thought.

Catherine put on a beret and adjusted it carefully. She squinted knowingly.

"Oh zere you are. I am zo charmed to meet you."

She held out her hand with her fingers pointing down.

Gabrielle hesitated. Catherine wiggled her fingers. Gabrielle finally reached up and grabbed them and let go.

"Yeah, like that," Audra said. "No one really knows how to shake hands that way."

"Oh, you are zilly!" Catherine said. "It is wonderful to be here to meet you."

"Why thank you," Audra said. "Are you famous? I bet you are!"

"Your questions are so amu-zing. As you know I am ze professional assistant to world famous supermodel Akasha of Prague, Czechoslovakia."

"Supermodel?" Gabrielle said.

"*Oui.* You two both of you have come all the way over from Moscow to make sure Akasha, along with her best friend Rikki from Beirut, who is alzo of course a supermodel, are not ideologically contaminated by the Americans with zer counter-revolutionary television and motion pictures. Akasha is only confused by politics and economics."

"Akasha?" Gabrielle said. "Rikki?"

"*Da,*" Audra said. "Zere vill be no defection."

Catherine nodded grimly. "Ze conzequences would be most unfortunate."

Gabrielle leaned over to let Audra whisper in her ear.

"Our families vud be sent to labor camp."

"Zere vill be no problem. I am certain," Catherine said.

Gabrielle adopted an equally grim expression. "No problems."

"As professional assistant I have many skills. I am expert French chef. I am well versed in international travel with special emphasis in traversing those nations trapped in the final desperate stage of dying capitalist system. Akasha's vants and needs are my vants and needs. Also I have received training in art of self-defense including extensive instruczen with automatic weapons. Thus safe passage across ze heart-breaking landscape of pre-collapse America iz assured."

Gabrielle covered her mouth and tried to keep a straight face.

Audra nodded enthusiastically. "Ve vill be among the last to see America before it vanishes forever. I am very much forward looking to the visit to Disneyland!"

"Da. And Hollyvud."

Gabrielle closed her eyes. "That's a lot to remember. Are you doing a French accent or a Russian accent?"

"I vill now explain ze Protocol of Prague," Catherine said, squinting.

Gabrielle saw Rushel and Samantha coming up the walkway, arm in arm. They paused.

"Do not speak to Akasha. Never attempt to touch Akasha. Never hand anything to Akasha. Do you understand?"

"Da," Audra said. She nudged Gabrielle.

"Da," Gabrielle said trying to copy her accent. It was pretty good, she thought, although Catherine's fake accent had drifted a bit. She didn't care.

Catherine speaking with an accent was really sexy.

"You vill make sure Akasha is protected from corrupting influences, of course, however your main job, as I stated before, is to prevent her from defecting. Americans have agents everyvere."

"Everyvere!" Audra agreed heartily. "Zay are zo devious!"

"Of course, vunce ve get into restaurant, ve zhuld be safe. Our goal is to achieve entrance. Remain focused on zis."

"Da."

"Da," Gabrielle said.

"I am personally looking forward to establishing lasting bond with oppressed restaurant verkers. Ve vill plan overthrow of mercantilist exploiters. Is enjoyable pastime."

Gabrielle couldn't stand it any longer.

"Where are you getting all this?"

Catherine laughed and her hand went to her cheek. "I lived in France for six months," she said in her normal voice.

"France?"

"Paris. You kind of pick it up." She glanced behind her. "Along with a pile of other stuff." She held out her hand. "You may come now," she said gently into the darkness. "Tactical situation iz stable."

Rushel and Samantha came out of the shadows. Gabrielle felt shock then realized it was just part of the game. Just go along with it, she thought.

Rushel, face set in a petulant frown, was staring at them wide-eyed as if taking the measure of her captors. She held her head high. Samantha was holding her right arm and whispering in her ear. Rushel was wearing an oversized white t-shirt with the tails hanging out and over it a men's white dress shirt, top three buttons undone, and the sleeves rolled up. It was luminous in the dark. She was also wearing a black men's tie loosely knotted, like a scarf. She still had on her original jeans but had switched shoes with Catherine and was wearing the Reebok sneakers without socks. She whispered something to a very attentive Samantha without taking her eyes off Catherine and Audra.

Samantha had not changed her white sweater and skirt. There was only the addition, like Rushel, of a tie worn like a scarf. Metallic blue. She spoke. "Zhe is hungry now." Rushel whispered to her again. "Zhe vants hamburger. Just like ze Americans have."

Catherine sighed and shook her head. "Hamburger is symbol of decadence." Then she smiled indulgently. "Akasha may of course have anything she desires."

A car turned the corner and headed in their direction. Headlights swept over them.

"Tactical," Audra said quietly. They all froze.

The Volvo passed and made a right.

Audra nodded.

"Very good. Now up sidevalk ve go."

Catherine and Audra led the way. Rushel and Samantha were right behind them, Samantha never letting go of Rushel's arm, her mouth always close to her ear. Rushel walked slowly, arms at her sides, looking like an unwilling participant. She scuffed her sneakers. Gabrielle, taking up the rear, thought Rushel looked like she was being dragged along, a spoiled child forced to do some awful chore.

Gabrielle thought Rushel was really good. Fearful glances mixed with impatience and when Catherine spoke, a look of exasperation.

"Every sing you see around you is *fake*," Catherine said. "All is lie. Zees buildings. Zee silly automobiles. All impossible. Zay fool no one."

Gabrielle noticed her accent was getting thicker. Still couldn't tell if it was supposed to be French or Russian.

"Is all propaganda show put on by oppressive American authorities," Audra said breathlessly, "who are under control of multinational corporations. They are ze real power."

"You haf learned vell."

"Thank you, Comrade! I haf question."

Catherine sighed. She shrugged. "Vat is question?"

"Ven ve came to America I looked out vindow of airliner."

Catherine looked angry. "You ver told not to do zat."

"But I wanted to see, Comrade Catherine, and."

"Your complete lack of initiative and imagination were vy you ver chosen for zis assignment. Vat has happened to you?"

"I became curious. So I looked."

"Oh," Catherine said mournfully. "Elena."

"Comrade Catherine, is not lie! All ze buildings are real! Filled with wonderful zings! And ze automobiles, Comrade, millions and millions of zem in lines stretching to ze horizon! And ze houses, I saw zem, huge houses where every vun has zer own room and vis out need to share bathroom vit four or five families. And ze apartments, even very small, zay have hot vater and electricity and a kitchen..."

"Nyet! You could not have zeen all zat from vindow! You are victim of brain vashing."

"But Comrade."

"*Nothing* exceeds the treachery of ze Americans. Is greatest evil in all of vurld. Upon return to ze motherland you vill report to reeducation camp."

"Oh but no please."

"Following reeducation you and entire family vill be zent to gulag."

Audra stared straight ahead. "I vill accept my punishment."

Catherine wiped her eyes. "Yet another pervectly good apparatchik ruined by Elvis Prezley, Coca-cola, and Tingles potato zhips."

"But I love ze Tingles!"

"Da. Every vun does. If only zat, I vud over look. But, my dear apparatchik, *zere is no room in socialist reality for Elvis."*

Audra gasped and wiped away a tear.

"Comrade!"

"I am zorry. Is truth."

Samantha turned her face away from Rushel's ear and cleared her throat.

"Yes, Rikki?"

"She vants both of you to stop talking. We are at restaurant."

Gabrielle could just see the man, standing at a podium in the open doorway, framed by lots of dark varnished wood. There was a light fixture on the wall close to him with a small blue bulb encased in a thick angular glass cover. It cast tiny rainbows onto the man's stiff white shirt.

Audra whispered, "Sunglasses."

"But I can't see," Gabrielle whispered back. "Dang." She took off her glasses and slipped on the plastic sunglasses. She stepped back and got behind Samantha.

Catherine stepped into the doorway, frowning. Rushel seemed to count to herself and then came up on Catherine's right. She gave her head and shoulder a toss and made her hair swing wide. Gabrielle saw the man's eyes widen.

Rushel looked at Catherine and said with an impatient tone, "*Dlaczego jesteś taki powolny?"*

Samantha, at Catherine's left, said, "She is already bored." Then she went back to Rushel's side. Rushel looked sternly into the foggy distance. Showing off her profile, Gabrielle figured. She thought she knew what the basic strategy was. Distract the target, usually male, using Rushel's attributes and when their attention is divided, a quick jab. A verbal jab, using attributes of Catherine and Audra. Me, I guess I would just punch the guy, Gabrielle thought, but their way is better. Maybe.

Catherine said, pronouncing carefully, "This is supermodel Akasha. From Prague. She vants to have dinner. Are you open?"

"Yes, ma'am. We are open," the man said.

Gabrielle thought his voice was strained, high-pitched and unpleasant.

"However," he said.

"How much?"

"Ma'am?"

"For ticket. How much?"

Samantha brought out a handful of money, the bills crumpled into a ball. A twenty was visible, just sticking out. Catherine pulled it out with a skeptical look, shrugged, and held it out to the man. His eyes went to the money and back to Rushel's hair. Then Gabrielle, squinting, thought he seemed to sigh internally and his eyes went firmly back to the money. When he reached for it Catherine held it higher.

"Vich vun? Of zis charming imaginary play money."

"Well, if you don't mind." He pointed at the twenty.

"Ah." Catherine hesitated. "Now ve go in?"

The man nodded.

"Oh. Kay." She let him take the twenty.

"Very good." He took a paper from the podium. "Your table is in the process of being cleared so if you please bear with us we will be seating you in just a few minutes."

"Eh? Ve go in?"

"Just a few minutes."

"Ve go in now."

"But."

"Now. Or you give money back."

Samantha, scowling, held out the wad of bills again. The edge of a hundred was prominent. The man stared at it. Catherine held up her hand and Samantha quickly put the money away. The man followed it with his eyes.

"*Chcę iść do* Denny's," Rushel said.

The man blinked at Rushel and Samantha and said, "Right this way."

"Oh. Kay," Catherine said with a smug smile. She followed him inside. Rushel, with Samantha on her arm, was right behind her. Audra kept expressionless behind her sunglasses and gave a thumbs up. Gabrielle walked behind her, bumped into the podium and started it rocking. Several pencils rolled out of it and clattered on the tile.

"Criminy." She whipped off the sunglasses, rubbed her eyes, and put on her spectacles. Audra was almost out of sight around an awkward corner of heavy walnut paneling. Gabrielle hurried to catch up and entered the main dining room. She stopped in surprise.

Fourteen. There were fourteen oval tables of three different sizes covered with deep red table cloths. Forty-one people sat at the tables. There were sixty-two wine glasses and sixty-four water glasses. The silverware. That was tricky. There was a tug on her sleeve. It was Catherine.

"Stay with us, Goddess."

Gabrielle closed her eyes for a moment. The dining room smelled of burnt coffee and perspiration overlaid with the acrid scent of a cigar.

"Here's your chair," Audra said. She pulled back a black painted chair with a thick cushion. The man had led them to a large-sized table beside the kitchen door. A small table was wedged between it and the back wall. The two people seated there watched them unobtrusively around their wine glasses. Gabrielle tried and could not catch them at it.

As Rushel and Samantha sat Gabrielle got the sense they were being scanned by almost everyone in the room. Rushel was to Audra's left at the end of the table close to the wall. When her chair bumped the small table behind her Rushel said, "Sorry." The man simply smiled at her.

He had sandy blonde hair and was wearing a gray sport coat with leather patches on the elbows. His partner, seated across from him, had short black hair which curled around her chin. She was wearing a trim black leather jacket and a string of pearls. She raised her eyebrows and took a sip of wine.

Gabrielle sat with Catherine to her left, across from Rushel. Samantha took a seat at the opposite end, the point most exposed to the room and closest to the kitchen's double doors.

Gabrielle tried to analyze the seating arrangement. Rushel was facing the room and attracting most of the attention, drawing it away from the others. *Away from me*, she thought. *Audra couldn't shield Rushel from view the way she tried in the sandwich shop, but this is a different situation. So that, while they're staring at her, Samantha can detect and deal with any actual physical threats. And at the same time Samantha's long black hair is stealing some of the attention and adding to the confusion. So what roles are Catherine and Audra playing?* This also seemed ripe for analysis.

Just as she thought that, she caught the man with the elbow patches looking at her. He made it seem completely casual and random but Gabrielle knew he had just given her a real once over. They were both doing it. His female companion had been a bit more discrete in using her wine glass as a cover and checking them all out from the corner of her eyes. Gabrielle saw them smile at each other.

Rushel seemed to sense these interactions, Gabrielle thought, and decided to break it up.

"*Chcę zjeść obiad!*" she said loudly into the room. All the murmuring ceased. Gabrielle saw a table of men, all in dark suits, look at Rushel and nod appreciatively. One of them, a man with a heavy beard, grinned hugely. As if he were looking at a new sports car, Gabrielle thought. She saw this was the guy with the cigar. The man from the front door walked in with a water pitcher and began refilling glasses. One of the men asked him a question and when he answered she picked out, 'Akasha' and 'Prague'.

The grinning man turned all the way around in his chair and lifted his glass of water in a toast. "Ah! Akasha!" The others did the same.

"*Nie chcę, żebyśż na mnie patrzył!*" Rushel said not quite as loudly.

Now Samantha turned around.

"Akasha says thank you for your kind gesture and she hopes you have vonderful evening in your lovely small American town by the sea."

The men all said thank you in subdued voices. The grinning man now began staring at Samantha.

"And now I must have menu. Akasha is very hungry."

There was widespread agreement around the room. Discussions ensued with impatient tones. Grinning man said something to the maître d who, judging by the wrinkling of his forehead seemed worried about something. Bathed in rainbow glints from the chandelier, still holding the pitcher, he walked quickly through the kitchen doors. As they swung shut, raised voices were audible. Gabrielle couldn't understand them.

"Good luck getting a menu," the grinning man said.

Catherine straightened up in her chair. She looked at Samantha, who was also surprised.

"What the hell," Catherine whispered. She leaned to her left to try to see into the kitchen. There was shouting.

"And I just noticed something," Samantha said. "No one is eating. And there don't seem to be any waiters."

Catherine sighed. "This may not have been the best idea."

Gabrielle regarded the table set with silverware and cloth napkins. They all had water in heavy goblets. Very well, she thought, this may be it. She cleared her throat. Catherine nodded. They all clasped hands on the table cloth and closed their eyes. Gabrielle heard the dining room go silent again.

Catherine spoke clearly. "Creator of all things, this is Catherine. Thank you for the wonderful meal we are about to receive. And even if we don't, because I picked such a crappy-ass restaurant, thank you for the wonderful glasses of water. And for the love of my family. Please keep them safe. And as always, thank you for that day in Paris."

In surprise, Gabrielle opened her eyes. It was just in time to see the man with leather patches smile at his partner and mouth the word, *Marvelous.*

Then he stopped smiling, taken aback. Samantha was staring at him.

"Well, that's it for now I guess. I'll be talking to you again soon. So shall it be."

They all said, "So shall it be. Amen."

Conversation resumed in the large room and there was the clinking of water glasses. A loud crash came from the kitchen. Gabrielle visualized a whole tray of plates and glasses hitting the floor. There was more incomprehensible shouting.

Audra half turned to look and as she did the man with the leather patches pushed his chair back and bumped her arm. Audra's wrist hit her water glass and it tipped over, soaking the table cloth.

"Good lord!" the man said. Gabrielle thought she detected an English accent.

"John, do be careful," his dining partner said. She also sounded English. Gabrielle liked the way her curling hair framed her dark eyes. Gabrielle thought she was very attractive. And those eyes didn't miss a thing.

"Of course, my dear. I'm so terribly sorry."

"Oh, don't worry about it," Audra said. "It was my fault."

"My dear wonderful young woman, I assure you it was entirely my fault. All due to my innate clumsiness which is only increasing with age."

"And he was never terribly graceful to begin with," his partner said.

"Which I'm certain is why they made me an officer. Do less damage that way, you know. You must accept my apology."

Audra, Gabrielle thought seemed almost hypnotized by the man's voice.

"I. Of course."

"You do?"

"Yes."

"Wonderful!" He took a deep breath. "What a relief. My name is John."

"Audra."

"Audra! How perfectly charming. Allow me to introduce my lovely partner Emma."

She raised her wine glass.

"John, Emma, it's very nice to meet you."

Catherine cleared her throat.

Audra said, "And this is my family."

Gabrielle saw John and Emma come to attention at the word 'family'. They're being very polite about it, she thought, but they are studying us.

"Samantha," Audra said.

Samantha nodded, barely smiling.

"Also known as Rikki."

"Ah, Samantha," John said. "Or Rikki."

"This is Catherine."

"Just Catherine," Catherine said. "That's fine."

"Catherine," John said.

"This is Persephone Gabrielle."

Gabrielle saw Emma raise her eyebrows and then quickly reset them to normal.

"Charmed," John said after a split second delay.

"And this is Rushel. Or Akasha if you prefer."

"Rushel. Wonderful."

Rushel looked at him sideways.

"And that would be the famous supermodel Akasha I have have heard so much about recently?"

Rushel winkled her forehead.

"Akasha does not understand you," Samantha said in her funny accent.

John gave her an uncertain look.

"Well, it's just that, if you don't mind, I couldn't help but notice you said she was from Prague and yet I could have sworn she was just now speaking Polish."

Catherine laughed.

Audra turned to look at Rushel. Rushel frowned at her.

"I thought it was rather good Polish. Passionate."

Rushel shrugged. "Why thank you."

Now Emma laughed. "Oh this is smashing!"

"You mean." John gave the room a furtive glance. "So not from Prague, then?"

"Washington state."

"Excellent! Shh."

"Oh, we wouldn't dream of it," Emma said.

"Perish the thought." John gave a professional nod to Samantha.

"Yes," Emma said.

"Thank you for allowing us to witness it."

"Our pleasure, John," Audra said. Gabrielle saw Samantha struggle not to roll her eyes.

"There was something that just occurred to me."

"John," Emma said with a warning tone.

"It's just that, well, if you've had training, and by that I mean in the service, you know, for example during the war."

"Now, John. The wine."

"There are certain aspects of training which quite involuntarily stick with you."

Emma sighed. "They're not interested in the war, John."

"Of course not, my dear. It just popped into my head. These days I am but a lowly philosophy professor laboring, unappreciated for the most part, at a university you have undoubtedly never heard of."

"Smithson," Emma said. "Somewhat north of here."

"I've heard of it," Catherine said.

"They have me teach the history of religion, that sort of thing. But let me ask, have any of you been in the service?"

Military service? Gabrielle thought. What a funny question. Aren't we all too young...

"Yes," Samantha said.

Catherine gave her a serious look. Almost angry. Audra was doing the same thing.

John just nodded at her.

Samantha locked eyes with Catherine then looked at John. "It was irregular, you could say."

"Ah. Then Rikki," he said in an attempt to break the suddenly tense mood, "You will probably understand."

Samantha smiled at 'Rikki'. "Understand what?"

"My analysis of your command structure."

Gabrielle felt herself blush as John nodded at her.

"The commander. With the unusual name."

"*John.*"

"You had the position rather forced upon you."

"Good lord, John. They are not here to be interrogated by you. Please forgive him. When he's had more than one glass of wine he turns into."

"Someone even more charming than ever."

"I fancy," Emma persisted, "he's playing a make believe role. John: Highly Regarded Analyst for Her Majesty. Instead of obscure teacher at obscure school."

"With tenure."

"Yes, and with worn out leather patches on your worn out, ever so tweedy jacket."

John, grinning, now nodded at Catherine. "First officer." Then Audra. "Intelligence officer." This made Audra smile. "Security officer." Samantha accepted the designation with a slight tip of her head. "And finally." To Rushel: "Your secret weapon."

Rushel wiggled in her chair. "I am kind of a bombshell."

Gabrielle saw Audra and Samantha exchange a quick look at this.

"You certainly are," Emma said. "John's quite finished now, aren't you dearest?"

John drained his wine and picked up the nearly full bottle.

"You're the most interesting people we've ever met here in all these years," Emma said. "See, now I'm doing it."

"You're pretty interesting yourself, Emma," Audra said.

Now Emma smiled. Gabrielle thought she was dazzling.

"What a lovely thing to say. Wasn't that lovely, John?"

"They're lovely people."

"Yes. It's this area. It's mostly."

"Old," John said.

Gabrielle risked a glance at the tables behind her. The grinning man and his companions were now staring at Rushel as if she were something good to eat. Like a piece of meat. Rushel seemed to sense this and reactivated her supermodel frown.

"Geezers." Emma wrinkled her nose. "Old is so tiresome. And then here you all are all of a sudden. Young and beautiful and on your own."

John seemed to get a thought. "So no boys at all, then?"

Gabrielle watched his reaction as they all shook their heads. Emma, wine glass at her lips, made a slow nod, wide-eyed.

"Really?" he said in what seemed to Gabrielle a very English manner.

Audra leaned back in her chair. "I like boys just fine."

"You do?"

"I just have no desire to see them naked."

"My dear wonderful young woman." He picked up his wine glass. "We have something very important in common." He raised his glass in a toast and Audra did the same with her empty water goblet.

"Why this is shocking," Emma said. "All they have is water. John."

"Quite right." He reached with the bottle and poured wine into Audra's glass. "Much better. One injustice rectified. Now if you will all simply pass me your glasses."

"Sure," Catherine said. She slid her still full goblet across the table and did the same with Gabrielle's and Samantha's. Rushel handed her glass to him. Water sloshed over the rim.

"Oops."

"No need to be careful, Akasha." One by one he dumped the water glasses onto the floor in the space between their table and the wall.

Emma began to giggle.

"Look John. You made a clean spot."

The water made a puddle on the thin red carpeting and flowed onto the linoleum in front of the kitchen door.

Audra and Rushel were surprised and both tried to catch themselves to keep from laughing. Catherine and Samantha, Gabrielle saw, watched with little reaction. Samantha gave her a slightly raised eyebrow shrug, as if to say, I knew something like this was going to happen.

John poured equal amounts of wine into each glass, about an ounce each. He held the bottle upside down to get the last drop. Then he got out of his chair and gave them all their glasses back. Gabrielle noted he did not mix them up.

John remained standing and raised his glass again. "To our fascinating new friends," he said.

Gabrielle raised her glass with the others but did not drink. She licked the heavy wine from her lips.

Audra brought her glass up again. "And to our new friends, John and Emma."

"Here here." Emma drained her glass.

Someone at a table on the far side of the room called out, "Pardon me, but how did you manage wine?"

"Quite simple really," John said as he sat down.

"We brought it from home," Emma called back.

There was appreciative murmuring.

"Only one bottle, sorry."

Gabrielle heard raised voices from the kitchen again and she realized it had been several minutes since she had seen the maître d. Catherine got up and went to the kitchen door. She pushed it open an inch and listened. The shouting continued. Catherine sat back down, looking rather sad.

"Now, Commander." John set aside the wine glass. "Did I hear your name correctly?"

"Well, no." Gabrielle winced as Catherine gripped her arm just under the table.

Audra happily spoke up. "This is the Goddess Persephone."

"Persephone?" John said. "The bringer of destruction?"

Rushel nodded. "Robert Graves."

"Quite."

"Not sure I agree with him."

"She's already destroyed a nightclub and a big house in Pasadena," Audra said cheerfully. Then she saw the expression on Catherine's face and stopped smiling.

"I didn't," Gabrielle started to say.

"The proprietors of this place had better watch their step then."

"It's become quite wretched," Emma said.

"Yes. Wretched."

Catherine leaned close. "We may as well go. I heard them yelling."

"You could understand them?" Gabrielle said.

"They're all speaking German."

"I thought this was a French restaurant."

"Melinda said it was. Maybe they're new owners. Anyway the head chef took off with all the money a week ago. They were hoping to get enough business over the next month to see them through but the suppliers cut them off."

"Wow."

"Yeah. That's it. I've seen this a couple times. They have no food to serve. I heard the guy say all they have is leftover stuff like frozen hamburgers. They were arguing about who was going to take it. They're getting ready to split."

Upon hearing that, Gabrielle saw her course of action clearly. Audra was looking at her in alarm.

"I've never destroyed anything."

Before Audra could respond, Gabrielle stood up.

"I need you to come with me," she said to Catherine.

"Do," Catherine said. "I." She stood up again.

Gabrielle went to the kitchen doors The other diners all turned to watch.

"This is much better than tv," someone said and there was subdued laughter.

Catherine spoke into her ear.

"It's just that I never know what you're going to do."

"It's always perfectly obvious to me. What to do."

"Okay. Well."

"If I believe it, they will believe it."

"Believe."

Gabrielle couldn't help grinning. "I know that because I've seen it. It actually works." Then she remembered. I've done something like this before, she thought. But that was completely different. She felt herself blushing again. Her palms were sweaty. "I didn't know you spoke German."

"Eh. *Un bissen*," Catherine said.

"Is that German?"

"It means *a little*. What must I believe?"

"I have to do the job right. Just the right sequence," Gabrielle said. Her ears felt stopped up. She calmed her breathing. She spoke softly to Samantha. "Rikki, would you ask Akasha to join us?"

Samantha and Rushel stared at each other for an instant and stood up. Rushel activated her supermodel face and glared at the room. She came around the table and Samantha took her arm as before and with a toss of her long black hair began whispering into her ear. For the first time Gabrielle could hear what Samantha was saying.

"*Madha nefeal?*"

Gabrielle had no idea what language that was. Apache? She shook her head sharply.

"Thank you for coming."

Samantha whispered. Rushel nodded. Audra stood directly behind her, still upset. Catherine got even closer on her left. Sealed from the crowd Gabrielle thought, they're all playing these roles and now I will too. So, what would be a good name? Right, that one.

"It is time to tell you ze truth," Gabrielle said softly. "I, Svetlana, am ze American agent."

Audra gasped. Catherine raised her eyebrows and squinted. Samantha smiled and whispered. Rushel looked at her in surprise.

"I work for Central Intelligence Agency. I am prepared to offer Akasha political asylum. She may bring any of her companions along with her. She will be provided..."

"Your plan vill fail," Catherine said in her Russian accent. "Our capabilities far exceed yours, lowly agent."

"Akasha and her friends will be allowed to stay in a large house in Hollyvud."

"Hollyvud!" Audra breathed. "Comrade."

"In a small Hollyvud neighborhood called Malibu, right on ze beach."

Rushel asked Samantha a question.

"*Czy to jest blisko Disneylandu?*"

"She wants to know if this Malibu is close to Disneyland."

"Right next door."

Audra tugged on Catherine's sweater sleeve. "Comrade, Disneyland!"

"Silence, weak-minded apparatchik. Do not be seduced by the sinister and evil Americans. You are disciplined soldier in inexorable global march of socialist peace and prosperity which inevitably results from total political, cultural, and economic domination. Also, remember your family."

"I'm actually not zat crazy about zem," Audra said. "Have you ever met my mother?"

Rushel closed her eyes and turned her head away. Her shoulders shook.

Samantha whispered something incomprehensible which Gabrielle translated as, *keep it going*, and then said, "And my family sold me into slavery when I was sixteen. Zey can rot in gulag."

Gabrielle thought Samantha sounded almost serious although that made no sense.

"Your families vill not be harmed," Gabrielle said.

"Enjoy your fantasy," Catherine said.

"Comrade Catherine, do you really believe I am only American agent in your country? *That* is a fantasy."

Catherine's hands flew up to her face. "The Politburo!"

"Yes." Whatever the heck that is. "You are making correct decision."

Rushel lifted her chin imperiously. "*Zabierz mnie do bezpiecznego domu. Ale pierwszy hamburger.*"

"Akasha choses Malibu and Disneyland," Samantha said.

Audra bounced on her feet. "Oh thank you, beautiful Akasha!"

"*Nie ma problem, kieszonkowa mysz.*"

"And also hamburger. Just like Americans have."

Catherine laughed. "Ha! Hamburger! Here is your downfall, Svetlana, right between your treacherous eyes."

Gabrielle tried to create a fierce expression, or at least defiant.

"Hamburger at strange German/French restaurant that is going out of business."

"Maybe not going out of business."

"Oh, honey."

Samantha coughed and looked at her feet. Rushel patted her back.

"I am tip of ze spear," Catherine said. "I am highly experienced member of worldwide vanguard of the socialist proletariat of the future. I am expert in failure."

"Hamburger is only a play my devious American mind thought up," Gabrielle said. "Make sure ve have everything."

They all checked the table behind them. Catherine retrieved her beret, trying not to make eye contact, in the soft light, with intently observing John and Emma.

"Remember when we had adventures, John?"

"Yes, Emma, dearest. So many adventures."

"Are we getting old, John?"

"We will always be young in spirit."

"What a lovely and evasive answer."

"One of the reasons you married me."

"Yes but not the most important reason, John."

"Of course not, dearest. Venice, if I may say so."

"You bastard."

They clinked glasses.

Smiling to herself, Catherine put the beret on and adjusted the strands of blonde hair that poked out over her ears. At kitchen door she said, "Now what, Svetlana? Zere is no going back."

"Yes, Comrade Catherine. I am Persephone Svetlana. I am," she thought furiously, "bringer of creative approach to problem."

Gabrielle pushed open the kitchen door and they all followed her in.

She saw stainless steel counters with steel legs and heavy steel shelves lining the walls. The counters and shelves were empty. There was a flat griddle, black and clean, and a large range made of cast iron. Pots and pans hung on racks. There was nothing cooking. A man stood halfway out an open door, his back to them. It was the front man. He was talking to someone in the back alley.

"Oh, too late," Gabrielle said. "Maybe."

Cold air was flowing into the kitchen. The man outside, a big guy in a white t-shirt, was speaking intently and waving his hands. A cook, perhaps. He stopped talking. From his widened eyes, Gabrielle knew he had seen Rushel. No going back. She hoped her glasses were on straight. Front man saw her.

Gabrielle held her chin up. Her heart began to pound. What's the first thing I say, she thought. Iron Curtain. Supermodel. Poland. Prague. Menu. Destruction. Creation. Intelligence. Central. Her heart was crashing against her ribs and each beat made her ears pop. This is what it feels like to faint, she thought. I'm going face down on that tile floor that hasn't been mopped in weeks. Here I go.

She tried to swallow and could not. She cleared her throat. Front man didn't move, just raised his eyebrows.

"I know you are having problems," Gabrielle said. "But I have reqvest." The fake accent makes this a lot easier, she thought. *Weird.* Concentrate.

"Yes, ma'am?" Front man said.

The guy in the t-shirt stared hard at her and then Rushel, then back to her.

"That." Gabrielle tipped her head back. "Is famous supermodel Akasha. She is all the way from Prague. There is two things she wanted in America. To go to Disneyland. And to have hamburger. A real hamburger like you have. We don't have this on the other side."

He straightened his shoulders and said, "Yes, the famous Akasha. Well."

"She will pay with this." Gabrielle took the large gold coin from her pocket and held it out by the edges. The man tentatively opened his hand and she dropped it onto his palm. The weight of it surprised him.

"Is only money she has. She sneaked it out of country. If they know she has it she is never allowed to leave again."

"That's terrible," he said. "Oh but this."

T-shirt guy craned his neck to see.

"A Krugerrand."

"Whaat?" t-shirt guy said.

"But this," front man said.

"Is worth almost three hundred of American currency dollars. Iz real one, I assure you."

"I am honored by this, um."

"Svetlana."

"Of course, Svetlana. This is not legal currency in the U.S. but that's beside the point. We have no way of making change at this time." He pressed his thumb into the coin. He frowned.

"Krugerrand is alloy of gold and copper so is very hard. I do not understand phrase change make."

"It's remarkable." The coin seemed to be making him nervous. "It simply means the remainder after the bill is deducted. A hamburger for Akasha and your party would come to approximately forty-five dollars. I would have to give you back over two hundred." He held the Krugerrand out to her. "We simply can't handle it."

Gabrielle kept her arms at her sides and her eyes on the man's face. "Change. Ah. Yes we have this. You must keep change."

"It's far too much." He dangled the coin.

Gabrielle avoided looking at the shiny gold.

"She is not permitted to possess money. She is not permitted to possess Krugerrand. It vill all be taken. All she wants is hamburger." She got close enough to whisper. "Please. Look at her. She is like little girl."

The man risked a glance at Rushel.

"You keep," Gabrielle said, "and she gets hamburger, yes?"

"Yes!" T-shirt man snatched the coin.

He had a slightly different kind of accent, Gabrielle thought. He gave a command out the back door in a brusque tone. Another man answered and appeared pulling a large plastic ice chest. It was so big it had wheels and a long handle. He had a gray shirt and hollow pockmarked cheeks. T-shirt guy spoke two sentences in what Gabrielle assumed was German and the heavy chest was brought into the kitchen. Ice chest guy seemed to notice Rushel and then just looked down.

They were on the way out, Gabrielle thought. They were leaving. It was that close. Then she had another idea. She stepped backwards, not wanting to turn her back on the guys, and said to Samantha, "What would Akasha say to offering everyone in restaurant a hamburger also?"

Samantha whispered and Rushel said, "*Oczywiście.*" Samantha nodded.

Gabrielle spoke to the front man who was pulling frozen food from the chest.

"Excuse me. Do you have enough, do you think, to give all in room a hamburger if zey are wanting one? Akasha would not eat alone in front of zem."

Front man locked eyes with T-shirt guy, who nodded, peering at Gabrielle.

"Hey," he said. "Who are you?" German accent but easy to understand. "Why are you doing this?" He gave the coin a toss with his large hand. "This is real. I've seen these things before. So, is this a gag?"

Gabrielle thought, this is it. She held her head up and tried to make her eyebrows rise. "Gag?" She heard Samantha mutter something. She took the opening. "Ah. No gag. Is for you to keep."

"It's just that I have trouble believing this."

Gabrielle tried to look puzzled. "Akasha desires it. She has her own way of doing zings." She straightened her shoulders and tugged her sweatshirt tight. "All we vant is hamburger for everyvun. Zen ve leave. Yes or no."

"Hell yes." He jammed the Krugerrand into his pocket then he said to front man, "Solves a lot of problems."

"All right zen."

Rushel stepped forward to the center of the floor and said, "*Jestem wdzięczny. Dziękuję Ci.*" Her voice cracked.

The big guy gave a curt nod.

Ice chest said, "What'd she say?" Southern accent.

T-shirt guy shrugged. "Come on, get moving."

Front man looked delighted. More than that. Astonished. I'll start thinking of him as the maître d, she thought. He believes. So should I.

He walked past them, smiled at Rushel, and went into the dining room. She heard him begin to speak in a loud voice.

Catherine whispered, "If I hadn't seen that with my own eyes..."

The sound of clapping mixed with a few cheers interrupted her. Gabrielle went to the double doors to peek but Samantha hissed. Ice chest was staring at them, mouth half open. T-shirt spoke in a clipped voice. Ice chest flinched and continued to stare, angry now.

"Hm." Catherine crossed her arms and stared back. "Ze tragedy of ze American proletariat. His kind vill not survive ze revolution."

Ice chest looked away, blinking.

Gabrielle felt a tug on her sleeve. It was Rushel. She pointed at the kitchen doors. They were going back in. Catherine nodded and maintained her stance.

Ice chest concentrated on the grill under the gaze of t-shirt.

That's someone who doesn't believe, Gabrielle thought. He doesn't believe at all. Not in Akasha, not in anything.

With this last thought came a twinge of fear. Then Rushel pushed open the double doors and cheering began.

The hamburger was delicious. Samantha slipped her patty to Catherine and had a lettuce and onion sandwich.

With all eyes on her, Rushel made a show of it. She lifted off the top bun and, scowling, examined the components. Lettuce. Onion. There was quiet laughter at this. The entire room waited silently and she put the burger back together and took a big bite. When she smiled and looked surprised the room applauded.

Grinning man lifted his glass of water again. "Welcome to America!"

Rushel smiled and waved back, the imperious supermodel face set aside.

Audra was hungry and quietly finished half of her's. She bumped shoulders with Gabrielle. "This is really good," she whispered.

"Hm hm." Gabrielle checked all the corners of the room but John and Emma were nowhere to be seen.

"What's the game plan, Svetlana? Do we just break character and bug out like I guess those two did?"

Gabrielle, wondering what 'break character' meant, thought it was pretty simple. She whispered her idea to Audra who stared into the distance, seemed to think through the steps, and surprised her by saying, "Okay, good."

Gabrielle told Catherine the plan. She whispered it to Samantha who raised her eyebrows and made a professional nod. Then she passed it across the table to Rushel. Their quiet acceptance made Gabrielle nervous. She knew why.

It's all on me, she thought, and she shook back her shoulders. Just pick the right moment and do it. But first let everyone finish eating.

Besides, she thought, this constant anxiety and fear before I do anything lately, I'm getting used to it.

I kind of like it.

She gave the dining room a quick scan. They were all concentrating on eating and talking to each other. She saw a couple empty tables now. The heavy layer of smoke had dissipated.

Then Audra was finished and also Samantha. Catherine wrapped up the remaining quarter of her burger in the cloth napkin and tucked it into her jeans pocket. Rushel, taking tiny bites and chewing slowly, had half left. She also scanned the room and lifted one shoulder. The diners had stopped watching her.

Gabrielle waited three beats and nodded.

Rushel wrapped her burger in her napkin and, eyes averted, gorgeous hair hanging straight down, stood up. Samantha did the same. Rushel came around the table and they both went through the kitchen doors. Only a few seemed to notice. Gabrielle waited. She saw one of the doors move in a gust of air as the back alley door opened and closed. She counted to ten and pushed her chair back. Audra did the same. They both stood.

"Ve will be right back, Comrade Catherine."

Catherine frowned at them. "Do not be too long, my apparatchiks."

"Of course not, Comrade Catherine."

"It vill go on your permanent record. Bear zat in mind."

"Comrade."

"Whatzever you are planning."

"Comrade."

With Audra at her side, Gabrielle pushed open the kitchen doors and stepped in. They let the doors close behind them. Rushel and Samantha were gone out the back. T-shirt guy was also gone and Ice Chest was chopping up an onion on the counter. His knife scritched on the stainless steel. He turned away from them after a furtive glance.

Gabrielle peeked back through gap between the kitchen doors. Catherine was sitting with her hands in her lap, a stern expression on her face. The count of diners watching her was now seven.

Audra whispered, "Like zis." She crossed her arms and pulled them up in a belligerent gesture. She lifted her chin and cocked her head.

"Right," Gabrielle said. "Just a few seconds."

Catherine, on the edge of her seat, turned her beret in her hands. She nervously checked the kitchen doors and then the front door. Half the room was now watching her.

Back in the kitchen. "Ready?"

"Yep."

They pushed the doors open and there was a collective gasp. They approached Catherine and simultaneously crossed their arms and cocked their heads. Catherine's eyes were fearful.

"It iz over," Gabrielle said softly. The dining room fell silent.

"What? *No.*"

"She iz gone."

"You lie!"

"Ha!" Audra said. She had a smug, off-center smile.

"Already she iz in Malibu," Gabrielle said.

More gasps from the closest diners. They repeated what she said to those behind them.

Catherine stood abruptly. Her beret fell to the floor. Her left knee buckled. She put her hands on her temples and unfocused her eyes. "You have ruined everyzing."

"Yes, everyzing."

"But you fool. You are also doomed."

"Ve are staying," Audra said. "Ve will be at Disneyland Hotel which is in Hollyvood."

"But is not real! It cannot be real! Our scientists have concluzzively proved the impozzibility of Disneyland."

"Now who iz fool," Gabrielle snapped.

"Ze retrieval team," Catherine said with a sudden remembering.

"Canceled. By me."

"No. Impozzible."

"Ve have capabilities you have not yet been even dreaming of."

Catherine looked confused. She shook her head.

Audra sighed. "Abandon your fantasy of vorld conquest and join us."

"Vy vud I quit. Ve are vinning."

"You vill be blamed for losing the great Akasha."

"I vill explain to them."

"Explain?" Audra said in astonishment. "They vill make example of you. You vill be made to convess while crawling on broken glass in front of color television cameras as your family throws rotten potatoes at your head and denounces you. Then you vill be soaked in petrol, shot twice in back of head, lit on fire, and thrown out vindow of tventieth floor. They vill say you killed yourzelf from shame."

"Sounds about right," Catherine said.

"The spot where your lifeless body hits ground vill become terrifying historical landmark and buzloads of school children vill be required to point and spit on it as they sing ze *Internationale* in celebration of your horrible death and as varning of their inevitable fate upon even ze slightest deviation from total obedience to ze State."

"Got it."

"Certainly, Comrade Catherine. I often vizzualize such things."

Catherine picked up her beret. "So Disneyland iz real?"

"See for yourself," Gabrielle said. "I mean, zee."

Catherine put on her beret and carefully adjusted it. She wiped her eyes. "I vill never zee home again."

"None of us vill," Audra said. "You must be strong. Now ve are splitting."

Audra turned smartly and pushed through the doors. Voices in the dining room exclaimed and grew louder. Gabrielle took Catherine's arm in her's.

"The Central Intelligence Agency. Zey are hiring?"

"Da, Comrade."

"Gud. You lead vay as I update resume."

They walked quickly through the small kitchen and upon reaching the back door began to run.

"Hey, your burgers were a big hit!" Catherine yelled at Ice Chest. "Hope that acne gets better!"

Laughing, they angled right into the dark alley and headed for the street ablaze with light in the cold night fog. They reached the sidewalk together and Gabrielle's breath caught as Catherine's arms stole around her waist. She was pulled back in to the shadows.

"Not so fast."

Gabrielle didn't try to speak as Catherine pushed her firmly against a brick wall and fitted her body fully onto her's. Catherine's hands left her waist and moved up. Gabrielle closed her eyes and felt Catherine's mouth directly over her lips, kissing her as she spoke.

"That was incredible," she whispered.

"*You* were incredible. How did you do all that? I don't know what I did. Nothing. I was guessing."

"All you guesses were perfect."

Cars passed and a couple walked past the end of the alley.

"I was so scared."

"You can handle it."

They breathed together for a while.

"Doing anything later?"

Gabrielle ran her hands under Catherine's silk sweater and caressed the bare skin of her back. "I was hoping we could get together."

"You staying at that motel?"

"Yeah, I'll be there."

"Maybe I'll see you."

Gabrielle hugged Catherine as tightly as she could. "Hard to wait that long."

"I know," she said and they finally kissed fully. This went on until they heard a car horn, at least a block away. In a corner of her mind, Gabrielle recognized it.

Catherine sighed. "Who is beeping?"

Gabrielle couldn't help but giggle.

"This place isn't so bad," Catherine said.

"The alley?"

"I mean, look how clean it is."

"It is clean."

"The whole town is just really clean," Catherine said and they kissed again. Catherine freed one hand and pulled up her sweater. Gabrielle unzipped her sweatshirt and started unbuttoning the heavy flannel shirt.

"God damn it, hurry up," Catherine whispered.

Gabrielle stifled another giggle. She tried to hurry but the new flannel was really stiff. Catherine impatiently clasped her face in both hands and kissed her forcefully. Gabrielle, before she closed her eyes again, saw car headlights sweep past the alley entrance. The headlights swung back and stopped, shining on their faces. The car was pointed right down the alley. She heard doors opening. Catherine dropped her sweater.

"Hey! You can't do that here!" It was Rushel.

Gabrielle moved from the wall with Catherine resisting.

"Is that my car?"

"Of course it's your car." Catherine pushed her back against the wall and began kissing her neck.

Her VW was sitting perpendicular to the sidewalk, front tires touching the curb. A black Mercedes rolled slowly past, faces frowning at them.

Gabrielle felt her pocket. Keys still there. She lost concentration. What Catherine was doing was making her feet tingle.

"Uh, we're kind of illegally parked," Rushel said.

Catherine looked up. "What?"

"We're about to be arrested and thrown in jail."

"As long as we're in the same cell." She gave Gabrielle's neck a final kiss. "I'm not finished with that spot."

"Oh," Gabrielle managed to say.

"Along with a bunch of other spots."

Rushel held out her hands. "Come along, children. Take my hands so you don't get lost again."

They walked out of the dark alley holding hands. Gabrielle saw Samantha behind the wheel. She let go of Rushel and slid into the back seat. Audra smiled at her. "You'll have to scrunch over," Catherine said as she got in and pulled the front seat back. Gabrielle was compressed between them.

"This is comfortable," she said as Audra snuggled. "You have a key?"

"Sure." Samantha's smile was bright in the green dash lights.

"We all do," Audra said.

"Really? Good." It was, she thought.

"All right, look. I'm sorry," Catherine said. "That place was not a great idea. It looked promising but I was wrong."

"It's all right," Rushel said.

"It was kind of fun," Samantha said.

"And we now have a new business if we want to pursue it," Audra said. "Cold War dinner theater! It would be a *blast*."

"Exhausting." Rushel sighed.

"And you were good," she said to Gabrielle. "I now have ideas. Many ideas."

"Oh?"

"We did manage to help them." Samantha started the car.

"You don't think I should have done that?" Gabrielle said.

"That was a goddess-level decision," Catherine said. "That place has major problems."

"It might work."

"I trust your judgment. Okay, let's blow this joint and go back to our seedy motel and get drunk."

Samantha put the car in reverse. Smooth, Gabrielle thought, she's getting better and maybe it was futile but I feel better helping those people, even poor Ice Chest. I feel better not carrying around that gold coin. I doubt M would disapprove. It's almost like something she would do herself. Also I'm going to get drunk in a motel room with my friends.

When Audra looked away Catherine rubbed her knee and they backed away from the alley.

The parking lot of the Sunrise Inn was full to overflowing and a row of pickups and old cars lined the shoulder of the highway. There were shadowy figures of people standing on the walkway outside the rooms.

"Hm," Samantha said, "Let's see. Ah, a nice quiet Sunday evening out on the highway surrounded by hookers and drug dealers."

The VW bounced over the large hole in the driveway And Samantha rolled past the closely packed cars.

"What the hell," Catherine said.

"Nobody left anything in the rooms, right?" Audra said. Rushel shook her head. At the end of the long building their parking spot was occupied by a white Jaguar with tinted windows.

"Did they rent our room out from under us?" Catherine leaned forward.

"Curtains haven't been moved," Samantha said. "Wait, okay, I know."

She drove past the end of the building and circled left behind it, off the pavement, onto the dirt courtyard. Gabrielle realized what she was going to do. Samantha backed up to their unit's odd back door until the bumper touched it and the thin wood bowed in.

"Perfect," Rushel said.

Samantha cut the engine and headlights and the car settled into the darkness.

"That door scared me," Catherine said.

Samantha opened her door. "You all wait here. I have the key. Be right back."

After Samantha walked around the corner where the stucco had been chipped and crushed at fender level, Audra said, "Just realized ours is the only room with a back door."

"Clientele?" Rushel said.

"Nice and private," Catherine said.

A rim of light appeared at the bottom of the door. Gabrielle felt Catherine's hand playfully work its way into her pants pocket.

"Such a flimsy door, though," Gabrielle said.

"Has all the earmarks of a pothead project, "Audra said.

"Pothead. Huh."

"Oh yeah." Rushel turned around. "They were probably going to build an addition to the room."

"An extra bedroom," Audra said. "This would be the best room in the whole place. They could charge double."

"And they went to the hardware store," Rushel said, "and bought a door and got so excited they had to get high and then they cut a big hole in the wall and suddenly realized they forgot the whole floor part, you know, and walls. This made them upset so they had to get high."

"Concrete. Framing. So complicated."

"Numbers. Calculations. Yikes. Better get high."

"Then they finally concluded they didn't have enough money anyway after buying all the pot. This made them sad," Audra made her voice tearful.

"Better get high."

"And they had to get their cousin, the one with the actual tools, to fix the big hole only he got confused, due to being high, and installed the door instead. And here we are."

Gabrielle had to cover her mouth and laughed so hard she blew her nose on the back of her hand.

"Here," Rushel said and pulled a napkin from her pocket. "Glad I stole this."

"Thanks. Ew."

"It just seemed like a stolen napkin kind of evening."

"Yes." Gabrielle was laughing again.

"It'd be funnier if we were high," Audra said. "Not that I would know."

"Of course not, Pocket Mouse. So you better get high."

"We do have wine," Catherine said. "Don't have to worry about the cops with wine."

"True," Audra said. "Of course here the cops would be high."

"And wine is probably better if you're high," Rushel said.

Audra nodded. "Better get high then."

"It's amazing that every situation in life compels you to get high."

There was the crunch of shoes on gravel. Samantha leaned over the windshield.

"What's so funny? Didn't you see the light? Room's okay."

Rushel opened her door. "Where'd you go?"

Audra pushed the driver's seat forward and climbed out. Gabrielle felt Catherine's hand reluctantly withdraw from her pocket. Then Catherine gracefully extended her legs and simply stepped out of the back seat. Gabrielle slid over and tried to exit the car the same way and hit her head on the sharp edge of the roof.

"Ah! Crap!"

Catherine put her hand on the spot. "Be careful!"

I'll never be like her, Gabrielle thought as the pain faded. I'll never be poised or balanced. It's like dancing. I'll always be the girl who bumps into things.

"It's all right," Catherine said, reading her mind. She kissed her forehead.

"So what took you so long?" Rushel said.

Audra stood beside Samantha. "Another thirty seconds and we would have activated worry mode."

"Thank you. I had to walk down and talk to the ladies."

"Those people standing around?" Gabrielle said.

"Were they," Audra said.

"Who I thought they were?" Rushel said.

"Yeah, they're hookers. Not much happening on a Sunday. Kind of looked like they were making a movie in one of the rooms. They had lights set up. I had to let them know we were just staying here for a night. You know. It's a business territory thing. They checked us out pretty good as we drove past them. One of them said, who's the blonde in the beret? That bitch is *hot*."

"Big business around here, I bet." Catherine grabbed the handle of her picnic basket and lifted it out of the back compartment.

Samantha looked at the back of the motel.

"It is. Not necessarily this place exactly but it is a high dollar zone. They seemed all right. The one I talked to said if any of us wants a hand job we'd get a special rate. Anything more they have to charge us the usual."

Gabrielle found it interesting this did not make her blush.

"That's good to know," Catherine said.

"It has been a while," Audra said.

"Let's all go have drink and talk about this."

Gabrielle locked up her car, double checked that the doors were really latched, and they all walked hand in hand around the end of the building into the weak yellow glow of their room's porch light.

Eight doors down, there was a group of women standing on the walkway. Two turned to look at them. The closest, a petite blonde, was wearing a short, stylish skirt and flats. Right behind her was a dark haired woman in a long black dress which was slit up the sides all the way to her armpits, no straps. As she turned, Gabrielle clearly saw thigh high black boots and no underwear.

The blonde woman waved in a friendly way. The dark haired one just stared.

Now Gabrielle felt herself blush. Samantha waved back. They all went into the room and Rushel closed the door firmly.

"Gee," Audra said.

"Yep," Samantha said.

Catherine sat the large basket on the small table and unhooked the wooden clasp. She unfolded one side cover and took out two bottles of white wine and a corkscrew with a thin retracted handle. From another section she took out wine glasses tufted with tissue paper. She expertly dusted them off and inspected each one for smudges. Then she took the corkscrew, with its compact lever tool on one end, and opened one bottle. Chardonnay, Gabrielle saw. She poured wine making sure each glass got the same amount.

"All right," she said.

Audra sighed. "Wow."

"What?"

"You know what time it is? Seven-thirty.

Gabrielle checked her watch in surprise. "I thought it was the middle of the night."

"I know."

"The whole evening lies ahead. Sheesh. Think I'll lie down for a bit," Rushel said. She took a glass of wine.

Gabrielle did the same. Samantha and Audra got theirs and Catherine, satisfied, picked up the last one. No one spoke. They gently clinked their glasses together making sure every glass touched all the others.

"That was insane. What we did," Audra said. She took a tiny sip.

"My Polish was getting rusty so it definitely worked out." Rushel gulped hers.

Gabrielle tried to sip and ended up gulping also. "We might be able to get into Disneyland for free."

Samantha shrugged. "We've never actually tried that."

"It's something to think about," Audra said. "That would be something." Another tiny sip. "This has to be the last motel in the country that doesn't have a tv."

"Judging by the socio-economic environment," Samantha said, "you're not supposed to sit around watching tv."

"No," Catherine said. Her glass was already half empty Gabrielle was startled to see. "You're supposed to get wasted. And."

"And what?" Audra said.

"Oh I don't know."

"I do," Samantha said. "Contribute to the local economy like a good consumer."

"I know who I'd like to consume. She was cute."

"But the one in that dress," Rushel said.

"I must not think of it. I am psychologically unstable," Audra said and took a longer sip. "This lousy room is freezing. And I don't think we can all fit in this bed."

Samantha knew what to do. She pulled the mattress onto the floor leaving the bed springs on the metal frame. She spread the extra blanket out and set the two extra pillows there.

"Old trick. Now we can all sleep in a bed."

"Perfect," Rushel said.

"Ever so resourceful," Audra said. She set her glass down and sat on the box springs and took off her shoes. She rubbed her feet and then lay flat on her back. "Huh. This is better than the mattress part. And no stains."

"You really don't need both." Samantha arranged the blankets.

They all sat back against the wall propped up by pillows.

There was a loud thump against the wall to their right. Then they heard the toilet flush.

"I foresee no problems sleeping," Rushel said.

"Nope."

The table lamp left half the room in darkness. Vehicles came and went. Headlights played over the heavy curtains.

"My pillow smells," Rushel said, "like feet."

"Mine," Audra said, "smells like b.o."

"At least it doesn't smell like," Catherine said.

"Armpits," Audra said.

"Neck fat," Rushel said.

"A plumber's armpit s in August."

"A politician's neck fat. As he's getting."

"Handcuffed and whipped."

"Ohh," Audra said. "That would be a great movie. 'Harder, Wendy, harder!'"

"Wendy?" Gabrielle said into the dark room.

"That would be my porn name. Wendy Whiplash."

"We should go see exactly what that movie is and not pre-judge such hard working people."

"I think I know what the movie is," Samantha said. "And I really don't think we should get any closer."

"Scary?"

"We'd be the new girls. They'd tear you to pieces."

"Oh, well, never mind, I didn't really want to," Rushel said.

"Ne neither," Audra said.

"Just curious."

"Kind of curious."

"Okay." Gabrielle couldn't help it. "Porn name?"

"It's your stage name. Has to look good on a movie on the theater sign."

Catherine pushed herself up and opened the second bottle of wine. She refilled her glass and checked all the others. Samantha's and Audra's were still nearly full. She topped off Rushel's. Gabrielle held her glass up. It was empty.

"Also you don't want to shock the folks back home," Audra said.

"So Wendy Whiplash, I'm guessing, is into bondage?" Samantha said.

Gabrielle shifted her pillow. "Bondage?"

"Um."

Gabrielle saw Rushel blush. That's definitely a first, she thought.

"You get tied up," Audra said. She was not blushing. "Everything's padded. Padded handcuffs. Sometimes they use blindfolds and this rubber ball that gets strapped over your mouth so you can't talk."

"Oh my God. People do this?"

"Not a lot of people."

Samantha was laughing. "Some people need it."

"Dominant. Submissive." Rushel was struggling to look analytical, Gabrielle thought.

"Well," Gabrielle said, "that's interesting but I'm kind of sorry I asked."

"Oh, ask us anything," Samantha said.

"If we don't know the answer, we'll," Audra said.

"Immediately invent something," Rushel said.

"Right."

Gabrielle let Catherine refill her glass again. I'm drinking this way too fast. She thought. I always do that. Catherine's drinking a lot too. At home, Catherine always had a glass of wine but barely sipped it. Interesting I never noticed that before. Of course I do have an excuse. Being drunk.

"What's so funny?" Catherine was halfway through her second glass.

"I'll have to inform you later."

"Fine." She snuggled closer and pulled the blanket over their legs.

"But I do have a question," Gabrielle said. She was starting to feel warm all over. "Was that Apache you were speaking back there?" Catherine tugged on her belt loop, her usual warning signal, she thought, or maybe just nervousness.

"Oh that," Samantha said. "That was Arabic."

"Arabic, wow."

"I just remember a little. My Apache, though, that's *really* rusty." She thought for a moment. "Let's see. My friends are crazy and I love them."

"Aww," Rushel said.

"*Asdiqayiy majnunun. Wa'ana 'ahbuhum.* That's Arabic."

"Ohh." Gabrielle finished her wine. Catherine poured her another half glass.

"In Apache, well, um." She cleared her throat. "*Shii-shiich'oonii ma'gooɬkąą shįį shii nkásht'įį daabįį,* I think."

"That's amazing," Gabrielle said.

"I'm not sure that's right. Arabic's easy compared to Apache. Or any Athabaskan language. I need to see if I can relearn it."

"That reminds me. There was something I didn't understand."

Catherine pushed aside Gabrielle's pillow and got behind her, leaning on the wall. Gabrielle settled back. Catherine curled her arm around Gabrielle's chest and let her chin rest on her shoulder.

"You're out of control."

"I'm sorry." I'll ask her later, she thought. Her stomach growled and then her throat was filled with a burning sensation. "I'm not sure I like this wine."

"Then don't drink it."

"I already drank it. Oh no." Gabrielle felt her stomach cramp. "Uh oh."

"Really?"

"Yeah." She pushed herself up and threw off the blanket.

"This is pretty strong," Audra said.

"Then don't you drink it either."

"Too late, Comrade."

Gabrielle looked at the bathroom. The memory of the bathtub at home flowed into her mind.

"This way."

Catherine took her arm and led her to the door.

"Outside, I guess," Gabrielle said.

"Are you all right?" Rushel said.

"Urp," Gabrielle managed to say. On the walkway she was startled by cold, wet air and loud voices and laughter in the darkness at the far end of the building.

"No, not that way." Catherine steered her left past the corner. "Your car. Come on."

Gabrielle stumbled off the concrete onto the gravel. They went around the building and at her car in the lightless courtyard she put both hands on the edge of the roof. She lowered her head and breathed rapidly. The cold air seemed to settle her stomach.

"Every time I drink wine too fast I swear to myself I'm never going to do it again."

"And a few days later you can't wait to get drunk." Catherine rubbed her back.

"You were drinking."

"I know."

"More than usual."

"Normally." Catherine hugged Gabrielle from behind and pulled up her shirt. Her hands were almost hot. "I get the girl to drink the wine, then I get the girl."

"Ah."

"I'm very calculating."

The back seat was as accommodating as always. The rear bumper made a barely audible sound rubbing against the motel room's back door.

Later, when they went back around the corner, a car in the parking lot began honking its horn. A female voice yelled from a car window.

"Audra! Auuudra!"

Catherine stood behind Gabrielle as the car rolled by. Newer Datsun. Gabrielle could see blonde hair.

"Oh my," Catherine said almost laughing.

"Is that?" Gabrielle said.

The motel room door opened hesitantly and Audra stepped out looking shocked. She waved at the car. "This place is crazy," she breathed.

The Datsun stopped. It was Melinda, wearing an old sweatshirt and well-worn jeans. Her flip flops crunched on the gravel.

"Ha. You *are* here," she said loudly. "I've been driving back and forth, back and forth." She giggled. "Hi!"

Audra, Rushel and Samantha behind her, said, "Hey."

Rushel whispered into her ear. Then she gave her a tiny push.

"How come it's so dark in there?" Melinda said.

"The lamp's," Audra said, "not very good."

Shoulders back, she stepped off the walkway and went to her. They looked at the motel seemed to share a joke. Then Audra began talking and Melinda listened, fascinated. Then they both got into the Datsun.

"We'll be right back," Melinda called out. "Gonna look at a place."

Rushel waved at them. "All right. Don't forget where we are."

There was no room to turn about so Melinda backed the car up all the way along the motel. She paused at the room where women were standing around and Gabrielle saw her lean out and talk to one of them. Then she made her way to the highway.

"Gee. Melinda," Catherine said.

"She just needs to get out of her rut," Rushel said. "Well, I'm tired. And it's freezing out here."

They all went back into the room. Rushel and Samantha lay on the box springs and Catherine spread the blanket out again on the mattress. In a minute, they were all under covers in the dark room.

Samantha spoke. "Do you suppose we'll ever see her again?"

"We've lost her," Catherine said.

"She'd better have good stories to tell when she gets back," Rushel said.

Gabrielle slipped off her clothes and lay on her left side and Catherine nestled behind her, the chill turning to warm under the smelly blanket. She set her glasses next to her pillow and, surprisingly comfortable, fell asleep.

The rattle of the doorknob awakened her.

It was much later. The night had changed. Deeper now, she thought. She saw the form of Audra framed in the doorway. Then the blanket next to her was gently thrown off and Rushel got up. In the near total darkness, the two had a whispered conversation. It sounded like an argument. Audra went to the bathroom and closed the door. Gabrielle heard the shower run. Rushel went back to her side of the springs, next to Samantha who had not stirred.

Rushel was waiting up for her all this time, Gabrielle thought. And she made her take a shower.

She closed her eyes, not sure what to make of this, and intended right then to analyze this fascinating situation. But Catherine pulled her closer and these thoughts dissolved. Gabrielle went back to sleep in perfect contentment.

She opened her eyes to Audra's face inches away.

"You agree, right?" Audra said, smiling.

"Oh." Gabrielle felt for her glasses. Audra handed them to her. "Agree?"

There was faint light coming through the curtains. Catherine was at the small table arranging paper cups and taking items from the basket. Her yellow windbreaker was zipped all the way up.

"This is my plan," Audra said. "So whatever I say goes. I am in charge pursuant to the plan. Which is mine."

Gabrielle noticed Catherine was giving Audra an annoyed look. So pretty normal.

"No matter how crazy," Audra said.

"Crazy?" Gabrielle sat up keeping the blanket wrapped around her. The cups on the table looked like coffee cups. Catherine carried one over to her.

"As long as it's not too crazy," Gabrielle said.

"There's no such thing as too crazy. That's just the way it is. Audra's law." Her smile became a grin.

Gabrielle sipped the coffee. Pretty good.

"Free continental breakfast in the office," Catherine said. "Apparently that guy knows his coffee."

"So this is a continental breakfast." From the voices, Samantha and Rushel were both in the bathroom.

"Technically should include a pastry. It's okay, though."

Gabrielle took a big gulp. "All right."

"All right?" Audra looked relieved.

"All right."

"Good. We have to have a meeting but first do not take a shower."

"Okay."

"Or brush your teeth. Or your hair."

"Really?"

"Trust me. Okay. Coffee. Bathroom. Then meeting."

Gabrielle leaned back against the wall with her cup. Sleeping on a mattress on the floor was as comfortable as anything. Then she wondered if Audra was going to tell her where she went last night. And Melinda. She was intensely curious but she knew she could never ask. She sighed and waited. The red t-shirt would be appropriate for today. And no socks.

When she got out of the bathroom – she had washed her face only and having Audra telling her not to take a shower made her really want to take a shower – they were standing in a circle around the rickety wooden chair placed in the middle of the room. Audra turned the chair towards her. Gabrielle felt the familiar surge of her heart and tried not to hesitate. She sat in the chair and clasped her hands.

"No need to be nervous," Rushel said.

"Let's not lie to the Goddess," Catherine said.

Gabrielle closed her eyes.

Audra stood directly in front of her. "Like some more coffee?"

"No, thank you."

"Last night," Audra said, "was a portent. A sign. The Prague Protocol is a trick for getting past the doorman. That's all. We've never put on a show before. Like I said, Cold War dinner theater. We improvised the whole thing. It was nuts. Ridiculous. And it worked. They believed it. Some, you could see, didn't want to, but even they ended up believing."

Gabrielle thought, not everyone.

"So if enough believe, this will work," Samantha said. Not quite a question.

"Yes. That was our greatest achievement as a team. And the day after tomorrow, we have to top it. By we, I mean you. We've already planted the seed. They want to believe. Proof: we had to buy Melinda a new mirror. Your job, Goddess, on Wednesday, is to set the hook. In person."

"You're mixing metaphors like crazy," Rushel said.

"I *am* a mixed metaphor."

Rushel beamed. "Good comeback, Pocket Mouse."

"Thank you. Now, Goddess, your hair."

Samantha had a nice hairbrush with a wooden handle. *Fuller* was stamped on it. They all liked to borrow it. She took it out of the leather satchel, stood behind Gabrielle, and started brushing her hair straight back and down. Professional, Gabrielle thought. It felt good. Her skin tightened down the back of her neck.

"This can be incredibly simple," Audra said. "Just a very few key signals. This, like this, is good. The main thing is, you're not trying to be attractive to boys."

"Actually, I'm not trying to be attractive to anyone."

"We noticed," Rushel said.

"I mean, I wasn't." Gabrielle looked up at them "I am now."

"This would work. Straight back off your forehead. When your hair brushes the sides of your face and frames your eyes it's considered alluring. Boys love it."

"What about bangs?" Catherine fingered the artfully cut hair above her eyes.

"Bangs also. But this all about signaling. You, we already know."

"So I can keep banging?"

"Bang your brains out."

Gabrielle laughed as Samantha brushed her hair harder.

"But what I was thinking was let's not take chances. Send a clear signal. Unmistakable."

Audra reached out and Samantha gave her the hairbrush.

"Like this."

With the brush she made a part an inch above Gabrielle's left ear and gently brushed the rest of her to the right in a big wave. It wouldn't lay flat on top and a good fraction wasn't long enough to make it all the way down to her shoulder and it curled up, out of control.

"Brush it a lot, should be okay."

"Um," Gabrielle said. Samantha gave her a small mirror with a silver handle. "I look like I just kissed a Tesla coil."

Rushel laughed.

"I guessing that has something to do with electricity," Audra said. "This is why you don't wash your hair. You need it to stick. Keep brushing and it should do what you want."

"And what is it she wants, again?" Catherine said.

"You want to look extreme. And not superficially. Not a t-shirt with the f-word on it. That's just wearing something extreme. You want to be seen as actually being extreme. Dangerous."

"She *is* dangerous. In a way," Samantha said.

"You don't smoke, do you?"

"God no."

"You think you could fake it?"

Gabrielle sighed as Audra continues to brush her hair all to one side.

"Try sneering."

"I don't know how, I don't think."

"Like you smelled something terrible," Rushel said.

"Holly's armpits," Audra said.

Gabrielle laughed and wrinkled her nose. "Like this?"

Audra sighed. "No."

"Well I don't know then."

She heard Samantha rummaging in her satchel. She handed Audra something. Some sort of makeup, she thought.

"Hm," Catherine said.

Great, Gabrielle thought with dread. She fingered the leather necklace. The thought of wearing any kind of makeup made her uncomfortable.

Audra studied the small bottle then stepped back and studied Gabrielle. "This is tricky."

"Eyeliner." Samantha continued to search through her satchel.

"Yes." Audra unscrewed the top and pulled out the tiny brush. She put it back. "I mean, makeup in general. It's a problem. Might be construed as an attempt to look punk. They kind of like punk attitude but they consider punk chicks to be girly girls trying to look tough. One of Patricia's hobbies used to be going to punk nightclubs and starting fights. I've seen her knock out punk chicks with one punch. Huh." She set the eyeliner on the table. "The real problem, Goddess, is you're just too damn cute." She crossed her arms. "Too cute, they just want to do you. And then beat you up. Try to look tough, they take it as a challenge. Then beat you up. But *extreme*. How to do it." Thinking, she pointed at her. "You're smart. You're interesting. They know for a fact you don't take shit from anyone, just ask Patricia. You're going your own way in life. Dissatisfied with who you are, it looks like you're going to make a move. They have reached out to you in their own perverted way but that's very recent. Now you suddenly appear at their door. They would hesitate. You tricked Holly before and they'll never forget that. Why would they invite you in?"

Samantha leaned over Gabrielle and whispered in Audra's ear. Audra's eyes widened and her mouth fell open.

"Yes. *Genius.* It would work," she said in awe.

Catherine abruptly looked worried. "What are you doing?"

Audra grinned and whispered into Catherine's ear.

"That is insane. You can't."

Gabrielle looked at them in near panic. Samantha and Audra grinned. Rushel shook her head.

"What?" Gabrielle said. "What?"

"I'm not gonna lie to you, Miss. There's gonna be pain."

It was an interesting device. Simple and compact. Constructed of anodized aluminum and stainless steel. A gun-like configuration. An adjusting knob, a spring. A trigger. An efficient design which she could appreciate as an engineer. No unnecessary components. The device held in front of her had one function: puncture skin.

The man displayed it proudly and considerately turned it from side to side in the grainy light of a bare bulb.

Gabrielle thought, he wants me fully grasp what is going to happen. He wants me to fully grasp in full consciousness my impending doom. She forced herself to breathe normally and remain expressionless.

The man in his hulking black and red plaid coat smelled of cigarettes and had too much hair. Head, ears, neck, arms, hands. Black curly hair. And a thick mustache and unshaved cheeks. But he moved with a measured intelligence and actually had a nice smile and a slow gravelly voice.

"Now, in the normal course of events," he said, "we use this for earlobes. It will work on other areas but because of its bulky nature it is not ideal. There is another instrument for that which I do not possess at this time. Gives one a bit more control. On this part of the body, your actual face, control is to be desired. If you really must have a nose piercing we'll have to be very careful."

"A ring," Audra said. "She wants a nose ring."

Gabrielle closed her eyes and leaned back in the old barber chair. Her hands were cold and she could not get them warm.

"Yesss," he said. "We are getting more demand for that."

"Right here." Audra put the tip of her index finger on the edge of her right nostril. "I mean left." She switched sides. "Left side."

"Left."

"Far back. You know, discreet."

"All right."

"And not a stud. Has to be a ring."

The man gave Audra a sideways look and said to Gabrielle, "Miss, you cool with all this?"

Miss. I like Miss, Gabrielle thought.

"Yes, sir."

"Oh, I ain't no sir. Just call me Clarence."

"All right. Thank you, Clarence. Yes, I want a nose ring, small and discreet, right." She took a tiny mirror from the bare plywood counter. "May I? Right here." She pointed at the edge of her left nostril with her little finger.

Clarence took a felt pen from his shirt pocket and uncapped it. It had a very fine tip. He slid his red barstool to her side.

"I can tell you. The usual spot is right here."

He hovered the tip of the pen over the edge of her nose as she watched in the mirror.

"Couldn't it be lower, closer to the rim?" And thus harder to see, she thought.

"It has to go in at a steep angle. Because of the internal structure," he said.

This made Gabrielle's stomach churn.

"Ah. I have been remiss. Let me show you." Clarence opened a drawer in his counter top organizer, below a big Harley-Davidson poster, and took out a thumb size bundle of gray cloth. "The ring we will use is in here. Sterile, as long as it is unopened. I have my own autoclave. Leaned to do this overseas." He ripped the tape holding the bundle together and set it on the plywood. "Just a moment." He got up and went to the back room.

Audra crossed her arms. "This guy's a pro. We got lucky," she whispered.

"Not luck," Samantha said. "Just clean living and good intentions."

Gabrielle forced herself to keep a straight face.

Clarence came back wearing latex gloves. They all but glowed at the end of his dark sleeves.

"Aw right. Let me show you now."

He unrolled the small bundle and revealed several tiny objects made of wire. One was a corkscrew, partially unwound. There was a simple open circle, D-shape. And there was a shiny pushpin with a wide head and very sharp point.

"The procedure is quite simple, Miss. We first determine the exact target location. How about right here?" He held the pen over her nostril. "It has to be about the angle I'm holding this."

Gabrielle looked in the mirror.

"About three millimeters back and down, please."

"Sure. Right here?" the pen did not waver.

"I'm going to say yes for now."

"Aw right." He gently touched the spot with the pen and left a mark that was barely visible.

Rushel let out her breath. Audra nodded.

"We load the stud into the piercer which I assure you has been thoroughly sterilized inside and out. The spring is pulled back. We swab the spot with alcohol and position the instrument. When the trigger is pulled the stud is pushed through the skin. It is just long enough to make it through and that's all. Nothing else will touched." Clarence swallowed.

Gabrielle breathed sharply. "Okay."

"Usually that's it. You leave the stud in place for up to three months while the skin heals. If it falls out, and it can, the skin will close up within twenty-four hours and it have to be repierced. But you want a ring only. So we will be immediately removing the stud and inserting one of these."

With tweezers he held up the D shaped wire.

"What do you think of that? That's titanium."

"Titanium? Really?" Gabrielle saw Rushel and Samantha exchange a smile.

"It's an interesting material, isn't it?" Clarence's eyes twinkled over his mustache.

"There's no clip. I thought there would be a spring of some kind. What holds it in?"

"No spring. It just hangs there. Titanium is guaranteed not to irritate the skin. That or solid gold. Anything else and there would be a problem with healing."

"Well that's good engineering. I like it."

"Simple's always best." Clarence sat back on the stool. "Just noticed you don't have your ears pierced. Unusual."

"I'm not what you'd call a girly girl."

"I hear ya. If you want we could set up a package deal."

"Just the nose today, I think."

"Aw right. Is this your final decision?"

"Yes. Right on that spot, please."

"Very well, Miss."

Clarence pulled the striker of the gun back. It clicked into the firing position. With tweezers he picked up the tiny stud and place the head into the socket, the sharp pin facing out. Gabrielle was relieved to see that Clarence's hand did not shake at all.

He stood up from the stool, cradling the gun in both hands, and shook back his heavy coat to loosen the sleeves. He took the top off a small glass bottle. It made a scraping sound. The smell of rubbing alcohol filled the dusty garage and Gabrielle's heart began to pound. Clarence carefully wiped the spot with a cotton ball. Cold, wet. He turned the knurled knob on the gun.

The skin of the 'working space', as Gabrielle thought of it, tightened. The forked receiver end pulled up within five millimeters of the open port of the barrel. Where the pin will come out, she thought. The forked part goes in my nose. The pin when released will go all the way through the side of my nostril ripping into the epidermis and cartilage and the mucus membrane full of blood vessels and nerve fibers. The steel point will be inside my nose. I could stick my finger into my nose and feel the point.

"You all right, Miss?"

"Sure. Go ahead."

She heard someone make an "Urp." Rushel, not a super strong stomach, and as she thought this the man put the piercing gun up to her face and smoothly inserted the forked receiver into her left nostril, aimed for three heartbeats and pulled the trigger.

She took a breath. He didn't lie, she thought, and I forgot to close my eyes.

"Bad?"

"Eh. It feels like a needle sticking in my nose."

"Aw right then, Here we go."

"What?"

Clarence pulled the stud out with the tweezers and in the same swift movement slipped the titanium ring into the hole.

Gabrielle wrinkled her nose and sniffed. She could feel it in there, definitely a foreign object in her nose. The sting faded quickly.

"Aren't a lot of pain receptors. Longs you don't fiddle with it."

"Huh. How do I look?"

"It's cute," Rushel said. "I didn't see any blood."

"It works on you," Samantha said.

"You look like one of them," Audra said.

Gabrielle nodded. "Okay. Let's get going."

"Goddess," they all said.

Clarence stared in confusion.

Gabrielle pushed herself up. "Thank you, sir."

Samantha paid him, fifteen ninety-five plus tip, so twenty even, and they quickly left the old garage.

Fresh misty air made it sting. Bending over made it sting. Breathing made it sting. Gabrielle sighed and fingered her necklace. As they were loading the car in the constant roar of morning traffic and asked Catherine, "So what do you think?"

Catherine stepped back and looked at her squarely. She leaned to the left then right. "I like that it's not shiny. That gray metal makes me think of computer stuff. Well, I will say this. It kind of makes you look like a different person. It's sexy."

"So I wasn't sexy before?"

"Not this way."

"What's this way?"

"It," she said, "it gives you the air of someone who hangs out at some seedy bar in Long Beach and the second I turn my back you'll try to cop a feel. Or grab my tits."

"Wow."

"The old Gabrielle would never do that. I would grab *her* tits."

Gabrielle considered this. She wasn't sure she liked it.

"So that means you don't want to grab my tits anymore."

"No, I want to grab them."

"It doesn't sound like it."

"I do. If we weren't standing next to the Pacific Coast Highway I would be all over you. Don't want to give those poor truck drivers a heart attack."

"You sure?"

"Gabrielle, right now I want to undress you with my tongue."

"Oh."

Gabrielle felt and hot flush run down her back. Samantha came out of the room with her satchel.

"We can't."

"Yeah."

"But I'm going to."

"It's."

Samantha opened the car and tossed her bag into the rear compartment.

She put her hands on her hips.

"This is just not the best place," she said.

"I agree with your brutally honest assessment," Catherine said.

"Shall we depart, then?"

"The Goddess will advise us."

"Thank you. I'm as hungry as I've ever been. Wasn't there a Denny's?"

"Yes."

"Let's go to Denny's for breakfast."

"Goddess."

"Hey you two," Catherine called. "We're going to Denny's."

Rushel and Audra cheered from the room.

"And Samantha, I would like you to drive."

Samantha nodded. "Goddess."

"Shifting gears is going to make my nose hurt."

Samantha looked into the distance. "Bathroom."

When she had gone, Catherine said, "This was a pretty good trip. We found a couple interesting restaurants, a neat bookstore, gave away hundreds of dollars in gold, and if I'm not mistaken everyone got laid."

"Oh, well, good," Gabrielle said. Then thought, Audra? Wow. And then thought, Rushel? Samantha?

"Holy cow."

"Yep."

"But wow."

Catherine shrugged. "People do it." Then she said, "Not them."

"Oh good."

"The old Rushel, yes. Not the new one."

"I was going to say."

Catherine, telepathic as always, patted her shoulder.

"Catherine, I'm so glad you're here."

"Sometimes it's better just to live for the moment."

"I'm not good at that."

"Pretty soon that'll be you."

"Me?" Gabrielle swallowed. "Oh I don't know."

Catherine's cheerful laughter rang across the parking lot. They all piled into the Volkswagen and Samantha drove them to Denny's which was filled the the aroma of bacon and coffee, conversation and chattering plates. The waitress curled her lip when she saw Gabrielle and Audra approved of this reaction. They had pancakes and scrambled eggs. They had to request extra maple syrup for the chrome wire syrup turntable. Gabrielle ate until she thought she was going to explode. When the bill came Audra grabbed it, to the surprise of Samantha, and left a twenty percent tip, four-fifty.

After a bathroom break they stopped at a Chevron and Gabrielle showed Samantha how the front hood opened. She winced at the gas price, seventy-two cents a gallon, but Samantha just pulled out a credit card.

Gabrielle felt a twinge of unease. They have credit cards? Where do the bills go? She forced herself not to speculate.

The attendant in a blue short sleeved shirt had an ear ring and a wispy beard. He ran the card through the imprinter and when Samantha signed it she gave him a wink.

Catherine sat in the same spot, left end of the back seat so as to be, as she said, on the safe inland pavement side of the car going south and as far as possible from looking straight down into the shrieking multi-thousand foot death plunge onto icy raging surf and razor sharp rocks covered with sharks and electric eels and sea scorpions.

Everyone thought this sounded reasonable.

Audra wanted the back window seat, for the express purpose of looking over the cliff, and Gabrielle sat in the middle.

And I have pretty good visibility, she thought. The gas gauge was pegged above F. She really liked that. Samantha was grinning at her in the mirror and she put the stick in first *very* precisely. They pulled out of the busy station and stopped in the left turn lane.

Rushel turned around and scanned everyone.

"It is important to realize what is now happening," she said as her hair tumbled.

The green arrow came on and Samantha smoothly accelerated onto the south bound highway. Gabrielle felt Catherine wiggle her right thigh and let herself nestle closer.

"For as long as we live this moment will never come again," Rushel said. "We will never be together like this again. Find a place in your memory, a protected place, and keep this moment safe there. In the years to come it will be a source of strength and a key component of your mental immune system as you live in the midst of a hostile world."

She turned back. They rolled out of the realm of concrete and power lines and entered a grove of towering trees shrouded in fog. Samantha turned on the heat and warm dusty air flowed into the car. Rushel turned around again. She was smiling.

"And now Audra has something to say."

Audra just stared. They bumped onto the old pavement.

"I do?"

Samantha laughed.

"Yes, Pocket Mouse. Tell us all about it."

Now Catherine laughed.

Audra cleared her throat. Gabrielle could see she was trying not to laugh also.

"Well, Melinda and I are going to be in a movie."

They all ooh'd and ahh'd and Samantha asked, "Super eight?"

"No." Audra rolled her eyes. "Sixteen millimeter."

"Nice. Sound?"

"I'm not sure."

"Was there a microphone on a pole?" Rushel said. "A tape recorder?"

"I guess not."

"That's okay," Samantha said. "They can add sound in later."

"*Oh*," Rushel said and began breathing heavily. "Oh, *God*, oh, God, oh baby, yeah like that, oh, *oh*, oh do me, oh yeah, *do* me. Cut. Print."

Audra shrugged. "Pretty much."

"Will we be able to see your face?" Catherine said.

"Huh. Let me think. Probably. Melinda for sure, they really liked her. But you know Yolanda is the real star."

"Of course," Samantha said laughing. "Melinda too, huh?"

"Now, Pocket Mouse," Rushel said. "With regards to Yolanda. Are there, if you don't mind my asking, any possibly identifying features we should know about?"

"Oh my God."

Catherine said, "So, Goddess, I know your hometown doesn't have porn shops but have you ever seen an adult movie?"

"No. I wouldn't even know where to go."

"Hollywood."

"Don't think I've ever been there."

"Eh," Samantha said. "I used to live there. It's all right."

Samantha's been everywhere, Gabrielle thought.

"Okay, now this movie," Rushel said. "Did they have a script? Or were they just making it up as they went?"

"Yes, there was a script. They only let me glance at it but one of the girls told me the basic story. And I saw the title."

"A title? Those guys are pros."

"The title is, *Apocalypse Blonde*."

"Oh."

"Uh huh. *Blonde is the way the world ends.* That's the sub whatever thing. See, there's this beautiful blonde woman and she dies mysteriously and her ghost returns and seduces women. Like everywhere. Cars, offices, out on the sidewalk in the fog. And it causes riots and destroys the world."

"Oh my goodness," Rushel said. "It's all female? Really?"

"So, there was no porn star," Samantha said, "with a really big you know? They always have those."

"That's a negatory. They paid me fifty bucks!"

Rushel stared at her wide-eyed.

"That tears it. Samantha, turn the car around."

"No can do."

She turned to Gabrielle. "Please Goddess, please, please, please."

"Of course not."

This made Catherine laugh but she wasn't sure why.

"We could make our own movie," Audra said.

"Oh for Pete's sake," Catherine said, still laughing.

"I mean, we do have the talent."

"Why thank you," Rushel said.

"You're welcome."

"Samantha," Gabrielle said, "Keep driving."

They laughed about the movie for miles. They went over the towering bridge, slowing for numerous people with cameras, diligent tourists undeterred by overcast skies. The sea stretched gray and icy blue, the horizon was dark and distant. The road climbed and they were once again amidst the cloud-topped hills, fence posts, and orange and pink flowers bright in the soft gloom. Rain pattered on the roof.

Gabrielle touched her necklace and then carefully her piercing. It had stopped hurting. All the anxiety she had been feeling about the week ahead had faded away. Spring, she thought, this is my spring. Gently rocking between Catherine and Audra she found a protected spot for the memory.

When they passed the gas station they all waved at Stanley and Samantha honked the horn. Stanley had moved his folding chair just inside the doorway of the booth. He waved back as if he had been expecting them.

They passed the cove where Audra said there might be another note, in a cave of some sort. No one wanted to stop.

On tight curves taking them right to the edge of the cliff, where the drop off was so precarious there was no room for a guardrail or even a warning sign, they all raised their hands and went "Whoaaaa!" as if on a roller coaster. Catherine covered her eyes. Audra tried to lean out.

"Shit, it is straight down."

"No, be quiet."

"I mean straight onto the rocks. You can see these huge waves just crashing."

"Shut up."

The highway flattened out and ran right to the edge of the shore. The ocean churned at high tide. Waves slamming the black tumbled boulders and black seawater sprayed across the pavement. Samantha laughed and drove straight through it.

They passed the gigantic old hilltop mansion and waved at the people in the visitor's parking lot. The area looked familiar to Gabrielle now.

I know the central coast now, she thought. The Big Sur coast. I know it quite well.

It was past three when they finally turned off Highway One. No one wanted lunch. Just head in.

"Everyone is homesick after one night," Rushel said.

"It makes sense because our home is so cool," Audra said.

"This whole trip has only reinforced to me how wonderful our home is," Gabrielle said. "As nice as all those places we saw were I wouldn't trade it for anything. Not even that whatchamacallit castle."

They all agreed and Samantha drove a bit faster past the estuary of green marsh grass sprinkled with elegant white egrets.

"We should take the tour up there some day. So we can gloat," Rushel said as they made the turn beachward.

"So we can laugh at them," Audra said.

"And we will laugh in a markedly condescending tone tinged with ironic pity."

"As befits the Von Stilts sisters. We are such brats," Audra said.

"As long as dear Daddy doesn't cut us off."

"What a chilling thought. Why would you even mention it?"

"I am in a dark and pensive mood, my dear sister," Rushel said.

"You are?"

"I miss my sweet jasmine flower."

"Aww." Samantha patted her knee. "We're almost there, see? Our eucalyptus trees."

"Yes," Rushel said, "And as always I can't help but wonder who in their right mind would plant millions of eucalyptus trees right here."

"Someone with a dream," Catherine said.

They bounced over the sand trap, drove through the open gate and stopped. Samantha got out and closed the gate and made sure it was latched. When she got back in she said, "I just felt like doing that."

"We trust your judgment," Catherine said,

As they rounded the final dune covered with chemise and sage, Catherine drew her breath in sharply. The sun was a golden shard just breaking under the vast seaward bank of coal black clouds. The sea glittered and the cirrus overhead turned red and orange, wispy flames sailing swiftly eastward.

For a moment in the bright light Gabrielle thought she could detect the curvature of the Earth. As she looked north where a sliver of green glass sky opened in the black clouds she thought I was just up there where the ancient mountains met the sea and stretched into infinity. When I woke up this morning I was up there and now I'm here. As she got out of the back seat she caught Catherine giving her a questioning look.

"It's all so incredible," Gabrielle said. "I don't think I'll ever understand it."

"Why would you want to?"

"We must never leave here," Audra said as she held the door. "This is where we belong."

"Of course. We will live here forever." Catherine unzipped her windbreaker.

"Forever," Audra said.

"Pantotiná," Rushel said. "It means everlasting."

"Shangri-La everlasting," Catherine said.

Gabrielle heard a rusty creak and Gislaine was standing at the screen door in a wide wash of golden sunlight raking the sandy boards. Gislaine's dark curly hair was unbound. Rushel walked up the steps.

"Sylvan historian."

"All-seeing prophet."

They met on the middle step and embraced and did not move as the car was unloaded around them. Audra, in the last of the light, closed the front door as quietly as she could.

The Winter Meeting

Low sharp sun in my eyes.

The car had a tendency to go diagonal on the ice. I could live with it but it was giving me vertigo and there was a stupid blinking light next to the fuel gauge, *Loss of traction*, it said.

Yeah no kidding.

At least it had stopped snowing. The wipers were heated so the windshield was sort of clear. The narrow mountain highway passed slowly, tediously, blank white snow banks on both sides higher than my head. The line of cars slowed, sped up, slowed. Snowboards and skis on rooftop racks. Pickups with lift kits, Subaru's, and lots of Audi's. Audi's everywhere. So different from southern California. There, all Mercedes. Here in the Sierra foothills an actual cultural break was unfolding before my eyes.

"This curve coming up is bad," PG said, strapped into her seat for once. I had insisted.

"They're all bad."

"Don't use the brakes.

"Easier said than done."

The grocery bags shifted in the back seat. We had stopped at the Safeway in Martell and PG had dropped four hundred on supplies.

"This will be a long one," she had said. Nothing else.

We were going to her secret hideout in the mountains, an old ski resort on its last legs. Just the sort of place no one would ever think someone like PG would go. Tahoe, Aspen, Vail, sure. But Rose Desirae? As I was waiting in the check-out line in the supermarket, I had slipped out my phone. It was described in several articles as 'scruffy', 'weather-beaten'. And in the comments: filthy, hopeless, junk pile. Permanent closure seemed inevitable but Rose Desirae kept going maybe just to spite them.

So that had to mean the people in the cars in front and behind were– had to be–the loyal Rose Desirae skiers. People who did not care about some article writer's opinion or internet commenters. They liked the place and to hell with everyone else. It was for all of them their secret hideout.

As a resident of Grimpen, Oklahoma, I admit I felt a sense of kinship.

The curve coming up was a big ice coated swooping dip and then climb. I could feel my bladder control failing.

"Don't use the brakes. Downshift. Never touch the brakes," PG said. "Never."

"Well thank you good advice okay."

Downshift to third into the curve, no change in speed, wait, it slowed a tiny bit and I could feel the rear starting to swing out, my guts twisted, and I knew what happens after that.

Loss of traction, spin out, uncontrolled urination, bounce off snow bank, slam into the Audi tailgating, get t-boned by the Audi oncoming. All that lovely German sheet metal trashed. Highway Patrol. Tow trucks. Insurance info. Screaming people. End of trip.

"Just," PG said into the car's warm interior.

"Yes, yes, okay."

Foot off brake pedal by huge force of will, I pulled the shift lever into second. The thing didn't want to do it. I could feel the trans do a gear-stripping thumping switch. The rattling engine revved up and the car lurched forward, grocery bags upended against my seat. The suspension bottomed out. And the car kept going straight. Perfectly straight. Huh. I drove out of the curve. My lower abdomen did not relax.

"See?"

"I never doubted you. I doubted me."

She laughed. I forced myself to keep quiet. She had let her hair grow out and without the bangs was almost unrecognizable. Same intense eyes.

We passed a pair of spun out SUV's. Dented fenders. Skis and coolers and beer cans lay spread out across the westbound lane. No one appeared injured. Several parka clad people stood on the edge of the snow bank, wallets in hand. Snowflakes blew across the highway in waves.

"This is pretty wild for a kid from Oklahoma."

"Oh, this isn't bad at all. Nice and clear."

"Yeah?"

"You can actually see the car in front of you. Rose Desirae can be a little extreme."

"You like to ski?"

"No. Never done it."

"Good."

"Why?"

"I was afraid I'd have to try it. Being wet and freezing does not appeal to me."

"Me neither. I just like the atmosphere of the place. You'll see."

"Oh, now I can't wait. So what will be be doing there? We have enough supplies for a week."

Our haul from that supermarket included an entire case of wine. Pinot Noir, some northern California label. She probably owned the winery and had completely forgotten. It would be in keeping with her recent behavior.

"I tell you everything that happens next. Everything. No matter how." She cut herself off and looked out her window. Self-possessed as always, her voice betrayed a certain anxiety. I thought it was completely un-PG. This was maddening.

It took an effort of will to keep from flooring it passing all the snowy cars. I almost did it. Poking along at twenty-five miles an hour, brake lights constantly blinking, was seriously frustrating. Through a stand of towering trees, the entrance approached. There was a final turn off into a reverse bank apparently designed to make big vehicles spin out. The main road, if you could call it that, continued east into the snow, unplowed. I made a testicle-compressing, descending right turn as slowly as I could. The stupid traction light kept blinking at me. We went down in a flurry of ice headlight crystals. And she said.

"Hey, it's still there."

"What is?"

"The stop sign. See? Usually someone slides into it. They have a bunch of new signs on poles ready to go. Must be a slow season."

I steered down the long central snow encrusted road past empty cabins.

The Resort at Rose Desirae, as the sign called it, was a collection of two condominium buildings, a central check-in station and a rather large three story hotel-like structure. A few windows there glowed warmly. The rest were dark, ice rimmed.

Several vehicles sat permanently encased in snow near the check-in pull out. The snow marker poles, with reflective tape for the plow drivers, were all bent to the ground.

Those two condo buildings, now that I looked, were lightless and cold. Blank windows devoid of blinds or curtains stared into the winter sky. They don't have power, I thought, they are out of business. Damn.

"This does not look all that great."

"Just pull in there."

"All right."

Snow began to fall. Huge wet flakes plopped onto the windshield, the wipers immediately froze up. The light was fading, the sky was a luminous icy violet. Other cars sped off down the road, out of sight. Private homes? My destination was the main check-in, the door framed by massive columns of ice at least two feet across. There was a parking spot against a huge snow wall. The car surged over the compacted ice left by the previous vehicle. I killed the engine. The wipers stopped in mid wipe encrusted with ice. I really had to pee.

"They have restrooms?" I unclipped the seatbelt and slid out. There was snow pouring in the half open window. The car, heater blasting, echoed like a phone booth. But the snow. It shushed. I hate being shushed.

Snow, shushing snow, was everywhere. Down my shirt, in my socks. I covered the back of my neck but it got down my shirt. A snowflake went up my nose and I sneezed.

She shrugged. "They did last time. Go in and left by the drinking fountain."

"Right, thanks, I'll be right back."

"Take your time. I'll get everything. I just glad the power's on."

"The," I said. "Does it not."

"They have problems, electricity-wise. It's kind of interesting."

"Okay. Okay, I'll be back."

"Go ahead, I'll get everything."

The low-ceiling lobby of Check-in had a rock fireplace with a nice fire going. Propane. Two sofas before it cradled unconscious skiers in bright ski coats. Tight fitting and uncomfortable looking. But they slept on with skis and poles stacked around them. The floor was also rock, uneven and wet, and I stumbled. Sighing, I pushed open the door to the men's room.

There was one stall and two sinks. As I opened the stall door the toilet flushed itself. I stepped in and it flushed again. Both sinks, apparently equipped with motion sensors, started running. They stopped and started.

"I guess it just does that," I said to the flushing toilet.

PG, cheeks glowing, was waiting for me.

"We can go on up. They'll bring everything.

"Hey, that's nice."

"One of the perks of being a semi-celebrity."

"Wouldn't say semi."

She rolled her eyes.

"We go right through here."

She pulled on a sheet of plywood attached to the wall beside the drinking fountain. There was ice built up around the edges.

"That?"

"That's the door."

"Sure they're not just fixing the wall?"

"No, the wall collapsed a few years ago. This is to keep the cold out. Works sometimes. You just pull on it."

"Really. It –"

The four by eight sheet hinged out. There was a string of light bulbs leading down a hallway.

"The wall looks funny."

"Ice."

"That's ice up there?"

"Whole thing is ice. An ice tunnel. It's the only way to get across. Our building is over there. We're walking on ice, too."

"And this is safe?"

"Not at all."

We stepped in. The tunnel made a sharp turn thirty steps in.

"They get confused sometimes," she said.

"You mean they can't find the other building when they're making the tunnel?"

"You need a good sense of direction."

"What happens if they miss?"

"The Drop Off. Part of the Crystal Canyon fault."

"And I'll bet it really drops off."

"Only fifteen hundred feet. But that's never happened."

"Let's just."

"Keep going."

Just around the bend, PG stopped. She was looking at the ice floor.

"I'm not too late," she said.

There were yellow marks on the ice. A series of circles, lines, and curves all, as far as I could tell, created by peeing.

"That's some serious control," I said. My breath hung in front of my face.

"Tradition."

We kept walking. The tunnel climbed and the ceiling lowered. I defected swinging light bulbs.

"Where we're walking was the old parking garage before the collapse. They just let it fill in with snow."

Another sheep of plywood confronted us after a final turn. We walked up ice steps. PG pushed the wet, splintery door and we entered what looked like a basement storeroom. Piles of red safety cones, an empty 55 gallon drum, snow shovels in neat rows leaning against tall lockers. Plastic milk crates held disassembled door knobs and towel bars and toilet paper holders. Coffee cups and coffee maker parts and dusty light bulbs.

"In the summer this is all just open to the sky."

"This place is," I said, "unusual."

"People in Rose Desirae have their own way of doing things."

I followed her to concrete steps.

"For example. The sign in the tunnel was good news."

"Someone peed good news?"

"I was kind of depressed thinking I missed the car-b-que but the sign showed me I was twenty-four hours off. I must have made a mistake with the Julian date. Don't know how I did that. So it's today. We're just in time. This is working out perfectly."

"A big bar-b-que in a snowstorm?"

"Car-b-que. Every winter they set fire to a car as a way of thanking the gods for the great skiing. The date varies depending on the orbit of Venus. Why are you looking at me like that?"

"They burn a car."

"It's donated. Tax deductible."

At our suite, PG tipped the two guys a hundred each for bringing up her luggage, all the groceries, the case of wine, and my backpack.

"Whoa, thanks PG!" Long blond hair, perpetual grin.

"Well, you both earned it. I just got here. Do you know where it's going to be?"

"Yuh," said the other. Hulky. Black beard. "At the grave."

"Yeah. Classic."

They both nodded.

"Okay. I gotta get ready. See you both there."

I saw them five-fiving in the hall.

The suite was straight out of the eighties. Carpeting in warm Navaho mosaic. The coffee table was a chopped off canoe with a glass top. Full kitchen. I got the downstairs bedroom. PG got the loft. White shag carpeting up there.

The unit had no tv, no phone.

I got out my notebook.

PG turned up the thermostat by the fireplace. The propane ignited with a wump. She sat on the sofa, perfectly self possessed, and watched me. There seemed at that moment nothing extraneous about her, no loose ends. Lost in thought she looked out the dark window, a quiet child watching the snow fall. I hoped she wasn't planning on going outside in those boating shoes but I knew better.

There was a bunch of stuff that needed to go in the fridge. We sat there. I continued jotting down notes. After a few minutes I had to use the bathroom and when I came back out she was gone.

Coat and boots back on, I made sure I had my key and opened the door. A naked woman stood there in the hallway.

"Oh gosh sorry," she said. "I have the wrong room."

"Well, that depends, doesn't it."

She had black hair that just tickled her shoulders. Her blue eyes wandered back and forth. I kept my eyes on her face, mostly.

"It does?"

"She's not here. And I have to go. I could tell her you came by."

"You could?"

"Sure. What's your name?"

"Oh *my* name. Felicity. She's not here? Dang. I wanted to."

"Yes, ma'am."

"You know."

"Oh, yes ma'am. I know."

I stepped into the hall and made sure the door was locked.

"All right, Felicity, nice meeting you."

I walked quickly away from the naked woman and with a effort did not look back. This is work, I told myself.

"Okay," she said. "Dang."

Stairs at the end of the hall led down to a brick patio partially cleared of snow. A trio of snowboarders huddled there. There wore coats that hung straight to their knees and were all drinking from large paper cups. I smelled red wine. The wind drove tiny particles of ice into my face.

"PG come by here?"

"Just missed her." Middle-aged guy with a gray stubble beard.

"Trying to catch up with her."

Younger guy pointed. His white coat was printed with cartoon bunnies.

"She went that way. Go down the steel steps and across the drive and you'll see this massive snow bank and just go through the second tunnel. That's Housekeeping. Think she went in there."

"She had a whole case of wine," the third one said, a young woman. Tufts of blonde hair escaped her knit cap.

I thanked them and went that way.

There was a light over the stairs at least. The staircase was a slope of solidified snow with an occasional foothold. I went down sideways never letting go of the railing and my hands were frozen and numb in seconds.

Away from the main building it was so dark I could not see where to put my feet. The jagged ice kept turning my ankles. An Audi rolled by and in its headlights I saw the snow bank. I picked my way to the second opening barely visible beneath the overhanging snow. Light was spilling from an door jammed open by ice.

I slipped through the door. I smelled hot coffee, doughnuts, wet socks. I sniffed.

"Hey." It was a woman behind a desk. Black knit cap, piercing eyes.

"Oh, hey, sorry to bother you." The walls were covered with schedules and labor department posters.

"That's okay." She sipped from a paper cup.

"I was looking for PG."

"You're that guy, huh? Go through that door, go left then left again until you see the carpeting change from the last flood. That's Building Maintenance."

"All right, thank you."

"Yowzer."

"Huh?"

"What do you mean huh?" She sipped again.

Building Maintenance was a bright room with six steel desks all clean and unused except one. A guy in a black jacket was reading his phone as he leaned back in a big chair. The nameplate on the desk said Stan D. There was a cup brimming with wine in the center of his desk calendar. He scratched his beard.

"Lodging," he said without looking up. "Keep going that way until you see the green sign. Can't miss it."

"It's not another tunnel is it?"

"Oh yeah. Don't worry. Power hasn't gone out in weeks."

In the warm cookie baking Lodging office, a young woman stood over a large printer which was spitting out sheets of paper at a rapid pace. She gave it a kick.

"Oh my God."

"Press stop." Sounded like a sewing machine wired into a dishwasher.

"Where the heck is stop?"

"Push all the buttons."

She did so with both hands. The machine clattered and fell silent. She wiped her eyes.

"Wow. Thanks."

"You need a new printer."

"Yeah *that's* not gonna happen."

A heavy oak door cracked open. I caught a glimpse of a well-appointed private office. A female voice rang out.

"Rocky! I need the reports!"

"Well I'm sorry but this stupid printer! It's stupid!"

A head poked out. It was Felicity.

"Use the printer in Housekeeping."

"She doesn't like me."

"Not everyone has to like you."

"She looks at me."

"Boiler room has a printer."

"Oh right. Stupid printer."

"It's so stupid," Felicity said and slammed her door.

Rocky got her phone and went to a rusty door. She covered her head with a gray shawl.

"She probably there," she said.

I rushed over.

"Thank you so much."

She went back to her desk and lifted a hat. Underneath was a paper cup of wine. She brought to her lips.

"Mm. You get yours?"

"No."

"Well don't worry. Come on."

She led me into a stairwell, steel steps, no hand rail. It smelled of cookies baking and something electric burning out. We went up at least six flights, seven steps each. That meant three floors, I thought. Finally on the final landing there was a door propped open with a rock. From inside the sound of electric motors and fans. And laughter.

Rocky pushed the door open. I stood still and listened and realized something.

Never heard PG laugh like that before. An actual belly laugh.

She was sitting on a folding chair beside a man in a heavy nylon coat who was sitting on the floor. He was leaning back on a boiler box as big as a car. There was a control panel with dials and lights. The fan in the boiler filled the room with noise.

"Hey Mike, gonna use your printer," Rocky said.

"Rock, for you, anything."

Mike was roughly seventy and had a thin gray beard.

"You're gonna get in trouble talkin' like that."

Rocky pointed her phone and a tiny laser printer began purring on a side table.

"Stick around and watch," Mike said. He kicked an air vent and it swung open. Freezing air and a flurry of snow blew in. Darkness had settled over the world outside.

"Gotta get back." Rocky cradled her reports.

"It's going to be incredible this year. Guess whose car it is?"

"I already know that. It's Monica's."

"Monica, really?" PG said, then to me, "Head chef. But wasn't her car?"

"Yep," Mike said.

"She worked so hard for it."

"Hit a bear."

"Oh no! Wow, poor bear."

"It was okay. She told me the bear gave her the finger and ran off. Her nice electric car was totaled. And the worst part."

"She was so proud of it."

"Her insurance would not cover it."

"Shit."

"No coverage for colliding with a wild animal."

"Sucks," Rocky said.

PG handed me a big paper cup of wine. She clinked her cup. I took a big gulp. "So the car-b-que is a vehicle," she said, "that has a battery bank. A huge bank of lithium ion batteries."

"Do not dispose in fire, right?" Rocky said.

"Yeah." PG sipped. "Wonder if this has ever been done before. They know not to stand too close?"

"Gonna be wild," Mike said.

"All right, I'll watch." Rocky tucked the printouts under her sweater.

"How will they ignite it?" PG said.

"Thermite charge right on top of – whoa!"

In the vast night outside a bright blue spark burst into life. A geyser of flames shot straight up. I could make out the outlines of a car, maybe a hundred yards off. A heavy thump reached us.

"Hurts my eyes," Rocky said.

Something spun up and away, burning furiously. The geyser of flames turned inward and became a steady red and yellow. I heard deep popping.

"That was the driver's seat," Mike said. "Now it's melting through. Here we go!"

The vehicle became a ball of fire too bright to look at and I saw a large fragment get tossed straight up like a piece of paper. Silhouetted skiers ran away as fast as they could through the deep snow. That was the roof, I thought, they've really underestimated.

The explosion was as loud as a shotgun. Rocky screamed. Even Mike looked worried. PG watched over the rim of her cup, happy and satisfied.

Incandescent fragment of white hot burning lithium ion batteries erupted in an expanding, symmetrical blossom. One of the fragments smashed into the stand of trees beside the parking lot. The upper branches immediately burst into flames.

"Oh shit." It was Mike.

Three flaming meteors as bright as the sun arced in our direction. Two went out but the third made a brilliant, graceful dive right into the snow field above the tunnel. It burned itself into the snow and smoke gushed from the crater.

"Ah," Mike said.

"Dang." Rocky had her phone out. "Forgot to press record."

"Look!"

A building was burning at the far edge of the resort. A fireball had passed through a gap in the trees.

"Hell," Rocky said. "That's not Employee Housing, is it?"

"No, looks beyond that. Oh I know!"

The lights flickered and went out. The boiler fan and pump shut down with a series of hiccups that sounded like a cat puking and the room fell silent.

"Powerhouse," PG said in the total darkness.

"So," I said. "This place runs on generators?"

"Yeah, we're way off the grid," Mike said. He clapped. "Free men, drink this! Greatest car-b-que of all time!"

"Rocky, may I borrow your phone?" PG held her hand out.

An hour later in our suite, PG poured herself a cup of wine by candlelight.

"Backup generator will be here within twelve hours. Twenty-four tops. If the highway stays open."

"Fireplace works," I said. "That's a relief."

"The propane system has its own power. One of the few things they got right."

"Well PG, this place is unique."

PG turned to the stove and slowly stirred a small pot. Soup, but I couldn't tell what kind.

"It was first settled a couple years after the Civil War. The Miwok avoided this area. They had legends about how the rocks could move. And the spirit or entity that controlled them was nothing to mess with.

"But a pioneer named Arthur Rose Desirae, founder of a cult called The Concordance, moved right in with about thirty followers."

"Cults again."

"It's a recurring theme."

"Totally California, I must say. Glad the stove works on propane."

"Yep. Tomato soup and grilled cheese sandwiches."

She laughed as my stomach growled and she started grating cheese.

I got my notebook ready. The fireplace ticked like a clock as it warmed and the wind whistled in the old windows. We set our plates on the hearth and after our simple dinner she began to speak in her soft, precise voice.

"This will be our last meeting. But if you're up for it there's something I'd like you to see in about a month. Depends on the weather. Could I contact you? It would be short notice."

"Of course."

She looked into the darkness and smiled in the blue flames of the gas fireplace.

"You never ask questions."

I smiled back even though I knew she couldn't see me.

She collected the dishes and put them in the sink. Then she sat on the hearth, warming her back.

"Do you believe what I've told you so far?"

"Yes."

"You sure? The box of gold coins. The die-off." She got up and spread a towel on the rock surface to sit on. "The backpack. Do you believe that? Miranda Street?"

"I don't understand it but I believe you."

"I don't want to leave anything out. But this last part you might find challenging."

"All right."

"Just wanted to warn you." Now she was grinning. "February and March, nineteen seventy-nine. This was the most intense period of my entire life. Emotionally. Physically."

I opened my notebook and got out my pencil, a mechanical pencil of a brand recommend by her.

"I have all the time in the world."

She relaxed and her face grew distant as she spoke into the dark room.

And long into that night and for the next seven days as the snow fell and my hand cramped from effort she told me the rest of the story, the long fourth and final chapter of the Persephone Gate.

Shangri-La παντοτινά and Beyond the Gates of L

Gabrielle smelled fresh bread and garlic.

The whole dining table was covered with a bedspread. Catherine skeptically lifted it off. There was a white porcelain bowl full of soup and serving dishes with vegetables and sandwiches.

"It *can't* be," she said.

"What can't be?" Gislaine said. "There's roast tomato soup with garlic croutons. Broccoli which I steamed and sprinkled with Parmesan and put under the broiler. And grilled cheese sandwiches," she said.

Gabrielle's mouth watered. The sandwiches had big grill marks on them and melted cheese had run onto the plates.

"I didn't think you all'd want to cook after driving all day. Pretty much just a snack. So, Goddess, what happened? You look like you tripped and fell face first into a jewelry store."

"It's an experiment."

"She was trying to get her ears pierced but Audra distracted her and the guy zapped her nose."

"So it's Audra's fault. I'm not worried then. Well, are you hungry?"

Catherine took a spoonful of the tomato soup, sniffed it, and then tasted it. "It's great."

"There's no need to look surprised."

"You can't cook."

"I cook all the time."

They both gave Gabrielle a puzzled look as she laughed.

"Sorry, long story," she said, and left the bright kitchen and went into the warm library and sat on the floor beside Audra who was moving the pointer around the computer screen with the box.

"Hello, Tess, did you miss me?" She made the little arrow move to her voice. "*Oh, Audra, I missed you so much!*"

"There's probably a second microphone," Gabrielle whispered.

"Don't worry, I remember. We should try hooking Tess up to the phone. Especially since it's free."

"I can't wait to try that. Radio Shack has everything. We need batteries for the light also."

"You and Radio Shack. Does it still hurt?"

"Only when I touch it. And I can't stop touching it."

"It always come down to touching, doesn't it."

"What?" Rushel came into the room. She turned on the two floor lamps and closed the curtains.

"Advisory. Second microphone."

"Right. We better find it. But." Rushel clasped her hands. "Don't worry about that for now. I just found out something that is so cool. Actually, it was in *Wired*. At the book store. You'll *never* guess." She bounced on her heels.

"Okay," Audra said. "What?"

Rushel giggled. She lifted the button box from the computer case.

"This device. Do you know what it's actual name is? The actual official name?"

"The pointer manipulator," Gabrielle said and grinned at Rushel. She positively bubbly, she thought.

"The selector box?" Audra said.

"Nope. This." She held it in the palm of her hand. "Is a *mouse*."

"Ohh!"

"Oh my God that's adorable," Gabrielle said.

"I know, it's so cute!"

"Dere's a little mousey!" Audra petted the bulky mouse.

"I love computers!" Rushel patted the mouse also.

Samantha and Catherine hurried into the room.

"Are you all right?" Catherine said.

"This thing," Audra said. "It moves the pointer on the screen."

"Yes?" Samantha said warily.

"It's called a *mouse*," Rushel said, still beaming.

"Oh my God that is so cute!"

"I know! It's so cute!"

"More like a gerbil, I would say," Catherine said. "Or a Guinea pig."

Audra nodded. "Fairly hefty for a little mousey mouse."

"It is cute, though." Catherine petted it with the others. "She's my widdle friend wif her widdle tail that is soo long."

Gislaine rushed in.

"Are you all drunk? That was fast."

Audra held it up. "All right. This thing."

"Do you know what it's called?" Rushel said.

"Sure. That's a mouse."

"What?" Audra gaped at her.

"Wow," Gabrielle said.

"That's a mouse."

"You know that?" Rushel said. "*Gosh.*"

"I'm sorry."

"How do you know that?"

"I just know it."

"No one just knows it."

"Well, I read it somewhere, like *Time*. And I remember thinking, that is so *cute*."

"It's adorable."

"It *is*. Who would've though those guys could come up with something so cute."

"What guys?" Audra said.

"The computer guys."

"I suppose there may be a few computer girls," Catherine said.

"Well I can tell you for a fact there will soon be two more computer girls," Rushel said.

"That's right," Gabrielle said. "I'll be hardware and you'll be software."

"Yes. I just love that. *Soft*ware. It's so clever. I love everything about it. It's a deal." She stuck out her hand.

Gabrielle shook hands with Rushel. Rushel crossed her arms and smiled.

That felt real, Gabrielle thought. A real deal.

"Who knows what will happen." Rushel said.

That night as she lay between Catherine and Samantha in the warm fresh bread smelling house Gabrielle dreamed again of the quiet street under the clear blue lightening sky. She searched for the correct house knowing that she must find it before the sun rose and that when she did an important question would be answered and she could finally finally stop searching.

She was so weary. Her legs were tired and her feet were heavy. There were many overgrown hedges and trees and all the houses with their dark mute windows were indistinct and she felt fear. The sun was coming up. She knew everything would be lost in the sun.

The wind began to blow, soft and warm but strong. It tore at her clothes.

She became aware of a presence behind her. Something huge was directly behind her. She froze and did not want to look. She knew it was *immense*, a vast intellect, and she could feel its attention like a focused beam on the back of her head. It paused there and moved on.

Then the cold feeling faded and she dared to turn. Something moved in the street, several houses away, a spot of gray on the unbroken blackness. It ran into the bushes. Scampered, more like.

It was a cat.

The wind picked up and the branches of the trees began to whip.

The fear returned. Every muscle in her body tensed.

The wind pushed her away, the houses fell into total darkness in a vacuum. Her hands tried to grasp but found only emptiness.

I'm leaving the sun forever, she knew. I will never see the sun again.

The fear was replaced by a great sadness. She gasped in free fall and woke up. Tears were running down her face.

In the warm bedroom, Catherine slept peacefully to her right. Samantha stirred.

Gabrielle felt Samantha's arms around her and the void faded into ordinary darkness. She shuddered, chilled.

"It's all right," Samantha whispered. "It's just watching. I don't know why. That's all it does. Don't be afraid."

Gabrielle swallowed. The shuddering stopped. Samantha pulled the blanket back over them.

Good, she thought, just watching. And she fell back to sleep.

In the morning, Catherine made waffles with blueberries.

Gabrielle, feeling very rested, gulped her coffee. She kept looking at Samantha, absolutely certain there was a question she wanted ask her if she could only remember what the heck it was.

Samantha sipped her tea and gazed out the windows at the gray morning.

"I had the strangest dream," Rushel said.

Gabrielle stared at her.

"I was on a street right before dawn and there was a cat. And it talked to me but I couldn't understand it."

"The cat talked?" Audra said.

"Not with words."

"Well of course not."

Gabrielle poured herself more coffee and closed her eyes, frustrated. She knew she had a dream too. But what was it? How can my mind not be under my complete control, she thought. It's *my mind*. There are secret places, corridors forbidden to me. But inside me. This is so unacceptable.

She gulped her coffee.

"And it was windy." Rushel said.

"In the dream?" Audra said with her mouth full.

"Really strong wind, too. I don't think I've ever felt wind in a dream. It was scary. Really scary."

"That would be scary," Audra said. "Because what if."

"You got carried away," Rushel said. "Where would you go?"

"Into nothing. Holy cow. Could you get back?"

"No more talking about this!" Catherine said. "Just finish your waffles which I labored on for hours."

"Thank you, Catherine," Rushel said.

"Yes, thank you," Audra said.

Gabrielle gulped her coffee again as Samantha smiled at her.

A bright sunlit morning and Gabrielle was glad to be back in school however jogging made her nose hurt again. She was afraid it was bleeding but nothing showed up on her fingertip as she ran past the swine unit. It was the swine unit at least once a week now and the warmer weather made the run much more memorable.

"We really need a new route," one of her fellow joggers said breathlessly.

Gabrielle passed her on the dirt trail. Cynthia, she thought, embarrassed at not being sure. Or Monica. In electives it was usually not worth the effort to learn names. You were unlikely to ever see them again. But still.

Gabrielle expressed her agreement and she saw Cynthia/Monica's gaze go directly to the nose ring and turn quickly away with a look of fear.

Back in the gym, Dr. Swanson stood in her office doorway. Her deeply wrinkled face was creased in a smile. A skeptical smile, Gabrielle thought, or maybe that's what Audra meant by a *sneer*.

No shower, per Audra's orders, but she had no intention of doing that anyway. She exited the sock-smelling door-slamming locker room as quickly as possible.

As she entered Advanced Topics, Dr. Rimmler was writing on the board. Grades again. She opened her spiral notebook (Rushel had her backpack) and Dr. Rimmler saw her.

His mouth fell open and he instantly looked away and closed his eyes. He finished writing out a line of numbers and set the chalk down. He nodded his head as if counting.

There were only five students remaining in Advanced Topics and they were all looking at her. Daniel raised his eyebrows questioningly.

Gabrielle kept her face neutral.

Dr. Rimmler, having composed himself, said, "The countdown to the final has begun. Yes, the quarter system is relentless. Or you could look at it another way: The pain will soon be over. Here is where the class stands to date."

A	B	C	D	F
100	89			59
96				57

"There are two weeks of regular classes left. This week followed by a week of review and then finals week. That's not a lot of time. However." He put his finger on the *F* column. "Those of you who find yourself in this position please keep something in mind. You are both borderline it would seem. A decent showing on the final will bump you up to here." He pointed at *D*. "An excellent showing will propel you to here." *C*.

"You are all engineers in this class, while you're here, and this is one of the most advanced and difficult classes offered by this school in any subject.

You made it this far. Engineers do not give up when faced with a problem. Perhaps you simply need a new perspective. Perhaps the solution is right in front of you. Take full advantage of review week. Only one of you can safely skip review week and we all know who that is."

Gabrielle felt herself blush as the other four students laughed softly.

Dr. Rimmler looked at her.

"You're still Gabrielle?"

Surprised she answered instantly. "Yes."

"So Gabrielle is Gabrielle."

"Yes." She smiled.

"One other question. Doesn't that hurt?"

Gabrielle laughed. "No, not anymore."

"You sure?"

"Yes, this is." She looked at her fellow students. "This is just a game I'm playing."

The guys started at her silently. Daniel nodded. She pointed at the ring. "It's titanium."

"Whoa," Daniel said and the guy behind her said, "Cool!"

"Huh." Dr. Rimmler said. "Good. Now." He erased the grades. "That's the past and this is the future." He wrote out: *Quantum tunneling in p/n junctions: the floating gate transistor*, and beneath, *Non-volatile computer memory*.

Gabrielle felt her pulse spike.

"Now you're talking," she whispered and Daniel grinned.

For the rest of that day not a single thought of disco dances, gold coins, or hidden microphones crossed her mind. She was taken with the idea of computer memory, stable and requiring no power, which you could theoretically carry around in your pocket.

Conceivably, she thought as she came out of the library and headed for the Burger Bar oblivious to the stares of the other students, it could be a simple memory module you plugged into your home computer, somehow, and it could contain entire books. Huge amounts of data. Digital video could actually happen. A movie in your pocket. And the processor. That would be different.

She stood still on the inner campus drive where a sprinkler was repeatedly spraying water on a dry corner of the lawn beside the English building. The sprinkler ticked in a short arc and reset with a rapid stutter. Water splashed onto her shoes. Students with backpacks over their shoulders flowed around her.

Gabrielle felt a tightness in her chest.

Her optical processor, big as a table top, filled the four-dimensional space of her mind's eye. As before, the flat processor folded and curled upon itself while sections detached, rotated, reintegrated. Her vision was incomplete there but.

She remembered to breathe. It was too much. So many sharp turns and connections.

Water sprayed over her feet again from the cheerfully clacking sprinkler.

And then she saw it. There it was.

"I know how to do it," she said.

The reciprocating sprinkler sent droplets of water across the lawn in a repeating pattern. A *stochastic* pattern. She thought: droplets of aluminum oxide fused into a wave guide. Irregular. Would these irregularities be a problem? Build up structures. Spray. Place. Put. Microscopic droplets.

Gabrielle was vaguely aware of sunlight, air, sound. In her mind's eye a completely new kind of optical transistor, built of tiny sapphire spheres, took shape. She made the effort to cement it in her memory.

She walked across the road to the lawn, making T-square wielding students abruptly change course. A shudder ran down the length of her body. She looked down at the sprinkler and said, "Thank you."

A scrub jay zoomed by in a flurry of feathers and whisper-sang to her but she could not understand what she said.

At the Burger Bar the cook let the toothpick fall from his mouth when he saw her as the four students in line ahead turned to see. The closest, a young woman in a black t-shirt stared at the nose ring for a good thirty seconds until her face turned bright red. She tucked her new briefcase under her arm and pretended to cough.

Gosh, even her knuckles are red, Gabrielle thought, how embarrassing. Nice briefcase, though.

She smiled and stared back.

When it was her turn, the cook took another toothpick from a box and held it while stroking his chin.

"I can't quite put my finger on it but you look different somehow."

"I lost weight."

"That's it. Good job."

"Thank you."

"Um. Cheddar burger?"

Gabrielle pulled her last three dollars out of her pocket. After this I'll have sixty-five cents left, she thought. At least I don't have to worry about going to the grocery store or gas. Or clothes shopping.

A cold finger touched the back of her neck.

Rent, she thought. It's due Monday. Not like it's a lot but what am I doing? Have to go to the bank.

"Cheddar burger?"

"Yes, thank you."

"And no fries?"

"No, no fries. Thanks."

"Because then all that weight. Blam! Right back." He raised his eyebrows under the paper cap. "Right?"

"That's so true. Blam. I mean, no blam please."

He grinned and slapped a hamburger patty on the grill.

Keep it, she thought. It's so cheap. And I told Rosie I would stay until June. She probably needs the money, such as it is. And *damn*. In the glove compartment. She shook her head.

"The note. Why can't I remember that?"

Grill guy turned and said, "Hm?"

"Sorry. I'm just talking to myself."

He said seriously, "Highly creative people do that."

"Oh, well, then I'm fine."

"See? There you go."

"There I go."

She went back to the Stacks with her cheddar burger and spent the remainder of the afternoon going over her notes for Advanced Topics, her Shakespeare class, and Intro to Philosophy. For Shakespeare she decided to do her term paper on the Sonnets. The professor of that class was a gentleman with a slow growling voice and very thick glasses who sometimes smoked a pipe in class. Leather jacket with black turtleneck sweater. Gabrielle noticed he liked it when students asked questions. Any question. His eyes would light up behind those lenses and he would launch into an impassioned lecture as an answer. Didn't matter what the question was. Shakespeare, the price of gas, President Carter. Any sign of actual mental activity in the classroom, since the normal behavior of students in humanities classes was to sit motionless and in total silence as if meekly accepting punishment, was appreciated.

Gabrielle knew it was crazy to use the Sonnets instead of *Macbeth* which everyone else was doing. But you looked for crazy. Crazy was an attempt to leave the conventional behind and explore the boundaries. More than likely there was nothing there but you had to look.

The bare fluorescents were giving her a headache.

She touched the titanium piercing. She could wiggle it without it stinging. She put away Shakespeare and opened Philosophy. Still no ideas for her paper. And a presentation? Standing in front of the class? She closed Philosophy with a frustrated sigh.

At least Advanced Topics was okay. The floating gate transistor was very cool with the floating gate itself being completely utterly crazy. But her lawn sprinkler inspired idea? Crazy enough? She began to sketch out the mechanism in her notebook. She kept her cheddar burger hidden on the plywood seat and took a bite whenever the area was clear of roving student assistants.

Gabrielle sat on the floor before the fire in the middle room with her math homework. She leaned close to her paper with her glasses folded neatly by her elbow. The hearth was the perfect height and the heat from the grate felt really good. Higher level math always made her hands cold.

Rushel sat on the hearth next to her and poked the burning split oak and watched Gabrielle solve equations. She kept pulled her hair back with a toss of her head. She smelled of apples and mint.

"I think I understand this part," Rushel said as Gabrielle finished a long problem. "There's a procedure you follow. You solve for x or y. But this part with the square root sign and all the exponents. I don't know what's going on there."

"That's just algebra."

"Algebra."

"Calculus isn't very hard."

"No, it looks like fun."

"It is. You didn't have to take math at all?"

"Just one required class. Introductory Algebra for Students Who Need All Their Fingers and Toes to Count to Ten. And I'm only exaggerating a little."

"I had to take that class." Audra set out a pile of paper on the bench seat beside Rushel. She had a box of felt pens, five colors. "It was awful. I am not numerical."

"Well I need to become numerical," Rushel said. "I'm a computer science major now."

"My mind still reels at that," Audra said.

"It's very exciting. I had no idea it even existed. A whole new world. But this math class of yours looks pretty challenging."

"It's not that bad. Started out rigorous but the professor just disappeared and the sub is a lot easier."

"Whoa." Audra began coloring in her dance flyers. Red for the girl's dress, blue for the guy's jacket. Then red and orange for the big letters smoothing out the stair-step lines. *Disco's Last Blast!*

"That never happens."

The room began to smell of ink.

"The new guy, Javier, is a bit slow."

"Javier?"

"Yeah, no one knows his last name."

"Huh. Good." Audra uncapped the green pen and traced out the line at the bottom of the flyer. *Period Attire Requested.* "Here." She slid it over.

Gabrielle didn't want to touch it. She touched it.

"So this is the thing?"

"This. And your nose. Your hair. I have confidence."

"I don't feel confident."

"Have you been practicing?"

"What should I have been practicing?"

"Sneering."

"Well. No."

"And rolling your eyes."

Rushel said, "Everything is just so boring and stupid."

"So incredibly stupid," Audra said. "The whole world. God, so stupid."

"And you are so tired of it."

"Sick to death of it. But, you know, your house here is really nice, Patricia. So much better than that stupid place at the beach with all that stupid sand. I mean, the roof leaks and the septic tank is clogged."

"Oh. Gross."

"So incredibly gross," Rushel said. "And they can't afford to fix anything. And they're going to get the electricity cut off. And they're all so mean. And stupid."

"So incredibly stupid," Audra said.

"So anyway," Rushel said. "It was nice finally meeting you all and like you know I'll see you all at the dance. It'll be *great*. There'll be a DJ and everything. Open bar, too. I mean, we couldn't put that in the flyer, you know. But yeah, totally open bar. Oh, could I like you know use your bathroom? It's such an incredibly long drive out there."

"Bathroom's right across from the pantry," Audra said.

"I'm absolutely certain you can do this."

"Okay." Gabrielle felt the skin tighten on the back of her head.

"Keep your hair like this. No shower. Don't brush your teeth. Wear dirty clothes. It's better to be smelly. Puts them at ease. Seven o'clock."

"Seven?"

"Knock on the door at seven."

"My last class gets out at four. I'll just wait until seven. I won't come home. I guess I could just go to the library for a while."

"You still have your room?"

"Oh sure. Right."

"Like something you half remember from your previous life," Rushel said.

"For tactical purposes I recommend you keep it," Audra said.

"I intend to." Yes, must keep it, she thought.

"Good. One more thing."

Gabrielle put her glasses back on and sighed.

"Go ahead."

"They're paranoid to a degree difficult for normal Earth people to comprehend. Even if they believe what you say they might want to test you. I wouldn't worry about it too much."

"A test." Now Gabrielle felt her stomach churn.

"I really doubt this will happen. But if it does, could be anything. Usually pretty awful."

"Like what?"

"Eat a bug. Drink someone's pee. Touch, you know, shit."

"Oh. No."

"They want to see how tough you are. And they just like to humiliate people. It's their main source of fun."

"Will this count for anything?" Gabrielle touched her nose ring.

"Yes. Because of that my hope is it will not be a low level pee test. They'll see that and get creative. Patricia is pretty good at torture. She's talented. One of the Susans, I forget which one, they tested by making her strip to her underwear and crawl all the way around the police station rolling an egg with a spoon, saying, I'm sorry egg, I'm sorry egg. In broad daylight. She got sent off for seventy-two hours psychiatric observation."

Gabrielle held her stomach.

"Wait. I think that was the Susan that got knocked up."

"They cast her out?"

"Not sure what happened to her," Rushel said. "Just kind of messed up in general."

"Great."

"But like I said, I doubt they'll go that far. Keep the goal firmly in mind. We must succeed."

"Yes," Gabrielle said. She took a deep breath. "It will all be worth it."

Wednesday morning was clear and cool and the low golden sun became a rainbow glint in Gabrielle's glasses as she drove. The dance flyer was tucked in a file folder and covered with a towel lying flat on the back seat. She couldn't help turning and checking the towel every minute.

It felt odd to be alone in the car. Because of a schedule change at College Costs Less, Rushel and Gislaine needed to be ferried around by Audra. The grocery store was down to only five employees and the rumor was the place was going out of business. None of the places in that little shopping center looked like they were doing well. The furniture store was pretty quiet and its eternal 'Sale' signs were dusty and torn. The small pharmacy had empty shelves and burned out lights. But the downtown seemed to be getting busier. No more empty buildings and a lot more traffic.

The Volkswagen bumped along the highway and she began to mentally review the route from school to her old house with an eye for avoiding the traffic.

She braked for slow vehicles in front of her. This was common now, she thought, just like Los Angeles. So leave earlier. A half hour would do it but she would have to contend with the near impossibility of getting Rushel to hurry up in the bathroom.

Gabrielle had to park in the furthest corner of the upper lot. She gripped her spiral notebook tightly and jogged to Shakespeare.

Halfway through the class she realized no one was noticing her new appearance. She began to relax. She went to the student union and sat at the counter beside the bowling alley and did her simple math homework. The constant noise made concentrating easy.

Then she jotted down ideas for her Shakespeare paper. She was writing about the Sonnets because they sounded intriguing and yet she couldn't quite tell what they were all about. Her thinking was if they were *that* mysterious she could write almost anything and it would be considered all right.

So I'm playing a trick, she thought. There's no final answer to these things. It's all interpretation. Of course I can't go completely off the wall, I have to reason my way through.

Or at least make it sound like reason. Which would make it b.s.

That, she did not like. She vowed to make her crazy ideas adhere to reason which would of course mean they were not crazy.

She closed the notebook. That's literature for you.

She opened Introduction to Philosophy. She looked at her notes. She closed Introduction to Philosophy.

Hell, she thought. Who needs a perfect GPA anyway?

She gathered her notebooks into a neat pile, took off her glasses, and rested her head on them.

She sat up. She saw it. There were goosebumps on her arms. She concentrated on Rushel's anthology book of philosophers, on the table of contents. There it was. She mentally turned to the chapter. The page appeared instantly in her mind's eye. She began rereading it. Parmenides.

I will do a presentation, she thought. Blank faced, she stared into the crashing bowling alley and visualized her plans.

Anti-climactic, she thought, just great.

There was a substitute professor in Philosophy who informed them that Dr. Townsend would return on Friday at which point their papers would be due or if doing a presentation be ready to give it at that time.

No Andrea, either, she noticed.

The sub wrote, "I am Dr. Mike" with blue chalk. He was a tall man with hollow cheeks who smiled continuously.

"Uh will there uh be anyone giving a uh presen uh tation?" he said slowly.

Gabrielle raised her hand and all eight students turned to look. Annie looked away quickly. Flannel shirt guy, puzzled, stared at her nose as if seeing something that could not exist.

"Just uh one? That uh doesn't sound like uh a problem. Does uh anyone uh have a question uh about uh the material? I would uh be more than uh happy to explain uh these sometimes hard to uh understand uh topics."

No one moved. There was a classroom-wide holding of breath. Gabrielle sensed a high probability of early class dismissal.

"In that uh case," Dr. Mike said. "Let us begin uh with Lacan. No uh doubt you are all uh familiar uh with him uh so just a quick uh review."

Flannel shirt guy let his shoulders slump in defeat. Annie tapped her pencil on her desk.

Gabrielle sighed. Familiar with him, yes. Unfortunately.

Dr. Mike wrote "Lacan" on the board in pink chalk.

Gabrielle wrote *Bibble-babble comma Post Modern Flapdoodle semi-colon Gobbledygook* in her notebook and began making a mark every time Dr. Mike said "Uh." She liked *flapdoodle.* Her dad had said it sometimes. So did Audra.

She knew it would look like she was taking notes. By the end of the class the count of "Uh" was two hundred thirty-one.

After Dr. Mike had left the long-haired student who never raised his head and turned in his seat.

"Now I know for certain we're being punished. I just don't know for what."

With her right temple pounding, Gabrielle walked slowly back uphill to her car. In the driver's seat, as usual, she immediately felt better. She took off her glasses, pressed the sides of her head, and breathed slowly five times. The sun disappeared behind low clouds. The hill to the west was shrouded in fog.

Driving to her old house was a nearly automatic sequence of shifting, accelerating, braking. It made her feel comfortable and sad at the same time. She thought the eucalyptus and palm trees looked different against the swiftly darkening sky. And the pavement was bumpier.

Her street was fully lined with parked cars and when she got to her house she stopped abruptly. There were two cars in her driveway and she didn't know either one. A new metallic green Pinto and a red Chevy Vega. She went to the end of the street and made a left thinking, who in their right mind would buy a Vega? She found a parking spot on a short connecting street between a Ford station wagon and a low-slung sports car.

She checked the folder under the towel and locked up the car. She spent a moment looking at the sports car. *Lotus.*

This whole area is changing, she thought. She stuffed her hands into her sweatshirt and walked up the sidewalk. She dashed across the street, rounded the corner and approached her house slowly just as the streetlights came on. The second story was brightly lit.

That's just not right, she thought.

When she reached her front yard of patchy grass she stared in confusion. The front curtains were open wide. She knew they were screwed down to make them student-proof but they had been pulled back and tied off. She could see the whole parlor. There was the bookcase with its empty vase and the picture of the sailing ship in the back frame. The tv set was still

on casting its bluish light over the room but there was no one in the sofa or
the big chair.

"Oh this is all wrong," she muttered and then stopped again. There was
a flicker of orange light. She walked up to the window. A fire was burning
in the fireplace. There was even a stack of firewood on the hearth.

"Someone's gonna get in trouble for that."

She went around to the driveway and the kitchen door and beheld
another strange sight. Mrs. Rosenberg's house was also brightly lit. The
stained glass window with the bullet hole was shining colorfully over the
dark porch.

Gabrielle said, "Wow," and turned the kitchen door knob. It was locked.
She blinked. "What."

The kitchen kitchen light came on and a dark shadow filled the
prismatic door window. The knob rattle and the door snapped open. A tall
man stood silhouetted by the bare bulb on the ceiling.

At least that was the same, Gabrielle thought.

"Hi," the guy said. Student, she could tell. Blonde hair.

"They fixed the lock?"

Gabrielle stepped up onto the stoop. The student did not move.

"Can I help you?"

"You must be new."

"Not that new."

"I live here."

"Sorry, I've never seen you before." He leaned over her.

"I'm the girl who lives in the basement."

"No one lives down there."

"I do. Over two years."

"Wait, wait. Right. Sorry."

Gabrielle held up her right arm as a shield and stepped into the kitchen.
The guy took a stumbling step back.

"The lady mentioned your name. I forget."

"Is Elliot here?"

"Elliot?"

"Good grief, who lives here now? The lady. Mrs. Rosenberg, right?"

"The owner, I guess. Didn't get her name."

Gabrielle thought, maybe this guy is just really dumb. She saw her
coffee percolator beside the sink. Not stolen yet. But the fridge. She yanked
opened the freezer and confirmed here fears. Empty.

"All right. All my stuff is gone."

"You mean the steaks and." His eyes lost focus.

"Yeah."

"That came with the house they said."

"What? Who said?"

The counter was covered with crusty stains. The whole kitchen smelled like an armpit.

"The owner lady. If you're the girl in the basement she said it couldn't possibly be yours because you don't know how to cook. So she said we could have it."

Gabrielle slammed the freezer shut and the white bulbous refrigerator rocked on its uneven feet.

"So Elliot is gone. What about Brian? Or Mark?"

There was a candy wrapper and tissue paper on the floor. Brian was fanatical about sweeping.

The guy grinned and shook back his blonde hair. "I'm not very good with names."

Gabrielle nodded slowly. "Okay. That's fine. That was almost a hundred bucks worth of food."

"We had a party. It was really good."

She looked at him in exasperation.

"I'm going to go watch tv."

Gabrielle closed her eyes for a moment and then went to her bathroom. There was a pile of wet towels on the floor. There was dried toothpaste on the edge of the sink and a disposable razor was stuck in it. And the water in the toilet was yellow.

"I may be getting mad," she said.

She flushed and wiped down the seat with the tiny bit of toilet paper left on the roll. It wasn't nearly enough and she dropped the blob in the water. Oh well, she thought, what did Samantha call it? Hovering? My leg muscles should be in good shape from jogging, right? Let's see if I can do it.

It was easy. She vowed to hover more often.

She went downstairs to the basement in familiar darkness. Her room was mostly unchanged. Her bed was still there, her box of projects/ nightstand and gooseneck study lamp still alongside. The washer and dryer were both piled high with laundry. Blue jeans and flannel shirts and wads of wet socks. She poked through it. All boy's stuff. Nothing but boys. She sat on the end of her bed with a sigh.

Tomorrow, she thought, have to go to the bank and cash a check. Twenty should be enough. Make sure to get a ten, a five, and five ones. Well, make one of the ones in quarters. Then I need an envelope. Samantha should have envelopes.

She checked her watch. *5:57.*

She finger combed her hair. Greasy. She smelled her armpits. Fragrant. She pulled the collar of her t-shirt out. Pretty good odor in general. She wiggled the titanium ring. Stinging and swollen. She knew she had to employ the salt solution from the mimeographed handout Clarence gave her but that was no good for right now. Put ice on it. Or, since her check of the freezer had shown no ice cube trays, scrape a bit of the frost build-up on the walls. Disgusting but ice is ice.

Going up her wooden steps she heard the kitchen door slam. Male voices, too loud. And one of the voices she knew. She opened the hall door and there was Elliot, his back to her, talking to the tall student.

"Huh?" Elliot said in annoyance, a tone she had never heard from him before.

"That girl from the basement came back," the student said. "She's *really weird.*"

"Basement?" Elliot turned and saw her. He broke into a grin. "Hey! There you are! I was getting worried about you."

"Hi, Elliot. I'm fine."

"Yes?"

"I've been staying somewhere else."

"Considering what happened I don't blame you."

"Brian and Mark are gone? What happened."

"Did you get the note?" He backed up and cocked his head. "Not bad!"

"Thanks." The note again.

"Did that?"

"Thought it was time for a change."

"But that. Did that hurt? Been thinking along those lines."

"*You* have?"

"Sure, why not? Hey, they fixed the lock as I'm sure you noticed so."

"I need a key."

"You need a key."

Elliot turned to the tall student, who had been watching them with a bewildered expression, and said slowly, "Jason, could Gabrielle borrow your door key for a minute? She'll give it right back."

"Yeah, okay."

He dug a key ring out of his pocket and handed it to her.

"She just needs the door key, Jason."

"Yeah, okay." He took the ring back, pried a silver key off and dropped it into her hand.

"Thank you," Gabrielle said. He looked different. His beard had grown in a bit more. He seemed more mature.

"She'll give it right back," he said.

"Yeah, okay. I'm going to watch tv."

Jason went back to the parlor and turned up the sound. *The Flintstones* were on.

Elliot smiled at Gabrielle shaking her head. They stood at the kitchen sink, out of Jason's hearing.

"So who lives here now?"

"Well, I'm still on the back porch."

"Of course."

"Then there's Eric, Brandon, Tim, Alan, and Jason."

"Seven?"

"Yeah." He sounded tired.

"Wow."

"They all showed up one weekend when I was gone and I'm afraid they stole all your stuff in the freezer."

"I noticed."

"I'll get them to pay you back. Don't worry."

"That would be great."

"Now, you have to tell me about this." He pointed at her nose.

Gabrielle laughed.

"It's a long story and I will tell you. But I have an appointment I can't be late for." She checked her watch and rubbed her temples. "Like right now."

"In the middle of the night?"

"Uh huh."

"This is absolutely fascinating."

"Elliot, if I told you everything you'd think I was insane."

Elliot laughed. "I would never think that."

"No, you would."

"Okay," he said, still laughing. "You still live here, right?"

"Yes." Gabrielle had the strong feeling this was a lie. She was lying to Elliot. Unless she wasn't. Shit, she thought.

"Okay. Good." He peeked around the corner to the parlor. "Jason! Gabrielle gave you the key back, right?"

"Oh. Huh?" Jason said, thinking.

"Just double checking."

"Oh yeah. Sure."

Elliot gave her a thumbs up.

"Oh my God," Gabrielle whispered.

"Now you have a key." He tipped his head in Jason's direction. "Full ride scholarship. Room, board, everything."

"What?"

"I'm serious. Golf."

"There is such a thing?" Gabrielle had to stifle a laugh. "So they pay for all the golf textbooks?"

He shrugged. "Sounds like something from *Saturday Night Live*."

Gabrielle was vaguely aware this was a tv show and had of course never seen it.

"Really!"

"Don't worry. We'll get him another key. Some day."

"Well, thanks." Gabrielle let her head tip back. "I better go. Can't be late." She felt a sharp sudden awareness that they were alone in the kitchen, she was standing too close to him, and letting her head tip back was an invitation to...

Gabrielle stepped away and turned just as Elliot started to lean forward. He recovered instantly.

"Thanks for the key," she said at the door.

"But, you're back, right?"

She couldn't help hesitate.

"Yes." She pulled the door open before he could come closer.

"Good luck with your appointment."

Gabrielle made a quick wave goodbye and stepped out of the warm kitchen and into the cold, foggy night. It was only six-thirty and that meant there was plenty of time to get nervous but with Elliot at home clearly waiting in the house was not an option. She would have to tell him she wasn't interested. She would have to tell him.

"Nothing," she said to the streetlight. She didn't want to have to tell Elliot anything. She didn't want to hurt his feelings. Why were boys like that, she thought. Why can't they tell? And what was going on with Mrs. Rosenberg?

By the time she got to her car and saw the towel on the back seat all thoughts of the note in the glove compartment slipped away.

Just go in, she thought. No hesitating. No back and forth. Walk up and knock. Just like that.

She took a deep breath and started the car. L's house was five minutes away.

Be fluid. That's the word. A light touch. Be above it all. Who will even be there? I can handle anything.

She locked her knees.

"Don't throw up. Don't throw up."

She rested her head on the steering wheel. Cold plastic felt good. The nausea faded. The knot in her stomach remained. She unclenched her legs, grabbed hold of the wheel, and pulled out.

She decided to approach the house from a different direction. She went up one block then left past cars and pickups glistening wet under streetlight beams filtered through swaying dripping trees. She stayed in second. The street was so narrow and hemmed in with parked vehicles there were barely two lanes. At a stop sign she slowed to a walk and did not stop. It was impossible to see cross traffic or even headlights until you were in the middle of the intersection so there was no point in stopping, she figured. And she thought of a way to use the jammed parking conditions to her advantage.

Through another intersection.

A student on a ten-speed flashed by missing her front bumper by inches.

Down a block then left again. She was now past their house. She made a U-turn and was now coming upon them from the west, the opposite side from the path of gardenias.

Then she was on their street. Old yellowish streetlights. Her pulse spiked. She pulled over at a wide driveway to let a car pass. Black Mustang.

Seven houses down, L's house was under the last streetlight.

The vehicles parked along the street caught her attention. There were several Japanese cars, all undented and without rust. A pickup with a rack of ladders. Halfway down the unmistakable grill of a BMW. And the street itself. There were parking spots. Several houses had no vehicles in front of them. Garages. No sidewalks. Walkways went from front doors right to the curb. The bushes and trees were trimmed. Not much cover.

She looked at her watch. *7:06.*

Thinking about it wasn't making it better, she thought. She pulled out of the driveway and proceeded slowly. There was an empty space in front of their next door neighbor. She slipped into it and killed the engine.

L's house was lovely she had to admit now that she could see it without the benefit of wine and vodka. It had a picket fence with a double gate and a wide front porch framed by boxy pillars tapered at the top. Macramé nets held red clay pots overflowing with flowers. White clapboards and varnished trim.

Windows, all brightly illuminated, had clean white closed curtains. There was a driveway with a strip of grass running down the middle. No cars in the drive. Brand new Mercedes at the curb. Dove gray. About a hundred fifty of those coins, she thought. They spend money like that?

"Yeah," she said. "M's money."

She opened her door and got out and pushed her seat forward. She threw off the towel and grabbed the file folder and took out the flyer. She slammed her door shut and shoved her keys as far into her pocket as she could until they poked her thigh. She held the flyer to her chest and went to their walkway.

Movement down the street. She half crouched, ready to run, expecting to see a bear. Something flew through the glow of the streetlight, made instant course corrections and vanished into the darkness only to reappear with wings fully extended. Then snapping back, then falling in the mist.

A bat. She tried to take a deep breath. Just a bat.

No sound came from L's house. She walked up the brick path and stopped at the gates. She put her hand on the painted wood. Wet and splintery.

She turned her head to listen but there was no train horn.

The stick-on letter L was still where she remembered. And so were the marks where the other letters had been scraped off. She took her hand away and took a step back.

A drop of sweat ran down her forehead and she wiped it off so it wouldn't get on her glasses.

She pulled her hair down. Her straggly hair was now also wet as well as sticky. She touched the ring.

Another step back. She put the flyer under her sweatshirt flat on her stomach.

"I love Catherine. I love Samantha. I love Audra."

She walked back to the gate and took hold. No train horn split the night.

"I love Rushel. I love Gislaine."

She pushed the gates open and stepped inside.

"And I love M. I love M."

Five steps to the porch. Up onto the painted boards, heel to toe. The wood did not creak. The house was silent.

They're not home, she thought. Or maybe they're all asleep with the lights on. Yes.

She shook her head.

Their front door was new polished oak. There was an oval window, beveled ground glass. No movement behind it.

"All right," she whispered.

She made a fist and raised it.

And gasped as music blasted her. Fantastic volume. Coming through the door, through the walls. A fast grinding guitar sound, she guessed. She opened her mouth and felt the music in her teeth. The curtains over the window to her left moved to the beat. The power to do that, she thought. Thousands of watts. In a living room.

Lyrics started. Woman's voice, totally clear. A beautiful strong voice. She was singing about a fish. That's what it sounded like.

Another voice behind her. Male, barely audible. There was a man in a white t-shirt on the porch of the house across the street a couple doors down. He was yelling and pointing at her. He put both hands to his mouth and yelled, a faint dribble of sound. The fish song swamped him.

Gabrielle could not understand him but there was no mystery. She shrugged and gave a short wave back.

The man held an arm straight out, turned his hand palm up, and made a fist. Except for the middle finger. He retreated back through his door and slammed it, a pitiful noise.

The song continued into an instrumental part and Gabrielle thought, now or never. She knocked on the door. The music absorbed the sound completely. She knocked again hard enough to make her knuckles sting. Something shifted behind the oval window.

She pounded as hard as she could with the side of her fist. Three times. Her hand went numb. She shook it. The music cut off with an electrical pop. A lock rattled in the head throbbing silence. The door was pulled open and someone stood there, back lit.

"Hey *fuckbrain*, what did I tell you about trespassing!"

It was Patricia. She looked at Gabrielle, sneered, then looked up and down the porch. The porch light snapped on.

"Hey," Gabrielle said and lifted one shoulder.

There were others in the living room standing still. Sentinels. Gabrielle with an effort did not look at them.

Patricia, wearing all black, smiled and looked her up and down. She let go of the doorknob and walked around her. Gabrielle watched without moving.

Patricia studied her. She examined her threadbare boating shoes, her jeans, her dirty hair. When she saw the nose ring her eyebrows arched and her expression instantly hardened. She tipped her head sideways and peered at it from a couple inches away. The smile returned.

She saw that it was real, Gabrielle thought.

Patricia wrinkled her nose and made her own silver nose ring wiggle. She put her hands on Gabrielle's shoulders and let her fingers run, tickling, down Gabrielle's arms to the elbows. She leaned close.

"What a wonderful surprise," she said in a soft, seductive voice.

People now filled the open doorway. It's all of them Gabrielle thought in near panic.

"Everyone, look who's here. It's the Goddess."

Holly, also dressed in a black leotard, stared with an unhappy expression. Debbie, in a green sweater, seemed confused. Tall Susan smiled over Holly's shoulder. Pretty Susan and New Susan took turns peeking around Debbie. They both wore black turtlenecks and their heads seemed disembodied.

"This is disappointing," Holly said. "I was all set to cut off some guy's balls."

"And add them to our collection," Debbie said.

Patricia held up one finger.

"Let's focus on *this* now."

Holly sighed loudly and exchanged a look with Debbie.

"Gabrielle," Patricia said. "What are you doing here?"

Gabrielle felt Patricia looking past her to the street as she took the flyer from under her sweatshirt.

"Well, you know, I just wanted to make sure you knew about this."

She held the paper out and all their heads bent to see. Holly's brow furrowed.

"They're putting on this, you know, dance because it's like the end of disco."

Holly looked up in surprise then anger.

"So." Gabrielle let her head tip to one side. "It should be pretty big. There's going to be a professional DJ. Oh, and they couldn't put it on the flyer but there's going to be an open bar."

Pretty Susan and New Susan both said, "Oh! Wow!" Debbie raised her eyebrows. Holly held her hand out. Gabrielle gave her the flyer.

Holly ran he fingers over the red and green ink.

She's recognizing something, Gabrielle thought.

Holly, studying the flyer, backed up into the living room. Tall Susan backed up in sync.

"So," Gabrielle said, "you should like come to the dance, you know." Oh, sounding pretty weak, she thought.

Patricia got behind her, put her hands again on Gabrielle's shoulders and pushed her firmly across the threshold into the house.

Low ceiling, all painted white. Hundred watt bulbs in table lamps. Along one wall, bookshelves of white Formica. Each shelf was full of potted plants leaning at a different angle. Twenty-nine of them. Green leaves and green vines. There were more plants hanging in more macramé in the two back corners. They had white flowers.

Along the other wall was a long white leather couch, a glass coffee table in front.

The wall in front of her had a doorway into the kitchen. One both sides of this opening were cases of dark wood as tall as she was and three feet wide. She saw that the front of each case was a plastic mesh. They were huge speakers. Wires as thick as her car's battery cables ran from them through jagged holes in the ceiling.

She coughed. Someone was smoking. There were two overflowing ashtrays on the coffee table.

Gabrielle's right shoe snagged the thick white carpeting and she stumbled. Tall Susan smiled.

"Thanks for inviting me in," Gabrielle said. Patricia's hands were still on her shoulders.

"You're polite," Patricia said. "Sorry I yelled at you. Thought you were the neighbors. He's a bit of an asshole. Holly?"

Holly stepped back in from the kitchen, the flyer in both hands. She raised her sharp chin.

"Your opinion?"

"This is bullshit." Holly let the flyer drop to the floor. "It's a trick."

Gabrielle's heart began to pound again. They heard us, she thought. There are microphones everywhere. Patricia exhaled on the back of her neck. Then something touched her right ear. Patricia's tongue.

"I'm so sorry," Patricia whispered. "What are we going to do now, Holly? What on Earth?"

"This is a grave violation of our sovereignty."

"But instead of becoming angry."

"Think of this as an opportunity."

"An opportunity to do the right thing."

"To do *good*."

Gabrielle snapped her right shoulder back as hard as she could and gave Patricia a glancing blow to her cheek. Almost got her in the nose again, she thought as she spun around.

"Fine, shit, don't come to the fucking dance. Who cares." Am I sneering, she thought, is that sneering?

With Patricia off balance she side stepped and went to the open front door. Debbie and New Susan were standing there. A wreath of smoke around Debbie's face. Holly cleared her throat and they both took a step forward. Patricia grabbed the sweatshirt hood and tugged. Gabrielle came away from the door.

"And this was looking like a boring Wednesday," Patricia said. "There's nothing on tv."

Debbie and New Susan sat on the couch and resumed smoking.

"This is much better than tv."

It was Tall Susan in the kitchen. Gabrielle heard water running in the sink. I have to get in there, she thought. Make a right turn. The pantry.

"I know what you're doing," Holly said. "You thought you could fool us?" She was standing with her black-clad arms at her sides. With one black stockinged toe she turned the flyer around on the carpet. "It's so transparent. I thought you were the smart girls."

Patricia closed the front door and turned the brass deadbolt. She went to the coffee table and got her cigarette from the ashtray.

Locked in, Gabrielle forced herself not to cough.

"What do you mean?"

"The fact that she sent you is pretty chicken," Holly said.

Gabrielle could read all the emotions in Holly's face. Hope. Despair. Fear. But hope was winning.

"Chickenshit," New Susan said.

"Shut up," Holly snapped. "When you see her tell her it won't work. We are not getting back together."

Gabrielle felt a weight lift from her chest. She tried not to show any reaction.

"Well, I don't know anything about that. But they are definitely having a dance."

"At some house."

"Yeah, it's a huge house."

Holly laughed. "Because it's the end of disco."

When she's smiling she's beautiful, Gabrielle thought.

"That's what she said." Gabrielle put emphasis on *she*. "I mean, I don't."

"Disco is *not* over."

"All right."

"You know," Debbie said from the sofa. Her voice was husky. "If you went you could show them."

"It would be so much fun," New Susan said.

"If it's true." Pretty Susan came in from the kitchen, dishtowel in hand. Tall Susan stood in the doorway.

"It's true."

"An open bar," Debbie said skeptically.

"Yeah. And a real DJ."

Pretty Susan was staring hard at her.

"What's the trick?"

Gabrielle sighed. "Like I said, if you don't want to come don't come."

Pretty Susan thought hard. She picked up the flyer. Holly and Patricia watched her.

"Why would you drive all the way from the beach to give us this?"

"I just wanted to get out of there."

Patricia crossed her arms. "Is the Goddess of the smart girls not happy?"

"I'm perfectly happy."

"Doesn't look like it," New Susan said and Debbie elbowed her.

Pretty Susan turned to Holly.

"In my opinion we should go. Depending, of course."

Holly nodded seriously. "Very well."

Patricia said, "Hmm. Okay."

New Susan bounced on the sofa.

Debbie lit another cigarette.

Gabrielle took a deep breath and relaxed. Gosh, that was easy, she thought. I shouldn't have been so worried. All I had to do was mess up my hair, not take showers, and get my nose pierced. Which was really easy now that I think about it.

Gabrielle smiled and said, "Depending on what?" They were all staring at her. She felt her chest tighten again.

"Well," Patricia said. "We call it the Prague Protocol."

Gabrielle froze in surprise.

"It's a series of tests we've developed."

"We have to be sure. You understand," Holly said.

"There are issues of operational security," Pretty Susan said.

Gabrielle thought furiously.

"Why do you call it, uh." She put her shaking hands in her pockets.

"During the war – that would be the Second World War," Patricia said, "which they don't teach anymore because it's all Vietnam all the time, the Resistance in Czechoslovakia had a way of ferreting out German spies. It was brutal by our soft, civilized standards.

"For instance, you are part of a cell. You have several partners. You have no knowledge of other cells. Instructions come in the form of mysterious messages written on certain walls in chalk. Strings of numbers employing a mathematical code. The Germans, thinking themselves superior in all ways, don't even notice."

Fascinated despite her intense fear, Gabrielle said, "What was the code?"

Holly laughed. "We knew that would get your attention."

"The details are still top secret even now." Patricia nodded at Gabrielle's raised eyebrows. "Yes, it was that good. Take the number from the wall and the current date and perform some function on them. All calculated by hand, of course. Combine them somehow with secret numbers known only to that cell. The Germans would never be able to spoof it."

Gabrielle had never heard the word *spoof* before. She listened intently.

"The resulting number would be what the next operation was. Blowing up train tracks, maybe, and where the explosives were stashed. But the Prague Protocol, actually, had nothing to do with mathematics, did it, Holly."

"Absolutely not."

"It was cold blooded murder," Pretty Susan said, grinning. Her black eye was almost back to normal.

New Susan was watching avidly while Debbie looked pained. Well, she is supposed to be the normal one, Gabrielle thought. She started to feel cold. Patricia came close behind her and spoke softly into her ear.

"When a cell found a prospective Resistance fighter they administered a simple test. He was brought blindfolded into a basement. They took off the blindfold. In the middle of the room was a German prisoner tied to a chair, gagged, but eyes uncovered. He's seen our faces, they tell the recruit. He must be eliminated. You do it. They would hand him a rock, about fist size, not very big. They would watch. If the recruit hesitated too much it meant he was a spy and they shot him. If he went at it with too much enthusiasm it meant he was a psycho and psycho meant stupid. And they shot him. If he went about it in a businesslike manner, a soldier-like manner, well, he passed the test and usually kept the rock as a trophy. The German prisoner died no matter what."

Holly came to Gabrielle's side and whispered, "Hate is the key. Hate is the perfect state of being. Hate protects you from harm."

Holly's perfume was overwhelming. Gabrielle saw black spots.

"They had to be sure, you see," Holly said. "If they were found out they would be immediately executed. Then the S.S. would go to their house in the middle of the night and force everyone into the street. To be on the safe side, their next door neighbors were subjected to the same punishment. Everyone into the street. The old people and young girls and children and aunts and uncles and especially young men. They were forced into a group while the Germans dragged out the people from the other houses in their nightclothes to watch.

"The command was given. Wailing babies were ripped from the arms of their mothers and dropped to the cobblestones. They were killed by rifle butts or bayonets."

Gabrielle's eyes filled with tears.

"Young children were made to face their parents while their little throats were slit, one by one. Their bodies were tossed into a pile. Young attractive women got special treatment. Their clothes were cut off. Naked and freezing, their hands were tied behind their backs. They probably cried, I imagine. Don't worry. They weren't raped."

Gabrielle shuddered as Patricia ran her fingers through her hair and across the back of her neck.

"Fraternizing with the locals was forbidden," Holly said. "They were untermenschen."

"They were what?" Gabrielle said.

Holly's cheek brushed hers.

"Subhuman," she whispered. "Animals. You can do anything you want to animals. The beautiful young women had chains fastened to their wrists behind their backs and they were hoisted into the air by a crane, dislocating their shoulders, and as they screamed and cried and begged the lovely blonde boys of the special S.S. squad took razor sharp knives and slit them open from breastbone to belly button. From years of practice they knew how to avoid the larger blood vessels so it took the young women a long time to die as their insides fell out onto the street. After they were gone, the remainder of the Resistance family and their neighbors were herded into a tight group and machine guns mowed them down. The other neighbors still in their nightclothes were forced to load the bodies onto horse-drawn wagons."

"All that for one member of one cell," Patricia said .

"As you can easily imagine," Holly whispered, "the people came to hate the Resistance more than the Germans. How about that."

Gabrielle gasped as Holly kissed her neck softly. Holly's mouth opened. Gabrielle felt Holly's teeth pressing sharply into her skin and in surprise she moaned. Holly took her mouth away and the place was cold with her saliva.

"We can begin the test now," she said.

Patricia stepped into Gabrielle's field of view.

"The Prague Protocol has three levels," she said. "First Level: the Tail of the Kite. You have sex with one of us while we all watch. You will be judged on your ability to take pleasure."

Gabrielle felt her knees shake.

"Level two. The Candy Store. You will have sex with all of us at the same time. You will be judged on your ability to take pleasure and inflict pain."

Tall Susan began to laugh in the shadowy living room.

"Level three. The Dark Lottery. You must accomplish a task chosen at random by our lottery machine," Patricia said. "We will now vote. This is a democracy, not a cult."

Debbie and New Susan stood up. Tall Susan came in from the kitchen and stood behind Pretty Susan.

Gabrielle's thoughts were jumbled. She liked Tall Susan's dark hair. It was short and feathered around the sides of her face and made her look even taller. There was a metallic taste in her mouth.

"Sisters, who among you desires Level One?" Patricia said in a soft voice.

Tall Susan raised her hand just over Pretty Susan's shoulder and wiggled her fingers. No one moved. Pretty Susan rolled her eyes.

"Level Two?"

New Susan's right hand shot up. She waved.

"Hmm," Patricia said. "Level Three?"

Holly, Pretty Susan, and Debbie raised their hands. Patricia raised her hand also.

"The Dark Lottery," Holly said into Gabrielle's ear.

"Yes," Pretty Susan hissed.

Patricia left Gabrielle's side. "Debbie, be a hot piece of ass and please fetch the machine. Susan, honey, would you please get drinks for everyone. Including yourself, of course."

New Susan said, "Sure!" and looked at Gabrielle. "Do you like vodka?"

Gabrielle like she was waking up from a dream.

"I love it."

"I know, me too! I'll be right back."

Holly, behind her, wrapped both arms around her neck in a double choke hold. Her perfume created a throbbing knot in Gabrielle left temple.

"Have a seat," she whispered and pushed.

Gabrielle crab walked around the coffee table, Holly gripped her shoulders, turned her around. Gabrielle bent her knees and sat on the edge of the sofa cushion.

"Stay put."

Holly went into the kitchen with Patricia leaving only Tall Susan in the living room. She leaned against one of the speakers.

"We've all done it," she said.

"You've all done tasks?" The only fun they have, Gabrielle thought.

"Yeah, I never vote for it. I only want to have sex. But I never win."

Gabrielle liked listening to her accent.

"What are, uh, what did you have to do?"

"Wasn't too bad. Had to seduce a professor. Didn't matter who. Pick one and fuck 'em."

"Huh."

Gabrielle thought of Dr. Swanson. Dr. Rimmler. She tried not to grimace.

"Know what the funny part was? I'm not a student. Never have been. Made it a bit tricky. They gave me forty-eight hours or I'm gone. Back to South Africa."

Ah.

"Know what I did? I was desperate. The clock was running. I found the lot where the faculty parked and I sat and waited. Wore a very thin shirt. Contemplated things. I mean, male or female, you know?"

The was a loud thump in the wall. Gabrielle heard Debbie's voice swearing.

"Uh oh, here she comes. The machine. Anyway."

New Susan came in from the kitchen with a tray of glasses. The stuff in the glasses was bright blue.

"Here we go!" New Susan put two small napkins on the coffee table and set the drinks on them. She gave a glass to Tall Susan. "Just something I whipped up."

"Thank you, Susan, it looks really good," Gabrielle said.

"Wow. You really are polite."

Gabrielle picked up the glass. The drink, thick as a milk shake, smelled like bubble gum. She sipped. Tasted like bubble gum with an extra something.

"Ah ha," Tall Susan said. She raised her glass. "Utter destruction to the enemy."

Sure thing. Gabrielle raised her glass.

"Utter destruction."

Tall Susan grinned and took a huge gulp of her drink, then another. She set her empty glass on the speaker.

Gabrielle took another sip, it was just so sweet, then another. Liquid candy mints with fifty percent alcohol. Tall Susan was watching.

"This is really good."

She took a deep breath and drank half the glass. Go fast, she thought. She dumped the rest of the glass into her mouth and swallowed. There was sudden sharp pain in her forehead to match the perfume headache.

"Yeah, it's too cold init. That bitch." Tall Susan closed her eyes.

From the kitchen came a heavy thump, a nasty scraping, and more swearing. Gabrielle heard a door open. Back porch, she thought. Her eyes didn't want to focus. Then Tall Susan was right next to her. She threw her leg over Gabrielle's knees.

"I'm *so* glad you came. This is going to be such fun no matter what the task is."

Gabrielle felt Tall Susan's fingers comb through her hair. She tried not to respond but a rogue wave of tingling ran down her back.

Now Susan rushed back in with a pitcher of the blue stuff.

"No, no, you're supposed to sip it. Do you have any idea how much vodka is in this?"

New Susan sat on Gabrielle's other side and handed her a full glass.

"Sip. So good."

Tall Susan intercepted the glass and drank half of it.

"You know what else is good?" she said.

Gabrielle gasped as Tall Susan's ice cold lips brushed the side of her neck.

"If you puke again I not cleaning it up."

"Thank you, Susan, that's good to know. Don't you think it's funny?"

"What? You know if you get any kind of bump I have just the stuff for it."

"Bump?" Gabrielle said as Tall Susan began making sucking sounds on her collarbone.

"Mm. You like that, don't you," Tall Susan said.

"Where your ring comes out. I forget what it's called."

"Oh, well, I think it's okay for now." Gabrielle gasped as Tall Susan lightly gripped skin in her teeth and then released.

"Keloid," Tall Susan said thickly.

"That's it. There's this oil from trees and it's great."

"Okay, thank you."

"You're welcome. It's just that it looks like you might be getting one. You know, if you want to get it on you should go in a bedroom. What's funny?"

Tall Susan began kissing the palm of Gabrielle's right hand. She paused and licked the wet spot she made.

"Awful lot of Susans aren't there?" she said. "Ever wonder about that? A bedroom."

"It's a coincidence."

Gabrielle felt Tall Susan's hand slip between her legs,

"*I* think there's a plan. I wish I were smart enough to figure it out. But you know right now I'm curious to see what the rest of Gabrielle tastes like. So let's all take our drinks into the bedroom and we can all solve this delicious mystery together."

New Susan took a sip then another sip. "Bedroom? Me?"

"Delicious," Gabrielle said. Tall Susan's hand moved further in. "But me?"

"Of course you, silly. Now, don't you think Susan is cute?"

"She's very cute."

"I know. Those blue eyes. Those luscious lips. Delectable."

Tall Susan suddenly leaned over making a purring sound and forced her tongue into Gabrielle's mouth.

Gabrielle thought, at least she brushed her teeth. Tall Susan opened her mouth fully and Gabrielle felt her hand pull out and move under her sweatshirt.

"Finally I have you," Tall Susan said.

Gabrielle thought, whatever they want I have to go along with it. I'm surprised I'm not blushing. She is really good looking however she's.

Someone sighed loudly.

"Not all that bright."

"We leave them alone for ten seconds," Patricia said.

Tall Susan lifted herself off of Gabrielle.

"Just think of it as a fuckin' test," she said.

"Unauthorized," New Susan said.

"What? That's the stupidest thing I've ever heard."

Gabrielle stood up with Tall Susan's hand still on her knee. Her glasses slipped to the end of her nose and her head swirled.

"Now what happens?" she said. Also, she thought, I'm getting used to being drunk. Like, every day.

Patricia looked at her appraisingly, unsmiling.

"Susan, Susan, get your lovely asses off the couch. Let's go."

Gabrielle stepped around the coffee table and the Susans gripped her upper arms and pulled firmly. They followed Patricia into the kitchen. She slapped a wall switch.

The kitchen surprised her. White counter tops and cabinet. A new refrigerator, also gleaming white. The sink was wide and had a jointed faucet dangling over it. Walls and window sills all painted bright white. Harsh light came from a glass globe. That's like two hundred watts, she thought. Gee, there's no table or chairs. Guess everyone sits on the floor. Cross-legged. Like first grade.

She giggled.

Patricia snapped her head around then continued.

"It's not funny," New Susan whispered. "There's nothing funny."

"Oh, I think that statement is erroneous," Gabrielle said.

The Susans looked at each other. Patricia had stopped in the short hallway which led to the bedrooms, back door, and bathroom. Gabrielle saw the edge of a sink. At Patricia's side was another door, painted white. It was odd-sized. Narrower than the others. All I have to do is open it for one second, she thought. The Susans increased their hold. One second.

"You can't talk," Tall Susan said.

"We're going to the Shrine," New Susan said.

"Oh of course we are," Gabrielle said seriously. She was propelled past the pantry, close enough to touch. Simple cut-glass doorknob. No deadbolt.

They guided her left. The back door was open before her. There were candles outside in the darkness. Dozens of candles.

"At least that's something. No lock, I mean," Gabrielle said. Cold air hit her face.

"Shh!"

Gabrielle was pushed down wooden steps into the night. A curving path was lined with candles all burning in the foggy air, She couldn't see where she was stepping. Concrete then grass then dirt. They came to a thick juniper hedge. She could smell gardenias.

Gabrielle felt an immediate surge of fear like a knife in the ribs. Those horrible flowers. She made her feet stop. Both Susans pushed on her arms. Gabrielle tried to turn, she wanted to run. She the sudden certain feeling the man with no face was behind the hedge. Fingernails dug into her skin.

"No, I don't want to," Gabrielle breathed.

Tall Susan sighed. "Look, it's too late."

"No. No."

"Well," New Susan said.

"Yep," Tall Susan said.

They lifted Gabrielle by the armpits and carried her down the curving path to where candles had been laid out in concentric rings. The dark shrine.

There were silent shapes. People in charcoal gray robes stood around the inner ring. Their faces were hidden by hoods. They seemed to turn in her direction.

For an instant Gabrielle thought she saw other robed figures, many others, countless shapes, enough to fill a stadium. She made herself *count*. She blinked and the rows of figures faded into the lightless abyss.

She was set on her feet in the center of the circle. She heard New Susan panting and shook off their hands with a rough shrug. The Susans backed away.

There are four of them, she thought, just four. Only four.

Gabrielle tried to think clearly. With her heart thudding in her chest she said, "You know, the robes and all, this is definitely a copyright violation."

"*Shut up*," said one of the hooded figures.

Gabrielle couldn't tell who it was. Not Holly, or Debbie. Patricia? Don't think so.

A fifth hooded person walked into the candle light pulling something on wheels. Tall Susan in her robe, she thought. She was sure.

The thing on wheels was a round shape under a thick gray sheet. It stopped in front of her.

She risked looking behind her. New Susan and Tall Susan in their regular black clothes stood a few feet back, arms at their sides.

Then I'm counting wrong, she thought, or there is someone new. Or.

The sheet was torn from the wheeled object. It was wire wheel three feet in diameter. No, a wire cage with a central axle. There were round objects inside the cage. She knew what this was. She had seen one almost exactly like at the Fourth of July carnival in Covina Park. Just not as big.

"Bingo," she whispered.

The one who had yelled at her turned its empty hooded face towards her and she braced herself for another scolding. The machine started. The cage began to rotate, the object inside began to cascade and tumble with a rushing sound. A bright floodlight came on shining straight up from the base.

The objects were red and sounded hollow. They weren't ping pong balls with letters. She thought they looked like those plastic snap-apart Easter eggs for children. For Easter egg hunts. Except instead of gumballs or Hershey's Kisses they contained tasks.

There must be fifty of sixty of them, she thought. She looked away quickly to keep from trying to *count* them. And thought.

This is more impressive than I imagined. They actually sat down and came up fifty or sixty grotesque, sickening, humiliating tasks to torture people with. Assuming there are no duplicates. That's a lot of work. It would take days to do that. So how long per task....

She closed her eyes tightly.

Stay *here*, she thought. You have to stay here.

Okay. How bad could it be? As long as it doesn't involve something disgusting. Like bugs. Or being naked in public. Or hurting something. She was suddenly gripped by a wave of helplessness. One of the hooded figures laughed.

Ah, *there's* Holly. That one.

The cage slowed. The tumbling plastic eggs made a low continuous growl.

"Gabrielle, this is your time of choosing."

The unfamiliar voice again. The hooded person raised their hand. The bingo machine stopped, reversed direction for one turn, then came to rest. The person tending it, Debbie, Gabrielle was almost positive, opened a small trap in the wire. A red egg popped out. The figure held it up for Holly, who giggled again under her hood.

They did this twice more. Now Holly held three of the eggs. The floodlight was turned off and the machine was pulled behind the hedge.

In faint candlelight, Gabrielle struggled to see. Holly stepped in front of her, hands held out. The three eggs looked black.

Gabrielle tried to look under Holly's hood. She had no face.

Holly began to rapidly shuffle the eggs in her hands. They made a sound like sandpaper on a balloon.

"All your life you knew you were different," she said. The voice was not Holly's. Gabrielle stared at the faceless figure in shock.

"You knew you didn't fit in. You knew you were better than everyone around you. You felt anger, contempt, and loneliness. Where could I go, you wondered, where the people would be as good as I am? As smart as I am?"

"Educated," said a figure behind her.

"As witty," said another. Patricia?

"As sexy." Debbie.

"As strong," said the unknown voice with the eggs. "Choose."

The fifth figure came from behind.

"Choose now!" The new voice again.

Gabrielle reached out, pulled back, then snatched the egg in the middle. It felt warm. The not-Holly held up the other two eggs and wiggled them as if to say, *nyahh, nyahh, you blew it.*

The new voice behind her said, "The task is in your hand. Complete the task and you will become one of us, the human beings. Fail your task and you will be cast out. You will wander the Earth the rest of your days, bereft of love or friendship. You will wander forever in the darkness outside lighted windows vainly trying to see the life within. Do you understand?"

Gabrielle nodded.

"There is one important condition you should be made aware of. As a human being you will be hated by your lessors, by the fleas of the world.

We tower over them, all the unfortunate little people, and sometimes sadly it is necessary to exercise our strength and crush one of them. Sometimes the fleas leave us no choice. This of course leads to more hatred from them. But when action is required, you must act. Failure to do your duty will result in your being cast out. All your human privileges will be immediately revoked." The person took a deep breath. "Do you accept this condition?"

Gabrielle held her voice steady. "Yes." She heard Tall Susan gasp.

The figure pointed at not-Holly. One of the eggs was twisted open and a slip of paper taken out.

"Gabrielle, this is one of the tasks you did not choose."

"While wearing only a black lace bra," the figures said, in Patricia's voice. "Sneak up behind the president of the university and pull his pants down. Then kiss him on the cheek."

Gabrielle let out her breath.

The other egg was opened. The figure now spoke in Debbie's voice.

"This task you also did not choose. While sitting in a comfortable chair before a warm fire, sip a cup of hot cocoa. Those cute little marshmallows are optional."

Gabrielle mouth fell open.

The figure laughed. Now it sounded like Holly again.

"Oh, bad luck. What an easy one, huh?"

All the hooded figures came around. Gabrielle looked at each in turn. They were all wearing flat black masks under the hoods. The effect was one of infinite depth. She almost expected to see stars.

"Open it and learn your task, Gabrielle."

"Open it," said another. Holly again.

"Open it, Gabrielle." They were all Holly.

Gabrielle thought, do it fast. Don't give them time to gloat. She gave the egg a twist and it made a cracking sound. She used her fingernail to pry it open and dug out the piece of paper. It was rolled up like a little scroll. She dropped the egg halves and unrolled it. There was single sentence. Gabrielle read it and felt relief then embarrassment. And then a kind of grief for her and Catherine. She tried to swallow but her throat was dry.

A muffled giggle.

"Well, Goddess, what does it say?"

"Choose your lover and do it in the middle of 101."

New Susan gasped and squealed simultaneously.

"You have forty-eight hours to complete your task."

"Tonight."

In her mind's eye, Gabrielle played back the the run of the freeway through town, both directions. Foot access. Lack of visibility to drivers, to police. Easy escape. Hurry.

"It could be..."

"Tonight. Right now." Quick, while they're off balance. "You. I choose you." She pointed at New Susan.

New Susan covered her mouth. Tall Susan's face fell and she looked away.

Gabrielle thought furiously. This was a long shot.

"The overpass at the north end of town. Where the big trees are. You can walk down." She wasn't sure if this was true. She put her hands on her hips. "All right?"

New Susan blurted out, "I know that spot! It's perfect!"

The figure seemed to shrug in annoyance.

"Gabrielle. Go wait in the living room," they said. The new voice again.

"I'm fine right here. Do we have a deal?"

The figure did not move.

"Doesn't that sound okay? I don't see why we can't proceed. Just let me use the bathroom."

She heard a long exhale under the hood. There was a whisper.

"I didn't get that."

"Fine."

"Great. This will be tightly focused task-specific operational sex in the middle of 101. As I see it, set-up, execute, confirm, and validate." Doubletalk. Gabrielle caught herself. Don't crack up.

One of the figures uttered, "Cool."

"Validate?" said another.

"Yes. Confirm and validate orgasm. No faking allowed."

New Susan gasped again. "I would never do that!"

"Of course not," Tall Susan patted her back. She still looked hurt.

"I play my part in the pleasure continuum like I'm supposed to," New Susan said.

"And you're very good."

"Thank you."

Continuum? Gabrielle decided against rolling her eyes.

"Can we go inside now? I really have to pee."

The hooded figures walked out of the circle of candles in a line and were quickly invisible in the dark. About where the Carriage House had been, she knew.

New Susan walked back up the path. Tall Susan came beside her.

"Kinda thought you might pick me," Tall Susan said softly.

Gabrielle whispered, "I didn't pick you because I like you." At least that's not a lie, she thought.

"Oh."

They walked hand in hand up the porch steps and into the dark hallway. The kitchen light popped on.

"Now just wait a minute," Tall Susan said. She closed the back door.

Gabrielle was startled by a loud thump. A plate hitting the floor. There was the sound of someone choking. Tall Susan swore.

Gabrielle, in the short hall, poked her head into the kitchen. Pretty Susan was bent over the sink. Her blonde hair clung to her wet collar and her body convulsed and she vomited.

Tall Susan turned on the water, took a look, then switched on the garbage disposer.

The disposer was loud. Pretty Susan upchucked again.

Gabrielle pulled back. The pantry's glass door knob was at her elbow. If it's locked, she thought, it's *mission:fail*. She quickly looked into the bathroom and then across the kitchen to the living room. No sign of New Susan and the hood people were still outside. She heard a voice just outside the back door.

She grasped the doorknob and the sharp edges dug into her palm. She twisted. It wouldn't move. She pushed the door down and twisted again. The knob turned. She pushed the door open a a light came on inside. They have to see that, she thought. The garbage disposer was turned off. In the ringing silence Gabrielle forced herself to *counting:override*. She looked into the panty for one heartbeat then closed as fast and quietly as she could. The light inside went out just as the back door opened.

Gabrielle let go of the knob, the warped pantry door only half seated, and she clasped her hands over her stomach.

Holly, in black leotards, appeared beside her.

"What are you doing?"

"Watching Susan throw up."

"No, I mean."

Patricia rushed past them.

"God damn it! We eat in here! And now the sink!"

Pretty Susan, gray-faced, held a dishtowel over her mouth and stumbled into the living room. The front of her t-shirt was dripping wet. Gabrielle heard the hall door slam. She smelled the sink and her stomach flip-flopped.

"I'm not cleaning this up," Tall Susan said.

Patricia glared at her. Holly crossed her arms.

"I wasn't the one who had a bowl of cornflakes for dinner using milk that should have been thrown out a month ago. Susan can clean this up herself. If she doesn't die."

"You can't leave it like this."

"I said no."

Tall Susan walked past Gabrielle and Holly to the bathroom and slammed the door. Holly went to the sink and looked in.

"Is that?"

"I think so," Patricia said. She picked up a spoon and fished something out.

Gabrielle could see a small cylindrical object soaked with green fluid.

"Um," Holly said and swiftly withdrew to the living room and went through the hall door. Patricia stood in the middle of the kitchen. She tapped her foot.

Intensely curious to see what could possibly gross out Holly, Gabrielle took a couple steps in.

"I wouldn't," Patricia said.

Gabrielle was close enough to see that the cylindrical objects had a string dangling. Patricia let out an exasperated sigh and went past Gabrielle to the bathroom. She knocked on the door.

"Susan. Honey. Why." She closed her eyes. "There is a big mass of tampons clogging up the kitchen sink. Used tampons. Did you do that?"

The bathroom door opened and Patricia went in. There were muffled voices. Not yelling, she noted, more like crying.

Alone in the brightly lit kitchen, Gabrielle took a deep breath and peeked into the sink. The tampons looked like a ball of soggy cotton snakes, streaked with brown stains, sitting in half a foot of lumpy green water. Cornflakes, she thought. But no blood. Well, very little.

"This is just like that lab full of freshmen," she said. "Don't think. Just do what you have to do."

She opened the cabinets and saw what she wanted. She pulled on rubber glooves and consciously not hesitating plunged her right hand into the opaque green water. She found the opening to the disposer. She felt around it. There were a few tampon shapes but they weren't the clog. She touched something soft and pushed with her middle finger. She pinched the mass and tugged. There was a loud gurgle and the sink began to drain. She carefully pulled the mass out. It was black fabric with a black strap. She spread it out on the counter as the vomit drained away.

She knew what the fabric was. She turned on the water and rinsed it off. She took off the gloves.

"Silk. Black silk in the sink," she said. But what was it? Panties? There's not enough material, she thought.

There was a single triangular piece with a tangle of elastic straps. She looked at the triangular part. There was something metallic stuck to it.

She lifted her glasses. It was a tiny silver pin in the shape of a heart.

She glanced at the bathroom door. She checked the living room door.

She shoved the G-string still wet into her front pocket.

Then she cleaned the sink keeping the tampons corralled. She looked around the kitchen. They believe in appliances, she thought. Big shiny toaster with four slots next to a big countertop over. *Convection*, it said, something new. Closest to the fridge was another boxy unit.

A microwave. A new style with a digital display and a keypad. It showed the time. *12:15.*

She checked her Timex in surprise. *8:02.*

She automatically wanted to set the clock and looked closely at the keypad. Something moved inside the microwave. There was dark object that twitched. She pushed the latch.

546

A mouse ran out onto the counter, turned right, and shot lightning fast behind an array of storage containers. The containers were surrounded by bits of spaghetti and rice. She could see the mouse's pink tail behind a jar of macaroni.

She carefully turned back.

At the edge of the open microwave's door, another mouse sat watching her. Dark gray fur. Long tail. It held perfectly still.

"If I were you, I'd get out of here," Gabrielle whispered.

The mouse launched itself from the oven and hit the floor with a solid plop.

"Ow."

It was gone in a an instant around the corner by the pantry. She heard the pantry door rustle.

Take another look, she thought. It's right there. You have the whole place to yourself. The memory of the pantry interior swam before her. She knew she's have to concentrate to see it. Later, she thought. Don't start now. Don't forget where you are. Don't push your luck.

She wiggled the nose ring.

A toilet flushed. Patricia and Tall Susan came out of the bathroom followed by Debbie.

Gabrielle felt the hair stand up on the back of her neck. Had she been in there the whole time?

Debbie's eyes rose to hers. She smiled.

"Do you still have to pee?"

"Yeah. Um."

"You okay?"

"Sure."

Debbie waved her in. Gabrielle tried to toss her hair back but it was too oily and it stuck to the sides of her head.

"Thanks."

Gabrielle stepped into the bathroom, closed the door, and sighed with relief. There was another door next to the shower. The other half of the living room, she thought, just calm down.

It took her a full minute sitting on the toilet to pee. As she was washing her hands she had the urge to open the antique mirror medicine cabinet. What the hell is in there? But they'll hear it, she knew. Her fingers tickled the chrome frame. She flushed the toilet and opened it.

It was disappointing. Aspirin. Dental floss. A red toothbrush. Normal stuff. No hypodermic needles. No drugs. Not even a loaded handgun. She giggled and flushed the toilet again to mask the click of the magnetic latch.

As she turned the bathroom doorknob music started playing loudly. Not the fish song but the same group, the same strong female voice. Gabrielle listened, acutely aware of her lack of pop culture knowledge. This song was about a man who did magic. She kind of liked it, just maybe not so loud. She could feel the beat in her ribcage.

She opened the door to see New Susan at the microwave oven. Susan had washed her hair. Tousled blonde tresses reached her waist in a damp wave over the sheer black nylon.

She did that for me, Gabrielle thought. Those blue eyes.

Picking her nose, New Susan took out a large glass bowl. She tore open a box of spaghetti dropped it into the bowl. Then she poured red sauce from an economy size jar. She gave it a shake and put it into the oven. Gabrielle could see numerous mouse droppings on the oven surface. New Susan slammed the door shut, keyed in 10 minutes on the display, and hit start.

"I never knew you could do that," Gabrielle said.

"Oh I use the microwave for everything." She wiped her hands on her pants and flipped her hair behind her ears. "It kinda doesn't work that great all the time."

Gabrielle could see the sauce start to bubble. There was the strong smell of burning garlic.

"It smells really good, doesn't it," Gabrielle said.

"Yeah. I'm like so hungry. I just need to eat a little."

"Sure."

"And then we can go." She smiled. "You know."

Gabrielle swallowed. "I'm kind of hungry too."

"Oh we have lots of stuff. Help yourself. Check the fridge. Do you like hot dogs?"

"I love hot dogs."

New Susan laughed. "I like the way you talk."

"Thank you."

New Susan pulled the white fridge door open with a jerk of her whole body. The bulb inside was very bright. Gabrielle saw a gallon of orange juice and a carton of milk lying on its side. The milk had covered the shelf it was on and made a puddle on the bottom surface. There were patches of green mold on its edges. There were empty jelly jars and on a side shelf a pile of crushed eggs. The shells were a solidified mass and the yolky contents a dry yellow film on the glass. There were mouse droppings everywhere. Her attention was drawn to a shriveled silver-gray twist of desiccated leather which lay next to a stack of styrofoam trays.

She leaned closer. The twisted object had tiny legs.

Gabrielle took a deep breath.

"Is that a lizard?"

New Susan giggled. "Not anymore." She took a hot dog from an open package.

Gabrielle forced herself not to look at it.

New Susan opened the microwave door. The fan stopped. The display showed seven minutes remaining.

"Just stick it in here for a few seconds."

She started to set the hot dog down amidst the mouse droppings.

"Wait."

"What?"

"Just wait. Um."

"Why?"

"Do you have any paper towels?"

"You don't need them."

"But."

"It's fine."

New Susan plopped the hot dog down and slammed the door and hit the button.

Gabrielle stomach lurched. She tried to see if the hot dog was touching anything but the metal window grid was too dense.

"It's so cool to watch them. Right? They like swell up and like burst open and all the juices come out. Like it's exploding from an atomic bomb or something. Like if an atomic bomb went off right there that's what you'd look like. Just your guts all coming out and all cooked inside."

"Uh huh."

New Susan counted down thirty seconds and popped the door open. The hot dog had indeed split open and was sizzling loudly. She picked it up.

"Here you go. Ow! Now I am absolutely the hungriest I have ever been in my life."

Gabrielle held out her hand and caught the dripping thing. It burned.

"Thanks." Don't see anything sticking to it, she thought. She bit off the top where it had a puckered look.

"Nice metaphor." Holly, right behind her.

Gabrielle nodded and swallowed without chewing.

"Susan, what are you doing? Cooking dinner? Get moving."

Holly's voice was gentle but her eyes were angry.

"But I'm really hungry!"

A stream of smoke was coming out of the microwave.

"Here you can have this," Gabrielle said. "I'm like you know full."

"Wow, thanks. Are you sure?"

"Oh yeah. Here."

Gabrielle set the hot dog in her hand. She saw it then. A black speck. Right where her thumb had been.

New Susan ate the whole thing in two bites then one by one licked all of her fingers with a kissing sound.

Debbie came in from the hallway. She had put on a bright red sweater. She eyed the unlatched panty door and paused. She turned the glass knob and pulled it shut with a bang. Patricia came in from the back door and they exchanged a look.

Gabrielle's heart started pounding. She focused on the floor. There was a pile of coffee grounds by the sink. Also a carrot and half an apple.

Debbie and Patricia spoke in quick barely audible murmurs.

Holly reached around her shoulders and clawed off her leotard top and stood topless. Gabrielle stared and wasn't quite sure what she was seeing until the light caught them. Rings. More piercings, she thought, and they are in her –

Gabrielle turned to the refrigerator.

She felt Holly's hands on her shoulders. Then Holly gripped her hair and tugged playfully. Gabrielle half turned.

Don't show a reaction, she thought.

Holly's expressive, swiftly changing face had abandoned hope and latched onto a much stronger emotion.

"The best part of my personality," she said, "you could say, my defining factor, is honesty." Her eyes seethed with anger. "I know how smart you are. I have your transcripts. You get straight As in advanced math and engineering classes. So you're almost as smart as my beloved. I also know she put you up to this. You're just not the type to do this on your own. However, if I'm honest with myself, I know I can be fooled."

Holly pulled on her hair until it felt the scalp was being ripped out. Gabrielle gritted her teeth.

"I would never lie to you, Gabrielle. If what you are doing is in any way a trick, you will devoutly wish you had never been born."

Holly let go. Gabrielle didn't move. Holly shifted enough to cause one of nipple rings to brush Gabrielle's arm. It was cold as ice.

"I'm not very happy in the English department," she said wistfully. "It's beginning to feel like waste of time. And no one here understands me. No one knows me. No one sees the world the way I do. It's as if I'm way up high looking down at all of you and there's no one up here with me anymore. So I'm alone. See? That's how honest I am. I accept my loneliness. I accept."

Gabrielle saw tears in her eyes.

"There will never be another. She belongs to the past. I need to let her go. I need to accept my life of loneliness."

Gabrielle saw sadness, even despair, in her face. And behind it all a substrate of anger. And then she was gone.

In the living room the huge speakers fell silent. Gabrielle could hear someone vomiting in the bathroom. A mouse ran between her feet and vanished under the fridge.

New Susan's eyes sparkled.

"Okay. Let's go have sex!"

New Susan got in the back seat and she bounced until the springs twanged. Pretty Susan rode shotgun. The smell of New Susan's shampoo was heavy in the tiny interior. Lavender and cigarette smoke. The night had turned cold, almost freezing, and no one rolled their window down.

Maybe the freeway will be quiet, Gabrielle thought. She sighed.

Sure.

As she pulled out, Pretty Susan said, "Holly likes you." Her straight blonde hair was combed smoothly to the left side of her head and then cut in a straight line angled up from her chin. Gabrielle thought it was a very sexy futuristic look.

"She likes me? I thought she was gonna kill me."

"Oh, no."

New Susan started bouncing on the seat again. The whole car shook.

"Oh my God!" Pretty Susan said.

"It feels good!" She kept bouncing.

"You'd think getting hit in the head with a two-by-four would feel good."

"Depends!" She paused bouncing. "She was pulling your hair. That means you have a shot with her."

Gabrielle missed shifting into third.

"Me? Holly?"

She held the stick in neutral. What street am I on?

"You definitely do."

"Not saying you should," Pretty Susan said.

"As you would know."

"Shut up. You gonna stop?"

Gabrielle slammed the brakes the car came to rest past a stop sign.

New Susan laughed.

Gabrielle looked both ways. Closely parked cars with barely one lane in the street.

"Never done that before."

"That would kind of sum up this whole day for you, huh?" Pretty Susan said.

Gabrielle looked at her with a feeling of surprise. So, not stupid.

"Yes."

"My advice about Holly is, don't. But if you do, you know, because you're overcome with lust."

"As you would know," New Susan said and leaned between the seats. "Big time lust."

Pretty Susan sighed.

New Susan continued. "Lusty lust all over the place. Every time you turned a corner."

"Shit."

"There they'd be. There were so many orgasms lying around I was tripping over them."

Gabrielle laughed. "That does sound like a lot."

"Oh, I mean they were on the walls."

"Ah," Gabrielle said. "The sticky kind."

As New Susan laughed Pretty Susan gave her a sharp look. "Sticky," she said softly. "Anyway, my advice is do not get involved. Waste of time."

Gabrielle wasn't clear. "Emotionally involved."

"Yep. It's always all about her. She does you, it's about her. You do her, it's still about her. What people say on tv is about her. The weather is about her."

"Wow. Well I have no intention."

"You don't know."

Gabrielle nodded just to nod.

"No really. Listen. You don't know. You might."

Gabrielle felt New Susan's hand steal between the seats and settle on her right leg.

"This is going to be so good. Let's do it now."

Gabrielle tried to concentrate on driving. She was all turned around beneath the nighttime overcast sky. Her mental map refused to come into focus. Most of the stores were dark and the parking lots empty wet asphalt. She looked for street signs.

Bianca, one sign said. Not familiar. It looked like not much more than a dark alley. It was lined with antique cars, one for sure a Ford Model A. There was one streetlight, the old type with a big yellowish bulb.

"How about that," she said as they passed. But that wasn't anything, she thought. That street.

"What?" Pretty Susan said quickly.

"Right back there. You never know what you're going to see driving around this town at night." One of the other cars had looked like a Bentley from the twenties. She suddenly knew where she was.

"I didn't see anything."

"There was..."

"This is the most boring-ass stupid cow town I have ever lived in. Nothing but hick farmers or idiot college students."

"Like you could even get into college," New Susan said.

"That place? It's like a big high school. They have cheerleaders."

"It's a lot harder than you think."

Pretty Susan laughed. "Is it gonna be much farther?"

"We're almost there," Gabrielle said. "Just past that gas station."

A threadbare gas station appeared in the fog. Only one fluorescent glowed over the pumps.

"See?" Pretty Susan pointed. "Nothing's open all night in this stupid place. Even the gas stations close. That's how you know you're in a cow town."

New Susan made a couple bounces.

"Oh! I just thought of something. You want to know your secret name?"

Gabrielle's hand slipped off the steering wheel.

"My what?" No, she thought, no.

"I'll tell you if you want."

Pretty Susan made a coughing sound which could have been laughter. "Secret," she mumbled.

"My secret name," Gabrielle said. "Well, um, maybe." The world would end, she thought, right here and now.

"I can't tell you how I know but I know, okay? It's..."

"Wait!" Gabrielle's knee bumped the stick knocked the VW into neutral with a nasty clank. The engine roared.

"Smashing Elektra! That's it. Isn't that great?"

"Smashing." Gabrielle wiped her face.

"That's really cool, isn't it."

"Smashing. Really." She dropped the car back into second.

"I know! We all really liked it."

"Uh huh." You all would, she thought.

New Susan, let down by her reaction, sat back.

"Susan, you know, it's not what I expected. I don't know."

"I think it's great."

"Well the Elektra part's good."

"But the Smashing! I mean, we all laughed." She caught herself.

"I'm just a little surprised."

"Okay."

Gabrielle made a left under a towering stand of eucalyptus. They went alongside a waist-high concrete wall and were instantly over the freeway, the four lanes good twenty feet below. A steady stream of bright headlights and shadowy vehicles flowed through the fog.

"We're right over it."

"Perfect!" New Susan said.

"Huh," Pretty Susan said. She turned her head from side to side, frowning. "Where is like the trees in the way. Like the sun."

Gabrielle looked at her and stopped the car on the shoulder. She killed the engine and headlights. All the houses were dark. What time was it? Student cars lined the curbs. Probably not super picky about parking, she hoped, but not going to be here long anyway.

The nose ring started itching and she carefully tapped it.

Do it fast, no fooling around. Then with a heavy feeling in her stomach she thought, this is ridiculous, Catherine. What am I doing?

Pretty Susan popped her door open, got out and slammed the seat forward much harder than necessary. New Susan bounced on the seat and let the springs propel her out the door. She giggled.

"Wow, Gabrielle. Down there?"

Gabrielle got out. Where? She stuffed the keys into her pocket. She said to Pretty Susan, "Could you."

"What?"

"Close your door."

"What?"

"The car door. Close it."

New Susan rolled her eyes and reached around and closed the door. She gave Gabrielle a look.

Pretty Susan shrugged and said, "We can study the sound."

The air was chill and heavy with smell of dripping eucalyptus trees and diesel exhaust. The cars and trucks hushed and rumbled on the slick pavement. The ground dropped away steeply under a rusty chain-link fence. There were no footholds Gabrielle could see going down, just compacted dirt with clumps of ice plant. At the bottom the dirt became the two westbound lanes where old pickups and delivery vans and eighteen wheelers passed every ten seconds. In the center of the freeway the looming bulk of the concrete support column flared out in the inky darkness beneath the overpass. The massive base of the column was surrounded by deflector guardrails of galvanized steel. They formed a wedge shaped protected space of just the right size and just out of range of the lone streetlight poking up beside the gas station.

"Right there, right? Yeah, I can't believe I never noticed this before."

"I just kind of remembered it."

"Nice."

New Susan put her arms around Gabrielle's waist and pulled her tight. Both of her hands found their way to her buttocks and massaged. She kissed Gabrielle on the corner of her mouth.

Gabrielle found she almost liked New Susan. Type 2, with the 'constant hungry' look, but all she could think of was *mouse turd*. And kept her mouth closed.

"Whoa," Pretty Susan said. "Hot." She stared into the fog.

New Susan's dark blue eyes flickered across Gabrielle's face.

"I thought you..."

Multiple conflicting thought processes collided and fused in Gabrielle's mind: You have no choice. New Susan is kind of cute. I'm not feeling anything. For*get* this. There's no getting out of it. They are looking at you. I don't think I can do it. You must do something *right now.*

Gabrielle wiped her forehead and gripped New Susan by the arms then caught herself. Gentle, she thought. She caressed her forearms and then her elbows.

New Susan looked uncertain and closed her eyes. Her breath deepened.

Gabrielle felt her body relax and slipped her fingers under the sleeves of the black t-shirt. New Susan's akin was warm and delicately soft. She trembled.

"My hands are cold. Sorry."

"It's," New Susan said.

Gabrielle took a deep breath. Analyze it, she thought. Step by step. I've never done that to this. An interesting idea occurred to her. She thrust her hands all the way under New Susan's sleeves and pulled her close. She smelled the side of her neck and exhaled into her ear. New Susan responded by forcefully rubbing Gabrielle backside.

Pretty Susan said, "Huh. Okay."

Another protocol, Gabrielle thought. I'll think about it that way. In outline form. The Gabrielle Protocol. This made her laugh and New Susan laughed also and began running the tip of her tongue along her jaw.

Linear style.

Foreplay: Sexy it most definitely was.

Nodes of Attraction.

Visual: Long blonde hair, blue eyes, slender waist. Type 2 lips, clean teeth.

Olfactory: Hair recently washed. Sweat on her neck. Gabrielle had no idea why sweat was sexy. It was same with Catherine and Samantha and this thought almost broke her concentration.

Tactile: Silky smooth skin of upper arms. Body heat radiating from her chest.

Behavioral: Throaty laugh. Nice smile. Likes to cuddle, I think.

Physiological: Um.

Gabrielle dug her hands into New Susan's shoulders. This made New Susan tip her head back and Gabrielle dove in and sucked on her neck. She got a tiny bit of skin between her teeth and pinched gently. New Susan made a high-pitched squeal.

Gabrielle continued the outline. Ok, what happens.

Physiological: Arousal. Might be past this stage. Probably. SR: *P:* Plateau. Yes. And then *O.* Version 1.0. Stick to that.

Gabrielle stopped and laughed.

Breathing hard, New Susan whispered, "What is it?"

"It's true. What everyone tells me. I never believed it but now I do." She cradled New Susan face in her hands. "I think too much." And she kissed her as hard as she could.

They leaned against a palm tree behind a large Fuchsia with sweet smelling flowers. It was very dark. Gabrielle slowed down as New Susan sped up. Gabrielle got there first anyway. New Susan cried. Actual tears.

"That always happens," she said. "Don't know why."

Gabrielle held her and stroked her hair.

Pretty Susan said," Huh, all right, but it doesn't count."

Gabrielle, annoyed, said, "How could that not count?"

Pretty Susan pointed down the slope past the ragged edge of the chain-link fence. An eighteen wheeler passed with a muted roar.

New Susan giggle. "We're supposed to be in the middle of 101."

"Oh come on."

"We'll have to do it again, I guess."

"I really don't want to go across the freeway."

"Me neither."

Gabrielle sighed as New Susan nestled against her.

Pretty Susan, arms at her sides, was gazing up at the overcast sky and nodding to herself.

"What is it with her," she whispered.

"She's just listening to the voices in her head."

"No kidding."

"They tell her what to do and stuff."

"My God."

"She told me once the voices sang to her at night. I always thought that would be kind of nice."

As long as the voices don't tell you to burn the house down or drain the brake fluid from someone's MG. Ok, she thought, no point in waiting.

New Susan sensed a change in her posture.

"It's really quiet here, isn't it. Let's just stay here for a while."

"Not a single car has gone by this whole time. It's super quiet."

"Super quiet."

Pretty Susan was standing in the middle of the street. Her head was tipped back and her mouth was moving as if she were having a conversation.

"She does that all the time."

Gabrielle disengaged herself.

"People just drive around her."

Gabrielle grabbed Pretty Susan's arm and pulled her gently to the shoulder. Pretty Susan's feet scuffed and she made a tsk sound.

"How'd we do?" Gabrielle said.

Pretty Susan looked at her blankly.

"Susan and I just had sex right down there. We almost got run over by a cement truck. Weren't you watching?"

New Susan gasped and stared.

Pretty Susan frowned.

"So," Gabrielle said, "we can go now, right?"

Pretty Susan shook her head. "Do you think I'm an idiot?" she said thickly.

"No, of course not. You're definitely smarter than the average Golf major."

"What does that even mean?"

"It means here we go. Come *on*."

Gabrielle held out her hand and New Susan took it. At the fence they both sat on the cold dirt and pushed themselves under the chain-link. Their jeans made a grabbling sound.

New Susan wriggled and laughed.

"This is like being a kid again!"

She tugged her hair from a knot of twisted wire.

"Yeah, huh. I guess we can just slide down." Getting back up will be a different story, she thought and craned her neck and looked up.

"I know! Whoa!" New Susan's Keds scrabbled on the gravel.

They both bent their knees and slid down.

"That was fun! Wow!"

A speeding Continental flashed by, a black boxy shape.

"Careful!"

"Wow! Did you see that? He was going like a hundred!"

Gabrielle slid on her pants and stopped at a Ficus tree. The poor thing was half bent over. She pushed her hands down and pushed and took two giant steps to the bottom. New Susan held her arms wide and caught herself at the edge of the pavement just as a Chevy van roared by. The side of the van was covered by a painting of a topless woman reclining on a rainbow. She was holding up her bikini top with one hand and waving it like a flag. The driver gunned it and honked the horn.

New Susan yelled. "Nice tits!"

Gabrielle saw the brake lights flash. She tensed and got ready to run up the hillside. The van accelerated and in a few seconds was out of sight around the curve.

"Oh my God I think he heard me."

"Kind of looked like it."

"I don't usually screw guys in vans."

"You should never do that."

"Why not?"

"Because."

"You don't like guys?"

"Not that way."

"But never?"

"No never."

"Wow, Gabrielle. You're really weird."

Gabrielle waited for another huge semi to go by. The roar was deafening.

"What if the guy is a psycho?"

"No way."

"What if he kidnaps you?"

"Why?"

"I don't know. Guys are crazy. It happens all the time in L.A."

"Really? Wow."

"Right. So don't get in vans with strangers."

"Okay, I won't."

"Promise."

"I promise. I really like you," New Susan said shyly.

"Thanks." Gabrielle shook her head from the mental gear shifting.

"Do you like me?"

"Of course I do." She had to admit it.

"I don't usually do it with guys. I want you to know that."

"Well, good."

"It's just that sometimes." New Susan's eyes widened and she looked intently behind Gabrielle at the westbound lanes. "Okay, now! Now!" And she darted across the freeway and hopped the guardrail. "Come on!" Her voice came from the shadows.

Gabrielle saw there were actually no headlights visible coming westbound and only an occasional vehicle eastbound. She stepped into the lane.

And of course, she thought, that one car over there will be the CHP.

She took another step. It felt like a very wrong thing to do.

A pair of headlights appeared in the fog. Dim and yellow. She could hear the engine. Rough and limping.

"Oh my God, Gabrielle!" came New Susan's voice.

Gabrielle listened to the blood pounding in her ears. She forced her feet to move. Eight steps. Her face was numb. New Susan grabbed her sweatshirt and pulled her against the wet steel of the guardrail. The gray overcast was blotted out by the lightless concrete of the overpass.

A red pickup passed with a sputter creating a raucous echo in the hollow space. Acrid exhaust fumes seemed to hand in the air next to her. Gabrielle choked and coughed. Her hands hit masses of flowers. The guardrail chilled her hands and the sharp edge cut her fingers It was almost too high to climb over. How had New Susan done it?

"You have longer legs than me."

Gabrielle got her right leg over, balanced on the edge, and swung left leg up.

"You are like so slow."

"This thing hurts." Gabrielle perched on the guardrail.

"You're such a baby."

"Oh, I'm..."

"Wait. Stay there."

New Susan pushed Gabrielle knees apart then put her hands around her waist.

"Perfect height."

Gabrielle kept hold of the steel edge. New Susan began to kiss her neck.

"So you're a student?"

"Uh huh," New Susan murmured.

"What," Gabrielle said before being cut off by a huge roar. A flatbed in the westbound lane loaded with sections of sewer pipe blasted by close behind her. The shock wave shoved her more tightly into New Susan's embrace then the vacuum instantly yanked her back and she swayed out over the pavement. She gripped the guardrail as hard as she could unable to balance.

"I got you," New Susan said laughing. "I should've done this a long time ago."

"Uh huh, sure." Good thing I peed, Gabrielle thought. It felt like her left hand was bleeding.

More headlights appeared in the mist. A mini truck with a plastic camper shell and another old clunker pickup, both thankfully in the right lane but still very loud.

Oh you can forget this, Gabrielle thought.

"This is great," she said.

New Susan burrowed deeply. "I just love the way your neck smells. I just love it." Her breathing became heavy and rhythmic.

Gabrielle stared into the darkness over New Susan's shoulder and began to breathe heavily also. She didn't want to let go of the guardrail. New Susan didn't seem to be paying close attention and she let herself be gently rocked.

"Oh," Gabrielle said. She rolled her eyes. "Oh my God. Oh."

New Susan moaned loud enough to be heard over a passing delivery van with tall white sides. She saw a stylized logo of a plate of food and the sign, 'Darla's Restaurant Supply. Nobody Beats Our Meat!'

Gabrielle felt New Susan's body tense and shudder. She was panting. Gabrielle tipped back causing New Susan to raise her chin and kissed her. She waited until New Susan seemed short of breath before pulling back.

"Susan, you're incredible," Gabrielle whispered. Her hands were almost numb. She slipped off the guardrail and let blood flow back into her arms.

New Susan stretched.

"I know."

Gabrielle could barely make out the dirt slope they had slid down. Traffic was even more sparse now. She didn't want to look at her watch. Long after midnight. The knot in her stomach relaxed a bit.

Still, Catherine.

The knot came back. Different. Colder. But first things first. Run across the freeway. Climb the hill somehow. *Get out of here.*

"Let's get back to the car. Where's Susan anyway?"

"Oh she's afraid of heights."

"What heights?"

"Any heights. Like she wouldn't even go to the edge of the street right there."

"She's not there? So she's not watching?"

"She's probably just leaning against your car."

"Listening to the voices."

"Yeah."

"So they keep her company," Gabrielle said.

"Oh sure."

New Susan dug into her pants pocket. She pulled out a plastic lighter and a small plastic bag which she unfolded.

"So all this?" Gabrielle waved her arms. She couldn't help it. "We didn't have to."

"What?"

"Come *on* before the police show up."

"Why would they show up?" New Susan took a small object from the bag and pinched it. The plastic bag she dropped and it blew away in the fog. She clicked the lighter then lit the end of the small object. She puffed on the other end, exhaled, and held it out to Gabrielle.

"Here," she said in a choked voice, "you need to get high."

Gabrielle felt her throat close up. The smell was incredibly strong, that awful burning t-shirt smell.

"You're kidding."

"No, it's good stuff." She waggled the joint. "Hurry."

"Thanks," Gabrielle said. It came out as a croak. No way out, she thought. I should've run when I had the chance. I always hesitate. I'm just not cut out for this.

"Oh my God you are so slow."

New Susan turned her hand upside down and stuck the end of the joint between Gabrielle's lips. Gabrielle tried to pinch it the same way. She could tell there was a technique to it. Her stomach did a flip flop and she cleared her throat.

Just get it over with. Like everything else. Like getting your nose pierced, she thought with dismay.

She could not see exactly how you were supposed to do it. The end of the joint barely between her lips was too small to actually suck on. She had a sudden idea. Fake it. Inhale around the thing. How bad could it be? Besides, I'm almost invisible here. It's perfectly safe.

She scrounged up her face as New Susan had done and breathed in strongly. An inch from her face the lit end flared brightly. And a massive surge of smoke filled her mouth and, before she could react, her lungs and sinuses. It was acrid, pungent, weirdly cold, and she couldn't smell it anymore. Wide-eyed she held her breath for two heartbeats then let it out. She was shocked to see the stream of smoke issue from her mouth twisting and turning like a ghostly snake against the blackness. She was surprised she didn't feel the urge to cough. She handed the joint back.

"Sheesh, use it all why don't you." New Susan quickly took another hit.

Gabrielle inhaled cold night air.

I did it, she thought. I did it by not thinking.

Her throat seized and a huge coughing fit hit her, a nasty dry hack, and she felt a knot of acidic phlegm make its way into her mouth.

As New Susan laughed and exhaled another cloud of smoke, Gabrielle bent over. In the corner of her eye she saw headlights approach on the eastbound side. Very bright headlights. As she spit the car locked up its brakes and slid to a stop well past the overpass. Gabrielle clearly saw the letters on the trunk. *Highway Patrol.*

The police car reversed and Gabrielle was hit by a massive impact across her chest and an instant later was lying flat on her back in the westbound lanes, her feet on the guardrail. New Susan was already at the hill and starting to climb.

Gabrielle rolled, got her feet down. More headlights were directly in front of her, high up, another big rig coming fast. Everything was suddenly bathed in flashing red light.

Gabrielle rolled all the way over and crawled into the path of the approaching eighteen wheeler then got to her feet and ran to the shoulder. She heard the CHP unit peel out. The flashing red lights were enveloped by the mist.

She knew the center divider was impossible to cross, he couldn't make a quick U-turn. *He has to go all the way,* she shivered on the edge of the dirt, *miles to an exit and come flying back.* She tried to figure it. *We have...*

New Susan shoved down past her, back to the freeway.

"I dropped it! Oh my God help me look!"

New Susan stepped into the headlight beams of the semi and plopped to her knees on the pavement. Her backside caught the light and the driver saw her at that instant. The truck's engine dropped to idle, no time for horn, too late to turn, the brakes shrieked at maximum extension and the entire truck and trailer passed over New Susan like a howling metal dragon.

Gabrielle could've reached out and touched it.

Pretty Susan screamed at the top of the hill.

Then the eighteen wheeler was past, brakes locked up. The tires emitted a thunderous rumble and black smoke. The cab did a crazy wobble and snapped hard to the left. The big front fender slammed into the trailer and the whole vehicle, a huge mass now governed by the laws of momentum and inertia, slid on the damp pavement under the eucalyptus trees until it was almost out of sight on the curving freeway. It lurched to a stop in the shadows between streetlights.

Gabrielle coughed. Burning rubber. *Jackknifed,* she thought.

She was afraid to look down at what was certainly the hideously mangled body of New Susan.

Funny, she thought. *I really don't care. My life is over. Never even made it to twenty-one. Poor truck driver. Hope he doesn't get in too much trouble.*

Gabrielle felt a wave of warmth envelope her from head to toe.

And then a ghostly figure rose before her, long hair streaming away.

Beautiful, Gabrielle thought. *But.*

"Wow," New Susan said, "that was like incredibly interesting."

"Oh, gosh," Gabrielle said. "You're still here."

"Like machines. You know? They are fantastic. Like, the human mind."

"The human mind creates meaning where none existed before," Gabrielle said.

"That is so cool."

"I thought you were dead."

"Why?"

They both walked easily up the hill. Pretty Susan was standing in the middle of the street holding her face in her hands. Her shirt was wet. She was drooling.

"Look at her," Gabrielle said. There was something so adorable about Pretty Susan. She wanted to hug the dickens out of her.

"I know," New Susan said. "What can you do?"

"Wow. I feel sorry for the truck driver."

"Yeah. Oh well."

"You know we should probably get out of here."

"But I like it here. I love all these trees."

"The trees are unbelievable."

"Unbelievable."

Gabrielle fished her keys out of her pocket. It took extra long because her pocket seemed a whole lot bigger than before. It was like whole world in there and she kind of got lost for a moment. She held the keys up to the light.

"That's just so interesting," she said.

"The key? That's your whole life right there."

"Right! It's like all the little scratches and the way it's worn on the end is a record of my whole life."

"So don't lose it!" New Susan said nearly in tears.

"Oh, I never would lose it," Gabrielle said and looked at the red lights illuminating the upper branches of the trees. She thought it was amazingly beautiful. Then a powerful spotlight swept the area including the broken down fence just above her head.

"Wow, who is that?"

Gabrielle threw her arms out and stopped New Susan before she stepped into the beam of light.

"Our course of action is clear." Gabrielle remembered something. A speeding car with letters on it. The spotlight went out.

"You really are," New Susan said.

"I are?" Gabrielle giggled.

"Smart. Like super smart. That's why you're so slow. Because you're always thinking."

"We just have to hold very still for a few minutes. The police officer will have to go help that truck driver."

"What truck driver?"

The warm, inviting, ocean of peace and confused thinking was slowly receding from her mind.

"The guy who was driving the truck that ran you over."

"Bullshit."

"No, that's him."

"Nobody ran me over. I'm pretty sure I'd remember something like that."

"Uh, forget what I said about holding still."

"Holding? I'm not holding."

Gabrielle took New Susan's hand and guided her to the Volkswagen. She opened the driver's door and pushed the seat back and gently pushed New Susan in.

"My feet are mixed up," she said.

As New Susan untangled her feet Gabrielle went to the middle of the street and put her arms around Pretty Susan's waist. Gabrielle took a step and Pretty Susan followed, still talking silently, and she led her to the car.

"No," New Susan said.

"Susan be nice to Susan."

Gabrielle pushed the seat back until it clicked. Quiet, she thought. She got in her seat and pulled the door not quite shut. No slamming. Key in ignition. Here comes a little noise, stick in neutral, clutch in.

She turned the key and the engine caught. Then first gear. She pulled away from the shoulder, went through a stop sign, and made a sharp right onto the street that ran perpendicular to the freeway. All the houses were dark.

"I can't see," New Susan said.

"You can see."

"But the front lights."

"Nope."

No headlights. Second gear. No brake pedal. The end of the street approached. Go right.

As she coasted to the corner trying to visualize the unfamiliar path ahead she turned the wheel and looked over her shoulder. There was someone standing at the spot where the chain-link fence met the street. Where they had been parked. A dark clothed figure. There was a spark. Flashlight.

Gabrielle held her breath, feet off pedals. As they rounded the corner did that distant figure look up?

It was quite possible.

They might have seen the car. Must consider the possibility. The possibility of being arrested and put in jail. Thrown into jail. Tossed like a sack of garbage into jail.

Still, she thought, no way he saw the license or any details, not even the color.

The stupidblanket was gone now. Her thoughts were cold and crisp.

Blanket or ocean. Which *is* it. Headlights on.

With the Susans quiet, she drove past the sleeping houses until she encountered a street she recognized. She went left and entered the university. The loop road was deserted, the red brick dorms all dark except for a few brightly lit windows. Yep, finals are almost here, she thought, checking the mirrors.

She circumnavigated the school and went out the back road, then left again onto the still busy street and headed for the center of town.

Just another car amidst all the traffic.

The freeway approached. They passed over and she saw nothing unusual on the foggy lanes. No flashing lights, no police cars. The truck would have to be a quarter mile east, she thought, out of range.

Gabrielle let her breath out. Her hands shivered on the steering wheel.

"I'm really hungry," New Susan said. "Aren't you hungry?"

The thought of eating made Gabrielle abdominal muscles cramp up.

"I don't think anything's open, Susan."

They stopped at a red light. A Continental covered with rust motored by followed by two compacts. One of the compacts was a blue Toyota Corona. Gabrielle sat up in surprise. Watching over me? Following me?

She calmed herself. There could be more than one blue Corona. Except she knew there wasn't.

"Told you," Pretty Susan muttered.

New Susan snapped, "Yes you did. Stop talking. Why do you have to talk now?"

Gabrielle made a right off the busy street then a quick left. Nothing moved on the streets. She got nervous again.

"Almost home."

"But I'm really hungry."

"Aren't there hot dogs left?"

"No."

"Yes, in the freezer," Pretty Susan said.

"Right! I totally forgot."

"Good. See." Gabrielle made the turn onto L's street. "I really need to get home. All my classes tomorrow are crazy." The street was just like she left it. Fog-diffused streetlights with bats. No music blasting. Cars parked tight on the curbs.

"Oh, yeah. Me too."

"Classes," Pretty Susan sniffed. "Like little kids."

"Not everyone is rich like you. I want to graduate and get a job. A real job."

Rich? Gabrielle thought. Well now.

"Susan, I never knew you were a student."

She slowed for L's driveway. The MG was still there and right beside it was a shiny black Mercedes two-seater. Flawless, she thought.

"What's your major? English?"

"Eww! Oh my God!"

Pretty Susan started laughing.

"What about me made you think I was an English major? Do I walk around with my head up my ass?"

"No, no, of course not," Gabrielle said, laughing.

"Do I wear all black and sit staring at the wall and then just start crying for no reason? Do I hang around the student union annoying the living shit out of everyone with petitions like to, I don't know, please stop the United States from being so good at everything because other countries are like sad and shit? Do I seem like that kind of student?"

Gabrielle stopped the car at the driveway and pulled the handbrake.

"Aren't you kind of describing an Art major?"

"Ah. No. See Art majors know they're screwed. There are no jobs for Art majors. They know that. So they are totally into starting businesses and being self-sufficient. It's all they talk about."

"Right." Did Elliot ever talk about that? she thought.

"The absolute lowest major. You know what that is, right?" New Susan said.

"Hm. Home Economics?"

"Surprisingly no. They teach you how to cook and sew. They know how to make clothes."

"Oh, huh. Yeah that would be useful. How about Political Science?"

"Ha. Like that's a science. Still not lowest."

"Gee, I don't know."

"Education."

"Really?"

"God, they're *idiots*. Can't add two plus two? Confused about who the President is? Not sure about the whole Earth orbiting the Sun thing? Here. We'll make you a teacher."

"Wow, it's really that bad? But there must be some smart ones."

"You're so far above them it's not even funny. I'm Biochemistry, by the way. Third year."

"Not bad." Pretty damn good, Gabrielle thought. She opened her door and got out.

"I'm interested in enzyme function. But I might get into genetics. My senior project is on RNA and the replication complex."

New Susan gave Pretty Susan a nudge. She looked up as if walking from a nap and clambered out.

Standing in the cold mist, New Susan said, "You can come in if you want."

Pretty Susan was already going in the front door and resuming her silent conversation.

"Thanks. But."

"You have to study."

"Actually just need to sleep."

"Sleep has its place, I guess."

New Susan hugged her and went up the steps.

"Don't forget Saturday," Gabrielle said.

"Oh! I won't!"

"Disco's Last Blast."

"That's so cool! I have to figure out what to wear."

"Should be really fun."

"So much fun! Thanks for inviting me."

"Sure. You're all invited. Well. See you."

"Okay!"

New Susan waved and closed the door. L's house was dark and quiet. A curtain twitched in the last window. Gabrielle made sure not to stare and got back in her car.

She wanted to get out of visual range. She pulled away and turned right at the corner and stopped at the first open spot, in front of another Victorian mansion. There were real estate signs in the windows. She switched off the headlights and sat still.

"That actually all happened."

The windshield fogged. The surge of mental clarity had dissipated. She did definitely feel she needed to take a shower. The awful pot smell was gone, she thought, but she couldn't be sure. Maybe other people can smell it. Just great.

"So back to the beach because you can forget about taking a shower at Mrs. Rosenberg's with boy's underwear in the sink." She laughed and put the car in gear. "I don't even want to get undressed there."

There was movement in the dark street. She froze. A figure in flowing white was walking toward her in the middle of the lane. The figure held out their arms and ghostly white sleeves caught the breeze and fluttered. It was Tall Susan. As she passed the Volkswagen, Gabrielle saw that her eyes were closed and her feet were bare. She seemed to glide over the pavement.

Feeling her way, Gabrielle thought. It's like I don't find this crazy anymore.

When Tall Susan was out of sight she got out of there.

On the empty valley highway, buffeted by the wind, she remembered to drive as normally as possible. No need to notice the old VW cruising along at the exact speed limit. She didn't relax until she reached the eucalyptus grove and its welcoming no longer scary fingerlike branches and shreds of bark drifting across the road. The adventurous kangaroo mice played in her headlights and she smiled as if they were old friends. The gate was open for her. That was a good sign. She latched it securely behind her and feeling everything at home was fine rounded the last curve. She stopped in her tracks.

Every light was on. All the windows were bright. The glaring bare bulb of the porch light. The floodlights shining up at the dunes. And all the curtains and blinds were open.

She saw Gislaine pass by one of the library windows then double back. As she stopped beside Audra's car, the front door opened and Catherine and Samantha came onto the porch. Catherine walked quickly down the steps and stopped at the edge of the sand as if unwilling to get far from the house.

Gabrielle shut down her car and got out into the early morning salt air. She could feel the surf thrumming under her feet. Somewhere behind her in the immensity of the night a blackbird began to sing.

"Where the hell have you been? Do you know what time it is? We've been worried sick."

"Sorry." Gabrielle checked her watch. *2:51.* "I guess I lost track."

"Yes, you did." Catherine held out her hand.

"But they, you know, they had me do this task. It."

"What?"

"It was awful."

Samantha came down and put her arms around Gabrielle shoulders and led her to Catherine, who pulled her close. Samantha put her arms around them both.

"All right. You're home," Catherine said, nose wrinkling. "And we know what you've been doing."

"Yes we do," Samantha said.

"I can explain." Gabrielle settled into the warmth of Samantha who ran her fingers through her hair. "You have all the lights on because you're waiting for me?"

"No. That's why we have to get back inside," Catherine said.

"It's all right, I'm sure now," Samantha said.

"I would feel better not being out here."

"What is it?" Gabrielle scanned the chaparral and saw nothing move in the porch light. The blackbird continued its song, unseen, insistent.

"Listen to that," Catherine whispered. "Can we please."

They walked into the house together and Samantha shut the door firmly and clicked the lock. She turned off the floorlamps.

In the kitchen Catherine turned off the under-counter lights and flipped the floodlight switches. The sage and Manzanita outside went pitch dark.

"You had the blinds open in the middle of the night," Gabrielle said. She heard the toilet flush in the new bathroom.

"We thought there was something outside," Samantha said. "Probably someone's dog running around."

Catherine pushed them both towards the hallway door.

"Bedtime."

Gabrielle could hear fear in her voice.

"Okay. But don't I have to take a shower?"

"We were just kidding," Samantha said. "Weren't we."

"Yes, we were. I want everyone in bed. No staying up all night."

"You know, I've never done that," Gabrielle said. She sensed it was not a good time for questions. She unzipped her sweatshirt and as she stepped into the hall the bathroom door opened.

Rushel and Audra came out. Gislaine came out of the end bedroom.

"I'm sorry," Rushel said. "I lost your backpack." Her face was drawn and her eyes distant. There were rough gray patches on both of her cheeks.

Gislaine slipped her arm around Rushel's and pulled her away on the soft carpeting. At their bedroom door, Rushel turned back.

"I understand now," she said. Her eyes were intense. "It makes sense. You have to pay to see the mysteries. I just wanted to see. So I paid." Her voice drifted off.

Gislaine guided her away into the bedroom and closed the door.

Audra let out her breath.

"Well, good night." Audra went into the living room. "I'll be in here."

Gabrielle, with Catherine hugging her, was taken to her room. Samantha undressed them both, carefully removing Gabrielle's glasses, and tucked them into bed.

Samantha spent several minutes looking out the window at the lightless dunes then took off her tunic and slipped under the blanket but remained perched, Gabrielle noticed, on the edge of the bed.

She's going to stay up all night, she thought, as Catherine's arm around her waist relaxed and warm tickle of breath on her breast bone became slow and regular.

Well fat chance I'm going to be able to get to sleep, she thought, not after a day like this. I am frazzled. And I have a headache from the diesel fumes. And the sun's going to be up any minute now. Any minute.

Bleary eyed, Gabrielle stumbled to the shower in darkness. She had been able to slide out of bed without waking Catherine. Samantha had vanished.

Nevertheless, after a quick shower, using a lot of soap, and getting dressed in her jeans and blue t-shirt and clean socks, Catherine was already in the kitchen in her cut-offs, hands on hips before the coffee maker. The curved window framed a panoramic view of ash gray chaparral and deep blue sky scattered with stars.

Audra was still curled up in her chair completely covered by her green blanket. Gislaine was sitting at the table with her notebook. She flipped pages back and forth and made marks with her fountain pen. She smiled.

"You're up early."

"I'm surprised I slept at all. It was either get up or sleep all day. And I can't. Thank you."

Catherine set a large cup of coffee on the counter for her.

"That's a bit more than usual," she said. "And I made it stronger. Mustn't fall asleep behind the wheel."

"Perfect." Gabrielle sipped and peered out at the ridge of dunes. A small bird took flight into the wind, hovered, and veered off sharply.

"She's out there," Catherine said.

"What is she doing?"

"She never says. And I never ask."

Gabrielle gulped her coffee.

"Gislaine, how is Rushel?"

"Fine," Audra said from under her blanket.

Gislaine set her pen down. "She needs to rest. So she'll take the day off from school. And so will you," she said in Audra's direction.

"Thank God." Audra settled into the cushions.

Gabrielle wanted to ask but she could see Gislaine was thinking.

"Everything Rushel told me will be in this notebook," Gislaine said. "It's the only unused notebook I have. Mostly unused," she said. She lifted it up. The cover was bright red with a heavy crease from top to bottom. "This was originally going to be my notes about movies. I like to write about things like that. So the first page. See?"

Gabrielle lifted up her glasses.

My Favorite Movies and Why I Like Them.

"Writing helps you organize your thoughts," Gabrielle said.

"Reading helps me think. But writing does far more. I didn't become fully conscious as a human being until I started writing." She closed the notebook and capped her pen. "Any time you want to look, feel free. You know where I keep everything. I'd better check on her."

"Tell her I'm worried about her."

"I will."

"I have to ask. Those marks on her cheeks. Did that just happen? What is that?"

Gislaine whispered, "I believe it's frostbite. I'll be right back."

"Gislaine, wait. There was something else from last night," Gabrielle said, remembering, looking at the red notebook. More than anything at that moment she wanted to open it. "Bianca."

Audra threw off her blanket and sat up. Gislaine stared in surprise. The pen fell out of her hand.

Catherine smiled and sipped her coffee.

"I keep telling you."

"Well, I think I'll get going," Gabrielle said. "I'll try to be home early."

"How the *hell*," Audra said.

"Audra honey," Catherine said. "There's no fucking swearing at breakfast."

"Sorry."

Gabrielle held out her hand and Catherine took it. They walked through the middle room and library and when they got outside, Catherine hugged her. Their shoes scuffed on the sandy porch.

"They haven't told me anything. I have no idea what that word means. It's just that every now and then we all get a reminder of why you're the Goddess. Also."

Catherine turned her head sideways and they kissed until Gabrielle had to signal lack of air. Catherine looked down shyly.

"With all the crazy stuff going on we didn't get a chance to, you know."

Gabrielle said, "Yes, that's true," and slipped her hand from Catherine's lower back up and under her shirt. More silk. "I'll be home as soon as I can."

"Okay."

"I wish I didn't have to go but."

"I'll be right here." Catherine smiled. "Are you okay to drive?"

"Uh, actually." Gabrielle felt her whole body flush.

Catherine made a purring sound and said, "Just hold that thought."

"I will."

"All day?"

Gabrielle cleared her throat. "Watch me."

Catherine untangled herself and brushed back her hair, luminous in her black shirt. "I can't wait."

"Me neither."

Catherine looked her up and down and without diverting her gaze backed into the open doorway. She closed the door gently.

Under a clear sky Gabrielle was on the long valley highway again and doing just fine, thinking about Catherine, steering around the larger potholes, until she did something she rarely did. She turned on the radio.

The speaker under the dashboard hissed and crackled. She turned the tuning knob on the little AM unit from one end of the band to the other. And as usual the only station she could get was at about 1400 kHz and the announcer's voice came in loud and clear.

Oh right, she thought, this guy. Audra's favorite. The guy was pretty funny but. She shook her head. She just wasn't in the mood. As she moved to turn the thing off the guy said in his deep voice, "Are we awake yet on the central coast? How about *now*." And a song started. "Donna Summer, *she* seems to be awake. Maybe because, *I Feel Love*."

I don't want to listen to music right now, she thought. But she hesitated.

There was something about the beat. The speed of it. Or, what was it, the melody? I know zip about music, she thought. I kind of like this, though.

As Donna Summer sang, her thoughts returned to Catherine's kiss. The VW bounced. She checked the mirror. No vehicles in sight behind. And the oncoming traffic, they wouldn't be able to see anything. She looked at the stick with its shiny knob.

Got a ways to go. No shifting required.

She giggled.

"Actually there is some shifting required."

Her left hand gripped the wheel. She turned the radio up. *I Feel Love* filled the car. She wiggled into the seat. The sun came up over the distant hills and, blinded, she wanted to flip the visor down but she didn't have a free hand. The road ahead was smear of dazzling golden sunlight and prismatic arcs filled her glasses. She turned her head to the left and concentrated on the centerline to stay in the lane.

The song reached a long shuddering climax and Gabrielle rested her head and bumped her glasses up.

In the instant before the wire frames dropped back down she saw through the glare. The swiftly approaching shadow filled the windshield and blocked the sun. Reflexively, she yanked the steering wheel down with her left hand and swerved into the oncoming lane and the bumper of the VW grazed the fender of the stopped cement truck making sound as loud as a gunshot. The concrete chute sticking out of the back went by like a cold steel wave.

Back into the blinding sunlight and fully on the wrong side of the road she passed the long line of cars and trucks. The highway curved right and it was impossible to see ahead. She tried in panic to hit the brakes and her foot slipped off the small, badly worn rubber pedal and instead jammed the accelerator.

She ducked her head and tried to see what her feet were doing. Her right shoe was jammed between the gas pedal and the central hump and the engine screamed.

Another shadow passed on her left. It was a blue pickup and it bounced on the gravel shoulder. Then a new Toyota went by.

Her left hand panic-gripping the wheel and she thought, nice car.

The sun was now at an angle and she saw all the oncoming vehicles steering out of her way onto the highway shoulder, one after the other. Pickups and big four door Buicks and Chevys flashed past.

Her left turn was coming up and she was traveling almost seventy. Wind whistled past the wing window. The traffic light was blinking red.

So the thing malfunctioned and went to stop-light mode and traffic is backed up and I'm going way too fast to stop so I have to turn, she thought. I can't hit someone, I *can't*.

She saw the other cars freeze as the drivers saw the red VW careening towards them. She pulled her right leg up as hard as she could and her shoe came off, still jammed. She kicked the stupid thing and the gas pedal at last popped up. The engine dropped to a growl and she lurched forward and tried to brake. Her old sock slipped right off.

She was at the intersection. No time to get her right hand free. She could see the face of the driver directly in front of her. It was a woman with glasses, hands on top of the steering wheel, mouth open in surprise.

Gabrielle saw the path she had to take, a sharp left with a target just beyond a yellow Volvo with ugly fog lights in the left turn lane. The Volvo driver had not seen her. She could see he was looking straight ahead. Wondering why no one's moving, she thought. Is it my turn to go?

She shifted her hand all the way over to the right side of the steering wheel.

In the final two seconds as she entered the intersection the Volvo pulled out. The guy turned his head in shock. She cut him off going just under forty and hauled the wheel over as hard as she could. The Volkswagen Beetle made a maneuver Gabrielle did not know was possible. The left side of the car lifted into the air and pirouetted on two tires. Gabrielle was thrown to the right and came completely out of her seat. She saw the world go sideways, she felt herself floating, the view out the front made a sharp swing rightward, and the car slammed down, her head bounced against the side window, and she was now headed eastward into the sun again at a sedate thirty miles an hour. Someone laid on their horn.

Gabrielle thought frantically as she pulled her hand free. Did I hit that guy? Didn't hear anything. But.

No one following. *Get out of here now.*

She pulled the stick into second and floored it then slammed third and accelerated away from the valley highway. The horn faded into the distance.

Gasping, she powered past green fields and volcanic hillsides and was soon back among the suburban houses. She made a random right thinking it might be a good idea to get off the main east-west street. Filter through downtown, she thought.

She panted and rolled down her window as she drove through an area of student housing. The street was lined with parked cars, their windshields still covered with dew. She was the only moving thing and this made her nervous. So she made another right and then left, then right again, onto the narrow road she knew would take her into the heart of downtown with its sweeping three lane one-way thoroughfares, one heading west, one heading east.

One more left and she was home free. Still no one following. She let herself relax a little. Her arms and shoulders were sore and there was a lump on the side of her head from the window. The tall downtown buildings loomed, still dark. One more street. Or was it two?

It felt like her right foot was bleeding. She figured that sock was ruined. So I have one usable pair of socks, she thought. One.

She drove through the red light at a steady forty.

She was halfway down the shadowy block before she realized what she had done. The red light shined accusingly in her side mirror.

"Run," she said. "Run."

Gabrielle got a green light at the next intersection and made a left.

Good, she thought.

She was now headed east on one of the big three-lane streets, the westbound one. With the sun hitting her square in the face again she missed seeing large arrows painted on the pavement indicating the correct direction, the way she had come.

She could instantly tell something was wrong. The stores and restaurants looked funny. It was a long block. She took her foot off the gas. At the upcoming intersection three lanes of headlights glared at her.

"Oh," she breathed, "oh, oh." Her hands froze on the wheel.

Problem: You are going the wrong way on a one-way street in the center of town.

Solution: Make a big U-turn or shoot into one of the connecting streets. There were pluses and minuses to each approach. On the one hand…

"Gahh!"

Gabrielle stuck it into second and popped the clutch and made a diagonal beeline across all three lanes to an intersecting street. She saw the backlit faces of the drivers all turn to watch. When she was out of their visual range she booked it and headed generally in the direction of the school on streets she had never seen before. She deliberately did not check her mirrors in the early slanting light.

The buildings and trees began to look familiar again. She knew where she was. She turned off and entered the huge south parking lot close to the theater and the new gym. Hers was the solitary car except for that rusty Dodge van still parked close to the gym restrooms.

In the cold winter sunlight, Gabrielle carefully parked five spaces from the van. She made sure the stick was in neutral, pulled up the hand brake, pushed in the headlight knob, and switched off the engine. Then she vomited up all of Catherine's coffee onto the steering wheel and the floor mat. Her abdominal muscles twitched and cramped. She puked up mucus and then she puked up a weird green fluid and then air like a violent hiccup.

She wiped her mouth with her hands and wiped her hands on the passenger seat. She rested her head on the wet steering wheel and stared at the puddle. She spit and cleared her throat.

"If I had hit that truck that chute would have ripped my head off and I would have had plenty of time to think, hey, my head was just ripped off and I'm dead now. And the cops and ambulance guys would've looked in and seen my head ripped off body and noticed how my hand was stuck in my pants and they would've known exactly what had happened. Fuck. Fuck. Fuck."

She rolled her window down and saw that the back doors of the Dodge van were open. A pair of sandal-clad feet poked out of the van, then legs in old jeans, then scooting on his bottom, the rest of him. He had light brown hair that reached to his waist and a tie-dyed shirt of many colors. No beard, Gabrielle noticed

Looks harmless. Keep key in ignition.

"God, this place."

He saw she was looking and smiled and waved. He had a large white
towel in his hands. A she walked up to the VW his eyes widened and he
stopped with a sandal slap.

"Hey," he said. "It's none of my business but I had a feeling you could
use this."

"Yes, thank you. How'd you know?" Gabrielle took the clean smelling
towel and wiped off the steering wheel.

"Just a feeling." He bobbed his head and his hair swung.

Gabrielle dropped the towel on the mat and mopped with her feet. The
sock on her right foot was wet. She sighed.

"My name's Thomas, landscape architecture and." He stepped back and
spread his arms. "Whoa, that's wild."

Gabrielle looked left and right.

"What?"

"It's none of my business but your aura is like on fire, man."

"My," Gabrielle said thinking, quick, give him back the towel and park
up by the library, "Aura?"

"Yeah! It's okay if you don't believe but your aura is like shooting these
blue laser beams."

"Lasers? Really?"

"Most everyone's aura is like this glow and there are colors that don't
like exist in secular reality so I can't describe them but man I'm telling
you yours is totally different. Like a whole other level. There's this three
dimensional effect. It's none of my business but did something like major
happen to you recently?"

Gabrielle tried not to stare at Thomas. "Kind of."

Thomas glanced uneasily at the line of cars beginning to enter the lot.

"Sorry to hear that."

"Oh I'm okay."

"You're actually more than okay. Your aura is like interdimensional.
There are massive power surges. You have like major power."

"Really?" Maybe Rushel could take a look, Gabrielle thought.

"Your aura is acting like a force field. Cool. Look, I kinda know how this
sounds to engineering majors but just read Castaneda. Dude's got it dialed
in."

Now Gabrielle really stared at him. "How."

A young woman in a brand new white Pinto pulled into the spot on
Gabrielle's right. The woman looked at Thomas, open-mouthed.

Thomas's smile returned. Gabrielle saw he had perfect teeth.

"Like I said it's none of my business but like could I ask. Who are you?"

"I am the Goddess Persephone Gabrielle."

"I knew it was something like that."

"Yep."

Thomas shrugged. "Why don't you just wave your hand and get rid of all that?"

"I'm trying to become a human being."

The girl in the white Pinto finally turned off her engine and got out with an equally new backpack, white with a cutout flower pattern. Rich kid.

"Hey," Thomas said to her. "Nice."

The girl froze with a terrified look for several seconds then walked quickly away across the patchy grass field.

Gabrielle said, "Probably frosh."

"Nah, she's just picking up *my* aura. I'm very dark and mysterious. My question is," he said, "if you don't mind."

"Not at all."

"Okay. A human being. My question is, why?"

There was something about Thomas that made Gabrielle want to trust him. There's no trickery in him, she thought. No games. Not this guy. He really believes.

Then she saw Thomas's gaze leave her face and center on her breasts.

Or maybe he's trying to bamboozle me, she thought. Well, I do know how to handle this situation. Don't I? She wondered what the effect would be if she just told him.

"Thomas, it's very simple. There's this woman and I love her. And the only way I can be with her is by becoming human."

Thomas's eyes glazed over. He looked like he was processing.

"As a goddess you can do whatever you want, of course."

"It's actually complicated."

Thomas thought some more.

"Even for you?"

"Especially for me."

"I understand. So even a goddess does not possess the key to the human heart."

He turned and walked away.

Gabrielle, startled, heard him mutter.

"Maybe there isn't one."

Without looking back he hopped into his van and shut the doors with a rattling slam.

Gabrielle, feeling off balance, rolled up her window and snatched the keys from the ignition. She found her right shoe and slipped it on over the wet sock.

She left the towel on the floor. There was a lot to soak up. Then she locked the door and headed for the student union. Maybe the restrooms were open.

She glanced back for a final position check. All the spaces around her car were already filled in with new Toyotas and Datsuns. Her Volkswagen didn't stand out, she thought, in any way. No reason to notice it. Right?

Feeling unburdened, she stepped light and quick and the sun did the rainbow thing in her glasses again.

After washing her face she felt even better. She zipped her sweatshirt all the way up over her wet t-shirt. It was still early, *7:10*, and she didn't want to spend twenty minutes waiting for math class sitting in the hallway so she stood in front of the eight foot tall bulletin boards. All the boards had one of Audra's dance posters.

She turned her attention back to the notices. On the board titled 'Housing' there were many notices for people looking for rooms. Basements, porches, tents on the lawn, any possible place to sleep. The section for housing vacancies was empty. She was a little curious what rents were like now. Well, she thought, I could always just ask around. She shrugged. Not something she had to worry about.

The board labeled 'Employment' was also empty. Just a collection of push pins. No jobs.

The board titled 'Buy and Sell' on the other hand was jammed with For Sale notices. Stereos, speakers, and all kinds of musical instruments. Violins, cellos, flutes. An entire corner was covered with ads for guitars.

Gabrielle looked through the window of the craft center. The potting wheels waited in the dark. She tried to think of where she was, schedule-wise.

"Winter quarter, still. Right?" Her breath fogged the glass. "And this is Thursday."

A guy walking past stopped with a screech of his running shoes. He had very red eyes and his backpack hung open. The zipper had been ripped off.

"You mean Wednesday," he said.

"No, it's Thursday."

"Has to be Wednesday."

She pulled back her sleeve and uncovered her Timex.

"I can't read that." His gaze wandered from her wrist to the red tile floor. "What does it say?"

"It says Thursday."

"Okay, I believe you." The guy wiped tears from his face. "But it's still January, at least."

"Oh." Gabrielle tugged her sleeve down. "Come on."

"What?"

"It's the end of February. March is next week. Then finals."

"Finals." He staggered back. "Next week."

"Week after next." Another bamboozler? First he was staring at the nose ring. He's staring at my chest now. "Well, good luck. See you at the dance on Saturday." She put her finger on the poster. "Everyone's going. I mean like everyone, man."

He looked around in confusion. "I don't know how to dance."

Gabrielle walked fast towards the east exit.

"That won't stop you, right?"

Out on the cold plaza she heard him laugh. "Period attire. That's funny."
Then the doors closed.

Gabrielle walked briskly out of the plaza. Before she turned the corner
at the bookstore, she took look back. The concrete planters with their new
young trees. The Burger Bar. Am I leaving?

She hurried on.

The whispering pines were silent, heavy and wet. She entered the
Science building and went past the hall of tiny faculty offices, each door
decorated with schedules and favorite comics from the Sunday papers.
Peanuts. B.C.

In the echoing hall, she went over her classes, end-of-quarter mode.

Philosophy. Presentation tomorrow. She still wasn't sure what it was
going to be about. Not quite sure.

Shakespeare. I'll work on the paper today, she thought. I still don't
know what I'm doing but I will figure it out today. Has to be today. *Today.*

Advanced Topics. Only the final exam remaining. All but finished. She
was already missing Dr. Rimmler just a little.

Jogging. Just show up for the remaining classes then Physical Education
will be forever finished forever. She felt better just thinking that.

"Especially after such a stressful morning. Stressful. That's the word."

Still laughing, she entered the northwest wing of Science and walked
past Geology. Beside the department door there was a five foot high mural,
hand-drawn, illustrating the newly rehabilitated theory of plate tectonics.
And there was a boxed display of minerals all neatly labeled including
a large hexagonal quartz crystal, nearly transparent. Both had the air of
student projects.

She walked past Chemistry with its constant smell of solvents. Her
most vivid memory of chemistry was from her freshman year. It was the
lab section of an accelerated sequence intended for Physics majors, heavy
on math. In this lab, she made soap, she made nylon (which came out like a
mass of brittle hair), and she made a spectroscope.

At the end of a cardboard tube, tape two razor blades edge to edge
leaving a tiny slit. At the other end attach a fingernail size bit of clear plastic
which was covered with tiny grooves, a diffraction grating. Shine sunlight
through the grating and a rainbow emerges. Pass the bright red light of a
neon discharge tube through it and a series of red lines appears. All the
same color, all different intensities, like a glowing barcode. These were the
emission lines of the neon atoms zapped with high voltage, the electrons
falling back into their orbitals and giving up precise amounts of energy.
Quanta.

Gabrielle remembered looking into that cardboard tube in astonishment.

I can actually see it, she had thought, I had no idea you could see it. The
electrons are doing that. Those little electrons.

There had been an extensive collection of discharge tubes, all looking like stuff from the nineteen-fifties, and she had begged the instructor (short blonde hair, glasses) to try others. Argon. Nitrogen. And oxygen, a weird green. The instructor, she remembered, had switched the tubes without hesitation, all the while with a knowing, observant look.

I've seen the quantum structure, she had thought. The structure of reality.

She had walked out of that class in a mild state of shock thinking it was so complex, it was so beautiful, it was so powerful, it was *so complex.*

She remembered, lost in thought, bumping into a drinking fountain and dropping her backpack, brand new then, and turning red even though no one saw.

Gabrielle paused. The drinking fountain was still there. She recognized nothing else.

She walked quickly past Biology. She hated the smells, whatever they were, preservatives for dead things, and didn't want to run into New Susan. What did Bio majors *do* anyway?

She went out the Science door and walked across a courtyard and went into a larger, newer building. She held her head up. Was the light subtly brighter? She was in the realm of Engineering.

She diverted her path to go one last time through the Triple-E area, the L-shaped wing full of labs. Mostly empty, the place still had an electric smell.

"How much time did I spend here," she said. "Years."

She shook her head. Her memories were jumbled, as if it had all happened to a different person.

The labs were staged in progression. You worked your way up the hall. Circuit analysis. Energy conversion. Semiconductors. Integrated circuits.

Pilgrim's progress, someone had said, or was it just *grim's.*

That first quarter she remembered as from a far distance. The faces of her fellow freshmen, so excited then. Nervous, but excited. She categorized the faces. There was a progression there, also.

Multiple threads: Knucklingdown. Fatigue. Fear. Resignation. Dropout.

Or: Youaremakingit. Success+relief. Competition. Whosthatgirl?

She smiled at that last one.

But all the ones who dropped out. What became of them, those faces she would never see again?

It had all moved so fast. Intense learning. The math was not hard but some of the concepts were new. *Impedance?* Fall back on particle physics, the Feynman method. Fall back on chemistry, the home economics of engineering, cooking and sewing.

And it was physical. You made things with your hands. Devices which had to work.

You learned construction techniques. Gabrielle remembered solder fumes and glaring lights. Headaches every day. Drilling printed circuit boards. Wire strippers, schematics. Power supplies with bad grounds that would destroy your expensive integrated circuits.

It was all about real world applications. 'Real world' was a phrase used a lot.

It progressed. Analog electronics. Then digital, the big new thing.

This was digital:

"Like stepping out of the fog into the sunlight of a broad highland at the beginning of spring where the sky is a sharp blue and the rushing streams clear cold and fast. The wind tugs at your sleeves. Impatient. We need to get moving. See those snowy mountains up there? See *way* up there? From up there you can see everything. Industry. Commerce. The whole world. The *future.* That's digital. That's where we're going. Right now."

"Thanks, Dr. Rimmler," she said.

Suddenly, it seemed, she was finished.

Then oops. All those dumb electives.

Well, *heck.*

She walked out of the place without looking back.

At the math classroom, she joined her fellow students leaning against the hallway walls, backpacks at their feet. Gabrielle could see it was still nearly the whole class from the beginning of the term. Only three or four casualties, she counted. She was rather proud of them.

Partial differential equations weren't exactly musical comedy, as her first math instructor once said. Ms. Black. White hair. A small tattoo on her inner right wrist, a Chinese character, very unusual. Her memory of that was crystal clear. Have to look that thing up someday, she thought.

A young woman ten feet away gave her a long serious look. (Back row, multiple ear piercings, type 1, zero interaction with her.) Gabrielle did not stare back. No one else looked at her, no one said a word.

Javier rounded the corner. He was wearing a plaid sports jacket with leather elbow patches. He adjusted his glasses and squinted at the keys in his hand.

Outside of a few acquaintances in her core major classes Gabrielle couldn't remember making a single friend in all her years in college. And now with one last quarter still to go, she realized viscerally it was over. Graduation was no longer just a vague idea from the distant future. The end was in sight. And she was finished with it. Over it, as Gislaine said.

She rested her head against the wall. Get a job as soon as possible, she thought with a conviction that jolted her. After all, I promised Mom. No graduate school. No more of this.

School, all of school, was now becoming part the past and the place was going on without her.

"So shall it be," she whispered.

Javier dropped the keys.

"You'd think I'd know which key it was by now. But I don't," he said.

"This is the worst quarter ever, eh?"

No one said a word.

That afternoon, library, Stacks, fourth floor, back corner study desk.

Gabrielle stared at the blank sheet of paper she had gotten from the student at the checkout counter who found it fascinating she was not carrying anything except a pencil.

"Shakespeare. What is it with this guy?"

The Sonnets, she thought. A hundred fifty-four of them. Five page term paper. She knew she could get away with analyzing a single sonnet. The structure, rhyme scheme, the shift in mood many of them had around lines eight to twelve. The professor would like that just fine. But the idea of discovering a hidden meaning, a secret order, was hard to let go of. Why did he write them? A message to someone? A real person? She knew there were whole shelves of books on the Sonnets. She did not want to so much as glance at them. Copying someone else's opinion seemed like cheating. She brought up Sonnet 1 in her mind. Figure it out, she thought. *Do it.*

Gabrielle stared at the blank sheet of paper.

Two hours and ten minutes later, as a student pushed a reshelving cart of books past her desk, she finally saw it.

"They are going to hate this," she said and smiled. She picked up her pencil and started writing notes. Just the main points, she thought, flesh it out at home. And have to get the citations right. She shook her head.

"Right in front of me the whole time."

A Sonnet is a poem consisting of three groups of four lines, quatrains, *concluding with a two line section, a* couplet. *Each quatrain has an independent rhyme pattern...*

A sentence or so about the layout of a sonnet, then,

The first seventeen of Shakespeare's sonnets has the poet trying to talk someone into having children. This someone is young and called fair, called a youth. A young man.

"You don't say," Gabrielle whispered.

The youth is considered beautiful, which is one of the alternate meanings of fair, the other being blonde or light-haired. The poet starts out diplomatically then really gets on his case.

Forty winters, tomb, die alone.

In Sonnet 18, the poet compares the fair youth to a summer's day. It is a love poem.

What exactly is the evidence that the poet of the Sonnets, the speaker, is a man? Did everyone just assume this? My contention is that Shakespeare's speaker is a woman, a woman of middle age for Elizabethan times, probably about forty years old and a commoner. The beautiful youth is of a higher social status, some sort of aristocrat.

I see two possibilities.

One, the speaker of the Sonnets is one of Shakespeare's dramatic characters. He was a playwright, after all. He created hundreds of characters.

Or two, the speaker really is Shakespeare. And Shakespeare is a woman.

Hm, she thought.

Evidence: Language of the early Sonnets.

Love of beauty. Sensual language. Desire for children. Awareness of time passing/death. Sensitivity to slights.

Gabrielle rummaged through the Sonnets in her mind. Page after page came into focus. Maybe stick with the first idea. The speaker is a woman. I'm not going for a dissertation here.

The later Sonnets are concerned with a different person, a woman with black hair. There is a change in tone. Less yearning after beauty. More interest in adult relationships. Lying. Cheating. Forgiveness. Resignation.

The poet seems to say I love my mistress the way she is, for her real qualities, not some idealized fantasy woman with snow white skin, golden hair, and rosy cheeks.

Mistress' eyes are nothing like the sun. Hair like black wire. Voice not musical. Her breasts are dun (compared to snowy).Her cheeks are not rosy. She does not exactly smell like perfume, either. [130].

I contend the poet is a woman who is unswayed by the romantic conventions of the period. Conventions created by men. She will be her own person who loves as she sees fit.

Gabrielle wanted to try using the computer to write it out. It would be so much better to use the word processor, and just thinking 'word processor' gave her a shiver of excitement. No noisy typewriter, no correction fluid.

She stood up and immediately felt dizzy. She checked her watch. She had been sitting for almost four hours. She folded the paper and tucked it safely into her pocket.

Walking across the inner campus she could feel the increased energy of the other students with the end of the quarter in sight. Everyone was walking a bit faster with serious and determined expressions. Carrying no backpack or books she attracted a few curious looks.

Gabrielle felt light on her feet in the low sunlight. She crossed the lawn in front of the new gym and rounded the corner of the theater. And froze. Flashing red lights.

There was a police car parked behind her VW blocking her in.

Gabrielle made a one eighty and went quickly back to the corner of the theater. Fighting spasms in her stomach, she tried to look relaxed and peeked through the leafy branches of a newly planted tree.

She drew back in relief. The flashing lights were on a tow truck. And it was a campus police car. They were towing Thomas's van.

Gabrielle let herself lean back against the concrete wall. Her stomach was still cramping. She made herself breathe normally.

The student union, she thought, go over there. Right across the street.

Gabrielle fought the urge to peek again. She went into the union and sat on one of the padded benches and watched the crashing clashing bowling alley. It was very noisy and looked like fun. There were lines of students waiting for their turn. Another class.

Bowling was one of the P.E. classes which were all but impossible to get into along with tennis and billiards. She figured you had to have inside help to enroll, unlike jogging. Anyone could get into jogging.

She wondered if there was a now a bowling major. And bowling scholarships. And expensive bowling textbooks.

When half an hour had elapsed Gabrielle left the union and crossed the quiet street to the theater. She peeked around the corner. The campus police car, the tow truck, and the ancient van of Thomas were gone.

She felt for her keys.

On top of being stupid I have also been careless, she thought. I have not been keeping a lookout. She had not sighted any black-clad girls and she chalked this up to sheer luck. Get a grip.

Her engine had a new tapping sound. It grated on her nerves as she approached the fateful intersection and signaled for a right. She held her breath as she turned. Would screaming police cars swoop down on her, would she be ordered out of the car at gunpoint?

She made the turn and drove home with the sun once again in her eyes.

As she stopped the VW on the sand, Catherine came out onto the porch. Gabrielle got out and saw her face and held up her hands.

Catherine ran down the steps and hugged her.

"What on Earth happened? Are you all right?"

"I'm okay. How is Rushel?"

"She fine. You're not. Here."

As they sat on the porch steps Gabrielle thought, maybe she can see my aura. That would explain a lot.

She told Catherine everything.

Catherine put her face in her hands.

"It was all my fault."

"It could not have been your fault."

"I should have nailed you in the shower."

"Oh. Well."

Seagulls cried overhead in agreement.

"Uh huh. See? All right, new rules. You cannot leave the house in the morning without, hmm, what shall we call it."

"I know what to call it." Gabrielle grinned.

"I mean what word."

"There's about a million words."

"We need a new word. A word just for us. Give me a while. In the meantime."

Gabrielle closed her eyes as Catherine turned her head sideways and kissed her.

"Snog," she said. "Snug. Snugtussle."

"That's cute. Snugtussle."

"Yeah, too cute. I'll work on it."

"So will I."

Catherine's eyes were a sharper blue than before, Gabrielle thought. Maybe it's just the light. Maybe I'm just seeing more clearly.

The seagulls wheeled in the clear evening sky and a snowy plover hopped unnoticed onto the step next to them. The sun slipped behind the fog on the horizon and bright Venus appeared just under the eave a hand width from elusive Mercury. Gabrielle stomach growled and Catherine laughed into the side of her neck and licked the edge of her jaw. The snowy plover departed.

"There's so much I want to tell you," Gabrielle said.

"I suppose language has it's uses. Not now though."

A while later they both heard a door slam inside. Catherine sighed.

"That's my cue. Just a few finishing touches here and there."

"They're probably starving."

"Won't kill 'em."

"Gislaine does know how to cook."

"Yeah, that's right." She pushed herself up and her knees cracked. "My left foot is asleep." She wiggled her toes.

Gabrielle took her foot in both hands and massaged.

"Oh. Uh," Catherine said. "That's. I was going."

"You like this?"

"Uh." Catherine leaned against the door balancing on her right foot.

"No kidding," Gabrielle said and pressed her thumb into the bottom of Catherine's foot and made a rolling motion.

"No. No," Catherine said. "Not now."

"Oh come on."

"Later." Catherine swallowed hard.

"All right." Gabrielle ran the tips of her fingers across the arch where there was no sand sticking. Catherine jerked her foot up.

"Oh my God!"

"You're so ticklish!"

"I have never been tickled in my life!" She opened the screen door. "Never!"

"We'll see about that."

"You think so, huh?"

As an answer Gabrielle leaned forward from the step and ran her fingertips up Catherine's bare thigh. Catherine slapped her hand away and, laughing, jumped into the library.

It was Rushel's turn.

The table was set with water and wine and full plates of spaghetti covered with Catherine's vegetarian sauce. The house smelled of roasted garlic and fresh baked bread. Gabrielle felt Samantha squeeze her right hand with a nervous urgency while Audra's grip was relaxed. Or was it fearful, she wondered. And Rushel. The patches on her face were gone. So she's all right, she hoped.

"I feel strong," Rushel said. "Here joined with my family while outside the great darkness of the universe stretches to infinity. For a brief moment we are together, enjoying the warmth of your spirit. Thank you for the wonderful meal we are about to enjoy. No matter what happens in the future, no matter what far flung place we find ourselves, we will always be grateful for this time. So shall it be."

As Gabrielle said, "So shall it be," with the others Audra released her hand and Samantha increased her grip to a painful level. When she opened her eyes, Gislaine's cheeks were wet with tears. Audra was still holding Rushel's hand.

Catherine glanced around the table, focused on Rushel, then picked up her wine glass and drained it in two big gulps. Then she picked up her fork and dug into her spaghetti. Samantha let her hand go and patted it in apology and also started eating.

I guess we're not going to talk about it, Gabrielle thought. She twirled spaghetti onto her fork and put the whole garlic sauce saturated bite into her mouth.

"Cathrun, nis is rilly goo!"

"Why nank oo!" Catherine said with her mouth full. She poured herself more wine.

"I wuv d!" Samantha agreed and sucked a strand of spaghetti with a loud slurp. She wiped her mouth. "It. Sorry."

Rushel laughed, a real belly laugh, and Gabrielle sat back in relief.

"I'm starving," Rushel said. "I love the roasted garlic."

"It's the real trick," Catherine said.

"It really is." Rushel got three strands of spaghetti tangled on her fork and awkwardly examined them. Then she slowly put them in her mouth and chewed. She looked around the table. "What? I'm just using my noodle."

Gislaine sighed and rolled her eyes.

"That pun was absolutely foul, Audra groused," Audra said.

"Oh cut it out, Rushel said sharply," Rushel said.

"Your sense of humor is back to normal. Our survival is now in doubt."

"Pocket Mouse, I've asked you at least a million times to please stop exaggerating."

"Say please."

"I said please."

"Are these the peas?"

"There are no peas."

Catherine and Samantha laughed. The tension broken, Gislaine sipped her water and took a tiny bite of her food, mirroring Rushel. Audra began to pick at her spaghetti, remaining observant, and did not speak.

After the table had been cleared – "Just put everything in the sink, Catherine said cleanly," Catherine said – Gabrielle sat down before the computer with a cup of coffee and was soon joined by Audra who made sure the fan-folded paper was positioned correctly in the printer. Rushel came in and looked over her shoulder. She reached around and pushed the big button on the back and Gabrielle heard the hard drive spin up.

"I still can't believe that, "she said.

The opening screen flashed on. *Tess.*

"The memory? Makes funny noises as it's booting up."

"As it what?"

"Booting. It was in that magazine. It's pulling itself up by its own bootstraps."

Gabrielle laughed. "I guess that's right. Self-start up."

Rushel explained how to start the *Write* program and how to adjust the margins. Gabrielle was afraid to mess something up but they both reassured her that was very difficult. The operating system had never had a problem in all the hours they had used it.

The thought of an electronic computer having an *operating system* so complex it could catch errors and correct itself made Gabrielle's entire body tingle. It was practically a living thing. And seeing the letters appear on the small screen as she typed gave her a thrilling feeling of power.

"It's great, isn't it?" Rushel said.

She typed her name at the top of the field. The black letters surrounded by the gray silver screen had a weird kind of authority, as if to say surely everything written here is very important indeed and should be treated as such. The thought made her hesitate.

"It had better be good, right?" she said. "It had better be the best Shakespeare term paper ever because I wrote it on a computer. And if I make a mistake all I have to do is use the *mouse* to place the *cursor* in the right spot and correct it."

"Don't you feel like you could write *anything*?" Rushel said.

Gabrielle unfolded her page of notes.

"Wow, Goddess, you took notes," Audra said.

"I like the Sonnets. But I'm a numbers person, not a Shakespeare person."

Rushel said, "You can be any kind of person you want."

Audra shook her head.

"My dear lovely Rushel. You are still thinking like a liberal arts major."

"The hell I am."

"We've had this argument many times. My I offer an example? I can*not* be a tall, blonde supermodel of eastern European extraction with an IQ of eleventy point five billion no matter how much I may want. And *you* cannot be a petite, green-eyed future lawyer of Italian and Irish heritage renowned for her spectacular verbal pyrotechnics. With curly bouncy black hair. That's just the way it is."

"My dear lovely yet mistaken Audra."

"Oh yeah?"

"I'm thinking like what I now am. I am a computer science major. If you would please remember exactly what I said. You can be any *kind* of person you want."

"Hm."

"Which is to say it a role one plays. You could play the role of model if you wanted. If you lost your mind."

"Sure."

"So you agree with me. You could be a model."

"No, I agree I could lose my mind."

"Pocket Mouse, be serious."

"I am the most serious person in the entire world. Doesn't mean I have to act serious."

"Well, good."

"So you think you could be a lawyer kind of person?"

Rushel stood up straight and put her hand over her mouth. She made a sound like a sob and shook her hair loose.

"Your honor, my client can't be the bank robber on that security video. You have the wrong red-headed, albino, seven foot tall, multiple amputee Norwegian. I rest my case."

"The sick part is that would have a fifty-fifty chance of working, depending on the judge."

"Judge Simone."

"Oh."

"About thirty-eight, auburn hair, blue-eyes. You know."

"Sure." Audra rolled her eyes.

"I'm telling you, you just need to get out there. That reminds me. Have you called Melinda yet?"

"I said I would."

"Yes?"

"And I did. From one of those tiny phone booths in the Science building."

"Those things are ridiculous," Gabrielle said.

"Yeah. Too small even for me. You have to suck up your stomach."

"So how'd it go?" Rushel said.

"Carl answered. I hung up on him."

"Tragic Carl. He knows the jig is up. Just keep trying. Don't hang up next time. Tell him you're a lawyer for the small business association and you need to talk to Melinda."

"What business association?"

"Doesn't matter. Fake it."

"Hm."

"Hm, hm. Now let's let the Goddess do her homework."

"Wait," Gabrielle said. "There's something I have to show you. This week has been a little hectic."

"Understatement of the year," Audra said.

"Yep. And I just had an idea of how to do it."

Audra and Rushel exchanged a puzzled look. Gabrielle held a finger to her lips and started typing on the computer.

There might be microphones in every room maybe even outside.

Rushel gasped.

And I saw only 8 of those boxes in their pantry.

Audra started to speak and caught herself. She knelt and angrily typed, **Then we get those 8.**

Gabrielle nodded and wrote, **All right. is everything ready at disco's house?**

Yes, Audra typed. **We go set up sat afternoon.**

Gabrielle: **Good. I really tried to sell it.**

Audra: **What did they make you do? You seemed a bit stunned last night.**

Gabrielle: **it's really embarrassing.**

Audra: **Actually you seemed wasted. Humiliation is their main hobby, right?**

Gabrielle: **They stole Rushel's ideas. They had robes.**

The lines of text now filled the frame and when Gabrielle hit carriage return they all scrolled up. It was mind boggling.

Audra: **Of course they did. They are incapable of coming up with anything on their own.**

Rushel reached between them.

Really creepy.

Audra: **They're certain they are the smartest people in the world. That's why we can trick them. You know what this is fun!**

Gabrielle: **I know! I did learn something there.**

Audra: **I'm afraid to ask.**

Gabrielle: **I can sort of see why you like pot.**

Audra burst into laughter.

Rushel: **I do not like pot!**

Audra: **Of course not.**

Rushel: **I don't!**

Audra: **Someone is awfully defensive.**

Gabrielle: **Rushel I have a question about the secret names.**

Rushel gasped: **No! No!**

Gabrielle: **I need to know.** She backspaced over that and typed, **Just a general question.**

Rushel, reluctantly: **Ok.**

Gabrielle: **Do the secret names consist of one word or more than one word?**

Rushel: **1 word. I have decreed it.**

Gabrielle: **Thanks. That's all I wanted to know.**

Rushel: **You scared me.**

Gabrielle: **Sorry. I won't do it again.**

Rushel let out her breath: **Good.**

Rushel left the library and they heard the middle bathroom door close.

Gabrielle: **How is Rushel?**

Audra looked over her shoulder: **Not sure.**

Gabrielle: **I have to ask.**

Audra: **It's all right. The Goddess should know.** She looked over her shoulder again. **She disappeared for six hours. GG was hysterical. Sorry**

They heard the toilet flush. Audra backspaced over her sentence.

The bathroom door opened and Rushel walked into the kitchen.

Audra: **It's like Deanna. She has to work it out.** She backspaced again. **She can drive you crazy.**

Gabrielle: **I just remembered my term paper style sheet was in my backpack. Would you happen to have something like that I could use?**

Audra: **Oh sure. Yeah you have to get the end notes exactly right. You know we don't have to be typing this.**

Gabrielle: **I know. I just like it.**

Audra: **If we all had our own computers could we send messages to each other?**

Gabrielle: **Sure I've seen it. 'email'**

"Neat!" Audra said. "Email. God that's cool. So these computers are what, ten, fifteen thousand? No sweat."

"We should all get one. In a few years a computer like this might be under five thousand."

"Well, we'll just hold off a bit then," Audra said as she went into the middle room. A moment later she returned with her backpack. She unzipped the main compartment and took out a three ring binder.

"My English composition archives. All the style sheets and guidelines I've ever gotten. You could study the evolution of the semi-colon in the California State University system. It's rather fascinating."

"Nice. So organized."

"I have to be. I can't keep everything in my head."

"Actually, I can't do that as much as I used to."

"Whoa! So you're like burnt out? No way!"

"Shakespeare did it to me."

"That bastard."

"Once I finish this paper, that's it. No more English classes."

"You're lucky. I have to take classes in writing *legal* English. They actually train you to be obfuscatory."

Gabrielle laughed. Then she remembered. It felt like a lump of ice had materialized in her stomach.

"What?"

"My presentation is tomorrow. I completely forgot."

"What class is this?"

"Introduction to Philosophy for Non-Humanities Majors."

Audra laughed. "Oh right. Can't believe that name."

"Yeah. Sometimes it's interesting. Mostly pretty silly. The professor likes that word. Obfus. What was it?"

"Obfuscatory. It has fusca in it. Hey! You fusca!"

"Ah. Fusca you!"

"Fusca off, man!"

"Okay, must work."

"Fusca that."

"I'm going to be up all night now. Fusca me."

Audra giggled and retreated to the kitchen.

Gabrielle scrolled down the textbox. Everything they had typed to each other was still there. She wished there was some way to save it all. She moved the mouse pointer around the menu on the top line.

"Wait a minute. Of course I can save it. It's a computer."

She carefully put the cursor over the **Housekeeping** menu item and clicked the button. A drop down list assembled itself in the blink of an eye. She carefully moved the pointer to **Save**, clicked, and the word blinked several times in acknowledgement. Another box came into being. She stopped to examine it. She clicked the pointer on a line labeled **Filename** and the blinking text cursor appeared.

The hard drive made a fascinating whirring sound and the box disappeared from the screen.

"Guess it's in there." Then she had a thought. She looked around the room and found the box of floppy disks on the high shelf over the middle room door.

Audra, she thought. The label on the box does say to keep away from *low level* magnetic fields. The disk had a bright red and white sleeve enclosing a plastic disk with a dark brown coating. It looked just like magnetic tape. The disk moved easily when she wiggled it with her finger.

She considered the size and shape of the drive box with its lever and thought about getting a screwdriver and taking the cover off. But it seemed fairly obvious how you were supposed to insert it.

The whole thing was interesting but she found herself thinking, this is all just a stopgap solution like the laser disk player. Little electric motors. It all seemed so *kudgy*.

"Problems can be solved," she said. She inserted the five and a quarter inch floppy disk into the drive and turned the lever. Someone cleared their throat behind her.

Catherine was standing at the door with a silver tray. She smiled.

"Having fun with *Tess*?"

"*Tess* is very complex and she takes everything literally."

"Challenging."

Catherine set the tray on the floor by Gabrielle's chair. There was the coffee carafe and ice cream in a silver bowl.

"You're going to need this later," she said. "And that's espresso ice cream."

"Thank you. I guess I will be working late. I think I have a good angle on the Sonnets, though."

Gabrielle leaned forward and Catherine massaged her shoulders. She knows exactly how to do that, she thought as her whole body flushed.

"Um," Catherine said. "I don't mean your homework. I mean later."

"Oh."

"So don't stay up too late."

Samantha entered, barefoot, and knelt next to *Tess*, fluffing her bathrobe.

"You're still working?"

"I haven't even started."

Samantha tipped her head sideways and kissed her, letting her hair drape the keyboard.

"Don't wear yourself out."

Gabrielle started to speak but Samantha kissed her again, slowly and softly, then got up and stood next to Catherine. They put their arms around each other's waists.

"We'll be awake," Samantha said. "Whenever you want to come to bed."

Catherine said, "The Sonnets. Interesting."

"Challenging."

"We will speak on this."

As she watched them leave the library together, Gabrielle thought, well what are you waiting for? Start writing.

She turned back to *Tess* and cleared the *window*, as Rushel called it, and started a new file in the word processor.

Title page first, she remembered. In the upper right corner she wrote her name and

English 312
Survey of Shakespeare
Dr Garland

Now the title. She spaced down and wrote,

The Voice of the Sonnets

She spaced down again.

"Okay. All right. Nothing fancy, just get to the point," she said. She ate a spoonful of the espresso ice cream and gulped lukewarm coffee.

As always, Gabrielle had no problem visualizing the structure of her term paper. In her mind's eye the words and phrases all had their own colors and polarity and they jostled and organized themselves like chaotic swarms of carbon and oxygen atoms.

Nothing was still, everything was movement. The words underwent a phase change and became sentences. Topic idea. Explanation. Evidence. Ideas had mass. Opinions had spin. A sentence of words extended ideas and opinion. A sentence was a vector. The vector was force times mass raised to the power of spin on a line, a heading, and the destination was *meaning*. That was the desired result. Circle *meaning* to receive full credit.

The whole procedure gave her a splitting headache. Her left eye twitched.

"God, I hate writing."

It is my contention the voice of Shakespeare's Sonnets, the voice which is speaking, is a dramatic character, not Shakespeare himself. Why would we assume that William Shakespeare, master playwright, would insert himself into his work? The Sonnets are not autobiographical.

My contention is that Shakespeare's speaker is a woman, a woman of middle age for Elizabethan times, probably about forty years old and a commoner. The beautiful youth is of a higher social status, some sort of aristocrat or noble.

Taken as a whole they constitute a new form of dramatic presentation. I will show that the voice of the Sonnets is a female character of great scope. To my knowledge this character is not given a name. I will refer to her [she grinned] **as *Holly*.**

Gabrielle wasn't sure she should use *italics* in a term paper. None of Audra's style sheets mentioned them. But she liked the look of it.

The evidence that the speaker is female is distributed across most of the first one hundred [backspace] **across Sonnets 1 through 128** [backspace] **across all the Sonnets in a remarkably subtle way, that is, the sensibility of the voice itself.**

"Nothing fancy, Gabrielle," Gabrielle said.

The sensibility of the voice, *Holly*, is decidedly female in the following ways.

Sonnet 1: Desire for children. The speaker is addressing someone unnamed, a fair youth, a young man who is considered beautiful, and encouraging him to have offspring.

"From fairest creatures we desire increase,

"That thereby beauty's rose might never die"

Sonnet 2: Sensitivity to passage of time. Someday, you will be an old person of forty and when you look upon your fair child you will feel warmth even when it is cold.

"This were to be new made when thou art old,

"And see thy blood warm when thou feel'st it cold"

Sonnet 3: *Holly* can see the fair youth's mother in him.

"Thou art thy mother's glass, and she in thee

"Calls back the lovely April of her prime"

This is an important clue. *Holly* knew the youth's mother when she was young. They were contemporaries. I believe this shows *Holly* was very close to the youth but not a family member. Childhood friends with his mom? Did the youth's mother marry into the highborn family while maintaining the friendship with *Holly*? This could make *Holly* an informal 'aunt.' Because this is serious nagging.

Sonnet 4: You, *Holly* says, are being selfish by not sharing your beauty.

"For having traffic with thyself alone,

"Thou of thyself thy sweet self dost deceive."

Yes, stop having traffic with thyself," Gabrielle said, and blushed. "Stupid Shakespeare."

Holly's feelings change.

Sonnet 17 seems to say, if you don't have children you will still live on in my poems.

"But were some child of yours alive that time,

"You should live twice,-- in it and in my rhyme"

This leads directly to the next phase. *Holly* seems to feel if he doesn't want to get married maybe I have a chance. Intense yearning for the young man's beauty consumes her. Sonnet 18:

"Shall I compare thee to a summer's day?

"Thou art more lovely and more temperate"

And

"But thy eternal summer shall not fade"

Finally Holly says forget about having kids, fair youth, I love you.

Her love evolves further. Time passes, an ongoing anxiety of hers. Our mysterious speaker *Holly* loves the young man because he looked like, and had the behavioral characteristics, of a woman in men's clothing. Interestingly, Sonnet 20 has a unique line pattern, eleven syllables each instead of ten. And line eleven itself states "But since she prick'd thee out for woman's pleasure." So a woman with a little something extra just for woman's pleasure. A woman with certain male physical attributes. A master and mistress at the same time. Was *Holly*, as we might say in the late twentieth century, exploring her sexuality?

Then a sea change. Holly is cast out.

Sonnet 29:

"When, in disgrace with fortune and men's eyes,

"I all alone beweep my outcast state"

Holly **is an older woman in love with someone much younger and from a higher social level. There is no hope. But she does not regret it and when she thinks about her love she feels**

"Like to the lark at break of day arising"

Gabrielle sat back and stretched. She saw the conclusion. The sense Gabrielle got from 125 was the speaker letting go of the young man. Not saying goodbye, just placing him off to the side of her heart. She wrote about 125 and 126 then said, "Time to cut to the chase, as Audra might sayeth."

*S***he discovers someone new. A woman with black hair and dark eyes.** *Holly* **argues her new friend is beautiful despite being so different from the standards of female beauty of the time, standards created by men, that is, snow white skin with rosy cheeks, golden blonde hair, blue eyes.** *Holly's* **feeling toward the dark haired woman are more complex than the yearning she felt for the young man.**

Sonnet 128:

"How oft, when thou, my music, music play'st,

"Upon that blessed wood whose motion sounds

"With thy sweet fingers, when thou gently sway'st"

Wood? Motion? Sway'st? If I said what I thought was really going on here I would get expelled. Does *Holly* **dream of having male parts now? Let me just say their relationship is very sensual and definitely physical. The idea is reinforced by Sonnet 129:**

"Mad in pursuit and in possession so;

"Had, having, and in quest to have, extreme"

Finally, in Sonnet 138, a resolution.

"On both sides thus is simple truth suppress'd"

Holly, **knowing the dark eyed lady is dishonest, is happy just to be with her. The usual male behavior would be to try to possess her but** *Holly* **gives no mind to that at all. Cheating, lying, and lack of standard beauty, these problems are conquered by love; the acceptance of and by a flawed human being perhaps the ultimate goal.**

Gabrielle sat up and checked her watch. *11:29.* The house had been quiet and dark around her for hours. She could feel the surf from across the dunes.

She saved the 'document' and was relieved that seemed to work. Then she checked the printer sitting on the table behind *Tess.* The paper looked straight, the little holes were engaged in the sprockets. The switch was in the on position.

"Okay. If this doesn't work I'll have to type it out which really will take all night."

She selected the **Edit** menu item and in the drop down box clicked **Print**. The hard drive buzzed. The printer made a thump and the paper jolted. Then nothing.

"Okay. Maybe not."

Gabrielle jumped back a foot as the printer began to make a sound like a tiny machine gun, a spitting crackling playing card in the spokes sound. The fan-fold paper was yanked and yanked again. She adjusted her glasses. She saw her name printed in the corner of the first page. The letters were made of little dots of ink. The print head moved right and instantly revered course.

"It prints in both directions. I have never seen that before."

Audra entered the library in her hooded robe and pink slippers. She rubbed her eyes.

"Bi-directional printing," she said. "Oh, the metaphors."

"Sorry I woke you up."

"I wasn't really asleep. I'm glad you're using the computer."

"It makes me nervous. Not sure why."

"*Tess* belongs to you, you know."

"I know. I'll work up to it."

They watched the noisy printer finish. Gabrielle tore off the last page at the perforations as carefully as she could.

"All right. So I know how to do it." Her watch said midnight. "Almost done."

Audra yawned and pointed back into the living room. The flashlight glowed. She spoke in a whisper.

"I'm glad to see you've bounced back. Even eight of those things is almost seven hundred thousand dollars." She looked back. "It's off. Checking every few minutes as usual."

"I wonder where Catherine hid them," Gabrielle said. "The coins we recovered."

"Recovered, yeah, that's the word. Where no one will ever find them. You sure you're all right? Any contact with them can cause lasting psychic damage."

"Well, New Susan got run over by a truck," she said as Audra laughed. "The police almost caught us. They had black robes with some sort of radio sound system. They could change voices so I couldn't tell who was who."

"That's new. They do like to spend money."

"In their front room they had these gigantic speakers. Biggest I've ever seen. They were playing this song so loud I couldn't hear my own voice. I kind of liked it, though."

"What was it?"

"I don't know. It was about fish."

Audra frowned and shrugged. Then she grinned mischievously.

"Any second now."

They both watched the flashlight. Audra counted down from ten and the light came on. A yellowish beam splashed up the wall.

"Needs batteries again," Gabrielle whispered.

"Saturday night, we rip it out," Audra whispered back. She took a deep breath. "Good!" she said stridently.

Gabrielle covered her ears.

"We have an understanding!" Audra continued loudly. "Monday morning you pack your things up and get out, never to return. Is that clear?"

Gabrielle made a sniffle. "Okay," she said weakly.

Audra made a fist at the corner of her eye.

Gabrielle nodded and sobbed. She rolled her eyes. It sounded weak even to her.

Audra made a thumbs up.

"Tears won't help you now. Go on!" she yelled. "You sleep outside. And not on the porch either. On the dirt. With the snakes and the." Her eyes flicked back and forth. "Blood sucking centipedes."

"Can I at least use the bathroom?" Gabrielle made her voice tremble.

"What do you think bushes are for? Go on! Go!" Audra opened the front door and then slammed it shut. She pointed again. "The light went out the I instant I did that."

"Wow." Gabrielle wondered if it had been New Susan. She didn't like the idea of tricking her. She thought there must be some way of explaining this all to her.

"The hook is set," Audra said and laughed.

Samantha was in the doorway, arms folded over her robe.

"Audra, you're really mean. Gabrielle, you can sleep in our room if you want. We'll protect you from the snakes. How is the term paper going?"

"Thank you. I'm just checking for typos then a final print out."

"So not much longer? Catherine wanted me to ask."

"Just a few minutes."

"All right. She said be sure and drink the coffee."

Gabrielle looked at her in surprise. Samantha raised her eyebrows and walked back into the darkened house.

"Coffee?" Audra said. "What about the coffee?"

"It's just coffee."

"Then why did she say that?"

"I'm not sure."

"Okay, well, I'm not drinking any."

"I'll just have a sip. Helps with my headache." Gabrielle began checking the printout. 'Dot matrix' was not very legible.

"It's great for headaches. But even just that you won't be able to sleep.

I know I wouldn't. You'll be jazzed all night. Anyway. Good night." Audra wiggled the front door deadbolt and yawned again. "We're good. No snakes getting in."

"Are there snakes?"

"There are always snakes."

Audra's slippers scuffed through the middle room and one of the reclining chairs creaked.

Gabrielle rubbed her eyes and then her temples. She took off her glasses and held the printout close. The tiny dots swam in and out of focus. She read to the end and then backwards to the beginning, a proofreading trick her mother had taught her. No mistakes. She hoped the professor would accept a computer printout. Too late now, she thought, and I'm tired of worrying about it.

She separated the pages and made sure they were in order. She dug into her pocket. She had a paperclip she found on the sidewalk outside the Administration building and had saved it just for this purpose. She set her term paper on top of the monitor.

"Okay. Finished. Now."

The presentation. Philosophy.

She went into the dark kitchen and located two items she needed and set them on the counter. She knew her presentation was going to be a little unorganized. She was winging it. But heck, she thought, the Philosophy Department. Would they even notice?

She shut down *Tess.* The process was intriguing. It made her pulse race to think this was going to be her life now. She was anxious to get to it.

She filled her coffee cup from the carafe. It was the perfect temperature for gulping. She drank two cups and switched off the floor lamp. House completely dark, she walked past Audra bundled up on her chair. In the hallway she stopped before her bedroom door. She remembered.

She went quietly into her bathroom and shut the door. She turned on the little green night light by the sink. She dug way down in her pocket and pulled out the flattened, compressed lump.

I cleaned it, right? she thought. She sniffed it. Smelled clean. Smelled like damp silk. She untangled the G-string and laid it out on the edge of the sink. The heart shaped pin was still dangling. She tried to smooth it, the little triangle part. It had to be absolutely clean. She lifted up her glasses. The delicately stitched edge had a crisp look. Looks brand new, she thought. Unused. Whose was it? What in the world happened there? I can never tell anyone how I got this. I need to make up a story.

She took her clothes off. She rubbed the strings, actually thin flat strips, against the porcelain. She tried to visualize how they were supposed to be configured. The topology. Under and through? Then she saw it. Simple. She tied one side, pulled it snug, not too tight. Redo knot, yes, right there. Uh, yeah. She tied the other side and tugged everything into position and checked the mirror. "Now who's prick'd out," she said and turned out the nightlight.

She sighed. My hips are the wrong shape, this won't work, it feels funny. She shook her hair loose.

And then all the coffee kicked in.

Gabrielle had a bleary-eyed breakfast of orange juice followed by coffee while Audra and Rushel waited in the car. When she grabbed the two items from the counter, Catherine reached over and stroked the back of her hand.

"You're running late," Catherine said.

"I know, I'm." Gabrielle put the two items into her sweatshirt pockets.

"Hm. You're never late. It's puzzling."

Samantha got up from the dining table strewn with papers and stood behind Gabrielle and wrapped her arms around her waist.

"I know why she's late," Samantha said.

Catherine came around the counter. She looked pointedly at the hall door.

"Gislaine's taking a shower," Samantha said and gently pulled Gabrielle away from the counter.

Catherine stepped into the space and pressed her body firmly into Gabrielle's. Samantha reached out and pulled Catherine tighter. Gabrielle looked up into Catherine's eyes and they breathed together. Then Gabrielle couldn't stand it and she giggled.

"Someone was a bad girl last night," Samantha said softly.

"A very very bad girl," Catherine said. She kissed Samantha over Gabrielle's shoulder. "My knee will never be the same."

"String burn," Samantha whispered.

Gabrielle with Catherine's breasts fully on her's managed to say, "Sorry."

Catherine began to kiss the side of her neck. "Oh, never apologize," she said into Gabrielle's hairline.

Outside, someone beeped the Volkswagen's horn.

Samantha whispered into Gabrielle's ear, "You're going to concentrate on driving, right? We insist you stay safe."

"I'll," Gabrielle said.

"Hm?" Catherine kissed her.

The horn beeped again.

"That one sounded like an editorial comment," Samantha said.

They both stepped back and Gabrielle swayed.

"Have a nice day at school," Catherine said. "When you get home come on over and we can play some more."

"Okay," Gabrielle said. "Can your friend Samantha come over and play, too?"

"Oh, we'll have to ask but probably."

"I really liked playing with her."

"We noticed." Catherine grinned and closed her eyes. "All right. School, young lady."

Gabrielle sighed as they both kissed her on the cheek. Then they guided her out of the kitchen.

"You have your lunch, I see. And you have your pencil? The modern day genius college girl is never without her pencil. And her term paper. Study hard."

"And be good," Samantha said.

"Oh I think it's far too late for that," Catherine said sadly.

At the front door, Gabrielle made a stern effort to get the smile off her face. Catherine and Samantha opened the door and pushed her through and closed it firmly. Audra and Rushel watched from the VW.

When Gabrielle opened the driver's door, she said, "Sorry."

Audra, in the back, stared straight out the side window.

"We're going to have to park at College Costs Less and walk in about a mile."

"Friday's usually aren't too bad," Rushel said. Her voice was breathy and she held her knees close together.

"Wait," Audra said. "Have you *ever* driven a car to school and tried to find a place to park? Driven round and round each lot and there's nothing and it's five minutes to class so you drive over the curb and park on the tiny grass area next to the farm store and it knocks your muffler loose and they tow your car while you're taking the midterm plus they charge you for breaking a sprinkler head?"

"No."

"I didn't think so."

Gabrielle started the engine and they headed down the sandy road.

"It is something I have observed. Friday's are light traffic-wise."

"I guess we'll see."

"Also," Rushel continued, "this is the second to the last Friday before finals and thus will be even lighter due to the fact that so many students have given up. Sad, really."

"That's rather cynical of you."

"I'm a much harder person than I used to be."

"This is the result of changing majors. No longer are you a silly Liberal Arts goof off."

"It's possible you are not wrong."

"Possible?"

Rushel sighed. "Goddess, could you step on it?"

Gabrielle powered her car onto the pavement and they sped through the hanging forest into the gathering fog.

From the big lot by the theater they walked slowly and watchfully to the postal kiosk on the inner road. Backpack laden students of all ages streamed around them, sober and businesslike in their Earth tone shirts and plaid coats. All the students stared at Rushel as they passed.

They stood under the messy tree. Fog dripped from the red leaves. Audra let her backpack slip off her shoulder.

"Listen," Audra said.

Gabrielle heard the steady shush of denim and a gravely crunch of athletic shoes. Rushel scanned the area.

"Pocket Mouse, is this like the time you heard a voice telling you to get a bikini wax? Remember, I had to sit on you."

"A what?" Gabrielle said. She checked her watch.

"No, listen. What aren't you hearing?"

"I guess no one's talking."

"Or laughing. Or singing," Rushel said.

"My math professor said it's the worst quarter ever."

"Really."

A guy in a gray sweatshirt, hood pulled over his head, walked by holding a wad of tissue over his nose. He sneezed and stumbled and started coughing as he passed.

"Nothing's gonna stop him," Rushel said softly. "Look, it's finals. Students are serious here. This isn't some creepy joke party school."

"There is such a thing?" Gabrielle opened her folder and checked her paper again. She tucked it back under her sweatshirt.

"Oh, yeah. Like Santa Barbara. You don't want that on your résumé."

"Never even considered that place."

"Me neither."

"Why did you pick this school? You could've gone anywhere."

"This is where my dad went to college."

"Ah. Sure."

"Mechanical engineering. Class of fifty-eight."

"Nineteen fifty-eight. Just think of that. A lost world."

Audra swung her backpack over her shoulder.

"Everything's set for tomorrow. Disco will be expecting us. He is super excited. The DJ will be there at five to set up so we should all get there about then."

"Sid?" Rushel grinned.

"Uh huh."

"Will his sister be there?"

"She always is."

"Really."

"The dance will officially start at seven just as it's getting totally dark."

Gabrielle felt her nervousness spike.

"What will I be doing?"

"Oh." Audra shrugged. "Well, nothing. Disco's roomies can move furniture if needed. Sid shouldn't need any help. He has his system perfected pretty much. So we just wait for them all to show up. Catherine will be there. I'll be on tactical. The three big girls will be on operational standby."

"Whoa," Rushel whispered.

"You could be dancing, you know, if you want."

"Dancing. I don't know."

"Not required."

"You're the best, Audra," Rushel said.

Audra wiped her forehead. "My finals schedule is awful. How about you two?"

"Easy," Gabrielle said.

"Piece of cake," Rushel said. "I finish Wednesday morning."

"Jeez." Audra closed her eyes. "My last final is Thursday at seven-thirty."

"Oh, you're done before lunch," Rushel said.

"That's seven-thirty in the evening."

"I never heard of that before," Gabrielle said. "So you get out when?"

"Nine-thirty at night. At least it's an easy class. *Contracts and the Supreme Court's Nightmare.*"

Gabrielle shook her head.

"Your classes are incomprehensible to me."

Audra smiled grimly. "That's definitely intentional on their part." She pulled her backpack tight. "Goddess, Rushel, I hope you both have a nice day. Good luck with your term paper."

"Thank you. I hope you have a nice day also."

"Thank you," Rushel said. "My adorable electron, thank you for all your hard work and I hope you also have a nice day."

"I'm really more of a semiconductor this morning. I feel doped. But thank you. We meet here at the usual time?"

"Okay," Rushel said with a absent minded lilt. She walked away from the messy tree towards the center of campus.

When she was out of sight, Gabrielle said, "Audra."

"She'll be fine."

Gabrielle could hear the concern in her voice.

"Well," she said. "How about you?"

Audra half shrugged and looked away, her brow furrowed. "I'm the strong one. Strong and solitary. You, Goddess, on the other hand."

"I know. Nuts."

"I hope you know what you're doing."

Gabrielle stood under the tree and watched Audra strike off towards the upper campus, slipping into the flow of students like a traveler jumping onto an airport escalator,

"I don't think I have any idea what I'm doing," she said and let these thoughts percolate. "I love this."

She gripped the folder and headed for the library the long way, a roundabout route through Science, which kept her safely away from the doors of the old gym.

Andrea gave her presentation first.

She stood behind the front desk with her eyes closed. Professor Townsend took position at the back corner. He leaned against the wall. Gabrielle watched him in her peripheral vision, trying not to turn her head, and she caught him staring at her.

Right, she thought, how could I have forgotten.

She plucked the ring from her nose and hesitated. She decided to just hold it. Keep it pinched. Do not drop it. She mentally thanked Townsend for reminding her.

Then she caught Annie looking at her. Annie immediately tried to cover this up by shifting in her seat. She shook her head.

"Andrea," Townsend said, "will now give her presentation."

Andrea's thick black hair had been pulled back severely and tied into a pony tail with what looked like multiple layers of white tape. She was wearing an oversize jacket, charcoal gray, with the sleeves pushed up to her elbows. She had a bandage wrapped around her left wrist and there were dark circles under her eyes.

"My name is Andrea. I'm majoring in Physics." Her voice was clear, her eyes unfocused. "My presentation is about the nature of consciousness. Atoms and molecules do not possess consciousness. A cell in my body, composed of atoms and molecules, does not possess consciousness. If, as some scientist suggested, consciousness is an emergent property of interacting cells, neurons, then it is obviously an illusion, like an ephemeral wave on the ocean. How can interacting neurons create a conscious experience? A shadow of a bird passing over the grass is not the bird. When I say I know something, this is not true. There is no 'I.'

Gabrielle shook her head. What the hell?

"It took me awhile to figure this out. You know what? Once I did, I felt better. And I'll tell you why. If I am not real then pain is not real. And I can prove it."

Andrea slapped her left hand on the desk, palm down, and from a back pocket pulled out a large knife. She held the point of the knife over the back of her hand. The blade was long, crooked and rusty. Her hand shook and the point glinted in the dull fluorescent lights.

All the students sat back in their seats. The long haired guy took his head off the desk. Annie gasped.

"Proof shall consist of the following. I will run the blade of this knife through my hand into the desk. I will feel no pain. Everyone clear on this?"

Gabrielle saw the big guy tense and look at Annie who was motionless. Townsend was still leaning against the wall. His expression was somewhat disapproving, Gabrielle saw, and not alarmed at all.

Andrea stared feverishly at the knife. She slowly raised it and held it poised over her hand.

"All right? I'll go slow and force the knife blade between the bones, severing ligaments and blood vessels. Any questions?" She looked at everyone. "Here goes!"

Her right arm tensed under the black sweater, she gritted her teeth, and the blade descended towards the back of her hand. The rusty point touched her smooth tanned skin and made a depression then pushed deeper. Gabrielle saw the point penetrate.

Annie emitted a strangled scream and the big guy jerked in his seat. Gabrielle thought he was going to jump up. The woman in the front of him, in her Army jacket, covered her face with her hands. Townsend still had not reacted.

Gabrielle did not move. Her stomach lurched but she thought, wait a minute. She squeezed the nose ring so hard the point of the wire jammed under her fingernail. She did not take her eyes off Andrea.

The blade was clearly cutting into Andrea's hand. Andrea was breathing loudly through her nose, mouth tightly closed. She was concentrating on the knife so intensely she was almost cross-eyed.

"Stop!" It was the long haired guy.

Andrea lifted the knife and frowned at him.

The big guy shook his head and exhaled. Annie's pen fell to the floor.

"Why?" Andrea said, holding the knife aloft. She sounded puzzled. Her eyes flashed.

"Uh, well, because."

"Because *why?*"

"I don't want you to hurt yourself." His voice was strong and clear.

"No, no, I already explained. I am an automaton. A mechanism. A mechanism can be damaged but not hurt."

He shook his straggly hair back.

"I don't think you're a mechanism."

"Why?" Her eyes drilled into him.

"You seem like a person."

"Seem?"

"Well, from where I'm sitting, as far as I can tell, you are a human being."

Andrea set the knife down.

"Appearances are inconclusive. My consciousness is a merely a simulation."

"So," he said, raising his index finger, "even though you seem to be conscious it's just an act, something like that?"

"Yes."

Gabrielle was beginning to detect a connection with her own

presentation. And that knife.

"If the simulation is perfect," he said. Gabrielle could almost hear his thoughts forming. "A perfect simulation of consciousness. Perfect, right? Wouldn't that necessarily include the capacity to feel pain? By definition." He shrugged. "I'm Computer Science."

Everyone in the classroom nodded. Smart man.

Andrea took a deep breath. "A simulation of pain is not pain."

"A perfect simulation would be indistinguishable from the real thing."

"I could control a simulation."

"Okay, now you're just begging the question because who is the 'I' that is doing the controlling?"

Gabrielle heard Professor Townsend say, "Hm," very softly. Andrea put the knife back in her hip pocket.

"The simul," she started to say. Then she said, "Thank you, that's all."

Andrea went to her seat in the front row and sat down.

The woman in the Army jacket let out a whistle then clamped her hand over her mouth.

After three heartbeats, Townsend said, "Andrea, thank you. That was very thought provoking."

"Thank you."

"All right. John. You're feeling better today?"

"Yes much better, Professor. Thank you for asking."

"Not at all. Okay, one more presentation and we'll be finished for the week. Be sure to drop off your papers before you leave. Um."

Gabrielle smiled as the Townsend looked at her, blank eyed.

"Gabrielle," she said.

"Yes. Sorry. Gabrielle will now give her presentation. Whenever you're ready." He leaned back against the wall.

Gabrielle felt the familiar uptick of her pulse rate and tightening of the muscles in her scalp. These physiological responses now had the effect of heightening her awareness instead of blanking out her mind in a fog of panic. Vision and hearing were sharper. And, she hoped, thought processes in general accelerated.

Not sure about that.

This doubt echoed in her mind as she stood up, still pinching the nose ring between thumb and finger. She left her pencil on her desk and walked to the front of the classroom.

With her back to the students she took the two items from her sweatshirt pocket and arranged them on the corner of the front desk. Then she turned and let them see.

Something sat there covered by one of Catherine's white napkins. They all watched her intently.

"I have been reading about an ancient Greek philosopher named Parmenides. He was born in 515 BC, which is just before the time of Socrates. Very little of his work survives but he was an important philosopher in his time. Plato named one of his Dialogues after him. We do have fragments of a poem he wrote called *On Nature.* In the preface, the narrator travels beyond the path of mortal men and receives instruction from a mysterious goddess."

"Persephone," Professor Townsend said.

"Yes?" Gabrielle answered. She immediately felt herself blushing and thought frantically, how could he know that? What the hell?

"Sorry. The goddess he encounters was thought to be either Persephone or Diké."

"Die kee." Gabrielle cleared her throat. She noticed John staring at her while Annie was grinning. "Right. Diké the Greek goddess of fair treatment. She always shown holding scales. The Romans gave her the blindfold and renamed her Justice. But this was way before the time of the Romans."

"Ah," John said.

Gabrielle's heart pounded against her ribs.

"What I found interesting was that Parmenides seemed to have discovered one of the fundamental laws of logic, the Law of Identity, well before anyone else. It's really very simple. He divided the universe into two realms. The Way of Truth and the Way of Opinion. The Way of Truth works like this."

She lifted the napkin from the object. Everyone leaned forward.

"What is, *is*, Parmenides said. It is not nothing. It has existence. And it is its own object. It is not something other than what it is. Someone tell me what this object is."

John looked from her face to the object and back again. Annie and the big guy exchanged another look. Andrea frowned severely while Army jacket woman nodded and raised her hand. Her gray streaked hair fell over her face.

"I know what it looks like," she said. Her voice was high and thin.

"Tell me what it is, not what it looks like. Feel free to come up an examine it."

The woman sat back. "Oh I don't know."

At this the big guy rolled his eyes and pushed himself up. He walked to the front, nodded at Gabrielle, and picked up the object. He hefted it and looked closely at the top and bottom. Then he set it back down and returned to his seat. He cleared his throat and raised his hand.

Gabrielle said, "Yes?"

"That is an apple," he said.

Andrea snapped her head around. "You don't know that."

"I'm pretty sure."

John raised his hand.

"It could be a simulation of an apple."

Gabrielle did not smile. "Examine it."

John seemed embarrassed by the idea.

"That's all right."

"Go ahead.

Gabrielle noticed Professor Townsend staring at her with a slight smile.

John stood up on wavering legs and stepped to the desk and leaned onto his elbows.

"Now then, let's see."

John had hollow cheeks and she saw his long hair wasn't blonde. It was colorless. She left terrible for making him stand up.

He put his face a few inches from the apple. He touched the stem then tipped it slightly and checked the bottom. Then he sniffed it.

"This is a shiny red apple. Either a real one or a good simulation."

"How good a simulation, John?" It was Annie.

"I'm prepared to say perfect. It smells wonderful. I guess I would have to taste it to be absolutely sure but."

Gabrielle came around John and said to Andrea, "May I borrow your knife for a second?"

Andrea smiled and pulled the knife out.

"Thank you," Gabrielle and quickly looked away. Andrea's eyes tracked her's. There was a cut on back of Andrea's left hand. Blood had dripped onto her desk. Gabrielle held her breath to keep her stomach from churning.

She set the apple on its side and cut out a thin wedge, the way her mother liked to. The knife was razor sharp. The aroma filled the classroom.

John watched her every move with fascination. He shifted his weight to his left elbow and took the slice.

"Thank you. Just a tiny taste. I'm supposed to avoid sweets."

He nibbled on the juicy apple wedge and his eyebrows rose.

Gabrielle took the opportunity to say, "A perfect simulation of an object would actually be the object itself. Indistinguishable, because the only information we have about the world comes to us via our senses. We have no other way of knowing. And our senses are limited. We have far from perfect awareness. So using only your human senses now tell me what the object is."

"It's an apple from the grocery store. Probably College Costs Less."

He ate the rest of the slice.

"You're absolutely sure?"

"No, but I'm sticking with it. And I guess I needed a snack. Thanks," John said breathlessly. He pivoted and sat back back down in a controlled slump. As he did Andrea snatched the knife back.

Gabrielle ignored her anger and set the apple straight.

"Ah," John said. "Yes. You're Rushie's friend aren't you."

"Um, yes. I am."

"Thought so. She's turning my department upside down. She's told me about you."

"Oh. Well," Gabrielle said. "Parmenides would say in the World of Truth this object has its own existence. It *is*. However we exist in another world, the World of Opinion, the world of appearances. We can detect truth with our senses and that's as far as it goes. It exists independently of our mind. Today we might just call it objective reality. In science we're used to this situation. We know we can understand the world even if we are stuck with our limited senses. We can't see the electrons around the atomic nucleus-"

"It's not there," Andrea said loudly. "It's not real."

"You don't think the apple is real?

Andrea sighed and smiled, a contemptuous sneer. "Little impulses from my senses do not mean anything. If we all agree on the parameters of the illusion, fine, it is still an illusion. I know that's the truth." She said the last word with a crooked twist of her mouth.

"All right, but all this 'knowing' you're doing. I thought you said your mind was a simulation."

Someone laughed out loud. It was Townsend. Andrea's shoulders slumped.

"I was just making a point," she said. "Besides, a simulated mind is still a mind."

"So you use the power of your mind, your will, simulated or not, to nullify whatever reality exists around you. You see a butterfly and you think, how beautiful, too bad I know it's not real. You destroy beauty, you destroy meaning, you destroy reality."

"No, look."

"Wouldn't it be better to create? I myself do this all the time. I'll give you an example. Andrea, you can see me, right?"

Andrea stared at her and blinked and shook her head.

"Am I visible?"

"Are you. Yes. You are."

"My name is Gabrielle. Who am I?"

"I guess you're Gabrielle."

"Don't guess."

"You are apparently someone named Gabrielle."

Sensing it would do no good to push Andrea any further, Gabrielle triggered her climactic stunt. She looked straight ahead, swung out her arms and in one smooth maneuver brought up and inserted the ring into her nose. She turned her head from side to side.

"Now who am I?"

Andrea frowned again. Someone cleared their throat.

"*Hot* Gabrielle."

It was John. He shrugged and smiled.

Gabrielle grinned at him.

"My point is simply that if even if I change my appearance, in truth, I'm the same person."

Andrea scoffed. "There is no objective reality. But you keep trying."

"All right I will."

Gabrielle picked up the apple and dropped it onto Andrea's head. It bounced with a hollow *bonk* sound and rolled under the desk.

Wide eyed, Andrea said, "Hey!" She bared her teeth.

"This concludes my presentation. Thank you."

John, Annie, the big guy, and Army jacket woman burst into applause. Professor Townsend pushed away from the wall.

"Okay," he said quickly. "Thank you, Gabrielle. Everyone have a nice weekend and I'll see you all on Monday. Our last week."

Gabrielle thought, do I need the apple? No. Do I need my pencil? No.

To the sound of notebooks closing Gabrielle avoided Andrea's furious glare and exited the classroom in a nice straight line.

"You just keep making friends."

Catherine was shoulder to shoulder with Samantha in front of *Tess*.

"I know."

Gabrielle squinted at the small computer screen. Samantha was using the *Calc* program which she referred to as a *spreadsheet*.

"She's a student?" Samantha adjusted the mouse. "She's the professor's girlfriend?"

"Not sure about that." Gabrielle saw that the title of the spreadsheet was 'M's Mess.'

"She follows him around like a puppy."

"Ah," Catherine said. "Different."

"This professor guy probably loves you now," Samantha said.

"I don't get that." Gabrielle rubbed her eyes.

"Did he come to her defense?"

"Nope. Just stood there."

"See. Andrea just got an update on her relationship status."

"A cold hard update," Catherine said. "Icy."

"That guy loves you for that. He didn't have the guts to do it himself. Andrea, on the other hand."

Catherine stroked her chin.

"Blind, all-consuming hatred that will never die."

Samantha let go of the mouse. "You know, hatred like that is bad. It can mess you up. You don't hate Andrea, do you?"

"Of course not."

"You sure?"

"Her ideas were silly. I don't feel anything about her."

"Is she cute?"

"Yeah, kind of."

They both looked at her.

"What?" Gabrielle said.

"How cute?"

"Long wavy dark hair. Large brown eyes. Nice chin."

"Chin?"

"I like chins. They're right next to lips."

"Please continue."

"Her lips are all right."

"Type?"

"Type two, pretty much."

Catherine said, "You were holding out on us, weren't you?"

"No. Well. I don't know."

Catherine laughed. "I see. You and Andrea. This whole entire semester quarter." She caught Samantha's expression. "Oh, here we go."

"Did Andrea actually cut herself?" Samantha said.

"Yes, I saw it."

"Was there blood?"

"Blood all over the desk."

Catherine sighed. "*Andrea.*"

"Unfortunately, that's very clear," Samantha said. "And it tells me everything I need to know about her so-called relationship."

Catherine shook her head. "Andrea."

Samantha smiled and said, "She's using self-inflicted pain to compensate."

"I really don't care about Andrea but compensate for what?"

"Total lack of whamblamming."

"Doinking deficit disorder," Catherine said seriously.

"We should," Samantha said as Gabrielle laughed, "help her. After all."

"Yes," Catherine said softy.

"It *is* what I used to do for a living."

"That's true."

"And I was pretty good if I do say so."

"You were well compensated by those nice ladies," Catherine said. "You still have the car, right?"

"Yes."

"That's good. You dare not drive it. Because."

"Because I always get in trouble."

"Yes you do. Big trouble." Catherine patted Samantha's arm. She said to Gabrielle, "It's a Lamborghini. It goes over two hundred miles per hour if you're not careful.

"Whoa."

Samantha dropped her head. "Yeah."

Catherine was grinning. "It goes faster than police helicopters. But not faster than Air Force helicopters."

"Army, actually."

"Right, yes. That was the Army, wasn't it."

"Yes."

"We have to get that all out and show her. There's a whole scrapbook. They had to land the helicopter on the highway to get her to stop." She rubbed Samantha's shoulders. "And what kind of helicopter was it? It was the best helicopter ever made in all of history."

"Apache. AH-64."

"That's right. A brand new *Apache* gunship on a test flight."

"Oh my God!" Gabrielle took Samantha's hands in her's.

"I'm still not sure why I did that."

"Yes you are," Catherine said gently. "You made progress. Overall, that was a good day for you. You got to drive really fast in your amazing car. You got to meet Jerry and Linda. There was Mike."

"Mike was the test pilot," Samantha said.

"Oh?"

"Yeah, he was cool. He wanted to hide the car behind some rocks but it was too late. I hid behind the pilot's seat. The cops got the car but we got it out in a couple days thanks to him. Turned out I was lucky. I was kind of accidentally almost on a military reservation. What was the name of it?"

"Oh. I forget," Catherine said. "Funny name. Area something."

"In Nevada. We got it out and drove it to a safe place. I think Mike just wanted to drive it."

"He wanted to drive a lot more than that."

"Hey." Samantha shrugged.

"And that," Catherine said, "is how you came to be in Los Angeles, in Hollywood, without a car. And the rest his history."

"Promise you'll tell the whole story someday," Gabrielle said as Samantha squeezed her hand. "Who was Jerry and Linda?"

"Jerry Brown and Linda Ronstadt.

"The Governor?"

"It was interesting. Also embarrassing. But listen, I'm speaking now as your Priestess. You can't let the situation with Andrea just twist in the wind."

Gabrielle sighed.

"Take control of events. You are the Goddess. Find her somehow and make it up to her."

"I will. I promise."

"Help her with math. Buy her lunch. Multiple orgasms. Whatever it takes. And I'll be happy to assist if you want. I know a few tricks."

Gabrielle spent a few moments thinking about what that would be like and said, "All right."

"Now I must get back to this. M's life in numbers." She patted the top of the monitor. "Shrinking numbers."

"It's not over yet," Catherine whispered.

"Technically, no."

"Let's go out to dinner," Catherine said abruptly. "Us three. Gislaine knows how to cook. It's her and Rushel here, right? Audra's in her law class."

"You two go," Samantha said. I'm at a critical point in tax year nineteen seventy-six. I'm gathering evidence that a certain trip to Paris was business related and therefore deductible."

"Oh my. Really?" Catherine leaned closer. "I have no idea how you do this. I wish I could understand it."

"It has its own language. Like a lot of things."

"Well I'm glad it's you."

"Thank you. Now you two go."

"We'll go together next time," Gabrielle said. "Next Friday."

"We can make it a Friday thing." Catherine stood up. "From now on."

Samantha nodded, eyes on the screen. "I like that idea. Doing something on Fridays would almost make it feel as if I have a regular work week."

"I've never had that," Catherine said. "My weeks were always crazy."

"In accounting they don't like crazy. They like boring."

"Even though you are far from boring."

"I feel myself becoming boring."

"*No.*"

"It's just as well."

"Next Friday we will do something unboring."

Samantha adjusted the mouse. "You're saying it's not too late?"

"I'm not sure."

"Please don't give up on me."

"I promise that with the help of a real Goddess I happen to know we will arrest your terrifying slide into boringness."

"Wow, I feel better already. See you later."

Catherine said seriously to Gabrielle, "Let us now go out to dinner."

Gabrielle said with a straight face. "Yes. Let us."

"Bathroom?"

"Yes."

"Me too!"

Gabrielle took a different route to town. She cut north along the tidal estuary, dotted with white egrets in the chill evening twilight and headed for Highway One. As she shifted she felt Catherine's hand sneak onto her thigh.

Catherine said, "This is the way we went that day."

"I remember. I like the estuary. I like looking at the bay."

The sun was below the horizon and the western clouds were gray and amber.

"Sure. But aren't we going." She pointed over her right shoulder.

"Yep. This way's a little roundabout."

"Is it because of."

"I suddenly just didn't want to go the usual way."

"Ah, I think I got it."

Gabrielle accelerated down the estuary road as it dropped and banked left. She took her foot off the gas and let momentum carry them between two steep hills, thick with dark green grass and trees. Close to the highway they got stuck behind a black Continental with tinted windows.

"That thing weighs as much as four of these."

"But it's not as intimate." Catherine pushed her hand deeper.

The Continental turned north in a slow, ponderous maneuver, Gabrielle made a quick right going south.

"Bet the back seat's comfortable," she said.

"True. You could really stretch out. We'd just need a chauffeur."

"Drive up and down the coast. Who's the chauffeur?"

"That would be Ilse from Reykjavik."

"Iceland. Okay."

"Being gently rocked in the back seat of a gigantic car by Ilse. That's a nice thought."

Gabrielle felt Catherine's hand move to her right knee. She tried to keep her eyes on the dark highway. Tendrils of fog swirled against the volcanic hills.

"A certain friend of ours told me something once. She said that we are always being hunted by invisible forces. Entities. They never rest, these things. They are absolutely real. Impersonal, like lightning, except intelligent. They feed on us."

Gabrielle risked a glance at her. "Invisible forces?" She kept the car in the lane.

"I've walked around your school a couple times There are a lot of stairs, aren't there. Steps. Let's say as part of your daily routine there is a certain set of concrete steps you walk down. You go that way every morning. The same time of day. It's perfectly safe. There is never a problem."

Gabrielle saw the lights of the town ahead. She felt relief amid the chill.

"And then one morning, a morning like any other, you trip and fall. As you lie on the concrete bleeding with a broken arm your mind races. How could I trip like that? Was it the steps? No, it was the invisible forces. *They* did it. They learned your routine like a hunter tracking deer and made you fall. You were an easy target. You thought you were safe but there is no safety. It could be a set of steps or a stretch of road. You take a shower every morning. One day you slip and break your neck. You always have a banana on your coffee break. One day for no apparent reason you choke to death on it.

"Safety is a myth, this certain friend said. Only arrogant ignorant humans believe in safety. Like a little mouse sunning itself on a rock while hawks circle overhead. Humans are prey. A food source."

"That sounds like her."

"I know, huh? The trick is think like a hunter. Be unpredictable. Throw them off your trail. Change your commute even if it's inconvenient. Alter your daily activities suddenly. Change the order of things you do. She said her grandfather told her all this while walking in the desert one morning. He taught her how to see them."

"You can see them?" Gabrielle felt the hair stand up on the back of her neck. She sped up.

Catherine shrugged. "Changing your route made me think of it. Samantha would approve."

They crested a hill and approached an intersection. The red and green traffic lights seemed dazzlingly bright. Gabrielle felt a bit comforted.

"So this is good," Catherine said. "This new route."

"Good. It feels good." Gabrielle looked at the dark sky as the signal turned green. Was the fog coming back again? How about a clear sky for once?

But the fog greeted them a quarter mile further in and the reassuring streetlights dimmed in the blowing droplets. Gabrielle began to get an idea of where she wanted to go. She thought where to park.

"Where are we going?" Catherine said.

Gabrielle looked at her in surprise and Catherine grinned.

"You forgot I can do that."

"Well, no, I."

"Yes, you did. Hm. This is like a date. Our first date. Have you given any thought to our date or are just winging it?"

"Winging it. But I have a flight plan."

Catherine laughed. "And I forgot how smart you are."

"It's been a very long week."

"Terrible week."

Gabrielle saw the street she wanted and stopped in a left turn lane.

Catherine looked puzzled but Gabrielle saw a familiar mischievous twinkle in her eyes.

"You're making a left however I believe downtown is to the right. You can almost but not quite see in the fog. And also I find the recurring fog rather hokey and theatrical. Please notify management."

"I am sick of the fog. I see things."

The light turned green and Gabrielle waited for a primer patched Toyota truck to sputter past. Three people were visible inside. Typical frosh vehicle, she thought, they shouldn't be out so late.

As she made the turn Catherine said, "It's only like six forty-five, right?"

Gabrielle put in second. "Five till."

"Not that late."

Gabrielle shook her head, as Catherine grinned, and she began to scan for side roads. She remembered it being on the right but sometimes, she knew, her memory randomly flipped orthogonals. Right for left or weird confusing mirror memories. She was certain, however, that it was west of the train trestle that cut across the street overhead. These were the same tracks that went behind her old house and she really liked that connection. On her current heading that strange street was before the trestle.

Gabrielle slowed. Each side of the street was lined with businesses and large trees. They passed several side streets lined with warmly lit houses. No antique cars or old style streetlights.

They went under the trestle. On the other side the fog and misty streetlights seemed the same. She got an idea.

"Do you see any police cars?"

Catherine's eyes widened. "Gosh." She twisted and looked around. "No police cars visible, not that I can see anything at all."

Gabrielle let off the gas and pushed in the clutch, waited for a westbound Camaro to pass, then killed the headlights and hauled the steering wheel all the way to the left. The VW made a wide U-turn and she slipped into a spot on the curb under spreading tree between two driveways. Perfect, she thought. Easy to get out and can't get blocked in. She switched off the engine.

"Had to throw off my pursuers," she said.

"I'm so glad I told you that story. I thought we were going to dinner."

"Oh we are."

"I don't see any eating establishments. I do see several motels, you saucy wench. Thou tempteth my better angel from my side."

"I hope so." They both got out. She considered telling Catherine about her insight about how the train tracks formed the actual boundary of the town. A circuit of steel. And parking here.

"It's better to park here. Unpredictable. No one can see us. Shakespeare."

"Okay. Yes, one of the Sonnets. Wasn't that your class?"

"Let's just walk down that way and see what we see."

"Very well."

They locked up the car and set off down the sidewalk. Streetlights were bright overhead. Farther down, much dimmer. They walked slowly, side by side, both keeping hands in jacket pockets.

"You have money?" Catherine said.

"I have money."

"Good. So do I."

Gabrielle glanced back up the street behind them. That was the spot, right over there. I must never go that way again, she thought, cringing.

Catherine bumped her shoulder.

"Must have been embarrassing," she said.

Gabrielle thought, I have to tell her. Put it all in one sentence and then say the sentence and be done with it. We're half a block up from the trestle. We're outside the boundary. If you say it out here in the clear the blackbirds will carry the words away forever.

She suddenly know that was true.

Catherine looked alarmed.

"They carried me into the backyard and made me play this weird lottery and a piece of paper in the plastic egg said do it in the middle of 101 so I did it with New Susan right back there and the Highway Patrol saw us and we barely got away."

They paused in the silent looming bulk of the train trestle.

Catherine said, "I have no idea which prostitute in training New Susan is so it doesn't count. Now. I'm really hungry. Let us continue walking."

Feeling greatly relieved, Gabrielle said, "All right," and they passed under the trestle. Catherine's windbreaker glowed. Inside, as Gabrielle now inescapably thought of it, the fog was thicker and colder. The tree shrouded buildings were dark and quiet, their windows watchful. The sidewalk was uneven and she stubbed her toe.

"I'm serious. I'm glad you told me. It doesn't count. Period."

"Okay."

"And we will never speak of it again."

Gabrielle nodded.

"You're agreeing without speaking, is that correct?"

Gabrielle nodded.

"Good. You're so clever. Friday night and this place is jumping, huh? Look!"

A Dodge station wagon with wood decal side panels passed them westbound while a Ford Cortina with a broken window went east.

"Incredible. Two cars at the same time? Why anything is possible tonight."

Gabrielle laughed and she saw this seemed to make Catherine happy.

They came to a corner and Catherine held out her arm. Gabrielle stopped. The street was empty.

"Wait. We'd better make sure to look *both ways.*"

They both looked left and right. Nothing moved on the wet pavement. She held her breath in surprise tugged her sleeve. When she took her hand out of her pocket Catherine grabbed it awkwardly.

She looked Catherine in the eyes. A wave of worry crossed her face and she took a deep breath.

"Now let's be careful," she said, "Okay run!"

Hand in hand they ran across the empty street and jumped together onto the curb. Catherine giggle and stopped. Gabrielle felt her carefully interlace her fingers. They continued walking, Gabrielle on the street side, and they dodged the branches of an overgrown Ficus tree with synchronized steps.

Gabrielle felt Catherine's hand tighten. Warm and restless.

"This town of yours. There's something about it."

"It's different every time I look."

"Yes. It has mysteries. I mean, look up there."

To their right the street rose. Houses with glowing windows marched away in the fog.

"There could be anything up there. What was it?"

"What was what?"

"You were looking for something pretty intently. Right around here."

They passed more closed shops and a gas station with rusty broken pumps. The wind gusted.

"It was nothing."

"Over there." Catherine looked across the street.

"It's not there." Gabrielle made a quick glance.

"What isn't there?"

Gabrielle made a mental sigh. "Just something funny I saw in the night. That night. It was a side street with a bunch of antique cars parked on it. That's all."

"You're sure you saw it?"

"Pretty sure. Maybe I was off."

"*Your* memory was off?" Catherine said incredulously.

"They made me drink something."

"Oh, God."

"It was blue. So, you know."

"Well, after that blue crap you should not have been driving. Come on. We'll keep an eye out."

They came to the busy street they had turned from and Gabrielle pushed the walk button. The light went green. Catherine let go of her hand and they walked quickly across the four lanes in front of a half dozen stopped cars. Mostly non-student cars, Gabrielle thought. Back in the pack someone honked their horn at them. Catherine turned to glare at the headlights.

"Horn blows, does the driver?"

Gabrielle saw a young couple in the first car burst into laughter. In the Granada next to them a man in a dark suit glowered. Catherine caught his gaze.

"Hey, gramps! Sorry I woke you up!"

Then she walked swiftly to the curb. Gabrielle had to jog to keep up. They stood in a shadowy doorway and waited. The light changed behind them and the cars moved through the intersection. The one Gabrielle suspected of being the honker was a Datsun mini truck.

"Frosh," she said.

Catherine said, "Humorous."

"Hm?"

"Your lip curled when you said that."

"I didn't mean to."

"You misplaced the subject."

"Words are not my thing."

"Neither mine are they."

Catherine took her hand as before. The sidewalk scrolled by.

"Did your professor like your Shakespeare paper?"

"I'll find out next week right before the final."

"Oh. I was just curious. I've read the Sonnets. I used to have them memorized. Well, the good ones."

"There are quite a few."

"There are."

They crossed another street. The evening was quiet and the trees lining the sidewalk rustled, voicelike, a half heard whisper.

Tall buildings rose, some four stories, with imposing entrances. The many windows were dark. They window shopped.

"You like Shakespeare?" Gabrielle said.

"I learned to like him."

"Yes. When I started reading the Sonnets, I mean really reading, I was surprised."

"Some of the plays can kill you," Catherine said.

Catherine stopped at a store selling woman's fashions. The manikins were decked out in sweaters. Young women, Gabrielle thought, college age with money. Definitely not me.

"Cute," she said.

"Preppy," Catherine said.

"Prep?"

"Can you believe it? Daddy was ever so cross when he found out I let Jocelyn borrow my BMW," Catherine said in a breathy voice. "I mean it was Spring Break and we were in Coco Beach which was so the place to be and we were getting pizza at Luigi's which has the greatest no-meat no-cheese no-crust pizza which everyone says is the greatest and Jocelyn saw Marion Quinepeg-Throckmorton drive by who just happens to be the captain of the rugby team and the hunkiest hunk of all time despite having a girl's name and Jocelyn had a meltdown *right there* and took the keys and God bless her she thought the 'R' on the shifter thing stood for 'Race' and she backed the BMW over the curb and through the windows and went right over these two girls and I kind of felt bad you know as a Smith girl myself but not overly because they were it turns out from Bryn Mawr however you pronounce that and the trust fund will pay for everything but the distribution isn't till the end of the quarter and Jocelyn, God bless her, is still waiting for the transplant. I mean can you just *believe* it?"

"That," Gabrielle said, "is amazing. Think I'll stick with my sweatshirt."

"You should stick with your sweatshirt."

"Good idea."

They kept walking. The sidewalk ended at a cross street. Gabrielle instantly recognized it as the spot where she ran the red light. As they stood on the corner Catherine gave her hand a squeeze.

"This town is full of landmines, isn't it. That just means you actually lived here. You were really here. This town has been imprinted with your spirit."

Gabrielle felt a wave of intense sadness wash over her.

"Not here much longer."

The bright green walk signal lit up and, communicating silently, they stepped off the curb. The street was empty.

"The danger is acting as if you've already left. You're still here. We are still here."

In the middle of the wide avenue Gabrielle stopped and Catherine turned to her. Gabrielle kissed her as the light turned red.

"It will be a beginning," Catherine said.

"I won't speak of endings."

"Good." Catherine smiled. "You know what? I think we're breaking the law."

"Then that will be imprinted here forever."

They reached the sidewalk under the red light and now Catherine stopped them.

"What is this place?"

"This is the Plaza."

"Ohh. Okay."

The Plaza was a long open space of red bricks shrouded in massive trees which obscured the few streetlights. It was dark and quiet.

"I don't know," Catherine said.

Gabrielle took her hand and they walked in.

The flow of bricks led to a landscaped pathway which led to a bridge. Other paths led into deeper darkness.

"I think there are restaurants over there," Gabrielle said. "We'll have to go around the block."

"Let's go over here."

They went to the bridge. There was the sound of water flowing in the nearly lightless void below. Gabrielle could just make out large boulders surrounded by shimmering black water.

"There's a creek," Catherine said, sounding puzzled.

"I completely forgot this was here."

"Interesting. You never forget."

"I think I've been here only once before and it was the second day. They had an orientation for new students. The Week of Welcome. They sort of rushed us all over the place."

"Frosh. You were frosh then."

"Yes."

Catherine laughed and it echoed in the dark hollow space. "It's hard to imagine."

"This was spring quarter. I was just seventeen."

"Were you scared?"

"A little. Everyone was nice but they pretty much ignored me. They were so much older. I was this little kid."

They gazed over the side of the bridge.

"I'll bet you were scared."

Gabrielle sighed. "All right, I'll tell you."

"I knew it."

"I handled everything. All the college stuff. My dad was in the hospital. I didn't want Mom to worry. I had already applied to here and got accepted right away. When Mr. Weber, my counselor, found out he was really mad. There were all sorts of grants and scholarships I could have applied for but I knew nothing about them. Too late. I graduated from high school in February. At least, I think I graduated. Well, I finished everything. It was such a hard time. I can't remember the sequence."

"You're not sure? You might be a high school dropout," Catherine said with a note of excitement.

No, Gabrielle thought. Damn it. She felt a twinge. An irregularity like that could be a problem. Could it? I'm about to graduate in June. I went all over that with the office. They check everything. Or did they?

"I did everything right, I know I did."

"Did you get a diploma?"

"No."

"Gabrielle."

"As long as you have the units, you graduate. There isn't any other step."

"Anyway, what happened?"

Something splashed in the water below them. Catherine moved away from the railing.

"I drove up here the Tuesday after my Dad's funeral. My first class was Thursday. So I had to find a place to stay. The dorms were way too expensive, like two hundred a month. I had a hundred and twenty-four dollars. I left the house kind of late in the day. Mom was upset."

"What? You left your mother by herself?"

"I had to go. I felt terrible but I had to."

"Gabrielle."

"I promised my dad. It was the last thing I said to him. He held my hand. He could hardly move. He said, when do you start. I told him and he said you have to go no matter what, no matter what. I leaned really close and said I promise, Dad, I promise. And he nodded and closed his eyes. And he died four days later."

"And you drove all the way up here on your own with no place to stay at the age of seventeen."

"Pretty minor problem."

Catherine pulled back.

"Death makes you angry."

The invisible stream murmured beneath their feet.

"He was thinking about you. It was very important to him that you not give up. And you did exactly what you promised. I'm sure your mom understood. If anyone knows you, she does. And mothers are strong, trust me. So there's no need to feel guilty."

"Thanks."

"It's pretty simple. And your father will always be with you. I have someone I feel like that about. And it's not my father as I'm sure you remember."

"I'm so sorry about that, Catherine."

"Oh no. I'm sorry you didn't get more time to spend with your dad. That's a tragedy. Me, I survived. I survived when no one thought I would. But you know what, you really have me fascinated now. After all that, what could possibly scare you?"

Gabriele took Catherine's hand and continued over the bridge. There was an amber streetlight almost lost in the trees and an empty sidewalk leading to the back patios of dark restaurants. They stopped at a broken gate under spots of light. The fog had deepened. Beyond the gate a crooked path stumbled down to the stream. They went that way.

"That first day," Gabrielle said, "when I got here the sun was already going down. The traffic made everything confusing. I knew the map so I found the campus okay and parked up above the redbrick dorms. I backed into a spot. I remember looking down at all those windows lit up. Long rows of windows so comfortable looking. Some already had plants hanging in them. Students had been checking in and I saw them carrying big speakers and suitcases. These two guys were going down the steps with a big bureau with about eight drawers. I guess they wanted their room to be organized. I sat there and watched them from the top row. It got to be night. The hills were right behind me. I had nothing to check in to and all my clothes were in a grocery bag."

"Center Market."

"Yeah. I had my blanket and pillow. I had my tool kit and a little pouch with a toothbrush."

"Did you have a hairbrush?"

"I forgot it."

"Just asking. Go on."

"I got out of the car and walked between the dorms and went to the student union building. It was so big and noisy. I mean, there's a bowling alley. And the students were all so much older and rushing around. No one was smiling.

"There was whole wall of bulletin boards and one was labeled housing and I really checked all the ads. Everything was really expensive. There were a bunch of students just reading everything.

"I was beginning to feel kind of lost. It was so dark outside and I had no place to go and I was worried about my car up by the hills. I hadn't had dinner but I wasn't hungry. I thought, just go to the restroom one last time and go back to the car and then in the morning, something. I could always live in my car.

"All the other students gave up. This one poor guy with smudgy glasses and messy hair, I swear he was crying. I still remember him. So I was the last one.

"And I turned to leave and a miracle happened."

Catherine gasped. "You never told me any of this before!"

"I never told anyone."

"What was the miracle?"

"This huge guy in a black coat came out of nowhere and bumped into me and stuck this tiny note on the board. Just slammed it in like he was mad. He had a black hat. I didn't see his face. His coat was this heavy wool and smelled like some chemical, super strong. Then he went straight out the door. I sneezed and looked at the note and it said, 'Basement by tracks -- $16.50/mo Ask for Mrs Rosenberg.' And the phone number.

"What!"

"You know what I did? I stole it."

"You little minx!"

"I still have it. And the push pin. The funny part was that smell. Dryer sheets."

"Oh my God! Rosie saved you!"

"That's what I told her once. She gave me this weird look. There's something going on with her lately."

"We have to get Rosie another present. And not a vase. Something big, like a new car."

Gabrielle laughed.

"That's fantastic." Catherine said. "This guy just materializes. Who was he?"

"Never found out. I didn't wait. I went to one of the pay phones and called right then. And she answered and told me to come over in the morning and gave me the address. It was really easy. She was nice. She was happy I wanted the room. I told her I would pay for the whole quarter, forty-nine fifty. Then I called my mom, she was so happy to hear me, and I told her I had a place to stay and it was pretty cheap. That was good, that call. I felt a lot better. I was so relieved. I had no idea how lucky I was. No idea at all."

Catherine smile faded. She braced herself.

"That wasn't it, was it."

"No. I don't want to tell it."

Catherine didn't move.

Gabrielle said, "Never told this to anyone either." She dug her hands into her pockets. "I'm freezing."

"Let's get out of here. Let's see if we can walk through."

"Wait. It's not very long," Gabrielle said. She thought her voice sounded weak and hollow.

"I was excited. I felt great even though my legs felt rubbery. I went back up the steps to my car. The wind was really blowing the tress around. I got the blanket and pillow from the compartment. I sat in the driver's seat. I was between streetlights and I could hardly see. Behind me were the hills. Total darkness. I thought, good. I can sleep better. I unfolded the blanket over me and took off my glasses. I opened the window an inch. I closed my eyes and leaned back.

"I thought, I can hold out, this will be fine. The Union will open at seven. I was so tired. I felt myself falling asleep and remembered. I pushed the door latch forward. That locks the door.

"The instant I did that a face appeared in the window. I froze. It was a boy with long hair and these black eyes. He stared at me and his mouth opened and closed and then he grabbed the door handle and yanked. He was naked. Completely naked. There was blood all over his chest.

"'Hey! Unlock it!'" he said, "'Come on!'"

"Another boy ran past on the right. Then a whole stream of them. They were all naked and they were covered with stuff. None of them talked or laughed. I could hear them all breathing hard. Then there were more, about twenty. They all stood around my car staring in at me. All these blank faces. My heart was pounding so hard it was making my ears pop. I held perfectly still. I. My mind was blank.

"The first guy hit the window with his fist.

"'I told you to unlock it you little asshole! We just want to talk to you.'

"Then he went crazy. He started pounding the roof of the car. It was so loud. He was making this grunting sound. I think I almost fainted.

"Then it got worse. All the other guys started hitting car on the roof and hood. There were up against the window, all these naked boy tits, you know? They rocked the car back and forth and all this time no one said anything. All these naked boys with their mouths open hitting my car and pushing it. That first guy grabbed the edge of the window with his fingertips and pulled really hard. He yelled. The pounding got faster. He pulled as hard as he could. He was going to break the glass. Then he was going to open the door and grab my arm with both hands and drag me out and I would fall on the ground in the dark surrounded by twenty naked boys who were all smeared with blood.

"The thought of that it was like I woke up.

"I hit the horn. I pushed the horn with both hands and held it. I just held it. He let go of the window and tripped back onto the car next to me. He yelled again and all the pounding stopped. I saw four or five run off. The rest watched him, like he was the leader. He just said, 'Fuck this,' and kicked the door with his bare feet and over the horn I heard him say, 'Ow!' He kind of limped away and in two seconds they were all gone. Vanished.

"I kept the horn going and got my glasses on and the key out and started the car, horn still going, and turned on the headlights. Didn't see anyone.

"I let off the horn and pulled out drove all around that parking lot. No one. I drove in circles through all the lots trying to calm down. I looked for another place to park but all the spots were taken and I sure as hell wasn't going back up there. I remembered the train station. I had gone past it. It wasn't far. I went down there and parked between two big trucks. It was perfect. Their restrooms were open all night. And I was really close to where I ended up living.

"Anyway, that's the time I was scared."

Catherine unclamped her hands from her mouth.

"Why the hell didn't you tell me this before? That's the most terrifying thing I've ever heard in my life. My God, Gabrielle, what did the police say?"

Gabrielle shrugged. "Never went to the police."

"Why the hell not?"

"What good would it do? They wouldn't've believed me anyway."

"You don't know that. A gang of naked rapists running through the hills. I think you'd get their attention. So you just acted like nothing happened?"

"I'm pretty sure I know what was going on. They weren't rapists."

"Oh, of course not. This was completely normal behavior."

"It was a fraternity doing an initiation. There's a word for it."

"Oh. Hazing. God. Fraternities. Disgusting. What if they had actually broken your window?"

"I just wanted to forget the whole thing."

"You can do that? Wow, not me."

"I got my little basement room and it was perfect. I never wanted to live on campus anyway."

"Then I showed up and ruined everything."

"You didn't ruin a thing." Just then, she remembered.

"What?"

"There's a note from Mrs. Rosenberg but I keep forgetting to read it."

"See? I'm a distraction."

"I have to admit that's true."

"Oh, yeah? How distracting? Do you realize all the time we've been standing here not one person has so much as walked by? Come on."

Catherine gathered up the front of Gabrielle's sweatshirt and pulled her to the crooked gate.

"It's nice and dark down there. I want to take your mind off that awful story."

Gabrielle was enveloped by her arms.

"You're shivering."

They went down the rocky stumbling path to the edge of the ink black stream. Away from the bridge the sound of the water echoed. They left the last of the faint light and stopped where the walls were made of old masonry. A few steps away the stream issued from a round ten-foot high tunnel opening of absolute darkness. They settled into a cleft in the ancient eroded wall. The air smelled of mud and wet leaves.

"I just realized something," Gabrielle said.

"That's my hand."

Gabrielle laughed but Catherine muffled it for a long moment.

"No, I mean the river. It runs under the town."

Catherine brought her head up.

"It's funny. I never thought of it that way," Gabrielle said. "But it's true."

They snuggled, backs against the wall.

"Awfully dark river, isn't it," Catherine said.

Gabrielle felt Catherine's fingers dig into her arm.

"What you do," Catherine said, "is hold perfectly still."

Gabrielle heard a splash deep inside the tunnel.

"They're attracted to motion. Or even thinking. So don't think of anything."

"Uh, Catherine."

"Hold absolutely still, don't even blink, and they'll lose track of you."

"I kind of don't want to," Gabrielle whispered.

"They move things. You can't see them directly."

There was another splash.

"That was closer, wasn't it." Catherine said.

"Yes."

"Hold still."

Gabrielle held her breath and pressed the back of her hand against the wall. The sharp corner of uneven brick poked the soft spot behind her ear. Her eyes were fully adapted to the dark and she could make out the surface of the stream three feet before her. Catherine clenched her arm again. There was another soft splash and this time Gabrielle thought she saw a ripple in the water. It looked like the water was surging and flowing around an obstruction. An obstruction that moved. She winced as Catherine's grip became painful.

Catherine abruptly released her arm and took a step forward.

"Ha! Gotcha!" she yelled. "Get out of here!"

Gabrielle, shocked, clearly saw a fist-size rock detach itself from the top of the bank and fall. It bounced twice and plopped into the middle of the stream. Catherine jerked back and reached behind her and snagged Gabrielle's sweatshirt.

"*Run*," she said in a choked voice.

They ran back up the rocky path, out of the stream channel, back over the bridge and out of the fog shrouded plaza. On the bricks, Gabrielle felt something snag her foot and she stumbled. The bricks were smooth and even. She got up and they kept running as fast as they could, laughing now, and they didn't stop until they reached the next street, full of traffic, where the lights were brighter, lights from busy restaurants, lights shining over welcoming recessed doorways from which Gabrielle could hear music.

Panting, they stopped in front of a bookstore and leaned back against the window beneath a green awning. A floodlight shone on a closed sign. The light spilled onto Catherine's face. Her eyes sparkled with excitement.

"I have," she breathed, "never done that before."

"That rock moved."

"I know!"

"But there was nothing there."

"There had to have been."

"And something tripped me."

"And something grabbed my sleeve."

"That might've been me."

"You were on the other side."

"When you yelled I nearly peed my pants."

"Sorry. I wanted to see what would happen."

"We made them mad."

"I can't wait to tell her. You don't think they'll follow us, do you?"

"Um."

"Hold still."

They held as motionless as they could, breathing hard, and watched the cars pass on the three lane street. Gabrielle began to count Volvos. The evening was chill in the absence of a breeze.

There was a wiggle in the ruffled edge of the heavy awning. The wiggle moved right, left, then stopped directly above them. Gabrielle cleared her throat.

"Could be raccoons."

"We all know from science there's no such thing as raccoons."

"Well, science is science. I have an idea."

"It had better be a Goddess-level idea because at this point."

"Yes?"

"We might be in trouble."

"My idea is let's go to some place where it's warm and well lit and there are a lot of people eating. It might confuse them. Also."

Gabrielle unzipped her sweatshirt and slipped it off.

"Yes!"

Catherine took off her windbreaker with a shuffle of her shoulders. They traded jackets and put them on.

"Hey, warm." Catherine zipped the sweatshirt up and thrust her hands into the pockets. "And it smells good. It smells like you." She shook her hair back. "I feel like soldering something."

Gabrielle put arms through the sleeves of the windbreaker. The nylon was crinkly and cool and her fingers barely poked out the end. The windbreaker billowed over her shoulders. She pulled the big plastic zipper halfway up.

"I feel protected in this," she said.

"Fits perfectly."

Gabrielle lifted the fabric and sniffed.

"Ah, garlic. One of my favorite things."

"Garlic? Never heard of it."

"It's wonderful. Would you like to learn about it?"

"Maybe," Catherine said. "I'm rather busy these days what with infiltrating evil lairs, living at the beach, and learning not to shift for myself."

"Sounds like you found a whole new world."

"Oh, yeah I suppose, but you know as a Goddess I just take it all in stride. This way."

Catherine suddenly began to walk quickly away from the bookstore. Gabrielle jogged to keep up. Catherine made an about-face.

"Now, this way."

They went back past the store and reached the intersection just as the light turned yellow. They ran across and Catherine tried to take Gabrielle's hand and caught the windbreaker sleeve instead. From a corner restaurant window heads turned to watch them as they jumped for the curb.

Gabrielle thought the inside of the restaurant sure looked good. Low light. Long stem glasses on dark tables. Candles in tubular crystal holders. All the men were wearing suits and ties. Catherine tugged her down the sidewalk.

"If you wore sunglasses," Catherine said, "we could say you were the well-known actress Stacey McStride looking for a place to celebrate her recent nomination at the Golden Orb Centennial Dinner Theater. That's in Hollister which is very close to Hollywood in the phonebook. Bet we could get in."

"Not that again."

Catherine scanned the street. "There's something you should know."

"What?"

"Now!"

Catherine ran straight off the sidewalk into the street behind a wave of large cars. She was in the middle lane before Gabrielle could think, don't hesitate, oh God, and she ran after her. She got five steps and bright headlights illuminated the yellow windbreaker. She did not look. Another three long steps and she turned sideways, and slipped between a parking meter and the sharp pointed nose of a green car with bulging front tires just as a Civic flashed by, it's little engine hitting a high wavering pitch.

Gabrielle thought, they hit the gas, they tried to hit me, and the green thing is the weirdest car I've ever seen.

"Whoa! Are you okay?"

Catherine took her arm and led her away from the curb and under another awning. Real Estate office. The doorknob was gold plated and dripping with dew.

"We've thrown them off our trail."

"All right, good." Gabrielle tried to catch her breath again.

"You don't normally run across streets dodging cars, right?"

"No, I don't. For some reason."

"*That's* why it will work. But look! Isn't this great? That's a Citroén!"

"Like, a lemon?"

"Everywhere you go in Paris you see these. I mean, this just says *France* to me. That whole part of my life. I never expected."

Gabrielle saw a distracted look cross Catherine's face and her scar became prominent, then faded back. She held out her hand.

"You know, walking around this town at night you see things."

"You do," Gabrielle said.

"The places all seem busy and no one is on the sidewalks. You're back to not asking questions."

"Yes."

"The time has come."

"It has?"

"To pick a restaurant. We seem to be in the dining district. I'm dizzy from imminent starvation."

"All right," Gabrielle said, nervous.

Catherine grinned. "Go ahead, Rib-eye."

Gabrielle stared in surprise.

"She told me."

"Good grief. Where is she, anyway?"

"Down south somewhere doing something. You're in charge of the date. Proceed."

There was the place with the candles and suits. *Fleet Street.* "Snootsville," Catherine said. There was a place set up like a garden with lots of ferns and round rocks on the counter. *Synergy.* "I don't know what that is, but tempura sounds good." There was place which looked like a classic diner. *Stan's.* "Burger and fries. Eh."

Mr. Wong's. "I like Chinese. Did you hear me?"

Juan's. "I did a research project on enchiladas They are like oxygen for me. Hello?"

Julie Kim. "Korean barbeque. I feel another research project coming up."

The Chocolate Enlightenment. "Chocolate pizza. Um, okay."

Tofu Palace. "I don't know. I have it all the time at home."

Professor Fusion's Laboratory. "Hungarian Chilean Thai food. Hey, that could work."

They reached the end of the long block. There was one restaurant remaining. Gabrielle thought the look of it was fairly standard. Recessed doorway, dark wood. But not snooty. And whatever they were cooking in there...

"Did you decide?"

"Yes. Right here."

"Really? Oh, yeah. *The Steakhouse at the End of the World.*"

"It smells good."

"It *does*," Catherine said. "And it is the end of the world. After you."

They stepped down through the open door. It was warm and the voices were soft and the carpeting was deep. There was classical music playing. The smell of grilling steaks made Gabrielle's mouth water. She stopped.

"It's too nice. I was wrong."

Catherine put her arms on her shoulders and gently nudged.

"This isn't *that* nice."

The young woman standing at the podium adjusted the bulky frames of her big glasses without looking up. She had short brown hair and was wearing a black sweater and absently scratched her left armpit.

"Corner location," Catherine said in a whisper. "Notice the walls. There's no dining room just rows of booths. I'll bet this used to be a pizza place. Cover everything up and give it a catchy name. And we are exactly the kind of customer they want."

"We are?" Gabrielle smoothed the windbreaker.

"Young and beautiful and rich. As long as we are dining here they are automatically cool and they know it. However they will have to earn their tip."

They approached the podium.

The young woman exhaled loudly and pretended to just notice them. Her smile was crooked.

"Party of," she said and scanned the empty foyer. "Two?" Her nametag read *Donette.*

Gabrielle felt Catherine foot tap her shoe.

"Yes," Catherine said. "And." She leaned closer, locking eyes with Donette. "Do you have any booths that are, you know, kind of private? I mean, they all seem fine except that some, you know, look straight into neighboring booths or the kitchen. Do you have any that don't look straight into other booths like that?"

Donette took two menus from the podium.

"A booth that doesn't look straight," she said thoughtfully, "into other booths. Let me show you what we have. We're not that full."

"Thank you so much."

They followed Donette to the back of the place. Gabrielle shook her head while Catherine grinned.

The booths had wooden framed dividers and Gabrielle thought they all looked private, only every other occupied. Mostly families, she saw. No students. She knew what that meant. Expensive.

Donette stopped at the last booth. The wall opposite was taken up by a station for dirty dishes and a door labeled *Ladies*.

"Best I can do. It looks straight at the woman's restroom."

"It's perfect," Catherine said.

"And the little boy's room is clear on the other side so you shouldn't be bothered."

Gabrielle slid onto the seat, her back to the restaurant, and Catherine slid in opposite her.

"We really appreciate it," Gabrielle said.

Donette beamed at her and set the menus before them. Gabrielle quickly checked the prices. The dinners went from twelve to twenty-four dollars. She relaxed a bit.

"Our special this evening," Donette said and took out an order pad, "is the rib-eye."

Catherine coughed loudly.

"Only ten ninety-nine, which includes your choice of our end-of-the-world fries or our apocalyptic onion rings, as well as a medium green salad. Would you like a few minutes?"

"Oh I'm ready," Catherine said. "I would like the rib-eye special with the terrifying French fries, oil and vinegar dressing. And to drink, I'd like a glass of whatever mid-range Merlot you'd recommend."

"Of course. Very good." Donette jotted quickly. "We just got in something new in a Merlot from up north. *Vallejo Seme du Flube.*"

"That's Merlot, all right. Intriguing. Steak with Merlot just says California to me."

Donette nodded. "Oh, and how would you like your steak cooked?"

"Well done, please."

"Really?"

"I know, it's almost sacrilege but it's how I was trained. In France they cook the heck out of beef. On the other hand, they use unpasteurized milk everywhere."

"France, wow," Donette said. She raised her eyebrows. "Didn't know that about the milk. And have you decided?"

Gabrielle looked up from the menu. She had made a complete scan. Dinners, entrees, sides, extras, beverages, deserts. It told a story, just like a sonnet, she thought. Vectors again? A meal was appetite factored by grilled New York strip/rib-eye/spencer/sirloin and fried onion rings crispy golden brown and roasted green beans on a plate with a fork and a knife, each a vector of *intent*. No. She started over. Appetite times steak and onion rings raised to power of hunger. And the result was what? Simple. Hunger satisfied. But was there *meaning*? She felt her idea fray. In a larger social context there might be *meaning* to a meal otherwise eating food primarily belonged in the category of bodily functions. Wait. A bodily function with an established and extensive social context. A different kind of appetite. A real *hunger*. So not so much Shakespeare as.

"Sex," she said.

Catherine was wide-eyed. "It is a blast watching you read a menu."

Gabrielle felt herself blush big time. Eyes down she said, "New York strip steak, medium rare, onion rings, the same oil and vinegar dressing, and a glass of *Chalone* Pinot Noir, seventy-six if you have it, otherwise I trust your judgment."

Donette nodded rapidly. "Got it. No problem." She beamed at Gabrielle again. "Thanks. Your server will be right back with your drinks." She took the menus and retreated towards the kitchen.

Catherine was sitting straight upright.

"I never know what you're going to do."

She picked up her paper placemat and scooped her silverware into her napkin and slid out of the booth.

Gabrielle moved over as Catherine sat beside her.

"And the funny thing is I always know what you're thinking. You may think that's a contradiction." She set out her silverware. "You might be right. Now we're invisible unless some lady needs to pee and if that happens and she sees us snuggling we simply smile knowingly."

Gabrielle moved her right thigh to be fully against Catherine's.

"Pinot, huh? Good choice."

"I think I saw an ad for it in one of Gislaine's magazines."

"Hm. We'll do a little wine tasting."

"That would be wonderful."

Gabrielle saw the familiar impish look cross Catherine's face. She looked over her shoulder and then turned back. Gabrielle sat back as she leaned over and held her face in close front of her's.

"Where do we go after here? By the way, if you kiss me and someone sees us we'll probably go to jail."

Gabrielle let her lips brush Catherine's cheek.

"I shouldn't drive after drinking wine," she said. "And no way will I kiss you."

"No, you shouldn't. Drive, I mean."

"Do you think we could make it back to one of those motels?"

"So much walking."

"About eight minutes."

"You might have to carry me."

"You could ride piggyback."

Catherine's eyes flickered back and forth. "Hold that thought." She sat straight.

Gabrielle heard footsteps approaching. A waiter in a black shirt carrying a tray walked past them and stopped at the restroom door. He seemed to study the sign in confusion. 'Ladies.' Then he caught sight of them. There were two full glasses of wine on the tray.

"Oh, right," he muttered.

He set small square napkins on the table by the silverware then carefully set the wine glasses on them. The rich red wine trembled at the brims.

"I always forget there's a booth back here. My name is Absalom and I will be your server this evening."

Gabrielle noted Catherine was studying him with a serious evaluating expression.

"Hi, Absalom," she said evenly.

"Hi. Oh. Uh, Donette said if you can tell which glass is Merlot and which is Pinot Noir she will give you fifty percent off all drinks." He shrugged.

"Half off?" Gabrielle said.

"Tell Donette she has a deal."

Catherine pushed the glass in front of her to the left. Gabrielle took hold of it. She pulled the other glass in front of her.

"That one's Pinot and this is the Merlot."

Absalom's smile vanished.

"That's right," he said. "You know."

"You know how I know, Absalom?" Catherine tapped her forehead. "It's all up here."

"All right. Well." He held up the serving tray like a shield. "Um. I'll go tell her. Your dinners will be ready shortly. In the meantime, please enjoy the end of the world."

"Thank you," Gabrielle said.

Absalom walked quickly away, scuffing his heels.

"Unusual name," Gabrielle said.

"About the only thing he's got going for him. Anyway, Donette likes you."

Gabrielle giggled as Catherine pushed her full wine over to her's until they clinked.

"Cheers. Don't want to spill."

Catherine lifted herself up and leaned over the table and sipped from her glass with a loud slurp.

"There's two glasses worth. Cheers."

Gabrielle pushed herself up and made a noisy sip. The dark red wine was surprisingly light tasting, not bitter and acidic. She made another sip.

"Try this."

Gabrielle leaned over Catherine's plate and sipped from her glass.

Heavier, with a different fruity flavor. It made her mouth pucker slightly.

"Pinot Noir would be perfect for something like roast beef," Catherine said. "We'll see how well it pairs with grilled steak. Depends how the steak is seasoned."

"I'm really not sure I can distinguish the flavors you can. It all tastes wonderful. I don't have your talent."

"Just takes practice."

"This kind of practice is fun."

"Yeah, this is enough to get fairly wasted. Donette's plan is to get you drunk and then steal you away from me using her ample charms."

"You mean those glasses? Donette is free to eat her heart out." Gabrielle noticed Catherine wasn't smiling. She drank too fast, she thought. "There are wineries all over the place. You could be a manager. Wouldn't that be better than working in a restaurant?"

"In some ways." Catherine turned her glass in the napkin. "I love to cook. Preparing food for people is an act of grace. It's my way of forgiving the world. Someone told me that once, years ago."

Gabrielle took another sip. "She never talks about herself."

"She deflects."

"Yes. She does. It's, like, all third person."

"Just ask her. Ask her anything and she will tell you." Catherine took a large sip. "You know." She shrugged. "It's the same with me."

Gabrielle's mind filled with questions. How did Samantha save her life? What was that day in Paris? Then she knew what she wanted to ask. A question that seemed key. She took another big sip of wine. Catherine was watching her with pensive amusement. They locked eyes for a long moment.

Better be the correct question, she thought.

Then they heard scuffing feet.

The salads came in bowls the size of a tea cup. Catherine scowled at her's.

Gabrielle picked her's apart. There were bits of lettuce and shredded carrots and at the bottom three bean sprouts awash in the oil and vinegar dressing. She ate the whole thing in two bites and sipped the dressing, tangy and sweet.

Catherine held up a bean sprout on her fork and examined it.

"Theoretically, this could be good sign," she said. ""Why should they care about the salad course. It's a steakhouse, right? They could at least give you croutons." She bit the sprout off her fork. "I must be really hungry."

"I love the dressing."

"It *is* good. Nice acidity. Kind of tastes like a cleanse."

Gabrielle slurped her salad cup. "Is that something from France?"

"They like to do it."

"A cleanse you drink?" Gabrielle had never heard of such a thing. "How would that work?"

"It doesn't. They think it does. Everyone's always worried about their liver." Catherine gulped her wine. "For some reason."

"I guess if you drink wine all the time."

"Oh constantly."

"But how could you know if your liver's getting cleaned?"

"You can't. It's all in their heads. I had fun with this. I couldn't help it. I made my own cleanse. I was famous, briefly."

"I should probably try it."

"Eh. Another twenty years of guzzling Pinot, maybe."

"So you tricked people into drinking your liver cleanse?"

"They *wanted* to be tricked. My Goddess, as your Priestess it is my duty to tell you this is a constant in human life."

They heard the kitchen door squeak and a rattle of plates.

"Lemon juice. A teaspoon of olive oil. Cinnamon, the cheap stuff. Habanero sauce. And a jigger of vodka. That's one dose." She unfolded her napkin.

Gabrielle laughed. "Vodka in a liver cleanse?"

"The All American Jimmy Carter California Cleanse. Pretty popular."

"Wait. Jimmy Carter?"

"This was the fall of seventy-six. They were all pulling for him. And they all liked California."

"It sounds like one of Debbie's drinks."

"Debbie's Colonic Purifier or the Jimmy Carter Cleanse."

"About the same."

Absalom stepped sideways into view carrying a large serving tray.

"Here we go," he said. "There is no escape. There is no tomorrow. The apocalypse is upon you." He set the tray on the unoccupied side of the table and took away the salad cups. "Rib-eye? And New York strip." He set their plates before them and then departed sideways.

They were the largest dinner plates Gabrielle had ever seen and, amazingly, not round. They were rectangles of porcelain, sixteen by twelve inches. Her strip steak had a surface area roughly equal to one of her spiral-bound notebooks and took up a third of the plate. There was a tiny wooden tag stuck in the edge. Med-Rare it said in burned in letters. A campfire smoke smell came from it and mingled with the rich charred aroma of the steak itself. Then there were the onion rings. Three of them, each at least eight inches across, perfectly golden brown. No, ten inches, she thought.

"Catherine, this is I don't know."

"Remarkable."

"This is enough food for a week. There are onions this big?"

And covering the final third of the plate was a thick slice of toasted bread and a ceramic bowl of melted butter.

"This is really," Catherine said, "unexpected. Golly."

Her rib-eye, Gabrielle estimated, was an amazing one and a half inches thick. The French fries were much too big to be called fries. Long potato wedges, light and crispy looking. And her toasted bread had grill marks and smelled strongly of garlic.

"All right. This is a lot," Catherine said. "Well done, Goddess."

"This is great! I've never even seen plates like these before."

"All right!" It was Absalom with a wine bottle balanced in the palm of each hand. "Don't worry. This is on the house." He skillfully tipped over both bottles and refilled each of their glasses to the brim.

"Wow," Gabrielle said. "Thanks!"

"Good job there, Abbie."

"You are welcome. I practice a lot. Now, do we have everything? Ah yes, one last item."

He slipped the bottles onto the table and waved his hands like a magician. From a pocket at his waist he produced two long objects in paper sleeves and set them next to each plate. "Your knives. Very sharp."

"Gosh," Catherine said.

"Eat, drink, and be merry for the world ends tomorrow."

Absalom walked quickly away.

"Why does everyone keep saying that?"

"Something in the air. Wonder if he left the bottles on purpose."

"That's a lot of wine."

"Too much."

"Way too much." Gabrielle took a big gulp of her Pinot and unwrapped the steak knife. "Look at that."

"Like a giant razor blade."

Catherine made a cut through the center of her steak.

"Definitely well done. Surprising."

"I could shave my legs with this."

"You could shave a lot of things."

"And it all smells so good."

Gabrielle gulped her wine again and bit into an onion ring.

"Mm."

Mm mm," Catherine said. "Sip."

"Mm."

Gabrielle thought it was the best steak she had ever eaten. Warm, juicy, slightly pink in the middle, the beef was so tender it barely required chewing. A bite then a bite of the sweet crunchy onion rings then the toasted bread. Melted butter ran down her chin.

Catherine, a potato wedge in her lips, daubed the butter with her napkin.

"The steak in grocery stores is never this good. Restaurants get it all. Otherwise we could eat like this at home all the time."

"It melts in my mouth," Gabrielle said.

"That's the standard. For a lot of things."

"I'm eating too much."

"You'll be much healthier."

"I guess I do feel better."

"Your body is finally getting what it needs. You were very deprived before."

"Plus eating the right things."

"That's a big part of it."

"Things."

"Multiple things."

When Gabrielle's steak was half gone, she pushed her plate away.

"I might be full."

She picked up her wine glass. How many glasses? She thought. She had no memory. Because they keep refilling it. It's one continuous glass of wine that never runs out. And once again I'm in trouble.

She set the glass down and tried to focus on her fork.

Catherine was smiling at her.

"You have nothing to worry about."

"Yes, I do."

"You can tell me."

"You're both so much older and more experienced than me in every way. I can't even imagine what your lives have been like. I feel like a little kid sometimes. You must think I'm an idiot. I feel like an idiot."

"Actually I was referring to your drinking problem."

"I know! I'm an alcoholic at age twenty."

"When you get drunk first thing in the morning every day you're officially an alcoholic. You're not even close. Yet."

"Okay. Good." Gabrielle nibbled her bread.

"You're the one who's going to be rich and famous. That's Rushel's prophesy and she has never been disproven."

"What has she prophesized?"

"You're her first."

"Oh. Well then that's right. Can't be disproven."

"That's how we see it. We certainly don't think of you as a little kid."

"Okay. Thank you. I still feel like that, though." She took a bite of her last onion ring. "And I do definitely have to become rich."

"Why do you have to?" Catherine chewed a slice of her well done rib-eye.

"I already owe Audra a million dollars."

"Audra?" She laughed. "Now *I* need a drink."

"Just think of the interest on a million dollars."

"I can't think of a million anything."

"It's a lot. The interest."

"Let's not worry about Audra right now."

"All right." Gabrielle's mind returned to the question without quite meaning to and she said it out loud. "How did you become interested in Shakespeare's sonnets?"

Catherine looked down. Gabrielle saw her frown in a resigned way.

"Normally," Gabrielle said, "students need high voltage shocks to get them to read Shakespeare. That's what my professor said. No one laughed. I kind of like him."

"Well, your witty professor is wrong."

Catherine drained her glass and picked up the bottle. Still half full. She poured the deep red wine slowly until it reached the brim again in a glistening bead. She pushed her plate away with two thirds of the steak remaining, and pulled her glass close.

"This was a long time ago. I was a different person then. I have been six different people, counting the current one. The Catherine you know has existed from December twenty-first, nineteen seventy-six, to now. In the time of the Sonnets I was at the very end of the second Catherine. I didn't know it was the end, but it was."

"I was in the ninth grade. Briony High School. Spring semester. I was in love for the first time. I knew what it was. I thought a lot about my feelings. In this one way, I am like you.

"I fell in love on March twelve, nineteen sixty-seven. Her name was Tamara. She was a senior. The first time I saw her she was just waiting in the hallway for some class. That face. I studied her. She was going to be valedictorian. She worked so hard. I would see her in the library at lunch. I was frosh. We never had a class together, of course. I would just see her.

"She was tall and had long brown hair, never in a ponytail. Her eyes were hazel. I was only close enough to see her eyes once. Exactly once.

"I followed her around in the library to find out what books she was checking out. I never tried to sit next to her. That would have been impossible. She was always surrounded by her senior friends, mostly boys, all so much older and bigger.

"I came up right behind her once in the checkout line. She had a book. I saw the word 'Shakespeare.' I saw her in profile as she walked away. She was perfect.

"She never looked at me, of course.

"But her friends noticed me. I caught them watching me once. They laughed to themselves.

"I told you I was disfigured. I never told you the details. I'll have you know I was kind of famous.

"The chainsaw hit my cheekbone and because my dad had been left handed his grip was bad and the blade ran to the left and into my upper jaw. The other way it would've gone into my eye socket and torn out my left eye. It ripped out most of my cheekbone anyway and my upper baby teeth. And all the skin and nerves and muscles.

"I healed. My teeth came back eventually. My eyes were all right. There was a long indentation that stretched up and that entire area of my face drooped. It looked like my face had been made of clay and got melted or something.

"There was nothing that could be done. It was pain all the time and terrible smells and my face. The doctor was good. He helped. He tried to reconstruct it. This was nineteen fifty-nine, I think. He showed me how to do exercises. He was a good guy. Then my aunt wouldn't let me go anymore.

"She hated me. My dad's sister. Stuck with a disfigured two-year-old. She got money from our relatives, especially older aunt. She was single. I remember her boyfriends, lots of boyfriends. It took me years to figure out what was going on.

"I got old enough for kindergarten. The other kids."

Catherine picked up her glass and emptied it in three gulps.

"Fuck them. Fuck. Them."

She filled her glass as before, to the very brim.

"I made it to ninth grade. I had no friends. I was the ugly girl. Famous, see? I kept to myself. They all ignored me except for when I would walk down the hallway between classes, where all the lockers were, and the other kids would make vomiting sounds behind my back. It was the girls who did that.

"I got the sense the boys kind of liked me a little. This thought scared me and I tried not to think about it.

"I saw in a magazine a blonde actress in Paris. She wearing a beret. It just looked so French. I pestered my aunt for months to buy me one. You've seen it. If I arrange it just right I can deflect your eyes away from my face and onto my hair spilling attractively over my shoulders. Plus I liked wearing a hat.

"I had my own world. I was the only one in it. Tamara shattered it completely into tiny pieces lost forever.

"Well, I left the checkout line and put the movie star magazine back and went to English literature and there on the Shakespeare shelf a book was missing. I put my hand there where her hand had been and grabbed the book next to it. Didn't look at it. I checked it out. The librarian, Mrs. Grein, just frowned at me and stamped it.

"See, if beauty equals virtue and goodness, ugliness must equal evil. That's the rule.

"I ran out of there. Everyone looked away from me as usual. I tucked the book in my sweater as far down as I could.

"I ran out of the school even though I had three classes left. I never skipped class. My GPA was three point eight. I ran through the snow alongside the parking lot past the dead trees and into the alley behind the stores on the main street. This was my usual route home. I tried never to walk on the sidewalks. I hid behind the dumpster for the boot repair shop, it smelled really good, and took the book out. The cover was dark green with gold letters. The *Sonnets of Shakespeare*. Edited by Catherine Smalley. Catherine. It was meant to be. I read the first one right there. From fairer creatures we desire increase that thereby beauty's rose might never die. I didn't quite understand it but I started crying. Beauty's rose. I ran the rest of the way home and hid the book under my pillow. I couldn't let my aunt see it. Every now and then she would ransack my room and throw out all my things, even my clothes.

"I read it in secret at night under my blanket with a tiny penlight I had found. I really tried to understand them but it was hard. So adult. He infers things. He talks around subjects. Kind of cold and aloof, I thought. And he talks about a youth. A fair youth. So it's a man going on about a young attractive man. As you can imagine, I thought this was confusing and if Mrs. Grein had known about it she would've banned Shakespeare from the school. I'll bet I'm the only person in Briony, Colorado, to have ever read all one hundred fifty-four Sonnets. Ever.

"I kept the book. I still have it.

"I'm not saying I got everything. A lot I couldn't figure out. But old Will could be clear as crystal when he wanted to be.

"Number twenty-nine. You know that one?"

Gabrielle nodded. She pushed her glass away. There was an intensity in Catherine's eyes she had never seen before.

"When in disgrace with fortune and in men's eyes I all alone beweep my outcast state. I thought, that's *me*. How did he know? Somehow he knew what I was going through. He must know everything about life.

"So I kept reading under my blanket. I was beginning to understand. I kept seeing Tamara off in the distance. I kept running down back alleys where no one could see me.

"Then I got to sonnet one-sixteen. It goes, let me not to the marriage of true minds admit impediments. And I just saw it. I guess it was that word.

"I knew no one would ever love me. The idea was ridiculous. It was impossible. Under my blanket with my tiny light I remember I laughed because it was so obvious. Why would I think such a thing? After all, they weren't wrong. I really was the ugly girl.

"I would spend my life alone. I knew this. No one would know me. Every day when I got home there would be no one there. I would never have an engagement ring or a wedding. I was simply not one of those people.

"You know, I still don't have a word for those people. Them.

"They all seem to find it so easy, right? You see them everywhere. I mean, the world is infested with them. All the happy couples. Girlfriends and wives. I vowed I would never go where they go. I vowed to avoid them. It's like their happiness had a stink only I could smell.

"I thought really hard. I tried to see the angles. I had to figure it out.

"If I ever accomplished anything important there would be no one to tell. If I got sick there would be no one to take care of me.

"Well then, I would do it all. I knew I was smart. No one would be there to help me when my car broke down? Then my car would never break down. No one to take care of me when I got sick? Simple. I would never get sick. *I* would take care of *me*. And I definitely would accomplish something important.

"By the time I finished that book I had lost all interest in love, as you call it. It did not apply to me in any way. I hid the book behind the heater vent in my room right next to my safe deposit box. The furnace had been broken for years so it was all right.

"My safe deposit box was a breath mint tin where I kept my money. I had a weekend job at a pizza place in town. Aunt knew nothing about it. They hired me because I knew a trick to make pizza crust really crispy – it involves baking soda – so they hired me even though I was too young. They made me always stay in the back. Don't need the customers throwing up. Seventy-five cents an hour. I never spent a penny.

"I saw Tamara a few more times after that and felt nothing. I sat in the library and stared at the wall. I guess even though I knew the truth of things I wasn't quite ready.

"Then something incredible happened. And the amazing thing was I have my aunt to thank for it.

"I was getting my history book from my locker. The end of lunch break. It was raining hard and the halls were jammed. I went to my locker the same time every day right before the bell. Back then I didn't know to alter my route. I slammed the locker shut and there was someone standing right there. I think I almost screamed. She was tall. Tamara was a head taller than me. I looked up. Those hazel eyes were gazing into mine.

"'Oh there you are,'" she said.

"It was her. She was talking to me. I couldn't move. Close up her hair was so silky. And her voice was deep. She got really close.

"'I just wanted to say I think your beret is adorable.'

"She loomed over me.

"'Thanks,' I think I said.

"Her two friends crowded me on my left, both wearing navy blue sweaters. Cindy and Mindy. I noticed something for the first time. They were all wearing a silver stud in their right ear lobe. Just the one.

"'I used to see you all the time and then you were gone. My friends and I, well, you're not mad at me, are you?'"

Gabrielle saw Catherine smile and then nod to herself.

"On my sixth birthday my aunt made me a birthday cake. It had two layers and chocolate icing. She put six candles on it and lit them with a big wooden match. I remember I clapped my hands as she sang happy birthday to me. My face was swollen from a doctor's appointment and the back of my head hurt where a kid hit me with a rock. They were always throwing rocks at me. But I remember how good that chocolate smelled. Then my aunt pulled out a chair and stepped up onto the table, pulled up her skirt, hitched up one leg and peed on my cake. She put the candles out. Then she laughed and climbed down and went to her bedroom with her bottle of wine.

"I ate the cake anyway. The whole thing. It was my birthday. Mine. You know what, Goddess? Best damn birthday cake I ever had.

"I stared as hard as I could into Tamara's eyes and said, 'Why would I be mad?' There was the tiniest little twitch in those eyes.

"'You were following me around like a puppy and I ignored you. That's why.'

"Mindy made this snort.

"I shook my head. 'Don't know what you mean.'

"'Yes you do,' Cindy said. 'We have standards.'

"'Yeah.' Mindy said. She was always so smart. And by smart I mean a bovine halfwit. Close up I could see the beginnings of a pretty good mustache.

"Tamara raised her hand to silence them.

"'You thought I would like you? You?' She laughed.

"Cindy and Mindy laughed and edged closer. I kept my mouth shut.

"'The ugly girl thought Tamara would like her,' Tamara said. 'You stupid disgusting little idiot with your horrible face right out of a nightmare.'

"I may have rolled my eyes. Aunt said far worse things to me every day. Tamara hesitated and I sensed a turning. This was her? My vow to remove myself from the world of – puke – love now seemed very smart and correct.

"'I have to go,' I said.

"'You're not going anywhere,' Cindy said. She had really crooked teeth and lisped when she tried to talk tough.

"Tamara took a deep breath and said, 'If we ever catch you following us, ugly girl, we will –'

"'Get out of my way or I'll slice your cheek open with this piece of broken glass I have in my hand and everyone will be able to see inside your mouth with blood all over your teeth and a big flap of dead skin hanging down with swarms of flies laying eggs on it.'

"'You're crazy!' Mindy spat out.

"'And then after I cut your face open I'll drop my pants and shit down your throat.'

"Tamara backed up a step.

"'Ew!' Mindy said.

"'You're psycho!' Cindy screamed.

"'I'm not kidding. There will be blood everywhere. Get out of my way.'

"Tamara raised her hand again. The bell rang.

"'You two go down there,' she commanded. 'See if you can find Claire. She owes me three dollars from last week.'

"'*Tamara*,' Cindy whined. God, I wanted to punch her. Mindy made her signature snorting sound. They both went down the hall, almost empty now.

"Tamara came really close and I froze. Was she going to hit me? I considered where I would hit her first. That perfect nose. She looked me up and down. She smiled in this crooked way.

"'You have absolutely beautiful eyes. Did you know that?'

"I did?"

"'Look, I have this boyfriend. My mom insisted.'

"Kids ran by. The boys all looked at Tamara.

"'You're tough. I like that.' She smiled. 'I know you work at that pizza place.'

"I just stared at her. Her eyes flicked over my face.

"'Don't worry about that. Nobody cares about that.'

"I dropped my history book. She pulled away.

"'Well I better get going. Late again.'

"'Me, too.'

"'I'll see you.' She smiled at me. And she walked away.

"I was shaking but I was more certain than ever. I left my history book on the concrete and went down the corridor and across the quad by the dead trees and out past the parking lot. I crossed the street without looking. I got home and went to my room and just stopped.

"My aunt had once again thrown everything away. Stripped the room bare. Always wondered what triggered it that time. I had suspicions. I got a nice sweater from older aunt at Christmas. It had reindeer on it. She got nothing. Also, I had a poster taped to my wall. It was a great picture of Paris with the Eiffel Tower all lit up at dusk. She hated France. That was gone. She could've been getting even for those things. But I think it was my training bra. I think that did it. I was growing up. Funny thing, she bought it for me. I imagined she burned it in the backyard.

"My closet and my three-drawer bureau were empty. My blanket and pillow were gone. Just a bare mattress. No sign of my tiny flashlight.

"My heart started pounding. I saw that the heater vent had been moved. I pulled it open.

"It was all still there. I grabbed my safe deposit box and the green book.

"I had my yellow cotton button-up sweater, a white t-shirt, my plaid skirt, old socks with stains around the toes, and my blue sneakers. And my beret. And three hundred seven dollars and thirty-five cents.

"No coat anymore. Not even a jacket. No underwear except what I had on. I knew all my clothes were probably jammed into our trashcan behind the shed, however, every time she did this before, the four previous times, she had taken scissors and cut everything into little pieces. So I wasn't inclined to check.

"I took a last look at my room. So small, but it had been mine. My bed, my closet, my window with the gray curtains full of holes. Through my window the world outside was bright and hazy. It looked cold. It was always cold. Too bad. I was going.

"I left the front door hanging open. I walked down the street, book under my arm, safe deposit box tucked into the tiny pocket in my skirt. Turned left and then went down the main street. The bus station was at the south end of town. I felt I should hurry. I hurried.

"Past the Texaco station with the wrinkly old man who always stared at me like he was angry and past the boot repair shop. I always liked the way their dumpster smelled. I knew I would miss that place. Past the little office where aunt worked. Something title, whatever that is. Didn't see her car, this stupid orange Chevy, so I relaxed a bit and walked even faster. Past the pizza place. I waved goodbye, the only time I did. Then it was empty lots and the town park all brown grass and scraggly trees. Always the same guy sitting on the bench. Used to be an old guy in filthy clothes. He had become a young guy with long hair. Same clothes.

"The sky was clear blue and the air was cool and dry. I took a deep breath. It smelled clean now. Spring was just around the corner. I was as excited as I'd ever been. There were roses in the front yard of the little house beside the bus station. I went over and smelled them. They were white and yellow and I wanted to pick one but I didn't. I walked up the steps of the bus station and pushed the glass door open and there was a big sign with a picture of a running dog and a long list of destinations and ticket prices. I was the only one in the place and I stood there for a while. To my complete surprise I had enough money to go anywhere I wanted. Anywhere in the country. And that's what I did.

"I was a runaway and that day I started a new life. I was happy for the very first time. I was in control.

"I never saw Tamara again. You probably think she was a creep but I have to say, when I think of her, I can't help but remember this one line. Thy eternal summer shall not fade. That face. I really feel that about her, wherever she is.

"And that's why I learned Shakespeare's Sonnets," Catherine said.

Gabrielle slid over the bench and hugged her. She felt Catherine sob softly.

"Let's get out of here."

Without further speaking they drank the rest of their wine, full glasses, and got doggie bags for the leftover steaks. Then they paid the bill, $34.21, and Catherine went back to the table and slipped a five under a bottle of steak sauce. Donette was nowhere to be seen. It took Absalom three tries to get the cash register to work and he wished them a happy end of the world.

Outside the air had become warm and they found themselves on an unknown street lined with dark buildings.

They both walked slowly.

"Oh, we drank too much," Catherine said. She waved her arms.

"It's really different. Like, there's no up and," Gabrielle said. The streetlights spun around. "Oh!"

She nearly tripped over a bike rack and bumped into a light post. There was a flyer taped to it. She lifted up her glasses and focused on it and laughed.

"Look! Wow!"

"Even for you, Goddess, you are *way* too drunk."

"This is fantastic. Read it. Look."

"Read? Oh, you optimist." Catherine was swaying. "What does it say?"

"Uh, well, it says there's thing called disco having a last blast and we are all invited."

"Oh, right. That whole disco dance craze from the olden days."

"There's gonna be a *lot* of people."

"Yeah. It's going out of control. But. In twenty-four."

"Hours?"

"That's what I said. That will be *it*. Success or failure. That Audra. What a talented young lady."

Gabrielle pressed the flyer's masking tape firmly on the pole.

"I could not have made a poster like this."

Fog swirled and vanished about the sidewalk. Wind cool and warm.

"I really admire her," Catherine said. "Some days I want to drown her in the bathtub but I admire her."

"She is definitely loveable."

"She loves you."

Gabrielle turned away.

"You know that, right?"

Gabrielle nodded.

"But you don't love her. You love me. Even after I told you that story. I *explained* it. If you loved her it would all be so much simpler."

"Samantha loves you. And I love you. No one tells me how I feel."

"It was better when I was just the ugly girl no one cared about. It really was. Okay, listen. Are you listening?"

"I'm listening."

"As long as we're on the subject of me, I must tell you there are two more stories. The Catherine that started at the Greyhound bus station in Briony, Colorado ended in Hollywood one day. In the winter. And that Catherine ended in Paris. If for some reason you want me to I will tell you those stories. As long as we're on the subject of me."

"Yes. Yes. I mean whenever you want."

"All right. It's a deal. You know, Samantha's stories are much more interesting. There's kidnapping and international intrigue and machine guns and tornados. You couldn't put it in a movie. No one would believe it."

Gabrielle snapped most of the way out of her fuzzy wine head.

"Did you say tornados?"

"Uh huh. Speaking of tricks, you have to trick her."

"Into telling the stories?"

"Yeah." Catherine. "It's tricky."

Gabrielle laughed. "Good job almost changing the subject."

"Oh. It didn't work?"

"No. You never told me who you love."

Catherine stared and started to speak. She shook her head.

"Such is your cleverness you phrased that as a statement instead of a question."

"It's my training."

"No one gets to ask me that. Not you, not Samantha. She already knows that rule and now you do too."

"Then," Gabrielle said half in fear, "it's a good thing I did not ask."

"Right. Yes. Shall we continue to walk down the sidewalk?"

"Where are we?"

"The answer will be forthcoming as we walk. You make my head spin. You and your adamantine logic."

"Adamantine? *Wicked.*"

"Did you say wicked?"

Gabrielle out "Oof" as Catherine grabbed her by the arm and pulled her off the sidewalk into a dark narrow alley. The streetlights angled in only a few steps and except for a small light over a door at the far end, they were lost in shadows. The walls of the alley were old brick, unbroken by other doors or windows. Gabrielle stood arms outstretched and her fingertips almost brushed opposite walls. Catherine unzipped her windbreaker.

"I can't stand it anymore," she said.

Gabrielle gasped as Catherine's teeth grazed the side of her neck. Her eyes watered. Catherine's breath was so hot. Gabrielle let herself be pushed back and her hair snagged on the alley wall. Catherine was kissing her ear and leaning in, bracing herself on the wall. Catherine made a sudden sound.

"What?" Gabrielle whispered.

"Sorry. Something jabbed me."

"Your hand?"

"Yeah. What." Catherine moved her head to one side. "It's sticky. *Ew.*"

"My hair's caught on something."

"I can't see it. Wait. It's all over my hand." Catherine peered closely at the brick wall. "It's gum. Bubblegum."

Gabrielle moved forward and the yellow windbreaker peeled away with a wet sucking sound. Her hair was tugged painfully.

"Ow! My hair is stuck in *gum*?"

"It's all over the wall." Catherine's voice had a note of panic. "Here. Careful."

She yanked on the stuck lock of hair.

"Ow!"

"Sorry. It's in your hair."

"There's gum in my hair? What? How can there be so much gum? Good grief!"

"We'll just cut it out."

"I have to *cut* my *hair*. Who the hell puts gum all over a brick wall?"

"Look," Catherine said with a shuddery voice. "Stay in the middle."

"I can see it now." Gabrielle wiped her hands on her jeans. Her fingers were sticky. "It's *everywhere*."

Catherine said in a stunned voice. "This is the most insanely disgusting thing I've ever seen. I, I can't stay here."

She ran for the back alley entrance. Gabrielle also ran. The windbreaker billowed around her like a sail. Catherine stopped in the connecting alley and held her hands over her heart.

"I'm sorry."

"Don't be. Is it really in my hair."

"Yeah," Catherine said sadly.

"What *was* that?"

They walked behind the buildings towards the lighted sidewalk a block away. There were aluminum beer kegs in neat stacks. Their feet sloshed aromatic alley water in a choppy wave.

"It's such a college student thing to do, forgive me for saying that."

"Really bored college students," Gabrielle said.

"Bored and crazy."

Gabrielle nodded. "Art majors."

"And I was in such a great mood."

"I admit it was looking good."

"Festive."

"Well." Catherine took a step. "Maybe we can... You coming?"

"Anon." Gabrielle found the sticky lump in her hair and tried to isolate it. Her fingers now smelled of bubblegum. She caught up to Catherine and they walked side by side out of the back alley and onto another street. There was no traffic at all. Stars gleamed above the darkened buildings.

"Anon?"

"Just something I remember."

"I like it."

They walked a block in silence. At a corner, they looked both ways and crossed on a red light, Gabrielle nervous, Catherine insouciant.

"What else do you remember?" Catherine said. "Wait. *That's* a dumb question."

"Some of it just seemed so accurate it made me crack up."

"The Sonnets, you mean? Like what?"

"I don't know."

"Go ahead."

"There was one."

Catherine grinned. "You better tell me."

"Well," Gabrielle said, "When my love swears she is made of truth I do believe her, though I know she lies."

"Ah."

"That she might think me some untutored youth unlearned in the world's false subtleties."

"Hm."

"Although she knows my days are past the best."

"No."

"Simply I credit her false speaking tongue."

"Keep talking."

"Therefore, I lie with her and she with me and in our faults by lies we flattered be."

Catherine nodded. They kept walking.

"Love," Catherine said suddenly, "is too young to know what conscience is, yet who knows not conscience is born of love?"

Gabrielle realized, I don't know this one. Uh oh.

"Then, gentle cheater, urge not my amiss lest guilty of my faults thy sweet self prove."

"And now I'm blushing again," Gabrielle said.

"Proud of this pride, she is contented thy poor drudge to be, to stand in thy affairs, fall by thy side."

They went up two streets. In the distance, Gabrielle could just make out the railroad trestle.

"You're not a drudge. But that was a good one."

"Thank you. Back in the day old Will got around okay, I'd say. Where are we going?"

"Nowhere."

"It's been a fun date so far. I haven't talked so much in years. I have to ask you a serious question now."

Gabrielle cleared her throat. "Sure."

"All right. Here it is. I'll have you know I have never told anyone I love them. Not ever. Do you somehow imagine that I actually love you in secret but, I don't know, I'm afraid to say it? That's the question."

"No, I don't think that."

"Why not? It would make perfect sense."

"You're mysterious. I want to know you. Most of the time I don't even have a clue how you're going to react to something I say. I'm not trying to get anything from you."

"You're not?"

Catherine's face was lost in shadows. Gabrielle couldn't tell if she was really angry. She couldn't see the scar. Well, she thought, here goes.

"All I have is love so I give it. I don't know how to take."

Catherine turned away quickly and Gabrielle was afraid she had said something wrong. Then in the sharp darkness she saw her smile.

"We named you well."

"Name? You mean."

"Oh my God!" she clamped her hands over her mouth. "It was the wine. The wine did it."

"Did what?"

"Nothing! I didn't say anything. Not a thing."

"Sure." Gabrielle forced herself not to laugh.

"You heard nothing."

"Don't know what you're talking about. Heard?"

"Thanks. Sorry. One more slip like that and it's back to sleeping on a bench at the bus station." She took a deep breath. "You wanna go to a motel?"

Gabrielle said yes and enjoyed the familiar feeling of not knowing what was going to happen next, even though she knew. Catherine picked a tiny place almost lost behind a stand of trees. The glowing windows looked expectant and secretive. After that, they paid no more attention to their surroundings and the night, already deep, became a far abyss, silent and trackless.

At the end of the world there were blackbirds.

Audra called the order of battle.

She set a salt shaker at one end of the dining table.

"Disco's house."

A pepper shaker was placed at the other end.

"L's house. And this." The small red sugar bowl. "This is the Volkswagen."

Gabrielle stood behind her chair. She was impressed by how nervous everyone seemed. Samantha seemed very distracted, almost distraught. She knew Samantha had used the phone early. She had heard the wine cellar door slam as the sun was coming up. And Catherine was studying her, too.

"This is the day. We move at sunset. Samantha driving the VW. Rushel and Gislaine are with you."

She slid the sugar bowl over to the pepper shaker.

"Go to L's street. Go around the block to the west and park in front of that house where they never mow the lawn. That's seven houses down, same side of the street. They won't notice you there and they never drive west from their house, only east, so no one will spot you. Like drug-addled barnyard creatures they're not very observant but we have to be careful. They can be unpredictable. So I'm sorry. Your job is hard. You wait for the signal."

Gislaine picked up her pen. "Signal?"

Catherine raised her hand. "Is it going to be a spotlight projecting the outline of a bat on low clouds?"

"No."

"Wow, could we do that?" Samantha said, smiling for the first time. "That would be *neat*."

Audra sighed. "The signal will be as follows. When all of them are at the dance, every single one, I will go into Disco's kitchen and make a phone call."

"He has a phone in the kitchen?" Gislaine said.

"Just like my former residence," Gabrielle said.

"These old places that's where they put it," Audra said. "I will call the Porch People and when they answer I will hang up."

"Hold on," Rushel raised her hand.

"Right," Gabrielle said. "Them."

"In the early evening, the people across the street always come out and sit on the porch if it's not raining. Their name is Devonshire. They never wanted to talk to me. I found out about them by going through their trash. That's how I got their number."

"You went," Gislaine said, "through their trash?"

Rushel laughed.

"I was an asshole in those days."

"And then you changed your ways," Rushel said, "and started being adorable."

"Thank you."

"That sounds more like a goal," Catherine said. "You know. For the distant future."

Audra shrugged. "Fine. When the Porch People get up to answer the phone that's the signal. Park in L's driveway, leave the engine running, open the front door with the crowbar, and get the eight boxes from the pantry. You must not drop them."

Rushel exhaled. "Right."

They were all silent.

"I don't know." Catherine looked at Gabrielle.

"They always leave one person to watch the house and since New Susan is their latest addition, and has the lowest seniority, she'll get the job. The Goddess, sorry to be crass, completed their task with New Susan. That was a nice bit of luck if you believe in luck which I don't. That was the Goddess in action."

Catherine, Samantha, Gislaine, and Rushel all murmured, "Goddess."

"The influence of Persephone Gabrielle will prove stronger than the influence of L. Good *will* triumph over evil. New Susan will go to the dance.

"When you get to their house, you have to move fast. If our two resident dancing queens fail to show up they will all become suspicious and send someone back to check their house. Your arrival at the dance will mean we have succeeded. After that who cares what they think."

Audra looked at them all.

"If we fail, this is what will happen. M will be ruined. She's almost broke as it is. A middle-aged woman with no recent job experience. She quit that aerospace job ten years ago. Property taxes on this house are delinquent. Even with Prop Thirteen it comes to five thousand dollars, very past due. The only reason we have food to eat is because we take it from College Costs Less."

"Steal," Gislaine said.

"Borrow," Rushel said. "We could pay them back somehow."

Audra said, "And there's another problem, a whole new situation, which we just found out about. And it's bad."

"Wait, hold on," Gabrielle said. "Samantha. What's wrong?"

Audra, grim, sat down.

"Samantha," Catherine said softly. "I've never seen you like this."

"I'm not certain yet," Samantha said. "Because it's Saturday. But my bank has an automated telephone information system. You enter your account number and a recorded voice will tell you your balance and any recent activity. Since we got the phone I have been using it to check on my savings. Thursday, I had eighty-eighty thousand, nine hundred fifty-five dollars in my account. This morning, it said my balance is zero dollars. It was all transferred."

They all stared in shock. Gabrielle sat and took Samantha's hands in her's.

"Good *God*," Catherine said, seething.

"How is that possible?" Gislaine said. "They have to be able to do something."

"Maybe. But usually," Samantha said in a quivering voice, "if the money's gone it's gone. My bank is in France. So no insurance. I'm sure they withdrew it all right away. I doubt the police over there would do anything."

Catherine hugged Samantha and they all sat stunned.

"It was my fault," Samantha said.

"*What?*" Gislaine slapped her pen down.

"It was the phone. They give you a customer code and you dial that in, then your account number. They don't have the touch-tone phones very much yet. You dial it and the computer over there counts the clicks, right? Well, guess what. Anyone can count the clicks."

"God damn them," Rushel said.

"Look, it's only money. But you know. All that sex for nothing."

"*Sammie.*"

"Your life savings," Catherine said.

"There are more developments," Audra said. "Do you want me to tell them?"

"No. I will," Samantha said. Gabrielle joined Catherine in hugging her.

"It's about our house down south," Audra said. "We now have a pretty good idea of what happened."

"Yes, you remember M talking about what a great deal she got on that mortgage?" Samantha said.

They all nodded.

"She did mention that to me," Gabrielle said.

"See, she met someone in a bar. That place in Long Beach."

"Oh M," Rushel sighed.

"Yes, even young innocent Rushel here," Audra said, "a mere college student, can see where this is going."

"*Innocent?*"

"Who just happened to work at a mortgage company. Felicity Home Loan. And they got to know each other, you know."

"Good lord," Catherine said. She kissed Samantha's cheek. "We are children. We are going to lose."

"And M got a fantastic rate. Two percent. The going rate was about eleven. Well, Felicity Home Loan does not exist. The bank which funded the loan, Inner California, does not exist."

"Ew," Gislaine said. "*In her* California."

They all moaned.

"Last time she was here," Samantha said, "she let a little detail slip. We were discussing the situation, a situation I now know I was woefully ignorant of, and she said something about that person. This detail allowed me to unravel the whole thing. She was walking out of the middle room, muttering to herself. She can't have realized I overheard. She said, 'Goddamn redhead.'"

"Right," Gislaine put her hands over her face.

"*Susan.*" Catherine almost spit.

Audra crossed her arms. "The one Susan the Goddess has not met. Although I'm certain she has seen you."

"The extra one wearing a hood. They all had hoods on. Tall."

"Yeah," Gislaine said. "M and redheads."

"Hood," Rushel said with a sick look.

"At L's house. Black hoods over their faces. And they had this radio speaker system so they could switch voices."

"God that's creepy."

"So M, God bless her, got a big loan to build a house. Four hundred seventy-five thousand dollars."

Catherine and Rushel moaned. Gabrielle felt her stomach clench. Eighteen times the value of her Mom's house.

"The money came from L. What a great prank. Let M build her dream house then walk in and take it away from her. M found out somehow. Maybe she half suspected. The morning the demolition crew showed up

L instantly counterattacked. She sold the mortgage to a huge bank in Germany. A very real bank. And she did it so quickly."

Samantha shook her head.

"Remember the thunderbolt. So M destroyed her house on which she had spent all but fourteen thousand dollars of that gigantic loan. She now has a vacant lot and massive debt she has no hope of repaying."

Catherine interrupted. "Use those coins to make the mortgage payments. And the taxes here. It would be a waste because there's no more house but it would get the bank off our backs."

"That's a good idea. M has no idea we have those coins. If she had known. Well. It's too late now."

"What is?" Rushel looked nauseous.

Samantha took a deep breath.

"Last Tuesday M filed for bankruptcy. But before she did that she filed a quit claim and deeded this house here to someone. When that bank in Germany tries to seize her assets they will get a vacant lot and maybe her savings and probably her Jeep. They usually don't go after your car but tearing down a brand new house is kind of extreme.

"So this place is protected and off the radar of huge German banks. M just has to go through the bankruptcy proceedings. I would say we're okay for now."

"We are not okay," Audra said. "Protected? L will now target this house directly. She's this close to destroying M completely and there's no reason for her to hold back. She's undoubtedly seriously angry her little prank didn't come off and she lost all that money. If we expect to keep living here we have to damage her ability to attack us."

"I have to admit," Catherine said.

"We are not dealing with a normal person who just happens to be upset about something. I lived with them for a year. If you try to defuse the situation, try to conciliatory, they see it as a sign of weakness. Attack them first. Attack. Make it really hurt. It's the only way to make them stop.

"And I can't even imagine how M feels. Her dream house ruined. Her family threatened. And why do you think she could never get a teaching job? There are God knows how many universities in Los Angeles. She's highly qualified. She's very attractive. The other professors would drool over her. But then there's an anonymous phone call to the personnel department. Or a letter with no return address. M is impossible to get along with. M is a plagiarist. Who would take a chance on her?"

"All right," Gislaine said.

Gabrielle raised her hand.

"The Goddess does not need to raise her hand."

"Oh. Lifelong habit."

"Goddess," Audra said.

"I have a question. Who did she deed the house to? A relative?"

"No relatives. Well, there's a brother somewhere," Samantha said. "She deeded the house to Gislaine."

Gislaine gasped and stared.

Audra dropped into her seat.

"How about that?" Catherine said. "What's your grandmother gonna say?"

Gabrielle saw tears in Gislaine's eyes, and thought, glad it wasn't me.

"She'll probably call the police. It's her answer to everything. God damn M. Her and her games."

"Game or not, it's important to remember this is perfectly legal and what's filed is filed. At some point you could deed it back to her. Or not. I'm assuming that's the ultimate idea however no one can force you. You are now a homeowner."

"What do I have to do? Gislaine capped her pen and closed her notebook.

"I'm not sure what to make of this," Audra said.

"Not a thing," Samantha said.

"Do I have to go to city hall."

"Nope. It's a County deal. But nope."

"Has anything changed?" Audra said. "Or is this game changing?"

Gabrielle thought a lot had changed.

"I think," she said, "we should honor M's wishes and think of this house as now belonging to Gislaine."

"Oh my God." Gislaine uncapped her pen and began writing.

"Then next week we take some of M's money and pay the back taxes. I doubt she would object."

"Goddess," Samantha said. "I can take care of that."

Rushel went around the table and hugged Gislaine from behind. Gislaine did not pause in her writing. Her pen made a soft smooth whisper on the paper.

"And I agree with Audra," Gabrielle continued. "Even if we're protected from that bank we are now directly in L's sights. They already invaded us to install those microphones. We could be surrounded by booby-traps."

Gabrielle saw they were all watching her intently. Samantha's eyes drilled into her's.

"I don't want to wait to find out what their plans are. We have a plan. We have a great plan."

She made a sharp nod.

"We fight."

Audra leaned over the table and Gabrielle took her hand. Catherine and Samantha did the same. Rushel reached over and put her hand on top of theirs. Gislaine put her pen down and put her hand on Rushel's.

"So shall it be," Gislaine said softly and Gabrielle could sense the fear in her voice.

Audra said. "We leave at sunset. Let's start getting ready."

Rushel put her hands on her hips.

"Hair," she said. "Maximum impact."

"Six hours," Audra said. "Is that enough time?"

"*Barely.*" Rushel headed for the large bathroom."

"How about you?" Gabrielle said to Samantha

"Oh it's easy for me. Just wash and dry. Three hours tops. However, the Goddess needs something to wear."

"I have nothing to wear."

"You definitely have something to wear," Audra said. "Right this way."

Gabrielle sighed. "A dress."

"You can't disco in old jeans."

"I guess not."

"Don't like dresses either. Where I come from wearing pants is frowned upon after you get out of high school. You're supposed to be a lady. So I have a couple skirts and a pretty good collection of dancing attire. And everything will fit you no problem."

"I don't have any dresses. I did get a nice wool skirt for my birthday once. I don't remember ever wearing it."

"Your parents gave you a skirt?"

"Oh, no, it was from my aunt in Houston. She was always sending me girly stuff."

"You're even more of a tomboy than me."

"I don't like that."

"Me neither."

"I'm just me. I guess I'm not a lady."

"You could fake it."

"Kind of tired of faking things."

"Just this."

"All right."

"This will be it."

"All right."

"Good. I also have some great jumpsuits. Satin. They are really fun. But otherwise." She opened her closet.

Gabrielle sighed. "A dress."

"Are they all like this?"

Gabrielle held up the black polyester, sequin covered garment balled up in the palm of her hand. She spread it open.

"It's slit up the side to my belly button."

"Your legs have to be free to do moves."

Gabrielle held the dress up to her side with a feeling excitement mixed with muted panic. It was a skimpy one piece bathing suit with long, she thought of the word, *bangles* dangling down.

"So the jumpsuits are perfect. See?"

A jumpsuit consisted of pants with a connecting halter top. The pants legs were widely flared at the ankles and the top, she thought was rather revealing. One was made of shimmering bright purple fabric, one was a stiff silver cloth that looked like a suit of armor, and the last was slender and a deep blue.

Audra was smiling at her.

"Figured you'd like that one."

"It's beautiful. Although I feel naked without sleeves. And bare shoulders."

"You also need a wrap. See?"

Audra unrolled a black scarf. Sequins made a snowflake pattern on it. She draped it around her shoulders.

"You wear this wrap outside then when you get to the coat check guy you take it off real slinky and say, hi." Audra batted her eyes. "Could you be a sweetie and put this somewhere where it won't touch the ground?" She blinked rapidly. "Thanks so much."

"I don't know about that."

"I like to lead them on. I never let them touch me though."

"Can I try this on? Doesn't that backfire sometimes?"

"Sure, here, it has a zipper. It's microscopic. Sometimes they follow me around. I just outrun them."

"You're not afraid of hurting their feelings, you know, breaking their hearts?"

"Oh right. How would that be possible? I've never broken anyone's heart."

Gabrielle said nothing as she slipped into the skintight navy blue jumpsuit and it fit snugly around her waist and even had a bra-like structure.

"Really makes them stick out, huh?"

"Uh, yeah."

"That's on purpose."

"God."

"You're supposed to pick the one you want, jiggle them in their face, an activity also known as dancing, then go somewhere dark and do it."

"Audra."

"That's the whole point of a dance. *You* don't have to do a thing. All that matters is they see you. Especially you know who."

"I feel like an idiot. What if someone asks me? I can't dance."

"You are pretty hot in that thing."

Gabrielle bounced on her heels. The flared out pants nicely covered her feet. I can wear my regular shoes, she thought.

"Yeah, shake it! We need to get serious about your hair now."

"This is kind of fun. Ah."

"What?"

"Just had a great idea."

"As long as no transistors are involved."

"Ha, you'll see."

"No batteries either."

Gabrielle went to the hall. From the large bathroom came the sound of laughter and running water.

"Middle bathroom."

In the living room a whistle came from one of the reclining chairs. Catherine pushed herself up. She was wearing a bright pink mini-skirt and a filmy, equally pink top. The top was not transparent, however, every detail of her body was discernable. She held one of her long tanned legs out in a stance.

"*Look* at you," she said.

"Me? Gosh."

Catherine was almost glowing.

"That's the pinkest pink."

"Thought I should try to deflect attention from you. Just waiting for room to open up in the hair salon."

"Oh, right, yeah, hair. Wait here."

Gabrielle found what she wanted in the bottom vanity drawer. She quickly put it on. Back in the living room, she said, "Ask me to dance."

Catherine clasped her hands over her stomach.

"Oh, hi, I was like watching you and, well, like all the boys are icky and I really like your bosom about to explode from Audra's underdeveloped high school outfit she got at that thrift store in Oakland and I wanted to ask you to dance and maybe we could go do something later."

"Ohh," Gabrielle said. "I'm sorry." She lifted up her right pants leg to reveal an Ace bandage wrapped around her ankle. "See? I can't dance."

"Hey, slick. You twisted your ankle."

"It's awful. But I still wanted to go. So here I am. I'll just watch."

"Perfect."

"We could still do something later if you want."

"Okay, sure," Catherine said in a breathy voice. "I like to pull zippers open with my teeth and sometimes I catch my hair and it hurts but I don't care because it feels so good. We could do that or I don't know."

When Gabrielle stopped laughing she said, "I can't wait."

"Me either. Are you leaving it in?"

"It? Oh." Her hand went to her nose. "Good question. I think I should."

"You should. The boys will find it fascinating."

"Thanks."

Audra came into the room wearing her bright purple jumpsuit. She shook her head and her hair bounced luxuriously. She said, "Maintain focus."

"You light up the whole room," Gabrielle said.

"Oh, I know. Does your car have gas?"

"Three quarters of a tank. Where is the crowbar?"

"Under the front seat. Good. It's the details that get you when you're pulling a heist. Hair time."

"I was here first," Catherine said. "Are they done yet?"

"I can hear Rushel singing so no."

"That girl and her hair."

"On a certain level the entire world is Rushel's little plaything. I feel lucky to know her," Audra said. "Same with you, Goddess. When you're out in the real world and you need a lawyer."

"You're hired."

"Really?"

"Starting now."

After a moment of surprise Audra extended her hand and they shook on it. Catherine watched carefully.

"That was real, wasn't it."

As real as a brush rabbit that turned into a kitten, Gabrielle thought. As real as an invisible force that knocked a rock into a creek. As real as a backpack that came flying out of nowhere to break the screen door. As real as an apple hitting your head.

"As real as anything."

By three-thirty, everyone was done with their hair and by four-thirty final clothing arrangements were complete. They all stood behind their chairs at the dining table. Gabrielle wished she had a camera. She concentrated on remembering. Audra in her purple jumpsuit, Catherine and Gislaine in mini-skirts and sandals, both wearing necklaces of chunky plastic jewels. Classic California hippie party attire being, Gabrielle decided, acceptable disco costumes. Samantha was wearing a flowing bright blue dress, slit up the sides to her belly button as was the norm, and platform shoes. She gave her hair a test toss and studied its behavior. The long black strands cascaded over her shoulders and brushed her ankles.

"Wella?" Catherine asked."

"L'Oréal."

Rushel fanned her hair out with both hands and the last of the sunlight created a golden halo. She had on a sleeveless white dress that hugged her body without being revealing. It was slit up the sides to above her knees and made her look even taller somehow. Audra beamed at her proudly.

Rushel said softly, "Well done, Priestesses. Goddess, we won't disappoint you."

Gabrielle cleared her throat. "You're all so beautiful."

"Whatever happens tonight," Audra said, "we will always treasure this moment and out time together. Our love for each other will never diminish.

For as long as I live you will be my family."

They all said, "So shall it be."

Beyond the curved glass doors the sand dunes were in shadow. Nearby a gull cried in alarm.

"Sunset," Catherine said.

Samantha took a deep breath.

"I feel like smashing something. Who's with me?"

Off the long valley road they made the left together towards town and Gabrielle, sitting in the back seat as Audra drove, forced herself not to worry about her Volkswagen, headlights steady behind them. Samantha was an excellent driver. She trusted Samantha implicitly. She hoped Samantha wasn't riding the clutch.

"Clutches are easy," she said and felt better.

"What?" Audra met her gaze in the mirror.

"Your car is perfectly safe," Catherine said without turning.

Both vehicles cruised beneath the overpass and reached the center of town. Waiting at one of the eight traffic signals – Audra had planned the route exactly – Gabrielle refused the look at the red light.

It all looks different, she thought. I guess I've already left. I've already said goodbye.

She caught Audra's worried glance in the mirror and sat up straight. Maintain focus.

On the other side of town the Volkswagen peeled away and disappeared on the long street which led behind L's house. Would the Porch People even be out tonight? It was clear and cool. The breeze had a bite. Gabrielle pressed her satin clad legs together and gripped the gray seat fabric.

Audra rolled through a stop sign and made a sharp left in third gear. The engine lugged. They slipped around a slow Chevy pickup. Two blocks from Disco's street.

"Throwing off pursuers?" Catherine said.

"Confusing any observers."

Gabrielle saw the street coming up. A brand new Saab was stopped in front of them in the left lane and a Mercedes was waiting to make the same turn on the other side. The Saab, turn signals a bright yellow, was waiting for a long line of cars to make a right onto the street. The line of headlights stretched at least two block, Gabrielle saw.

Audra jerked her Corona to the right lane, popped the clutch, and came abeam of the Saab. Gabrielle could not count the number of people in it. Couples? She got the impression of a lot of hair. Permed, curly, feathered hair.

They saw why no one was moving.

"Sweet mother of God," Catherine said tightly.

"Yes!" Audra pounded the steering wheel. "Yes!"

Disco's steep street was a sea of taillights and headlights and flashing turn signals all going nowhere. Near the top of the hill a bright floodlight flashed red and pink and blue.

"Disco colors," Gabrielle said. "Look at that."

"That's Sid! We have to get up there. We're already late. Hang on!"

Audra slammed her car into reverse and spun the wheel. Someone laid on their horn, a little Honda, which passed on the right.

"Anybody else back there?"

Audra revved the engine and popped the clutch again. The Toyota lurched backwards over the curb. The rear bumper scraped and the car bounced up and over the sidewalk and plowed through a hedge. Gabrielle was lifted off her seat and watched the branches scrape her window. They came to a stop across three parking spaces of a real estate office. *Jim's Properties* the modest sign said, the windows thankfully dark.

"You okay?" Catherine said.

"Huh?" Gabrielle was dizzy.

"We gotta go." Audra yanked the parking brake and snapped off the engine. "Neither of you has a purse, right?"

"Never," Catherine said.

"I left everything at home," Gabrielle said. "Do we need money? I don't even have my license."

"Oh, no. If you don't have it you can't lose it."

"Why would we lose anything," Catherine said.

"Sometimes these things get out of hand. Sometimes."

Audra took the key out of the ignition, a single bare key, and slipped it into her bodice. There was a snap.

"Secret pocket."

"Well I guess that's better than taping it to your boob."

They all opened their doors.

"There's another place I could put it."

Audra got out and tipped her seat forward. Gabrielle stuck a leg out. Someone whistled from a passing car and beeped their horn.

"I wouldn't want to lose my virginity to a piece of brass." Catherine slammed her door. "Locked."

Gabrielle stood and draped the scarf around her shoulders. Traffic roared past them.

"I like this." The sky to the west was blood red fading to gray. The air was warm and cool.

Audra closed her door. "Well."

"You're nervous," Gabrielle said.

"You're going to stop traffic in that."

"Just wait till I get warmed up," Catherine said. "Observe."

Catherine stepped off the curb into the lane and put her hands on her hips. A big Dodge pickup locked up its rear wheels skidded to within five feet of her. She glared at the truck, and tossed her hair, and continued across the street to where the Saab sat, blinker blinking. The truck driver gunned it and sped off.

Catherine smiled at the occupants of the Saab and waved.

"Whadaya waitin' for? Come on!"

All of the Saab doors opened at once. A trio of women clambered out of the rear seat. They were wearing shimmering jumpsuits, one red, one white, and one blue. They shook out their dark hair as three more women got out behind them. They all had long blonde hair, identical white dresses, and shoes with long stiletto heels. Gabrielle winced as they walked, ankles bowing. Then four more got out of the front, guys this time. They slowly unfolded themselves. Black jackets and white shirts with extra wide collars. They hurried after the young women.

"Sheesh, it's like *Doctor Who*," Audra said. "Oh right, the dance contest!" She stepped off the curb.

"Look both ways." Gabrielle jogged to catch up.

"I never look both ways. Just one way."

They reached the Saab and Audra closed the rear passenger doors. She leaned into the front and spoke to the driver.

"No use sitting here. Park on a side street and walk in."

Audra caught herself. Gabrielle peeked over her shoulder. The driver, also in a black jacket with wide lapels, looked like a school kid.

"Okay, how old are you?" Audra said.

"Why?" he said, a high young voice.

"Just answer the question."

"I'm almost fourteen."

"Almost, huh? Like in two years?"

"No."

"You're twelve. This your dad's car?"

"No."

"Your mom? Oh wait. That's Givenchy. This is your big sister's car. Your parents gave it to her when she graduated high school. She's a student here, right?"

"How'd... Yeah."

"What's your name?"

"Steinmetz."

"No I mean." Audra held up her hand. "Your parents are college professors, aren't they." She shrugged. "Nice outfit."

"Thanks!" he said. "I like your dress. It really shows off your –"

Audra slammed the door. The Saab pulled away with a chirp of the tires. They waited for a huge flatbed truck to pass then ran for the curb.

Gabrielle, sweating, said, "That was a kid!"

"Yeah. By the time this night is over I'm going to be middle-aged."

They walked slowly up the hill. The suburban darkness was alive with laughter and blaring radio music and the narrow street was full of revving engines. There were groups of brightly dressed people on the sidewalk and the shadowy lawns of the neighboring houses. And something else. Gabrielle could smell it.

"Better than booze, in my opinion," Audra said. "But I expect a truckload of booze. I also expect the cops. Can't block the street like this. Oh well, they'll find out."

Two houses from Disco's, with its color changing floodlight, a girl in a frilly pink dress stumbled from behind a hedge and fell face down on the sidewalk in front of them. Her shoulders heaved. She was laughing uncontrollably. Audra leaned over her.

"Coke or 'ludes? Amyl nitrate? Poppers?"

The girl coughed and kept laughing.

They walked around her as three satin-clad women burst from the hedge, all giggling, and knelt down. A car hit the horn in the street.

The crowd in Disco's front yard spread over the sidewalk into the street.

"*Look* at all that hair," Gabrielle said.

"Are your eyes watering? All that hair spray, one tiny spark. Vomp. Spontaneous disco combustion."

"Audra, this is completely insane."

"I am so glad you are on my side now. Look out."

They reached the corner of Disco's patchy grass yard. The crowd was watching the closed front door. Most of the males turned to look at them. There were whistles. Gabrielle took a step back and got behind Audra. All of the women close to them tossed their hair, frowning, a collective surge of frothy curled locks glinting gold and silver in the floodlight.

"Fifty-eight," Gabrielle whispered.

Audra nodded. "And multiples of that waiting in cars. Plus whoever's inside. Why aren't they going in? Where's Sid? That's his car."

There was a huge convertible in Disco's steep driveway, a white Continental with wide flat tail fins. Blood red leather upholstery. What is that, Gabrielle thought, a sixty-four? And at least a four twenty-five, maybe bigger.

Gabrielle saw the front curtains twitch. The front door opened an inch and was slammed shut. One of the guys yelled, "Oh come on! Let's go!" to applause.

"I can't wait to meet Sid. What a car."

"You'll love him. I want to marry him."

"No kidding."

"Or his sister. I want to marry her, too."

Gabrielle laughed. "Rushel mentioned her."

"Storm."

"Her name is Storm?"

"You name your kid something like that it's a lot to live up to."

"What?"

Audra took Gabrielle's hand and they went up the driveway to the edge of the crowd. Audra elbowed a tall guy wearing a tuxedo. He stumbled from the porch steps.

"Oh sorry."

"Geez!"

"Well?"

There were rumblings as they climbed the eight steps. The front row of the crowd, all angry glittery eye-shadowed women in long dresses and fluorescent jumpsuits, leaned forward menacingly. On the far side, Gabrielle saw a familiar scowling face.

Gabrielle felt the urge to run. Audra gripped her hand tighter. The front door sprang open and Catherine stood there, bare legs in the floodlight turning from red to hot pink. More whistles.

"Where the hell have you been? Here she is, Sid! Just a couple minutes, folks!"

As the crowd grumbled, Audra stopped at the threshold.

"I forgot to warn you."

"All right." Gabrielle felt her pulse rate spike the way it did in the German restaurant. She tried to swallow and could not.

"It's Disco's roommates."

"Oh. Those guys? I saw them."

"That was only a few. There's a lot more. Over twenty."

"How. Well, okay."

"But."

"But what?"

"They're not the problem. They're mostly Aggies. Mostly."

"Aggies are all right. I think I just saw Patricia."

"Okay good. Yeah they're just regular guys. It's his two newest roommates that are the problem. The Aggies tried to warm him but you know Disco, can't say no."

Gabrielle took a fast look at the unhappy crowd below, tossed her hair as fiercely as she could, and stepped in to the large, low ceiling room. A super parlor, she thought. It opened to an even bigger living room which smelled of furniture polish. There was an elegant curved staircase at the end. A mirror ball was suspended from the ceiling. It rotated slowly in darkness over a massive walnut dining table set for – she couldn't help it – sixteen places.

There was a wooden podium with a gooseneck microphone and big boxes on tripods spray painted flat black. High power speakers. And a tall thin frame covered with a gray sheet. What's that? she thought.

Two people were working intently at the podium, a man in a shiny metallic-looking suit and a tall woman in a white sleeveless dress. They both seemed to be deliberately trying to ignore two blonde women who were talking to them.

Gabrielle whispered, "Is that Storm?"

"Yep."

"Gosh."

Audra laughed and the man in the shiny suit looked up and spread his arms.

"Counselor!"

Audra ran to him.

"Your Honor!"

Gabrielle watched with delight as Sid gave Audra a bear hug, lifted her off the floor, and swung her full circle. She giggled the whole time then Storm did the same.

"You've lost weight," Storm said.

"Stress."

"Oh, poor baby." Storm hugged her again.

The two blonde women regarded them sternly. One was wearing thick eyeglasses and the other had a wispy bald spot on the very top of her head.

"Sidney," Eyeglasses said. "*Sidney*. My *word*, whoever you are, please do not interrupt."

"Whoever?" Audra said, Gabrielle estimated at eighty percent max volume. "I am?"

"There is no need to raise your voice. I have cancelled the dance effective immediately." She refolded her arms.

"Sondra, right? And you're Clementine? Both of you stop talking."

"You can't just."

"Stop! Sid, this is my best friend, Gabrielle, star of electronic engineering and computers. Gabrielle, may I introduce my friend and mentor Sidney Parkinson, Stanford law student extraordinaire and his sister Storm. Physics department Berkeley." Audra grinned. "Both originally from Ohio."

Gabrielle shook hands with Storm and Sid, whose eyes went directly to her nose ring.

"It was a gag," she said. "I haven't even had it a week."

"There nothing wrong with that at all," Storm said. "I like it."

Gabrielle thought Sid didn't seem so sure.

"You know what that is?" he said. "That's punk."

"I've heard of punk." She wrinkled her nose. "It itches."

"Yeah, punk's the next big thing. Unless pop wins. It won't be rock, definitely. Then there's rap, that's the real wild card. But Counselor, I have to tell you, I don't think it's the end of disco. We've never been busier."

"We're going up and down the coast every weekend," Storm said. "It's exhausting."

"This time next year I'll be able to put a down payment on a place in Palo Alto. You could stay with us."

"It would be so much fun," Storm said.

"Okay! That's fantastic! Oh my God I have to tell you about Rushel. You know what she did?"

Sid raised his finger. "Hm. Created a new religion?"

Gabrielle felt herself blush and saw that Sid instantly noticed.

"She changed her major. You'll never guess to what."

"No more finger painting?" Storm said.

"Computer science!"

"Hey, yeah."

"I know. It's weird. It makes perfect sense. She's been taking math classes in secret."

"Gotta keep that stuff secret from her advisor, huh," Sid said.

"Math and science. She'd get in trouble with all the slackers."

"Oh my," Storm laughed.

"So Gabrielle will make the computers and Rushel will program them. It's perfect."

"And you can be their attorney. Whew. When you go public I want in on the IPO." Sid seemed genuinely impressed.

"No problem," Gabrielle said, thinking what's an IPO, and was startled by a loud knock on the door.

Catherine reached for the doorknob then hesitated.

"Where is Rushie, anyway?" Storm said. "I want to dance with that girl. We'll set this place on fire."

Holy cow, Gabrielle thought.

The front door flew open and a young woman entered. It took Gabrielle several seconds to recognize Pretty Susan. She had bleached her hair dead white and was wearing a rainbow striped dress with a neckline that reached her navel.

"Is this where the dance is?" she said with only slight slurring.

"No!" Sondra said.

"Yes! Come on, Susan. Sondra. You can't cancel anything," Audra said calmly. "Are you mental? Are you trying to make me mad? Who do you think you are?"

"I am a graduate student in Child Development. I don't want there to be a dance."

"So what? Why should anyone care what you want? Are you the reason the God damned furniture hasn't been moved?"

"Oh," Clementine said, "you're being very masculine."

Sid covered his mouth to laugh.

"You're both Education majors," Gabrielle said. "Huh."

"Counselor, I am one hundred present ready to go. Just say the word."

"Thank you, your Honor. I'll bet everyone's in the kitchen."

"That's where the booze is, so yes ma'am."

"Very well." Audra gave Sondra and Clementine a puzzled look. "Why would you do this? You are deliberately trying to make me angry."

"The issues are too complex for your limited understanding," Sondra said.

"You're doing this on purpose because you are a couple of ivory tower chickenheads. That's Phillip K. Dick, by the way. Hm."

Gabrielle followed Audra to the kitchen door. Behind them, Sondra began to berate Sid.

"Sidney, listen to me."

"Yes, ma'am."

"It pains me to see a young Black man like you being treated this way."

"I assure you they are treating me very well."

Clementine said, "That's just false consciousness," in her monotonic, condescending voice.

"They're treating me very well, too," Storm said. "That's not false anything."

"As a Black woman," Clementine said, "you are subject to discrimination and oppression on a culturally and perceptually sub-aware level."

"Honey, anyone messes with me, as a Black woman, I kick their ass. Problem solved."

"Thus are many problems solved," Sid said.

"Oh, I don't think violence is the answer."

"Really? We're still talking about planet Earth, right?"

At the kitchen door, Audra stopped suddenly. She was breathing in sharp gasps, gulping air. She made fists.

"Heart palpitations," she said. "I am maintaining a rational outlook."

"Yes," Gabrielle said.

"I am in control of my emotions."

She shook her shoulders back.

"Stand in the doorway but do not enter. As your Priestess it is my duty to protect you."

"All right. Is there anything I can do?"

"Just observe."

"I will."

"I'm doing pretty good, don't you think? I'm handling it, right?"

"Yes you are."

Audra pushed the kitchen door open. Gabrielle saw multiple cowboy hats under a bright bare ceiling bulb. Audra held her hands out and the crowd of Aggies parted respectfully, a receding wave of flannel. All conversation ceased.

The tile countertop was completely covered with large bottles of alcohol, some clear, some amber. Round and rectangular, all labeled on the necks with official looking tags. Gabrielle blinked.

Audra grabbed a big square bottle and held it up to the light. Then she tossed it underhand into the sink. It exploded in a shower of glass and whiskey. One of the guys cried out in pain.

"That was a half-gallon of Jack Daniels. Get out there and start moving furniture or so help me God I will trash *everything*."

She picked up another bottle, something clear.

"No, wait!" one of them said.

"Start moving."

One in a white shirt and black hat peered out the kitchen door.

"Well, now, Sondra..."

"Sondra is an idiot. Sondra isn't in charge of anything. I am in charge. You do what I say. It's very simple. Tequila."

She slammed the bottle into the sink and it shattered with a loud pop. Tequila spouted to the ceiling.

Several of the guys said, "Whoa!" The rest nodded sadly.

"Besides, have you even looked out front? Have you seen the girls out there? They're unbelievable. And they're all drunk. What kind of guys *are* you? Start with the table. Put it outside on the lawn. Then the chairs. Go." She snatched another bottle, clear and rectangular, and hefted it like a club. "Go!"

Black hat laughed.

"All right, all right. Jeez, Audra. Even though it's disco. I mean."

"It will be great." She kept the bottle raised.

"Yeah, well, come on," he said to the others. "That table's blamed heavy."

"Thanks, Travis."

Audra tucked the bottle of vodka under her arm walked backwards to the door and held it open. The guys filed out in a rumble of boots. Gabrielle heard Sondra shout. The final guy out, dirty jeans, dark green flannel, said, "Uh oh," and stopped.

Sondra stood at the head of the dining table, arms crossed. She shook her head at Travis. Travis backed up.

Audra threw the bottle underhand with a snap of her wrist and it made a graceful half turn and hit Sondra on her right cheekbone with a sharp plink.

Sondra said, "Hi!" and fell backwards onto the hardwood floor where Pretty Susan was sitting cross-legged.

Travis shrugged, tipped his hat, and began pulling the massive table. Four of the guys pitched in and the table started moving towards the front door.

Audra retrieved the bottle and went to Pretty Susan. Sondra moaned, curled up. Her Birkenstocks clumped.

"Here, Susan. All for you, honey."

"Gosh. Stolichnaya. Thanks, Audra."

Audra got up and went to a shocked open-mouthed Clementine, got behind her, and pushed her around the slowly moving table to the front door.

"Open the door, Clemmie, and go out on the porch."

"No, no, I can't." Her sneakers squeaked.

"Just turn the knob. See? Now pull it open."

Angry voices and perfume flooded in.

"You've been very very sick. How do you feel now?"

Clementine stepped through the doorway and the floodlight illuminated her face, sky blue turning amber.

"I feel fine," she said, confused.

Gabrielle followed as Audra shoved Clementine out of the house and then put her arm around her waist.

"Thank you all for being so patient!" Audra raised her hand palm out. The angry voices subsided. "We had a delay in setting up because of the surprise return of Clementine from her first round of chemotherapy."

There were many 'Ah's." Clementine stared at Audra.

"She told me herself just now she feels *fine*. We all decided that this dance should be dedicated to her. So welcome to Clementine's Disco's Last Blast!"

There was a wave of applause. Someone yelled, "Yay, Clementine!"

Clementine said, "Oh, well, thank you."

Travis appeared at the doorway angling the legs of the table through.

"Our DJ is none other than the famous Sid Parkinson from Planet Hollywood!"

As the crowd applauded, Gabrielle spotted Tall Susan and Debbie at the very back. Sid came up beside her.

"Hi, nice to meet you by the way, Gabrielle."

Gabrielle shook his hand. "Thanks, nice meeting you too. I love your jacket."

"It's a bit much, I know. I have a bunch of them. There's a store that sells them. Kind of a disco department store."

"That sounds exactly like Hollywood."

"It's wonderful. It's who I am." He held up his index finger. "We need to reestablish momentum. I could use your help."

"Sure, anything."

"Hold this." Sid handed her a flat block of wood and a mallet. A gavel.

"Like this?"

"Perfect. Come with me."

They went onto the porch and the concentrated attention felt like sunlight on Gabrielle's face. She held up the gavel and block like an offering.

Sid said, "Uh huh," and took the gavel.

Scattered applause turned to cheering. Music began playing inside.

"On behalf of Clementine and all the great people who call this place home, welcome. My name is Sid and you may address me as Your Honor."

There were whistles and applause.

"And I hereby declare this party." He slammed the gavel onto the block.

"Started!"

Gabrielle, hands stinging, took cover behind Audra as the first row, all female, bounded up the steps with loud platform shoes giggling.

"*The Sound of Philadelphia*," Audra said.

"Storm's the programmer these days."

Sid nodded at the brightly dressed people passing.

"I really like…"

"Hey!" It was a guy in a white dress shirt and square oversized sunglasses. His black hair was brushed straight back, also square looking. "The sign said open bar. The people of my temple need a drink. So where the hell is it?"

"Well, Mister Rude Dude," Audra said. "That door straight back there. Just go on in and…"

Temple man instantly pushed past her and a girl in a tight pink leotard hissed at him. "*Pig.*"

"Open bar," Sid said. "You're playing with fire, Counselor."

"Necessary."

"Why's that?"

"I want maximum excitement, maximum interest."

"Hm. All right." Sid scanned the crowd. "Pieces are falling into place. There's something I've been meaning to ask you. Will *she* be here?"

"I'm counting on it."

"See, you don't like disco very much so this whole thing made no sense. This is all one of your schemes, isn't it."

"At this time I am unable to respond to that inquiry. *She* will be fashionably late as always."

"Uh huh. Well, I'm ready for her. Also, I should tell you, we have a friend who has been following us around. Storm knows him from Berkeley. Probably following Storm around would be more accurate. He may show up."

"You don't mean Kenneth, do you?"

"Ah, you remember."

"He seemed okay. Kind of, you know, off beat."

"Yeah, he's into odd stuff these days. Just warning you. Shall we?"

Gabrielle, burning to ask Audra questions, followed them back inside. Storm was at the podium with its built-in cassette player. Two guys, both with big mustaches and wide lapels, were talking to her.

"Oh, don't worry. I'm pretty sure the Bee Gees will be around, she said.

"*Turn the Beat Around*?" one of them said.

"Sure. Good idea. I'll put it, let's say, fifth."

"Great, thanks!"

The dining room had been cleared of furniture except for a tall display cabinet against the back wall. Plates and glasses were visible through windows in the doors. A hutch, right? Gabrielle thought. The hutch swayed when people walked close to it. She could feel the floorboards springing.

Storm smiled at her.

"Tell me your favorite song and we'll play it, Gabrielle."

"Thanks but I don't have a favorite."

"Oh you don't?"

"I don't know anything about music. Or what's popular. Or anything. And it's been proven I can't even dance."

"Hang around with Audra. She'll teach you."

"I have learned a lot from her."

Audra was kneeling next to Sondra who was cross-legged in the far corner.

"Sondra. Keep ice on it. There was a huge fight in the kitchen. There's broken glass all over the place. I think they were trying to hit Travis."

"Ta. Travis?"

"Yeah, here sip this. I got it from Susan."

Pretty Susan wiggled her fingers at them.

"It burns. Is Travis okay?"

"Just sip. It's tonic water from Russia. You'll feel better. And Travis totally kicked their asses. It was something."

"Thanks, Audra. Wow."

"Sure thing, sweetie."

Storm turned down the volume as the song ended. She took the cassette out and set it in a long tray full of other tapes. There were three of the trays, all custom made of varnished wood, on tripods like the speakers. All the cassettes were the same generic white plastic and had a Dymo label on the top edge. Gabrielle saw *B-G*, *Donna*, and at the very bottom, *ABBA*. She tried not to count but there were too many distractions. Three hundred eighty tapes and the sharp, easy to read labels with band names followed by letters, a code. *B-G SA*. Song title, maybe. She filed away the blizzard of data as Storm watched her with a puzzled look.

"Audra figured all this out. This is her system. One song per tape, all cued up. When it finishes just turn it it over and it's ready to go again."

"Professional."

"That's her. She showed me how to do things I never thought I could do. My life would be so different without her."

Sid rushed up.

"How do I look?"

"Great!" Gabrielle said. "Your Honor."

"You look like my crazy brother."

"Then everything's perfect. Music?"

Storm slid the heavy tray back.

"All cued up, Your Honor."

"Well done, Audio Engineer. Ah, good choice."

Sid flipped a hidden switch and red and blue and gold spotlights lit up the rotating mirror ball. The dancers cheered and clapped. People were five deep along the walls.

Gabrielle saw the first tape was labeled *B-G SBD*.

"Normally we would build up to this," Storm said. She put the tape into the player. She nodded and there was a click. "Hit it."

Sid produced a microphone from an inside pocket. There was a short wire antenna. The crowd cheered and began swaying. The sound of breaking glass from the kitchen filled in the background.

Gabrielle felt a tug on her sleeve. Catherine pulled her back into the shadows by the hutch.

"Don't you think this is exciting?"

"I had no idea it would be like this!"

"Bigger then high school, huh?"

"Oh, I never went."

"Never? This is your very first dance?" Catherine looked around the jammed raucous living room. "Pretty crazy introduction."

Clementine squeezed between two students in matching polyester tuxedos. One guy tried to look down her blouse. Clementine's face was strained.

"There you are. You're Audra's friend, right? You have to do something. There's blood all over the kitchen floor and the toilet is completely stopped up. They're using the sink. Boys." She covered her mouth at the word. "Boys are picking girls up and holding them over the sink so they can pee."

"What great guys!" Catherine said.

"*No.*" Her voice was anguished. "You have to do something."

"Thank you, Clementine. I will," Gabrielle said.

"You will." She sniffled. "You're the adult, I can tell. Also, the police have blocked the street."

"All according to plan, my Clemmie," Catherine said.

Clementine sniffled again, brow knotted, and crab-walked away along the wall.

Gabrielle scanned the loud room. "That wasn't part of the plan," she said. Audra was standing at the kitchen door.

"It sure wasn't. Who are we missing?"

"Most of them."

"Shit."

Sid cleared his throat and the speakers popped.

"Ladies and gentlemen. Dance fans. Music fans. Sports fans, and *Star Trek* fans."

In the back someone cheered.

"Welcome to Disco's Last Blast. Always a great pleasure to once again find myself on California's beautiful central coast. The rolling hills in the clean air, the ocean, the beaches, and the lovely town filled with fewer Black people per square mile than Provo, Utah."

Audra started laughing. Many people in the crowd said, "Aww."

A guy in an expensive looking silver suit stepped up and patted Sid on the back.

"You Honor, what can we do to help?" he said loudly.

"It's very simple, young man. It's very simple."

There was a click and the hiss of a tape beginning.

"All you have to do is." Bee Gees began pulsing from the speakers. "*Start dancing.*"

The crowd let out a whoop and arms reached into the air to the beat. Elbows jostled, glittering platform shoes swung out and pivoted. The center of the super-parlor was full of dancing couples. They found their space and grinned at each other. A young woman in a red velvet halter top snapped her head from side to side and her short black hair spun out in a tight fan.

Gabrielle could feel the floor dip almost like the deck of a boat. The hutch rocked and the top bumped into the wall.

She thought a silent command: no one notice me. I am a wall flower. I do not belong here. It does look like fun, though.

She backed up further and dodged a satin-clad arm and solid chain bracelet. Her hand caught something and there was a giggle.

"Oh, hi."

Gabrielle slumped against the wainscoting.

"Hey, Susan," she said.

"You don't wanna dance?" Pretty Susan's eyes were not tracking together. The vodka bottle was down by a quarter. "I'll dance with you. Girls can dance with girls all they want. No one will care. Girls can get away with anything."

"Can't dance. See?" Gabrielle lifted her right jumpsuit's leg.

"Oh. That looks fake."

"No, it's real."

"Does it hurt?"

"It's pretty sore. Ow." Gabrielle let the blue silk drop. She saw that Sid was watching the dancers carefully, even critically. He wants to keep the momentum going, she surmised. So it's all a kind of performance. The dancers are his performers. There's so much about everything I don't know.

Through a brief gap in the twirling bodies she saw the guy in the silver suit shake Sid's hand. They laughed.

So that was a set-up, she thought. Everything could be an act and you have to go along with it. You have to. So when it's me doing the acting. Pretty Susan took a swig of the vodka and held up the bottle.

Gabrielle sighed. "Thanks." She sloshed the vodka between her lips with her tongue tightly pressed to them. Hardly any got in. She got a big thumbs up from a couple dancing close to her. As usual it tasted like electrical contact cleaner. She thought of something and gave the bottle back.

The Bee Gees song ended and she used the relative quiet to ask, "Where is everybody? I saw Susan and Debbie."

The next song started and the dancers cheered the opening notes which turned into a singer making an exaggerated laughing growl. Sid switched on the his microphone.

"So I noticed this big school you have here, what's it called, tech something. Tech? So I thought a little *Love Machine* might be the ticket"

More cheering followed by even more dancers shoving their way into the parlor. Beside the front door, Gabrielle glimpsed a guy in a pink jacket lying face down. A girl in a fluorescent blue skirt and shoes with clear plastic heels danced directly over his head. The heels gouged the floor an inch from his ear. Gabrielle saw that the heels were full of water. And was that a goldfish?

"Susan might not be coming," Pretty Susan said.

"Susan?"

"Holly told her to watch the house."

"Watch the house." Gabrielle's heart sank.

"Yeah, who knows why. Holly is so hung up on that. I'm getting tired of her. No one's gonna mess with the house."

"And Susan really wanted to come," Gabrielle said thinking, we're screwed.

"If she can sneak in without Holly seeing her everything will be fine. One thing I've noticed about Holly over the years." She took another big gulp of the vodka.

Gabrielle waited a moment. A frosh-looking girl in green satin danced by making robotic arm movements. She's dancing alone, Gabrielle thought. I wish I could do that. Like Audra that time.

Gabrielle felt her whole body flush. She shook her head. This whole thing is a disaster. I cannot keep up. Maintain focus.

"What?" she said.

"What?"

"What about Holly?"

"What about her?"

"You said you noticed something about her."

'Oh. She's an asshole."

A tall guy in a John Deere hat elbowed through the mass of dancers and said, "Care to dance?"

Gabrielle, over the music, shrugged and said, "Sorry. Can't." She showed the Ace bandage.

"Oh, that sucks!"

"I know I just watch."

"Well aww right," he said and tipped his hat. He walked back along the wall towards the kitchen.

"Bet Audra's in the kitchen," Gabrielle said. "Have to tell her."

"What?" Pretty Susan said. "And she only pays attention to herself. It's

like other people aren't real to her. If she wants something from you she'll
be super nice until she gets what she wants and then, boom, you don't exist
anymore. You want my advice?"

"Sure." About eight ounces of vodka and Pretty Susan's almost coherent,
Gabrielle thought. Must take advantage of this somehow.

"Bang her and dump her. Trust me. It's the only way to get her goat."

"Susan, I don't know about that. I mean, yeah."

"Those shoulders."

"Uh huh." And those thighs. "Where is L right now?"

"L.A."

The robot song ended. Gabrielle decided to risk it.

"What's the real reason she hates M so much?"

Pretty Susan studied the vodka bottle. Gabrielle strained to hear her.

"Something happened a long time ago. I always wondered how I
would've reacted."

"Reacted to what?"

"Well, there was a third party."

"You mean T?"

"No not him. God. That poor guy. He was cute, though, so I kind of."

"Susan." Gabrielle shook her head. "So someone…"

Sid began announcing the next song and the dancers applauded as he
spoke.

"Isn't that funny," Pretty Susan said. "They're all clapping at themselves
for dancing so wonderfully." Another mouthful. "And then."

Pretty Susan's eyes went out of sync again.

"And then?" Gabrielle said.

"What? You didn't know any of this, did you? Don't feel bad. None of
you did, of this I'm certain." She closed her eyes and her forehead furrowed.
"You'd be surprised what I know about you. What does tofu taste like,
anyway? I'm gonna puke."

Gabrielle backed away, heart pounding. They heard everything, she
thought. Cut the circuit in the wine cellar. It's too late but cut it. She tried to
think as *I Love The Nightlife* started up.

But this. This is safe. It has to be. We knew about the microphone.
Except, she thought with a surge of panic, they have radio sound systems in
those robes. They have the ability. There could be transmitters all over the
house. Rushel, Samantha, and Gislaine, they could be walking into a trap.

"This is completely out of control."

She went along the wall and passed the rocking hutch as dancers
screamed behind her and a loud male voice shouted "Ew!" She skirted past
Storm and Sid and sidestepped the speaker stands. The kitchen door opened
a crack and a tall unsmiling man with long gray hair peeked out at the line
of dancers. The line stretched across the width of the parlor and out the
front door.

"Yeah?" he said to the first in line, a student in a purple frock and bright red fez.

"Yuh, could I have like two margaritas?"

"We got whiskey. That okay?"

"Yuh."

The man closed the door and ten seconds later reappeared with two plastic cups brimming with a deep amber fluid. Oh, that's a lot, Gabrielle thought, that's way too...

"Thanks." The student's eyes lit up.

"Put the cups in a trash can. Next."

Right behind her, Gabrielle heard Sid's amplified laughter as the song ended. The dancers once again applauded.

"Ladies and gentlemen, our special event of the evening has arrived."

More cheering. The line to the kitchen door shifted feet impatiently.

"Yeah?"

"Three martinis and make one of them extra dirty," said a middle-aged man in tight blue sweater with a crocodile logo.

"We got whiskey. That okay?"

The man sighed.

"That's all we got."

"Very well."

"I'll give you extra." The Gray Man closed the door and Gabrielle counted fifteen before it opened again. He had three large plastic cups of whiskey and carefully transferred them to the man's grasping hands. "Here ya go. Put the cups in a trash can."

"Thanks. And here."

He had a business card between his fingers.

"Jim's Properties. Right down the street. If you ever contemplate selling."

"'Preciate it." He took the card and stuffed it in a pocket. "I'll be in touch. Next. Yeah?"

A woman in a slim gray jacket with padded shoulders stepped up. Her black hair was cut in severe straight bangs that covered her eyebrows and she clutched a black leather purse.

"Shot of whiskey, neat," she said.

"All right." He didn't blink. Again the kitchen door closed and this time wait was longer. The man stuck his head out.

"No more whiskey. Tequila okay?"

"How can you be out?"

"Drank it all."

"Huh. Well, tequila than."

"All right. Here."

He handed her a large cup half full of tequila.

"That's too much."

"What?"

"I only wanted a shot. This is more like ten."

"Yeah. Put the cup in a trash can. Next."

The woman turned to Gabrielle while a mustached guy in a pink tux, a girlfriend on each arm, put in his order. More tequila.

"Hi," the woman said. Her eyes focused on the nose ring. "Could you help me? I haven't quite descended into the depths of alcoholism yet. Would you like some of this? I'd hate to throw it out."

Gabrielle said, "Sure," and then to the Gray Man said, "Is Audra in there?"

"Who?"

Gabrielle held out her hand. So tall. She wiggled her fingers.

He smiled. "Oh sure. Hang on." The kitchen door closed.

Gabrielle gripped the slippery plastic cup as it was pressed into her hands. She took a tiny sip.

"Hm Differential roller bearing cleaner."

"What? Thanks. Have more. My name's Alice."

She stuck her hand out, fingers hanging down limply.

What does she want me to do, kiss her hand? Gabrielle thought. She coughed and a drop of tequila escaped her lips.

"I'm Gabrielle."

She gripped Alice's fingers. She didn't know how else to do it.

"So nice to meet you, Gabrielle. I'm so sorry."

She daubed Gabrielle's chin with a tissue from her purse.

Someone cleared their throat loudly enough to be heard over *Ladies Night*. Audra took Gabrielle arm as she gave the cup back.

"Sorry, business in the kitchen."

Alice turned quickly away and pretended to brush the hair from her eyes.

"Don't look down," Audra said as the Gray Man opened the door for them. Gabrielle looked down.

The floor was covered with a smear of blood which stretched from the avocado green fridge to the chipped porcelain sink piled high with empty liquor bottles. There was a blood soaked wad of clothing in the corner. She saw blood on the ceiling, a long scarlet spray. She saw thirty-nine unopened liquor bottles on the counter. And two cardboard boxes with a vodka label. All but two of the Aggies had departed. One guy was lining up plastic cups and one was sloshing tequila into them from a bulky rectangular bottle. The Gray Man turned his head.

"Four."

The Aggies handed him four full cups. Four new cups were set out.

There were people visible through the back door window, just outside. The back yard was full of disco-clad partiers. And there was another group, all wearing black leather jackets, just out of the light. A face there tracked her as she peered and Gabrielle felt a chill.

"Pretty fun, huh? He'll be fine. Nicked an artery. Guy named Thomas. Landscape Architecture."

"Oh no, poor Thomas!" Gabrielle felt like laughing and she covered her mouth.

"You'd think I'd be used to this." Audra pointed at the blood. "Right?"

"I have to tell you. It's bad news. It's Susan."

"Not now." Audra glanced at the back door. There was a face in the window.

"Susan, out there, gets almost understandable when she's..."

Audra grabbed both of her arms and turned her away from the back door.

"And *that's* how I knew it couldn't really be a flying raccoon!" she said loudly. "Isn't that completely in*sane*? Oh, no way! What a surprise! Where did *you* come from?"

Gabrielle saw New Susan stepping through the back door. She was smiling conspiratorially and her eyes were bloodshot.

"Audra! Gabrielle! I parked on the next street had to climb over four fences. There was this dog! See?"

New Susan was wearing a gold foil miniskirt and a black silk leotard top under a short white disco jacket. Her blonde hair tumbled over her shoulders and sparkled in the dull kitchen light. She pointed at her right calf. There was a welt oozing blood onto her Reeboks. She giggled and sneezed.

"As long as she doesn't see me, I'm cool. There are really weird people in the back yard. Really, really weird."

She sneezed again.

"Thai stick. Oh my God!"

"Pretty high, huh?" Audra said.

"I am so high. I am so incredibly high. I mean I can see the whole west coast. Is she here? Have you seen her? Her car's parked at the corner."

"It is?" Audra looked at Gabrielle.

"Oh my God I love Thelma Houston!"

She raised her hands over her head and began swaying her hips. She snapped her fingers to the beat. Gabrielle thought the guy with the tequila bottle was going to start drooling.

Audra said softly, "What did you want to tell me?"

"Doesn't matter. I thought we were in trouble."

"Well, she's still not here."

"Her car's here."

"I need to actually see her."

"I just thought of something else. Where's Disco?"

Audra looked surprised. "Yeah."

"Upstairs maybe?"

"Doing his hair."

As Gabrielle laughed, Audra's smile faded.

"Who was that out there?"

"Oh. No one."

"Uh huh. What were you doing?"

"I just. I don't know."

"Are you trying to be the world's easiest pickup? Here, drink this quart of tequila while I feel around for your zipper."

"I was just being nice."

"There is no nice. You can't be nice. Be like Rushel. She is your teacher. You are not nice. You are a terrifying guided missile of sexuality and whomever you target will be utterly destroyed by your orgasmic power."

"I don't feel sexy." Gabrielle swallowed. Mouth sure is dry, she thought.

"You are very sexy."

"All right." She flipped her hair back. "I am a sex missile."

"In the males you inspire fearful lust. In the females, lustful fear. And lust. Some of the females."

"What's the percentage?"

"Higher than you think."

As they both laughed again, New Susan's hand went right and her elbow knocked over a large clear bottle. It collided with a row of empties and they dominoed onto the floor. The clatter made Gabrielle's ears ring.

"Oh my God, I'm sorry!"

"That's all right, hon," Cups said.

Bottles continued to stare at her legs, a silly grin on his face.

"Thanks, you're really nice."

"Nah. Here, have a drink."

"Okay!" New Susan gulped a half cup of vodka.

Gabrielle heard Sid's mic click on. She peeked out the kitchen door. The couples were clearing the center of the parlor. Clementine walked by and stood behind Sid. She had a manila folder. Storm faded out the song. *Don't Leave Me This Way.*

"Oh, I know what this is," Gabrielle said.

"Ladies and gentlemen. Disco fans, well done."

The room applauded.

"What a momentous evening we have planned for you." He lifted the gavel over his head. "You are rarin' to go, all warmed up. The dance contest starts *now.*"

As the gavel hit the podium the crowd cheered. Outside a car horn blared and Gabrielle saw flashing lights shining on the living room window frame, red and amber. She slipped away from the kitchen door and went past the line of people waiting for booze and went out onto the porch.

The flashing lights were on a tow truck at the bottom of the hill. The street was now clear of cars. No sign of police cars. In the deep mist, the dining room table was being loaded onto the back of an ancient pickup by two guys with long dirty hair. A third guy carried two of the dining chairs to another old truck. All the overflow dancers seemed to have gone to the back yard. Where they'd have access to alcohol, she thought, and could pee in the bushes.

Inside, Sid announced the prizes.

"The runners up, and there will be two of them, two, will each receive a pair of matching Shake-It shirts in metallic silk."

Gabrielle squinted. What it shirts?

The dancers applauded as Storm held up a shirt that looked like stitched together strands of Christmas tree tinsel.

Gabrielle had the urge to scratch her armpits.

"Second place. Oh, by the way, this is my new assistant, Clementine, ladies and gentlemen."

Clementine opened the folder and took out a dark green slip of paper. She held up the money.

"Fifty dollars! And first place."

Clementine held up a crisp bill. The dancers close enough to see all said, "Whoa!"

"One hundred dollars in cold hard cash. An actual one hundred dollar bill will be awarded to the first place couple."

The room erupted in applause again.

Gabrielle heard the sound of breaking glass from the kitchen again and everyone laughed. There was a yell and slamming door.

"Isn't that fantastic?" Sid continued. "Now just for a moment let's get technical here on the high-tech central coast. We have something *amazing* to show you. An absolutely ground breaking system. I believe I will let the genius inventor describe it. And I'm not calling her that just because she's my sister. Ladies and gentlemen, my I introduce, Storm!"

There was a chorus of cheers and whistles.

"Thank you," Storm said as Sid gave her the mic. The parlor became totally silent. "In our dance contest, *you* are the judges. Your applause and cheers will determine the winner. We wanted to be as objective as possible and I created a system to do just that. I call it."

She pulled a string and the sheet fell from the tall thin frame. There were rows of plastic button extending up four feet. Six per horizontal row, forty rows, two hundred forty. Gabrielle couldn't help it. And what looked like a numerical display at the top.

The crowd made a collective, "Ahh!"

"The Digital Acoustic Response Analyzer."

Gabrielle said, "Wow," as the dancers applauded and rows of buttons lit up, am ascending ladder flickering lights, green at the bottom, then amber. As the applause continued and the rows came one in sequence the display on top came to life. It read *2.0* in sharp red dots. As the applause subsided, the rows went off but the display retained its reading.

"It will keep showing the score until I reset it." Storm looked at the number. "Two point zero? Really? Do you have any idea how much work it was to make this thing?"

"Come on, ladies and gentlemen!" Sid boomed and the bars shot up almost half way. *4.8.* The crowd laughed and the bars flickered up and down with each wave of sound. Sid took the mic back.

"As you can see, my sister is a tough grader. Had anyone ever gotten a perfect ten?"

"I don't think so."

"Well perhaps tonight will be different. I just feel it. I can feel the energy about to be *unleashed.*"

Storm pushed a button and the score went to *0.0.*

"Are we ready, Engineer?"

"Ready."

"Let the contest *begin.*" He gave the podium a knock with the gavel. "One hundred dollars first place. Fifty dollars second place. Genuine Shake-It shirts for two runners up. Who wants to go first? Just come on up and tell me your names and the song, whatever you want, we have everything. We have all songs. Don't we?"

"We do," Storm said.

"All right! Step right up."

No one moved under the swirling spots of light from the mirror ball.

Gabrielle nodded to herself. Can't blame them, she thought, now this acoustic level display. Very cool. I'll bet she's using...

She felt a hand on her shoulder.

It was Elliot. He had a nearly empty cup of something clear. And, Gabrielle saw, he was clean shaven. She remembered the last time he had taken such drastic action. It was a major stress indicator. It had been finals week two quarters back. He had to write a two page research paper for his kite flying class and stayed up two nights in a row. At the time she remembered thinking that was hysterically funny. She shook her head.

"I had no idea you were going to be here," he said. He rocked on his heels. "I'm really glad."

Gabriele first confused thought was, Elliot likes disco? Also, am I like this when I'm drunk? Oh dear.

There was applause from the end of the room as a couple made their way to the center of the dance area. Gabrielle glanced at them. Graduate students, office-oriented majors. They spoke to Sid and *Shake Your Groove Thing* began to play. The couple danced rather slowly, she thought. The guy, in a black tux, carefully twirled his partner, a young woman in a blue dress. The dress did not have the usual slits up the side and she had to move her feet in tiny fast steps. And Gabrielle didn't think they were keeping up with the music at all.

Elliot took a sharp breath.

"I just wanted to say it's been great having you as a roommate. Housemate."

Gabrielle, alarmed, said, "Elliot, are you."

The crowd applauded .

"Cindy and Mike, ladies and gentlemen," Sid announced. One person cheered and the acoustic display reached *2.9* and fell back.

"All right, wonderful. Thank you, Cindy and Mike, for being the first and therefore the bravest. Now, who wants to be next?"

Elliot backed away. His eyes went down.

"Elliot, wait. What in the world is going on in our house? Are you moving? Where's Mrs. Rosenberg?"

He looked at his cup.

"Everything's changing," he said.

Elliot slipped into the crowd without looking back.

The second couple began dancing to *Funkytown*. The guy got his platform shoe caught on the girl's high heel and fell flat on his back. In the uproar, Gabrielle lost track of her longtime housemate. The kitchen, she thought, he's sneaking out the back. He can't just leave.

As the acoustic display hit *4.4* and Sid said, "Doris and Drew, ladies and gentlemen!" Gabrielle elbowed her way to the back wall and went towards the kitchen. Hands waved in her face to the beat of *More More More* and someone grabbed her arm. She pulled away sharply and some guy said nasally "Hey come on!" He smelled like piss.

From the kitchen door the line stretched to the far end of the parlor and doubled back. They all glared at her.

"I have to get in."

Gray Man gave a brimming cup of something brown to a girl with silver hair and a pink heart drawn on her cheek. He opened the door.

Gabrielle sidestepped in. She tossed her hair at the hostile onlookers.

Audra was still standing next to the big black telephone in the relative quiet. She had a cup of something amber in her hand. Elliot was nowhere to be seen. It was Cups and Bottles and Gray Man. And New Susan dancing by herself in the corner.

He's gone, she thought. He was like a ghost who materialized just long enough to say goodbye.

The dancers cheered the next contestants.

"Jocelyn and Marcia and Jason," Sid announced.

Audra shook her head. "Kids these days."

"You're drinking?"

"Just a little."

"Don't drink."

"I was really nervous, okay?"

"This works or it doesn't work."

"How can you be so calm about it?"

"In engineering you learn exactly how mistakes are made. You get to be an expert in all the ways you can screw up. And everyone screws up. It's a major learning mechanism. It's really what school is for because in the real world."

"There's no room for failure."

"No, there isn't."

"Well then I can plainly see an advantage the legal profession has over engineering. If your flying saucer won't fly it's super obvious there's been a failure. But if your class action lawsuit against the manufacturers of flying saucers gets thrown out you simply claim miscarriage of justice and refile. Keep the ball in the air. It's kind of like a baseball game with endless innings. Give me enough time and I can change reality. Then I win."

Outside, the applause was loud.

"Five point four, Ladies and gentlemen!"

Gabrielle turned sharply.

"You change reality?"

"Legal reality," Audra said. "What's he doing?"

"Real reality versus legal reality."

"If you believe it, it's real."

"So belief versus actual knowledge."

"You've been talking to Samantha. She knows. Most people just go with belief. It's less work."

There was a sudden surge of applause and cheering.

New Susan jumped up and down.

"Oh my God, this is so exciting! Look, look!"

Audra laughed. "Here we go." She looked at the telephone.

Gabrielle peeked out the door with New Susan.

Sid was rummaging through the cassette organizer. Storm was standing back, shaking her head. The dancers had stopped and some applauded. The students closest to her had sweaty faces and damp hair. It was a guy in a white business shirt and black waiter's vest and his partner, robot-dancing girl, both breathing heavily. There was a drop of perspiration on the end of her nose and she blew it off. They both laughed.

Sid slammed a tape into the player.

She thought Sid looked more than nervous. He looked frantic. Storm looked exasperated.

More cheers from the front yard. Loud steps on the porch. Gabrielle held her breath.

"Wow," New Susan said. "I'll just peek under your arm."

"Okay," Gabrielle said.

The front door sprang open and whacked against the wall. A shocked silence fell over the room. Two women in black leather jackets walked in, side by side. Their black boots were authoritative on the hardwood. It was Patricia and Debbie. Their hair was slicked back and both wore heavy eyeliner. They scanned the room, scowling, then nodded to each other. They both took two steps in leaving just enough room for a third person to squeeze through. It was Tall Susan in a gray robe. Gabrielle could see her short black hair under the familiar hood. Tall Susan held up a cut-glass decanter with a bulb pump began to spray perfume into the room. Dancers nearby waved away the strong scent of *Subterfuge*. A guy with a full cup sneezed and Patricia elbowed him. Tequila splashed onto the wall.

Gabrielle said back into the kitchen, "You have to see this!"

"Oh, I know," Audra said.

A song began to play.

"*Heaven Must be Missing an Angel*, ladies and gentlemen," Sid announced.

As Audra laughed loudly, a shadow fell across the threshold.

Then Holly was standing there, backlit by the bright red floodlight turning fire orange. She placed her left foot inside, poised and angled. She was wearing a form-fitting halter top of gold streamers which barely concealed her body. Her hair was now a dark blonde with bleached stripes. Gabrielle thought it looked longer than before. Her left shoe sparkled. There was a flashing light in the heel, a light bulb or tiny xenon flash. It flashed again. The crowd gasped.

Holly, unsmiling, stepped through the doorway. The dress reflected the moving lights flamboyantly. Her gaze found Sid, frozen behind the podium. Both her heels flashed as she walked towards him. Each flash was greeted with applause.

Gabrielle, focused on Holly, started as New Susan pulled away from her side with a gulping sound. There were new voices in the kitchen behind her.

Holly smiled at Sid. He smiled grimly back and the music volume faded. Everyone in the room watched, dots of lights sweeping over their faces.

"Hi, Sid. Good to see you again."

Sid had a blank look. Storm kicked his feet.

"Right," Sid said. "Holly."

"I'm not too late for the dance contest, am I?" she said slowly, no longer smiling. She stared at Storm who smiled mildly back.

"No, not at all. Absolutely not."

"Good. I would be upset otherwise."

"No need to be upset. No need at all."

"Have you played it yet?"

"No, ma'am."

"You won't play it until I say so, right?"

"No, ma'am."

Gabrielle heard Audra say, "Uh." She turned and froze.

In the kitchen there was a man right behind her. His leering face was a few inches from hers. His head was shaved off except for a row of hair from his forehead to his collar. What's the word for that? Hair like that? The Mohawk was tinted blue and razor blades were dangling from his ears. The man grinned. His teeth had been filed to sharp points. His eyes were bright yellow.

There was a girl next to him in a matching leather jacket. Her head had been neatly shaved, clean and shiny, on one side. The other side had luxurious curly black locks reaching to her navel. Fine silver chains in a spider web configuration hung from one ear. One eyebrow was missing. She had on tarnished wire glass frames, no lenses. Her expression was blank with boredom.

"Pardon me," the man said, "but we are a wandering band of disco fans. Could you tell me where I might find the open bar of song and legend? My friends and I have come a long way and we are very very thirsty. We were wondering if we could get a drink before participating in the contest."

He continued to grin.

"Did I startle you, Miss?"

"Why no," Gabrielle said. "The bar is right behind you."

"Thank you so much. My name is Slake and this is my partner, Slash."

"Nice meeting you. I'm Persephone."

Slake's grin increased. "*Diamond.* Wonderful to meet you. Well, we're off for a drink, then. Won't you join us?"

This close, Gabrielle could see the points of his teeth were merely cleverly painted on. And contact lenses. She shuddered.

"Don't mind if I do."

Slake snapped his fingers and there were loud footsteps on the back porch. Heavy boots, black leather jackets. Black pants. Levi's with the tags ripped off. The first guy had a face painted white with stripes. Then a totally bald young woman. No eyebrows at all. Her head had writing on the side. *Insert Tongue Here*, with an arrow pointing to her ear. There was a red Mohawk and a woman with dead white hair greased into points. Chains hung from pockets.

Gabrielle counted ten of them. Students? She couldn't tell. One guy was obviously middle-aged. There was something weirdly familiar about him.

In the crowded kitchen, the Aggie she thought of as Cups said, "You look like about as much of a disco fan as I am." The other Aggies laughed.

"Oh you do me an injustice, mate," Slake said. "I'm a philosophy major. Dancing is all I ever think about. The music speaks to my soul."

"Is that right?"

"I become free. And most of all."

Slash walked around from the counter with ten pint bottles of vodka in her arms.

"Most of all, the feel of her hand in mine."

Slash tsk'd and handed the bottles out.

"What happened to your teeth?"

"Born that way."

"Whoa."

Audra cleared her throat.

"They answered."

"Urp." New Susan, back pressed as hard as possible against the refrigerator, covered her mouth.

Gabrielle said, "The Porch."

"Gonna puke," New Susan said. She lunged for the kitchen door and her Reeboks slipped on the blood and she fell face forward. Her head slammed the door open. Gabrielle saw a gold dress.

Holly sneered. Her lips curled when she saw the punks.

"This your idea of a joke, Goddess?"

"No, sorry." Don't look down, she thought. Do not look down.

"Yes, it was a joke," Audra said.

Holly's expression softened.

"Why don't you just calm down, Holly. You're here to have fun, right?"

Holly's gaze flickered away from Audra.

"She's right. I'm sorry, Gabrielle," Holly said.

Stunned, Gabrielle said, "Okay." Holly's eyes were bloodshot.

New Susan lifted her head and made a loud hiccup. Then she vomited vodka and tequila onto Holly's left shoe. There was a snapping sound and a blue spark. A stream of smoke issued from between Holly's toes.

"Oh *yeah.*" It was Slash. She giggled.

Holly's half smile turned to puzzlement.

"Oh, you poor thing," she said. "Why don't –"

Her eyes widened.

"You! Susan! Susan get up!"

New Susan coughed.

"Susan, you can't be here. Get back to the house right now. Where did you park?"

New Susan moaned and tried to stand. Her knee slipped in the bloody vomit.

"I just wanted to dance, Holly. *Guy,* can't I even have one dance?"

"Someone always has to watch the house. You know that. You're being very irresponsible. Stand up."

Holly lifted New Susan easily by the armpits. Slake gasped, Slash elbowed him.

"Fine, look Susan, we're going back right now. You can't possibly drive. My car is right out front. Come on."

In the parlor, another couple was talking to Sid. Storm hit reset and the display went to *0.0.*

Gabrielle saw Audra staring at the phone. She had never seen her panicked before. Her stomach lurched.

"Oh no," Audra whispered.

Gabrielle jumped over the spreading puddle of vomit and out of the kitchen.

Holly and New Susan were already at the front door. The other dancers backed away from them.

"Sid," Holly called back. "I'll be back in one minute." She smiled coldly at him. "You got that?"

Sid waved. "Don't worry." The next contestants were perusing the cassette organizer.

Gabrielle ran across the empty dance floor with an idea partially formed in her mind. She couldn't feel her feet. Her heart began slamming against her ribs. All the dancers stared at her

What am I doing, she thought. I don't know how. I don't know how to dance. I can't dance.

She slid to a stop in front of Sid.

"I'm next," she said. "I'm the next contestant."

Holly and New Susan went out the door.

We've already lost, Gabrielle thought, it's too late.

"Please, please, I'm next."

"Well," Sid said. "Just you? I don't know."

Gabrielle went to the cassette organizer. With both hands she shoved the male contestant away.

"Whoa, not so fast, beautiful!"

First row, second to front, she remembered, the first music group. She pinched out the tape and went to the tape deck. Sid had not moved. She hit the button and the player opened and she dropped the cassette in. The Dymo label on the edge read *ABBA DANCING QUEEN*. She snapped the door shut.

He had seen the title.

"No," Sid said, "no way. I can't."

"Please, Sid, hurry."

Gabrielle ran to the center of the dance floor. Her ears popped. Her hands tingled. Her vision and grew dim around the edges. Every head turned towards her. Audra appeared at the kitchen door.

Sid saw Audra. They locked eyes. Audra nodded.

"*Damn* it." Sid punched play.

In the hummingbird moment between two heartbeats, Gabrielle tried to remember, have I even heard this song before? Without volition, a data structure assembled itself in her mind, as towering and complex as the structure for Human Sexuality. She glimpsed categories and topics.

Storytelling: Beginning/Induction.

Desire/Conflict. Mystery/Search. Loss/Recovery. Resolution/Ending.

Movement: Emotion. Acting: Happy when sad. The Beat as Character.

Only vaguely aware everyone in the room was staring at her, she thought, So there's a way to figure it out. I could generate a—

Music blasted from the speakers at full volume. Piano, very fast, thumb running down the keys. It blanked out all other sound.

Or I could, she thought, feeling buoyant and energized, I could just move to the music. Some. How.

She spun on her heels.

That was *late.* You're already behind. Get *on* it. Also, definitely never heard this song before. About a girl who goes dancing Friday night. She knows she's the best, the object of desire.

Gabrielle made exaggerated arm movements and remembered to smile. Most of the surrounding faces smiled back.

She made another spin then a gesture she thought of as scolding or mocking all the while moving her legs and hips to the beat. Robot Girl had made this move. That made it okay. The music mellowed a bit. There was a line about being seventeen and she thought, I was a freshman here then.

She knew she had no hope of correlating the dance moves with the story of the song but figured no one would notice. Having the music so loud helped and so did the swirling lights. It was almost a protective feeling. A shield. She made a chugging motion and turned full circle and when she was facing a terrified looking Sid, a fist hit her between the shoulder blades. Her glasses slid to the end of her nose.

Hands grasped her right arm painfully and yanked hard. Gabrielle came face to face with Holly.

"You again! God, I *hate* you! You ruin everything! This is *my* song!"

Holly's voice came out in a hiss. Her eyes were red and full of tears. The song continued amid shouts. A woman laughed hysterically.

Gabrielle's instantaneous thought, now I'm inside *her* defenses.

She slipped her left hand around Holly's waist, gripped the gold streamers, and pulled her close. Holly gasped angrily and released her powerful hold. Gabrielle's back throbbed. With her now free sore right arm she pointed straight up, made what she hoped was exaggerated hip moves to a change in the music and tried to get Holly to turn. Holly stood still, rigid, arms at her sides. Her eyes remained fixed and her face was wet.

Gabriele calculated the song was a third done just past. She leaned back as the music tempo slowed and let both hands run down Holly's forearms. She took both of her hands in her's. There was loud whistling and laughter.

Gabrielle anticipated a burst of music and tried a move she had seen several of the young women attempt. It was tricky. She let go of Holly's left hand and spun herself counterclockwise holding her right hand in the center of her chest inducing a one arm hug.

Holly hissed in her ear, "*No.*"

Gabrielle turned to face her. She stood on tip toe and whispered in Holly's ear, "You are an object of desire."

Holly's eyes widened. She seemed to smile.

Gabrielle gasped as Holly took her left hand. She did the spin-hug move again and this time Holly pulled her painfully tight.

"You know nothing about me and you never will," she said. "No one will."

Gabrielle was spun out and she let her free arm point up as Holly roughly yanked her back in and stuck her left leg out. Gabrielle was turned backwards and tripped. Holly caught her as she dipped. There were loud cheers and over the music the sound of a car horn outside. Then continued cheering and applause.

Gabrielle felt Holly's already iron grip tighten as the cheers grew louder. That's what she loves, a part of her mind relayed while simultaneously another part said, look out!

Holly effortlessly pulled her upright and Gabrielle stood there under the mirror ball for two dizzy heartbeats. The she remembered to keep moving and began doing the fist-shoulder maneuver, as she thought of it, and Holly did the same. Holly now looked more puzzled than angry and they danced like that, face to face, until the music changed again.

Final third, Gabrielle thought. Interesting that the song's main theme was about not being nice. Dip! Do the dip! The song built to a conclusion.

She put her right foot as forward as she could and reached out with her left hand. Holly pulled back then leaned into it, rolling her eyes. Gabrielle placed her left hand in the small of Holly's back and turned herself to the left. Holly let herself be turned around, smiling crookedly, and let her arms hang down. There was a chorus of "Whoa!"

Holly dipped.

Gabrielle gasped and strained her entire body. She staggered and her left knee buckled and she tried to counterbalance by leaning back. Holly was now horizontal. Her taut cheek twitched.

"Wow," Holly said. "You suck."

Gabrielle dropped her on the floor.

Someone laughed then choked it off.

Holly grinned in astonishment.

Sid's mic clicked on.

"Holly and Gabrielle, ladies and gentlemen!"

There was an embarrassed pause and then the room exploded onto cheers and whistles. Holly quickly got to her feet and waved, turned full circle.

Gabrielle saw the acoustic display hit *8.0.* Holly grabbed her arm and lifted it up like a prizefighter. *8.6.*

Gabrielle twisted her wrist away.

"The high score of the night, everybody! Good job, Holly and Gabrielle! Now we're cooking!" Sid said to raucous laughter. "Who will be the next talented contestants?"

Holly stood in the center of the dance floor, a figure of animated sparling gold, and continued to smile at the crowd. Glad to be ignored,

Gabrielle pushed her glasses up and slipped sideways towards the kitchen. She didn't see Audra or Catherine. The front door of the house still hung open. She wanted to see outside – was New Susan still on the porch – when excited applause again ran through the dancers. Someone let out a loud drunken "Whoa!" A female voice yelled, "All right!" There were clumping footsteps on the grand staircase.

Sid and Storm turned to look.

Gabrielle, exhausted and sweaty, stood amidst the milling dancers and rubbed her temples.

Sheesh, now what?

Disco was coming down the stairs. White jacket and wide, sharply pointed lapels, white vest, contrasting black unbuttoned shirt, tight white pants with flared cuffs and brown leather shoes with extended heels. His blonde hair bounced on his shoulders with each step. He paused at the bottom.

A woman standing beside her said, "Oh!" There was more applause with an undercurrent of female voices. The crowd parted before him creating a path to the dance floor.

Holly slowly turned, hands on hips. Disco locked eyes with her. They stepped towards each other. Holly shook out her hair. Disco took a slip of paper from his vest pocket and gave it to Sid.

Sid nodded and gave the note a thumbs up.

Disco stepped close to Holly and held out his hand, palm up. Holly waited two beats then with careful deliberation put her hand on top of his. Delicately, Gabrielle thought, as she watched, fascinated. The crowd fell silent under the dots of light.

Poised, hand in hand, Holly and Disco both turned their heads toward Sid, who nodded. Holly nodded. Sid pushed a button and a song began to play. There was a wave of applause.

This was a song Gabrielle remembered hearing. The music was beautiful but she didn't much like the lyrics. So I'm more than a sex object to you? *Got it.* Good for dancing, though. A different mode. Much smoother. Unchoppy. The crowd "Ahh'd" in anticipation.

Disco started with a dip and held Holly easily. Then he gracefully lifted her and they spun away from each other still clasping hands. They reeled each other in.

Gabrielle found it hard to keep track. Now I don't feel so bad, she thought. I could never be this good.

Disco seemed light on his feet, almost weightless, his movements were so fluid. And Holly was a dazzling sight as she did a pirouette back into his arms, a huge smile on her face. Then they did a multistep maneuver perfectly timed to the music. The crowd surged forward and Gabrielle found herself in the back alone.

The room of dancers applauded as Disco spun Holly and then pointed at the ceiling like that movie poster.

The front door slammed shut and this made Disco nearly lose his concentration. Holly seemed to step up her dancing to counter the distraction. As the song reached its climax Gabrielle saw Sid scowl at something.

All the punks had exited the kitchen and were standing in a line, a phalanx of black leather. The kitchen door opened and one of the Aggies peered out. Then a tall man in a black turtleneck sweater pushed through and headed for the podium. Gabrielle felt a hand on her sleeve. She turned to see a blood stained dress.

"It's all over." It was Gislaine.

Another hand grabbed her other arm.

"You all think you're so smart." It was Patricia.

Patricia's hand was slapped away. Rushel and Samantha came close on both sides.

Samantha whispered in her left ear.

"The situation has changed."

Rushel whispered in her right ear, "Sorry about your car."

Their dresses were both splashed with mud. Rushel's fingernails were broken and there was a deep cut on the back of her hand.

"It's nothing," she said.

"Look at all this," Samantha said. "Gosh, what did we miss?"

"Everything," Rushel said. "Dang."

"We'd better catch up."

"Time is of the essence."

"Good luck." Samantha extended her hand.

Rushel shook it.

"You too."

The tall man made his way along the wall to Storm, who crossed her arms and shook her head. Sid did not look happy, Gabrielle thought. The man stood beside the acoustic analyzer, pulsing with light, and frowned.

Holly did another spin-out and return with an instant repeat and there was a collective gasp from the crowd.

Gabrielle heard a giggle directly behind her and the sound of a vodka bottle being uncapped in the darkness. Then a woman turned and let out a sharp scream. Now all the people around her looked. The women were either disgusted or half smiled, the guys openly hostile. Gabrielle finally looked.

Slake and Slash were gulping their vodka. They locked eyes with each other. Slake jammed the empty in his back pocket.

"Are you ready, love?"

"Sure." Slash tossed her bottle sidehand.

Gabrielle saw it coming but it was too close to react. The bottle hit her right temple. She held on to her glasses in the sharp pain.

Slash gurgled with laughter. "Yeah, you're a genius."

It was the voice.

"Andrea."

They pushed past her and the dancers flinched in revulsion.

More Than a Woman faded.

Holly and Disco did a final dip and then bowed. The crowd seemed to take a deep breath then exploded in cheers and applause and whistles. Holly looked ecstatic, her face was shiny with sweat and tears. Disco stood, arms at his sides, and watched her.

"Let's hear it for Holly and Darren, ladies and gentlemen! All right!"

The acoustic analyzer hit *9.0* then *9.2*. The dancers began to chant "Holly, Holly!"

9.6.

A woman screamed as Slake and Slash, hand in hand, stepped onto the dance floor.

9.9. A strobe light began to flash.

Holly waved both hands and made a full circle and stopped. The cheering and clapping was choked off.

The eight remaining punks elbowed through the crowd. They all smelled like dryer sheets. In the swirling lights, the pudgy older one caught her attention again.

Oh it *can't* be, Gabrielle thought in amazement.

Holly's smile disappeared. The surrounding faces were horrified. Or fascinated, Gabrielle thought.

"What's this," Holly said. "Who are you?"

"Why, we are the next contestants, aren't we?"

"Yeah," Andrea said, sneering.

"Did she bring you?"

"No one brought us, oh beautiful one." He grinned big again.

"You're lying. Get out."

Andrea said, "We have as much right to be here as you."

The Aggies, in a chorus of cowboy boots, filed out of the kitchen and took flanking position behind the punks. A dozen dance couples took this as a cue to retreat to the far wall.

Disco, hands on hips, said, "It's ogghey up hont ants."

Holly stared at him.

"Thank you, sir," Slake said. "My good man, I would like to request a song."

Sid cleared his throat.

"Of course. And what are your names?"

"Slake and Slash. And our song. Disco Inferno."

"Oh please," Holly said.

"Slake and Slash, ladies and gentlemen."

The crowd stood in uneasy silence. The strobe light continued to pulse,

9.9 on the display. Storm, at the cassette tray, muttered to the tall man. He shook his head.

Samantha, swinging her hair, came up to the bald woman.

"May I?" she said.

"What?" the woman said, annoyed.

"Insert my tongue?"

"Um"

"I really want to." She tossed her ankle length hair again. "Please."

The woman smiled. "Go ahead."

As Samantha leaned in the pudgy punk yelled, "Hey!"

I know that voice, Gabrielle thought.

Disco Inferno began to play.

Andrea slapped Slake and it was as loud as a balloon popping. Several tuxedoed guys shouted, "Oh!" Slake grinned and slapped Andrea. She slapped him again and he slapped her to the beat.

The tall man shouted over the music.

"Listen! Y'all listen to Ken!"

His voice boomed.

"Disco's demise, is worse than advertised! Storm and Sid are cool, they're takin' you to school! So enjoy the disco dance, you little fancy pants!"

Storm yelled, "Kenneth!"

Gabrielle saw Sid put his head in his hands.

Andrea shrugged. Slake shrugged.

Kenneth said, "If you're gonna rap."

Slake slapped Andrea.

"Don't fall into the trap."

Andrea slapped Slake.

"Big change is a comin', you gonna get a drumim'!" Kenneth said then clapped.

All the Aggies took a step forward. Slake and Andrea slapped each other quickly and there was uneasy laughter.

"Ha, ha! To the man named Slake! We know those teeth are fake! The lady with the hair! Is makin' you a dare!"

"Wait, I get it!" Rushel, in the front row, shouted. "Monty Python!"

Slake gaped at her hair, slack-jawed. Andrea glared at him, furious.

"Hey!"

Andrea slapped him hard enough to make him stagger. His shock turned to anger.

"N*ot* Monty Python." He pulled the vodka bottle from his pocket and threw it at the acoustic display. "*Rage!*"

The display, still showing 9.9, toppled and fell.

"God *damn* it! That's my perfect score!" Holly said and laid a right cross on the bridge of Slake's nose at the exact instant Andrea's hand hit his cheek. Slake went down with a wet cough.

Andrea yelped, "Ow!" and shook her hand.

"Oh shut up!" Holly socked her in the jaw.

As Andrea screamed the punks threw their vodka bottles in the general direction of the podium. Sid ducked. Storm opened her hand and caught one. The music volume hit maximum and *Disco Inferno* roared.

An Aggie stuck out his leg, grabbed a bottle thrower, and yanked him backward. Tripped, the punk went down with a grunt. One of the taller punks began throwing punches at an Aggie in a white hat. The Aggie stood still as the blows hit his face then he seemed to just straighten out his arm. The punk keeled over backwards. The rest of the Aggies collectively shrugged and began throwing punches at whatever punk happened to be nearby. The bald woman threw her bottle and managed to knock off a cowboy hat. The guy put it back on, tipped it towards her, then went back to swinging at two punks, both with Mohawks. Pudgy-punk shoved Samantha and she responded instantly with a left jab to his eye socket and kicked his feet out from under him. He fell to the floor like sack of potatoes.

My professors are dropping like flies, Gabrielle thought. Do not laugh.

Through the melee, Holly locked eyes on her. Patricia and Debbie were beside her. Andrea and Slake were kneeling. They also stared.

Gabrielle stared back, hands on hips.

"Look!" Holly shouted. "She evil!"

"She *brilliant!*" Slake grinned again.

Samantha and Rushel appeared and stood shoulder to shoulder like a shield. She detected a familiar perfume and knew Catherine was behind her.

A vodka bottle sailed across the room and hit the mirror ball. It broke free and crashed at Andrea's feet with a shower of sharp silver bits. The punks howled in triumph. The glass door hutch rocked a final time, tipped forward, and smashed with a thunderous impact. The house trembled.

The fighting seemed to reach a peak. An Aggie was on the floor getting kicked by a team of punks. Two Aggies had ganged up on one of the Mohawks and were sequentially pounding his face.

The regular dancers, lining the wall, seemed to be cheering the Aggies although the punks had fans too, Gabrielle noted.

A couple of tuxedos had joined in to throw punches at a scrawny punk with pink spiked hair. Weak and pathetically telegraphed punches, Gabrielle thought. The scrawny punk was laughing as the blows fell. She saw a female dancer, head down, pummeling one of the Aggies. It was Robot Girl and the Aggie fended off the hits with the palms of his hands.

When one of the punks got slammed face first into the big parlor window she felt a tug on her dress. Catherine began to pull her backwards.

"Time to make like a tree," Samantha said and they walked in formation to the front door as punks and Aggies and dancers ran around them. Catherine put on the brakes. The bald woman stood at the threshold.

"Hey, Cindyloo, get outa the way," Catherine said.

She gazed calmly back. Without eyebrows her face was weirdly expressionless. A vodka bottle struck her in the chin and she fell backwards.

Gabrielle saw Storm waving.

"Good shot!" Rushel said. "I'll call you!"

Storm gave her a thumbs up.

Gabrielle took a final glance back. Sid stood at the podium, rubbing his temples, as Sondra and Clementine yelled at him. Disco was leaning against the wall, wide-eyed.

Holly, Patricia, Debbie, Tall Susan, and Pretty Susan were huddled by the remains of the hutch, conversing intently. Debbie glowered at them.

Three Aggies slammed a punk against the big window and the sash fell out and shattered. The punk went out head first into the rose bushes. More crashing issued from the kitchen along with wild laughter and screaming.

Gabrielle jogged as Rushel and Catherine hustled her out of the house.

Fog had rolled in and the streetlights were shrouded. Dancers milled on the lawn and shuffled down the steep driveway, laughing, high heels and platform shoes skittering drunkenly.

Audra was talking to someone in a parked car. She waved urgently.

"Those guys wouldn't last ten seconds in London," Samantha said. "We're down there. Just turn right." She pointed down the hill. The cross street was invisible in the fog.

Samantha saw a cowboy hat lying on the lawn and picked it up. Black with a silver strap. She put it on and tipped it back with a finger. "Well, aw right."

"Haay," Rushel said, admiring.

Gabrielle headed for Audra and said, "Where's Gislaine? What happened?"

"It's not serious," Samantha said.

"Don't be long," Rushel said.

They both walked quickly down the hill, arm in arm.

The car Audra was standing next to was the yellow and blue Saab.

Steinmetz, tux unbuttoned, was pounding on the driver's window.

"Lady, you're in my car!"

"Maybe you can talk to her," Audra said.

New Susan was in the driver's seat. She was searching the pockets of her disco jacket. She saw Gabrielle.

"I can't find my keys!"

"Susan, you're in the wrong car."

"But oh my God I can't find them." She held her head. "I have to watch the house!"

"Unlock the door and I'll help you look."

"Where *are* they? I have to get back!"

"Susan."

New Susan grabbed the handbrake.

"No, Susan, don't touch that!"

New Susan twisted in the seat and the handbrake went off with a snap.

"Ow! My funny bone!"

The Saab began rolling backwards. Steinmetz tried to grasp the edge of the door with his fingertips. The right front tire scraped the curb and Gabrielle thought for a second that might stop it but the hill was too steep and the tire climbed implacably over the concrete. Then the Saab began to roll very fast. Steinmetz had to let go.

"Oh my God this is so stupid," New Susan said as she vanished.

The passenger door scraped the fender of a BMW and then the Saab went straight and accelerated backwards down the middle of the street at terrifying speed and disappeared into the fog. Gabrielle heard another loud metal on metal scrape and then a long blast of a car horn and screeching tires. There was a crash, a massive sound she felt in her stomach, followed by silence.

In the darkness, a blackbird made a comment.

"We should go," Audra said.

Gabrielle walked with Audra and Catherine across the street. Several guys ran downhill, their open jackets flying.

"Too late, disco dudes," Audra said.

Steinmetz yelled, "Thanks a lot, lady!"

"What did *I* do?"

"*Keep moving*," Audra whispered.

Gabrielle heard a distant siren.

"You're car's okay, kid, trust me," Audra said. "Don't slow down. We will continue to walk along the wet sidewalk in a calm and orderly manner. We will go downhill and turn right."

"Yes we will," Gabrielle said.

"And I'm sure Susan is just peachy."

"Didn't we park right at the bottom of this hill?" Catherine said.

"Yes, but if that thing crashed into my car it would be the worst possible disaster therefore it didn't happen. Plan for the best and the best will come to pass."

"Let's try that."

Disco's house faded into the fog. Gabrielle could just make out Sid loading equipment into the back of his Continental. The window diving punk was still embedded in the roses. Several guys were peeing in the hedge by the doorway. The bald woman was still sitting on the grass, heads in hands.

Audra did not look back.

"We'll make it up to them."

"Poor Sid and Storm."

"Both of them. And Disco. All of them. Keep walking. We must not remain at the scene."

Arms linked warmly, they walked down the hill. At step forty-two, Gabrielle began to see flashing red lights in the dark fog. A fire engine and a police car materialized. There were firemen in front of the strip mall.

"I'm trying to make sense of what I'm seeing," Catherine said.

Lights from the fire engine illuminated the front of *Jim's Properties*. There was a neat hole in the hedge. The car parked just inside, Pontiac GT, had a pushed in windshield and dented roof. The front end of the Saab was just visible inside the office. It had punched through the window and come to rest in a nest of filing cabinets. Gabrielle saw maps and signs. A new Selectric was wedged under a tire.

"See? That ugly thing is perfectly fine in there," Audra said. "Now."

"Better get your car before more cops come," Catherine said.

"Yeah, you both better go. I'll catch up."

They all tried to see into the fog.

"I don't see any of them."

"That means they're safe."

Audra ran across the street. Gabrielle saw her change her movements subtly. Shorter, faster steps. Hands waving. She knew what it was. Girly Mode. Should be effective on firemen, she thought.

Sure enough, in a few seconds Audra was waving thank you to the guys. She got into her car, the headlights came on, and she began backing out of the ruined strip mall.

Catherine tugged and they walked arm in arm away from Disco's street.

"That was my first dance," Gabrielle said.

Catherine thought for a moment. "We should put on a dance. Oh! A dance on the beach!"

"In the moonlight."

"We'd have to be very selective. I'm thinking, no punks."

Gabrielle laughed.

"My philosophy class is going to be interesting next week. When someone shaves half their head I don't recognize them."

"You knew that one?"

"That was Andrea."

Catherine laughed. "I think I'm going to enroll in your crazy school. You got some pretty good action going."

Gabrielle heard a familiar engine approaching.

"I don't know why but I don't feel anything."

"You're in shock."

Audra's car pulled up. They both got in. Audra drove on slowly, without speaking, and scrutinized every side street.

"What about Rushel?"

"Huh? Oh, she said sorry about your car."

"Sorry for what?"

"Didn't say. Normally I'd be worried but I don't feel anything."

"Finally." Audra said.

She jerked the Toyota to the right. It was a street of closed up repair shops and small houses. Gabrielle saw her VW facing the wrong way, next to a pile of old tires. Gislaine, Rushel, and Samantha, still wearing the cowboy hat, were leaning on the hood. Gabrielle looked between them and saw no obvious damage.

All three of them were smiling.

Audra stopped close, head to head. The small houses were dark, curtains motionless.

Gabrielle got out first. Gislaine held out her hand.

"Nope," she said. "You stay there."

"Okay. What happened?"

Rushel said to Samantha, "You want to tell her?"

"You should tell her."

"Not me. How about you?"

"I suppose I could," Gislaine said.

"Oh my God, cut to the chase," Audra said as she got out.

"I could never do that. You'd miss all the suspense and fun and stuff. I have to tell it my way."

As Catherine laughed, Gabrielle said, "That would be fine."

"We got to the street and there was a perfect place to park three houses down. Samantha turned off the car. The people were sitting on the porch.

"We saw Holly's car pull out. Only one car left at that point. The MG. And we thought, uh oh. Susan's not going."

"Nope," Samantha said.

"That hat looks *really* good on you," Catherine said.

"Much obliged."

As Gabrielle laughed, Gislaine said, "However, as soon as Holly's Mercedes was out of sight the MG took off."

"Perfect," Rushel said.

"So we waited. And waited."

"And waited," Samantha said.

"After a while, the Porch People started getting a little restless and we thought, well, it's a bust. But we waited. Finally they both got up and opened their door and."

"Our hearts sank."

"And in that instant."

"We heard the phone ring," Rushel said.

"Samantha fired up the car and we zipped into their driveway. Samantha left the motor running and got the crowbar. The Porch People came back and watched."

"I opened their front door," Samantha said.

"She jammed the crowbar into the space between the knob and deadbolt and pushed it all the way over and the door popped open in a dramatic shower of splintered wood."

"That's what I said. Their house stank. It smelled like wet towels and ashtrays. Also, even in the dark I could tell, the carpeting was really dirty. The light came on. I found the pantry."

"There they were," Gislaine said. "Eight boxes on the back shelf with cans of soup."

"Pork and wild rice," Rushel said. "And they had a whole shelf of canned meat like little bits of chicken."

"They can't cook real food," Audra said. "They think it's too girly."

"Samantha handed me a box and I almost dropped it. It was really heavy! And it had sharp edges too."

"We forgot gloves," Rushel said.

"We took turned taking them to the car. We set them on the floor in the back. Samantha got the last one and."

"I felt something," Samantha said.

On the street behind them a police car roared past, lights flashing.

"I felt the wall move. I tugged on the shelf and there was a click. The whole thing opened out. There were more shelves. They were full."

"There were more than eight," Rushel said. "There were ninety-six."

"Ah!" Audra gasped. "The whole thing!"

"So we made an assembly line."

"Bucket brigade. But these boxes, I have to tell you."

"What?"

"Lighter. A lot lighter."

"What? You mean empty?"

"Don't think so," Samantha said. "Different, though. Those first eight were about as heavy as the one we opened. Maybe these are just partly full, maybe something other than, you know."

They stood away from the VW.

"Even lighter there were still a lot of them. We got as many as we could fit. Ninety, had to leave six. I was afraid the tires would blow out."

"God," Audra said. "Good God."

In amazement, Gabrielle checked her car. It was riding several inches lower and the rear tires were squished looking. The entire back seat area was a mass of gray titanium boxes. They came up to the windows.

"It seemed like a good idea to stay away from the main street."

Audra coughed.

"So, along with who knows how many vials of Russian nerve agent, this is probably right now the most valuable and dangerous vehicle in the entire world." She tipped her hat. "Boy howdy."

"Put half in my car," Audra said. "And let's get out of here."

They wouldn't let Gabrielle help at first but she insisted when she saw how tired they all were. The boxes were definitely lighter. She estimated less than ten pounds. Cold with very sharp edges. Her hands were quickly sore and cold.

"This is titanium. If they were empty they'd be light as a feather. So something's in there."

Gasping with exertion, Audra said, "All right. Put them down here." They filled her back floor then they started sliding them onto the seat.

Gislaine tried to assist and nearly dropped one.

"My arms are falling off," she said.

"Just rest," Gabrielle said.

Her lower back was screaming and there were welts on her hands. She tried to keep up with Catherine whose face was shiny with sweat. Her legs were as strong and muscular as ever.

Finally Samantha said, "Okay stop. That's fifty."

Rushel slumped over the hood of the Toyota. Audra moaned and lay flat on the driveway.

"Just gimme a second."

Gabrielle tried to straighten up but it hurt too much so she walked bent over to Samantha who handed her the keys.

Audra sat up. She brushed a leaf out of her hair.

"Enough resting. We have to get out of here."

Catherine pushed herself up. "Back to Shangri-La."

Samantha and Rushel and Gislaine got into Audra's car.

"We'll follow you," Audra said. "Don't stop for anything. Not the cops, not world war three."

"All right," Gabrielle said, startled at how grim Audra looked.

As they drove to the cross street, Catherine locked eyes with her.

"I know," she said. "It feels like we crossed a line."

They turned right, Audra close behind, and the foggy avenue in the rear view mirror was full of flashing red lights. No one noticed the two old cars slipping away.

Exhausted and sore, they unloaded the cars under moonbright clouds streaming just out of reach overhead. The watchful dunes hummed in the wind. They stacked the boxes on the bench seats in the middle room and Catherine covered them with wool blankets. All blinds and curtains were shut and lights extinguished.

Audra peeked between the slats of the vertical blinds beside the dining table, eyes fixed on the swirling night outside.

"Well, I'm going to take a shower," Gabrielle said. "What is it?"

"Now we wait." Audra swallowed tensely. "For the thunderbolt."

Gabrielle stepped back.

"I'm going to stay up. I might go outside. Up on the hill."

"Can I help?"

"We're safe for tonight. It's all the nights to come that worry me."

After her shower, Gabrielle lay between Catherine and Samantha and listened to the crashing of the surf and the pounding of her heart and did not sleep until the world lightened and a snowy plover sat on the sill and trilled its delicate song. It sounded like a warning.

"Do we have any idea where she is?"

"She wouldn't say. Down south."

"What is she doing? Looking for a job?"

"She's kind of given up on all that. Probably holding up liquor stores."

"We have to tell her. We can't just wait."

"We have to wait. Is the gate definitely locked?"

"You locked it."

"Oh. I don't remember doing that. Then we're good."

"We have to open them. I have to see."

"Too dangerous."

"I can't stand this."

"We have to wait."

Sunday, Gabrielle saw little of Audra, who left early in her car. She returned at noon. Then with Samantha they both patrolled the dunes around the gate.

Catherine studied her card catalog, put it away, then got it back out and studied it. Rushel and Gislaine sat on the front steps and whispered to each other then went for a walk on the beach.

No one looked at the shapes under the blankets.

Gabrielle went over her Volkswagen in the hazy winter sunlight.

Half a tank left. Oil: okay. Air and gas filters: time to change. Front tires had too much wear on the outer edges. Were they damaged from having about a thousand pounds in the back seat? No way to tell.

Inside, she pulled up the back seat and examined the battery. This was what she had been worried about. All that weight on the seat could have forced the springs into contact with the battery terminals. She had heard of Beetles catching fire from that. And she saw scratches on the top of the battery but the terminals, protected by heavy plastic shields installed at the insistence of her father, were untouched.

Thanks Dad, she thought, and let the seat down. She had to smile. Her father could never imagined what he had been protecting her from.

She sat in the driver's seat and dusted the dashboard with one of Catherine's napkins. She opened the glove box and a small envelope fell out.

She strained and picked it up.

"Rosie. Damn it. It's been, what, three weeks? So much has happened."

Gabriellle, it said in Mrs. Rosenberg's spiky printing. She used her thumbnail to open the flap. It smelled faintly of vanilla. No perfume, though.

To Gabriellle,

    This is a special note just for you. I'm not going to be doing this anymore. The reason is I'm to old and I just don't want to. I want you to know you were my best tenant ever all these years. You were never late with the rent and also you never complained even though you had good reason (I see everything)

    I have this company taking things over. They are kind of new. They have a name I can't remember right now. They might raise your rent a little – sorry it is out of my hands – but they promised me not very much. I told them to give you a good deal. And they might change a few other things. Everything changes. Change is good. My own mother said that to me. Then she died. Calvin Coolidge was president. I was about your age. Change stinks, you ask me.

    I didn't mean to go on so long like this. I'm going to miss you. Please write to me at this address.

    Natasha Alicia Eiger-Rosenberg

    PS Say hi to Catherine for me!

The address was in Florida. Gabrielle held the note for a moment.

"I'm going to miss you too." She closed up the car and went inside.

Catherine took one look at her and grew alarmed. Gabrielle handed her the note.

"Mrs. Rosenberg is gone."

Catherine gasped in shock.

"She retired. She moved to Florida."

"Scare me to death." She unfolded the note. "God bless her."

"She says hi."

Catherine giggled. "Natasha?"

"I know."

"Oo la la!"

"They're going to raise my rent."

"Oh." Catherine's breath caught. "She's going to miss you. Well, you're not even paying twenty bucks a month so you know."

"I guess. Elliot's gone, too."

"Boy."

Catherine set the note on the dining table and hugged her.

"The security officer is doing a perimeter check with the intelligence officer. Wanna take a nap?"

They moved the bed in front of the big window and watched the clouds.

"That one looks like a gargoyle on Notre Dame, up on the second level. See the tongue sticking out?"

"I was going to say woodchuck. But I see the tongue."

"I always wondered what a woodchuck looked like."

"Guess they look like gargoyles."

"We're in trouble now," Catherine said and pulled away.

"We were in trouble before."

"Not like this. Who knows what they're plotting."

"We knew this would happen."

"Let's get out of here. We could go up there. The river. No one else knows about it. It has everything. We could build a house. You and Samantha could build anything."

"Can't just leave."

"It's what M would do, believe me."

"We'll just have to handle it."

"What if you can't?"

"Then I don't know."

Catherine got up.

"Can't stand not knowing."

She went to the bathroom.

"Dinner will be at seven-thirty," she said. "But I don't know."

At dinner, no one said grace. Catherine gave them all a spoonful of scrambled eggs, boiled carrots, and except for Samantha, hamburger patties.

Gabrielle thought she was hungry but after the first bite her appetite vanished. She put her fork down.

Samantha also set her fork down.

"Why don't you go first?" she said to Audra.

"The situation is this. They are hunkered down at their house. A scan of their cars shows Patricia and Holly are preparing to travel. Susan was released from the hospital this morning. No sign of the rest but they're probably just waiting for orders from the Reptile Queen." Audra sipped her water.

"Our security here," Samantha said, "is not good. A good push will break down the gate. If they showed up right now and came in and started grabbing those things –"

"They don't think that way," Audra said. "They are far too clever and smart and everything to take the direct approach."

"Get those things out of here," Catherine said.

"They radiate evil," Rushel said. "Bury them out there. No one would ever find them."

"We have time. In my opinion," Audra said.

"The bottom line is we have to wait," Gabrielle said. "For her."

Everyone nodded.

"If she doesn't show up this week we bury them."

"Good," Catherine said. They all slept solidly that night. Sheer exhaustion, Gabrielle thought, plus making that decision. They're looking to me again.

She shifted her thoughts to school. Still a student. She tried to remember what the hell her schedule was. Classes? Finals?

"Right, all that," she whispered.

Samantha, who liked the new position of the bed, was curled around her protectively while Catherine was perched on the edge of the mattress ready to hit the ground running.

This could all work out, she thought. In a couple days everything will be fine. Reading her mind in the cold night, Samantha murmured and pulled her closer.

Monday, English went smoothly in review mode. It was the last regular week of the quarter and Gabrielle found herself getting nervous about the calculus final. Been slacking off, she thought. All too easy.

The professor apologized for the upcoming final because it was going to be multiple choice which, he explained, went against everything he believed in as a practicing scholar.

This made her nervous. She mentally sighed as the professor handed back their term papers. I either know it or I don't, she thought, or whatever.

There was long note on her paper's title page.

> *Good use of evidence and I thought your conclusions were*
> *logical, if controversial. The best kind! I enjoyed reading your paper.*
> *A*
> *PS The entire department is envious of your computer! We will*
> *be forced to update the style sheet. I suppose change is inevitable.*
> *What do you think?*

Blushing a bit, she tucked the paper into her notebook. Logical and controversial. Maybe that's my secret name.

The professor was the first out the door at the end of the class and there was the usual chorus of zippers. Outside in the hall, there was raucous laughter.

Pulse thudding hollowly, Gabrielle peeked out. There was a group of students at the end of the corridor, a tight circle of backpacks, looking at something on the wall. A female student said. "Ew!"

One of the guys saw her approach and said, "No, don't look!" and laughed.

There were slashing lines of paint on the wall, blood red, wet and dripping to the linoleum. It was a drawing of a naked female in a squat, knees out, hovering over a smaller figure. The smaller figure, doll size, also naked, had large breasts and eyeglasses. A trickle of red dots was issuing from between the legs of the large figure and hitting the smaller one. It looked like splashing.

They did this just now while I was in class, she thought.

She looked up and down the hallway and studied the streaming students. At the stairs she stopped, unable to see around the corner.

"Just go," she whispered.

On the inner campus road with hours to go before Philosophy, she considered her options. Library: jammed, even the Stacks, with last minute crammers. Student union: nearly deserted. So I would stand out like a sore thumb, she thought. I could hang out in the labs, help the first years. They certainly need it. And they wouldn't dare enter Engineering. All that math? Terrifying.

But I think I want to stay out of buildings. Just how I feel. Find a place outside.

She went to the plaza and sat on the planter where Catherine found her that day, under the shade of the eucalyptus tree. She could see the Burger Bar and bookstore and part of the inner road.

"Pretty soon this will all blow over," she said, still observing the students carefully. Winter coats were being replaced by sweatshirts. Summer clothes were peeking out from the Earth tones. She shoved her hands deep in her pockets.

At a quarter to one, she figured that was enough. She was sore from sitting and she had to pee. She went back to the English building, second floor, and used the restroom. There were no messages scratched into the mirror, no wall paintings. She leaned against the wall outside the Philosophy classroom.

This, she was looking forward to.

In the stream of passing students she heard a laugh. Annie and the big guy walked up.

"You survived!" he said. "I saw you there. What the hell *was* that?"

Gabrielle stared at him for a second.

"Yes. I was there."

"Wow," Annie said.

"It was just supposed to be a dance. I have a friend who's crazy about disco."

"*God.*"

"About twenty people got arrested and a helicopter crashed," the big guy said. "Somebody lassoed it from a roof."

"That's incredible!" Annie said.

"Gosh," Gabrielle said. "A helicopter."

"It's like the biggest riot on the town's history."

"*God.*"

Should I tell them who else was there, she thought. It's already too complicated.

She looked at her watch.

"I guess we could go in. No one in there."

"You know, they weren't there Friday either," Annie said.

"They all gave up maybe." the big guy said.

They sat in their seats.

"Wasn't it poetry?" Gabrielle said. "Modern poetry."

"The boundaries of my soul encased in filth, man," Annie said.

"Whoa. Deep." The big guy nodded solemnly.

Gabrielle laughed. Why couldn't they have been like this from the beginning? she thought.

"Rage, man," she said. "Rage at the empty vodka bottles."

"Ha! There were vodka bottles everywhere!"

"They were throwing them."

"I can't believe I missed it," Annie said.

"Missed what?"

Professor Townsend walked in followed by John and the remaining students. The woman in the old Army jacket. The young woman with the massive glasses.

No Andrea.

The professor seemed to be the same somewhat overweight, bearded guy as always. She couldn't see any indication of being punched and body slammed by Samantha.

"There was a rather out of control party," Annie said.

Townsend nodded with a stiff smile. He opened the grade book on the front table and made marks with a pen.

"I saw a little of it," the big guy said. "Apparently a helicopter crashed."

"Ho!" John said.

Gabrielle froze as Townsend locked eyes with her.

"A helicopter," he said. "That would've been something to see." He smiled and shrugged.

Gabrielle nodded back.

"All right then."

He closed the grade book and looked at his hands.

"Thank you all for coming today. Because you are here, you are hereby excused from classes this Wednesday and Friday and are also excused from the final exam next week. You will all receive an A."

There were stifled gasps.

"You know, I requested this class," Townsend said. "No, I demanded it. You should not assume that because I'm teaching this stuff that I agree with it. I know you think it's all so silly. Ridiculous. Drivel. Here's the thing. It's not. It's dangerous. You should think of this class as a training exercise or as a warning.

"There is a war going on. A war against rationality, against reason. A war against reality. And from here on out it's only going to get worse.

"I'm already revamping the course for next quarter based on your responses. I think I can do better. So, I've enjoyed attempting to teach you this quarter. You're a challenging bunch which is to be expected from young people who are almost too smart for their own good.

"I'll tell you one thing. That bit with the apple? I'm stealing that. To tell you the truth, in this particular case, I don't think it worked. You can't reason with someone who has abandoned reason. But it was a noble effort. I'm trying to come up with a good name for it. How about Gabrielle's Gambit?"

Annie clapped and the big guy said, "Yeah!" with a thumb's up.

"What do you think?" Townsend said the Gabrielle.

She couldn't help grinning.

"Sounds good, Dr. Townsend."

"All right. Good luck with all your classes and tests and have a nice quarter break. If you ever want to discuss anything you know where my office is. See you around."

Townsend piled up the grade book and briefcase and walked quickly out the door.

No one moved.

"Oddest class ever," John said.

"Has it been sixty seconds?" It was gray haired Army jacket woman.

"Almost," Annie said.

"Run."

Laughing, they packed up and left the classroom. Gabrielle as usual waited to be the last one out. As usual, no one spoke to her.

Between classes, the hallways were quiet and she took her time leaving. At the front door of the building, she paused watching the students walking by. Down the road in the direction of the library she saw the rapidly walking figure of Dr Townsend. A fast half step behind him was a female student with a heavily loaded backpack and long dark hair swinging from half her head.

Gabrielle waited until they were out of sight then she pushed the door open and went the other way, to her car.

"Nothing. Nothing at all," Gabrielle said.

The sun was already gone behind the scudding off shore clouds. They coasted past the towering trees and through the small town. The light stayed green just long enough.

"Good," Audra said.

"Not good," Rushel said. "I'd much rather know where they are."

"No sign of any of their vehicles. They're not following us."

At the gate, Gabrielle made sure it was locked behind them. She ran her fingers over the carved letters.

All I want to do is protect this, she thought. And them.

Catherine and Samantha looked tired and frazzled but a long shower together proved beneficial. Dinner was toast with jam and tea without sugar.

That night everyone slept with leaden heaviness, energy and adrenaline and emotions utterly flat lined.

Gabrielle was the first up. She gulped coffee.
"Easy day," she said. "Absolutely easy."
There was a surprise in her jogging class. Instead of the sign-in sheet there was a note on Dr. Swanson's office door.

> *To Intermediate Jogging pupils,*
> *This will be your final class session. Print your name at the bottom of this sheet to make sure you are counted. If you wish you may use the Swine Unit as your jogging target but it is not required. As in any class, what you get out of it is proportional to what you contribute. Consider this a real world demonstration. Good luck. - Swanson*

Gabrielle wrote her name. That's it, she thought. I can go. She read the note again and smiled. Swanson was her usual sarcastic self.
Not wrong, either.
One last time in the deserted locker room she switched to her running shoes. Then she jogged up to the Swine Unit and back. She was alone on the trail and barely broke a sweat. That alone was something, she knew. She decided she would miss the smell.
Back in her regular Top Siders, she put her ancient running shoes on top of her notebook and tucked it under her arm and walked out of the locker room.
"No more P.E," she said. "Never again will I have to take a P.E. class. Finished for all time."
She felt a minor celebration was in order. She pulled out her money. Three ones. Perfect.
She entered the student union plaza. Her heart sank a little. There was a line at the Burger Bar.
"Oh who cares."
The line was not long. The bowling alley and pool tables were silent and there was no music playing. She got behind a guy wearing short pants, a silk shirt, and a backpack with fake fur shoulder straps. She tried not to get too close. A guy with black frame glasses got behind her and stared at the nose ring.
She looked around the large room to the wall of bulletin boards. The Employment section had only a few notices while For Sale was saturated. The Housing board had only a smattering and a female student in a pink neck brace was scrutinizing it and taking notes.
Gabrielle turned attention to the menu. There was a new item under her favorite *Cheddar*. Her mouth began to water. *Super Cheddar.*

She saw the cook was her old friend with the toothpick. He was working hard by himself to handle this crazy pre-lunch rush. She watched the next customer, a young woman with short, layered hair like that ice skater, order a Monterrey burger, fries, onion rings, and a large Coke. Gabrielle winced. Enough calories for a week.

The guy with the furry backpack ordered a plain burger and root beer. Gabrielle shook her head. Who doesn't like cheese? Boring.

The cook saw her and grinned. Gabrielle saw his eyes go to the nose ring and his expression became slightly quizzical for a second. He grinned again.

"Hey! There you are. Before you order your usual I would like to point out our new burger. The Super Cheddar."

"I saw."

"Well, you inspired it. It's a bit more."

"I only have three dollars."

"That's perfect. With tax it would be two eighty-seven. Want to try it?"

"Yeah, sure. I inspired it?"

"You certainly did." He adjusted the toothpick. "Watch this."

He slipped a hamburger patty onto the grill and it sizzled. He checked his watch. He flipped it and put a thick slice of cheese on it and then a second slice. The layer of cheese was thicker than the burger. Then he covered it with an aluminum lid.

"Trust me," he said.

He took a split roll and put it on the griddle to toast. He lifted the lid and peeked.

"Ho ho! It worked!"

All the cheese had melted over the burger and flowed onto the griddle and become cooked and crispy. He quickly assembled the Super Cheddar and wrapped it up.

"Wow," Gabrielle said and there were several ohhs and ahhs from the line. She dug the three dollars from her pocket and when she looked up there was someone standing directly in front of her.

It was the girl with the pink neck brace. She had come in the exit. The brace made her cheeks puff up. Her eyes were red and there was a bruise in the center of her forehead. She wiped back her oily blonde hair.

"I just have a question," she said. "You don't mind if I ask you a question, do you?"

"Susan," Gabrielle said.

"I thought you were my friend but that was a lie, wasn't it. I thought you liked us. I thought you were on our side but that was a lie, too. The dance was a lie. Everything was a lie. I got thrown out. You probably think that's funny."

New Susan wiped her nose. The Burger Bar was totally silent.

"My God!" she shouted. "I had *sex* with you and that was a lie. You cheat, you're so smart, right, you cheat on every test. You lie and cheat on everything. Everyone knows that. How do you live? That's the question. How do you live being such a fucking asshole?"

She calmly picked up her backpack.

"Anyway, that's all. Goodbye."

New Susan exited into the plaza and brushed past several students who had been listening.

Gabrielle kept her back to the people in the line and held out her three dollars. The cook was half grimacing, half smiling.

"Sorry."

"Oh, no." He got her change.

Gabrielle picked up the Super Cheddar.

"There was this party, well, dance, on Saturday and it got a little crazy."

"The helicopter! I heard about that! Did she?"

"Her, you know."

"Yeah, whoa."

"That actually happened?" It was Glasses Guy. "A helicopter made a crash landing in a swimming pool?"

Gabrielle shrugged. "Yep."

"Man!"

She took that as her cue and left the Burger Bar without a backwards glance. She went to her spot on the planter, unwrapped the burger and nibbled on the crispy cheese, stomach clenched. She tried to understand the avalanche of emotions that was close to paralyzing her.

Sorry, New Susan, she thought. She had never betrayed anyone, not consciously. They had stolen from her friends and broken into their house. They spent months spying. Knowing all that did not make her feel better. And what was all that other stuff about cheating? It was infuriating. They were spreading horrible rumors about her and to who? Were they telling this crap to, her professors? Who would believe it?

"No one." She took a big bite of the Super Cheddar. Wonderful.

It was possible, she knew, that New Susan in the Burger Bar was just another one of their performances. Maybe.

Just an few days left in the quarter. Time was running out for them to try something big. She finished the burger and wiped her hands on her jeans. She was getting beginning of a feeling.

Everything was going to be all right.

"I'm being followed," Audra said.

Wednesday. Audra was waiting for her in the hall after Shakespeare.

"Come on," she said. "I just got an idea. What happened there?"

She pointed at the shiny new paint which almost covered the red drawing.

"Someone left me a message."

Audra nodded and looked up and down the crowded hallway. They went out to the front steps.

"I can't spot them. So here's my idea."

Gabrielle looked around them, alarmed.

"Followed?"

"Out of the corner of my eye. They're good."

"Them?"

"Don't think so. Like I've said a million times they're just not that smart. When's your next class?"

"I'm finished."

"Really? That's perfect. My idea is, we draw them out in the open. We go off campus."

On the inner campus road, she brushed back her hair.

"So let us walk to your car in a normal manner."

"All right."

"Not too fast."

"No."

They walked slowly, side by side, away from the English building.

"God, next week is going to be terrible."

"You told me. Your finals are something."

"And now this."

"What do they look like?"

"I keep seeing someone in a dark suit."

"Like a professor?"

"No. Can't tell if they're male or female. They stay far away. Every time I look in their direction they're just turning their head away. It's happened four times. Always the same distance."

They passed the mail kiosk and the maintenance building with its green lawn. Students in light jackets and sweatshirts and neatly bundled backpacks streamed around them. The street was long and curved.

"Don't look back," Audra said.

"Are they there?" Gabrielle fought the urge to turn.

"Maybe, I don't know, can't tell."

"Audra."

"Just don't look back."

They got to the library plaza. All the benches were full.

"Car's this way," Gabrielle said still only looking straight ahead.

"Let's go around back."

They went to the alley between the Stacks and the massive Architecture building.

My friends the dumpsters, Gabrielle thought and patted one.

"Over here!"

Audra dashed around a concrete pillar. Gabrielle got behind her and they peeked back.

Passing students with T-squares shook their heads at them. The main entrance was thronged.

"Give it a minute. When it quiets down," Audra said. "There!"

In the glare of the bright low sun, Gabrielle squinted at the spot where the road emerged from the trees around the kiosk. Someone in dark clothes was standing in the shadows under the branches. The figure stepped back slowly behind a tree,

"Wow. This is scary."

"Uh huh." Audra laughed. "I know. What do you suppose would happen if we just started running towards them."

"No, don't."

"Just run right at them screaming."

"Not sure I want to know."

"Yeah. So, we continue."

Audra stood and straightened out her flannel shirt. They walked leisurely away from Architecture and went back to the library plaza then up the sidewalk to the upper lot.

"Don't look."

"I wasn't going to."

"You looked like you were."

"I can't stand this. Who *are* they?"

"We just need to get a look at them."

At the car, she looked back. A full lot of student's cars. More Japanese these days for sure, she thought. But no creepy follower. No one at all.

Audra got in and slammed her door.

"I just thought of the perfect place. Proceed nonchalantly."

Gabrielle backed up.

"Always wondered what that meant."

"It's just something people say on tv."

"Oh, tv."

"Yeah, I don't miss it."

"Me neither."

Gabrielle decided to stop talking. It was making her more nervous. She drove left on the main campus road and mentally said goodbye to the Swine Unit on the hill. She immediately thought, why did I do that?

At the light, Audra said, "We go into town."

They went south. No vehicles followed. Midmorning traffic was light. A Dodge van passed going north, rusty and primer gray. Is that a law, she thought, that all vans have primer all over them? A blue Datsun zipped around them. It had come from the back of College Costs Less. At the next light more cars joined them going south. Regular cars, Gabrielle saw. A little Toyota pickup. A black Ford four door. Real estate people, she figured.

Audra directed her to the three lane avenue where she had walked with Catherine. West, then down to the other three lane street. Gabrielle felt a

708

wave of embarrassment which was interrupted by Audra.

"Here. Right here."

Gabrielle slid into a spot in front of a clothing store.

"That place back there by the baby trees."

"Oh, that's the coffee place."

They locked the car. There was a parking meter. *Expired.*

"Screw it," Audra said. "Come on."

The window of the clothing store had manikins dressed in striped t-shirts and sun-visor hats. One of the manikins was petite in size and had curly black hair. Gabrielle looked away quickly.

"What?" Audra spun around. "What did you see?"

"Just something I remembered."

They were alone on the sidewalk. Vehicles hurried by and Audra scanned each one. Delivery trucks. A Pacer with cardboard for a rear window. A Vega belching smoke.

They walked past a café with two tiny sidewalk tables and benches made from old crates. There was a candle store which smelled of incense. A tiny place that looked like an old alley made into an art gallery with a shelf full of highly detailed wooden sculptures. One was a book on a stand draped by a ribbon, another a pair of boots complete with laces, all carved from solid wood. Then a restaurant.

"Hey, this is the coffee place," Gabrielle said.

"Tina's?"

The door said *Tina's Famous Ice Cream Factory, est. 1974.*

"I came here with Catherine. They had really good coffee and éclairs. All French everything, you know."

"Maybe the other street?"

"I remember those trees. Just planted." Baby trees.

Audra pushed open the door.

"Nothing yet."

"Maybe we lost them."

The ice cream store was cool and smelled of vanilla. A guy in a sky-blue jumpsuit was being handed ice cream in a plastic cup from a young woman wearing a paper hat. The ice cream was dark purple.

"Hi, look, free samples," the guy said.

"No way. This is the best ice cream place *ever.*" Audra said.

"Carbonized blackberry." He turned to Gabrielle. "Hi."

Gabrielle tried not to make eye contact.

"What?" she said.

He blinked and went to the table in the corner.

Tall tables and long legged chairs. The same, she thought.

Audra went to the counter.

"I would like a single scoop of Noble Chocolate Martyr, please, in a sugar cone."

The young woman said, "Sure," and looked at Gabrielle.

"Well."

"I got it," Audra said.

"How about Revolutionary Vanilla Antihero. Sugar cone."

"Single scoop?" Her shirt had a word printed dead center, *Phuque*, in old English letters.

"Yeah, thanks."

"Sure." She picked up the cones and scoop.

"I'd rather lose them," Gabrielle said. "Feels weird to be off campus."

"This whole week is weird. This is Wednesday? The whole week."

Ice cream cones in hand, they stepped out onto the sunny sidewalk. They walked west. They carefully clinked their cones together.

"That was good back there. You weren't nice." Audra licked her chocolate and looked up and down the street.

"Blue Boy?"

They both laughed and Gabrielle said, "Honestly, some guys are just nuts. I mean, at the dance."

"They're all kind of nuts."

"The guys I know in my major aren't like that. They might be assholes sometimes but they're not crazy."

"Women. Whenever you see guys acting really crazy it's usually because of a woman."

Gabrielle shook her head. They had stopped under the shady awning of another restaurant, Tubby's Vegetarian Burgers. Behind the window, a group of middle-aged women in red t-shirts printed with the hammer and sickle all held hands over a tiny round table.

"I'll bet if more women go into your major you'll start to see the guys acting crazy."

"Great. We're bad for guys, aren't we."

"We are. They should develop other interests."

Gabrielle laughed. A police car, lights flashing, stopped in midstreet several storefronts to their right then angled in. Another police car braked aggressively to their left. A third police car stopped directly in front of them and a fourth vehicle, a black Ford, screeched to a stop next to it. There was the sound of car doors slamming. A policeman appeared on the sidewalk by the art gallery. His hand was on his gun.

Gabrielle felt a tug on her arm. Audra took her ice cream cone.

"Listen to me."

Audra dropped both cones in the gutter.

"You two!"

Male voice behind them. A second cop was walking towards them. Their uniforms were black. They were scowling and staring hard at them.

"Stay where you are!"

Gabrielle, ears ringing, looked into Audra's eyes and saw fear.

"Listen to me," Audra said fiercely. "Don't say *anything*. You understand me? Not a word. Not a single word!"

"I said don't move!" the first cop screamed. He looked like a young guy. More doors slammed. Gabrielle could hear the police radio. People were gathering in doorways to watch.

Audra stepped away, eyes locked on hers. She nodded. Her expression became one of distain and she faced the first cop.

"Hey Callahan, I'm walking down the street with an ice cream cone. What's the big deal?" Her voice was loud but measured and steady.

The policeman stopped and hooked his thumb in his belt. His angry look did not change. Gabrielle saw his eyes look past her. The second policeman was only a few steps away. Older guy, she saw.

"Just hold still," the first one said in a normal voice.

Audra turned to the second cop and looked his uniform up and down. "County?"

The older policeman squinted at her. His hand remained on his gun. "Sheriff's department?"

He made no move.

"It's all right, Colombo, I give you permission to speak."

"One more word out of you," he said instantly, "and I handcuff you both."

Audra sighed and shrugged. Gabrielle gave her a wide-eyed *no*.

"That's fine. You're gonna do it anyway. You know how I know?"

She waved at the third police car which was blocking most of the street. Another policeman was talking to a woman in a black pantsuit. Gabrielle thought she looked about M's age. The policeman had a different manner about him. Maybe higher up in the organization.

"Well bless my soul if it isn't agent Stephanie of the FBI."

Stephanie had short sandy blonde hair and hollow cheeks. Her face was set in a taut frown.

"Please keep talking, Audra. All right."

The third policeman looked at the first two officers and said with a reluctant tone, "We're taking you both in. Let's go."

The first policeman took a step back and spoke in a piercing voice.

"Both of you. Place your hands on this window."

Gabrielle tried to breathe. Her legs shivered.

"You, with the glasses, place your left hand here."

He touched the restaurant window at eye level.

Gabrielle went to the window, feet numb, and pressed her left hand against the glass. The women at the table inside did not look up.

"Place your right hand here."

Gabrielle was now leaning on the window. *Tubby's* was at her chin.

"Now move your feet apart. Hold still."

Gabrielle braced herself. Her head pounded.

"Okay, good." He leaned close and said in a normal voice. "How old are you?"

"Twenty."

"Remember what I said!" Audra yelled.

The first policeman continued. "You are not under arrest. You are being taken in for questioning. But we have to frisk you. You understand? This is routine."

"We have to make sure you're not carrying hand grenades or machine guns. You know, the usual college student accessories these days," the second officer said.

"Samurai swords," the first one said. "All right, here goes. Start at the top."

Gabrielle felt herself blushing more then she had ever had in her life and the policeman patted her arms, left then right, barely touching the sweatshirt sleeves, then lower, armpits and along her sides. This made her flinch.

"Keep your hands on the window. Do not move."

Gabrielle breathed heavily through her mouth. Her vision was dimming. The sidewalk was full of people in both directions. She heard the click of a camera.

He patted her sides again down to the top of her jeans then once quickly under her breasts and then his hands were on her thighs and between her legs, all around her legs, then down to her ankles. His fingers probed around the tops of her shoes. He stood up straight.

In the window reflection she saw him wipe his forehead and talk a deep breath. He looked at the other policemen and rolled his eyes.

"All right," he said. "Stay where you are."

Gabrielle nodded. Get it together, she thought. Are you the Goddess or aren't you? Stop being weak. And never, never, never tell Mom this happened.

"All right, you saw how we did that," the second policeman said to Audra. "Place your left hand on the window here." He tapped the glass.

"I'm sorry. Where?" Audra said.

In the restaurant, the red-shirt women were gaping at them and clapping.

"I'm going to say it one more time. Put your left hand here."

"Um, I forget which is my left hand."

The crowd was now ten deep in both directions and all traffic had stopped. She could hear angry voices.

"Hurry up!" It was Stephanie.

The policeman tried to grab Audra's wrist and she pulled away.

"Hey, Steffie! Virginity still eating you up inside?"

As the crowd laughed, the policeman got hold of her right arm and pulled up. Audra gasped. Then he grabbed her shirt collar and pushed her against the window. Her forehead thumped the glass.

Someone yelled, "Bullshit! Leave her alone!" The angry voices grew louder.

He let go of her collar, got the handcuffs from his belt, and snapped then onto her wrist. Audra responded by holding her left arm straight out. Her fingers brushed Gabrielle's shoulder.

The policeman simply put his hand on her elbow and pulled down. Audra said, "Ah!" Then he got the cuffs on her and held her by the arm.

"See?" he said. "I can frisk you safely now."

Gabrielle sensed the first policeman behind her again.

"Look," he said, "it's safer this way. Safer for everyone. The trick is to relax. You're relaxed, aren't you?"

She shrugged. "Sure."

"Good. Lower your right arm and put your hand behind your back."

Gabrielle did so and immediately felt cold steel on her wrist. There was a click.

"Now do the same with your left arm."

She felt the handcuffs snap shut the second she brought her hand down. Her shoulders cramped and her nose started itching. Her glasses slid down her nose and she jerked her arm. He turned her around.

The crowd was a lot closer than she thought. The sidewalk was jammed with people, shoulder to shoulder, as far as she could see. There was shouting and jostling.

She was propelled into the street. The sun was blinding. Audra was pulled in a different direction.

"Stephanie! You can't be this dumb!" Audra shouted. "You're not going to get anything from her! She's using you!"

The first policeman took her by the arm to his car. She lost sight of Audra. The flashing lights hurt her eyes.

Here I go, she thought.

"Stop," the officer said. "Face the car."

Gabrielle felt the handcuffs tighten, then there was series of clicks and her hands were free.

"Hop in." He opened the door for her.

Gabrielle rubbed her wrists and pushed her glasses back up. He watched her with a neutral expression. In the sea of stopped cars someone laid on their horn. She got into the police car, heart racing and he closed the door solidly.

The police unit smelled of window cleaner and the passenger seat was as hard as a slab of steel. She slid around. There was no comfortable position.

Gabrielle was fascinated through her fear. There was a radio under the dash, Motorola, and a microphone with a coiled cord. The speaker made a continuous crackling sound. There was a panel with two rotary switches, lights and siren, maybe. And there was a pump action shotgun mounted vertically on the dashboard. Her leg was pressed against it. She jerked away from it as the officer got in.

"You all right?" The engine growled.

"Yes. Thanks." His nameplate said *Kirby*.

"Well, you were cooperating."

He steered into the center of the street and the cars in front pulled over and he hit the gas. Gabrielle slid back.

"We're happy to assist the FBI but this is our town not theirs."

They went through several red lights and turned into the parking area of a building Gabrielle could not remember ever having seen before. The lot had a high fence topped by coils of barbed wire. The walls of the building were windowless. There was single door, made of steel. He stopped with a chirp of the tires.

"Sit still." He came to her side. Gabrielle noticed suddenly her door did not have a latch or window crank. He opened the door for her and she got out. The radio made a crackling sound and he mumbled something into the mic.

"Just go over to that door and stand there, okay?"

Gabrielle went to the blank metal door. There was no knob. She heard a muffled buzzing.

"Hey," the policeman said as he got back in his unit. "What's your major, anyway?"

"Triple-E." The steel door opened.

He knew what that was. He let himself smile. "Yeah, I figured it wasn't Home-Ec." He dropped onto the seat and backed quickly out of the lot in a cloud of dust.

Another uniformed officer was standing in front of her.

"There you are. Did the officer explain what was happening?"

He was a very young guy. Not wearing a gun but he did have a black club hanging from his belt. Nameplate read *Smith*.

"Yes. He said I wasn't under arrest."

Gabrielle stepped into a hallway with a linoleum floor and bright lights protected by wire cages. There were seven doors, labeled A through G. A plastic folding chair sat between E and F.

The steel door snapped shut behind her. The hall had a sour onion smell.

"Is that what he said? See that chair?

"Sure."

"Sure. Sit in that chair and do not get up until instructed to do so."

Gabrielle felt the numbness return to her feet. She sat in the chair and it made a skittering noise.

The young officer stood just outside her eyesight.

"What is your name?"

Gabrielle stared at the blank wall in front of her.

"I said, what is your name?"

She made an effort to breathe normally. The door at the far end of the hall, D, had a frosted window. A shape moved behind it.

Smith spoke directly into her ear. His breath reeked of urine.

"Things can get uncomfortable for you."

He got directly behind her and put his hands on her shoulders. Gabrielle froze in shock.

"I'm sure you know what I mean."

He squeezed. She gritted her teeth and held perfectly still.

"Just admit it. Tell me your name and admit what you did. You're in a dangerous place. You have no idea what's really happening."

Gabrielle shot her right hand to her left shoulder and pinched the back of *Smith's* hand as hard as she could. She dug her thumbnail into his skin.

"Hey! Bitch!"

He yanked his hand away.

Beyond the frosted glass door there was a voice. Before Gabrielle could turn her head the steel door buzzed open and slammed shut. She gasped for air and wiped off her shoulders.

She stood up as the glass door opened.

Another officer stood there. He looked at her in surprise.

"Hey. How'd you get in here?" He had a Southern drawl. Narrow face. Ice chest, she thought. His nameplate said *Smith*. No club, no gun.

"Your guy let me in."

"Guy? I'm the guy. Where's Officer Kirby?"

"He took off."

Smith hurried to the steel door and opened it and scanned the parking area.

"Ah, no," he said. He let the door shut.

"His name tag said Smith."

"Eh? That opened the door? I'm the only Smith here." He stopped and looked at her in alarm. "Are you all right?"

"Well."

"What happened?"

"Nothing."

"Eh? Look, I'm the guy that's going to help you. Don't lie to me."

"Nothing."

He squinted and shook his head.

"You sure?"

"I'm sure."

He put his hands on his hips.

"All right. Yeah you're lying but you may as well have a seat. Not the greatest chair. Would you like a cup of coffee?"

Gabrielle sat in the folding chair. "Sure, thanks."

Smith opened the glass door with a key and as he went through she heard him muttering to himself. "Fuck me. I'm in deep shit. This is a major fuck up."

Gabrielle watched both doors, cranking her head from side to side. From a door behind her she heard the scrape of a chair and raised voices. Room B, she thought.

"Yeah, I'm in a dangerous place."

After a minute *Smith* came in with a styrofoam cup.

"It isn't very good."

"Thanks, that's okay."

Smith exited and the hallway was quiet.

The coffee was lukewarm and had a metallic taste. She liked it. As she sipped there were more voices from B room. A shape appeared in the frosted glass, taller than *Smith*.

The door opened slowly. It was the officer who had been talking to Stephanie. His eyes were red and tired looking. His nameplate read *Parley*.

"You see the door labeled B?" he said. "Open the door and go in. Go in there now."

Gabrielle stood up.

"I'd like to know where Audra is."

He nodded slightly.

"Just go in. It's unlocked. And close the door behind you."

Gabrielle left the cup on the chair and turned the knob of B door. It opened in. Parley watched her. She saw a small square room. More lights in cages, the edge of a steel table, and another door opposite. She stepped in and closed the door behind her. She wiggled the knob. Locked.

A person sat in a chair, hunched over, their back to her. They were wearing a white leather jacket. A small white purse lay on the table. It was familiar, as was the perfume which filled the space.

Gabrielle spoke in the hollow room.

"M, are you all right?"

She swiveled. Her short blonde hair artfully framed her face as before. She had it cut, Gabrielle thought.

"*You.* No I'm not all right. What."

"I have to tell you."

"What are you doing here? You of all people. What's going on?"

"I have to tell you what happened."

There was laughter beyond the inner door. M reacted sharply. Her eyes widened in fear.

"Gabrielle, listen." M backed up against the wall. There were beads of sweat on her forehead. "I'm going to ask you to do something because I know you can do it. You following me?"

"Yes, but."

"Keep your head," she whispered. "No matter what."

The inner door opened. A woman wearing all black and a shoulder bag walked in and closed the door behind her. She was startlingly beautiful. She saw Gabrielle and stared. Gabrielle stared back. After a time in which Gabrielle forgot to breathe the woman tore her eyes away.

"Hello, M," she said.

"L."

"And who have we here?"

M began to say, "Persephone" at the same instant Gabrielle started to say Gabrielle. They both halted on the first syllable.

"P," M said.

"PG," Gabrielle said.

L stared at her again.

"PG." She smiled. "So you get two letters?"

"Yes."

L set the black shoulder bag on the table.

"All right, M. Here's the situation. Agree to return everything and you walk out of here. Otherwise I knock on that door and they take you both to jail. Very simple."

M shook her head.

"Return what?" Gabrielle said.

"This is the wrong time and place for games, my dear."

"Gabrielle," M said. "You said there was something you wanted to tell me."

L studied both their faces.

"Oh, this is a revelation," she said.

"Yes," Gabrielle said. "We figured out where L was hiding all the money she stole from you."

"All?" L sniffed. "Oh, far from all, I assure you."

Gabrielle jumped on it.

"We figured out where L was hiding all the money she just now admitted to stealing from you."

L, surprised, grew angry and stepped back.

M said, "Huh."

"So we tricked them into leaving their house and we went in and took it. That's what happened. It's all in the middle room."

"Um. What is?"

"It's hundreds of gold coins."

M coughed and laughed.

"Gold! Of course. Makes sense. Can't very well trust the banks, right? Cash is so much better. God, L."

"M," L said.

"What a bizarre world you live in. I will never understand you."

"So true."

"I offered to give it to you. Thirty million. I was ready to write a check for the whole thing."

"Out of pity. It was my inheritance."

"You'd rather steal it."

"My rightful property."

"And, let's see if you remember, after you stole it, giving that poor man a heart attack, did you notice an absence of something? Think now. What did not happen?"

L stared at her.

"I know it's hard. You were never terribly bright. Everyone knows how you got that Ph.D. Harvard, wasn't it? PG?"

Gabrielle raised her eyebrows.

"Ph.D? Pleasing his dick."

L put her hands on the shoulder bag.

"I did not go to the authorities. I didn't call the cops. I didn't call the FBI, like that would do any good. Interpol investigated on their own but you know they came up empty. You got away with it. All you had to do was *nothing*. Just leave me alone. You had won. You got everything. But you wouldn't go away."

M took a deep breath.

"What would it take to make you stop?"

"One day I'll pick up the paper and read about your tragic suicide."

M laughed. "And why come back? Why not stay over there? Weren't you happy spending the money and humping your adorable Euro friends?"

"Europe is dead," L said. "They've lost it. They've given up. You can't really say that about the United States."

"I suppose not. I always figured you must have had help. High up. Patricia is a bright girl but it's really a matter of access, I would say. Just so I know, who helped you?"

L did not look up from her bag.

"DDR," she said softly.

"*Wow*, L. That makes perfect sense. East Germany. Thank you for telling me. Was she cute? The nice blonde German girl from the Ministry of Finance and Torture?"

"It wasn't like that."

"How unusual. I assume you had to have had something to sell and since we all know you don't have a soul..."

"Oh, M, you know those people. There's nothing they worship more than money. They have no idea what it is. They think it's magic. This makes them a bargain."

"And that's a lot of gold," M said. "You couldn't just stick it in a suitcase."

"Hundreds of pounds," Gabrielle said.

"There is that much gold in the middle room."

"Yes. I think that's what it is."

"And you are actually supposed to declare things like that in Customs.

But you smuggled it. What, walked through the airport with bags of the stuff?"

"It's in these boxes," Gabrielle said. "Metal boxes."

M looked at her in surprise then at L in anger.

"Even I didn't think you were this twisted, L. East German military equipment. How could you brings those things into the country?" M put her hands on her temples. "And they're in my house."

"Ninety of them," Gabrielle said, disconcerted. L was grinning at her.

"Fu—," M gasped. "You didn't drop any of them, did you?"

"They're Soviet, actually," L said. "Well, they paid for them."

"Oh, swell."

"M, there were so many times in Europe when I wished you were there beside me. You might have begun to understand why I see the world the way I do, in terms of basic biology, not the fantasy of a Judeo-Christian morality play. My way is reality, your way is science fiction. They are not like us. They're perfect in their madness. They have no mercy. They have no pity. There is *force*, there is *will*."

"There is evil."

"There are different points of view."

M sighed and said to Gabrielle, "Why didn't you tell me?"

"We had no idea where you were. We couldn't call you."

"Yes, M, really," L said. "A houseful of young ladies without so much as a telephone?" She winked.

Gabrielle said, "I found something one day. A phone line going into the house. We traced the wire. It went to a circuit, an amplifier. There was a microphone in the chandelier over the dining table. And there might be more."

M stared at L open mouthed.

"You bugged the house? Gosh, L, by your standards that's almost quaint."

"We used it against them," Gabrielle said. "I rigged up an indicator so we could tell when they were listening and we fed them fake information. That's how we tricked them into leaving their house."

"Wonderfully clever," L said. "Innovative. Resourceful. You are an excellent adversary."

"Thank you."

"Everything was fine, PG, until *you* came calling. M, where on Earth did you find this one?"

"I picked her up at the mall."

"You're right, PG. There's more than one microphone. There are eighteen. Wherever I was I could dial up the number and listen. Very high quality. It was like I was there in the bedroom with you." She grinned again. "Oh Catherine, oh Catherine, oh Catherine." She laughed.

Gabrielle turned away. She tried to force herself not to blush. Stay cold, she thought.

"I get how smart you are. But you made a terrible mistake."

Gabrielle made herself look L in the eyes.

"And M, it's all your fault for leaving them alone. Now, PG. This is your mistake. You said coins. Do you realize it yet? Tell M what you did. What you did with the box." L backed up and leaned against the door and crossed her arms. Her smile disappeared. "This will make it all worthwhile. Tell her while I watch."

M said, "What does she mean?"

Gabrielle tried to organize her thoughts.

"There was," she said. "When I first arrived at the house with Catherine at one point I sat on the bean bags in the library and there was one of those boxes on the floor underneath."

"Bean bags," L said.

"Rushel stole it from their house."

M shook her head. "Rushel?"

"She went there with Audra for something, to pick up clothes, and it was lying on the coffee table. She grabbed it."

"Millions of dollars being guarded by a collection of psychopaths and pot heads," M said.

"When they got back, and they were bringing it in, they dropped it and it landed on the bean bags. They just left it there."

"Bean bags," L said, nodding slowly. "Continue."

"I tried to figure out what it was. I weighed it on the bathroom scale so I knew what was inside. Then after I thought about it I had a good idea how to open it."

"No. You cannot open them," M said. "Gabrielle, they're incredibly dangerous."

"I made an induction coil from the lamp cords."

"No," M said.

"We threw it in the ocean."

"You realize how close you came to killing yourself and your friends," L said.

"Yes."

"Not to mention ruining a very nice part of California. You could tell it was gold from the weight but you had to open it to know it was in the form of coins. Too bad you said that. There you all were in that isolated house. No television. No radio. No phone that you knew of. Not even a mailbox. No newspapers. And who would think of checking the newsstands when you were in town?"

M let out a long moan.

"Oh my God. The die-off. You caused it. And they."

L laughed again.

"You idiot college girls."

"I have made my decision," L said. She unzipped the shoulder bag and reached inside. Gabrielle saw her grip something bulky. She pulled out a titanium box and held it up.

"Empty, they weigh almost nothing."

"You brought one of those things into a police station," M said.

"Thought I might have to show those boys what all the fuss was about. And Stephanie had never seen one. Not going to do that now. Change of plan. Both of you. Pay very close attention. I'm going to show you exactly once."

She set the box flat on the table then tipped it onto one edge.

"This corner. You noticed the mark there?"

"Yes," Gabrielle said.

"Of course you did. Place the carrier, the *Träger*, on its side with the mark on the upper left. Turn it like a square wheel to the left. Like this."

She tipped it over.

"*Eins.* Now keep going for a full rotation. *Zwei. Drei. Vier.* Then lay it flat away from you."

The box thumped to the table.

"It is now reset. Notice the position of the mark. Following so far? Now comes the tricky part. This is called the Dance of the Vanguard."

She picked up the box, carefully keeping it level then tipped it back.

"That's forty-five degrees. Level again."

She tipped it to the left.

"Thirty degrees. Hold that angle and tip back sixty dress from horizontal. Then, holding that angle, tip right to thirty. Now, without altering the angle in the slightest, rotate a horizontal three-sixty with the corner as the axis. It takes practice."

Gabrielle saw L's arms tremble as she pivoted the titanium box a full circle. From inside there was a whirring sound and three loud clicks. The lid popped up on its central post.

"Generally, that's how you open them. The induction coil is how you set them off, I now know. These are sometimes used for assassinations. See, the target feels privileged to receive the induction coil. It's built into this ugly stand. And there's a thirty minute delay. The poor target thinks they got away with it. This one's completely empty."

She plucked the lid off.

"Brilliant and horrible. How familiar," M said.

"I learned a lot of this only very recently," L said. "What you are doing is guiding a tiny ball bearing along a specific channel in a series of weighted cogs to what is termed its destination. One destination opens the lid, another activates a radio beacon, yet another sets off an explosive charge to kill the user. So it isn't always nerve gas. And there are other destinations I have no knowledge of.

"The genius who invented this was a sculptor living in Saxony-Anhalt.

He liked to make puzzle boxes. The authorities considered non-socialist art like puzzle boxes decadent and counterrevolutionary so they put him to work on these things. When he finished, they concluded his calling the unlocking procedure the Dance of the Vanguard was a wee bit sarcastic. They hate that most of all. So he was shot. They went to his village and made his wife and two daughters lie in the gutter face up and they were shot between the eyes and left there. Never hurts to remind the proles who's in charge, I guess.

"They took me to his unmarked grave beside a wheat field. They were trying to frighten me, to impress me with how ruthless they were. I think I ended up frightening them. Someday I'll tell you that story, PG. Suffice to say, they didn't like me."

"Oh L. I'm sure they liked you. How could they not?" M said.

"A few did, on the German side. I'm telling you this, PG, to give you a sense of how utterly insane they are. You should take them seriously. The Russians, primarily."

"In the basement of the house," Gabrielle said, "there are bottles of wine with Russian labels. The old rancher." She looked at M. "Did he have a connection to all this?"

"Oh," L said, smiling. "I'm sure that's just a coincidence." She winked again.

Gabrielle heard angry voice beyond the inner door.

"We have very little time," L said. "I'm going to tell you exactly what the situation is and what I'm going to do."

"You're going to tell the truth?" M said.

"Yes," L said with an air of exasperation.

"Aren't you afraid you'll burst into flames?"

Gabrielle couldn't help laughing but covered her mouth.

"In the DDR, there is always intrigue. After helping me, they took their cut, and I received the Träger I wanted, empty, along with an induction coil stand. I learned about the vial. Then they took them away to fill them, they said. I wasn't allowed to observe. They told me to only open them once I got home. What an odd condition, I thought. You see what they were doing."

"They're your kind of people, L."

"I was suspicious but at that point I had nothing to go on. Still, I could tell something was up. I decided to get even. Proactively, you could say. I used some of my own money."

M coughed.

"Sorry. I used some of the money I got from M and bought myself a friend in the Ministry. The Department of Interior Social Stability was the name of the office."

"What was she like?" M said

"Lovely. Innocent. Trusting. Greedy. Ambitious. Murderous. She became my assistant. She filled the Trägers with mostly their assets, I believe. She thought up the Krugerrand angle as a deflection. It was right up her alley."

"What happened to her? You throw her to the sharks?"

"She's here now, quite recently. I've yet to speak to her. You've met her, PG."

"I have?"

"You call her Tall Susan."

Gabrielle stared at her with naked incredulity.

"My advice? Never turn your back on her. She taught me the Dance and the real purpose of the ugly stand. As reward I got her out of that country.

"It all belongs to you now. I think the only one to have been sabotaged was the heaviest. The lighter ones probably not. Susan was not there to advise me. Audra and Rushel came by for a surprise visit. We had a little chat. I was set to open the thing but Rushel absconded with it. So she saved the day. For me, at least. If you encounter any more, you bury it. Three meters, away from water.

"One more thing. Ever so efficient Susan was the only one who went into the vaults to fill the Trägers. Serious intrigue going on there. See, the ones at the top, the military, the Party, they like to create private empires. Secret fortunes. Perhaps some old general collected assets for his retirement and never got to use it. And there it sat on some shelf. There wouldn't exactly be any records, naturally. They might not really even know what was missing. We can assume the heavy ones contain gold but the lighter ones? No idea what they contain. For your sake I hope something very valuable. I think you're going to need the money."

L took a deep breath and grinned at M, who was calm and firm but glassy-eyed.

"Gosh, M. You're rich again. However, I'm going to take a wild guess and say they now know it was a chemical weapon from behind the Iron Curtain that caused the die-off. So you might have some visitors poking around. You know, spooks. Then there's the DDR. Money is very important to them. It's their true religion. They might want it back, whatever it is. And it's not like you can hide it all under the *bean bags*." She laughed, a belly laugh. "How can you not love America? Well, ladies, I'm off. PG, you're more nefarious even than Holly. No doubt we will meet again. M, goodbye forever."

L slipped the box into the bag and knocked on the door.

"L," M whispered. "You're so dumb."

"Oh, and don't worry. As soon as I pay the horrid Stephanie she'll stop bothering you."

She knocked on the door again and it opened a crack. L put the bag over her shoulder and slipped out. As the door closed Gabrielle heard Stephanie's voice, stressed and angry, then L, calm and authoritative. Sensuous.

She shook her head. It affected me, too, she thought.

"M," she said. "M."

M's eyes were locked on the empty table.

"We'll get those things out of the house. We'll take them far away and bury them. Out in the desert."

M nodded.

"They'll be no sign they were ever there. And Samantha will know what to do with the coins. It's all your money. You don't believe her, do you? Good grief, all that?"

"Yes, that's great. We'll do it that way. Good idea."

"But you don't—"

The B door clicked loudly and *Smith* stood there. In the hallway, Audra, cup of coffee in hand, was talking to the older officer who had handcuffed her.

"But that's my mom," Audra was saying. "That's why I'm down here."

"Audra, makes me glad I'm down here, too. She might have a problem."

Audra smiled then started when she saw M.

M walked straight to the steel door. She stood there and brushed her hair back.

Audra walked quickly after her.

"Nice talking to you, Steve."

"Yeah, sure. Try and stay out of trouble, Audra."

Gabrielle went around *Smith* and stood behind Audra.

"Oh, yeah, Audra," the policeman said. "One thing. What kind of car do you drive?"

"Toyota Corona."

"It's not a red Volkswagen, is it?"

Gabrielle froze.

"Blue. Toyota Corona."

"Uh huh. So not a red Volkswagen?"

"Toyota."

Gabrielle faced the door as calmly as she could. M rapped on the steel and the buzzer went off. She pushed on the door with both hands, purse dangling from one arm. Sunlight flooded in.

In the parking lot, M walked quickly ahead to the chain link gate.

"M, you can't possibly believe her," Gabrielle said. "That's the most ridiculous stuff I've ever heard. What is she, Mrs. James Bond or something?"

"Huh?" Audra said.

"Sorry. My car," M said. She turned right at the sidewalk and walked faster. The toe of her loafer snagged a crack and she stumbled. She didn't look down. She kept walking.

"She made all that up to keep those girls from messing with them. The CIA is not coming to the house."

"Wait. Who?" Audra said.

She's running away from me, Gabrielle thought.

She stepped off the curb and Audra tugged her back.

"We'll meet her at the house," Audra said.

"I need to paint my car a different color."

M was already out of sight beyond parked cars and closely spaced trees

"So what happened to you, anyway?" Gabrielle said.

"Nothing really," Audra said. "Sat in a chair. Had really bad coffee. The officer. He's a crack up."

"Steve?"

"He showed me how to get out of handcuffs. He said it was a skill every modern girl should have. I heard yelling. Pretty sure I recognized the voices. Then they took me to that hallway."

Audra stopped. Her hair blew over her face and she brushed it back.

"Hold still," she said. "Just stand there."

Gabrielle halted. Traffic roared past them

"Remember, I am your counselor. And Priestess. And intelligence officer."

"Yes."

"You were in that room with her. Do you feel, right now, as if you've just escaped from a parallel universe where the laws of physics are different and the air has had the oxygen replaced with perfume and you believe there could actually really be flying raccoons?"

"Kind of."

"It's *her*. You have defenses but M does not. Breath normally. Your car is back this way."

"You're not supposed to be home yet."

Audra rushed into the house. Gabrielle walked slowly up the steps.

"A bunch of stuff happened."

"Do I want to know?"

"Those things."

"I want them out of here."

"Have you seen M?"

"She's back?"

Audra came out hugging a titanium box to her chest. Gabrielle took it from her and set it on the porch railing.

"One of the light ones," Audra said.

Gabrielle found the corner with the mark.

Catherine looked alarmed.

"What are you going to do?"

"Open it," Gabrielle said. "L showed me how."

"Who?"

Gabrielle set the box on its edge, marked corner upper left. She scratched the tiny indentation with her fingernail.

"It's mechanical."

Samantha and Gislaine came out the door.

"She's going to open it," Catherine said.

"You figured it out?" Gislaine said.

"L showed her," Audra said.

"L," Samantha said.

"Honey," Gislaine said. "Here's the thing. You can't trust her."

"I realize that. But she actually opened one in front of me and M in the police station."

"*Police* station?" Catherine said.

"M is here?" Gislaine said.

"We were both arrested," Audra said. "Downtown. We were both taken away in handcuffs. Almost started a riot. The FBI was there."

Gabrielle saw tears in Catherine's eyes as she hugged her.

"Are you all right?" she whispered.

"I think so. It wasn't fun."

"My God."

Catherine hugged her tighter for a moment. Then Samantha took her place. Gabrielle buried her face in Samantha's hair.

Catherine hugged Audra, who said, "I'm fine. Really."

"You don't have to act so tough all the time, Pocket Mouse," Catherine said.

Gabrielle was surprised to see tears in Audra's eyes as well.

"Oh, I don't think it's an act," Gislaine said.

"You're right. What was I thinking," Catherine said.

Gislaine leaned close to the box, keeping her hands away.

"Booby-trapped?"

"Yeah," Gabrielle said. "You tip it in a very specific way. There's a mechanism with a ball bearing that has three destinations, as she called them. One, box opens. Two, activates radio beacon. Three, explosive charge kills the user."

"Shit," Gislaine said. "Where do these things come from? Who would make something like this?"

"She told us a long story about them. She called them Trägers."

"Carriers," Samantha said. "German."

"How many languages do know, anyway," Audra said.

"*Nür zwölf order dreizehn.*"

"Oh. Thank you."

"*Bitte.*"

"I have no reason to think L told us the truth."

"No, she thinks truth is a weakness," Audra said. "Because in principle truth exits in the real world independent of her mind. She can't control it. In her fantasy world she gets to be a god. Not the same thing as being a goddess, I should point out."

"Of course," Gabrielle said. "There might be elements of truth."

"Woven into a story," Gislaine said "Everything is an elaborate story."

"With her as hero," Samantha said.

"It's easy to get caught up in her fantasies," Audra said. "A lot of people have. M is very susceptible. We all might be doing it right now."

Gabrielle turned the box to be in line with the railing.

"The one I saw in Holly's locker, they wanted me to see it."

"Yes," Samantha said.

"There was no other reason for it to be in there. And the one Rushel took was set out for her to see but she messed up their plans by stealing it. No one ever expected Rushel to do something like that. Then I really messed up their plans by opening it. Even worse, I opened it the wrong way which caused the capsule to go off."

"You mean the," Catherine said.

"Now, according to her, only that one had the capsule. Someone over there was trying to double cross her."

"Where?" Gislaine got her pen out.

"East Germany."

They all said, "Ew!"

"It was the heaviest of them all. They intended her to use this induction coil device to open it which would have killed her and everyone in the house."

"If you believe her," Catherine said.

"My idea is let's bypass L and her stories and open them all. If any others have that capsule we can dispose of it. She told us how. And I can research that to see if she's lying. Russian nerve gas. Still don't believe it. I think she made that up."

"You don't think that caused the die-off?" Samantha said.

"How could one drop of anything do that much damage?"

"Don't know."

"A coincidence?" Audra said. "I could go to the County. They might tell me what they're found. That guy liked me."

"Now you're thinking like her," Catherine said.

Audra shrugged. "Am I cute or aren't I?"

Gabrielle said, "I was going to take this out to the dunes."

"Why not open it here?" Samantha said.

"If you believe her, if I do it wrong it can explode."

"Then don't do it wrong." Catherine's gaze was steady.

"We've been over this before, Goddess," Gislaine said.

Audra crossed her arms.

"Whatever it is we face it together."

With tears in her eyes, Gabrielle said, "Here goes." She rolled the box to the right letting each side thump on the old redwood. "One complete rotation, now flat." She let it back down being careful not to turn it in any way. "Now it's reset. Okay." She rubbed her hands. "Now the hard part."

Gabrielle picked the box up level and stepped away from the railing. The edges bit into her palms. Her right shoulder was still sore from doing the dip with Holly and the tendons there screamed. She began to breathe hard.

"Is there any way we can help?" Samantha quickly moved in and gently supported the box with her long fingers.

"See the corner there with the mark? Orient on that."

"Okay."

"Tip it back forth-five degrees with the axis of rotation where my left thumb is. Then level again."

With Samantha's help the box seemed almost weightless. Gabrielle thought, better remember it correctly. Forty-five back, level, thirty left, forty-five back again, hard over right thirty.

"Easy so far," Samantha said.

Gabrielle could see her arm muscles quivering. Hurry, she thought.

"One maneuver left. Holding it at just this angle rotate full circle with that corner as the axis."

"I don't see what that will do."

"Me neither but it's what she did. My idea is we just walk it around. See that nail in the board there?" She tapped the porch with her shoe. "It's directly under the corner now."

"Left?"

"Right. I mean right. To the right."

"Counterclockwise?"

"Yes, looking down."

"All right. Ready?"

"Ready. Uh, ready."

"If you make me laugh I gonna drop it," Samantha said.

"Sorry. Real slow. Three, two, one."

They both stepped heel to toe around the nail head.

"This is kind of fun," Samantha said.

"She called it the Dance of the Vanguard."

Catherine laughed. "Oh *brother*."

The lid popped open.

"Wow!" Gislaine wrote faster.

"Let's set it on the railing."

Samantha flexed her arms. "Not the worst workout."

Gabrielle held her painful hands together then rubbed her shoulders. "All right." She pulled the lid off.

Samantha laughed. "That bitch."

"What?" Catherine didn't move.

"Don't tell me," Audra said.

"Well," Gabrielle said. "No gold coins. Looks like metal cylinders. Six of them."

Audra sighed loudly.

"It's dusty," Gabrielle said. She blew some of it away. The six cylinders were held in by screwed-in clips. Phillips head screws, she thought. Finally something I recognize.

"They're stamped," Samantha said. "Serial numbers?"

"Wow," Audra said, holding her head.

Gabrielle turned the lid over.

"And no glass capsule."

"Lead weights?" Audra said.

"No nerve gas?" Gislaine said. "Good, right?"

"Everything's really dusty. And that's stainless steel. Six cylinders made in the shape of a roll of coins. And the end looks like it's threaded."

"This whole thing was a waste of time. I'm gonna puke," Audra said.

"We have to open all of them," Gabrielle said. "They can't be empty. Why would she go to the FBI? She could've just gone, ha ha, fooled you."

Samantha took a penny from her pocket and scraped the steel.

"Can I use your tools?" she said.

"Okay," Audra said. "I gotta go. I have to pick up Rushel at work."

"I'll go with you," Gabrielle said.

Audra shrugged.

She opened the hood of her car and got the tool pouch.

"Remember, supposedly that thing has an explosive charge."

Samantha untied the pouch.

"Just gonna check it out a little."

"I can't see where it could be but we should get rid of it."

"I'll take care of it," Catherine said.

"Bomb disposal," Samantha said.

"I have nerves of titanium."

Gabrielle laughed. Audra stared at the ground.

Rushel nodded grimly at the orange sun setting in the western fog bank.

"So we stole a half a ton of lead weights."

"Not heavy enough to be lead. They're very strange. And all dusty like they've been sitting on a shelf for years."

"So we're not even sure what they are."

"Nope."

"Double crosser gets double crossed." Rushel reached into the back and patted Audra's knee. "This has been a very strange winter quarter here at our lovely yet still reasonably priced state university, hasn't it, Pocket Mouse."

"A horrible disaster I may never recover from."

Audra took Rushel's hand and held it all the way back.

When the gate came into view under the wind whipped clouds,

Gabrielle slammed on the brakes. Catherine was standing in the middle of the road, backlit by the swirling sky. Her windbreaker billowed and riffled around her.

"Uh oh," Rushel said.

Catherine came to Gabrielle's window.

"I want to leave. Back up. Go back to the street."

"What?"

"She's back. She's... I can't stay here anymore. Those things."

"Things?" Audra said.

"It's just too much."

Catherine stumbled at the edge of the sagebrush. Gabrielle jumped out and went to her.

"What is it?"

Catherine seemed on the verge of panic.

"It's bad. It's bad."

Gabrielle looked at her imploringly.

"Can we just leave?" She sounded exhausted.

"We'll get it straightened out."

"It doesn't work that way." Catherine finally returned her gaze. "You don't believe me."

"We have to go in. And of course I believe you."

Catherine stepped away and her legs tensed. Gabrielle could see her pulse pounding in her throat. She noticed her cut-off jeans were soaking wet. Catherine spoke into Gabrielle's ear.

"Being smart isn't going to help you this time."

She got in the back.

Gabrielle stood in the wind, cold and warm, scented with invisible spring flowers. Nerves tingling, she slid into the driver's seat.

The black Jeep was sitting beside the patio wall. The screen door opened and slammed back against the jamb. M stepped out. Her hair was matted to her head. She was wearing an oversized white t-shirt and jeans with worn out knees. From the porch, she watched them get out of the Volkswagen.

"You said there was a phone. Where is it?"

"In the wine cellar."

M shook her head angrily.

"Why couldn't you put it in the house?"

"Sorry. We've been," Gabrielle said as M rushed past her. "Busy."

She heard M swear as she got a flashlight from the Jeep.

"Go on. Go back inside. Go *on*."

She disappeared around the corner.

Rushel and Audra went up the steps into the library. Catherine stood at the edge of the driveway where a brittlebush rattled its dry leaves. Her windbreaker glowed in the near darkness.

"Catherine?"

"I'm not going in there."

"What *is* it?"

"No. I'm fine out here." Her voice was feathery in the wind.

"Do you want me to stay out here with you?"

"You better not."

Samantha and Gislaine came down and took Gabrielle by the arms. Samantha held out her hand to Catherine. Catherine shook her head. Samantha held her hand steady. Catherine turned away.

Gabrielle was taken through the library and into the middle room. Down-pointing gooseneck lamps made circles of lights on the carpeting. The stacks of metal boxes were in disarray. The blankets lay in a pile.

"She just got here," Gislaine said.

"We have to show you," Samantha said. "I opened seven."

Audra came in from the kitchen.

"You know," she said, "I'm starting to think Catherine has the right idea. Let's."

"Get the hell out of here," Rushel said.

"We have to show you," Gislaine said. "If you wouldn't mind entering our laboratory. In the kitchen."

Walking through the doorway, Gabrielle saw rows of steel cylinders on the counter, mottled and dusty under the halogens. There was also a row of water and wine glasses. The glasses were half filled by what looked like chips of broken glass. Funny looking glass.

"I used your tools." Samantha picked up a wine glass.

"What's that stuff?" Audra said. "Marbles?"

"We're keeping track of the serial numbers," Gislaine said. She dumped the contents of a glass onto the laminated tourist placemat of California adorned with pictures of oranges and avocados. "Do any of you know anything about diamonds?"

"Oh my." Audra rushed closer. "Goodness."

"Each box, each Träger, we've opened has one hundred diamonds. And they're fairly large, I think." Samantha shrugged and grinned. "I'm sure they're very valuable but I have no idea how much."

"A *lot*," Rushel said.

"More than gold?" Audra's nose was almost touching the placemat. "They're all really big. Look. That one's a half inch across. And that one, it's kind of bluish. I think that's something. Wow!"

"The boxes with the diamonds have a lead lining. To boost their weight, maybe."

"To block x-rays," Gabrielle said. "Eighty-two lightweight boxes. Eighty-two hundred diamonds. Interesting. What do you think, Samantha? What's L doing?"

"The boxes with the coins are perfectly clean inside. They're new, I think. L took some of M's money and bought a bunch of Krugerrands and other coins. The diamond carriers have a different feel. Older. And the way they're organized. I think they came out of long term storage somewhere."

"That fits in with what she said."

"L loves jewelry," Audra said. "It's an obsession. This makes perfect sense."

"So a government like East Germany has thousands of diamonds in little boxes." Gabrielle heard raised voices outside, one definitely Catherine.

"Diamonds would be even more untraceable than gold coins," Samantha said as she watched the front door. "It's not like those guys trust banks."

"Maybe this is how they pay spies," Gislaine said.

"L took M's money," Gabrielle said, "and got access. And bought them?"

"Stole," Audra said. "A skunk can't change its smell."

"Well, we don't know that for sure."

"Why would you doubt it?"

"In the police station that's exactly what she told us. I automatically did not believe her."

"For her, telling the truth is the ultimate deception."

"Let's keep opening," Samantha said.

"Is she still in the wine cellar?" Rushel said.

"Who is she be calling," Gabrielle said. "Who else *is* there? Does she know about all this?"

"She wouldn't let me explain," Samantha said. "I don't think she saw the diamonds."

"*Way* more valuable than gold," Rushel said. "I can probably find out in the library. If we thought ninety boxes of gold coins was about eight million dollars with diamonds it will be multiples of that."

"Multiples." Gabrielle tried to visualize it.

"Money changes people," Catherine said from the doorway. Gabrielle looked up sharply.

"M started off as a rich girl in Hollywood," Gislaine said. "Maybe she'll just go back to that."

"Hollywood," Gabrielle said.

They all heard a loud thump under the floor.

"She can't hear us, can she?" Gislaine paused in her writing.

"Nothing would surprise me," Gabrielle said. "This is amazing, Samantha."

"She's very handy," Catherine said. "She works on Lamborghinis."

"Of course." Gabrielle cleared her throat. "Are."

There was another thump from below.

Gabrielle felt Samantha's hand on hers.

"Dinner will be right now," Catherine said. "The table is already set."

"Oh yum," Samantha said.

"Let's hurry and have dinner, okay?" Catherine said.

They all had before them bowls of tomato soup, and they were the big bowls with straight sides, and large spoons. And grilled cheese sandwiches with deep grill marks. Melted cheese had run over the plates.

As Gabrielle slid into her seat, her mouth watering, Catherine stood.

"The Goddess is here. It's my turn. Please join hands."

Gabrielle took Audra and Samantha's hands.

"Close your eyes."

"But."

"Close them."

Gabrielle hesitated. She tried to comprehend Catherine's expression. Her scar was only slightly visible, however, so she wasn't too worried. She closed her eyes.

"In the beginning," Catherine said and stopped.

Gabrielle heard footsteps on the porch. The screen door slammed. There was a loud crash and a light bulb popped. Then shuffling shoes in the middle room. Then giggles. Gabrielle kept her eyes closed.

"In the beginning, we were all lost souls," Catherine said. Her voice quavered and grew calm. "Allow me to remind you of the details. Gislaine. You were a waitress with two college degrees disowned by her family living alone in an illegal converted garage in South Laguna. No bathroom. You used a bucket. Rushel. Junior college dropout. Pot head. Living in a trailer with potheads in that idiot's backyard. No water, no electricity. Your mother refused to speak to you."

Gabrielle heard quiet sobbing. It was Audra. The sounds from the middle room had stopped.

"Audra. Vandalism. Assault and battery. Drunk driving. Your parents threw you out. You lived in an abandoned shipping container at the waterfront. There were rats. You got food from dumpsters."

Catherine took a deep breath.

"Samantha. An escaped slave now call girl walking down a Hollywood sidewalk in worn out Candies. No residence. No car. A hundred twenty thousand in the bank under a fake name."

She paused.

"Okay. I admit that one's kind of cool."

They all laughed and Gabrielle felt Samantha squeeze her hand.

"Gabrielle. Living in silence in a basement. Soon to graduate to a lifetime of silence, not quite here, not quite alive. And Catherine. Assistant chef at a Hollywood restaurant and kept out of sight in the back because when customers saw her they got sick. A lifelong celibate. But don't feel sorry for her because she had recently discovered a new friend called heroin, a whole new kind of beauty, so it's not like she was going to be alive much longer anyway.

"That's who we were. And then, one by one, we found each other and it is my belief it was not random chance. It was intended. I don't know what's going to happen next but – "

"Don't worry, I know!"

Gabrielle was startled by M's voice. Drunk, she thought, very drunk. But her speech wasn't slurred. Sharper. A sudden realization hit her. M is a crazy drunk like me.

"Look at you all! This is so much *fun*."

"M, wait."

"Now everyone keep your eyes closed. Here, take my hands. Rushel. Catherine. Thank you. Finally, it's my turn."

Gabrielle felt Audra and Samantha tense up.

"In the beginning it was me," M said. "All me. And you know what's funny? It's still all me. What's going to happen next is, well, *me*. Not her anymore. I am finally released. It's been so long. I predict." She burped loudly. "Here's some advice, girls. If you find a bottle of old Russian wine in a cellar, do *not* drink it."

M vomited onto the dining table, a thick splashing, a long "*Urrp*." Gabrielle felt the front of her sweatshirt become soaked. Her hands were released but no one spoke. She couldn't breathe in the stench. Ancient vinegar, black mold, cat piss. She counted to five and opened her eyes.

Regurgitated red wine lay in a film on their their soup and was soaking into the sandwiches. Her spoon was half full of it.

M, cross-eyed, said, "Oopsie," and burped again. Her face went slack and she walked backwards through the door. Titanium boxes rattled to the carpeting.

Audra was the first to get up.

"We got it."

Catherine went to the sink and stood with her head down. Rushel hugged Gislaine and got dish towels and Samantha began piling up plates dripping with pink vomit.

They wouldn't let her help. Gabrielle reluctantly left the dining room. In the middle room, she walked around toppled boxes and the broken floor lamp. There was a puddle of vomit on the porch and she took a long step over it. M's Jeep was gone. The disturbed sand on the steps had a large wet area.

She stood on the bottom step. The chaparral flowers danced in the wind. She watched the cold night for a minute. Chilled, she shuddered and went back inside.

In the kitchen they still wouldn't permit her to help so she went to her room. Lying flat, her pounding heart made her shirt pulsate. Sometime later in the dark they came in and lay beside her but, later, she was never certain of this memory.

When she thought about it she concluded the whole thing could've been a dream.

Gabrielle woke to an empty house.

In her robe, she stood barefoot in the kitchen. Cold. Vacant. Gone for hours. She checked each room. Clothes still hung in closets. Certain items were missing. Catherine's sneakers and windbreaker. Samantha's sandals and tunic.

So they got dressed and left, she thought.

There was no note on the counter or fridge. The kitchen was perfectly clean. The neat stacks of coins and the glasses full of diamonds had not been moved.

She fished out a diamond as big as a marble, beautifully faceted. She lifted her glasses. The way it reflected light. What a fascinating object. She stuck it in her robe pocket.

In the middle room, the boxes lay in untidy stacks. She pulled up the blinds in the library. Her car sat where she had parked it. In the gray light, no other cars were visible. She opened the front door. The vomit had been scrubbed.

So what do I do, she thought. Thursday. Just PE. There's no other place to go.

She tossed the robe on the bed and got dressed and got all her remaining money from the top drawer. Eight dollars and a quarter. She wasn't hungry and did not want coffee. She left the front door unlocked.

She started the engine. Barely a half tank left. She rolled away from the house. She made sure the gate was locked behind her. She hesitated in the silence of the idling car. She didn't want to leave. It felt wrong to leave.

She left.

An hour earlier than usual, she got three dollars of gas and went to the campus by an illogical, circuitous route and easily found a spot by the theater. She had five dollars left. And then what? Access the savings account. $349.18, she knew. It would have to last.

She sat in the car as the sun warmed her and tried not to think the unthinkable.

Heading for the old gym, she caught herself. She stopped dead in the street.

Right, right, she thought with a weird shock. No more PE. I guess I forgot. How? Just the final in Advanced Topics next week. She let the hurrying students flow impatiently around her. She felt dizzy.

"Not thinking straight."

It was finished. The quarter was finished. She had no reason to be here. The Stacks. I'll go there. Just for a while. Then.

"I'll go home and they'll all be back."

There was a sign on the door to the Stacks. 'Closed No Access."

Gabrielle stared at it, mind empty of thoughts, until a student behind her spoke.

"You can't go in there," he said.

"Right." She rolled her eyes.

He didn't notice. Wrinkled t-shirt. *The Who.* Unwashed hair.

She walked away without looking back.

"They're tearing it out," he said. "It's all going away. Sucks. It was my favorite place in this whole dorkwad school."

"Mine too."

"Yeah, it's all rich kids now. Glad I'm almost out of here."

Out on the small library plaza, Gabrielle sat at the end of one of the concrete benches. The sun was warm and she began to sweat under her shirt. She shivered, chilled to the bone.

"I'll just sit here," she said.

Someone sat down next to her. Crinkly nylon. Bright yellow.

Gabrielle, surprised, did not move at first. Then she looked. Catherine's hair was matted to her head. Her eyes were dull. The scar was deeper than she had ever seen it before.

"I need to talk to you. It's important." She wiped her eyes.

Gabrielle kept her voice steady.

"All right."

"Let's go back to your car."

No questions. I'm back to that.

"I'm by the theater."

At the car, Gabrielle forced herself to not fumble the keys and unlocked Catherine's door first. Catherine made no move to get in until she slid into the driver's seat. She caught a glimpse of Catherine's face. The anger had been replaced by what looked like anguish. As she closed her door the anger returned.

"Go back to the house," she said.

"You said you wanted to talk to me."

"Are you deaf?" Catherine stared straight ahead.

"No, I'm not deaf."

"Drive to the house."

Gabrielle waited but Catherine would not look at her.

She got the car started and drove back the way she came. Still no blue Toyota in the grocery store parking lot. She went as fast as she dared. Catherine remained motionless, tense and silent, her hands folded on her lap.

As the wind gusted, Gabrielle hit the sand trap and accelerated to the gate. Whatever this is, she thought, let's get it over with. She hit the brakes. There was a small animal in the road. It ran into the sage. Not a brush rabbit.

"That was that kitten. Did I tell you?"

Catherine was looking at the spot where the kitten had been. Surprise and fear crossed her face.

"No," she said. She turned away with her hand on her cheek.

At the house, Catherine opened her door before the VW stopped
and went quickly into the house. She slammed the front door behind her.
Gabrielle took her time parking. No Jeep, no Toyota. Going up the porch
she saw Catherine's footprints on the sandy steps but no other disturbances
since early morning.

So it's just us, she thought.

She slowly turned the doorknob, half expecting it to be locked, and
stepped into the library. Cold, dark. The broken lamp lay where it had fallen.
In the middle room the boxes and blankets were untouched. She stood in
the doorway to the kitchen. The diamonds were still there. Catherine stood
at the end of the counter. Her hands were fists. Gabrielle was afraid to step
into the room.

She stepped into the room.

Catherine instantly went to the sink and picked up a water glass. She
opened her hand and it shattered on the porcelain. Gabrielle heard her
mutter and she angrily reached into the sink again. The tossed the broken
glass onto the kitchen floor and then another glass. She opened a drawer
and grabbed forks and spoons and with angry look dropped them calmly.
She jerked the silverware drawer out and the track broke and she pulled
it free. She dumped the remaining spoons and knives then dropped the
drawer. She methodically pulled out each drawer and did the same. Hand
towels. Spatulas. All the knives in a sharp clatter around her feet. Tongs.
Potholders.

"Catherine."

Catherine swept the coffee maker off the counter. The half full carafe
exploded. She then grabbed the handle of the microwave. The door popped
open. She slammed it shut.

"Fuck you."

She opened it and slammed it again.

"Fuck you, asshole."

She opened it yet again and with careful consideration dragged the
microwave off the counter. It crashed onto the scattered silver forks and
chef's knives. The door snapped off with a loud crack. She stepped over it
and opened the refrigerator.

"Catherine, stop."

"Stop? No one tells me what to do."

Catherine took a carton of milk, held it out, and dropped it. It split and
milk flowed under the dining table. More milk then a carton of orange juice,
cranberry juice, cream. Lettuce, a bunch of celery, leeks. A plastic drawer hit
the floor and styrofoam trays of hamburger, steaks, and fish slid out in a fan.
A large film wrapped package with writing that looked Japanese. Tofu.

"Why are you doing this?"

"Huh," Catherine said. She pushed open the sliding glass door. Sand
spilled onto the floor. "Maybe you're not as smart as they say you are. Ever

think that, Goddess? Ever think, maybe I'm kind of stupid."

She tossed the lettuce and celery outside. She did the same with all the trays of meat. Then she opened a drawer and, one by one, threw potatoes and onions out on to the sand. Tomatoes, apples, pears, and a double handful of garlic. The papery skin made a scratching sound.

"Hey, Jonathon Livingston asshole, come and get it!" She looked up. "Pretty funny, huh? Let's see. Ah yes."

Catherine opened all the upper cabinets. Dinner plates, bowls, serving platters, gravy boats, water glasses, wine glasses, were quickly pushed off their shelves.

"Catherine, stop. Please."

"I'm sorry, what?" Catherine dumped a bin of sugar on the floor. She picked up a box of salt and tore the top off.

"Please. Please stop. I'm asking you."

She set the box of salt on a stool.

"Good. See, you're learning. What I wanted to talk to you about is this." She took a deep breath. She clenched her hands on the counter and looked at a far corner of the living room. "You tried to trick me into saying I love you. I thought it was funny at the time. Oh look at her. Then it pissed me off. How dare you. You. You *kid*. And all that stuff I told you about me please just forget I said it."

Gabrielle tried to speak but no sound came out.

"We. None of us like you. We've been putting up with you but no more. We're all tired of you."

From the seething turmoil of emotions swamping her mind Gabrielle found the thread.

"You're lying," she said.

Catherine shook her head. "Look, Gabrielle."

"You don't think I'm smart, fine. But I can tell when you're lying."

"You can shut up now."

"Catherine, someone told you to say all that."

"No one tells me what to do."

"Someone told you what to say and you said it."

"You." Catherine grabbed a coffee cup. "*No* one." She threw it hard at the tile backsplash and it exploded into bits. "Get out. Go to your room, get your stupid things, and get out." She sounded weary.

"Cath—."

"Go. Hurry up." She kicked at the pile of dishes. She kicked a glass bowl into the living room. "Why are you standing there?"

Gabriele decided it would be best to say what she was thinking.

"I'm really scared. I don't know what I did to make you so mad. I don't understand all this. But if you want me to leave."

Catherine remained motionless.

Gabrielle walked to her room. Suddenly unsure of her balance she gripped the door jamb. My things, she thought. All right

She opened all the drawers of the bureau. Four t-shirts, two pairs of socks with multiple holes. A black silk sweater, silk undies.

Catherine went into the big bathroom and Gabrielle heard her knocking over stuff on the counter. Catherine rummaged through the medicine chest and slammed the mirror door so hard it shattered. Then she was in the bedroom. She tossed items onto the unfolded white bathrobe. Toothbrush. A tiny bottle of perfume.

"God, you're so slow."

"I'm sorry."

Catherine gathered up Gabrielle's clothes and dumped them onto the robe, then folded the robe over. She held the bundle up.

"See, wasn't that simple? Do I have to tell you everything? Take it!"

Hands tingling, Gabrielle took it.

"Remember where the front door is?"

Gabrielle carefully put one numb foot in front of the other. In the library, Catherine opened the front door and she hit the screen with the heel of her hand.

"There's your car. Get in your car and leave. And no matter what, never come back. You understand me? Never."

Gabrielle stepped over the threshold and Catherine instantly shut the door behind her. The deadbolt clicked and she heard Catherine's footsteps as she retreated to the kitchen, almost running.

She waited without knowing why and felt Catherine listening. Then she went down the steps and dropped the keys in the sand. The bundled robe slipped from her fingers also. Dizzy, she picked everything up.

She opened the car door and swung the bundle onto the passenger seat and got in. She turned the key and the Volkswagen lurched forward. Ears ringing, she pushed down the clutch. The engine caught, rough. Flooded it, said a voice in a distant crevice of her mind. She kept it in first and was around the corner dune before she thought to look back. The house was already out of sight.

Gabrielle made it to the pavement. She got past the eucalyptus grove. She rolled through the small town and onto the long valley road. She had little conscious awareness of these events. A small part of her mind operated the car. The rest was a raging cacophony of voices and crashing dinner plates. And Catherine's face.

It was hard to see. Her field of vision had contracted. She kept forgetting where her hands were or what gear the car was in. The traffic light loomed.

She pulled over and stopped. The noise in her mind did not let up. She began to feel cold.

So. Back, she thought. I have to go back. I have nowhere else to go.

Gabrielle shot onto the highway without looking and accelerated through the intersection as the light turned red. Horns blared behind her, she sped into the southern part of town. She felt like going fast as possible. She just had a feeling it might drown out the noise.

She roared past hotels and shopping centers and car dealerships. She veered around traffic and ran every red light she encountered. The freeway appeared. She coasted down to seventy. North or south? South, towards Los Angeles, would be admitting defeat so north it was. She dropped it into third and slalomed through three stop signs, almost on two wheels again, speed shifted and floored it up 101.

Past the drive-in movie place, *Invasion of the Body Snatchers*, past the town. Pastures and oak trees. Then the big hill, the long climb out of the coastal plain.

The car slowed in spite of maximum throttle and she settled in behind a gravel truck as a part of her consciousness rose above the noise and refused to destroy the engine by powering up the hill in first gear. Staring at the bumper of the truck her pulse slowed. The chill returned.

She crested the hill and passed the gravel truck and proceeded at legal speed into the interior of California. Dry hills, leafless trees, seemed to crawl by. A town passed then another.

On a curve the low sun caught her eye. Her ears popped. She looked at her watch. She looked at the gas gauge. *3:46.* Just above E.

I just feel like sleeping, she thought, To lie down with her head on a pillow was the best idea ever.

She reversed course at a county road and made her way back to the last town. She spent her last five on gas. In the restroom she was distantly interested to see that her urine was dark yellow, almost brown. Maybe I'm dying, she thought. But she knew it wouldn't be that easy.

Coasting back down the hill her worn tires whispered under the rushing wind. *Asunder, asunder.*

Her street was unchanged and utterly unfamiliar.

She found a spot in front of the house behind a new Saab.

"Someone has money," she said as she locked her door then remembered the bundle. Later, she thought.

She walked up the driveway and got out the key for the kitchen. When she reached the corner she heard a strange sound. It was the front door opening. She watched in surprise as a chubby guy came out and went down the walkway. The walkway was swept off and the lawn, still mostly brown, had been neatly mowed. She had no idea who the guy was. Student, but. White pants? She heard the tv playing and felt reassured.

The kitchen door was unlocked and the light was off. The window in the door rattled as always as she stepped in.

She recognized nothing in the kitchen. The old porcelain white refrigerator with its rounded off corners was gone. There was a new fridge with double doors. Sharp-edged. Dark gold color. The black Wedgewood stove had been replaced by a new glistening white model. It had a digital clock. There was a new toaster and new coffee maker, Mr. Coffee. The coffee maker had a clock, too. Gone was the massive old dial telephone. A lightweight clamshell model sat in its place on the phone book. She picked it up. Lighted touchtone keypad. And next to it was another device. She had to study it for a moment. Dual cassette tape player with another clock display. An answering machine. The oak kitchen table was now a glass disk with chrome legs strewn with papers and envelopes.

She heard laughter from the parlor. The right side of the room was dominated by a large color tv set in a wooden cabinet. The bright screen was alive with swirling colors. Gabrielle found it hard to look away. An animated logo appeared. *CNN*, said a deep announcer's voice.

She peeked a bit further. Multiple pairs of feet in socks. She stuck her whole head in. There were eight guys watching tv in the dark. Two were on the sofa, the reclining chairs were gone, the rest were sitting on the floor backs to the wall. The front door banged open and White Pants tromped in.

"Hey, whose red Volkswagen is that?"

"Mine," Gabrielle said. Nine heads snapped around.

One of the guys on the sofa laughed.

"Okay, *that* was funny," he said. "Are you?"

"I'm Gabrielle."

"Right. The girl in the basement. The lady told us."

"Mrs. Rosenberg?"

"Who? Hang on." He got up and went past her into the kitchen.

"All of you live here?" All the heads nodded. "There are ten in this house?"

"Lucky to get this," said the one closest. Thick glasses. "I was living in my car."

"Here's your mail. Nice to meet you. My name's Kai, by the way." Sharp chin. "First year Triple-E."

There were two envelopes. One had a return address of Cuesta Property Management.

Ah yes, the rent, she thought. Well, how bad could it be?

"Triple-E? Great, me too," she said, trying to sound interested. She tore open the first envelope. The other was an official looking letter from the university. She had no idea what it could be.

The envelope contained a single sheet of paper. A photocopied form letter. *Rental Agreement.* Her name was written in a space labeled, *Tenant.*

Location: 1255 Cat Creek Avenue.

Rental Rate: $345.75 per month.

Rent Due: First of the month.

Late Payment: Rent more than five days late will result in eviction.

Gabrielle had three thoughts. One, the rent for March was due today.

Two, the first payment will wipe out my savings. Three, the *fuck* I'm paying this. So I guess I'll be living in my car, also. Her ears ringing again it took her a moment to notice that Kai was talking.

"Anyway, I forgot," he said. "Your friend came by. I hope it was all right."

"What? Who?" she said in irritation.

"Your friend. She's down there now."

"Who?"

"Your blonde friend. She said you'd be surprised."

"Yeah." Gabrielle tried to keep hold of the letters. She's here. How'd she get here? I knew she was lying, I knew it.

She had to talk to her. She wanted to talk to her more than anything.

"All right, thank you," she said.

She went to the basement door. Light headed, she grabbed the knob. She let go and wiped her hands. Okay, she thought.

She opened the door and stepped onto the landing. There was a blonde woman sitting on her bed reading a magazine. The study lamp shone up. Gabrielle closed the door firmly and took the first tread.

"Catherine," she said watching her step.

"Oh, hi. Who's Catherine?"

Gabrielle stopped.

Linda had a new hairstyle, shorter and straighter, all brushed over to the right.

"This is where you live, huh? You told me it was tiny but dang."

"Linda."

"Are you upset I'm here? You are definitely upset." She dropped the magazine. *Vogue.*

Gabrielle tried to breathe.

"I'm not upset about you."

"But you are upset. Here sit down by the cozy clothes dryer and tell faithful sidekick Linda what's wrong. You don't want to sit down?"

"I'm too worked up.

"Wow. You are."

Gabrielle got to the final step and held onto the railing. She felt like she might throw up. Then she felt like laughing.

"It's great that you're here."

"You sure you're not upset about me?"

"No. God, no. Like, finally, someone who knows me."

Linda smiled and giggled.

"I thought I knew you. I had fun meeting your friends."

The knot returned to Gabrielle's stomach.

"My who?"

"They came into the restaurant. Patricia and Holly. And Debbie. Boy, Susan has red hair, doesn't she?"

Gabrielle stared at her.

"Anyway, it was lucky they ran into me. They were having trouble finding your house. Good thing your mom happened to be home yesterday. They were all there this morning – what?"

Gabrielle took the steps three at a time. She missed the top one and nailed her shin. She could feel bleeding. She stumbled into the cold dark kitchen. Blood was running in her shoe. She slid into the counter and grabbed the phone. The phonebook hit the floor. She punched her number, got the last digit wrong, hit the hanger and started over.

Linda was behind her.

"See. I knew it. You're upset I'm here."

The phone rang.

"Gabrielle."

Gabrielle held up her hand. Another ring.

"I don't understand. Is there."

"Linda."

"But they said."

The phone was picked up.

"Mom!"

She could hear breathing.

"Mom! Mom?"

"Ah. Hey you."

Female voice. Young. Amused. Then off to the side.

"Hey, everyone, guess who."

Gabrielle heard voices calling out.

"Patricia," she said through gritted teeth.

"Right. How's it going, lover?"

"You're in my house."

"You were in *my* house."

"Where's my mom?"

"Sitting on the sofa. We were watching the news before taking off. Traffic reports, you know."

"Let me talk to my mom."

"Oh don't be silly, you silly goose. Everything's fine. For now."

"*Patricia.*"

"Gabrielle, you've been holding out on us. Your mom is an absolute scream. We've been having a blast telling her all about this *torrid* affair you've been having with this hot blonde. Which turned into an intense threesome with a simply incredible Native American woman."

"Apache, you *ass*hole."

"Whatever. She's different, isn't she? We all had so much fun listening. Holly should be in your neck of the woods already. You might run into her. Oh, and someone wants to talk to you."

The phone jostled.

"Hi," said another female voice. A new voice, speaking low. "Gabrielle?"

"Who are you?"

"Well," she laughed. "I'm Susan. I guess I'm the one Susan you haven't met yet. First Susan, right? That's flattering. You know, Patricia, Debbie, and I stayed here last night. Your mom is super nice. Debbie slept on the couch. Patricia and I slept in your bed. We did it in your bed, Gabrielle. Isn't that hot?"

"Put my mom on the phone," Gabrielle said, face burning.

"I'm looking forward to meeting you."

"Put my mom on the phone or I'm going to hang up and call the Covina Police."

Linda gasped.

"Oh all right." Another laugh. "Bye!"

There was a long pause. She heard Patricia say, "Allison."

They're calling my mom by her first name she thought in a cold rage.

"Hi, Sweetie," her mother said.

"Mom!"

"I don't know why you didn't tell me, honey."

"Mom, look."

"You know you can talk to me about anything. Patricia, Susan, and Debbie are wonderful people, although we all agree." There was laughter in the background. "That Holly is a bit much."

Gabrielle felt a pressure building in her temples. She wiped the sweat from her face.

"That's true, Mom."

"What did you want to tell me?"

Gabrielle felt her stomach cramp again and there was a metallic taste in her mouth. A voice said, "Don't do it."

"What was that?"

"Oh, just that the quarter will be over in a week and I'll be back down."

"Oh. That's it?"

"That's it."

"Are you sure?"

Gabrielle could hear Eyewitness News playing. She pictured her mom in her bathrobe and slippers standing in the living room at the small end table, the round one, the perfect place for a phone. And Patricia and First Susan were standing right behind her.

"Everything's fine. It's been a long quarter."

There was another pause.

"All right, Sweetie. We'll talk when you get here."

"Sure."

"I love you."

"I love you, too, Mom. Oh, could I talk to Patricia again? I'll see you soon."

"Sure, Sweetie."

The phone changed hands again and she heard Patricia breathing. Waiting for Mom to sit back down by the tv out of earshot, she knew.

"Patricia!"

"Hi, Sweetie," Patricia said softly.

"Get out of my house."

"Maybe."

"Get out of my house and never bother my mother again."

"Oh, poor Gabrielle. Poor sad powerless Gabrielle. We can do anything we want. You'll find out very soon. You ruined everything. And no matter how long it takes, no matter what, we will get even. I do hope you understand me, Sweetie."

Gabrielle heard the plastic phone crack as she squeezed it.

"Still there? Well, gotta hit the road."

She heard First Susan call out, "See you!"

The line went dead.

Gabrielle dropped the phone on the counter.

"Okay," she said. "Okay."

Linda was backed up to the wall.

"So I shouldn't have."

"No."

"Done that."

"You couldn't know."

"They weren't your friends."

"Just the opposite."

"I'm so sorry, Gabrielle."

"It's my fault. I said the name of your restaurant under the chandelier."

"The what?"

"Everything all right?" It was one of the guys from the front room. Black eyebrows, black t-shirt. He and Kai and all the others crowded the doorway. "We heard the word police."

Gabrielle shook back her hair and hung up the phone. The guy saw her nose. Linda, she noticed, was also seeing it.

"Thanks. There's nothing you can do, really."

"We could beat the shit out of 'em."

Gabrielle grinned.

"Violence never solved anything," Kai said to universal eye rolling.

"Not solving anything, dude. Just beating the shit out of 'em."

"Thanks, but it doesn't matter. I can't afford to live here anymore anyway. They raised my rent so high I can't believe it."

Several said, "What?"

"Yeah, and it was due this morning which I didn't even know so now in five days they're going to evict me. I can live in my car. It's all right."

"Fuck 'em." It was White Pants. "Stay here anyway."

Kai gave him a squinty look for the bad word and said, "Yeah, don't worry about it."

"They're really slow." A guy in blue flannel. "Be a couple weeks before they notice."

"Okay." Gabrielle grinned again. They were all smiling now.

"The whole company is some guy and his girlfriend," said Black T-shirt. "Hospitality majors."

Gabrielle laughed. "What the heck is that?" She realized the Golf major was missing. "Thanks, I won't worry about it."

They're gone by now, she thought suddenly. My house is clear. I can call Mom back and warn her.

Most of the guys went back to the tv. Black T-shirt and Kai looked like they were about to say something.

"Well, I need to straighten out my room."

Don't call, said a voice. Her voice. She's alone in the house. Maybe never tell her. The thought surprised her.

Gabrielle ducked around the corner to her door.

"Audra was right. Your feelings can kill you."

Close behind, Linda said, "Who? Oh my God, Gabrielle. Those guys! They're like your private army!"

They went down the stairs side by side.

At the bottom, Gabrielle saw the other letter on the floor.

"May as well see what this is. Really dizzy."

"Well, no wonder. Have you eaten anything today?"

"Don't remember." Waking up in the empty house seemed like a lifetime in the past.

"So who were those girls? They told your mom all kinds of stories. I don't even want, you know, to say."

"I'll tell you everything, I promise. Ultimate pinkie swear."

They interlocked fingers. Gabrielle blinked away tears. She ripped open the envelope.

"You can't tell me now?"

"I don't know the ending yet."

She took out the single sheet of paper. She read the single paragraph. She sat on the bed.

"What is it?"

"We were expecting a thunderbolt."

"I don't know what you're talking about."

"February twenty-six, nineteen seventy-nine. From Assistant Administrator, Office of Student Evaluations and Records, Forensic Division. It says, 'Irregularities in your College of Engineering admission documentation have been brought to our attention. These irregularities are of a disqualifying nature. Therefore, beginning March one, nineteen seventy-nine, you are **suspended** from the University until further notice. A preliminary hearing has been scheduled at the following time: December fifth, eight a.m. in this office. Subsequently, all your courses preregistered for Spring Quarter have been canceled. If you have any questions, please contact this office. And so on."

"Gabrielle, this place is insane."

"I know."

"Is that real? What are you going to do?"

"Not sure."

"Which one?"

Gabrielle shrugged.

"Okay." Linda looked around the basement.

"This might be it. I've been kicked out of school."

I just feel cold, she thought. All emotions, rage, shame, terror of losing someone, all coalesced into a background roar. And she knew if she let it the roar would escalate into a shriek which would blank out the world. "So don't let it."

"Don't let what? They can't just kick you out."

"They can do anything they want."

"You still have that ugly green jacket? Who's they?"

"If this is them."

"Sounds bogus to me. I'm starving."

"I don't have any money."

"I have money. I'm rich."

"You're."

"Rich. Come on. Let's go somewhere like."

"McDonald's."

"And then let's go to a motel."

"Well."

"Because I don't think we're both gonna fit."

"In my bed. Yeah."

"Let's take my car."

"You have a new Saab nine hundred."

Talking about cars was a welcome distraction as they pulled out of McDonald's. The interior still had the new car smell, and leather seats. Gabrielle cradled two milkshakes she had talked Linda into, chocolate and strawberry. Plus an untouched apple pie in her pocket.

"It's not brand new. No way. My dad helped me. You remember what he called people who bought new cars?"

"Non-union product testers."

The Saab glowed in the streetlights.

"There was an ad in the paper. This old lady just didn't want it anymore."

"Nice."

"So I'm an old lady now."

They went to the south end of town. The Saab was fast and built like a tank. There were chain motels in a row and Linda eenie-minee'd one.

"Oh my God, I forgot your clothes and everything."

"That's okay. I really don't want to go back." Even though I have to, she thought.

The motel had two beds and a color tv. The bathroom had two little bars of soap on the counter, tiny plastic cups, and an extra roll of toilet paper. No health aides dispenser on the wall. And all the hot water you could want.

When she came out barefoot, Linda was curled up on the bed watching tv. The sound was barely audible. There was a cardboard box on the floor.

"Thought maybe you fell asleep in there."

"I've just been cold all day. Shivering. And my ears are stopped up."

"Uh huh. Here."

Linda rolled to the edge and reached into the box.

"What's that?"

"Vital supplies."

She took out a rectangular box. There was a plastic spigot sticking out of it.

"Isn't this cool? Wine in a box. Oh, look, disposable cups we can use. Perfect for cheap wine. I just went and bought it and they didn't card me or anything. Guess I look old. An old lady in a Saab. It's real."

The label on the box said, *White Wine.*

"Is it a Riesling? Or Chardonnay?"

"Whoa."

"I've learned a few things."

"Don't doubt it. Here."

After two sips of the sour wine Gabrielle felt warmer and almost relaxed. She sat on her bed. It was hard to focus on the tv. Her ears popped again and there was a rushing sound. It was the toilet flushing. Linda came out and turned off the tv.

"Okay, drink up."

"Okay." Gabrielle was surprised the see her cup was empty.

"Good girl."

Linda pulled back the covers of Gabrielle's bed.

"You just lie down now."

"Okay."

"Wait. Probably should take your pants off first."

"Good idea."

Linda laughed.

"The faithful sidekick is always the one with the good ideas. That's how it works. When the hero is in trouble, the sidekick comes to the rescue. Like now."

"Wow."

Gabrielle found the zipper challenging and it took a while. Linda watched patiently as she let her pants slip to the floor.

"Commando style, huh? Get in the bed, my hero."

Gabrielle saw the soft pillow come up and hit her head with a sigh. Where am I, she thought. Oh. Linda. The house. Catherine. Diamonds, gold, Catherine, M, rent, suspended. What is this I'm feeling? She thought.

"I'll tell you what you're feeling." Linda pulled the covers up.

"Did?" The blanket was thin. She curled up but the warmth from the shower was gone.

Linda switched off the table lamp. The curtains glowed. Linda got into her bed.

"You're in shock. That's what you're feeling."

"Is this what it feels like when you die?"

"I don't know."

"You're always honest, that's for sure."

Gabrielle," Linda whispered into the darkness. "What happened? Tell me what happened."

"You would never believe me. My friends don't like me anymore. And the others hate me."

"You mean Patricia? Them?"

"Yeah, those are L's girls. And Catherine."

"Who is that?"

"I love her but she doesn't love me."

"Oh."

"I love you too, Linda, just not like that."

"I see."

"She made me leave. I had to get my things and leave."

"What a jerk."

"I think she was lying. M made her. She said bad things to me."

"My God, I'm so sorry."

"I'm really cold."

"Hang on." Linda slipped out and came around to the other side of Gabrielle's bed. She pulled the covers back and got in.

Gabrielle closed her eyes as Linda's warm body fitted close behind her.

"You're ice cold. If this doesn't help, back to the hot shower."

"I feel much better. It's hard to think. Vathys. Stage seven."

"Huh? So what won't I believe?"

"Do you know about the die-off?"

"Um, yeah, I guess. It was in the news a while back."

"I did it."

"What?"

"Yeah. And the government of East Germany is hunting for me because we have all their diamonds and gold coins. And Audra's going to be in a porno movie. And I hit Andrea in the head with an apple. And I got handcuffed by the police. And New Susan crashed her car into a building.

Right through the window. Oh! And it was a Saab. Isn't that interesting?"

"You weren't kidding."

"That's nothing. There's a lot more. I just don't understand why she did that. I'm not selfish, I don't think."

"No, you're not."

"I really never thought I would find anyone. I thought, there's no one for me. How could there be? I will live my life alone. And then." Gabrielle suppressed a wave of sadness. "And then I thought maybe. Maybe there is."

"Go ahead and cry," Linda said.

"Selfish people cry. They didn't get what they want so they cry. She didn't want to go with me. I just."

Gabrielle fell asleep in mid-thought as Linda caressed her face.

The morning was cold with a faint sun in a milky sky and they drove slowly until they found a tiny doughnut place. They got coffee. Gabrielle, drained, nibbled on her McDonald's apple pie. Then Linda took her back to the house.

They stood on the wet sidewalk, hands in pockets.

"I have to get going." Linda had brushed her hair straight back and it kept getting loose from behind her ears.

"All right."

"I'll see you next week."

"Yeah. Probably Friday."

"Do you like it here?"

"I used to. Thanks for everything."

"I keep telling you. Did you know you talk in your sleep?"

"Oh."

"Uh huh. This is all because of that lady in the store, isn't it?"

"Yes. It is."

Linda looked away.

"It's not like I haven't thought about it. You know I've never had a boyfriend."

"What about Steve Laskowski in ninth grade?"

"Oh, he doesn't count."

"Sure looked like it counted."

"Nope."

"Okay."

"Let's discuss this next week."

"I'll call you when I get home," Gabrielle said and when she moved to hug her Linda hesitated a half heartbeat. Well, she thought, as Linda's arms encircled her.

Then Linda was in her car, waving, and gone around a corner. Gabrielle stood motionless until she got cold again.

"I'm right back where I was before. Nothing has changed," she said.

Then she said with absolute weariness, "Everything has changed."

She got the bundle of clothes. "At least everything's clean." She organized her shirts on her bed and put the robe on. So soft. Luxurious, that's the word, but it had a faint trace of Catherine's shampoo and she said to the bare rafters, "Yeah, no. Get rid of it." She put her hands in the pockets for the last time.

"Ah. *Right.*"

That afternoon, feeling much less weary, she walked to the school and went directly to the library. The place was jammed. She wanted current info, as current as possible. Periodicals? She went to the desk and waited for the librarian, a woman with thick glasses and a facial expression, Gabrielle knew, of someone who hated college students. Ms. Johnson, her nametag said. She directed the guy ahead of her, who was looking for information about sea otters, to the rows of encyclopedias with a sneering smile. Her eyes went to the rumpled sweatshirt, her unbrushed hair, and the ring.

"Yes?"

"Looking for any current information about diamonds, the jewelry kind. About the market. Prices, mostly."

"You too?"

Gabrielle thought, yep.

"Periodicals, door B, subsection violet, shelf azure." She raised her eyebrows.

"Oh of course." Gabrielle walked away.

Periodicals was a long room with nice carpeting. She easily found the azure shelf and pulled out a file box labeled, *Diamond Market World,* magazines printed in black and white. The latest issue was October, 1978. There were charts and graphs, all interesting, and she found what she wanted right away. Carats, clarity, cut. She put the helpful magazine back and headed straight out of the library. If Rushel was there she did not want to see her.

Next, the Science building. Biology would have it, she knew. Her watch said *1:11.*

Down an echoing hall of classrooms, all occupied, all with open doors. From each, soft, droning voices of professors. But not the last room. She walked by and did a scan. Full seats, no professor. Sophomores, she guessed. Young looking but without the nervous movements of first years and yet not bored like juniors and seniors. There was a name in the corner of the chalkboard. *Mrs Wilkinsen.*

And along the back counter, a row of analytical scales. Ten seconds would do it, she thought. I could just walk in, they wouldn't care. But I don't want anyone to see what I have.

She had another thought, a mischievous idea.

"I'm suspended," she said. "What can they do to me?"

She threw her head back and walked into the classroom. All eyes followed her. She smiled at them all, trying to look like a self-satisfied graduate student. She got a piece of chalk and wrote *Ms. Johnson.*

"Good morning, I'm Ms. Johnson."

The students smiled back.

"Mrs. Wilkinsen wanted me to tell you that today's class, which was going to be review, has been cancelled."

A sigh of relief issued from the students.

"Unless anyone has any questions?" She held up the chalk.

Widespread shaking of heads.

"In that case, good luck on the final and have a nice quarter break."

Several said thanks and they all packed up in a flurry of highly practiced activity. In less than a minute, the room was empty. Gabrielle walked between the desks.

She hit the power button on the closet scale, a midrange Ohaus. Student model but more than good enough. She zeroed the display and took the diamond from her pocket, checking to make sure no one was watching. She set the diamond in the center of the tray and closed the glass door. The display settled. Mind reeling, she grabbed the diamond, shoved it deep in her pocket.

"Well now."

She left the room and the Science building without looking back, once last time under the whispering pines. Goodbye, she thought.

Straight to the student union and the restrooms. The calculations completed themselves as she entered the stall.

One point seven five one seven grams. Two hundred milligrams per carat. So about eight and three quarters carats.

Now the price. Highly subjective judgment of clarity, cut, color. Anywhere from six thousand per carat to twenty-five. So fifty thousand to over two hundred thousand. That's the value of it, she thought. This bit of crystallized carbon.

"Shit. Why didn't I grab a handful of the stupid things? There were bigger ones, much bigger."

And the total. All of them. *Good God.* Eighty-two boxes at a hundred each equals eighty-two hundred diamonds. Average size? There were a lot of smaller ones. She guessed overall average size at three carats. Twenty-four thousand, six hundred carats. Might be low but.

She put her head between her knees.

One hundred forty-seven million at the low end to over six hundred million at the high end. *Dollars.*

Gabrielle had the sudden urge to drop the thing between her legs and flush. But it would pay off her mom's mortgage with a lot left over.

"Good."

I guess I am selfish, she thought. She didn't like this thought.

It was hard to sleep with all the extra feet overhead. All the laundry was outside her door. She had used the bathroom which was surprisingly clean and free of personal items. Her numerous new roommates were generally polite around her. They lowered their voices and didn't use bad words. They all stared at the ring as if in awe.

Gabrielle imagined what Catherine's reaction would've been. She could hear her voice.

"Those nice boys have never seen a girl like you."

"They won't stop staring."

"They're waiting for your command."

"Oh I don't think so."

"Trust me. If you were to sweetly request that someone go out and rebuild the engine of your car a huge fight would break out over who would get to do it."

"Yeah."

Gabrielle laughed under her blanket and then stopped. I'll never hear her voice again, she thought. Just like that and it's over.

Her chest tightened painfully and a deep shiver gripped her. She had no idea how she would make it through the night.

The dream returned.

A street of dark houses set behind hedges and trees. The clear sky was just lightening. The stars flickered. She recognized the houses and she knew she had never seen them before. The air was warm and still.

She knew the houses had been created for her. She turned full circle in the street. No cat scampering about.

She was anxious to find the house where her friends were, where she would be welcome. But she sensed herself drifting. Her feet no longer touched the pavement. She knew she was about to lose it forever and this filled her with terror.

Some unknown time in an endless night she awoke in total darkness and felt for her clothes. She left the house and walked the sleeping streets and paid no attention to where she was going. From nowhere, the small park lay before her. She went to the bench. Right here. She sat right here.

She waited for the sky to lighten but it didn't look anything like the dream.

Monday morning. Gabrielle smiled at Dr. Rimmler as he came down the office corridor. He smiled back and then grew concerned.

"Good to see you," he said. His sharp eyes bored into her's.

"There's a problem."

"What's the problem?" He unlocked his door.

"I got this letter. I guess it's real."

His eyes widened. "Real? Come on in."

Rimmler's office was a windowless box. Desk, bookshelves, side table with Selectric. Two office chairs with plastic wheels.

"Okay. Ready for the final?" When Gabrielle didn't smile he said, "Let's see this letter."

As Gabrielle gave it to him he continued to watch her face. Finally he pulled the paper out and read it.

Gabrielle was impressed. She had never seen Dr. Rimmler get angry before.

"This department. Never heard of it. The name here. Ward. Mean anything to you?"

"No, nothing."

"Well. Real? It looks *official.* You know I've been a professor here for eighteen years. I missed meeting your father by one quarter, I believe."

"Yes, you told me." Gabrielle smiled and this seemed to energize him.

"This is unmitigated horseshit. You ever hear the word matriculate? Funny old word. It means to enroll in a school and begin taking classes. Gabrielle, you matriculated years ago. If there was a problem with your admission, highly doubtful, the time for action has long since passed. Ancient history. If you're in, you're in. That simple."

"It says they canceled my classes. I was going to graduate."

"Yes." He read it again. He checked his watch. "Come on."

In the carpeted lobby of Administration, Rimmler studied a directory. He waved and smiled at the secretaries behind the main desk. They all seemed to know him. They went up to the third floor. Another directory. There was a room with three receptionists and behind them, closed office doors. The nameplate of the far left door read *Ward.* Rimmler spoke to the closest receptionist there.

"I'm here to see Ms. Ward."

"Do you have an appointment?" Her nameplate read *Tansy.*

"No, I do not."

"Well, if you'd like to make an appointment there may be something on Wednesday." She opened a large appointment book.

Rimmler said, "Is she here now?"

She looked at him blankly.

"I thought so."

Rimmler walked around her.

"Sir! You can't!"

"Oh, yeah?"

He opened the office door.

"Hey!" the receptionist said. She jumped up and tried to block him but Rimmler slipped into the office. Gabrielle could only see part of a bookcase and a framed diploma.

"Ms. Ward?" he said loudly. His voice filled the reception area.

"I'm sorry..." Tansy said.

Gabrielle heard another voice. Female. She couldn't make out the words. Tansy went back to her desk.

"Ms. Ward. I'm Mike Rimmler, professor, Department of Engineering. I demand an explanation of this."

Gabrielle could hear the rustle of paper and Ward's voice again. A dismissive tone.

"Ward," Rimmler said firmly. Gabrielle had to smile. No more 'Ms.'

"I am demanding you tell me the facts. As the academic advisor of Gabrielle Tyndall I am entitled to the facts that led to her being suspended."

Gabrielle heard Ward speak again. Low, as if deliberately trying not to be heard. She only hear Rimmler's side of the conversation.

"I do not intend to wait until December. You can tell me here and now or we can do this in the President's office. The President and I are on very good terms, Ward. You know why? Let me explain how universities work. Over the last four years I have been responsible for nine grants from industry, state, and federal governments totaling over forty million dollars. I can assure you the President will listen to me. Gabrielle Tyndall is not just one of our top students. She *is* the top. She is the star. And this is starting to feel like an attempt to harass her. There is no substance. That is what I will convey to the President."

Ward's voice again, argumentative.

"Trust me, Ward." Rimmler's voice was cutting. "We in the Engineering Department know what goes on in the outside world. We are not an ivory tower. This is all happening to Ms. Tyndall because she is gay. Admit it."

Gabrielle felt her entire body flush. The receptionists stared at her. The one at the third desk grinned and waved.

"Look, Susan. May I call you Susan? Gabrielle Tyndall isn't really suspended, is she? And her classes haven't been canceled –"

Gabrielle pushed open the door. She saw red. Cascading bright red hair. First Susan smiled at her from behind her desk. The smile became a look of hunger.

Rimmler, looking embarrassed, said, "We stand one hundred percent behind Gabrielle Tyndall."

"Dr. Rimmler, this won't do any good."

First Susan stared at her, ravenous.

"Oh, I disagree. Ward," he said sharply. "If this is something personal on your part my advice is start looking for a new job. I am leaving now for the President's office. I am not bluffing."

Rimmler ushered Gabrielle through the door and past the receptionists. She heard First Susan say, "Nice meeting you!"

In the hallway, Rimmler said, "Look, I'm sorry, I."

Gabrielle kissed him on the cheek.

"It won't do any good. They're in control."

"Control? Who's they?"

"My enemies."

Rimmler looked astounded.

"How could you have enemies? Even so, I assure you the President of the University is actually in control of the University."

"All right."

"Now, my instincts, honed by eighteen years of academic politics, tell me it would be better if I go alone to the President's office. How can I contact you? Do you have a phone at home?"

Gabrielle told him the number. "We even have an answering machine."

"Very good. Those things are useful. I will try to call before five but I can't be certain."

"Okay, Dr. Rimmler. Thank you so much for all this. I was so scared."

"You are our star student and this is criminal harassment. Ward is in deep trouble and she knows it. She's the one who is scared. If anything else happens along these lines, no matter how small, let me know right away."

"I will."

"Oh, and you never answered my question. Ready for the final?"

"Dr. Rimmler, your tests are too easy."

His laugh echoed down the hall. They shook hands and she waved goodbye as he got into the elevator for the top floor.

Then she walked back to the house checking over her shoulder the whole way.

The call came after she fell asleep. She listened to the tape in the morning. Rimmler spoke fast and to the point.

"Gabrielle, here is the situation. An investigation has been opened. The President was surprised and concerned. He said you should proceed as normal. Just ignore that letter and start spring quarter as always. Everything is all right. Okay? Come and see me any time."

Gabrielle pushed stop.

"Well, good," she said to the gurgling Mr. Coffee.

But she didn't believe it.

After withdrawing sixty dollars from her savings, it was a relief to be able to drive to school on Tuesday. She walked into her math final in a distracted state. Indifferently, she scanned her test paper. Just don't care, she thought. This state of mind seemed to help.

She finished quickly and sat in her chair thinking about what she was going to tell her mother. She was home by noon and found herself nervous about Thursday.

It was all too easy.

The final for Advanced Topics was at ten and when she came around the hallway corner she saw, uneasily, all her remaining classmates standing at the classroom door. Late? Dr. Rimmler was late for the final? She made herself breathe normally.

"I'm used to bad news," she whispered.

When Daniel saw her he said, "Ah, good."

"Good?" Gabrielle said.

"Was staring to worry about you too. He's gonna be late."

"I don't think that's ever happened before."

"Never," said Daniel's friend. Josh? Terrence? She barely knew their names.

"Something's up," Daniel said. "Went by his office and he was yelling into the phone. Something to do with the President."

Gabrielle stomach clenched.

"The President of the University?"

"I couldn't help eavesdrop. The President's taking a leave of absence. Don't know why. I mean, I don't know why Rimmler would be upset about that."

"It's because of me." Gabrielle said.

"Okay."

They all waited. Daniel smiled.

"She's not going to tell us."

"Gabrielle!" Josh said.

"Sorry. It's kind of serious."

"Well, heck," Daniel said.

They all heard familiar footsteps. Gabrielle felt better for a second. Then she saw him.

"Whoa, look," Josh whispered.

Shock, Gabrielle thought. That's what I looked like to Linda.

Rimmler, file folder in hand, walked mechanically, shoes shuffling. But shoulders back, head up. His eyes tracked the floor and he did not look up. He unlocked the door.

When they were all seated, he cleared his throat and said, "Ready for the final? Of course not. Here we go."

He handed out the file folder and then caught himself, took out the stack of tests, and handed them to a grim Daniel.

Gabrielle got her test and she had to smile. The first question was pure Rimmler.

While walking through the student union you find a 3x5 card on the floor. You pick it up and while sitting in the ice cream shop, draw the following shape with your pencil.

There was rectangle with a crossbar.

You fill in the outline with your pencil and with your DVM, which you always carry with you, measure the following values...

Gabrielle finished before the others, as usual. She knew she was going to miss this, Dr. Rimmler's blend of theory and real world materials. You actually can make a paper and pencil transistor while having ice cream.

The real world was the realm of engineering, as her father often said, and she wondered if she could maintain that ideal. At the moment, she doubted it. She got up with her test.

Rimmler struggled to look her in the eye.

"Dr. Rimmler, will you be in your office tomorrow morning?"

She thought he looked exhausted.

"Yes. Nine o'clock."

"I'll tell you everything. Thank you for trying."

She exited as quickly as she could and left the university.

Gabrielle dismantled her room.

With her study lamp on the floor, she placed all her clothes in her cardboard nightstand box. An old pair of jeans, a filmy blue top, the green jacket. Black sweater. All her bathroom items went into the box also. She made sure the River Arcady leaf, encased inside two paper plates wrapped in a napkin, was safe bundled in her shirts. All went into the robe and into the box. The *item* was transferred to her tackle box in her car. She wrapped it in a wad of toilet paper and tucked it next to a roll of solder. She made sure the hood of the Volkswagen was locked

In the kitchen, while her roommates watched tv, she gathered up her silverware, salt and pepper shakers, and the steak knife with the broken handle. No skillet or aluminum pot. She knew all her food was gone but she was happy to locate the coffee percolator in an upper cabinet. Her toaster was nowhere to be found.

That's it, she thought, going over every room in her mind. Good. It felt good.

She went back to the basement and sat on the bed.

"One more night to get through."

She slumped back and, fully clothed, pulled the old wool blanket over her. After a while she reached out and switched off the lamp. Lying on her side, shoulders tense, she fell asleep and did not dream.

She awoke in darkness, stretched, and swung her legs from under the blanket. She checked her watch. *5:31.*

It will do, she thought.

Cold and damp. She turned the lamp on. Her breath was a cloud swirling around her face. She spun the dial of the dryer and hit start. In a couple minutes the basement was tolerably above freezing and smelled of dryer sheets. She folded up her blanket.

She made a quick trip to her former bathroom. Shower? She figured no one cared what she smelled like anymore.

She flushed the cracked toilet for the last time.

Her plan was to drive to the campus and wait in the car until nine. Then after all that, home. She saw a glimmer of light in her frosted window. Still no one tromping above. She put her blanket and lamp in the box and carried it up the steps. She left her door wide open. In the kitchen, she looked around the place one last time. It was barely recognizable.

"So," she said. "I no longer live here."

The kitchen door she shut quietly.

The morning was misty and very cold. Ice filmed her windshield. The box just fit in the back seat. Driver's seat up, she got in. Something caught her attention.

The power lines behind the house were covered with birds. Blackbirds, dozens of them. They watched her in silence.

Senses suddenly alert, Gabrielle pulled her door shut and put the key in the ignition. A fluttery movement made her look up. There was piece of paper tucked under the wiper blade right in front of her.

She got out into the cold and lifted the wiper. She peeled the paper off the glass. There was writing on it, tiny writing in ink. She took off her glasses.

That other note is a lie, it read and under that, *PS I do not hate you.*

Gabrielle stepped back from her car. There was a second piece piece of paper under the right wiper, folded tightly and jammed into the bracket. She used her fingernails to get it loose. She unfolded it, the tiny wad becoming a full sheet of note paper.

Please come back. I don't know what happened to me. I was crazy. I beg you to forgive me. Everything will be like it was before.

Gabrielle please come home.   – C

She read the note again. And again. A lie? L would say that, wouldn't she. Why would Catherine lie like this? Is this all a game again?

Gabrielle read it again. And again.

She got back in her car and pulled out without looking. Through town and onto the long valley road, her heart tried to climb out of her chest.

Then the small town and the eucalyptus grove and out onto the foggy coastal plain. She got to the sand trap and slammed on the brakes.

The sand trap was gone. The sandy path was now a brutal slash through the sagebrush, twice as wide. She approached it slowly. The wet sand was compressed. Heavy equipment, she thought. Bulldozers. Trucks. God, what happened.

She feathered the clutch and started down the road at a crawl. She passed a pile of shattered old wood. The gate. She tried to think clearly. Before the final turn by the sand dune there was a car parked, a plain Ford sedan.

She went a few feet further. Another vehicle, a police car and in front of that, an ambulance. She kept going. She made the final turn. There were two old pickups. She barely glanced at them. Then the black Jeep. And a huge red fire engine. Fire hoses curled over the sand.

She tried to make sense of what she was seeing.

The house was a pile of blackened rubble. The patio wall had toppled and the roof had collapsed, spidery and charred. The porch, library, middle room, and kitchen were flattened and burned. A bright blue tarp was stretched over over a corner where the debris had been shoved into a heap. A policeman stood beside it. Smoke issued from several spots.

That's my room, she thought. Still burning. Her vision dimmed and she shook her head. There were two people on the other side of the Jeep. One was M, the other a tall man in a black suit.

The man said something and M turned sharply.

In the middle of the road, Gabrielle turned off the engine. She got out. Wet ashes, acrid burning wall board and carpeting. Her breath caught. The smell was overpowering. She coughed. M was looking at her in anger. The man, hands on hips, just watched.

Gabrielle approached them

Across the hood of the Jeep, M said, "Gabrielle, stop. You shouldn't be here. Go home. Go back to school."

"M. God. What have you done?" She saw the man look surprised at this. "You didn't have to."

"Gabrielle, go home."

"Why? You could've just run away like you always do."

"No."

The man held up his hand, looking sideways at M, and took an object from an inside pocket. It was a badge.

"Lieutenant Simmons. Miss, tell me your name, please."

"Gabrielle Tyndall."

"And what is your connection with this place, Miss Tyndall?"

"I lived here. Until last week."

"I see. Now."

"Gabrielle!"

"Ms. Martingale," he snapped.

Gabrielle watched M struggle to maintain composure. That's her name, she thought.

"Now, Miss Tyndall." The lieutenant was looking hard at M. "You said, you didn't have to. What did you mean by that?"

"I meant she didn't have to destroy the house."

"Destroy it? You mean deliberately destroy it?"

"Yes."

"Why would you think that? You think Ms. Martingale destroyed her own home?"

"She did it before."

M turned away. The lieutenant put his hands back on his hips.

"Ms. Martingale, you stand right there. Now, Miss Tyndall. Tell me what happened."

"She had a house in Pasadena. Up in the hills. I stayed overnight there. I went back a month later and it had been leveled. I still don't know why."

"There was a problem with the title," M said. "That's all you need to know, Gabrielle. Why don't *you* tell her what happened. She'll believe you."

The Lieutenant stared at her again.

"The situation here is a little different, Miss Tyndall," he said. "There seems to have been an explosion."

"Seems," M said.

"We're actually not in the business of guessing, Ms. Martingale. I sure you understand." He voice was solemn.

"Gabrielle, " M said. "Did Catherine ever mention smelling propane?"

"Yes." Gabrielle felt queasy.

"And did you ever do anything about it?"

"No, I," she said. "No."

"There was a leak and the gas built up. There was an explosion. Gabrielle listen."

"Yes." Gabrielle felt the world sway.

"Catherine was killed in the explosion. She's dead, Gabrielle."

"M."

"Please go home now. Please."

Gabrielle studied M's face. Red, puffy eyes. Quivering jaw muscles. Shirt untucked, one shoe untied.

"Bullshit," she said.

The Lieutenant was openly astonished.

"Forget it, M. I don't believe you."

"Gabrielle, please."

"So I'm supposed to believe that's Catherine under that blue sheet? All right."

Gabrielle walked to where the porch had been and stepped over the shattered boards of the steps. She went around the remnants of the bookcases and piles of sodden books and saw a beige box, crushed in the black ashes. *Tess.*

The blue tarp was at the edge of a hole where the middle bathroom had been. Wine cellar, she thought. She pushed through the heaps of burned wood, coughing. The policeman watched her approach and she saw him look past her.

Gabrielle got to the tarp. She set her feet into the blackened sand and gripped the edge with both hands.

"Was she a friend of yours?" the policeman said. He seemed very young to her.

"What?"

"My advice is, don't"

"Right."

Gabrielle lifted the tarp and threw it over. The smell of burning plastic clogged her lungs. She saw a long muscular leg pinned under blackened wood. No longer tan, now gray and mottled. She saw cut-off jeans and a yellow windbreaker torn to ribbons. Dead gray skin. A hand stuck out of the debris, arm twisted backward. The fingers were drawn up into a claw. She saw a tuft of blonde hair in the wrong place, attached to a crushed lump of matter. The words formed in her mind and for several seconds she refused to acknowledge them. Then she did.

That's her head, she thought. Her head was ripped off.

Gabrielle could not take her eyes off the strands of blonde hair. She was firmly turned away and incomprehensible voices were hollow in her ears. The policeman led her through the ruins. Her feet were numb. She kept stumbling. Her car swam up to her, it seemed, and she put both hands on the roof. Cold steel. She focused on the cold.

Her door was opened for her. Her head was ripped off.

Gabrielle sat on the edge of the driver's seat and the policeman spoke.

"Until you feel better. I'm really sorry. There's room to turn around here. You see it?"

Gabrielle nodded at him and pulled her legs in and closed the door. She dug the keys out of her pocket. She started the engine and as the policeman continued to talk and made a U-turn. The sagebrush scraped the fender loudly. Branches that had been turned into claws. She steered past the old pickups and kept the car moving over the rutted sand. At the pavement she dropped it into second.

Go fast, she thought. Just go.

She had trouble keeping in the lane. She went halfway onto the shoulder and more dry brush scraped the door. She saw the small town in the rear view mirror. She didn't remember driving through the light. Was it green, she wondered. On the long valley road the crosswind pushed her over the centerline and a horn honked.

She took her foot off the gas as the left turn came up fast and she remembered she no longer had to turn left. She suddenly didn't know the way home. There was a strip of bright poppies alongside a barbed wire fence and she steered onto it, only half off the highway. For a second she had to think which pedal was the brake. The engine stalled.

Traffic stopped beside her for the red light. There was a plumber's truck. Delivery van. Datsuns and Toyotas. She watched them, breathing hard, it was hard to breathe. Next her was an Impala with primer patches and a bad muffler. She rolled down her window. The exhaust fumes filled the Volkswagen and, combined with the noise of the muffler, created a screen of sensory overload. She wanted to pull it over her like a blanket.

"Hey!" The plumber's truck. Guy in passenger seat.

Gabrielle with an effort looked up. The plumber's assistant was in a clattery diesel truck, oxidized paint, and big white bumpers.

"You aww right?"

Gabrielle, eyes watering, nodded.

The light turned green and the line of cars began to move. The was a bad synchro whine from the truck as the driver forced it into gear. The sun poked through the fog.

"It's just that you don't look so good. I could call a tow truck if you want. Or I could call a ambulance."

Gabrielle stared at him.

"What did you say?"

The plumber's truck got moving with a roar.

"What?" he yelled.

Gabrielle watched them drive off. Her abdomen spasmed. She put both hands on her temples.

"God damn it. God," she said, "damn it."

Gabrielle laughed. Her entire body convulsed in laughter, She started the car and put in reverse and pushed down on the gas pedal as hard as she could. The engine screamed and all the sheet metal resonated in a single tone.

"Motherfucking son of a,"

She popped the clutch.

"*Bitch!*"

The Volkswagen launched backwards, her chest bounced off the steering wheel and gravel sprayed. She kept half in the lane and sideswiped the barbed wire fence and clipped a fence post doing thirty in reverse. Then she was clear of the line of vehicles. The smell of burning rubber filled the car and the foggy sun glared in her sweat smeared glasses, Gabrielle heard a sound behind the howl of the engine, a sound she could *feel*, emanating from somewhere deep down, a place never accessed before this moment.

Gabrielle growled, spun the wheel as hard and tromped on the clutch. The Volkswagen spun left, tires smoking on pavement and in the blink of an eye she was pointing the way she came in the wrong lane, She did not take her foot off the gas and steered around an oncoming station wagon locking up its brakes, got in the correct lane, speed shifted second, third, hit sixty and veered onto the shoulder and passed a Sparklett's Water truck. Fourth, the stick was *really* loose, she pushed on the gas until her leg lifted her from the seat.

Seventy, seventy-four. She swore at the speedometer. The car bounced on the rough asphalt. The front wheels shimmied.

She passed a funky van with a sea serpent painted on the side and a yellow Pinto emitting a trail of smoke. Pushing eighty on the downgrade heading for the sea, she passed the speed limit sign at the boundary of the small town. *25 MPH.* She swept by the towering eucalyptus sentinel trees. Oncoming traffic was heavy. Heads swiveled.

The intersection loomed, red light, a line of cars had just turned left in front of her heading for the short cut up to Highway One. The light went green and she hissed in triumph. Road was clear. Full throttle in.

She flew through the intersection at sixty-eight. At the corner convenience store a student on a ten-speed rode off the sidewalk almost into her path and she turned her head. Something registered in the corner of her eye. That line of cars that had just turned left. The one in the middle of the pack. Just went out of sight. The edge of its roof had a familiar shape. Very familiar.

"*Fuck.*"

She pulled up on the handle of the parking brake with all her strength. The rear tires locked up, the Volkswagen skidded left, she made a U-turn at thirty-five on two wheels again. Back through the cloud of her own tire smoke, red lights ahead, they were getting away, she hit the gap between a Volvo and a Honda, ran up onto the convenience store's parking lot right behind the student, floored it and went airborne off the curb with an impact that made her ass bounce onto the parking brake and her glasses slip to the end of her nose. Feet suspended over pedals, she managed to steer out of the way of a pickup loaded with ladders, got in the correct lane, slid back onto the seat and jammed the gas. What gear? Second, the engine roared, third, the street dipped and she saw the line of cars, now spaced out, and there, just rounding a curve, she saw it. Black Jeep doing the speed limit.

Gabrielle left it in third and accelerated. As the Jeep disappeared around the curve she saw there was no oncoming traffic and she got in the opposing lane and passed first a new Ford Capri and then a yellow Pinto. The Pinto honked its horn. She snapped back to the right lane as the estuary appeared. Not much farther.

She knew if they made it to Highway One she would lose them. They would simply pull away while she burned out her engine.

Going around the curve at seventy the Volkswagen threatened to lift off again and she worked the steering wheel.

The Jeep was directly ahead. She saw the on-ramp to Highway One.

They haven't seen me, she thought, *faster.*

Now she slammed fourth gear. The car surged. She was thrown back. She came up behind the Jeep, they saw her, the rear window flap moved. With one hand she whipped her car into the oncoming lane, missed a rusty Datsun, and passed them. She saw Samantha in profile.

She got in front of them, let go of the steering wheel and pulled up on the parking brake with both hands while pushing down on the brake pedal. Her face plowed into the dashboard. Her tires shrieked and there was a deeper screech. The Jeep hit her rear bumper, she was knocked off her seat again, the engine stalled.

Stunned, Gabrielle heaved herself back and stopped her still rolling car. Tire smoke obscured the windows. She looked behind her. The Jeep was angled into the shoulder. She put the VW in first so it wouldn't roll.

Gabrielle got out. She swayed. Blood dripped from her chin. She pushed her glasses up. The tire smoke blew away. She took a step and stumbled. Her right knee hurt like hell. She ignored it. The rear bumper had been punched into a v-shape. She smelled burning oil.

Samantha was visible in the driver's seat, M next to her, both motionless.

Her heart crashed against her ribs.

I was wrong, she thought. I was wrong.

Something moved in the rear of the Jeep. The back flap was tossed open and she saw a bare arm emerge.

Gabrielle ran as tears came.

Catherine stepped around the Jeep. Dark gray jacket and cut-off jeans. Her hair was shorter, matted and tangled. She glanced up then kept her eyes down. Her long legs were streaked with ashes.

Gabrielle laughed and she saw Catherine smile crookedly and she hugged her. Burning plastic and *Fracas*. She put her hand on Catherine's cheek where the scar was deepest and held it there.

M and Samantha were staring through the windshield. Cars passed slowly. The fog had returned.

She looked into Catherine's eyes. The blue into gold was still there. Catherine finally met her gaze.

"I loved you," Gabrielle said. "Goodbye."

Catherine's mouth opened. She said nothing.

Gabrielle backed away from her. She limped back to her car. Her face was cold and wet.

As she sat on the driver's seat, the passenger door opened.

"Listen to me," Catherine said. She sat.

Gabrielle didn't want to look at her.

"So I'm cast out."

"No, you are not cast out. Listen."

"I'm listening."

"Trueheart."

Now she looked at her.

"That's your secret name."

"Trueheart," Gabrielle said slowly. Her knee flared with pain and her neck was stiff. Her chin was still bleeding. Her heart missed a beat. She smiled. "But won't the world end?"

Catherine nodded. "It just did." She slammed her door. "Activate the vehicle."

Gabrielle didn't move for a moment then put the key in the ignition. She started the engine. There was a shadow over her door. Samantha was standing there.

"Can I sit in the back?"

Gabrielle got out and pushed her seat forward and Samantha got in. Standing in the street she watched M, alone in her Jeep. She was looking at the trees as if they were the most interesting thing in the world.

"M," Gabrielle said. She got in and pulled away. Highway One, just go.

Then the Jeep was lost in the fog and she felt all the muscles in her body relax for the first time in days.

"You have every right to hate us," Catherine said. "Rushel was *furious*."

"I don't know what to think. We can talk about things later."

"All right," Catherine said after a long pause.

They made it to the northbound on-ramp.

"Audra is missing," Samantha said.

"Missing? Maybe she just went home."

"She would never go home," Catherine said.

"No, she wouldn't. The campus police found her backpack in the parking lot, the one above the library. They found our phone number inside and called just as M was ripping the phone out."

Gabrielle looked at Samantha in the mirror.

The engine sputtered and Gabrielle gave it gas. It struggled to fifty-five.

"I got kicked out of school."

"What?" Catherine said.

"First Susan."

"How can she do that?"

"Not sure. My advisor is working on it. But I don't think so."

"Hell."

Gabrielle felt energy returning. Her temples stopped pounding.

"My engine's shot."

"I'd bet it would take you fifteen minutes to put a new engine in this thing."

"I can't afford it."

"Oh yes you can."

Gabrielle laughed.

"I can, huh?"

"Remember all the gold coins? Three hundred and fifty-nine of them left. You're sitting on them."

Gabrielle laughed again. The engine smoothed out.

"Catherine is very sneaky," Samantha said.

"You're telling me, Scooter."

Now Samantha laughed.

"Originally it was Wichita," Catherine said.

"What? How could you?"

"Yeah, once we thought about it, no."

"Kansas?" Gabrielle said.

"No, something else," Samantha said. "From a long time ago."

"Another mystery," Gabrielle said. "Catherine, your secret name is perfect for you."

"Yes it is," Samantha said. "Concasser."

"Oh brother."

"In French cuisine," Samantha said. "To chop, crush, or grind."

Gabrielle laughed. "Still think Audra's is the best. What do you think happened? Has she ever done anything like this before?"

"Never."

Rain dappled the windshield.

"We know they're capable of anything," Gabrielle said. "This feels bad. You think she just took off in her car without her backpack?"

"She would never do that," Samantha said. "Something happened. They're all gone, by the way. I checked their house. Deserted."

"Then we're going in the right direction," Catherine said. "We have gas. She always talked about going up Highway One."

"Yeah, with."

"Her. Right."

"Let's keep going then," Gabrielle said. "For now, let's concentrate on this, all right? Everything else can wait. We find Audra."

They both nodded.

"North it is."

Samantha said. "We should hurry."

Sorry Dr. Rimmler, Gabrielle thought. She wiped her face with her sweatshirt. The road ahead, a sharp gray line, stretched under low clouds. The path was obscured.

"I wonder what we'll see."

Stars Then and the Wind Steady at Her Back

M died at midnight on the first day of spring. PG was alone at her bedside holding her hands. M, sedated, started awake.

PG was surprised at the strength in those bony hands. She's hoarding her energy, she thought. Not much left.

"Gabrielle," M whispered.

PG leaned closer.

"I'm so sorry about Catherine."

"Oh, M. That was so long ago."

"No. You should have had more time."

M closed her eyes, wincing.

PG forced back tears.

"M, you were there at the very beginning. The beginning of my life. You rescued me."

M squeezed her hands in agreement. Then, eyes still closed, she smiled wryly as if she had just thought of a good joke. PG saw her struggle. M tugged her hand and PG put her ear close to her lips. M opened her eyes, breathed in and then out.

"Uncreate me."

PG, surprised, nodded, making sure M could see her nod.

M fell silent still smiling that smile and did not wake again.

Nearly two months after our winter meeting, PG contacted me. Early morning email from a public library in the Palm Springs area. A request to meet her in Santa Barbara again.

I shot back, "*Now hold on. How do I know you're not L? Or First Susan?*"

There was a delay during which I could easily imagine PG laughing her head off. Her message popped up. I did not blush. I'm used to this now.

"*According to DARPA agent Janice you have a tattoo on your left inner thigh. A rabbit running. I stopped her before she translated this for me. Now how would L know that?*"

I emailed back, "*I guess I believe you. And let us never talk about this again.*"

"*I have a serious request. Pick me up at the Marea rooftop garden bar tomorrow no later than 2pm. We will be driving north. Say yes and the tickets will be waiting for you at Will Rogers."*

Drop everything and fly across the country on the spur of the moment heading for an unknown destination. I realized I missed stuff like this.

"Yes."

Maybe Janice would be there.

The trick in my opinion is look like you care about your appearance but not to a degree it interferes with your work. Because work is very important to you. Work defines you as far as the world at large is concerned.

Flying into stormy weather along the central California coast, I figured I nailed it. Last shave, two days ago. Last haircut, three months ago. Sport coat? How about a dark gray jacket, not too golfy, worn fabric around the collar. A work jacket. Under that an expensive white dress shirt, tailored in fact. Blue jeans comfortably worn but no holes. (Brand new slacks get you pegged as management. Holes get you pegged as a coder. I refuse to be pegged.) Then nearly new hiking shoes, low cut, not clomping boots.

I overanalyze everything. It's a gift.

In this getup I strolled across the Marea parking lot, framed by palm trees against a dark sky, towards the side entrance PG told me about. To my right was the main entrance where I picked her up that day over a year ago now.

I saw what I guessed was the rooftop bar.

Potted palms and tall chairs behind a glass windscreen running along the artfully weathered brick wall of the two story wing. Under cloudy skies, two women were sitting at a café table up there, backs to me. They were joined by a third. PG in her leather jacket.

"There she is."

Couldn't tell if the saw me. I hurried and looked up at the women PG was talking to. One had shoulder length blonde hair, the other long black hair which I could easily imagine reached her ankles.

"Well, hello," I said.

Would I finally get to meet them? My pulse began to race as I went through the door. It was a restaurant, no signage at all, and all the empty tables had flowers. The smiling maitre'd directed me to wide oak stairs and I unzipped my jacket. The second floor was a quiet bar with a single large tv showing a sports talk show watched only by the bartender, a young woman with blue hair and a pink apron. A spiral staircase constructed of transparent crystal led up to the roof patio. I walked out into cool breezy air and a nice panorama of the Pacific. Your basic billion dollar view.

There they were at the far end of the patio. PG was not in sight.

I felt like I knew them. As I walked up they both smiled. The blonde one brushed back her wind tousled hair and cocked her head. The black haired one fixed me with a flat steely look. Nevertheless, I kept walking.

"This is a surprise and a great honor."

They stared at me.

"Catherine, Samantha, what a pleasure to finally meet you both."

They looked at each other.

"Oh, um, I think there's been a mistake," the blonde one said. "My name isn't Catherine." Her face became angry. "I'm Patricia."

The eyes of the black haired one bored into me.

"Yes," she said. "And I'm Holly."

She sprang up and lunged forward. Their table rocked.

I stumbled back. My chest tightened. I raised my hands as blood pounded in my ears.

The blonde one stood too.

"*Wow*," she said.

"Oh my God," the black haired one said.

"You weren't kidding, PG."

I regained my balance, barely. She was standing beside me. She gave the two a thumbs up. My face burned.

"Perfect," PG said. "Are you all right?"

"No."

Both women laughed.

"My name is really Jen." She tossed her blonde hair back again. "After that, could I buy you a drink?"

"Oh, yes ma'am."

"And I'm Susan," the black haired one said.

I looked at PG. She winked.

"I'd love to buy you a drink," she said to PG.

"We're just here for a conference," Jen said. She named one of the gigantic social media companies.

"Normally, I would love that but we have to be going."

"Okay," Susan said. She handed PG a business card. "Look me up anytime."

PG put the card in her pocket.

"PG, you sure we."

"We have to go."

I noticed she was carrying a long flat parcel wrapped in brown paper. I turned back to the two women.

"Jen, Susan, it really was nice, actually exciting, to meet you both."

"You're not gonna tell us," Jen said.

"Who Catherine and Samantha are?" Susan said. "Or Holly?"

"Or Patricia?"

"It will all be in his book."

"A book?"

"Yes, assuming I live long enough to finish it."

"Well you better live then," Susan said.

PG tugged my sleeve. A drop of rain hit my cheek. We waved goodbye and hurried down the spiral staircase.

"No one gave me their card," I said.

"I noticed."

"They finished each other's sentences."

"Yes they did."

And they weren't the right age. And no way was I going to say that.

In the car, I said, "My heart is still pounding."

PG set the parcel by her feet and pulled the seatbelt over her lap. Just held it.

"Nothing is as it seems," she said. "Everything is on purpose."

We put the Marea Hotel forever in the past and I accelerated onto the northbound 101.

"Head for Big Sur."

She closed her eyes in the jostling car and fell asleep sitting up.

A hundred miles on I made the transition to Highway One.

"PG, isn't this?"

"Yes. Keep going."

"All right."

Rain was falling in sheets and the gusting wind kept knocking me out of the lane. The hills and fields were green, oak trees just getting leaves. I cranked open the window and smelled flowers. We left all towns behind and the highway stretched out onto a sloping plain beside the white capped surging Pacific. So what lay beyond the verdant hills, I wondered. The trees shaped by the wind held secrets and the rain had a purpose.

Then past green pastures and rough barbed wire fences I saw something on our right, wreathed in clouds. It took a moment to comprehend.

"Oh, it really is a castle," I said and regretted it.

PG opened her eyes.

"Sorry."

"No, don't be silly."

"I've never seen it before."

"Yes." She smiled. Her cheeks were wet.

She was holding something tightly enclosed in her right hand.

The highway ran along the very edge of the shore. The *continent*. Pavement, pitched and potholed. The wipers cleared the ocean spray. A tiny cove of black rocks passed. There were dozens of huge sea lions, gray and leathery, basking in the rain.

Wind whipped the car. The air vents whistled. The highway climbed through a long switchback and then still higher. There were rocks in the roadway, some boulders big enough to take out the oil pan. I slalomed around them.

Rain inundated the car. It roared. The wipers could not clear the windshield, they just pushed waves of water back and forth. I slowed to a crawl.

"You have to go faster," she said.

"All right then."

I considered sticking my head out the window. I settled for keeping the centerline in the corner of my eye.

The rain eased up slightly and the wind increased. Tree branches sailed across our path.

"No other cars," I said.

"This is rather dangerous what we're doing."

Tiny settlements passed, empty and lightless. The road ran down to the sea then back up through a forest. Clouds enveloped the dramatic trees.

PG was sitting up straight as rivulets of rain flowed across her window.

"Get ready."

The road became narrower, it twisted and turned. The mountainside was a vertical rock wall and the sea cliff a shear drop off. Wind driven rocks slammed into the doors.

"This curve," PG said. "Right here. Slow."

Another switchback opened in front of us, a tight one, down fast and left.

"The shoulder right here."

I hit the brakes and the car slid onto the sandy gravel. I killed the engine. The wind sounded like a freight train. The car rocked.

PG picked up the parcel.

"This is the Place of Returning. It must be approached only on foot. Don't worry, it's not far at all."

"If you don't mind could I see what you're holding there?"

She opened her hand. On her palm was a gold ring.

"Go ahead," she said.

I picked it up as carefully as I could.

"My mother's wedding ring. And then it was my wedding ring."

The setting was three diamonds originally, I could see. One of the settings was empty.

"My mom was pregnant with me when she married my dad. One day after my dad died she noticed one of the diamonds was missing."

I set the ring back in her palm as the car was rocked again. Without a word PG opened her door, the wind whipped it, and she got out. I opened my door and lost my grip. Rain entered horizontally.

I got out. I shielded my eyes but it didn't help. I squinted in the half light. We were parked opposite a mountainous cove. Beyond ragged trees a quarter mile out was the sea. Across the highway, a hundred yards over, there was a steep hill angling up to a sharp peak. PG was already halfway there.

I ran after her, my jacket flapping.

The heart of the storm was upon us. Wind and rain impacting the cliff were being driven straight up in a monumental column of gray black clouds. I had to tear my eyes from the stupendous sight.

PG stopped at the base of the hill. A steep footpath led to the peak, the cliff edge. As I reached her, completely soaked, she finished unwrapping the parcel. It was a broken fragment of a pine board, blackened by salt and sun. She ran her hand over incised letters. *PERS.*

She hugged the last remnant of the Persephone Gate and started up the path. Her wet hair covered her face. Rain ran off her shoulders. I did not move.

At the path's end, the edge of the world, she stood and stared into the upwelling storm. She held the pine board up to her face and kissed it. Then she threw it into the roaring clouds and I saw it sail up and up, a spinning speck against the gray, and vanish.

She now held the ring in both hands and clasped it to her chest. She swayed and fell to her knees, inches from the drop off.

Panicked, I ran up the path. My scrabbling shoes got little traction on the wet gravel. Gasping, I stopped a few feet behind her.

PG opened her hand and kissed the ring. I could just hear.

"I love you. I love you. Goodbye. Goodbye."

She got to her feet, resolutely faced the storm, and threw the ring into the elemental abyss.

Two heartbeats later an object hit her face. A shiny speck, it bounced onto the wet rocks and tiny flowers. I kept my eyes on it and picked it up.

I set the ring on my open hand. PG stared in astonishment. There were now two empty settings.

"One diamond left," I said.

She took it with shaking hands and turned back to the storm as the wind howled. She nodded.

I guided her from the cliff. I risked looking down. Far below, straight down, furious waves crashed on black rocks and I felt suddenly dizzy. Now PG tugged me.

We walked arm in arm to the car. We were both sopping wet.

PG could not stop staring at the ring. I started the engine and got the heater going. We sat in silence for several minutes.

"Why is this called the Place of Returning?"

PG covered the ring with her other hand and again pressed it to her chest.

"That's the next part of the story," she said. She patted my arm.

With more than a little trepidation I got us moving and, as PG grinned, we drove up into the clouds, swiftly, with a following wind.

Mysterious Writer

It was the age of Orwell. It was the age of Heinlein. The old century had ended and so had history. The old certainties. In the new century nothing was certain. Empires augered in. Broken links and failed memories. Meme plagues and fifth generational warfare. Every idea, every word, had been weaponized.

Be a lot safer if I made no move at all.

Midwinter's night, PG style.

I stood stock still before the railroad trestle as a night freight crawled north. The old abutments were covered with flowering vines. No stars. The wind.

I could smell gardenias and jasmine. Eucalyptus. And *Fracas*.

"Are we watching the train?" Janice said.

"This is the boundary. Once we step over it."

"We turn into pumpkins?"

"We will be in her realm."

"If that's something from your project remember I haven't read it yet." Her dark as night eyes never missed a thing.

"You know a lot already."

"When they carried her out of the bedroom. That's as far as I got."

"Yes, too bad you had to leave early in Oklahoma."

"My job." She did not smile. Her pink sneakers were as luminous as the streak of purple in her hair.

"Yeah. Well, keep your eyes peeled. If you spot a blue backpack."

The train rumbled and couplings crashed. As reassuring as a familiar heartbeat.

She looked at me expectantly.

We walked under the trestle together. Janice scanned the area.

"Where are we going?"

"Straight ahead."

"I can't decide if you are charming or just a nut."

"A distinction without a difference. We're going to the end of the street."

She still wasn't smiling.

"Thank you for inviting me. I kind of liked Covina."

"Had to see it. It's where she's from."

"I could live there."

"Yeah?"

"This town reminds me of it. You putting it in your project?"

"Already have."

We kept walking. At a busy corner the light was green but I hung back. There was a speaker over the traffic light. A mechanical voice was counting down in an urgent tone. "Seven! Six!" it said.

"What?" Now she smiled.

The light went yellow and then red. Janice hit the walk button.

"This whole setup. I just don't like it," I said.

"You don't like pushing the walk button?" She was grinning.

"No, makes me want to jaywalk."

"You are so like her."

The light turned green.

"Walk!" the traffic light commanded.

"Bite me," Janice said to the machine.

"Ten! Nine!" it responded.

"See?" I refrained from laughing.

We jogged across. We were on a long block of stores and dining establishments.

"We are going to have dinner at some point, right?"

"Yes, just want to see a few more things."

"Because I'll pay."

We crossed another street. The shushing of passing cars echoed between the office buildings.

"Describe it," she said. "Covina."

"As if you plucked a small Kansas town from the prairie and dropped it, complete with diagonal parking, into an ocean of tract houses with dramatic snow-capped mountains in the background."

"Diagonal parking is the *best*," she said quietly.

We came to the end of the street. There was a large park before us. Brick walkway, many trees. The streetlights were hidden in the branches. It was darkness a few feet in.

"Right in there."

"Um, really?"

We walked into the shadows. The trees rustled. Something fluttered past my head. We came upon a branching path. There were steel handrails. I saw a wide opening, a lightless hole. Stairs led down.

"Yes. There it is. I have to see this."

"You're going down there?"

"Yeah, come on. Or wait here."

"No, lead the way."

I noticed her jacket was now fully unzipped.

"Happen to have a flashlight?"

She sighed.

"If you're going to be an urban adventurer you need more than a notebook. Here."

The beam of the LED was intense and focused.

"Dang."

"That's nothing."

The path led steeply down to sand and rocks. There was flowing water, couldn't tell how deep. Past an abutment I turned the light up. There was a large arched entrance of a tunnel in a rock wall. The river was issuing from it. Total darkness inside.

"Looks like it might be possible to walk in."

"You're not."

"No." Gave the pencil light back. "It's real. The water's flowing. Had to make sure."

"Okay. Is this something."

"Has to do with Rushel."

She stared at me and turned off the light. We listened to the running water. She bumped me with her elbow.

"Not the worst place for making out," she said. "I mean."

"Just a couple more places to see." We walked up the steep path to the handrails.

"You are not a typical guy."

"Thanks. Maybe."

Behind us someone coughed.

Janice hit the light. There were people in the tunnel entrance. I guessed three individuals ankle deep in the stream. They all turned away from the sudden light. Hair covered their faces. Black sweatshirts in shreds, wet cotton pants. Pajama bottoms.

Janice killed the light and pulled me by the sleeve until we were back on the sidewalk under an old style streetlamp. She zipped her jacket back up and stuck her hands in her pockets.

She looked at me and shook her head.

"Walk around this town at night and you never know what you're gonna see," I said.

She did not smile. As we walked past busy restaurants she bumped into me a couple times. I took her hand and we walked that way for a while.

The big three lane street was thronged with cars. Still no one else on the sidewalk. A little ways up, I stopped.

"Yes!" I said. "Not that I didn't believe it. But I have to see this."

"What?"

"Or rather I have to smell this."

The alley was so narrow I could touch both sides. I sniffed the wall.

"What *are* you doing?"

"Bubblegum."

"What? Oh."

She made no move to get closer.

"Well, that's certainly impressive. Look at it. Ten feet up."

"It's a cultural landmark."

"Only in California."

"Probably so."

Somewhere in here, I thought. I'll bet her hair is still stuck there. Janice squeezed my hand. We kept walking.

In PG's old neighborhood, nothing matched up except the small park with its bench. And the railroad station.

No sign of Cat Creek Avenue. I kind of did want to see Rosie's house. We rested in the shadows. My feet were sore.

"Not good?"

"Maybe she's protecting someone."

The sweat on the back of my neck chilled me. We walked north on a busy street and I tried to imagine the Volkswagen passing by, Catherine shifting. Had to have been close to here.

"You're so far away. How many more miles?"

"About two, according to her."

We walked past a large sign welcoming us to the University.

"Forty years. Nothing will be the same."

"You never know."

Fog rolled in from the west. I stared to get nervous. The parking lot where PG encountered Thomas was now an extensive dormitory compound complete with a sand filled beach volleyball setup.

"I think I know the spot. Well, where it used to be."

"What did she do here?"

"Puked her guts out."

Her laughter ran across the quiet street. The few students hurrying by turned their heads. Most were wearing either short pants or leggings, t-shirts tucked under sweats. Beach wear.

"Do you know where to go?"

"I memorized the old maps she gave me. I'm recognizing only a few buildings. That's Administration. That's the new gym."

"New?"

"Right across the street, that's the Student Union. Let's go over there."

It was a cast concrete building with cheerfully lit windows and colorful banners flapping in the cold wind. We walked down stairs and pushed through the doors. Students stared at Janice and she smiled at them. Their eyes mostly veered away from me, thankfully.

We were in a big two story room. A huge incongruous wall sealed off half the space. An open doorway led to a dark room. Bowling alley? It resounded with rock music. Looked like a night club. There was no row of bulletin boards. But there was, beside the far end doors, the Burger Bar. Except of course it was something else. Still an eating establishment at least.

Janice gripped my hand.

"Not pizza, please."

"No."

"We're going to a real restaurant. My legs are going to fall off."

"See that door right there, the exit? She stood right there. And so did New Susan."

"Right," Janice said. "Real name Susan Sloan."

"Ah."

"And you'll never guess what she's doing now."

"Okay. What?"

"Oh this is great."

"Come on."

"Maybe later."

We exited the Union. The concrete Activity Center was nowhere to be found. Also missing was the postal kiosk. We searched for the whispering pines and found them outside the Science building, currently silent. We found the u-shaped English building and went up the steps.

"The scale of the place. I need to feel it."

"Are you?"

"This is what she saw every day. From here she went to the library and Catherine was there. Now, this way, and we'll see if the crown jewel still exists."

I walked hand in hand with a serious unsmiling Janice to the old library, repurposed many years ago. But the windowless cube. That structure. I pointed.

"The Stacks."

"Can we get in?"

We went through the double doors and turned left and faced a blank wall. The door had been sealed off.

Janice peeked one by one into all the doorways in the lobby.

"So no Stacks?"

"Changed beyond recognition." This was really disappointing.

"Then we'll just have to rely on her memories. Okay?"

"One more important location on campus. The clock tower building."

"At least it's close. That looks like a gym from the nineteen forties. Are you getting what you wanted?"

"A lot smaller than I imagined. Yeah, I am. I know it's all very ordinary."

"Nothing is what it seems."

Janice wiped her face. Pretty long day.

"We go down here, see? Shortcut. Then the final stop."

"Then dinner, right?"

"At midnight on Halloween the clock strikes thirteen."

"Nothing about this is ordinary."

The path was narrow and lined with dark trees. We found ourselves on a busy street corner. We crossed, jogging. I tried to spot it. No College Costs Less and no McDonald's.

Janice studied everything. Sign, trees, my face.

"You're not asking any questions."

"Would you answer them?"

I knew the street. We headed south and descended. We left the bright shopping centers behind. After one block we were in the fog. Traffic dwindled. What time was it? Then I heard the freeway. The overpass materialized. Wet concrete. Headlights flashing the guardrail. I could see vague speeding shapes.

"Stop," Janice said. "I've never seen you like this before."

"No."

"What are you afraid of?" Weeds, chain link fence. "I'm not registering a threat."

"Maybe because it's not a threat. Just a door. Don't you remember?"

"Yes, and do you remember where I work? Don't worry about what I believe or don't believe."

"There was also Rushel."

"Her? Here? What about her?"

"I haven't read that notebook yet. All of a sudden it's freezing. Come on."

I started walking. Janice did not let go of my hand. I went fast so I wouldn't chicken out. We entered the overpass. I looked back. Fog obscured the street and the echoing sound of traffic faded. My heart started pounding. We got to the middle of the massive structure. Her hand was cold and sweaty and she let go.

She jogged ahead.

"Do me a favor," I said. Did she detect a threat now? "That street. Is it named Miranda?"

"No," she said, distracted.

"What's the matter?"

She ran back and grabbed my arm and pulled me from under the overpass.

On the other side, her face was strained and her hair soaked. She reached under her jacket. I heard a heavy thump.

"Get behind me." Her voice shivered.

I got behind her.

The chain link rattled and crashed. Other side of the street.

"See it? Right there."

I saw.

A dark shape moved. It had legs. It was moving away from us. A fast powerful saunter.

"Oh, no," I said.

"Stay be*hind* me."

"He got out. Good bear."

"Are you completely nuts? If it comes back I'll have no choice."

Fog came in waves, heavy and cold. Impenetrable.

"You don't have to worry. This is wonderful."

Janice gave me the kind of glance you give stupid civilians. The black bear was already almost out of sight, a quick moving shadow. It was galloping away.

"Just wait til I tell her. She will love this."

I wiped my forehead and rubbed the back of my neck. My whole body tingled. A train horn pierced the night over the entire town. Sharp, insistent.

"This is fine," I said, almost giddy. "Everything is fine. I'm so glad you were here to see this. What were you thinking for dinner? Kind of in the mood for Chinese."

The sky directly above was a robin egg's blue speckled with stars. The freezing metallic fog was gone. I smelled roses and green grass. This place, I thought. Door closed for now.

"There is so much you are not telling me. You and her. This is not over."

Flinty-eyed, she zipped her jacket. We walked into the town, hand in hand.

Later, as an owl questioned the night, Janice whispered in my ear.

"So describe it. Her town."

Her fingers massaged my temples.

"Not really ready."

"Just tell me what you're thinking. You owe me."

"You're right."

"And I paid for dinner."

"Yes, thanks. It's a little incoherent."

"Just like you." Her fingertips were subtle.

"The air," I said. "The air is scented with flowers. I made that part up and it turned out to be true.

"The wind never stops.

"It is a city of mysterious side streets and shadowy doorways. Steps lead to carpeted mezzanines and heavy doors with brass mail slots. Most of the doors are locked.

"The smiling young people in the stores and restaurants are unafraid to make eye contact. Confident. It is a city of business and chasing money. But it feels fragile, this money. I can't tell where it's coming from.

"No matter. Rebuilding upon rebuilding.

"The old working class town, the railroad and ranching town with its Spanish Mission and unpainted Victorian houses with tiny shed garages whose driveways have a strip of grass down the middle, that town still exists. Carefully preserved, maintained, passed down. I was impressed by how much of PG's town I was able to find, protected briefly from the rebuilding.

"It is a city of deep silence and underground rivers. The sky is blue even though the sun has set. Has it always been like this? An eternal twilight. You are lost and you don't care. If you find yourself in an empty room and you don't know how you got there or where you're going and you can tell the place is haunted but you can't see the ghost, it's really quite clear. You are the ghost.

"A rain swept downtown corner, a green left turn light, an avenue lined with overgrown trees. All paths lead into the foggy distance.

"Her spring, long ago, was just beginning. She knew she would never live in the town again. As she drove north with Catherine and Samantha she looked long into the rearview mirror."

Janice was gone in the morning. She left a note.

Sorry. Duty called. Thanks again for inviting me. Perhaps we will meet again one day.

Not unexpected. I knew what she really wanted. I checked out. No breakfast, no coffee. This was my last day. One stop left.

Her directions had been precise. Down the long valley road, through the small town, and at the designated traffic light I zeroed the odometer. The air became salty and electric. Down and through the eucalyptus grove. At two point four miles – the sand trap – I hit the brakes.

There was no sand trap. There was a stop sign and a paved street.

A Prius filled with students beeped at me blocking the road. I made the turn and proceeded slowly.

Then street curved and went up. Where the gate had been I could only guess. The final turn offered a view to the north, ocean and repeating dunes. The house was next. I braced myself and went around the hill.

Where M's house had stood there was now an outhouse built of cinderblocks. Beyond that, picnic tables and signs showing the trails through the sand.

I pulled in next to an RV with a puttering generator. I glanced, briefly, at the outhouse and headed for what looked like the main trail to the beach.

I quickly took off my jacket. The sand was coarse and brown and my shoes kept sinking in. PG mentioned once she thought it was the presence of tiny bits of sea shell that made it so damned fluid. I got on my knees. There they were.

When I reached the waves and I pulled off my shoes and stood there in my wet socks. Then I rolled them off. And I was walking barefoot on the beach. I stepped over drifts of seagull feathers and crab shells.

The air was balmy. Thunderheads were popping up to the east.

I stood at the edge of the hissing water. Each dune had trails around them and they all led to steep drop offs. I tried to imagine white robes in the wind.

I suppposed there could have been fragments of an old rubble foundation under that outhouse or in the jumbled field behind it. I certainly wasn't going to find anything. No remains of a wine cellar, no titanium boxes.

The wind shifted and the immense atmosphere of the shore hit me. It was hard not to gag. I gave a wide berth to a heap of kelp entwined with driftwood and the contorted blackened skeleton of a harbor seal, crawling with flies.

I walked north into the wind. I could see the three smokestacks of the power plant, shuttered now. A wave washed over my bare feet. Cold, warm. I picked up a broken shell and tried to see the life within, as she would.

My phone rang and I swore. Then I saw who it was and I swore again. I got ready for bad news.

"Mrs. Findley, good to hear from you."

"Oh. Hello?" Her whispery voice was hard to distinguish from the surf.

"Hello, Mrs. Findley, can you hear me?"

"They took it. They just took it."

"All right now. What did they take?"

"Your car. From the garage. They broke the door."

"The Volkswagen."

"Your little old red car. They had this truck. And they broke the door."

"The garage door. Now Mrs. Findley, are you all right?"

"Oh, I'm fine. I just looked through the curtains, you know. But they took it."

"You sure?"

"Yes, yes but."

"Now it was just an old car, Mrs. Findley, and those were dangerous people."

"Dangerous?" She laughed and this led to a bout of coughing. "It was a buncha girls." More laughing and coughing.

And did they ransack the house? The notebooks, my computer. Carissa's phone. I spun on the sand. I had to get out of here.

"Thank you for calling, Mrs. Findley, I'm glad you're."

Gone. Signal was nonexistent.

A flash startled me. Not a bright yellow windbreaker. The shell slipped from my fingers was lost. I swayed at the edge of the continent, dizzy then terrified. A fork of lightning ripped the dark sky apart.

Audra

The Rape of Things to Come

Audra folded her test paper lengthwise and wrote her name at the top. As always, the first to finish. She sat back and looked around the old stair-stepped, sixty seat lecture hall. Lightning flashed outside.

Thursday evening, *8:41.*

Her fellow students hunched over their desks scribbling all looked exhausted. She did not understand that. It was finished. You're all free now, she thought.

She stood, feeling light as a feather, and grabbed her backpack. She went swiftly down the aisle and plopped her test in front of the glowering professor. She smiled cheerfully.

"Thank you for a fascinating class, Professor Planchett. I still think you and the Supreme Court are wrong about *FCC vs. Pacifica* and I hope you can find the inner strength to admit it."

The professor's eyes lost focus behind his think glasses and his wrinkled face became grayer. He cleared his throat.

Audra paused two heartbeats. Then she smiled again and shouldered her backpack. She felt all fifty-nine sets of student's eyes on her as she pushed the door open. She thought she heard one of the guys whistle softly.

Down the hallway, she slammed the main doors open. Outside. The weight of the quarter was finally lifted and she took a deep breath of the night air. Then the weight of everything else came crashing down. As lightning flickered across the sky, she had two thoughts.

Don't obsess about it. It will work itself out, it has to. I'll explain everything to her. It will be fine, eventually.

And then, I'm gonna get wet.

Climbing the steps to the upper lot above the new library construction site she saw lightning over the hills to the east. She heard cheers and applause. The streetlights all went dark and there was more cheering. There was a group of people on the sidewalk above. They were watching the storm.

She rolled her eyes. She had to walk past them. Her car was up in the northeast corner.

Lightning crawled over the hills and formed multiple bolts in the black sky, all in silence.

The people applauded appreciatively. Audra thought they looked like staff, maybe TA's.

"Ah, Spielberg!" one guy said.

There was cheering at this. Another bolt snaked out of the sky.

"You could really see the Scorsese influence in that one," a man in a suit exclaimed. He saw Audra. He had a round face and a tiny mustache.

"Well, good evening! Quite a show, isn't it?"

Audra stared at him flatly.

"This may be the most California thing I've ever seen," she said.

"Excellent!" he said and they all laughed and applauded.

Audra walked around them as still more lightning burst, distant and soundless. Their clapping followed her into the lightless upper parking lot.

She had parked next to a white, rust covered Ford Pickup. As she neared the end of the sidewalk the Ford became visible. The white truck sat alone in the last space.

Audra ran a few steps. It was so freaking dark. Her Toyota was gone.

"Oh God damn it! Shit!"

She ran to the spot where her car had been. She let the backpack slip off her shoulder. She tried to look around the lot. Few other cars, none Coronas.

"Maybe this is the wrong truck. *Damn* it."

Everything she owned was in that car. Every article of clothing, every book and paper for school, and all the money she had in the world. Two hundred ten in an Altoids tin.

In the center of the space she turned in all directions. Lightning flowed overhead and she heard idiots cheering.

Then she heard music. Car stereo, buzzy speakers, from the small staff lot a level fabove.

Black Betty.

There was thunder now mixed with the music. Audra threw her hands up. Who else had the key to the car? Only one person. Just her.

Oh careful, she thought.

She walked up the berm, pushed aside branches of sycamore and scrub oak, into the darkness. There it was, tucked into a niche where two hedges converged. Her blue car was ghostly in the lightning. The driver's door hung open. The dome light glowed orange.

She approached slowly and stood at the front bumper. There was no movement in the thick brush. The pounding music was weakening, the battery running down. She put her hand on the hood as lightning cast blue shadows. The hood was cold. Something scurried behind her. She held still.

"Okay, that's enough. *Ram Jam.* Sheesh."

She went around to the open door. Key hung in the ignition. She ejected the tape. The music cut off with a pop. She stood and turned three-sixty again.

"Holly! It's nineteen seventy-nine! Disco is *dead*!"

Rushing. Too late.

The fist that struck the side of her head arrived with the whisper of a blackbird's wing.

Audra felt so cold. It was so cold. Something was over her mouth and she could not move her hands. She was lying on her side. There was noise, car noise, and she was jostled roughly. Her breath whistled through her nostrils. She blinked. I'm blind, she thought wildly, then a faint light sprayed across the fabric of the seat back inches from her face. The side of her head throbbed and burned. She was so sleepy. So easy to fall sleep.

Audra forced herself to hold still and breathe. She smelled dust and urine. Her pants were wet. Her hands were tied behind her back. Something flexible and sticky and strong. She pulled one hand and then the other.

The car lurched. Her head exploded with pain. She didn't want to but she moaned.

There was another smell. Of course, she thought on the gray edge of consciousness. *Subterfuge.*

The driver downshifted and jacked the wheel then slammed fourth and wound up the engine. No other headlights passing. Far from town.

Audra heard a familiar giggle.

"Are you awake?" Holly said. "Make a sound so I know."

Her voice was lighthearted and amused. Audra felt fear now.

"Make a sound or I'll come back there."

Audra quickly hummed into the tape covering her mouth. Her chin rubbed the seat and as she turned her head a corner of the tape came loose.

"That's so good. Sorry, I know it's uncomfortable. It's your voice, Audra. Your voice has power over me so I fear it. Now what's happening is I've taken your advice. This is a spur of the moment thing but, as I've said so many times before, true spontaneity requires careful planning. Are you listening?"

Audra hummed again.

"You have a blanket and a pillow back there. Did something happen to your nice house at the beach?"

Holly giggled again and then sniffed.

"Now, I might become emotional and you know how I hate that."

Audra watched the gap between the front seats and she rubbed her chin. The tape began to stick to the fabric. She stopped. Go slow, she thought, expecting Holly's fist any second.

"Don't worry, not much farther."

The car skidded through another tight curve.

"I want to apologize for my behavior earlier. It's embarrassing for me to think about. It took some time for me to realize you were right and I let your wisdom guide me."

Holly drove without speaking for several minutes. Audra heard her clear her throat and thought, she's crying.

"You told me you had moved on. Well, Audra, so have I. Yes, I can tell you I have moved on. And what a thrilling, uplifting, spiritual feeling it is. Since this will be the last time we will ever be together I want to tell you everything I have done."

Audra pulled her right hand as hard and as quickly as she could. It felt like the tape stretched. She pulled again. She knew from the sea smell and the lack of traffic and all the curves they were somewhere on Highway One heading north.

How long was I out? she thought. Just get your damn hands loose and jump out. *If she suspects.*

"I have tried to cleanse myself of you, Audra, and this right now will be the final step. I found some of your things under the bed. Your green sweater and an old letter of yours. I was careful not to read the letter. I burned them both in the street. I found some pictures of you from years ago. The trip to Lake Tahoe, remember? I tore them into little bits and flushed them down the toilet. Each action made me feel more free.

"Watching your face swirling down the toilet I almost felt I could fly."

Audra pushed her cheek into the seat and dragged back. The tape pulled away from the corner of her mouth and she could breathe. Easy, easy, she thought, gasping. *Quiet.*

"And then school," Holly said. The car climbed. "In retrospect it was obvious. I took inspiration from your wonderful friend Rushel. You will be shocked to learn I am no longer in the English department. Are you shocked?"

Audra clamped her mouth shut.

"Mm mm!"

"Yes, I knew you would be. I had been thinking about it and now it seems so obvious. I have changed my major," Holly said, "to *Journalism.* It's perfect, Audra, don't you think? My concentration is Broadcast. My fellow Journalism majors are absolutely convinced they are the smartest people in the whole University. Smarter than the Physics majors, Biochemistry, Electronic Engineering. Such wonderful people."

She took her foot off the gas and they came to a stop.

"As you can imagine I fit right in. I may take over the place. What do you think? Did I make the right decision?"

"Mm mm!"

Her mouth uncovered, Audra kept pulling her hands. The tape was looser on her wrists where it had doubled up and cut her skin. It felt wet there.

Holly stopped the car and picked up something from the passenger seat. Audra froze. It was a block of wood. Holly placed the piece of two by four next to her right foot.

"We're finally here. Well, I don't want to make this any harder than it already is. No long drawn out goodbyes."

She got a second piece of wood and wedged it between the seat bracket and the clutch. The pedal was pushed to the firewall. This two by four had a long cotton cord tied to it.

Holly put the stick in neutral. She levered the first piece of wood onto the gas pedal. The engine clattered and shrieked. Holly leaned in and pushed the stick into reverse. She stood in the open door.

Audra pushed herself up against the seat.

"No, Holly! Not my car!"

Holly turned in surprise, her eyes wide. She smiled sweetly.

"Oh, you little scamp. Look at you there. Just look at you. You're not going to need a car ever again," Holly said and wiped her eyes.

Audra pulled her right hand with all her remaining strength. No good. Not coming loose. She kicked the door latch. It didn't budge.

Holly, cord in hand, spoke into the wind.

"Farewell, Audra, my beloved. Farewell, Audra Rachelle Rustichello of Falkirk, Washington. God speed you on your journey."

She reverently pulled the cord and the clutch popped. The screaming Toyota burned rubber in reverse. Audra, still kicking, was thrown against the seats and a half second later the rear end of the car was bounced up hard. Sagebrush scraped the floorboard. Then she was falling and though the rear window she saw stars arc up and then down. Down into nothing at all.

Holly crossed her arms and watched the old blue car containing her beloved bounce backwards over the brush on the shoulder of Highway One and slide smoothly over the cliff. The headlights vanished with a yellow streak. She heard a loud crack as a small tree was snapped off and then accelerating thrashing followed by silence for a single heartbeat. Then a final distant crash as the Toyota impacted the sea swept rocks a hundred feet below.

She uncrossed her arms. She held her face in her hands. She began walking south in the middle of the road and felt not the slightest inclination to look back.

The wind tousled her hair questioningly.

Holly imagined the cold sea taking everything into its eternal embrace. She walked faster, energized and carefree. Her heart swelled, finally unbound. She lifted her eyes to the stars in the moonless night.

"It's my world now."

Acknowledgements

The author would like to thank the following people for their indispensable assistance in the creation of *The Persephone Gate*:

Connie O'Dare Hall (for the idea of the *observations notebook*. Also, the whole 'initials' thing. Thanks, HB), Jessica Doss, Catherine Lee, Glenda Sweger, Samantha Calvillo, Molly Curtis, Valerie Johnson, Ralph L. Purfor, jr, Eric van Gelder, Karen Donohue, Paula Strande, Dixie Blakeley, Susan Rampenthal, Susie Schneider, Mary Lynne Myers, and Suzanne Bennett.

The secret of happiness is freedom. The secret of freedom is courage.
~ *Thucydides*

K.C. Russell // is the pen name of a writer currently living in northern California // is originally from Covina, California // is a graduate of California Polytechnic State University, San Luis Obispo, 1979 //

www.ingramcontent.com/pod-product-compliance
Lightning Source LLC
Chambersburg PA
CBHW071532120726
47907CB00014B/1505